Beyond Perfect

Beyond Perfect

Beyond Perfect
BY JENNIFER PETERSON

Far Above Rubies
BY BECKY MELBY AND CATHY WIENKE

Family Circle
BY JANET LEE BARTON

The Wedding's On
BY GAIL SATTLER

HeavenSent
from
Crossings

Beyond Perfect
Copyright © 2000 by Barbour Publishing, Inc.

Far Above Rubies
Copyright © 1997 by Barbour Publishing, Inc.

Family Circle
Copyright © 2001 by Barbour Publishing, Inc.

The Wedding's On
Copyright © 2002 by Barbour Publishing, Inc.

This edition was especially created in 2003 for Crossings by arrangement with
Barbour Publishing, Inc.

Published by Crossings Book Club, 401 Franklin Avenue, Garden City, New York
11530.

ISBN: 0-7394-3699-6

Printed in the United States of America

Beyond Perfect

Beyond Perfect

by Jennifer Peterson

1

"W hat is it?" Deborah Shaughnessy scrunched up her chocolate brown eyes and peered into the water-filled bowl.

"It's a goldfish, silly!" Cali Shaw laughed as she wadded up the torn wrapping paper that littered the floor.

"I know it's a fish, but why?" Deborah cautiously tapped a manicured nail on the side, trying to attract its attention.

"Well, let's see . . . When did God create the animals?" Cali put her forefinger to her chin and feigned introspection. "Hey, Chris, do you remember? Wasn't that the third day?"

Chris shook her head as she exited the kitchen area, holding a cake teeming with candles. "Nope, it was the fifth. Now, on the third day . . ."

"All right, already! I get it. I just want to know why you guys thought a goldfish was an appropriate twentieth birthday gift." Deborah raised her face from the bowl to their fake looks of disappointment.

"You mean you don't like him?" Cali questioned, wiping nonexistent tears from the sides of her eyes with great finesse.

"I'll bet she's afraid it'll meet the same fate as the African violets we got her last month. Now blow out your candles before we burn down this poor excuse for an apartment," Chris teased. As soon as Deborah had managed to extinguish twenty flaming wax clowns, Chris began slicing generous pieces of butter cake and placing them on paper plates. "By the way, Deb, when are you going to buy some real tableware—you know, the kind you don't throw away?"

3

"I move too much to buy nice plates. You know that. Besides, I could never decide on the perfect pattern. Sometimes I think roses would be nice, but then I see some wild splash of colors and designs. . . ." She glanced up to find knowing looks on her friends' faces. "But enough about that. What do you mean 'the same fate as the African violets?' Are you insinuating I can't take care of a fish?"

"Well," Chris said slowly, "I didn't think we were insinuating anything."

"Yeah, I'm pretty sure we just came right out and said it," Cali grinned, grabbing the fishbowl protectively. "This was just a joke, Deb. Your real present is still in the car. We know since you're a gal on the go and everything, that makes it hard to sustain any life-forms that can't survive on diet soda and toaster pastries."

Deborah stood and puffed up to her entire five-foot-six frame, her wide smile betraying her facade. "Now, you wait just a minute. The African violet was an accident. You and I all know only trained professionals should be allowed to keep such a plant." Chris and Cali rolled their eyes in unison. "And what about that Peace lily? I kept that guy alive for months!"

"But it never did bloom again, now, did it?" Chris's green eyes twinkled mischievously. Pulling her blond hair into a loose ponytail, she sat down with her cake and began to eat. "C'mon, Deb, sit down. You don't have to prove anything to us. We love you. It's your birthday, so sit and eat."

Deborah shook her auburn mane in defiance. "No way. Not until you admit that I can keep a fish." She crossed her arms and waited.

"Sweetie, we don't doubt that you can keep a fish. It's just that we're not sure how long the fish will be . . ." Cali paused, seeming to hunt for the most tactful words.

"Not only will that fish live," Deborah announced, punctuating her words with a finger, "he will flourish under my exquisite

4

care. Why, he already has a name, as far as I'm concerned. And a home." Grabbing the bowl, she proceeded to the kitchen area of her studio apartment. "Right here on top of the microwave! When I eat, so shall Gil eat!"

Deborah returned to the "living room" to the sound of muffled snickers. "You guys wait and see," she said with a grin. "Gil is now the new man in my life."

"Eat your cake, O Deborah, Mistress of Marine Biology." Chris shoved a piece of cake toward her. "You may keep the fish."

"Gil," Deborah insisted, sampling the dessert. "By the way, you two—this is fantastic. Much better than those pre-made jobs they sell at the supermarket."

"Deb, you are hopeless. Let's hope for Gil's sake you find some fish food. I don't want to come over here and find little bits of microwave burrito in his bowl."

"Don't worry, Cali. Gil and I will be just fine. You wait and see. If I'm wrong, I'll buy you both lunch at the restaurant of your choice."

"You're on, girlfriend. Hey! If we don't hurry, we're not going to make it to the movies."

❧

Sitting cross-legged on her shaggy orange love seat, Deborah surveyed her newest domestic conquest with a scrutinous eye. Having moved less than a week ago, she could already sense problems. The bulk of the dilemma lay in her inability to properly furnish the tiny apartment, but she felt she couldn't justify nice furniture without a nice home. So, she scoured flea markets and thrift shops, vowing to spend no more than thirty dollars on any given piece. She was particularly proud of the orange "monstrosity," as Cali called it. A true bargain! Naturally, that was more than likely due to its postdated style, but Deborah thought it was like snuggling into fourteen really big sheepdogs—orange sheepdogs that didn't drool or need to be fed.

The studio itself was larger than most she had viewed, boasting all the amenities from a full bathtub to a full stove, but something about it just wasn't right. It lacked certain warmth Chris had identified easily: "No central air." It was more than that, though. It was the same something fueling her from her last apartment—a one-bedroom joke—on to this one, and already, the flames ignited and attempted to propel her into yet another search for *"home."*

After her initial move from home at seventeen, having graduated early from high school due to astounding marks across the board, Deborah first tried the dorms, but found them insufferable. As soon as her birthday rolled around, she begged her parents to fly down to Kansas City and co-sign a lease for her. Her mother was the only one who could get away from work, so the two women searched the area for a suitable and safe alternative to the arranged living offered at the University of Kansas, some sixty miles away. Kathleen Shaughnessy had insisted on a month-to-month lease, saying that she feared her only daughter would feel "trapped and unable to live her young life to the fullest." Deborah knew this stemmed from her mother's own regrets, and yearned not to make the same mistakes as her parents.

Even now, Deborah could hear her mother's words of warning. *"Life offers you many choices. Too many, if you ask me. You needn't let it rush you, however. I don't want any child of mine making the same poor choices I did."*

Deborah had to admit, living in such a way allowed her to move on a whim, a luxury she had come to depend on. She was an excellent tenant, paying her rent on time and offering no major problems. Her references were impeccable, and she encountered little resistance when she decided to lease on her own. No, the problem, she determined, was that she had just not stumbled across her niche.

"That little Victorian place had a nice feel," she said aloud. "Too bad about the gas leak." She remembered the mauve throw rugs provided by the landlord. He had worried a great deal about her scratching his hardwood floors. Too bad he hadn't been so meticulous about the pipes to the stove.

There had been half a dozen places in between, and each of them had had its problems. Deborah, however, was determined not to be defeated by these minor setbacks. She believed when the right place came along—just like the right job and the right man—she would feel it. "The Sparkles," she called them—the tingling sensation she felt when she saw the right outfit or heard the right song. Logic seemed to dictate that such a feeling would translate into all areas of her life, providing a rational barometer for gauging her happiness.

Deborah slowly took in what modest decorations she possessed, mostly framed magazine pictures that had piqued her interest. Smiling, she settled her eyes on a small framed "photo" of a popular television leading man—a gift, she jokingly insisted, from her true love in Hollywood. Most of the remaining decor centered on tigers, her favorite animal due to its ferocious nature and cuddly appearance. *National Geographic* and other random nature publications provided stunning photographs, and a ragtag collection of stuffed animals and figurines covered every surface and inhabited each cubbyhole. Her last, but most necessary, addition was an eclectic montage of refrigerator magnets. Her grandmother had impressed upon her the domesticating effects of the tiny treasures. "Home just isn't home without refrigerator magnets," she had said. As of yet, they had proved to be miserably inefficient at their task.

Deciding to curl up with a novel for the evening, Deborah cozied herself into the awaiting embrace of her vibrantly colored couch. The hardback edition of this month's leading bestseller, *How to Fish Without a Boat,* promised Deborah an easy path to finding the desires of her heart. The caricature under the title showed a man with a reel, hanging out the door of a helicopter.

Make your life over in fifteen easy steps, the words pledged from beneath the drawing. On the back, Deborah saw the statement that caused her to buy the book in the first place. *You can't get what you want—until you know what you want.*

"You said it," she announced to the empty room.

Only a paragraph into the introduction, the phone rang, and instinctively she knew it was her parents' birthday call. She tossed the book aside and hurried across the room to catch the call on the third ring. "Hello?" Returning to the love seat, Deborah cradled the phone against her shoulder.

"Hi, Debbie. Happy birthday!" Kathleen Shaughnessy's jubilation oozed over the connection.

"Hi, Mom. How are you? How's Dad?"

"We're great, Debbie. How are you? What did you do for your birthday?"

"Well, Chris and Cali came over and we went to a movie. Oh, they got me a fish."

"A fish? Whatever for?"

"They said it was a joke, but that was only because they doubted my superior ability to enhance the lives of those around me, be they plant or animal," Deborah laughed.

"Oh, sweetie, I don't know about that. Do you really want to be tied down to a pet at your age? Won't that make it difficult for you to do all the things you want to do?"

"Mom, it's a fish, nothing more. It's not like I've become a halfway house for wayward animals. I can handle a fish."

"Oh, it starts out as a fish, and the next thing you know, you've got a cat. . . ."

"Tiger," Deborah corrected.

"Joke all you like, young lady, but I speak from experience. The little things combine to tie you down. What if you decide to study abroad? What will you do then? Today, the fish; tomorrow, it's a car payment and a mortgage and . . ." Kathleen stopped suddenly. "Debbie, I know you. You are filled with potential and dreams. I don't want you to exchange the life of perfection you could have, simply because you long for stability. You know your father and I married way too young for the very same reason. You know how much we struggled. Now, we made it work because it was the right thing to do, in the eyes of the world, our church, and our loved ones. But it's still hard. Likewise, you know I can't stand my job at the State. Your father can't stand his, either. But we settled into them because we felt we had no choice. I don't want that for you. You're so young."

Deborah listened intently, as she had for as long as she could remember. "I know you're right, Mama," she said soothingly. "It's only a fish. I promise it won't be more than that. Chris keeps fish, so if Gil gets to be too much . . ."

"Gil?"

"That's what I named him—you know, fish have gills, his name is Gil. . . . But anyway, what I'm trying to say is, I will be careful. I am waiting for the right opportunity to come along. I won't sell myself short. I promise. Please don't be upset on my birthday. Not over fish."

She heard her mother's deep sigh. A sigh of resignation. "I know you'll do the right thing, Deborah. I don't mean to overreact like that, but you're so important to me. I want all the things for you I couldn't have for myself. I want happiness, contentment, and fulfillment for you. That's all." Deborah could hear a garbled voice in the background and her mother's indistinguishable reply. "Oh, Daddy wanted me to tell you that he sent off the check yesterday. Now, if you need more, don't hesitate to call us. We want you to have everything that you need so you don't feel pressured to perform."

Ever since Deborah had moved out on her own, her parents sent her a thousand dollars, three times a year. They hoped to ease the consequences of her flighty nature, from security deposits to enrollment fees. Unknown to either of her parents, though, Deborah had only deposited the checks into a savings account, unable to justify using the money. Besides, she always had a job, whether in school or out, and usually did just fine where finances were concerned.

"Tell him thanks, Mom. And thank you. You know that I love you, right?"

"Of course. But don't you worry about me. Or your dad. We've made our beds, so we must lie in them, so the proverbial saying goes, right? Now, before I forget, I mailed your birthday present a couple of days ago. I still haven't figured out how long it takes mail to get from Oregon to Missouri, but it should be there by tomorrow. I hope you like it."

"I know I'll love it, Mom."

"Well, I need to go, but happy birthday again, and I love you so very much. Don't ever forget that. I'll try to call soon."

Deborah said her good-byes, hung up the phone, and walked over to her kitchen.

"Well, Gil," she said, stopping directly in front of the microwave, "you've managed to cause quite a little stir for a goldfish. Of course, the visual picture I get of being 'shackled' to you is pretty funny, if I do say so myself. Maybe I'll find something in my fishing book to straighten out the entire matter." She grinned. "Hey, that's pretty neat, huh? I've already got me a fish and I did it without a boat. I'd say I did pretty well for myself. Maybe I don't need the book."

idan McCullough stretched one hamstring, then the other, trying hard not to lose his balance. Moving to his shoulders, neck, and chest, he continued the routine he had developed almost ten years ago as a freshman in his high school weight-lifting class. Now, at twenty-five, he was definitely in good shape. Always having more of a gymnast's build than a linebacker's form, Aidan wasn't what one would call overly muscular. But, he was well defined and in good health, utilizing the body God had given him to the fullest. That was all that mattered to him.

He enjoyed working out in the early mornings, right after McCullough's Gym opened at 5:30. He remembered well trying to cajole his sister and brother-in-law to accompany him. "It's good business to practice what you preach," he lectured. As the gym's sole owner, he felt he had an obligation to mingle with his customers. However, at this time of day, they were all family.

"Hey, Sis, what's with the light weight? You're not going soft on me, are you?" Aidan's good-natured heckling made him one of the best personal trainers in the Metro area. His sister, Maureen, didn't seem to agree, at least not today.

"Hey, I don't see you pumping anything," she said, continuing to curl the light weight. "I distinctly recall that not twenty-four hours ago, Pastor Riley was saying something about dealing with the log in your own eye before moving on to hassle innocent patrons about their level of exertion."

"Uh-oh, what did you say to her, Aidan?" Tom Walsh entered

11

the gym just in time, apparently, to catch the end of his wife's lecture.

"I was simply encouraging in a competition-enhancing manner," Aidan replied, his hands up in a defensive nature.

"I'll bet that's what you tell all your clients. I'll bet it's even printed that way—word for word—in the brochure. Am I right?" Maureen stood and stretched her arms high over her fiery red ponytail.

"Well, perhaps, but you've got to admit—never before have truer words been strung together in the history of fitness training," he stated in mock solemnity.

"Give me a break!"

"Not after that pitiful thing you call a workout! To the track, fair maiden! You want a break around here, you gotta earn it."

After running a brisk mile, the threesome walked a few laps to cool down and headed back to the weight room. Maureen, begging off any further activity, due to an inexplicable bout of nausea, finished her cooldown while the men took turns spotting each other on the free weights. Tom and Aidan, feeling the full effects of their endorphins, headed down the stairs for a whirlwind match of racquetball after Maureen had showered and took control of the front desk.

The two men had been friends through high school, their passion for fitness ignited in the same class. Through the trials and victories of adolescence, the boys had grown into men, but more so, brothers. It seemed only natural that Tom would marry Aidan's older sister, two years their senior. The three were inseparable now, and while Aidan owned McCullough's Gym, Tom and Maureen helped run the day-to-day affairs and even taught a few classes.

Aidan insisted that Tom have a few clients to train in addition to teaching his basic tae-kwon-do class. He seemed to enjoy the discipline and routine, and Aidan had been complimented on

Tom's ability more than once. Aidan, himself, had to admit that Tom had a gift for instructing a wide range of ages in such a rigorous art. Maureen, always active and in great shape, taught the high- and low-impact aerobics, as well as a few of the trendier classes from time to time.

After a shower and shave, Tom and Aidan emerged from the locker room, laughing and joking, as always. Making their way up the stairs, they greeted familiar faces. "Hey, Aaron, how's it going?" Aidan stopped midstep and firmly shook the hand of the tall, blond man. His muscular, athletic frame revealed his devotion to McCullough's Gym. Aidan realized they had only worked one-on-one for a little over a year. It seemed like they had known each other forever.

"Pretty well, Trainer Man. How's business?"

"It's going smoothly. Mostly running on our faithful few. Of course, in a few months, the preholiday crowd will rush in, and all will be blissfully chaotic, until about March."

"I know you love it, though. I'll bet as a kid you messed up your room just so you could clean it," Aaron chuckled in a deep baritone voice.

"Hey, just for that, you've got one heavy-duty max-out day coming your way! You'd better hurry up and get ready!" The two parted and Aidan continued up the stairs, mentally planning out Aaron's personally guided workout. Since the man was obviously no stranger to exercise, Aaron had decided to utilize his appointments with Aidan only once a week, when he would lift his maximum amount in shorter sets in order to push his body closer and closer towards its peak performance. The other two workouts were at a more comfortable weight and pace, and Aidan's guidance was not required.

Rounding the corner and approaching the front desk, Aidan found Tom rubbing Maureen's shoulders as a pained expression washed over her face.

"You all right, Moe?" Aidan knew that his concern was unmistakable.

"You haven't called me that since I broke my ankle two summers ago," she murmured, attempting a smile. "I'm fine. That run this morning just took it out of me. I don't know what happened. I got sick right after you guys hit the showers, and my head feels like it's going to explode." Tom stopped the massage and lightly kissed the top of her head.

"Do you need to see the doctor?"

"No, no. Don't be silly. I'll be fine. Mr. Trainer there just worked me too hard. I didn't eat much of a breakfast, either. That's probably all it is. You know how easily I get sugar dives. Don't worry, guys." Maureen turned and accepted an elderly woman's membership card. Handing her a small, white towel emblazoned with McCullough's Gym, she smiled. "Have a good workout, Mrs. Wittenburg."

The woman grinned like a teenager. "I always do. How could I not, surrounded by all these handsome young men?" She poked Aidan in the side and giggled. "You know, you are the spitting image of your grandfather, Shawn. And he had such a delightful Irish brogue. All the girls would just swoon over him, you know. Your grandmother was the envy of us all!"

Aidan blushed ever so slightly and gently hugged her slight frame. "You're too kind, Mrs. Wittenburg. I've seen photographs of Grandpa McCullough, and I don't see any resemblance whatsoever when I look at my sorry mug."

Laughing heartily, she playfully slapped at his arm. Turning to Maureen, she whispered, "This one's too modest. We have to be careful with him, or he'll gratefully marry the first lass who sets her sights on him!"

"I don't think we'll have to worry about that, dear. Our Aidan knows his heavenly Father has the perfect woman already prepared for him. He's never been one to become overly smitten with a girl who happens to fall for his red-headed charms."

Mrs. Wittenburg smiled. "Well, that's good to know. Your grandfather was a man of God, too. I'm glad to see that the good looks aren't the only positive traits handed down in your family." With that, she headed off for the track, looking every inch the part in her pastel pink jogging suit and white name-brand sneakers.

"She's such a sweetheart," Maureen commented. "It's so neat to talk to her and hear about her memories—especially since she knows the family."

"I know. And I particularly enjoy the parts about how dashing I am," Aidan's green eyes smiled despite his efforts to keep a straight face.

"Don't you have a client, brother dear? I don't think I can take much more of your self-indulgence with this headache."

"It's understandable, Maureen. One is easily overwhelmed in the presence of greatness." After a grandiose bow, Aidan turned and laughed warmly all the way to the weight room.

❧

Aidan locked the doors to the gym and walked briskly to his car at the far end of the parking lot. Today had been particularly strenuous since Tom and Maureen took off early for a doctor's appointment. Maureen's condition wasn't improving, and Aidan worried that she might overwork herself, given her two classes each day. At the insistence of both men, Maureen relented and allowed Tom to call their physician. Aidan decided to fix dinner for the couple and closed McCullough's early on Friday, hoping that the break would help his sister recover from her ailment. Since the three of them refused to work on Sundays, he realized he was to face his first complete weekend in years.

Stopping at the grocery store, he chose the ingredients for a light meal of lemon-pepper whitefish and fresh green beans. Perhaps if there was enough time, he'd bake a loaf of honey-wheat bread, Maureen's favorite.

A few hours later, Aidan was laying out the finishing touches on the dining room table when the doorbell rang. Immediately after, the door of his duplex opened, and he was greeted by the contrasting expressions of his sister and brother-in-law.

"Mmm . . . It smells wonderful in here. I'm so glad Mom made you learn to cook, little brother. Ooh, is that honey-wheat bread?" she questioned, eyeing the freshly sliced loaf on the table.

"You bet. Only the best for my family. So, come on. What did the doctor say?"

"Oh, it can wait. I won't be able say much if I pass out from hunger."

Though it was against his better judgment, Aidan shrugged and gestured them to sit. "Tom, would you say grace?"

Distractedly, Tom nodded, and the family bowed their heads in prayer. "Father, I thank You for this time we have to share together. I ask for Your blessing upon this meal my brother has prepared and that it will nourish our bodies and spirits. I ask for Your healing hand to touch my wife. Keep her safe, Father, for You know I would be lost without her. Finally, I ask for You to bless and keep me. Make me into the strong and holy man You would have me be. In Your Son's precious name, amen."

"Amens" echoed from brother to sister, and Aidan's eyes rose expectantly. "So?"

Maureen's smile seemed a mile wide. "We're pregnant!"

Aidan mirrored his sister's elated expression, and then let out a victory cry. "I'm gonna be an uncle! Tom, Sis, congratulations!"

"But . . . ," Tom eyed his wife sorrowfully, "the sonogram shows she's pregnant with twins."

"Twins!" Aidan exclaimed. "That's wonderful news." He gave his brother-in-law a puzzled look. "Why do you sound so upset?"

"He's just being a worrywart," Maureen said, helping herself to some fish.

"The doctor said that because it's twins, the pregnancy will be classified as high-risk. Maureen's nearly two months along, but her strenuous exercise regimen made it impossible for her to know, and now. . . ."

Aidan's countenance fell. "Oh, Moe. Are you going to be all right?"

Maureen snorted in defiance. "You boys think I'm made of glass. I will be fine, but the doctor would rather I not teach aerobics."

"The doctor said under no circumstances were you to teach aerobics," Tom chimed in.

"Then she won't," Aidan assured.

Maureen's forehead wrinkled. "I would like to take some time off, if you think you can spare me. I am not going to sacrifice my health or the health of our babies by being foolish and not taking care of myself. That does include exercising." She held up her hand to silence the two men before they could speak. "Expectant mothers do it all the time. Light exercises are even encouraged. Perhaps I could teach a class like that."

Tom shook his head. "No. You heard the doctor. No more aerobics. Nothing high-impact and no weight training." He looked to Aidan for support. "He told her there were stretches and, of course, walking." He turned back to his wife. "I've never minded if you worked at the gym. You know I would never keep you from doing what you love. But I love you, and I don't want you to do any damage to yourself or to the babies."

"He's absolutely right," Aidan nodded in agreement. "The gym will be fine. I can find someone to teach your classes for nine months. Hey, ten months. Whatever you need. Just take care of yourself and let me worry about the gym."

"Actually, like Tom said, I am already eight weeks along. I

was so shocked! I figured from all the horror stories I'd be in the throes of morning sickness, but he said some women don't experience it at all! I should only need nine months, max. I want to spend time with the babies, obviously, but the gym is our home. Those people are our family. I can't think of a better environment to raise a child, let alone two! Perhaps this would be a good time to make plans for a nursery."

It was obvious to Aidan that no amount of medical worries could steal his sister's joy. All that they could do was offer it up to God and wait for His will to be revealed. He smiled and nodded. "Well, no sense in letting this good food go to waste. After all, you're eating for three now."

(3)

A knock at the door roused Deborah's attention away from her laptop computer. Struggling to jump up from her position on the floor, she hollered out, "I'll be right there!" Discovering that her legs were asleep from the knees down, Deborah couldn't help but laugh at her pathetic predicament. By the time she managed to limp to the door, tears were streaming down her face and her giggles had become uproarious. *It's like an* Incredible Journey *story,* she thought. *They'll feature this on motivational programming.* "Notice how poor Deborah can barely hobble to the door, yet through sheer determination and willpower, she succeeds."

Peering through the peephole, she saw the perplexed face of Chris Abernathy. "What is going on in there, Deb? Are you okay?"

After unlocking the dead bolt, Deborah allowed Chris to come inside. "My . . . legs . . . fell . . . asleep," she gasped, trying to catch her breath and stop laughing. "Was . . . trying . . . to . . . make it . . . to . . . the door." It was Chris's turn to laugh, and Deborah knew the young woman found her antics infinitely amusing. Almost as much as she, herself, did.

Soon, the two were laughing so hard at each other, they fell into the awaiting solace of the orange beast. Minutes passed before they could regain composure.

"Wow. How uncalled for was that?" Chris managed to sit up and then, to stand. Wiping tears from her eyes, she headed to the kitchen. "Hey, do you want me to bring you some water? You're probably pretty thirsty after all that. Wait a minute . . . Gil! You're still alive! Hooray!" Returning with two plastic convenience-store

19

cups, Chris finally said, "This should be something more substantial than water."

Deborah looked at her friend quizzically. "Why?"

"Because Gil is still alive. We should be celebrating in proper style."

Deborah frowned. "Sorry, I'm out of diet cola."

Chris laughed and settled back. "So what happened to you— to your legs?"

Deborah, now much calmer, smiled. "I was working on my résumé, and when I stood up to answer the door, both my legs had fallen asleep while I was sitting on the floor. I could barely drag myself across this vast wasteland of a living room." She took a long drink, then exhaled deeply. "Wow. We have more fun than people have a right to."

"What were you working on your résumé for? You have a job at the restaurant."

"Yeah, well, I quit." Abruptly, Deborah got up from the couch and returned to the computer screen. *Just let it go, Chris. . . .*

"You quit? Why?" Chris followed her over and sat down.

"I didn't want to be a trainer." Hoping Chris would leave it at that, she began to type in the last of her job description. "Would you look at that? It's hard to believe I've had seven pages worth of jobs in less than three years."

"Obviously, you have the perfect résumé times seven." Chris stretched out her long legs and flipped her pigtails over her shoulders.

"What are you talking about? It's hardly perfect." She silently read along, then added softly, more to herself than to Chris, "So much I haven't done yet. I still don't know what I like to do."

"What I mean is, the ideal résumé is supposed to be one page long. What are you going to do with seven pages? Don't you think that will look a little bad to your prospective employers?"

"Are you kidding? I'm an ideal employee. I can do almost

anything. I'm qualified for whatever they can throw at me, short of open-heart surgery and a few chemical engineering arenas. And as far as that goes, I can be trained. This way, I'm destined to find the perfect job. Then, my dear Christine, I can finally buy those dishes you so desperately want me to possess."

"What does the perfect job have to do with your buying dishes? Come to think of it, what does the perfect job have to do with anything?" Chris's frustrated curiosity seemed to be getting the better of her.

"Because, if I find the perfect job, the perfect apartment will not be far behind. And with those two areas secure, the perfect man is sure to follow." Deborah explained her plan as if it were the most logical thing in the world. And it was, at least in her world.

"Deb, don't you understand that God's plan for you is just that? You don't have to be in charge of all of this. You're going to drive yourself crazy. You can't keep all the balls in the air all the time. You want to juggle things that are beyond your control. Turn this over to prayer so it won't bother you so much." Chris's face reflected genuine concern.

"I don't expect you to understand. To you, life seems so black-and-white. You find solace in prayer, and believe me, I don't want to take that from you. Look, I don't want to argue. Please understand; this is just my way. You have your way." Deborah turned her attention back to the blinking cursor. "I think I'll be 'Debbie' for this round. It sounds . . . carefree and whimsical. Debbie Shaughnessy."

Chris slowly stood up and smiled sadly. "Look, Deb . . ."

"Debbie," she supplied, grinning from ear to ear.

"All right, Debbie. I know you think life is one big, multiple choice, no-wrong-answer placement test, but it's not. I say this not to be cruel, but to be truthful: I know I have chosen the one right way. The Bible backs me up, 100 percent. Now, that may not mean anything to you, but to me, it defines who I am, what I am, and what I can be. I guarantee you, your 'way' will only deceive you and leave you empty on this endless pursuit to attain perfection. And it's out there—don't get me wrong. But what you need is to have it in here," she said gently, placing a hand over her heart. "If you need me, if you have questions, I'm here for you. I will always love you—Deb, Debbie, or Deborah. God will too, regardless of how many pages your résumé is, or what name you choose to go by. I know you know the truth. I only hope you accept it soon."

Deborah could only watch in stunned amazement as Chris walked out the door of her apartment. It was the first time in her life anyone had ever spoken to her like that—with such peace, with such authority. Not even the pastors at all the churches she had attended. Definitely not her mother or her father. For once, Deborah was rendered speechless.

Aidan had just finished sterilizing all of the machines when the phone of the gym rang. "McCullough's," he answered, setting the spray bottle of alcohol and the used towel on the counter.

"Hey, Aidan, it's Maureen. How are things going? Did you get too many complaints about canceling my classes?"

"No, not really. I explained the situation in minimal detail to a few of the regular ladies. They were more concerned than irritated. They know that it must be a pretty big deal for the Aerobics Queen of the Greater Kansas City Area to back out on her subjects." Aidan smiled and began doodling on the notepad. He really did need to find a replacement teacher soon.

Maureen laughed and added, "Well, it's true. I love what I do. But I'm so excited about being a mother! Imagine!" Lowering her voice in a conspiratorial manner, she continued, "I'm sure you know Tom believes they'll be boys, but between you and me, I know they are girls. The McCullough women are famous for their firstborn girls—and with good reason, I might add. Look how stunning and intelligent we all turned out!"

"Yeah, well, we'll see. Don't forget, Tom's family is all boys. Perhaps that'll throw a bit of a curve into your genetic certainty." Aidan loved to tease her, ever since they were just toddlers. He marveled at the close relationship they shared, knowing that sibling rivalries destroyed a good number of family ties. Now with their parents' making a home in their ancestral Ireland, it was good to have her close.

"Well, you just wait and see, little brother. I wouldn't want you to waste your hard-earned money on light blue accessories for the nursery. But, back to business. Has anyone suggested a replacement for my time away? Maybe one of the women in the class could step up and take over."

"No, they all made it quite clear they weren't even remotely qualified to do what you do. Claimed you brought something 'extraspecial' to the class, and they definitely weren't prepared to deal with the disappointed masses when it became obvious they were mere imposters. All joking aside, though, I haven't found anyone here who feels comfortable with it, and I can't imagine bringing in an outsider to teach. We're all so close here, and it's not that I want to keep things segregated, but a new staff member is a big deal. I want someone who's going to be able to keep up with me, you know?"

"Yeah, you are quite a tough guy to work for; I'll give you that. Maybe that's why no one wants to take my position. Perhaps you've been too hard on me and the ladies have witnessed my abuse firsthand. 'Maureen, do this. Maureen, don't use those weights. Maureen, come run a mile with me. Maureen, call for take-out.' I tell you, in retrospect, I don't know how I managed to put up with you for so long," she sighed dramatically.

"Oh, poor girl. I know working here must have been sheer torture. Especially the way I forced you to teach both aerobics classes. And you were so against it," Aidan played along, his voice dripping with sarcastic concern. He remembered well trying to talk his headstrong older sister into teaching just one class, but she would hear nothing of it.

"All right, all right. Maybe you should just put an ad in the paper. Or better yet, ask Aaron. He's got a little sister. Maybe she can come teach. She always looks to be in great shape whenever she drops by with Aaron. Just like a cheerleader, all bubbly and cute. At any rate, let me know how it goes. I feel awful about leaving the gym with no substitute." Aidan could hear the regret in her voice, and his heart broke. *She truly loved it here,* he thought.

"Look, don't you worry about any of it. Tom and I will get it taken care of. You just rest. The place isn't the same without you, and you won't be forgotten, but I can surely find someone to teach your classes. I'll talk to you later, all right?"

"Okay, Aidan. Are you still coming by for dinner?"

"You bet. Talk to you then." As Aidan replaced the phone, he noticed Aaron striding confidently toward him.

"Hey, Aidan, my man. Overheard you saying you needed an aerobics instructor. Everything going well with Maureen?" Aaron's usually smiling mouth was turned down ever so slightly at the corners, belying his worry.

"Well, she and Tom just found out they're pregnant, and the doctor has labeled it 'high-risk' because it's twins. It's early on still, so there's not a big worry, but Maureen's taking it easy for a while. I'm actually glad you stopped by. Maureen mentioned your little sister might be a good candidate." Aidan leaned casually on the counter of the front desk, intent on hearing Aaron's answer.

"Who, Chris? Well, I wasn't thinking of her. She's not really into classroom-type exercise. She's more of a loner. Likes her biking, swimming, and tennis. She did tell me that a friend of hers is looking for a new job. The way I understand it, this gal's taken all kinds of physical education classes at KU and really seems to enjoy it. Maybe I could mention it to Chris and see what she says."

"Mr. Abernathy, you'd be a lifesaver. Any friend of your sister has to be salt of the earth. Definitely tell her about it. Let me know later if she's interested, and we'll set up an appointment. It'll give me time to pray about it and come up with a suitable job description. I took Maureen's position for granted, I'm learning. I guess she did more than just jump around all day, huh?"

Aaron smiled and grabbed the towel from around his neck. "Well, if you need my help, I can always answer phones or whatever on Saturdays. This is already my second home. Might as well pitch in and help out. If I didn't, my poor mother would be really disappointed. I gotta hit the showers, my man. I'll see you later."

Aidan playfully hit him on the shoulder. "Thanks, Aaron. I've got to get back to work, too."

§

After finishing her workout, Deborah printed out her résumés and placed the large stack of papers into a file. She liked to keep a good number of them with her in the car, in case she noticed a "HELP WANTED" sign while she was out and about. Cali and Chris always joked about it being like head shots for a model—always needed to have them close at hand for the big break.

Deciding to do a little "room" cleaning—she couldn't very well call it a house—Deborah changed into a pair of cutoff denim shorts and a modest tank top, advertising one of her previous employers. Emblazoned on the front in rainbow colors, it read Susan's Little Ones, a local day care run by a middle-aged woman from Deborah's church at the time. Unable to have children of her own, Susan had turned her sorrow into a booming business by caring for infants to preadolescents out of her home. Deborah remembered the job fondly, recalling the deep regret she felt upon quitting. Susan had assured her she would always have a job with Little Ones, no questions asked. Though the pained look in Susan's eyes stayed with her, her mother had been especially supportive of the decision to leave. *Perhaps someday,* she thought, *I can find a job that makes me as happy as Susan is.*

Today, though, was no time for reminiscing. Today, things must be cleaned and a job must be found. After sprinkling deodorizing powder on the carpet, Deborah began dusting her tigers to the beat of her portable stereo. She had just gone to plug in the vacuum when the phone rang. "Hi," she answered cheerfully.

"Hey, Debbie, it's Chris. Look, don't say anything for a minute. I just finished talking to my brother, and he said you could get a job at his gym. The owner's desperate for an aerobics instructor, and Aaron remembered my telling him about all your PE classes. So he mentioned this to Aidan—that's the owner—and he's interested! He wants you to call and set up an interview! Isn't that great?" Chris drew a deep breath, and Deborah had to giggle.

"Wow, and I thought I was long-winded. Thanks, Chris. That sounds perfect. And, now, the fact you made me join that gym with you should finally pay off! Just give me the number, and I'll call right now. I was only cleaning, anyway."

After Chris had given her all the information, Deborah asked, "So, this owner. Is he some old man who has been running it for hundreds of years?"

"No way, girlfriend. He's a good friend of Aaron's. I think they're about the same age. I've seen him before. Not what I'd consider gorgeous, but definitely a good guy. But never mind about all that. Just call and get yourself a job, girl! I'll be praying for you." Chris hung up and Deborah dialed the number to McCullough's Gym. A man answered.

"Hello, this is Debbie Shaughnessy. I hear you need an aerobics instructor."

*H*eaving a sigh of relief, Aidan placed the phone back in its cradle. Due to the astonishingly quick response to his need, Aidan felt sure God was completely in the midst of the entire ordeal. Sitting down on the weight bench, he breathed a quick prayer of thanks.

"Lord, I know You have already answered our prayers, and for that, I thank You. I ask if this woman is who You would have to replace my sister, You would give me a sure sign. Please know that it is Your will I desire, and help me to remember it, too. Amen."

Deciding to get in a quick workout before Ms. Shaughnessy arrived—she was due in less than half an hour—Aidan moved to the controlled weight machines in the main area of the gym. As he hurried through the workout, his mind was on the prospective employee. What sort of woman was she? Well, if she was a close friend of Aaron's sister, she would be barely a woman. Aaron's sister wasn't much more than nineteen or twenty. But, Debbie Shaughnessy held a confident tone in her voice—one that seemed to inherently demand the sort of respect derived from maturity and experience. He smiled slightly at the memory of their conversation. Never, he recalled, had she spoken of the position without subtly implying it was already hers. He liked that. She wasn't pushy, he decided. She just knew what she wanted. Just like he did.

ও

Deborah pulled into the parking lot not twenty minutes after she confirmed the interview with one Mr. Aidan McCullough. As she locked her car door, she took in her surroundings. McCullough's Gym stood alone, and the nearest business was a locally owned grocery store. She liked that it was open and freestanding. It seemed safer that way. It also made it feel more professional. *There is nothing quite so disturbing,* Deborah thought, *as a fitness center crammed right next door to a fast-food joint.*

As she walked toward the building, she admired the large windows and clean appearance. In bold blue-green letters, it read McCullough's Gym in a cross between print and script-style fonts. The main structure was painted white, and the front lawns were well-manicured and bursting with vividly colored flowers. To her surprise, upon entering, no one stood to greet her at the front desk. It, too, was in the same turquoise as that of the outside lettering, and Deborah found the designs within to be extremely crisp and upbeat. She could hear a popular song playing on the well-placed sound system. Everything about this business radiated order and precision. That made the lack of a desk person much more ironic, in her opinion.

Deborah, clutching her seven-page résumé, decided to have a look around. Behind the desk, she noted a track area. Picking up the sharp scent of chlorine, she walked over to a steam-covered window and found a large indoor pool in the adjoining room. Several patrons were swimming laps, completely oblivious to her watchful eye.

Backtracking toward the main reception area, she spied a stairway leading down, and assumed it led to the locker rooms. On either side, the walls displayed bulletin boards, full of class schedules, related events in the community, and random tips from popular fitness magazines. There was also a board devoted to action snapshots. Deborah scanned the happy faces of a women's aerobics class, then of a martial arts class. Many others consisted of individuals in the midst of their workout. She realized a number of the photos included a man of medium build, with sandy red hair and dark green eyes fringed with beautifully dark lashes. She was taken with his boyish good looks, reminding her of the movie stars who always play the kindhearted Everyman heroes. He was rarely photographed alone, but instead was candidly caught helping a child in the pool or hugging a grandmotherly woman. It reminded her of a family's photo album. McCullough's Gym definitely appeared to be a closely knit enterprise.

Just past the stairs, Deborah poked her head into an empty weight room attached to a large open area, probably where the classes were held. Noticing a doorway, Deborah proceeded into the main area, containing various cardiovascular and Universal equipment. A man occupied one machine, simulating a bench press. Upon closer inspection, she recognized him as the handsome redheaded man from the pictures. Realizing he was oblivious to her presence, Deborah watched him for a moment. *He must really be in a hurry,* she thought, wincing at the uncontrolled quickness with which he released the weight and allowed the plates to slam into each other. *Well, I may not work here yet, but I can't allow some obviously devoted patron to injure himself. Just a quick word of unsolicited correction, and I'll go find the office.*

Strolling confidently over to the machine, she positioned herself to look straight down at the man. "Hello, sir. I know you don't know me, but I couldn't help noticing you're improperly releasing the weight. You're just letting gravity take over instead of controlling it all the way down. I wouldn't want you to hurt yourself, or anything. Plus, if you do it the right way, you'll allow the muscles to work even harder, and that'll improve your results." Smiling broadly, Deborah took in the stunned expression on the man's face.

"I assure you I know how to lift weights, ma'am. I . . ."

"No, no. I wasn't trying to insinuate that you don't. It's just that I am pretty well versed in weight lifting and exercise in general. Here, hop up and let me show you what I mean." All but shoving the man out of the way, Deborah set her résumé on the floor and lay down on the bench. "Here, watch. Count it out. Lift and exhale, one, two, three, four, five. Hold, two, three, four, five. Bring it down and inhale, one, two, three, four, five. See?" Deborah sat up and waited for his response.

"That's what I was doing. I think you should know . . ."

"Nope. You were doing it like this—watch." Lying back down, Deborah lifted slowly, and brought the weight back down immediately, the plates making a loud "clank." "When you do it correctly, you shouldn't be able to hear the weight when it returns to its original position. Let that be your guide." She wasn't sure, but she thought the man blushed ever so slightly. "I didn't mean to embarrass you or anything. I just wanted to help." Extending her hand, she added, "I'm Debbie Shaughnessy."

The man returned the handshake and introduced himself. Deborah felt her face drain of all color when he stated simply, "I'm Aidan McCullough, the owner."

છે

As much as he wanted to remain indignant about her admonishment, Aidan couldn't help but be humbled. After all, she was right. He was rushing through the sets, and he knew better. And this way, he knew she had her facts straight. *Lord, the next time I pray for a sign, remind me to put some stipulations on it; but I must admit, You know how to cure a man of his pride!*

"Ms. Shaughnessy, it's good to see you. I'm sorry I wasn't out front to greet you, but you appear to have found your way around without too much of a problem." He was amused by her chagrin, but he knew he should apologize for his behavior. "Look, I didn't mean to make you feel bad. You were absolutely right. I wasn't using the proper technique, and while my muscles will probably survive, my pride was definitely injured. But that's no reason for you to hold back when it's obvious someone is going about something the wrong way. Especially when it can be as potentially dangerous as poorly executed weight lifting. I'll expect no less of you when you are here."

"You mean you'll still consider hiring me? You have to admit, that was an awful interview."

He could tell that she was still kicking herself, but he liked the edge of humor. "Yes, and you're right. That was not much of an interview, though its failure is mostly due to me. So how about we go out front and try again?" He accepted the proffered résumé and had to struggle to hide his surprise when he received not a page, but what felt like an entire ream of paper. Debbie nodded proudly and followed him back to the front desk.

Offering her a chair, Aidan sat down and began to scan the document. Over the pages, he found her beaming the same smile as when she appeared from nowhere at his machine. Apparently, her "novel" was something that registered an emotion quite unrelated to shame. This charmed him further, for reasons beyond his understanding.

"Let me begin by giving you a little information about myself and the gym. I've been running McCullough's for about three years now. My father decided to start a family-atmosphere gym fifteen years ago. When I graduated from college with a degree in physical therapy, he turned ownership over to me, and he and my mother relocated to Ireland, where my paternal great-grandfather was born. McCullough's Gym is a very prosperous business. My father wanted to maintain the highest quality of fitness facilities, and I feel the same way.

"Our clients are dedicated to improving their health and well-being, so we don't encounter a lot of improper use of equipment. You also won't find the gym very crowded. Our facilities are state of the art and meticulously maintained. We offer assistance to our clients, such as discounted family memberships, free junior gym for their children, and adjusted fees for individuals who are struggling with financial difficulties. We want everyone to feel as though this is their home away from home.

"As for me, I think of my apartment as my home away from home. I can't imagine doing anything else with my life. If you become part of our staff, you become part of our family. It's hard work, but it's incredibly rewarding.

"So, now that you know the basics about McCullough's, tell me a bit about yourself and why you want to work here. I see you have had a lot of experience, but most of it is unrelated to teaching an aerobics class." He leaned back in his chair, eager to hear her answer.

"Well, I've been attending the University of Kansas for two years, off and on. The bulk of my classes centered around physical education. For awhile, I thought I might major in physical therapy or something similar. I really enjoy exercise—especially aerobics. I was never graceful enough for dance classes, so the thought of jumping around to choreographed moves in a gym was as close as I could come." She laughed. The sound was melodic and genuine.

Aidan found himself mesmerized by her features. The bright, beaming smile. The deep brown eyes, eyes that always seemed to be amused, but in a way that said, "I know what you're up to." Her shoulder-length waves of auburn hair suggested a color Aidan thought could only be achieved in summer sunsets and autumn plumage. She had fair skin, porcelain-smooth and flushed slightly pink in her excitement.

He surveyed her outfit, a tasteful pantsuit of deep green. Her jewelry was modest, diamond solitaire earrings and a simple braided gold chain. Smiling, he recalled how eagerly she fell into the role of a trainer. He liked that she was not rendered a mannequin just because she had on a pair of pumps. In many ways, she reminded him of Maureen.

32

Realizing the awkward silence, Aidan coughed nervously. "I'm sorry. My thoughts were elsewhere."

He saw her soften. "Oh, were you thinking about your sister? I forgot that was why you needed me." She leaned forward, her dazzling eyes fixed on him. He was touched that she would recall his brief statement about Maureen during her call.

"Yes, well, in a roundabout way," he said, careful not to lie, nor reveal his appraisal. Quickly, he resumed the interview, "Let's continue. Would you be available to do reception work, light cleaning, and general instruction, as well as teach the two aerobics classes? It would equal anywhere from six to ten hours a day. Since there are just three of us—me, Maureen, and her husband Tom—we put in many long hours. We basically live here."

"I walked around quite a bit. I didn't see everything, though, so I have to ask—do we sleep downstairs, or will I have a cot in the back?" Debbie giggled. She then added seriously, "Yes, I will have total flexibility for the next nine months."

"I know it sounds like an overwhelming amount of work, and it is. But, believe me, it's a lot of fun, too. I don't want you to think you won't be appreciated. I just want to be completely up front about what the position requires." Aidan didn't want to scare her off—quite the contrary, he wanted her to agree more than anything—but he couldn't allow her to accept the job if she didn't understand all that it encompassed.

"It will be great here. Your sister probably helped out in a lot of ways that you've only begun to notice in her absence. At least, that's how it would be for me. It's like when my water pipes burst in my last apartment. I figured on no water, in the sense of no showers and no dishwashing; but the first time I went to refill the ice cube tray, I was baffled, trying to figure out what was going on. Not that your sister is anything like a water pipe, but you know what I mean."

Aidan nodded and chuckled. "Well, no, Maureen's not a pipe,

but I do understand your point." He liked this woman. Really liked her. But something was gnawing at the back of his mind. *It has to be dealt with,* he thought. Collecting his Interviewing Employer persona, he tried to make the inquiry seem as gentle as possible. "Ms. Shaughnessy—"

"Debbie. Please call me Debbie. Ms. Shaughnessy sounds like I should be teaching algebra instead of aerobics."

"All right, Debbie. Can you tell me about your previous jobs?"

"Definitely. Which one would you like to know about? There are quite a few, and I wouldn't want to bore you by going through them all." She seemed to have warmed to this topic, which was not what he expected.

"Well, that's what I'd like you to tell me about, Debbie. Why are there so many? Did you have personal conflicts? Religious conflicts?" Aidan waited anxiously for her reply.

"The issue is this, Aidan—may I call you Aidan?" He nodded, his impatience to know the young woman before him mounting inexplicably. "As I was saying, the issue is this: I loved all my jobs. I enjoyed everything I did, with the exception of my brief romp in factory work. I couldn't stand that. So monotonous. But everything else was terrific. They were all valuable learning experiences, and that's what I'm about. I want to learn everything so I can find my passion. I'm looking for the Sparkles, Aidan. Plain and simple." She acted as though her explanation cleared up the matter, but Aidan was more confused than before.

"Excuse me? The Sparkles?" He hoped he wouldn't be sorry. The last thing he wanted was for Debbie to be some New-Ager, tossing around "enlightened" terminology originating in some mystic's can of soda. He knew if that were the case, they could never work together. He would never insult his God with her foolishness.

"Oh, I'm sorry. That's something I came up with as a child. It's like, well, hmmm. What's your favorite song?"

Thrown, Aidan stammered. "Uh . . . it's 'Pachelbel's Canon in D.' Why?"

"Do you remember what it felt like the first time you ever heard it? The tingly feeling, like when your hand goes to sleep—only it's all over your whole body? That's the Sparkles. When you find something that's 'right,' you get them. That's what I'm looking for."

"Oh, I see. Well, do you have them now?" Immediately, he regretted his question. He found himself drawn to her and realized he wanted her to have her "Sparkles." *Lord, I don't know what's happening to me. Please guide me and help me not to be imprudent.*

"Well, I sort of got them out front, but I think I'm just excited to have a new job." Unoffended by the personal question, she paused. "So, do I have the job?"

"Just let me check your references, and I'll call you as soon as I know." Aidan was very interested to hear what her prior employers had to say about this enchanting young woman in search of the Sparkles.

5

*N*ervously, Aidan chewed on his pen cap as he waited for someone to answer his call. On the seventh ring, a tired voice answered, "Susan's Little Ones. Susan speaking."

Aidan immediately adjusted his posture. "Yes, my name is Aidan McCullough, and I am calling to get a reference on a Debbie Shaughnessy. Am I speaking with Susan Conner?"

"You are. What job has Deb applied for?" Susan's interest and affection were very evident.

"I'm the owner of McCullough's Gym, and I am hiring for an aerobics instructor-slash-desk help-slash-personal relations position." Chuckling mildly, he added, "It's really a mixture of positions, all melded into one. I called because she listed you as both a business and a personal reference. I'm wondering if you could answer a few questions about her performance for me."

"Of course! Deb's a wonderful girl. Just fabulous. I love her and so do the children. What would you like to know?"

How about everything? he thought wistfully. Instead, he answered, "Just the basics. Was she absent often?"

"No. Hardly ever. She came down sick with the flu right after she started, but other than that, she was here every day with a smile and ready to work."

"Would you hire her to work for you again?" He held his breath, fearing this woman would say no. Perhaps she knew something about Debbie's personality that caused her to flee from so many jobs. He dreaded the possibility that her numerous resig-

nations were the product of options offered by lenient management—"Quit, or we'll be forced to terminate you."

"Absolutely. In a heartbeat. I was so sad to see her go. I love
that girl. Deb has such a way about her. She's very friendly. Very
efficient. I actually told her when she left that she'd be welcome
back at any time. Gave her a total open-door policy. She can work
for a day or a month or a year. I don't have any qualms whatsoever.
No questions asked. It's so hard to find decent help in the child-
care industry when you're just a small business. Deb was top-
notch, despite her age. I think that actually gave her an edge over
me. Tons of energy, and the patience of a saint."

Susan paused, and Aidan waited for her to continue. He willed
himself to follow the proper guidelines of confidentiality, but his
mind was screaming, *Then why did you let her go?*

"Ms. Conner, can you tell me anything else about Ms. Shaughnessy?" Aidan hoped his voice wouldn't betray his tension, but he
couldn't understand why Debbie would leave. She obviously
thought highly of her employers—that much was evident in her
interview. But now, to know her employers esteemed her equally,
if not more so, he was at a loss. Why would anyone quit a job,
let alone fifteen, if she was so happy?

"I wish I knew what else to say, Mr. McCullough. I strongly
recommend her. She is a hard person to capture with words, as I
am sure you understand if you interviewed her. She's a free spirit,
but she's definitely a good worker. You'll come to love her almost
overnight. That's just how Deb is. She used to go to my church.
That's how we met. She had the entire congregation wrapped
around her little finger, though she would never take advantage
of anyone. I adored her."

"Then why did you let her quit?" Aidan winced as soon as the
words escaped his mouth. This was too personal. The etiquette of
questioning was such that he could ask whatever he liked, but she
was only obligated to tell him the basics. He knew better than to

ask, but he just couldn't get past all the positive endorsements. The employers were so full of praise for her performance, and he couldn't make the pieces fit together. *But it's none of my business,* he scolded himself. Now, it was too late. "Ms. Conner, I apologize. You don't have to answer."

"It's all right. I remember being just as frustrated as you are now when I was hiring her. As to why I 'let' her go, I assure you I did nothing of the sort. I begged her to stay. She said that while she loved the job, she feared it wasn't the perfect one for her. I had to respect that. I knew she wouldn't stay forever, but Deb's got it in her head that a promotion is equal to a lifetime contract. I truly believe she was scared. Scared to settle. I pray she's changed, but I know she's got God at a distance. As long as that is her way, she'll never know peace. I apologize if my opinion offends you, Mr. McCullough. You asked a question, and that's my answer. I do hope you hire her. I think you will be just as pleased with her as I was."

"No, Ma'am, I'm not offended at all. As a matter of fact, our beliefs are very similar, indeed." Aidan could hear the sound of children arguing in the background and Susan reprimanding them in a hushed manner.

"Mr. McCullough, I need to go. I trust the information I've given you will be sufficient."

"More than sufficient, Ms. Conner. Thank you for your time." As he hung up the phone, he was already well in prayer. *Lord, I guess I really could've botched that with my impulsive tongue. I don't know why this girl is so vexing to me. If she needs You in her life, I pray that You will use me in whatever manner that will glorify You most. Please conform me to Your will. In Jesus' name, amen.*

Checking the top of her résumé, Aidan dialed Debbie's number. She picked up on the first ring.

"Hello?"

"Debbie, this is Aidan at McCullough's Gym. I'm calling to let you know all your references came back positive. If you're still interested, we'd love to have you."

"Great! I am really looking forward to it. When can I start?"

"How about tonight, say four-thirty?"

"Sounds fabulous. I'll be there with barbells on." At that she giggled.

Aidan smiled. "All right; see you then." It was only after he began to tidy the desk area that he realized he had known her voice, simply by her "hello." And what a lovely voice it was.

❧

Deborah began dancing around her apartment in an invisible congo line, singing at the top of her lungs. "I just got a jah-OB! I just got a jah-ob!" It seemed odd that new employment would still thrill her, but it did. Twirling her way over to the closet, she selected her sportiest outfit. She opted for a heather gray tee shirt, boasting the University of Kansas's athletic department in navy blue, block letters and navy drawstring sweatpants. Realizing she still had over an hour before her scheduled start time, she called Chris.

"Guess who's a brand-new aerobics instructor?"

"Congratulations, Debbie! When do you start?"

"At four-thirty. How about a celebration supper?"

"Are you sure, Debbie? I would think the last thing you'd want to do is fill up before you need to go jump around for an hour."

"No, no! Tonight's only orientation. Paperwork and such."

"Then it sounds terrific. But it'll have to be my treat, of course."

"Of course! But we'd better hurry. I don't want to be late on my first day."

"Do you want me to come pick you up?"

"No, we'd better drive separately in case time gets away from us. I'm going to call Cali, so I'll let you go. Let's meet at that fifties' diner place by the movie store."

"Yum! See you there."

ঽ৶

At a quarter after four, Aidan looked up to find Debbie strolling confidently across the parking lot. She was dressed more casually, with her coppery ringlets caught up in a short ponytail. Shorter layers underneath escaped their confines and softened her appearance. He was relieved she didn't show up in the popular aerobic attire of cropped latex tops and painted-on leggings, but instead chose a more demure and functional outfit of good ole sweats and a light tee shirt. He opened the door for her and smiled. "Good evening, Debbie. You look like you're ready to go to work."

Her eyes were as dark and sweet as chocolate syrup. "Always!" she replied, winking playfully. "So what's the plan, Boss?"

"Well, I figured we'd get your paperwork filled out and get you acquainted with the patrons and the equipment."

"Hey, wait a minute. Do we have to call you 'Boss' now? When did this start?"

Aidan recognized the voice, thick with feigned confusion. "Debbie, this is my brother-in-law and best friend, Tom Smith." Leaning in closer, he whispered, "He also thinks he's funny. Just humor him."

"I heard that. Don't make me tell my wife on you." Cupping his hand beside his mouth, he pretended to yell in a childlike voice. "Maure-eee-en! Aidan's making fun of me!"

Aidan rolled his eyes, and Debbie laughed. He was glad to see her open and comfortable so quickly. "What do you say we get to work, Debbie?"

"Sounds like a plan. It was nice to meet you, Tom. Even if you are a tattletale."

Turning back to Tom, Aidan wagged a finger accusingly. "Looks like you've been found out, Mr. Smith. And so early in the evening, too."

Tom feigned a stricken look. "How can you resort to name-calling? I'm crushed!"

"I'm sorry, Tom." Debbie's face assumed a look of introspection. "Perhaps I'm not cut out to be an aerobics instructor, after all."

Tom began to protest, and Aidan feared his companion had offended the new hire. Debbie continued to nod thoughtfully. "Yes, I think I'm better suited for something else. That's it! I should definitely be an umpire."

Aidan wrinkled his eyebrows in confusion. "Why?"

Grinning with smug satisfaction, she stated matter-of-factly, "Because I call 'em like I see 'em."

Tom slapped his forehead with the palm of his hand. "Ugh. Maureen has got to meet this woman."

❧

Deborah watched Aidan as he briefly stopped her training to help an elderly woman decode the treadmill. He wore a loose, white tank top and a pair of hunter green gym shorts. *They're the same color as his eyes,* she thought.

Tenderly, he coached the woman on which programs would be most beneficial and showed her how to adjust the elevation and the speed. His medium frame bent over slightly to meet the grateful client's withering form. Deborah smiled. How could Chris say he wasn't attractive?

His hair wasn't quite wavy or straight. It was terra-cotta in color and caught the light beautifully. It seemed as though millions of tiny embers danced throughout his thick mane. It was almost long enough to be considered shaggy, but styled enough to excuse the long overdue need for a trim. He had a square jaw and a narrow, chiseled nose, sprinkled with freckles. And as for his physique, well, Deborah knew he followed his own advice. While he wasn't bulging with muscles, his arms and legs were lean and well defined. But what truly captured her attention was that smile. It was soft and sweet, almost hinting at embarrassment. She found she couldn't look at it without grinning like an idiot, herself.

"You ready to keep going?"

Aidan's voice shattered her concentration. For a moment, she felt her face grow hot. "Definitely. Let's press on."

"Well, over here, we have our bulletin boards," he said, stopping just short of the stairwell. "Here are the class schedules. These two classes, 'Lo-Gear' and 'Hi-Gear,' were Maureen's. They're the ones you'll be in charge of. We'll go ahead and take a snapshot of you and post it so the ladies will be able to put a name with a face. The classes are staggered so you will never have two on the same day. 'Low' meets only twice a week and 'High' meets every other day. We're not open on Sundays, so you'll always have at least one day off. Make sense so far?"

Deborah nodded eagerly, allowing her brain to sort and file the information.

"So when will the classes resume?" she asked, committing times and days to memory.

"Whenever you feel comfortable. But no later than next week." He smiled and added, "Of course, there's no pressure."

"No, no, naturally," Deborah countered good-naturedly. "I suppose my plan for saving the whales will need to be submitted in triplicate before I can assume any responsibilities."

Aidan chuckled and she briefly lost herself in the green depths of his eyes as she turned to face him. *Knock it off, Deb. You're acting like a silly teenager.* Her split-second chiding gave way to a spurt of energy, and she walked quickly to the next board.

"Are all of these pictures of regulars?" She hoped her inquiries would divert his attention back to the orientation and away from her dazed appearance moments before. Thankfully, Aidan didn't seem to notice. He joined her promptly, but his nearness made her suddenly woozy.

"Yes, they are. As I told you, we have a small, but loyal group of clients. This one here is of the low-impact class. The woman with the bright red hair is my sister." Deborah studied the tiny image, immediately recognizing a family resemblance. Smile and nod. Smile and nod. She forced herself to concentrate on the photos, rather than the musky scent of Aidan's aftershave.

"Let's move on. We'll have plenty of time to meet these fine folks in the flesh. I want to show you where you'll be teaching." Aidan's powerful strides made it difficult for her to keep up, but she appreciated the time to compose herself. She quickly looked from side to side, absorbing anything and everything that wasn't Aidan McCullough.

6

*S*o what do you think of the new girl?"

Aidan felt his face flush at Maureen's question. "She seems like she'll work out fine," he answered curtly, focusing undue attention on the blackened chicken breast before him.

"I should hope so, with the way the tops of your ears are blending with your hair, little brother. Anything you'd care to elaborate on?" Maureen cupped her chin in her hands and lifted her eyebrows expectantly.

"C'mon, Sis. It's the spicy food you're forcing me to eat. You know Cajun cooking turns my ears red." He hoped she would leave the subject alone, but deep down, he knew better.

"Yeah, right. Tell me about the woman who's taken my place at the gym, as well as in your affections. I've never seen you this worked up about a girl before. Except for Megan Tyler. Ah . . . fourth-grade love revisited." Her self-satisfied smile assured Aidan that the fight was far from over.

Tom attempted a rescue. "Hey, sweetie, tell us how the doctor's visit went."

"Nice try, hon, but I promise I'll still be pregnant after Aidan tells us about the cause of the sparkles in his eyes."

At the word "sparkles," Aidan promptly choked on a mouthful of milk. Quickly regaining his composure, he ran a hand through his thick hair and looked around, as though some external force had caused his accident. Maureen seemed to burst with laughter, and even Tom couldn't contain himself.

"What happened there, Aidan? I've never seen Cajun cooking

do that to you before. However, you did frequently experience similar problems when confronted about Miss Megan. Hmmm . . ."

Knowing he was backed into a corner, Aidan waved his white napkin in submission. "All right, all right. I'm smitten. But that's only because she's so mysterious."

Tom nodded emphatically. "And we boys do love a mystery. Especially redheaded ones with spunk." His hand darted out and tickled Maureen's unguarded side.

Maureen attempted to parry her husband's attack. "Now, calm down, you. Let the man continue. Aidan?"

"It's nothing, really. Her name is Debbie Shaughnessy. She's twenty, beautiful, and a job-hopper." Aidan took a bite of dirty rice and shrugged his shoulders. What more could he say about her?

"A job-hopper?" Maureen rolled her eyes. "You kids and your newfangled vocabulary. Please, Mr. McCullough, enlighten us."

"It's just what it sounds like. She hops from job to job, for no apparent reason. She's an employment frog, if you will. A vocational kangaroo. A . . ."

"Enough!" Maureen roared with laughter.

"What? I'm just trying to explain. That's what intrigues me. She's had fifteen jobs in two years, and from all I can gather, every one of her employers adored her. And she adored them!" Aidan shook his head, dazed by the facts once again.

"I don't see what the problem is, Aidan. Are you worried she'll leave the gym before I get back?"

"No, no. I should be, but honestly, Maureen, I'm not. I can't even give you a reason why. I just wonder what would drive her to abandon so many other jobs she clearly enjoyed. She told me she's looking for the "Sparkles"—you know, a tingly feeling that lets her know she's in the right place. I've never met anyone so obsessed with . . . well, I don't even know what to call it. I can't picture not having a straightforward plan that hinged on God's will. I can't fathom not knowing what I want to do." Aidan relaxed into the ladder-back chair and sighed. "I can't imagine what it would be like to be her."

"Maybe it's not so complicated as you're making it out to be," Maureen said tenderly. "Maybe she's just exploring her options. She's young. Now is the time for her to experience a myriad of different things in order to discover her passion."

"Could be. I just don't know how to define her. She appears to be very motivated and self-confident. She's quirky and fun-loving. And she's got a great sense of humor." Aidan felt his mind drifting off, bringing a picture of Debbie into focus.

"Looks like she's also got herself an Irish admirer, judging by that goofy grin on your face. When can I meet her?"

"Tomorrow morning. And if you mention this dinner or my fourth-grade year—in any capacity—you will rue the day, Mrs. Smith," he warned with false bravado.

"I wouldn't dream of it," Maureen assured, patting his forearm condescendingly. "Don't you worry. I won't reveal your latest crush to anyone. Except maybe to Mrs. Wittenburg. She's been worried about you, you know."

❧

With a skip in her step, Deborah made it to her apartment door. As soon as she got inside, the phone rang.

"Deborah," her mother asked, "how are you?"

Instantly, Deborah felt a dark cloud invade her enthusiasm. Why did it have to be her? Overwhelmed with guilt for her feelings, she dejectedly sought solace in her shaggy love seat. "Hi, Mom."

"I just called to tell you we won't be down next month, after all. The vacation time we requested was postponed due to a high workload. I know I've said it before, but I'll say it again—I can't stand that place! You know, I actually created a countdown to retirement. I keep it posted in my cubicle. It is quite a daunting number, when you see it written out, but I just take comfort in the fact that it's getting smaller day by day."

"Why don't you find something else to do, Mom? Maybe crafts or writing or church work." Deborah knew her efforts were in vain. Her mother and father wore their misery like badges of honor and reigned unchallenged as the Ultimate Martyrs of the State of Oregon.

"Oh, sweetie, it's too late for me to change jobs. Besides, I'd have to start all over, and I'd end up someplace worse than where I am. But mark my words, Deb, we are reaping what we have sown. God is punishing us for our faithlessness as young adults. We must endure this trial and recognize it for what it is—divine discipline. That's why I am constantly urging you to be careful and find the perfect job, and the perfect home. And," she lowered her voice considerably, "the perfect mate. You don't want to anger the Lord by not proceeding with caution. Don't throw yourself into the first supposedly good thing that comes along. You'll end up like me, baby, and I don't want that for you." Deborah closed her eyes. She recalled her mother's words from her youth.

"You must always remember to not anger the Lord. If you sin, you will be punished. Never forget to fear Him, for this is what He desires, Debbie."

She had been read stories from the Bible to reiterate this—the Flood, Sodom and Gomorrah, and so many others. Of course, Deborah never actually read them herself, but she didn't need to. No, she understood that she served the same vengeful God as her parents. She had no desire to do anything beyond the bare minimum to save her soul from hell.

"Deb, are you still there?" Her mother's voice sounded so strained, so tired. She longed to cry out to God and demand an answer as to why He punished those He claimed to love. She wanted to know why He caused her mother to suffer as she did, but she knew better than to question Him. Or Kathleen Shaughnessy.

"Yes, Mom, I'm here. I'm just really tired. I took a job at a fitness club here in Kansas City, and today was my first day." She held her breath, waiting for the inevitable interrogation.

"Did you let them know it would only be a temporary position for you? Do they understand you are still exploring your options? You did tell them that, didn't you, dear?"

"I didn't have to. It is only for a maximum of nine months. The owner's sister is out with a complicated pregnancy, and I will be filling in for her until the babies are born. They expect her to return full time as soon as possible. As I understand it, everyone was extremely sad to see her go. I don't think my being there will change their plans."

"Well, good. You are so precious to me. I love you, and I only want the best for you. I can say beyond any doubt, I don't think you will be happy working in some gym. But for now, it should be all right." Deborah was relieved her mother stopped so soon. She took advantage of her docile state and quickly said her good-byes.

Deciding to run a hot, soothing shower, Deborah locked the door and headed toward her makeshift bedroom, directly beyond her sparse living room setup. After quickly donning a terry-cloth robe, she stepped onto the cold tile floor of the bathroom. Fixing the temperature, she allowed the steaming streams of water to mingle with her tears.

Why does she upset me so much? Why do I feel so afraid all the time? I wish I could just talk to God, or scream at Him or something. I feel like walls and judges surround me, as though my life were some Olympic event. I feel so alone.

Half an hour later, she emerged feeling clean on the outside, but stale and dusty on the inside. She slipped her nightgown over her head, secured her robe, then selected a movie and sat down to watch it.

I love movies. You can just pop them in and fade off to another world.

Her thoughts were tinged with despondency. How often had she wished her life were a movie? A feature film promising resolution in less than two hours' time. Perhaps a lighthearted comedy, in which her mother and father could be happy—for themselves, as well as for her.

Her melancholy thoughts were interrupted by a light knock at the door. Through the peephole, she saw Cali and Chris holding bottles of soda and bags of microwave popcorn.

"Open up!" Cali shouted gruffly. "We know you're in there!"

Unlocking the dead bolt, Deborah consciously adjusted her countenance and flung the door open. "You'll never take me alive!" she cried in her best mobster impression. "Don't make a move, or the fish gets it."

Chris pushed her way inside, crying in mock desperation. "Gil, Gil, speak to me! Oh, no, he's in shock! He's frozen like this." She opened her eyes wide and rounded her mouth into an oval. "What did you do to him, you scoundrel!"

"I fed him microwave burritos." Deborah narrowed her eyes menacingly and enunciated her words slowly.

"You're a bad egg, Debbie Shaughnessy. Here, put this in the microwave for three minutes." Cali tossed a bag of popcorn at her and plopped down on the love seat. "How about we go couch shopping—soon." She picked at the orange strands, her face contorted in disgust. "This is so disco. It needs to be put out of its misery."

Deborah reached out and caressed the sofa lovingly. "Leave my sheepdogs alone, Cali. They're gonna grow up to be a big couch someday. Aren't you, fellas?" She stroked the back of the orange beast as though lovingly attending a favorite pet. "You'll see. Then you'll be sorry," she said, nodding to her friends. "I won't even let you have pick of the litter."

"Quick, tie her down. Now she's seriously lost it. Debbie, you can't talk to furniture. The men in the white coats will hear you and take you away." Chris handed her a glass of soda. "Here, just drink this and try to relax."

"So what are we watching? Not another musical!" Cali buried her head in her hands.

Deborah smiled and felt genuinely grateful for the distraction. *This pity party has definitely been cancelled.* "We can turn it off, and then I'll tell you all about my latest career."

"Yeah, how did it go with your new boss?"

"Well, he's super sweet. And his whole family thrives on sarcasm, so it seems."

"You should be right at home, then," Cali observed playfully.

"Definitely. Aidan showed me around the place and where my classes will be held. It was actually a lot of fun. I'm really looking forward to working there."

*D*riving south on I-35, Deborah decided she would have a fairly comfortable routine at the gym. Glancing down at the clock on her stereo faceplate, she smiled. This job afforded her more time off than she realized. She was scheduled to arrive at ten o'clock in the morning and would stay until seven in the evening. Although Chris had been aghast at the hours, Deborah relished them. Having been a waitress for the past four months, quitting times were no more than a loose suggestion. Sure, it might say you could leave at close, but that was rarely ever the case. However, the order and certainty created mixed feelings within her.

Aidan had promised to introduce her to Maureen today. He had called early this morning, and Deborah hadn't been able to get back to sleep. Heading into work an hour early, she mentally walked through a workout she had designed during her freshman year at KU. First, a five-minute warm-up of stretching. Then, ten minutes of cardio—probably a jog around the track. Next, on to arms and chest: bench presses, butterflies, dumbbell curls, and triceps extensions. Switch back to cardio for thirty minutes; stretch, then shower.

After parking, she jogged to the door and headed to the open area behind the weight room. The music was dynamic, and Deborah had to consciously force herself not to bounce during her warm-up.

"Hey, what's going on?"

"Just a little prework workout." Deborah looked up from her seated hamstring extension to smile at Aidan. She fluidly switched sides, then brought herself to a cross-legged position. "So when do I get to meet Maureen?" For some reason, she was especially excited about the encounter.

"Well, she should be here pretty soon. At least she'd better be. She promised to bring doughnuts."

Deborah rolled her eyes in disgust. "What a wonderful role model you are. Doughnuts in a fitness center. Ha!"

Aidan laughed. "I thought if anyone could appreciate the irony, it'd be you. So, what's next?"

Deborah perked up at the compliment and beamed a brighter smile. "I was going to get my blood flowing with a brief jog. Care to join me?" Realizing she wanted him to say yes, she inwardly cringed. *My emotions are running wild! This man is a temporary fixture in my life. I can't be getting all mushy and attached.* Even so, she felt as though she were walking on air as he accompanied her to the track.

"So, tell me about yourself." Aidan words were smooth despite the rapid pace of their run. *He's done this before,* she thought with a grin.

"What do you want to know? Although, I must warn you— government activities may create noticeable, yet unspeakable gaps in my personal history." She was glad that she had maintained her athleticism, for she blushed even imagining her huffing and puffing self beside his toned and well-kept physique.

"You are quite a kidder, you know that?"

"What are you talking about? I am known worldwide for my ineptitude in humor." She focused on the ground ten feet in front of her, but glanced Aidan's way ever so often.

"Yeah, right. Why don't you tell me about where you grew up?"

"You first."

"Okay. I grew up in Kansas City. I lived in Lee's Summit, really. I had a great house with a huge backyard and a fortress I built with Maureen. My folks were super people, and we were raised Protestant. We had a strong Irish heritage, like I told you— my Grandpa Shawn's parents immigrated here in 1913. Even though he was born an American, he was reared with a definite Irish flair. He brought up my dad the same way, and Maureen and I experienced the same cultural exposure."

"So I guess you ate a lot of potatoes as a child."

"You betcha. But don't forget corned beef and cabbage. My Grandma Beth could cook quite a meal. He met her in high school. Mrs. Wittenburg, one of our regulars, knew both of them from adolescence." Aidan looked around and nodded. "That's her on the treadmill. Can you see her?" Deborah strained and found a tiny, ancient-looking woman wearing a broad smile and pastel blue sweat suit.

"She looks sweet. Do you know her well?"

"Do I ever. She claims I'm the mirror image of my grandfather. She's trying to marry me off to somebody."

"Who?" Deborah would've kicked herself, if it weren't for the distinct possibility of falling down. *What do you care? Do you care?*

Aidan snickered. "I don't think she much cares about the 'who' as much as the 'when.' She's got a more detailed five-year plan than the United States Congress could ever dream of. I'd be careful if I were you. She may decide to play matchmaker with you, too. But, enough about me. It's your turn."

"Well, I was born and raised in Oregon. We lived in The Dalles, and my parents still drive back and forth to Portland every day for their jobs. It was not the most exciting place for a kid to grow up, but it was safe and quiet and had beautiful scenery."

"Why did you move to Kansas? I would think being close to the ocean would be too fantastic to abandon."

"Oh, I came here to go to school. My mother's sister went to KU, and since she's the only college graduate in the family, her school had the most appeal. Besides, my aunt is a great lady. Loads of fun. She's serious, like me." Deborah heard Aidan mutter in jest. "What? You don't believe I have an aunt?"

"No, no. I believe you do. I just can't imagine a family with two masters of wit. I'll bet your family reunions are a riot."

"Actually, the rest of them spend most of their time gawking at us like we have lobsters crawling out of our ears. We don't blend in very well. But anyway, I am an only child, and I've lived here in Kansas for three years now." Gradually slowing her jog, she altered to a fast walk.

"I'm getting ready to do my upper-body routine, so I guess I'll talk to you later, Aidan. I enjoyed the run. And the ridicule. No, really. That was fun for me. Honest. I enjoyed it. Almost as much as when I burn the roof of my mouth, but not quite." Deborah enjoyed bantering with him. It was a great pastime with almost anyone, but Aidan seemed to take it so well. He dished out a bit of his own, too. *It's good to have a little competition, even in a sport as twisted as this,* she mused.

"I'll head up to the front desk and relieve Tom. Just come on over as soon as you finish. No hurry. Wednesdays are usually slow for us. I'll holler if Maureen shows up before you're done. And thanks for letting me run with you. I had a good time, too. Though I'm at a loss for words to describe it, in light of your colorful comparison."

Deborah curtseyed daintily and replied, "Well, I thank you for the recognition. It's not every day one is acknowledged for his or her outstanding sarcasm with sarcasm. You just keep working on it, Aidan, and maybe someday, you'll be as good as I am." Turning abruptly, she strolled toward the Universal machines, filled with confidence. *This is going to be too much fun.*

The workout was incredibly invigorating, Deborah decided. Having quickly showered, she hurriedly readied herself for her day. She pulled on her shoes and smiled at herself in the mirror. Exercise never failed to energize her. She bounded out of the locker room and up the stairs.

Rounding the corner, she nearly ran headlong into Aidan and a petite woman. Choking back a laugh, Deborah decided this gal looked like a smaller, feminine version of Aidan in a bright red wig. Extending a hand, she launched into an introduction. "You must be Maureen. I'm Debbie Shaughnessy. And as I understand it, you claim this man as family."

"Yes, and yes, though I have been tempted to recant the latter statement." The woman chuckled and reached up to tousle Aidan's coppery hair. "But he's all right. He's a good little guy."

Deborah gasped in surprise as Aidan gingerly lifted Maureen and teased, "Little guy, eh? I beg to differ." Setting her back down, he smiled at Deborah. "Debbie, this is my big sister, Maureen Smith."

If Debbie had known them a little better she might have joked about the term "big" sister. Maureen had to be at least half a foot shorter than Debbie. Petite and delicately structured, there was nothing at all "big" about Aidan's sister. Realizing Aidan was still talking, Debbie quickly focused her attention back on her boss.

"She'll be instructing you on the finer points of our office work, as well as disclosing her valuable aerobic techniques and acumen. I'll let you two get acquainted."

Deborah relished the familial affection. With a pang of remorse, she regretted she had never known such tender relations with anyone in her family. Quickly disposing of the bitter recollection, she put on her best smile and followed Maureen's rapid gait.

"So, Aidan tells me you're more than qualified for this position. What sort of experience do you have?"

"I haven't taught any classes, per se. I created a few routines in college, and they were graded very highly. I structured the majority of my classes around physical education. I strongly thought about getting my degree in physical therapy."

"Ahh . . . you sound just like Aidan. It started out as a requirement for him, but it quickly blossomed into a passion. So what is your degree in?"

"Oh, I don't have a degree. I stopped attending KU a year ago. They make you declare a major in your junior year, and I hadn't even the remotest idea what that should be for me."

"Well, it certainly sounds like you do. Why didn't you just put down physical therapy and change it later if your path became clearer?"

"I don't know. I guess it just seemed too permanent. I'd hate to fulfill all those PE requirements, only to discover I preferred criminal law. I'd be in college for the rest of my life!" Deborah giggled, and hoped the joke would pacify her curious companion. Honestly, she didn't know what she wanted to do, and the fear of choosing incorrectly, only to live a life filled with divine punishment, nearly paralyzed her.

Maureen led them to a small room adjacent to the entrance. Deborah was surprised she had never seen it, given all her tours. "Have a seat. This is our workstation, if you will." Deborah sat down in a cushioned seat and rolled it up to the large oak table dominating the space. Glancing around, she found more bulletin boards, covered in photos, uplifting sentiments, and Bible verses. At least, Deborah assumed they were Bible verses. She recognized John 3:16 from her childhood Sunday school classes, and the others around it spoke of peace, joy, and eternal life. *It never ceases to amaze me how people pick and choose their biblical truths,* she thought cynically. *What about the rules? The repercussions? The fear of the Lord?* Obviously, this family was living a "Happy Jesus Fairy Tale," as her mother put it. Focusing on the perks, but never stopping to ponder the consequences.

Maureen busied herself in a large file cabinet. "Aidan wanted me to have you fill out the remainder of your paperwork. Here's the last of 'em." She handed Deborah the forms and a pen. "While you do that, I'll tell you about myself and my responsibilities."

"Sounds good," Deborah replied and began to fill in the blanks.

"I assume Aidan told you we grew up in the area and have worked for my father here at the gym. I married Tom—you know, Aidan's goofy blond shadow—when I was twenty-four. He'd been helping out Dad alongside Aidan since he was a freshman. They met through their high school weight-lifting class. Anyway, I've been teaching the aerobics classes full-time for three years. Aidan wanted the staff to be family, or as close to family as he could find. I recently found out I'm pregnant. In fact, we've having twins." She touched her stomach lovingly, causing a strange twinge in Debbie. It almost felt like envy, but that was preposterous. *There's no way I envy her,* Debbie thought. *She's tied down— her choices are made. Even if she's made the wrong ones, it's too late. She'll have to reap what she's sown.*

"Anyway," Maureen continued, "with the pregnancy considered high-risk, there'll be no more jumping around for me! That's where you come in. As I'm sure you know, you'll be filling my shoes for the next nine months, or at least until the babies are born and deemed healthy enough for me to bring here to work. Do you have any questions for me?" Maureen's candid nature caught Deborah off-guard. She was so open and so bubbly. *I wonder if it's her age . . . or maybe it's because she's married. What makes her so secure? Maybe it's because she found the right things for her,* Debbie reasoned. Perhaps when a person found the perfect mate and perfect home, her life just automatically lent itself to a happily-ever-after feeling.

Feeling rather embarrassed as she realized Maureen was just looking at her, Debbie tried to act nonchalant. "Well, yeah. I suppose I do have some questions. First off, I want to make sure I understand my position. I'll be teaching both classes and helping out with desk work and maintenance, right?" Maureen nodded. "Are you still going to be here?"

"Oh, definitely. You couldn't drag me away from this place. I may not be able to teach, but I can surely hand patrons a towel and a key! I also don't want you to be bombarded with the testosterone tsunami that dominates McCullough's Gym. I think you and I will be great friends. I don't have too many girlfriends. I really look forward to having you here." She placed a warm small hand over Deborah's. "So, anything else?"

"Do you want me to teach from your steps, or should I incorporate my own? I know classes can vary—some are devoted to one routine, and others thrive on a mix. I just don't want to step on your toes." Deborah affixed her signature to the last page and turned to face Maureen. She really did look like Aidan, only with more freckles on her nose and the tops of her cheeks. Her bright green eyes were full of life and her smile was full and sincere. Her pale complexion was very similar to Deborah's. Someone could mistake them for sisters, except for the contrast of Maureen's fiery mane, and her own darker auburn locks.

"You know, I am completely open to suggestion. I typically create one basic routine, and tailor it to three or four different songs. Sometimes I'll incorporate weights or a step-platform, but they are similar, simply because the students don't have to feel overwhelmed with learning a completely different set of moves. I want them to be able to focus on sweating." At that, Maureen winked. "I would love it if you felt comfortable enough to add to the class in that way. I would be more than happy to show you my notes and let you show me what you have in mind."

Deborah could feel her face light up. This was turning out to be better than she could ever imagine. A new job, and more importantly, a fantastic new friend.

8

*H*ey, ladies! May I have your attention for a moment?" Maureen clapped her hands at the front of the room where several women gathered for their aerobics class. Deborah stood at her side, self-assured and ready for her first class—Lo-Gear. "This very talented and experienced young woman has been gracious enough to devote the next nine months or so to picking up my slack." The women giggled at this, and Deborah surmised that the leotard-clad ensemble was in the know Softly, Maureen nudged her. "Introduce yourself, Debbie."

Deborah stepped forward, and waved. "Hi, gang. My name is Debbie Shaughnessy. I'm originally from Oregon, but I moved to this area to attend KU. I studied this sort of thing extensively, and Maureen has given me the green light to teach. But, don't worry—I don't plan to reorganize the hour. Maureen let me sneak a peek at her notes, and I added a few of my favorite routine pieces, so the pace will remain the same. I'd love to get your feedback, but feel free to address any comments or concerns to Maureen as well. I know I'm still a bit of a stranger."

Maureen nodded in agreement, "As some of you know, I'll continue to work the desk and assist in any other low-stress areas, as per my physician's instructions. Like Debbie said, you're welcome to pass your observations on to me. Now, let's get started."

Debbie was met with eager smiles and murmured affirmations. "Well, then, let's get going."

੨

Aidan watched in wonder as Debbie led her class in a series of strenuous moves. *The woman wasn't kidding when she said she was qualified,* he mused. From the weight room, he had a pretty clear view of her smiling face, her cinnamon-colored ponytail bobbing with the beat of the music. She looked at peace, despite the rigors of the routine. Shifting his gaze to the women, he was relieved to find them sweating along with her. Some were smiling, some were focused on their exercise. None lagged, however. He remembered Maureen's comments, a few hours before.

"She's good, Aidan. Better than I am, even. She's got a way with this sort of thing. She showed me her routines, her music selections, and even how my routines could be blended with hers, in order to make the ladies feel more at ease. I know you wanted her to start with my plans, but honestly, I feel like it will signal to the class, as well as to Debbie, that this is her baby now. Let's allow her to do it her way. I don't think we'll be sorry."

So far as he could see, he wasn't. His eyes traveled back to Debbie and a lopsided grin settled on his face. *She is something else,* he decided. *Unfortunately, I need to get back to work and stop drooling over the help.* Just as he turned to leave, he saw Maureen, staring right at him with a smile that threatened to take over her tiny countenance. "Uh-oh," he muttered softly. "Looks like big sister caught me. Well, if she sees what I see, she'll understand."

Aidan ambled toward the front desk, lost in his thoughts. For some reason, he found himself wishing Debbie would stay permanently . . . that this gym could be their gym. He could imagine her looking up to smile at him—for him—in the middle of her classes. He could picture himself teaching tiny replicas of themselves to exercise. What he saw, he realized, was a family.

"Aidan!"

The distinct masculine voice drew him out of his fantasy. "How are you, Aaron?" He completed the last few steps to the front desk and leaned nonchalantly on the counter.

"I'm great, man. I was wondering how Chris's little friend worked out for you. Is she still here?" Aaron looked around, and

Aidan assumed the question was genuine. For a split second, though, he thought Aaron was mocking her and her multitude of jobs. Somehow implying that if she were still here, it would be a miracle. Mentally, he chided himself to be more relaxed. Debbie was not his responsibility. He had no business defending her honor—whether slights on it were real or imagined.

"Yeah, she's been here about a week. She's teaching her first class tonight, with Maureen's guidance. Honestly, though, it didn't look like she needed it."

"Well, that's good to hear. So, without further ado, I am ready for my one-on-one training session with the esteemed and lauded Mr. McCullough." Aaron's eyes crinkled into tiny half-moons as he laughed heartily.

"When will you learn, Mr. Abernathy, that it is not wise to mock the one who determines your workout?" Aidan shook his head in false disappointment. He was grateful, though. Aaron's workouts existed solely in the metal jungle of the weight room. Even with his attention on his client and friend, he was still close enough to Debbie to sneak an appreciative glance her way.

ᕗᕉ

"So, how do you feel it went?" Deborah dried her forehead and neck with one of the tiny white towels Maureen thoughtfully supplied for the class. Deep down, she knew it went surprisingly well. The women introduced themselves afterwards, resembling multicolored waves in a sea of spandex and sweats. They were, in no uncertain terms, delighted with Deborah's addition to the McCullough's Gym family. But, for some reason, Deborah found her elation hinging upon Maureen's answer.

"Oh, honey, if you have to ask . . ." Maureen stopped and placed an arm around Deborah's shoulders. "You were fabulous. They loved the steps; they loved the music; they loved you. I was impressed. I know what I saw in the workstation, but it's even better on the floor."

Deborah soaked up the approval. It felt so wonderful to be told she was doing a good job. She also felt relieved to not be consumed with worry, wondering when the questions and requests for permanency would come. Before her thoughts could travel any further, Maureen continued.

"What do you say to dinner? My treat. You go and shower, and I'll arrange everything at the desk so the boys can easily finish up."

"Oh, that sounds great. I'm starved." Deborah pivoted in place and bent down to lock up the stereo.

"I was hoping we could talk a bit more, as well. Like I said, I want us to become friends. Outside of work. Even though we'll both be here from dawn till dusk. But, hey, you know what I mean." The women laughed, and Deborah hopped down the stairs and into the locker room.

"Debbie, hi!" Untying her shoes, Deborah craned her neck sideways.

"Uh, hi there! Were you in the class tonight?" Deborah's mind raced to identify the young woman.

"Oh, well, not technically. I came in with my sister. She's in Lo-Gear. I'm in Hi-Gear, so I came to check out your style." The perky brunette did resemble one of the women in the class tonight.

"I'm sorry; I'm horrible with names. I don't recall your sister's, though I can picture a woman a few years older than yourself who looked quite a bit like you." Deborah shook her hand.

"No problem. I'm Jessica Hunter. My sister was Leah. She has been in Maureen's class for years. I started going when I got into varsity cheerleading, about eight months ago. I'm the lead caller, you know. You've gotta be in shape, or before you know it some sophomore's staking a claim on your position. Anyway, I just wanted to say my hellos before tomorrow. It'll be pretty hectic for you, I'm sure."

"So I take it you approved of my routine?" Deborah could nearly smell the desperation in the girl. The need to be taken seriously. The desire to be seen as important and mature. Unfortunately, Deborah recognized the same practices in herself, even in their current conversation. *Tell me you liked me. Tell me you'll remember me. Tell me I mean something.* The exchange was oddly humorous, like two starving women confronting the other in search of sustenance.

"Yeah, I really thought it was intense. I look forward to tomorrow. Bye, now." Abruptly, Leah left, and Deborah sighed heavily. *I hope I'm not that obvious.* Preparing for a fast shower, Deborah attempted to put the razor-sharp realization behind her.

❧

"How'd it go?" Aidan asked as Maureen approached the entrance.

"Oh, like you don't know," she teased. "I saw you ogling the help."

"I was not ogling. I was observing from a distance."

"Uh-huh, sure. Do you always observe with that silly grin?" Aidan felt his face burn and awaited further humiliation. "I've never seen you observe me that way. Or Tom. Or Mrs. Wittenburg. Or the tae-kwon-do class. Or . . ."

"All right, Mrs. Smith. That's quite enough. We can talk about this after work."

"Oh, no, we can't. I won't be here."

Aidan scrutinized her suspiciously. "What do you mean, you won't be here? Where are you going?"

"Nowhere. Why should you care what Debbie and I do outside of work? It is almost seven. You promised us we would be off at seven, right?"

Aidan knew she was enjoying this way too much, but the bait was dangling before him. Try as he might, he couldn't help but bite. "You and Debbie? You're going somewhere with Debbie? I want to go!" His voice bordered on a whine, like that of a lovesick child. *Aidan, you will never live this moment down.* Somehow, all of his pretenses of indifference vanished like fog in the presence of the sun.

Maureen refused to face him, though he could make out her smirk. She busied herself with laying out the closing paperwork and writing down the remaining duties. "She's hungry. I'm hungry. Therefore, we're going to get something to eat. And no, you can't go, because I fully intend for you to be the main topic of conversation."

"What are you going to tell her, Maureen? Don't you say bad things about me. I'm in charge here. You can't talk badly about the boss." Aidan was busily grasping at invisible straws, yet he knew he was losing horribly.

"Don't you assert your power with me, little man. I know all about you. It seems like I'd be the very last on your list to alienate. You certainly don't want her to know about the way you sucked your thumb until you were ten. Or about the tea parties you begged me to let you attend. Or the way my purple plastic pony vanished and mysteriously appeared as the charge of your army men. Do I need to continue?"

Aidan shrunk into the chair as far as he could go. "No," he muttered dejectedly. As a quiet afterthought, he added, "I just liked horses. That was all."

"Good, because Debbie's been waiting behind you for the last five minutes, and I really don't want to make her wait any longer." Maureen stuck out her tongue.

"Debbie, I . . . I . . . ." Aidan spun the chair around and sucked in his breath. His ears threatened to ignite, and his words tumbled over each other and stuck in his throat causing him to choke.

But there was no Debbie. Only a laughing Maureen, sauntering like the winner of a cowboy shoot-out toward the stairway.

Turning before she descended, she hollered out, "Gotcha!"

Aidan could only chuckle. "I've got it bad. And she knows it. Am I ever in for it now."

&

Deborah brushed her damp hair and applied a light covering of makeup. She was thankful she had thought to bring a set of casual clothes. Briefly inspecting her outfit of khaki slacks and soft-knit yellow tank top, she decided it would do. After all, she didn't need to pull out all the stops on dinner with a girlfriend. *It's not like Aidan will be there,* she reasoned, catching herself by surprise.

Exiting the locker room with her gym bag nearly bursting, she found Maureen on her way down the steps. "I was beginning to worry about you. Thought maybe you went down the drain."

Deborah smiled. "No, I was just trying to make sure I looked presentable. Didn't want you to be ashamed of me."

"Never. But let's get out of here. I'm dying for some quesadillas. I know a terrific place. Loud enough for us to remain anonymous but quiet enough to hold a conversation. Do you want to ride with me?"

"That sounds great. Let me ditch this stuff in my car. Laundry day has arrived sooner than usual!"

9

Maureen's choice for dinner was located just off of 119th and Metcalf. Surprisingly, it was not very busy, and they were seated immediately. Deborah admired the numerous Tiffany-style lamps and antique decorations while Maureen ordered their beverages. When the waiter returned and placed the sodas in front of them, Deborah realized she hadn't even begun to look through the menu.

"Oh, I'm sorry. I've never been here before. Could we have a few more minutes?" Having been a waitress herself, she was especially sensitive to the needs of her servers, no matter where the restaurant was. She felt bad when she wasn't ready to order, but since the establishment was particularly "dead," as was the lingo, she didn't worry too much.

Before the man could leave, Maureen interjected. "Please bring us the quesadilla appetizer. I've been thinking about those for the last two hours."

"You bet, ma'am. I'll get those started right away, and if you need anything else, just holler. My name is Kevin."

"Well, hello there, Kevin. I'm Maureen and this is my dear friend Debbie. We're delighted to meet you." Deborah smiled and realized Maureen was just as outgoing in public as she was in the confines of the gym. Kevin grinned, and Deborah assumed that he enjoyed the banter. She knew she had loved spunky guests when she worked in restaurants.

As he walked away, Maureen propped her face with her hands. "So, what do you think?"

"I think it looks like way more fun here than at the place where

I waited tables. I love the decor. I know it's popular in these kinds of restaurants, but I really like the way they've used the antique pieces. Especially the mirrors. I think it's so clever how they put them in the old frames. It adds so much character." Deborah looked down at the large menu. "You're going to have to suggest something. There's no way I can read all of this in one sitting."

Maureen laughed. "They do have quite a selection. Here, I'll point out my favorites, and naturally, we'll ask Kevin's opinion when he returns with our appetizer. Umm . . . the burgers are great. The fajitas, too. Ohh . . . wait. Yes, there it is. Try this chicken dish. It's smothered in mushrooms, bacon, and Swiss cheese. I adore it."

"That does sound good. What're you having?" Deborah read through the side items, and Maureen flipped through the menu's numerous pages.

"Oh, I'll probably get the combo meal, with the barbecued ribs and chicken. I love barbecue. I guess that's why I stay in Kansas City. It's what we're famous for."

"Oh, that's right. I'm not too keen on local sites—just the food since I've worked at a bunch of restaurants, so you'll have to remind me of anything overly important. I'd hate to appear out of it."

"Not a problem. We'll make sure to visit the Nelson-Atkins Art Museum, and maybe walk through an exhibit at the Art Institute by the Plaza. It's amazing how a person can live here for years and years and never take advantage of what the city has to offer."

"That's me in a nutshell. I honestly know Lawrence better than I do my own neighborhood. I live by Westport, so I'm always scared to explore too much. Quite a few places I'd rather not be seen near, if you know what I mean."

Maureen nodded. "Yep, it's a big party down there. Of course, there are a lot of neat shops tucked away, too. I remember a shop that sold those little egg-shaped dolls—you know the ones that house progressively smaller dolls inside? Oh, what're they called?" Deborah shook her head, having racked her brain, yet unable to come up with the name. Maureen appeared to be in an equal quandary. "Never mind. You know what I mean. I found some really cute ones in there. They also had some beautiful Russian Orthodox icons. I loved to look at them. If you couldn't guess, I'm a bit of an art freak."

"Yes, I picked up on that. Of course, my powerful skills of perception are honed to a fine point." Deborah sipped her soda.

"So, what do you do for fun?"

"Not much, really. I spend time with my friends, Cali and Chris. I talk to my mom on the phone, though that's not always classified as fun."

"Why not?" Maureen's interest in her was evident.

"Oh, she and my father are not exactly leading an exciting life. They've worked at the same jobs ever since I was born."

"So, why don't they change careers? They can't be that old."

"Well, no, my parents married young and had me very early in the relationship. My mom claims she would end up worse off than she is now. Claims she's lying in the bed she made."

"Do you believe that's the truth?"

"What do you mean?" Deborah's curiosity was piqued.

"Well, I suppose my faith causes me to see that line of defense as weak. If your mother is miserable and feels it's her own fault, my answer would be to seek forgiveness and repent. Then, she can open herself up to allow God to create a new thing in her life. Isaiah speaks of that."

"Don't you believe that sins are punished? I believe that is what my mother is getting at. She and Dad didn't wait for God's timing. They forced His hand. Instead of waiting for 'right,' they settled for 'right now.' "

"Sure, I believe sins are punished. They're referred to as consequences. I don't doubt that sins have consequences. And yes, some are such that you live with them for the rest of your life, for example, having a child out of wedlock. The child won't disappear, simply because you repent; but you can allow God to use that to His glory, and therefore, it becomes a new thing. Something positive. He's known for using flawed and fallible human beings to spread His plan of redemption, you know."

"I'm not sure I agree. I believe God provides us with one shot to do it the right way. That's why we must be particularly careful to make sure we're on the right path. Otherwise, we'll end up like Job, and who wants that?"

"Job wasn't tested because he made a bad choice, Debbie. Job was tested to reveal God's sovereignty, even in the midst of hardship. Have you ever read it?"

Deborah could sense the question was genuine, not an attempt to make her feel dumb. Maureen seemed to honestly care about her, even though they'd only known each other a short while. Kevin arrived with the appetizer. *Just in time to get me off the hook,* she thought.

"Can I get you ladies something for dinner?"

Having decided to go with Maureen's suggestion, Deborah ordered first. Maureen quickly followed, and Kevin disappeared.

"So?"

"So what?" Deborah desperately wanted the conversation to shift, yet she was oddly intrigued.

"Have you read Job? If you've only relied on brief summaries and commentaries, then it's understandable that you feel as you do. Many people falsely believe that Job was being 'punished' rather that 'tested.' "

"I haven't read it, myself, but my mother quotes it often. I've never felt compelled to read it." Lowering her voice to a whisper, she added, "But I don't think it was fair."

"Is that a secret?" Maureen giggled, and Deborah felt herself panicking.

"No. Well, sort of. Yes. Okay. Yes, it is." Cautiously, quietly, she attempted to explain. "I don't want to anger God. Let's just leave it there."

Maureen frowned. "I hardly think I can, after that justification. You can't keep secrets from God. He knows your heart. If you have a question, God doesn't have a problem. You can't always expect an answer, though. Not the kind we as human beings are used to."

"I just don't think we have a right to question God. After all, He laid into Job for that sort of thing. 'Where were you when I created the world?' and such. I know my place." Deborah knew if it came down to quoting Scripture with this woman, she would surely lose. After all, Maureen had taken the time to pin numerous verses all around the gym's workroom. Or at least she'd had some part in it. Deep down, Deborah felt herself becoming defensive, and almost angry. "I know what I believe," she concluded forcefully.

"I don't doubt that, Debbie. And you're right. God did take issue with Job, only to demonstrate how He knows best. He alone created the universe and everything in it. But let me ask you something. Are you saved?"

Deborah rolled her eyes. "Well, of course I'm saved. I don't want to go to hell. I made sure I told God I was a sinner and begged for His forgiveness. I did that when I was six years old. My mother had me scared out of my little mind, that sometime in the middle of the night, the world would end, and if I wasn't right with the Lord, my little body was headed straight for the fiery lake."

Maureen smiled sadly. "Is that the only thing you believe you've secured? Is that all your relationship with the Father consists of? What about His Son? Or the Holy Spirit? What about the rich and fulfilling life He has in store for you?"

"What more is there, really? I know some Christians profess that Jesus is their best Friend, and life is all rosy. But at the heart of it all, I guarantee you, is the fear of the Lord. Or at least that's how it should be." Absentmindedly, she picked at a quesadilla. *Why is this woman so interested in why I became a Christian?*

"Debbie, I will admit, as a Christian, I am so very grateful God has granted me everlasting life. Not just so I don't go to hell, though. It's more than that. The fear of the Lord is definitely something to have. But what about the joy of the Lord? That's what I depend on. I get to spend eternity with my Lord and Savior. I get to sing His praises forever. I will finally meet my Creator face-to-face and be in the presence of the One who had written my name on His hand before the formation of the earth. But while I'm here, on this planet, I can enjoy a personal relationship with Him, because of Jesus' death and resurrection. He died so we could have a bridge to the Father. So we could be cleansed of our sins— something we could never accomplish on our own. Something so fantastic, our minds couldn't even fathom to ask for. Jesus lives in me. His Holy Spirit guides me and provides me with discernment and many other gifts. He can and will do the same for you. He loves you, Debbie. You are His daughter. What Father would be so calloused as to demand our love and devotion solely out of fear?"

Deborah was at a loss for words. She had never heard these things. Sure, Chris had mentioned similar topics, and she attended churches, filled with verbose preachers and loyal members. They sang of a friendship with Jesus, and of His abounding goodness. But she'd never really heard these things. Not directed at her. It was as though she had signed on for the basic plan of salvation, and everyone else had opted for the premium package. Those sorts of things weren't for her. Now, Maureen sat here, barely more than a stranger, and had somehow broken through to her very heart. Deborah felt embarrassed for sharing what she tried so hard to keep hidden.

"You're probably right. I only know my parents are convinced their suffering is due to the mistakes and impulsive acts of their youth. I know I don't want to have that kind of life. So I am careful to explore every avenue, and I am determined to wait until everything feels right. I tried to explain it to Aidan at my interview. It's what I call 'the Sparkles.' When I get those, I know God is signaling me that I have found the correct path. I envy your confidence, Maureen. I honestly do. I found myself wondering what made you so sure of yourself. If you're telling me your God is loving and merciful, I believe you. But I've heard enough stories from my childhood—direct from the Good Book—to assure me God is not to be crossed." Pausing to nibble a bit of tortilla, she sighed. "But, if it's all right with you, I'd prefer if we talked about something else. We can discuss this again sometime, but for now, let's just keep things light."

Maureen agreed, much to Deborah's relief. "You've got it. But I will definitely take you up on your rain check. Meanwhile, tell me how you like the job so far." She precariously transferred a gooey triangle to her plate. "Mmm . . . I just love these. They have got to be the best in town."

"You've got that right. I don't think I've ever tasted anything like them. I usually hate onions and yucky vegetables like that. And as to the job, well, I simply love it."

❧

"Thanks for the ride," Debbie said as she emerged from Maureen's car. The hour was getting late, and the day was catching up with her. Stifling a yawn, she added, "Now you get home and rest. I don't want you fainting on the interstate."

"I had a good time with you, Debbie. I'm sorry we had to leave so soon. This being pregnant thing is kind of a drag sometimes."

Maureen chuckled. "But I'm so excited most of the time I can barely wait for the little ones to show up! I guess they just like to remind me they're there by making me incredibly tired. I can tell they're going to be a handful already."

Deborah waved as Maureen drove off, and began to fish for her keys. From the shadows, a man emerged and hesitantly greeted her. "Uh, hi. I'm sorry to bother you, but my car battery's dead and there's no one to give me a jump start. Would you by any chance have a pair of cables?" The man's sheepish grin and docile manner set Deborah at ease.

"You bet I do. Here, let me get them out of the trunk." Deborah located the subject of her search and walked to the back of her car. Holding individual keys up to ascertain the correct one, she propped her leg on the bumper and balanced her purse on her knee.

"I really appreciate this. I finished working out, just as they were closing here. By the time I realized everyone had left, I was stranded. Missed my little sister's school play. I feel just awful. And I know it's got to be scary with some guy out in a dark parking lot coming from out of nowhere." He stood beside her, with his hand shoved deep into his pockets. Deborah finally opened the trunk and began rummaging for the jumper cables.

"Now, don't be silly. You seem like a nice enough guy. A victim of bad luck, maybe, but nice nonetheless. I can tell these things. You've got to trust your feelings. Ahh . . . here they are." Deborah bent down and reached deep into the back. "I've got . . ."

Suddenly, she felt a sharp blow to the back of her head. Swaying momentarily, she tried to lift her hand to her head.

"You shouldn't always trust your feelings, lady."

The man grabbed her purse. He ran off into the night, and she sank to the ground and felt herself spinning into velvety blackness.

$$10$$

"Where are you off to in such a hurry?" Maureen set her huge purse on the entryway table of her home. Obviously confused by the rapid actions, she watched as Aidan scurried around to locate shoes and keys.

"I forgot to set the alarm at the gym. I don't understand how I could've done such a thing! Three-year track record, blemished beyond repair! I locked the doors, you know, but didn't remember to . . ." Aidan opened the door wide and closed it behind him with a crash. The massive oak portal widened about three inches. Aidan sheepishly emerged. "Sorry. I am just so rattled. I'll be back in ten minutes, tops. Oh, say—how'd it go with Debbie?"

Maureen smiled smugly, hands on hips. Aidan nervously licked his lips. "I guess I'll find out when I get back."

"I should say so, darting out of here like a madman, only returning to ask about Debbie! What about your sister—your flesh and blood? Don't you want to know how I am?"

Aidan rolled his eyes. "Okay, I'm wrong. Sorry. I apologize for making you feel unimportant, sister dear. It's just that, well, after your 'prank,' I don't particularly feel like wondering about your well-being." Aidan stuck out his tongue and then became more serious. "But honestly, Sis, I gotta go. I promise to return for my lashings." Maureen just laughed, and Aidan sprinted to his car.

Lord, how could I do this? This isn't like me! I feel so irresponsible. Please don't let anything bad have happened. I realize it's just a place— just things, but Dad did so much to put the place together. I don't want to be the cause of it being destroyed. He took a deep breath and tried to steady his nerves as he merged into traffic.

I pray for Your will, Father, but I also beg for Your mercy. I realize the likelihood of a gym's getting robbed is next to nil in this neighborhood, but still, I am afraid. So, in keeping with the psalms, I will trust in You. Amen.

Aidan halfheartedly sang along with the radio and drummed his fingers against the steering wheel. "Come on, hurry," he pleaded to the driver in front of him, though it appeared to have done no good. Thankful that he and his family worked and lived in Overland Park, Aidan rejoiced when he arrived in the parking lot, five minutes later.

A shadowy outline of a car instantly claimed his attention. "How strange. What's that still doing here?" Shifting down to first gear, he inspected the vehicle from the safety of his own forest green SUV. The trunk was open, but seeing no one around, he stepped down off the baseboard and jogged to the front door of McCullough's. *I've got to get the alarm set before I can investigate this,* he thought warily.

Unlocking the door with a swift flick of the wrist, he leaned to the left and brushed a stubborn palm leaf out of his way. The plant's main purpose was to hide the alarm panel, and tonight, it seemed to be doing its job a little too well. Deftly, he punched in the code, and heard the high-pitched beep that assured him the system was armed.

Relieved, he quickly exited the gym and secured the door once again. He strolled back to his Suburban. Just as he opened its door, he noticed someone's body, prone on the ground.

"What's going on?" he wondered aloud. Stepping cautiously to the rear of the Cavalier, he looked down. His senses went into overdrive. This couldn't be happening. "Debbie?" He rolled her over gently.

"Oh, no. Debbie! Can you hear me? Debbie, come on, wake

up." Aidan felt like he'd had the wind knocked out of him. A set of keys dangled from the trunk, and Debbie lay unconscious with a small tote bag just out of hand's reach beside her on the ground.

Aidan leaned his ear over her mouth. *Good, she's breathing.* Carefully placing her arms at her sides, he positioned her as straight as possible. Somehow, it seemed an orderly thing to do. Somehow, it seemed to lessen the severity of the situation.

Inspecting the bright red tote, he realized it contained jumper cables. His mind reeled. Jumper cables? What was she doing with jumper cables? Had the car refused to start? He looked to the trunk and then back at Debbie's still form. Had she hit her head? Had she fallen?

He hurried back to his car and leaned over the driver's seat to grab his cell phone. Dialing 9-1-1, he hurried back to Debbie's side and held his breath until the operator picked up. "9-1-1, what is your emergency?"

"I'm over at McCullough's Gym, 11904 95th Street. We are just across the street from Oak Park Mall. I found a young woman in the parking lot, unconscious. She's twenty years old. I don't know if she's got a concussion or what."

"Sir, please stay calm. Let me repeat the address—" Aidan was grateful the woman promised him paramedics would be there soon. Within seconds, he could hear the sirens as they quickly approached.

"Thank you. I can hear them now. I'm going to try and wake her up." Not waiting to receive a reply, Aidan hung up. "Debbie, wake up and tell me what happened. Debbie, it's Aidan. Wake up, please." Squeezing her tiny hand, he hoped the pressure would cause her to awaken. He was rewarded with a small moan and a flutter of her eyelids.

"I'm . . . sorry . . ."

Aidan was puzzled at the words. "Debbie, what are you saying?" But instead of words, she only whimpered quietly. By this time, the paramedics were on the scene, much to Aidan's relief.

"Sir, please step aside until we can get her moved and stabilized." Aidan nodded helplessly. "Her name is Debbie."

Feeling at a loss, Aidan stepped back and called Tom and Maureen, so he wouldn't feel so useless.

"Hello?" Tom's voice betrayed his concern. Aidan knew the couple never received calls after nine at night, and this would come as a particular shock.

"Tom, it's Aidan. Look, I'm here at the gym. There's a problem. I found Debbie unconscious by her car. I called the ambulance, and they're here now. I'm going to ride with her to Overland Park Memorial, and I'll call as soon as I know anything."

"We'll be praying, Aidan. I'll tell Maureen right away."

"Thanks. I think they're ready to go, so I'll talk to you soon. Look, my Suburban and her Cavalier are over here, so I'll need you to give me a ride back. I hope that won't be a problem."

"Don't be silly. Of course I will. Go on ahead. We'll talk to you soon."

Aidan disconnected the call and walked back to where the EMTs were busy assessing Debbie's condition.

"Debbie, can you open your eyes? Open your eyes." One shined a penlight into her pupil, while another took her blood pressure and pulse.

Aidan watched helplessly as the men roused Debbie from her benumbed state. Her eyes struggled against leaden lids, and she continued to whimper unintelligibly. When she appeared awake, a barrage of commands ensued.

"Debbie, stick out your tongue. Thata girl. I need you to squeeze my fingers. No, no, both hands. At the same time. Good. Now move your legs for me. Can you wiggle your toes? Okay, now, what's your name? Can you tell me your name?"

"Deb . . . rah. Deborah Shaughnessy." She sounded like someone talking in her sleep, but Aidan was still delighted that the information was accurate.

"All right, Deborah Shaughnessy, do you know where we are?"

"No. Yes," she said, seeming to struggle with the question. "Work. Parking lot. My car . . ."

"That's right; we're in the parking lot of McCullough's Gym. Do you work here?"

"Yes."

"Good. Now, Deborah, do you know what today is? Can you tell me today's date?"

With some struggle, Debbie recited the data, and then sobbed softly.

Aidan felt as though thousands of tiny daggers were piercing his heart. *Father God, please touch her. Heal her. I am powerless to help her, and I can't stand it. Please wrap Your arms around her.*

The EMT turned his head toward Aidan. "Sir, we'll still take her over to the hospital to run more thorough tests, but it appears as though she was hit on the head with a heavy object. She has a knot on the back of her skull, which could indicate something more serious, but she's responding to our voices and commands. Neurologically, that's a good sign."

Aidan nodded as he struggled to listen. Gently laying a hand upon her arm, he offered up prayers as quickly as his mind would allow. *Please protect this woman, Lord. She's got a special place in my heart, though I don't understand why. Spare her life and allow her injuries to be minor, according to Your will and steadfast love. Envelop her in Your warm embrace, and calm her spirit. In Christ's precious name, I pray, amen.*

Before they lifted her into the ambulance, Aidan stood beside the frail body of the woman with whom he had become enamoured. He could feel a dull ache in his chest as he took in her pasty pallor and blood-tangled hair. "You're going to be all right. You just have to be."

Deborah struggled to push her eyes open. *Where am I? Why do I hurt all over?* Wincing painfully as the light filtering through venetian blinds assaulted her tender eyes, she attempted to roll onto her side. The back of her head throbbed—why? She forced herself to rouse and survey her room. She was in a hospital.

"A hospital? What's wrong with me? What happened?" Frantically, she raised her voice, beseeching someone—anyone—to answer.

There was a man.

Yes, she remembered a man. A man who needed help.

He hurt me.

No, surely not! He spoke of little sisters and missed school plays. He wouldn't have hurt her!

My feelings were wrong. He said so.

Suddenly, her mind raced back to earlier that evening.

Dinner with Maureen.

Why did the thought of dinner with Maureen fill her with such panic?

You spoke out against God. He is angry with you. You have been punished.

Tears began to sting her eyes. Yes. There was no other explanation. She was suffering at the hand of Almighty God, the One who heard her announce that His ways were unjust.

Softly, she cried. In a voice no stronger than a whisper, she begged for His mercy. "I'm sorry. I didn't mean it. I won't ask any more questions. I will be good. Please don't be angry with me."

Suddenly, a noise demanded her attention. "Aidan? What are you doing here?" She hoped he hadn't heard her crying. Certainly, she could not explain her tears.

His pale skin was aglow with the light of morning. A coppery five o'clock shadow dusted his chin. His emerald eyes were heavy with concern.

"I've been waiting for you to wake up. You've been in and out all night, and we've been praying for you just as long. How do you feel?"

She could sense his tenderness—both in his words and in his expression, but his mention of prayer caused her to frown. *God made this happen to me. Pray all you like, Aidan McCullough, but He doesn't care about me.*

"Oh, me, I'm fine. I've never felt better." *Yes, that's good. Banter. The sooner he believes I'm well, the sooner he'll leave. The sooner he leaves, the fewer questions he asks.* "Don't you need to get to work?"

"I can stay awhile."

"No. I want to be alone. Really, I do."

"Are you sure?"

"Yes. Go! You have other stuff to do, anyway."

He smiled, so she smiled. "Yeah, I suppose so. I haven't gotten any sleep, though, so I may wimp out and let Tom take the helm. I think I'm going to head on home, and go to bed. I'll tell the doctor you're awake."

Don't leave, Aidan. I'm scared. Please stay. Her childlike pleas echoed in her already-pounding head. She wanted to say the words—needed to say them, but she couldn't.

Reaching for the door, he turned to her, his lopsided smile melting her heart. "You gave me quite a scare, Ms. Shaughnessy. See that it doesn't happen again. I don't think I could take it. Oh, and I'll expect you back at work very soon." Deborah gave a weak salute.

"Aye-aye, Cap'n." She was silent for a moment and then added, "Thanks for staying with me, Aidan."

She watched as his eyes crinkled and his mouth upturned. "Are you kidding? I wouldn't have missed it for the world."

Pausing, he turned again. "The doctor said you'll need round-the-clock care for the next forty-eight hours. Do you have anybody who could stay with you?"

"Yeah, sure. Cali or Chris can do it." Suddenly, she remembered the two young women were out of town, with their church singles' weeklong retreat. *Oh, no. Now what? I can't deal with this. I know what he'll suggest. . . .*

"Is there a problem?"

Deborah assumed her displeasure registered on her face. "Sort of. They're both out of town. But, really, I'll be fine. I feel much better." Fighting the urge to cry out, she painfully raised herself up to a proper seated position.

"No, you don't. You are following doctor's orders or else. I can't have you missing classes." Though his eyes twinkled mischievously, Deborah could tell he was not entirely joking. "I'll have Tom run me back to the gym to get my Suburban, and then I'm taking you over to Maureen's. And I will hear no arguments."

"I'm a grown woman, Aidan. You will not—rather, you cannot—force me to go anywhere against my wishes. I said I will be fine. Now, please leave me alone!" She regretted her harsh tone and hated the hurt look that washed over Aidan's face. But she couldn't stay with Maureen. She would want to talk more about her faith. She would question her.

"We'll see about that." Unable to say another word, Deborah watched as Aidan flashed one last smile and exited the room.

(11)

*M*aureen sat with her legs tucked under her, working halfheartedly on a crossword puzzle. Aidan sipped his iced tea pensively—questions gnawing in the back of his mind. His sister's melancholy temperament didn't ease his anxieties.

"Hey, Moe, what's wrong?" He already knew the answer. It was the same reason for his tension: Debbie.

"It's nothing new, really. My soul just aches for Debbie." Aidan nodded sadly. Maureen sighed and set the paper on the coffee table. "You know, I don't expect us to be best friends after such a short time. I don't even expect her to be thankful for my efforts. I mean, gratitude is not why I agreed to watch her and make sure she was all right. I just . . . I guess I just thought that after our initial talk, I'd made a small dent in her armor."

Aidan turned to face his sister. He noticed tears brimming in her eyes. "What do you mean?" In all of the excitement, he had forgotten to ask about that fateful evening.

"Deb has some major issues with God. She believes He's some cosmic disciplinarian and nothing more. Her parents bombarded her with that philosophy. Aidan, she actually lowered her voice to a whisper to question Him. She feared if He knew what she was thinking and the questions she has, He would become angry and smite her."

"You explained to her those fears were unfounded, right?"

"Sure, but what good does that do? If she's not ready to see the truth, I certainly can't force her. And now, with the tragedy, I know she believes God punished her for her opinion. I don't know how I know, but I do. Deep down, my spirit is telling me, 'Maureen, she thinks God caused her to be mugged.' She won't say more than three words to me. She won't open up. It's as though the drawbridge has been raised and that is the end of it."

Aidan chewed his lip and closed his eyes. "She goes home tomorrow night, right?" Maureen offered a dejected affirmation. "And she'll need the rest of the week to recuperate, according to the doctor. Maybe she just needs some space. She's awfully independent. Maybe it grieves her to see herself incapacitated."

"Aidan, I know you want her to be just like you. I know that you've fallen for her and her whimsical, happy-go-lucky persona, but I'm discerning something quite the contrary. She's lost and alone and afraid. She's running as fast and furiously as she can to make sure everyone keeps his or her distance. You're expecting after today, she'll be laughing and joking with you like before, and I am warning you here and now—that won't be the case. Our faith is going to repel her."

"You can't be serious. If anything, it should comfort her to know we care and are praying for her."

"That's true. It should comfort her. But it won't. How has she reacted when we've prayed? Think about it. I thought she was going to spit fire when Tom suggested we lay hands on her. Remember?"

But I don't want to remember. The look in her eyes was that of a caged animal. Debbie's eyes had betrayed a terror that seemed unnatural under any circumstance, but certainly it didn't fit in an atmosphere of petitioning God for her well-being. Somehow, in their caring for her physically as well as spiritually, they had managed to alienate her. He had to admit God and Debbie were not to be mentioned in the same sentence. Ever.

"I've tried to talk with her. I've confronted the issue head-on, only to be frozen out of the room. Aidan, for your own sake, let her alone. Pray, petition, fast—whatever you feel you need to do—do it quietly. Don't allow yourself to make her a project in salvation. You're going to have to trust me on this." Maureen had laid a hand on his arm to soften the stern tone in her voice.

"I've got to get out of here. I need to be alone for awhile. Don't take this personally, Sis, but I can't be here anymore. I can't believe she's beyond hope. I refuse to leave Debbie to her misconceptions and defense mechanisms. She may hate me, and that's the last thing in the world I want her to feel for me, but if it means she knows the truth, then so be it." Rising to his feet, he ran a hand through his unkempt hair.

"Please don't think I want to abandon her," Maureen said. "That's not it. I just know there are times when God must perform the work Himself, as much as we believe we should be a part of it. Don't expect her to fall into your arms and praise you for your spiritual tenacity. And don't allow this to become more about you than God. You can't save her."

"Maureen, I know that."

"Do you really? I know you, Aidan. I know your heart breaks for hurting people. I don't believe for one second that you aren't regarding what I've told you about her as a righteous challenge. And that is not necessarily a bad thing. You are on fire for God. You love Him with your entire being, and I respect and admire you for that. But you must temper these qualities when you're dealing with Debbie. She's just as headstrong as you, and she feels no less justified in her beliefs than you do in yours. Don't beat her over the head with the Bible. Love her with your actions. Show her your faith—don't tell her about it. That's the only advice I can give you if you intend to pursue this."

"I understand what you're saying, Maureen. I do. But . . . oh, I don't know what I want to say. You'll need to wake her soon, and I don't feel like I can be here when you do. I need to clear my head."

He looked at his sister, and found her smiling sadly. "Go, little brother. Pray. And I will, too."

❧

Aidan bench-pressed the heavy weight, pushing out the aggression that festered within him. "Why won't she talk to me?" His questions came out in ragged spurts. Glad for the early morning sanctuary of the gym and thankful for the rare solitude, he allowed his anxieties and frustrations to drip out of his soul like the sweat from his body.

"It's been two months—two months! I can understand the first couple of weeks. Headaches, nausea, fine." He sat up and wiped his face with a towel and took a small drink from his water bottle. "But, why is she still so distant? I saved her life! She ought to at least talk to me." Feeling like a fool, he sighed. "Instead, I'm sitting here talking to myself."

He quickly walked to the track and immediately broke out into a fast-paced jog. "Lord, please. Show me what to do. Show me how to help her. I know she liked me. She enjoyed my company. And now, it's as though we're strangers. I just want her to know the truth! Please speak to my heart, guide me, fill me."

This is how God must feel toward us. In the Garden, we were able to walk and talk with Him and rejoice in His presence. We, too, enjoyed His company. But we strayed and chose to forsake His love. He saved us, yet we continue to distance Him—be ungrateful and self-reliant. He offers us the truth, yet we shut Him out and indulge our sinful urges and willful ways.

Aidan nearly tripped over his own feet. In a moment of consuming humility, he fell to his knees. "Father, forgive me for my selfish thoughts. How familiar this must sound to You! I struggle with the affections of one woman. One hurting, confused, and beautiful woman. You battle for the hearts of the ones You created, minute by minute. I care for her, Father. I do. Even in the midst of her angry actions and the rants of her sharp tongue. But how much greater is Your love! You see her. You know her pain, her worries. Forgive me for believing this was beyond You. Help me to choose Your perfect will over my own foolish desires. I want her to be Yours, Lord. I am laying her before Your throne, and begging for mercy on her behalf. Humble me, Father. Amen."

The realization made him tingle all over, as he felt the Holy Spirit fill him. He could feel the Lord's hand upon him and could sense His presence all around.

"Oh, Debbie. If you could only feel these Sparkles . . ."

❧

"Keep it up, ladies! You're doing great!" Deborah bounced from foot to foot as she led the Hi-Gear class. Focusing on the routine, rather than Aidan's stare, she proceeded into a complex number of moves involving the plastic exercise step. The song thudded in her brain, causing her to remember her injury, now almost three months in the past. Forcing a bright smile, she continued to urge the women before her.

"We're almost through. C'mon; count with me!" The room filled with the strained voices of the fifteen participants.

Within what felt like seconds, the forty-five-minute session concluded, and women lingered only long enough to express their approval of the intense workout.

"Great job, ladies. Next time we'll break in a new routine," Debbie announced. The women voiced their approval in nods or single-word comments. Glowing from the intense workout, they headed en masse to the showers.

Debbie lingered in the gym, picking up her things. She had no desire to make small talk with the women of her class. In fact, she had no desire to talk to anyone.

Picking up her towel, she blotted the dampness on her neck and shoulders. She could feel her collarbone through the towel. She figured she'd lost a good twelve pounds in the last few months. She liked to blame it on the intensity of her workouts, but she knew better. The turmoil of her life kept her from eating properly. Even Cali and Chris were concerned.

"I'm not going to worry about it," she muttered, tossing the towel over her shoulder. Waiting until the majority had showered and departed, Deborah made her way to the locker room, proficiently avoiding Aidan and Maureen.

She breathed a sigh of relief once she was inside the protective seclusion of the locker room. Her walls of defense came down just a little as she considered the sadness she'd witnessed in Aidan's eyes this morning. *I've hurt him,* she thought. Then just as quickly she pushed the thought aside. *No, he's hurt himself.* Yes, that was it. It made perfect sense.

Aren't you tired yet?

"Excuse me?" Deborah looked around, but found no one. "Great, the blow to my head has made me daffy." Unbraiding her sweat-dampened hair, she allowed herself to rest briefly on the wooden bench in the center of the room.

Why are you running away?

Angrily, she leaped to her feet. "Who's there? And what are you talking about? You have no idea why I do what I do." Whipping her head from side to side, she scrutinized the area. Still, she was alone. Unbidden tears began to fall as the disembodied voice continued.

I know you, Deborah. I know why you run. I know you're tired. I know . . .

"Leave me alone! Whoever you are, just shut up!" Sure she was losing her mind, Deborah began to cry harder.

You don't have to be afraid.

"Yes, I do. And I have to keep running. I have to keep going. Or it'll all fall apart. I know it will. And then what? Who's going to pick up the pieces then? I'll tell you who—me. And I don't have time for that." She could hear herself, sobbing like a child lost in a crowd. She could almost feel the fear that filled her words.

Shamed, she wiped her eyes roughly with the backs of her hands and started for the showers.

Come home, Deborah.

Stopping dead in her tracks, she clenched her fist. She'd had enough and readied herself for battle. "Ha! You show me home, and I'll gladly go there. Nowhere is home. Don't you know that? I don't get to have a home. I'm not worthy of a home. I'm not worthy of security and comfort. If you knew me at all, you'd definitely know that." Her sense of powerlessness gave way to bitterness and sarcasm. Closing her mind and binding her heart, she willed the unknown antagonist to be silent. But in the solace of the shower stall, she was overwhelmed with exhaustion and despair.

By the time she arrived home that evening, she'd made a decision. She needed a change. With only a week and a half left in the month. Deborah reconstructed her cardboard boxes and began to pack. Stopping momentarily in front of the microwave, she sprinkled a few flakes of food into Gil's bowl.

"Are you ready to move?" she asked. "I think you are. How about a one-bedroom place this time? I think that sounds good. Now, eat up, lest the trip exhaust your little fishy body."

Grabbing a cold soda from the refrigerator, she opened it and took a deep drink, and then she tied her hair into a loose ponytail at the nape of her neck.

She unfolded a newspaper from a few months prior and proceeded to wrap her breakables. Tomorrow, she'd find a new apartment. For once, she appreciated her mother's counsel and her subsequent compliance to live with thirty-day lease agreements. She had to leave this place. She needed a change—effective immediately.

eborah smoothed her skirt and reached for a hymnal. Flipping through until she found the selection, she rose simultaneously and began to sing along with the large congregation. As she sang, she glanced around herself, trying to discern a familiar face. How long had she been attending this church? Six months or so, she guessed. And still, the families who stood nearby were no more familiar to her than sitcom characters. The situation reminded her of the verses she recited. Somehow, the words were embedded in her subconscious, yet she couldn't recall their significance. As far as she was concerned, they were merely old warnings and threats—promises of retribution should she stray.

As the music concluded, she sat in the small pew. Next to her, a middle-aged couple smiled their greetings and passed her the register. Mechanically, she filled in her name and checked the "Regular Attendant" box. As the pastor walked up to the pulpit, she felt her mind switch to autopilot. She bowed her head when he began to pray, and murmured affirmations right along with the others. But the words evaporated as quickly as rubbing alcohol and left her with the same chilled sensation.

Deep down, she had to admit the reason she found her way to church every Sunday was the same reason she buckled her seat belt in the car. Protection. Insurance. Just in case. At first, she had found herself stirred by the pastor's words, just as she had in the many fellowships that preceded this one. But now, she felt nothing. Instead of focusing on Pastor LeBon's interpretation of the

Sermon on the Mount, she plotted her furniture-moving agenda. *Perhaps Cali can borrow her dad's truck . . .*

Deborah quickly ingested the sacraments of Communion. *Lord God, forgive me of my sins and lead me in righteousness. Amen.* Her prayer was rehearsed. The very same one her mother and father had taught her when she was a little girl. Remarkably similar to the salvation prayer they had begged her to recite. Deborah was startled at those memories. *So what? Why should I remember this now? What difference does it make why I prayed it? The point is I prayed it . . . right?* The mounting uncertainties in her life were threatening to drive her insane.

Today, the hour-long service seemed to drag into eternity. With stiff legs, she stood for the final invitational hymn. Keys in hand and purse securely on shoulder, she edged her way to the aisle and prepared to bolt out of the sanctuary as soon as the final note faded.

The music began and the words seemed to leap out from the pages. "Softly and tenderly, Jesus is calling."

She stopped singing and felt a nagging fear grow somewhere deep inside, and by the time they reached the chorus, Debbie found it nearly impossible to breathe.

"Come home, come home. Ye who are weary, come home."

It was just as the voice had encouraged her at work. "Come home." She closed the hymnal and felt her hands begin to tremble. *This is madness,* she thought. Pure and simple. It was all too much.

I won't let this defeat me. I won't! After the move, she promised herself, *it'll be time to find a new church.*

ॐ

Aidan sat, hunched over paperwork at the front desk, trying not to eavesdrop on Debbie's phone conversation. However, when she began to lament loudly, his attention was captured.

"Oh, no! What do you mean, you can't help? I really need this, Cali. You know I can't move a couch in my tiny car." Stealing a peek, Aidan noticed her face contorting in a strange mixture of frustration, sadness, and exasperation.

"I understand. I guess it can wait. The storage unit isn't going anywhere. Oh, well. Maybe next weekend, huh? Oh, yeah? Uh-huh . . . sure. Oh, by the way—do you have any new church suggestions? I think it's time to find a 'new pew,' if you know what I mean. Oh, Pastor LeBon is great, but I just don't feel fulfilled there."

She paused for a moment and her face contorted once again. "What do you mean, I'm the problem? Come on, girl. Don't be like that. Look, you know I love you. I just don't have time to discuss this with you. I do value your opinion. Just not now, okay? I'm at work, you know. Okay. Bye." When she hung up a bit too forcefully, Aidan bolstered his confidence.

"What's going on, Debbie? Anything I can help with?" *It's hard work, trying to appear nonchalant,* he decided. Nevertheless, he didn't want to frighten or put her off. Propping his head with his hand, he leaned against the wall and faced her. All the while, he prayed for a calmness of spirit.

"It's nothing."

Still as cool as November, he concluded. When would she drop this illogical grudge? "Now, don't be silly, Debbie. I was right here. What did you need to get done? Maybe I can help."

She sighed and focused her gaze on the palm tree. "Well, I'm trying to get my couch moved, along with some other boxes. Those, I can do myself. But my car won't move a couch. It's physically impossible. It'd be like asking a fish to pull a submarine. Not happening." She smiled, and Aidan's resolve fell to pieces.

Stammering, he finally managed to reply, "I could borrow Tom and Maureen's truck . . . if you wanted me to, that is." *Father, let her say yes. Let me help her. Let her see I'm not the bad guy.*

Much to his surprise, she agreed. "That would be really sweet of you, Aidan. I would really appreciate the help. My new apartment is looking pretty sparse. How about tomorrow night, after work?" Her shapely eyebrows arched, and her deep brown eyes grew large. Aidan felt his heart skip a beat when she pursed her lips apprehensively, acting as though she feared he'd say no. Instantly, he recognized his bargaining chip and, against his better judgment, he persisted.

"I'd be happy to—if you'll come to my church next Sunday."

"What?" He couldn't be sure, but he thought the response was not entirely hostile.

"Come to church with me, Debbie. I heard that part too." As an afterthought, he added, "Sorry. I'm not usually one to eavesdrop, but you were only, like, a foot away." He grinned broadly, hoping her curiosity would win out over her dismay.

She looked at her hands for a moment as if weighing the decision carefully. "All right, Aidan McCullough. But only because I need your help. And 'need' isn't even the right word. Your help will be convenient, nothing more. And I will go with you this once. And that is only because I am considering a new church home. Again, I stress the convenience of your offer, rather than the necessity."

Aidan struggled to hold back a hearty laugh. *Thank You, Lord. I won't let You down. I know this is an opportunity You have provided for me.* Nodding thoughtfully, he assured her of his understanding. Somehow, though, he was sure the radiance he felt coursing through his veins gave him away.

"So, should I follow you home tomorrow night? That way, I'll know where to pick you up, come Sunday." *Whoa, boy,* he chided. *Don't scare her away.*

"Yes, you can follow me home, and, no, I will follow you to your church on Sunday. I don't go anywhere without a visible means of escape." She paged through the jumbo-sized scheduling calendar on the desk and read over the information scribbled in. Aidan had a sneaking suspicion that this conversation had drawn to a close. Still, he could revel in his small victory, and he longed to tell Maureen. As far as Aidan was concerned, tomorrow night couldn't get here fast enough.

♨

Deborah unlocked the door of her new apartment and flopped onto a tiger-striped beanbag chair. It would be so good to have the Shaggy Orange Dogs back. Thoughts of the couch gave way to Aidan. Why was he still trying to be nice to her? Why didn't he leave her alone, after the way she had treated him? Shame burned her cheeks, as she recalled her behavior over the last ninety days.

"But I had to do it," she sighed. "I liked him too much. I liked Maureen too much. And I couldn't have that."

In her mind, she could see Aidan distinctly. His soft, wavy hair, and his intense emerald eyes filled her brain. She could picture his lean form, bedecked in a deep green running suit, helping a young man maintain proper form, or jogging alongside faithful patrons. She could hear his laugh and feel his warmth. How she longed to talk with him, and tell him her innermost secrets! Fearing rejection, yet longing for companionship, Deborah felt as though she were bound tightly. The heaviness in her chest and the whirling accusations of her mind showed no signs of dissipating.

"The move should've helped," she reasoned. "Why do I still feel so trapped? Perhaps I miss the girls. Maybe I should call them to come over." She walked over to her bookshelf and opened a classical music sampler. As soon as the CD began to spin, she dialed Cali's number. When no one answered, she tried Chris. Again, the ringing only yielded a brief, quirky phone message and a short rendition of "Jesu: Joy of Man's Desiring" in annoying beeps.

Left alone with her thoughts again, Deborah allowed herself

to focus inwardly. *So, I've got the new place and a little over five months left at my job. Nothing "feels" right yet. How much longer will God make me wait? Perhaps this is akin to "the sins of the father being revisited on their children." Mom and Dad were too quick to settle, and now, I'll be forced to wait until I'm old and wrinkled to find my perfect anything. But I'm doing the right things! Or so I thought. Why isn't anything panning out? How many more options do I have to run through? I can't keep doing everything! I'm so tired. Haven't I been through enough?*

Her train of thought jackknifed into hostile territory. Suddenly, her consciousness flooded with images and sensations from over three months ago. She knew she was still unable to cope with the trauma of her mugging, and barely mentioned it to anyone. When anyone broached the subject, she deftly incorporated it into a joke. She recalled breaking the news to Cali and Chris, who were devastated that they were out of town when she needed them.

"The worst of it is, I really liked that purse," she repeated, in perfect time with her memory. No one knew how much that moment had changed her life. It had knocked her off balance and forced her to reevaluate herself. That was not a welcomed situation. She kept replaying the night's events, hoping to find a logical explanation for her failed theory. *I could feel nothing out of the ordinary. He sounded sincere. I felt . . .*

She felt tears begin to trickle down her face and under her chin. "Why did You make that happen? I didn't mean to be insolent. And Maureen . . . she was sweet and knowledgeable. If You didn't want me to say anything, why did You let her ask the questions? Was it a test? If so, I obviously failed. And now, they think I'm a horrible person. They think I don't care about them. Which isn't true. I don't want to care about them, and that is completely different. Why do You want me to be alone?"

Regretting her brazen words, she immediately begged for forgiveness. "Please, Lord, I'm sorry. Don't be angry. I've learned my lesson. I won't ask any more questions. If I am to be alone for the rest of my life, so be it. I just thank You for not sending me to hell, which is all I ask. Amen."

With a throbbing headache, she stumbled back toward her tiny bedroom. With some trouble, she managed to navigate through the maze of boxes and promptly collapsed onto her goose-down comforter. The pain intensified into a migraine, the symptoms of which she could never recognize until it was too late. Holding a pillow over her face, she implored sleep to overtake her and simultaneously dreaded her dreams.

*T*he next morning, Aidan, Tom, and Maureen gathered at their usual time. Practically bursting with joy, Aidan ran circles around the young couple.

"Whoa, there. Did you have a little coffee this morning, or what?" Maureen was reduced to a fast-paced waddle, her tiny frame struggling to maintain balance. Aidan was amazed at how much time had actually lapsed since the family learned of the pregnancy. She was now twice her normal size and often complained of backaches, but she was still as feisty as ever.

"Not a drop. I'm just excited to be here. With you. And Tom." Aidan grinned from ear to ear.

Maureen rolled her eyes and rubbed her enlarged abdomen tenderly. "Even the girls got a kick out of that one. How about the truth?"

"What? You think I don't enjoy being with my family? I'm so wounded. Maureen, I would hope that you would know better than that. But still, I suppose I must confess . . ." Aidan stopped, attempting to heighten the dramatics. He watched as husband and wife exchanged wary glances.

"Out with it, Aidan." Tom cocked an eyebrow suspiciously.

"I'm helping Debbie move her couch tonight." A self-satisfied smile broke out. "And, she's gonna let me take her to our church."

"Is that all? I figured you'd discovered oil in your backyard, or something major."

"Come on, Maureen. This is a big deal. She has spent the past three months hating my guts."

"I don't believe that is entirely true, Aidan. If she hated you, wouldn't she quit? I know I would."

"Well, maybe not 'hate,' but certainly, you must admit, she has displayed a strong dislike when it comes to me."

"Aidan, it has very little to do with you. I thought you understood. Debbie's issues are with Debbie. Now, she may or may not know that. Either way, it's easier to lash out toward you than it is to own up to the possibility that she is dissatisfied with herself." Aidan shook his head, as if to keep his sister's words from penetrating his brain.

"Look, I'm not going to let you ruin this for me, Maureen. I am thrilled to pieces to be allowed access—no matter how small—into her life. She has agreed to go to church with me! I know Pastor Riley is just what she needs. The whole congregation will welcome her with open arms. Once she sees the truth—"

"What makes you so sure you are the one human being to get through to her, Aidan? I don't mean to sound harsh, but really! Surely, you are not the first person to share the gospel with her. It is hard for us to stand here, knowing what we know, and conceive what must be going on inside her head. How can she still feel as she does, when time and time again, I have expressed my beliefs? Because, Aidan, they are *my* beliefs. Until something occurs in her life to make the Lord real to her, we cannot force our testimony or our fellowship to affect her."

Aidan sighed. His sister was so wise, but somehow, on this particular subject, he couldn't help but feel she was misguided. He couldn't let a single opportunity pass him. Every chance he had, he would continue to chip away at Debbie's iron resolve until he was able to break through.

Before he could summon words to describe his convictions, Maureen continued, "I am so happy for you, being able to be salt and light in her world. That is truly a privilege. You get to see her every day. With my being at home most of the time, I only get to see her when she brings the weekly bookwork by. I still talk to her, though, and I still discern a quiet rage within her."

He knew it saddened her to say these things, yet he realized she was not one to give in to overreaction. "I believe you, Maureen. Honestly, I do. All I know is, God has placed me in her life for a reason. Perhaps it is to be like the relationship I have with Tom. I was able to lead him to Christ." Looking expectantly at his best friend, Aidan waited for his response and support.

"Uh, Aidan . . . I don't mean to burst your bubble, but the Holy Spirit led me to Christ. You were a vessel. You were definitely a part of the plan, but I could've just as easily been saved without ever having met you. God knows who belongs to Him. His plan doesn't come to a screeching halt just because you aren't available. If Debbie belongs to the Father, He'll get her. He may use you, but He certainly doesn't need you."

Aidan realized he couldn't have been more shocked if the couple told him they were from outer space. *Lord, how can they say this? I know You and You alone save, but I know that You used me. I played a small part in it. I had to have . . .*

Aidan searched the faces of the man and woman before him. Maureen's eyes were glistening with tears, pleading with him to understand. Tom's hazel-brown eyes were stern, yet compassionate.

"Aidan, I've believed this was the way you perceived things, ever since you learned of Debbie's difficulties," Maureen said. "I didn't want to say anything, because I didn't know your heart. Can you see why I said the things I did? Sweetie, you can't save her. You can't allow her beliefs and convictions about God to determine your faith. In your mind, if she was to come to God and see Him as the loving Father and Creator He is, that would most definitely mean a star by your name. But what if she doesn't? Does it mean Aidan McCullough is not near the Christian he thought he was? Will you be held responsible for her choices and decisions? Of course not! We don't earn commission on our converts. God desires a personal relationship with each one of His children. If you could somehow bypass that—somehow offer Debbie a condensed version of your faith—what a disservice you would be doing her!"

Feeling his cheeks and ears flame, Aidan lowered his gaze to the ground. *Could this be true? Could it be I am trying to share in the glory God solely deserves?* Dumbstruck, he excused himself to the workroom and locked the door.

He sat opposite the bulletin boards and read the verses tacked on them. Ephesians 2:8 and 9. "For it is by grace you have been saved . . . it is the gift of God—not by works, so that no man can boast."

John 14:6: " 'I am the way and the truth and the life. No one comes to the Father except through me.' "

Aidan's vision became blurred, and he could no longer make out the words. His tears fell steadily, first out of anger and betrayal, but after a time, they changed to the bitter tears of mourning and meekness.

"Lord, I don't know how long I've been this way. I don't know why I am this way. I can't believe I was so prideful as to take credit for Tom's salvation. I am appalled my plan for Debbie was no different. Please forgive me this, Father. I know if it were not for Your gift of the Holy Spirit, no one would be prompted to come to You. You are responsible for the whole conversion. You are so gracious to use cracked vessels, and I am honored that I could be a part of Your plan. Please humble me, Lord. Please allow Your light to shine through me. Let it be to Your glory. Help me to remove myself from the picture, and please fill me with Your Holy Spirit. It is in Your Son's precious and lifesaving name I pray. Amen."

Aidan rose from the padded chair and exited the workroom.

He knew his first order of business was to seek the forgiveness of his sister and brother-in-law. Then, he would focus on Debbie.

❧

Deborah awoke, startled. Her room was filled with early morning sunlight. She realized she wore the same clothes she had on yesterday. *The migraine,* she recalled. Propping her body up with both arms, she turned to see the glowing red numbers of her digital alarm clock.

"Nine-forty-five!" she screeched. "I still have to have a shower! I can't make it in fifteen minutes! There's no way." Pouncing out of bed, she ran down the hallway and frantically dialed McCullough's Gym.

"Good morning, McCullough's. This is Aidan; how may I help you?"

Great. Why did it have to be him? "Uh, hi. This is Debbie. I am going to be a little bit late. See, I had a migraine last night, and I didn't set my alarm. I woke up just a minute ago, and I still need to shower and . . ."

"Don't worry about it. You're fine. Just get here as soon as you can. The gang's still around from our workout this morning, so Maureen can probably sit in for a half hour or so."

"What's she doing there? I thought she was staying home until the babies were born." Despite the fact that such knowledge was immaterial at this point, she pursued it, finding herself worried about Maureen's well-being, and longing to connect with Aidan in a way that wasn't confrontational.

"Yeah, she had decided to do that, but she came in to walk the track with Tom this morning, and we all got to talking."

"Ah-ha," Deborah commented. "Look, I am really sorry about this. Are we still on for tonight?"

"You bet. Oh, and Debbie? You don't have to come to my church on Sunday. I'd be honored if you did, but you are welcome to go anywhere you like. I didn't mean to turn the matter of your couch into hostage-style negotiations."

"No, actually, I'm looking forward to it. I can't thank you enough for tonight. You'll understand why it is so desperately needed when you see my place. I'll let you go. I will be there in less than thirty minutes."

Relieved at Aidan's good nature and surprised by her confessed excitement about the new church, Deborah delighted in the 180-degree turn of the day, in simply a matter of minutes.

In twenty-two minutes flat, Deborah walked through the doors of the gym, practically breathless, but nonetheless, wearing a broad smile. "Good morning, Maureen! How are you feeling?" She stopped at the turquoise desk and flipped her hair over her shoulders.

"I'm great, Debbie. Big as a house, but great. How are you?"

"Oh, I'm late. I'm good, otherwise." Maureen's warm expression threatened to melt Deborah's heart, but she quickly moved on. "Hey, why don't you let me take over? You can go and head out, if you'd like. It has been quite awhile since I've seen you in here." Slipping behind her chair, Deborah deposited her large gym bag next to the built-in cabinets, and surveyed the calendar.

"I know it. I miss it so much sometimes, and then other days, I feel like it's a tremendous weight off of my shoulders. Today, I will most assuredly take you up on your offer, though." Deborah watched, unsure of how to help, as the woman struggled to rise to her feet.

"Whew! I know that was more of a workout than I've ever had in my life! It's a wonder I can still drive the truck! I'm going to say good-bye to Tom. I'll be right back." Deborah suppressed a giggle as the tiny woman headed down the hall, swaying back and forth like a human metronome.

"Hey, Red." The smooth voice resonating behind her made Deborah unsteady. Whipping around, she found herself staring at

Aidan's chest. Slowly lifting her face to meet his, her gaze was drawn immediately to his brilliant green eyes.

"Uh, hi, Aidan." Her heartbeat quickened and her senses screamed. *Must he stand so close?* she wondered. "What can I do for you, sir?"

Aidan only chuckled and shook his head.

"What's that supposed to mean?" Regaining some of her composure, she wrinkled her forehead questioningly. "Don't tell me you've been contemplating Maureen and Tom's additions and you've decided to make one of your own. And now—you need advice on what sort of pet to buy."

He laughed. "Yeah, that's it." Suddenly, he reached toward her. *He's going to kiss me. He's going to kiss me right here in front of everybody.* Holding her breath, she closed her eyes and jutted her chin forward. Seconds passed like hours.

"You all right?" Opening one eye slightly, she saw a confused Aidan holding a stack of printouts.

"Uh, yes. Yes, I'm fine. Just kind of tired, I suppose." *What is wrong with me? He's my boss. He's just a temporary boss. No matter how handsome he may be . . .* Deborah's thoughts reeled. She couldn't decipher her emotions, but there was no mistaking her rapid pulse and innermost thoughts. *I actually thought he'd do it! And, what's more, I think I wanted him to!*

"What are you thinking about?" Aidan cocked his head to one side, and Deborah thought he looked like a puppy, investigating a foreign insect.

Her cheeks flushed and her words caught in her throat, "Nothing, really. I guess I was contemplating my answer."

"To what?"

"To what kind of pet you should have. I don't see you as a dog person, really. I think the slobbering and the whining would get on your nerves. I see you as more a cat person. Yes, a nice calico kitten to play with. Cats are definitely my favorite. I love tigers, really. I have them all over my apartment." Deborah immediately bit her lower lip. *Nice going, Deb. Cats? He's going to think I'm crazy. Oh, wait. He already believes that. Yet, I am almost certain the look in his eye means something more.*

"Well, I'll keep that in mind." As he walked away, Deborah thought she saw his perfect lips break out in a beaming smile.

"What in the world must he think of me?" She exhaled sharply, as though she could relieve herself of her wild imagings.

(14)

*D*eborah pulled into her marked parking space and exited the car. As she waited, Aidan backed in next to her. Admonishing herself to stay calm, she walked toward her apartment and unlocked the door.

"Well, this is it. Not much, but definitely better than most I've had." Deborah forced herself to focus on business, rather than the simple fact that Aidan was inside her home. "I would like the couch to go here, against this wall, opposite the TV. Then, I can put the beanbag chair over here, by the closet."

Aidan nodded, and looked around. "So, you weren't joking about the whole tiger thing, huh?"

"Nope. I love them. I've been collecting them since I was in middle school." She walked toward her tiny kitchen and called to him. "Hey, come meet Gil!"

"If Gil is a tiger, I'm going to be very upset." Aidan rounded the corner and grinned.

"No way. Gil is my faithful goldfish. I have kept him alive for over five months now." The surge of pride she felt was not lost on Aidan.

"Congratulations, I think."

He seemed unsure of how to respond, so she elaborated, "Technically, he was a gag gift, but I kept him to prove something to Cali and Chris. They figured I would allow him to waste away to nothing, but I've shown them otherwise. When I eat, Gil eats."

"Poor fish must be starving then," Aidan said absentmindedly.

"What's that supposed to mean?" Debbie felt her defenses rising.

"I'm saying you've lost a good deal of weight since your accident."

Debbie laughed nervously. "Oh, that. It's just the aerobics. I used to weigh less when I dieted in college. This is nothing to worry about." She reached over for an open package of saltines and popped one in her mouth. Then she ceremonially sprinkled fish food into the tank. "See. A feast for kings. I have improved his quality of life a million times over. I'm just like that."

"I suppose you are." Deborah sensed more was behind the statement and felt herself blush. "Well, let's get over to the storage unit while we still have a little light."

They exited the kitchen, and Deborah gathered up her purse and keys.

"What have we here?" The amused tone in Aidan's voice was hard to miss. "Debbie, Debbie, Debbie. You never cease to entertain."

"What are you talking about?" she questioned, then realized where his gaze was fixed. "Ohh . . . that. That, dear Aidan, is aptly titled my Wall of Experience. See, these are all the name tags from every job I've ever had." Alongside him, she surveyed the corkboard hanging on the wall. "See, this one is from the restaurant I worked at during my first semester at KU. This one is from the supermarket. This one is from that little fashion shop by the supermarket. This is from a family-owned floral shop." Turning her attention from the board, she found that Aidan's gaze was on her, and not her souvenirs.

"Does my Wall not fascinate you, Mr. McCullough? Are you too good for my Wall?" She tried hard to choke down the emotion that threatened to overwhelm her. Something in his eyes—a mix of mirth and respect—caused her stomach to flip-flop. Focusing on her sense of humor, she attempted to laugh it off. "Well, I know when my guests are no longer interested. I can take a hint. You know, you're worse than Cali and Chris."

"Am I?" His soft tone and mischievous eyes unnerved her.

"Yes, you are." For a moment, silence reigned. Deborah's breathing became shallow, and soon, alarms began to sound within her brain. *Get out of here! Leave!* Clearing her throat, she ducked behind him. "We need to get going, don't you think?"

Aidan appeared to be embarrassed and nodded rapidly. "Yes. Do you want to just ride over with me? I'm not sure where we're going, and I would hate to get lost. You know how we men are. The authorities wouldn't find me until Christmas!"

Eased by the lightened mood, Deborah determined to put the awkward moment behind her. "That sounds like a good idea. I would hate to have to organize a search party tonight. Especially since I was so looking forward to having my couch."

After they had fastened their seat belts, Deborah began to direct Aidan toward their destination. Once he had successfully navigated his way to Troost, she began to get fidgety in the silence.

"So, tell me about your church, Aidan." The question shocked her, almost as much as it did Aidan, based on the dropping of his jaw.

"Uhh . . . it's nondenominational, which just means we believe in the essential biblical truths—you know, the Trinity, the death and resurrection of Christ, the forgiveness of sins, baptism, and so on. We don't rely on a person or any additional texts for our beliefs. Our pastor is a really special guy. His name is Erik Riley and his wife is the choir leader and piano player. Our worship is contemporary, and we take Communion once a month. We have some great Bible studies, too, led by the men and women within the congregation."

"Hmm . . . that sounds like it will be acceptable. Do you have pews or chairs?"

"Excuse me?"

"Pews or chairs. In the sanctuary."

"Pews. They were renovated last spring. Why?"

"No reason, really. I just particularly like churches with pews." Pausing as she scanned the area, she added, "Turn left up here. It's the one with the big padlock on the sign."

Aidan did as she instructed, and she guided him to the second row of units. "Stop at number fourteen. That's me." Jumping down to the pavement, she was suddenly grateful for her sweatshirt and jeans. The air had grown nippy and crisp in the near twilight. Deborah found it hard to believe it was almost fall. Aidan echoed her thoughts aloud.

"It's weird you would say that. I was just thinking it to myself. Guess we've got some sort of telepathic link, eh, Aidan?" His tender smile caused her to grin like an idiot. Laughing at herself, she located the key and unlocked the large garage-style door. Aidan erupted in merriment the minute she let go of the door guide.

"What's this all about?"

"What?" Looking around, Deborah could see nothing out of place. Her boxes were labeled and ready to be moved, and her orange-shag love seat was easily accessible.

"This," he said pointing to the yellow tape that divided the unit into equal halves. "And this." He gestured to the boxes and their appropriate categories. " 'Studio' and 'One-Bed?' What is it for?" His chuckles grew louder and more enthusiastic.

"I don't see what is so funny, Aidan. Is my organization amusing to you?" Deborah shook her head. "Boys."

"No, really. Why do you have it set up like this, Debbie? Don't you think this is a bit neurotic?"

If this is good-natured ribbing, I'd hate to see him when he wanted to be mean! "I have it this way because I move a lot. I have devised a plan to calculate what will and what will not fit into a studio apartment of normal size. My last studio was not of normal size, so I have moved to the one-bedroom, which you saw. I labeled and categorized my things so I would always have what I needed, no matter what size the apartment was." Deborah searched for the humor in the situation, yet she could find none.

"You are priceless, you know that? Sometimes I'm so glad I hired you on at the gym that I can barely see straight. Your sense of order far surpasses that of anyone I know. Honestly." Deborah's irritation grew as compliments increased.

"Look, here. I don't think it's wise for you to mock me. I'd knock it off, if I were you." She announced this a little more sternly than she had intended, yet she rationalized that, so long as she elicited an acceptable response, she couldn't complain. Her desire for self-preservation had to come before his feelings, no matter how much she had begun to care for him.

Aidan's jovial expression faded at her words. "Debbie, I was serious. I think you're incredible. Your way of looking at the world makes me smile. You amaze me. You brighten every day of my life. Do you honestly think I'd be here if I didn't care about you?"

Deborah bit her lip, trying to conjure an appropriate response. "Umm . . . okay. Sorry. I get a little overprotective of myself from time to time. Never mind me. You should hear me get started on retirement plans! I get downright vicious. I guess I am very passionate about my beliefs. Truce?" She held out her hand and awaited his acceptance. When he touched her, a rush of sensations made her dizzy.

Determined to circumvent another moment of tense silence, Deborah was the first to pull away. Immediately, she began to place numerous boxes into the bed of the truck. "Just let me know when you want to put the love seat in," she called behind her.

"Now is fine."

For the remainder of the evening, they worked in relative silence. Occasionally, a joke would be made and a forced laugh would follow, but Deborah maintained an air of frigidity that Aidan mirrored perfectly.

What am I supposed to do with you, Aidan McCullough? You're making me crazy!

&

"So, how did it go? Is she still going to go to church with you on Sunday?" Maureen asked, balancing a glass of milk on her swollen abdomen. "Hey, wait! Look at this! My girls are going to be models! They've already mastered balance, and we know they're going to be beautiful—what more is there?"

Aidan looked at the precariously positioned glass and applauded lightly. "Bravo, sister. Quite a great day in prenatal arts, dare I say."

A soft pillow hit him squarely in the face. Aidan sputtered briefly, but added, "What a talented family! You're a pitcher, your daughters are models . . . say, what do you do, Tom?"

The sandy-haired man laughed. "Most of the time, I feel like a referee for the two of you." Maureen shot him an inquisitive look.

"How many?"

"All right, you four. See what I mean?"

Aidan crossed his arms and sighed. "Well, I hardly think it's fair odds. I think she's cheating."

"You want to take them for awhile? Hmm?" Maureen's arms were wide in mock surrender.

"No, thanks. I'm sure there will be plenty of times when Uncle Aidan will be called on to save the day. I'd rather keep the whole arrangement fresh as long as possible."

"That's what I thought. And I am certain that Uncle Aidan will be of the spoiling persuasion, so the odds will lean in his favor in time."

He ruffled her hair and kissed the top of her head. "Well, family, I suppose I am going to be on my way. But in answer to your question, Maureen, I believe the evening went well, with the exception of Ms. Shaughnessy's becoming mighty sensitive over comments on her eccentric nature. As far as I know, everything is still as planned for Sunday."

Maureen eyed him suspiciously. "What else?" Aidan knew his older sister had learned to read his mannerisms as plainly as printed words. Usually, he didn't mind, but with the question of Debbie's feelings still so uncertain, he hesitated to comment on their brief, yet powerful encounters. However, he knew Maureen would no sooner let him leave than she would keep her opinions to herself. So, he continued, "I've got a feeling that Debbie likes me."

"Oh, yeah?" The couple seemed to perk up in unison.

"Yeah. She's been staring at me a lot more. I think that's a good thing." Try as he might, Aidan couldn't help but grin. *She cares for me! I know she does!* "Oh, and once, I caught her smiling at me like you caught me smiling at her. At least, I hope that's what I looked like."

"So, I take it you want me to have a talk with her, eh, little brother? You need me to feel her out for you?" Maureen's already glowing countenance beamed even brighter.

Aidan stuffed his hands deep into his pockets and nodded emphatically. "Yes, please."

15

*D*eborah knocked softly on the Smiths' front door. Clutching the weekly figures and other assorted paperwork, she waited for Maureen to answer. Minutes passed, and she became worried. "Maureen?" she called through the ornate oak door. Still nothing. Gingerly turning the knob, she was relieved to find it unlocked. Hesitant to enter, yet consumed with worst-case scenarios, she stepped into the entryway of their home.

"Maureen? Are you all right?" Surveying the living room, she found nothing amiss, so she continued on. She found herself offering up prayers for the woman's protection and well-being. *Lord, please keep Maureen safe. I try not to ask for too much, as I am sure You know, but this woman is important to me. Please let her and the babies be all right.* It felt odd to pray, and Deborah was surprised that it was a viable response in this troubling situation. Somehow, though, she felt comforted.

Familiar with the residence from her two-day rest, she hurried back toward Maureen's bedroom. The door was cracked, and she saw the woman lying on her back across the massive mattress.

"Maureen, it's Debbie. I brought you the books."

"Debbie? Oh, come on in. I was dozing and didn't hear you. I can't sit up, though. I was trying my shoes, and I guess I bent wrong."

Deborah stood by the bed and looked over the woman. "What happened? Are you hurt?" Cautiously, she sat on the edge and took Maureen's hand.

"I'm sure I'll be fine. I called the doctor, and he explained that

111

in my condition, given my original size, back injuries are highly probable. He said a week or two of bed rest, and then I can be up and about again. So, here I lie. This is the only comfortable position I've found so far." Maureen smiled.

Deborah moaned. "Oh, how awful! Can I get you anything? Aspirin? Ice pack?"

"No, I've taken what I can, and I don't have the energy to roll over for an ice pack!" Laughing, she suddenly winced. "Oh, that didn't feel good. So, no laughing, no sitting, no walking. Hmm . . . doesn't leave much to do, to my way of thinking. Say, Debbie, you wouldn't want to help me do the numbers, would you?"

Tucking a stray strand of wavy hair behind her ear, Deborah stood. "Sure, Maureen. Whatever you need. Just let me go grab a pen and a chair." *What if this is a trick? What if she really wants to talk about your beliefs? Do you want to set yourself up for that?* Deborah shook off the cynical inquiry of her mind.

No. She needs me, and I will help her. This woman has been kind to me, and I owe it to her to return the favor. Maureen wouldn't trick me! What a horrible thing to assume! As ludicrous as it seemed to argue with herself, Deborah nonetheless battled to silence her worried and antagonistic thoughts.

Locating the objects of her search, Deborah hurried back to Maureen's bedside and switched on the lights. Deborah read the numbers to Maureen who punched them into a calculator. The result was to be carried over into the last column, and this practice continued until daily totals yielded a weekly summation.

Deborah let out a heavy sigh. "Wow. It seems so simple with you here, but I know the minute I go to do it alone, I'll be overwhelmed and reduced to tears! Please tell me it took you a long time to understand all of this."

"Oh, definitely. I've never had the head for numbers that my brother has. Or Tom, for that matter. I'm more at ease with displays and flyers. You know, the creative side. I love to make the calendars for the public bulletin boards, and I enjoy making collages with the photos. But the bookwork is not so bad as it could be. Of course, you probably know that. Didn't you say you dabbled in accounting?"

Deborah nodded. "Yes, at the floral shop. It was a tiny thing, over by the corner of 45th and Roanoke. You know where I mean? Well, the staff was so short, by my second week, I was managing on my own, which included reconciling all of the figures. That was frightful compared to this."

"I am glad to hear our numbers aren't 'frightful'! At least I think I am. I suppose more frightful numbers might mean more patrons—but then again, we do all right for ourselves." She smiled, then asked, "So, tell me how things went today." Maureen attempted to stack a few pillows behind her head, but Deborah could hear the strained sounds she emitted.

"Here, let me help you." After Maureen was comfortable, Deborah drew her knees in to her chest and hugged her legs. "My day went pretty well, I think. Tonight was Hi-Gear, and the class did really well."

"How many of the women signed up again for the fall roster?"

"Oh, most, I think. A handful of ladies from the low-impact class crossed over, though, so we have a total of twenty-five, if I'm not mistaken."

"Fabulous! I am so glad they are sticking with it. You, too, Debbie. I'm particularly proud of you."

"Naturally!" Deborah giggled at her feigned conceit. "No, seriously. I do want to thank you for all of your support and encouragement. I know I have been difficult to get along with at times."

"Why do you say that, Debbie?"

She sighed sadly. "Oh, I know I was avoiding you, Aidan, and even Tom after my mugging. I just didn't want to face any of you, and I am sorry."

"Would you like to talk about it?" Maureen's gentle tone and the seclusion of the house seemed to persuade Deborah to say yes.

"I was just scared to care, you know? I feel like everything in my life is a test, and that leaves very little room for friendships."

"What about love? Don't you want to get married and have a family someday? Do you see that as a future for you?"

"I would love to have a relationship like you have with Tom. You two have really opened my eyes to what marriage can be. I figured most were like my parents'. You know, worrying all the time, having arguments over everything, and giving each other the cold shoulder half the time. I knew I didn't want misery."

"I can't say that I'd blame you, Debbie. But do you know why our relationship is appealing to you?"

Deborah shook her head. "Wait—God, right?"

"Yes."

"And?" Deborah waited for the inevitable sermon sure to follow.

"And what?"

"Aren't you going to tell me how God can do the same for me, and someday I will recognize His goodness and glory for myself? That my parents' situation has more to do with pride than it does with God, and we can't continually blame Him for everything that isn't perfect?" Deborah drew in a deep breath and paused. "Well?"

To her surprise, Maureen only smiled. "Sounds like you have already decided what you believe, Debbie. Those were all your words, not mine. Sure, I can discern a fragment or two probably came from our discussions, but overall, the sentiments are yours."

Deborah began to sputter. "Well, I . . . I, uh . . ."

"Debbie, it's okay. Calm down, and talk to me. I want to be your friend. I have, ever since you came on at the gym. I want us to be close. I know you don't have many friends, and certainly fewer mentors. I am in a similar situation. I think we could encourage one another to focus on the Father. I think we could giggle all night and eat chocolate, as well as many other productive activities. What do you say?"

Deborah tried to fight the tears welling up in her eyes. "It's so hard. And I'm so tired. I don't know what to believe, Maureen. I don't know what to think of you or your brother."

"What has Aidan done?"

"Nothing, really. Except be nice every time I am cruel. Or help me every time I need someone or something. But then again, he's making me go to church with him."

"He's making you? Are you sure about that, Debbie?" Maureen's eyes laughed, despite her full lips turned down in a frown.

Deborah rolled her eyes. "Well, he's not making me. He did tell me I didn't have to go, if I didn't want to."

"But you want to, don't you?" It was a soft question—one that Deborah could not refute.

"Yes, but I don't know why I want to go." Closing her eyes and laying her head against the backrest of the chair, she continued. "I don't know if I'm going to get what you guys have, or if I just want to be with Aidan." A blush crept over her cheeks, yet, she felt sure Maureen was the only person in the world she could confide in. She didn't dare peek to see if the bedridden woman's expression had changed.

"Well, I can assure you faith isn't handed out in tidy packages at our church, but we do have a forthright and knowledgeable pastor. I know he would be happy to hear your questions. I also know I would be more than happy to help you, and Aidan would be, as well. As far as your latter statement, I can't judge your motives. I can't even say I understand what you're getting at. Care to elaborate?"

"I can't. That's the problem. I don't even know what I'm getting at. There have been occasions when I feel something for him.

I don't know what it is, and it scares me. I doubt he even cares about me."

"I wouldn't be so sure, Debbie. Aidan wouldn't offer to take you to Grace Fellowship if he didn't care about you."

"I know he cares about my soul. But I think that's all I am to him. A conversion waiting to happen. A choir member in the making. Not as a woman. Not as . . ." Deborah couldn't continue. *What am I saying? And why am I saying it to his sister?* Suddenly, she extended her legs and stretched. "Look at the time. Whoa. I've got to get home. Are you going to be at the church on Sunday?"

"No, I've got to stay here. But how about you and Aidan come by afterwards for lunch? I think it would be good to have a review of the sermon, since I won't be there."

Deborah hesitated, but ultimately gave in. "That does sound pleasant. I guess I will see you Sunday afternoon."

"Oh, and Debbie?"

Turning from the doorway, she answered, "Uh-huh?"

"Go ahead and ride with Aidan after the service. Our driveway isn't big enough to hold four vehicles, especially since he drives that Monster Truck around everywhere."

"But, couldn't I park in the street?"

"You could, but I wouldn't recommend it."

"Why not?"

"Oh, just a mother's intuition, I suppose." The grin on Maureen's face was impossible to interpret. But, even though Deborah left the house feeling baffled, she had to admit she also felt slightly relieved.

16

*D*eborah arose early to prepare herself for the service. After showering and applying a light dusting of powder and a quick coat of mascara, she turned her attention to her wardrobe. The November chill had settled on the city. In order to fend off the breeze, Deborah opted for a floral navy skirt and a heavy cable-knit sweater that matched the beige centers of the tiny daisies on the fabric. Quickly tying the laces of her brown leather granny boots, she then gave herself a hasty appraisal.

"It'll have to do." She scattered a few flakes of food in Gil's bowl and nibbled a dry piece of toast as she waited for Aidan's knock. Thinking about what Aidan had said in regard to her weight loss, she quickly slathered butter on the toast and resumed eating. No sense giving him any more chance to comment.

At nine o'clock sharp, Aidan's heavy-handed knock roused Deb out of her thoughtful state of mind. He was here! She checked her hair in the mirror as she flew by and threw open the door before he had finished knocking.

"Uh, hello there. Are you ready to go?"

"Definitely. Would it be all right if I rode with you? Maureen wanted to have that big lunch afterwards, and so I figured it would be more economical to carpool to the service, and not just to their house."

"You're right. That does sound like a smarter choice." Deborah could sense his pleasure at her decision, yet he masked it with a no-nonsense reply. "So, did you mind riding in the Suburban? We could take your car, if you'd be more comfortable."

Deborah crossed her arms and smiled. "Nah. I'd think I'd feel fine in the Monster Truck."

"Monster Truck? You've been talking to Maureen, haven't you?" His eyes twinkled, and Deborah could feel their magnetism. Rather than reward him with an answer, she secured her purse strap on her shoulder and waited outside the door for him to catch up.

"Coming?" she called. *Hurry up, Aidan, before I lose my nerve.*

He joined her at once, and she was reduced to stammering her appreciation when he gallantly opened the passenger side door for her.

Settling into the rich, gray leather seats, she fastened her seat belt and listened intently to the tape playing on his stereo. "What is this?" she murmured. "It sounds like hymns—only faster."

"Yes, basically, that's what it is. They are remakes of popular praise songs. I like to listen to them on my way to church. It gets me in the mood for worship." Aidan looked over and smiled. Suddenly, his face contorted in dismay. "Oh no! You forgot your Bible! Do you want me to turn around?"

Embarrassed, Deborah fought to regain composure. "No, I don't bring a Bible. I was taught that it's rude to read during church. Besides, I thought you said your pastor was good. Won't he keep my attention?" She grinned, attempting to disarm Aidan's interrogation. Thankfully, he seemed satisfied.

"He sure will. This week, the sermon is about the family unit—our own physical families, and then our heavenly family. Pastor Riley gives us a sneak preview every week to entice us to attend. Of course, he's so dynamic, I can't imagine missing one without a good reason."

The couple pulled into the parking lot of Grace Fellowship some fifteen minutes later. Deborah guessed the service began at 9:30, given the number of empty spaces.

"It'll really get packed here in the next ten minutes or so. I usually come early so I don't have to park in the street. I'm excited our congregation has grown so much. I remember when I was a little boy, there weren't more than ten families—around fifty people or so—who attended. Now, I think the roster is up to five or six hundred."

"Are they going to build a bigger church?" Deborah watched as a multitude of vehicles converged on the tiny lot.

"Well, we'd like to, but the funds are low for such a thing. Besides a special offering, we are praying for a miracle. Of course, we know that when the time is right, our Father will provide."

Together, they walked into the foyer, and Deborah was soon enveloped in hug after hug. "Hi there! Welcome to Grace. My name is Marion Riley. What's yours?"

"I'm Debbie Shaughnessy. This is my first time here."

"Well, it's so good to have you. You couldn't have found a sweeter guide. Aidan, now you take good care of our sister."

Deborah looked perplexed. "Sister?" she whispered to Aidan, as soon as the perky brunette was out of earshot. "She thinks I'm Maureen? Doesn't she know she's pregnant?"

He laughed at her inquiry. "No, she knows you're not Maureen. Besides the whole baby thing, you've got a good five to six inches on her. But, just wait. You'll see. That's what the sermon is about. But, suffice it to say that all Christians are family, brothers and sisters." Aidan placed a warm hand on her back and helped guide her through the crowds. Deborah felt as though he'd caused her sweater to catch on fire, so she walked faster to escape the effect his blazing fingertips had on her.

Gesturing to a pew in the center of the middle section, Aidan motioned for her to enter the row first. Deborah shook her head. "I like to sit on the aisle." He slipped in, and she sat to his left. As the band tuned their instruments and the singers warmed up their voices, random individuals began to sing along. Soon, Aidan stood as well and began to sing. Tugging gently on his jacket, Deborah whispered, "Where are the hymnals?" Aidan smiled, and Deborah found herself grinning back, against her will. "What? Why are you laughing at me?"

The music grew louder, and Deborah could scarcely hear herself. Aidan pulled her to her feet and handed her a folded sheet of paper. Dipping his head near her ear, his breathy whisper sent shivers through her body. Or were they Sparkles? She didn't dare answer her own question.

"I'm not laughing at you, silly. You just make me smile, that's all. Here, we use these instead of hymnals. I grabbed one for you. I figured you wouldn't know to take one, and it was too loud to tell you."

He promptly resumed singing and left her to follow on her own. Scanning the lyrics, she made her best attempt to accompany the melody, and before she knew it, the Communion prayer was being offered. "Before we take some time to get our hearts right before the Lord's Supper, I would like to read a passage to you from 1 Corinthians, chapter eleven. If you would open your Bibles and read along with me, beginning at verse twenty-three." Aidan turned to the page and encouraged Deborah to read. She found it hard to look at the pages, having avoided them so successfully for so many years, but today she could not keep herself from ingesting their meaning.

"Verse twenty-seven states, 'Therefore, whoever eats the bread or drinks the cup of the Lord in an unworthy manner will be guilty of sinning against the body and blood of the Lord.' It goes on to say that without self-examination, we are eating and drinking judgments on ourselves." The pastor looked out into the congregation, and Deborah was sure he fixed his gaze directly onto her. "Are there those among you who feel that you are your own worst enemy? Is there anyone among you who understands this verse from firsthand experience? Perhaps you have come before the Lord without recognizing His sacrifice. Or as Paul puts it, 'without recognizing the body of the Lord.' I would encourage those of you with heavy hearts to allow the Holy Spirit to guide you in your decision to participate in the Lord's Supper. Forget about what your neighbor will think. Focus on Jesus. Get right with Him, and then partake."

Deborah did not partake of the bread and juice. Somehow, her thoughts were on the pastor's words of warning. As Aidan bowed his head in prayer, Deborah snatched up his Bible and continued to read. Silently mouthing the words, Deborah let the plate and cup pass her by.

᛫᛫

Aidan smiled as he watched an enraptured Debbie listen to the sermon. *Thank You, Father. Thank You that Pastor Riley is Your servant. Please allow Debbie's heart to be soft and tender and yielding to Your Spirit. Amen.*

As the final corporate prayer ended, the worship team began its invitation hymn. Aidan was surprised to see Debbie with purse in hand, edging her way to the aisle. *She's going to go forward! I can't believe it!*

But Debbie didn't go forward. As soon as the last refrain had been sung, her eyes seemed to plead with Aidan to hurry. He was barely able to keep her in sight, and in a matter of minutes, she had disappeared from his line of vision. Knowing she could find the SUV, he decided to thank Pastor Riley for his words and secure some notes for Maureen.

"Why, hello, Aidan. How are you today?" Pastor Riley's small hands covered Aidan's large one in a firm shake.

"I'm absolutely blessed, Pastor. Thank you for that awesome sermon. I was going to see if you had any extra notes I could pass along to Maureen. She's home with a strained back, and I know she will want to pick my brain about what was said. Of course, you know me; I'd be hard-pressed to tell her the specific verses."

"I could copy off my original notes. That is, if you think she could read my handwriting." The smaller man laughed and led Aidan back toward his office. "So, who was the young lady you had as a guest? My wife tells me she is very attractive, yet harbors the look of an abandoned animal. You wouldn't know anything about that, would you?"

Aidan smiled. "I just might. She's been working for me almost six months now. She's got some pretty mixed-up ideas about God, and through some discussions with Maureen, she has made it clear He's no more than a ticket out of hell and a dealer of cosmic consequences. I was hoping she would come to believe otherwise."

"Well, Aidan, you'd be surprised how many churchgoers and Christians believe the very same way. I know that to us, it seems foreign and downright foolish not to see the love and grace of our heavenly Father, but we must not be judges. I would like to talk to you about this more, but I do need to get back to the foyer." He handed Aidan a stack of copies.

"Thanks. I know Maureen and Tom will appreciate this." After saying his good-byes to several other families, Aidan made his way to the parking lot. He found Debbie standing by the door, her eyes darting around, panic-stricken.

"Debbie, over here!" He waved one arm in the air and watched as a smile broke out on her lovely face.

"Aidan, don't we have to hurry over to Maureen's?" Her voice was higher than usual, and Aidan could only nod.

"Yes, and we're headed there right this very minute. I had to get the sermon notes for her."

"Oh, all right."

"So, did you like the service?" Aidan pulled smoothly into traffic and headed east on 87th Street.

"It was fine. I just am starting to think your church isn't for me."

Aidan forced himself to remain on an even keel. "Well, maybe you should give it another try. First days are always hard."

"Actually, I was wondering if you'd prefer to let me keep the gym open on Sundays."

"What?" His mind screamed in unison with his mild exclamation. "No way. Your faith may mean very little to you, but I will have no part in working on the Lord's Day. It has been that way since my father opened the gym, and so long as I have a say in it, it will be that way forever. Is that clear?"

He hated to be so zealous in front of her, and he recalled Maureen's admonishment to do whatever he felt led to do, quietly. This was too much, though. He stole a glance and found her chewing her bottom lip and gazing out the window. Casually, she tucked her hair behind her ears, and he quietly prayed for guidance.

"I'm sorry, Debbie. I didn't mean to explode like that. It's just a real touchy subject for me." Aidan hoped she would look past this and enjoy the time with him. He knew he could think of no better way to spend his afternoon.

Silence continued until they pulled in the driveway of Tom and Maureen's house. As soon as he opened the door, the smell of roast beef and stewed vegetables filled his nostrils. There was even a hint of freshly brewed coffee to take the wintry sensation out of their bodies. It all seemed so inviting, and Aidan imagined with Debbie by his side, the two couples would spend many an afternoon in this very manner.

"Debbie! Aidan! How was the service?"

"Terrific, as always. Pastor Riley copied his notes for you. It is definitely something you and Tom will want to go over together."

"So, Debbie, did you enjoy it?" Aidan listened for her answer, and was delighted to hear her affirm his reply.

"It was just as Aidan said. I have a few questions, but it is nothing that a little bit of independent study won't remedy. Now, how about some of that delicious-smelling roast!" The four friends sat down around the table, and Tom offered the blessing. Soon, between mouthfuls of homemade mashed potatoes and juicy beef, the group was laughing and talking.

Debbie smiled as she said, "You know, I'm so glad you guys kept me around. I really enjoy your company. Your friendships mean more to me than I could ever put into words. Perhaps a song—a musical interlude, if you will—but never words." Aidan smiled at the woman by his side. He drank in the vision of her soft, coppery hair billowing around her face in perfect ringlets. He drowned in the chocolate depths of her eyes. For a moment, he was speechless.

"I don't know if 'friends' is the correct term for all of us. You and Aidan seem to be a little more than friends. He's moving your couch; you're going to church with him. . . ." Maureen enumerated examples of their closeness. Rather than chagrin, Aidan felt himself grow more and more curious about Debbie's response.

She briefly choked on a forkful of roast, but then chuckled. "No way. Aidan's just one of the girls. I do nothing differently with him than I would Cali or Chris. And he does nothing for me that they couldn't do. Or you, Maureen. You know, all I have is girl-friends."

Aidan's jaw dropped, and he struggled to maintain composure. The rest of the meal progressed in a similar manner, with the only exchanges of true emotion resulting from his and Maureen's eye contact.

Lord, what am I supposed to do with this?

❧

Deborah sat, "stuffed to the gills," as her aunt used to say, in the front seat of Aidan's SUV. "What's taking him so long in there?" she wondered aloud. Within seconds, Aidan bounded out to the Suburban and secured his seat belt. After a moment or two of silence, Deborah attempted to jumpstart the conversation. "Thanks for taking me."

"Ahh, it's nothing. You would've done the same for me. Or Cali, for that matter." His voice was curt and laden with sarcasm.

Oh, so that was it. Unsure of how to respond, Deborah said nothing. How could she explain her true feelings?

The remainder of the ride was tense. As soon as Aidan pulled in next to her Cavalier, she jumped down from the huge vehicle. "Well, thanks again, Aidan. I wouldn't mind going next week, if that's okay." Running as fast as the granny boots would allow, she slipped the key into the lock of her front door and twisted. The engine to the Suburban was still running. Focusing on the door handle, her thoughts raced. *Why won't he just go? Must he watch everything I do?*

Finally, the lock yielded, and she pulled the door open wide. All at once, two firm hands held her shoulders, and one pushed to spin her around.

"Aidan, I—" Deborah could only stare helplessly into his endless green eyes. Enfolding her in his arms, his mouth promptly demanded hers in a slow and tender kiss. Deborah felt her body melting against his, as her mind cried out, *Finally!*

Just as abruptly, he turned her loose. Halfway back to his vehicle, he turned. "When's the last time one of your girlfriends did that?" His face registered an emotion somewhere between frustration and self-satisfaction. Deborah, mouth agape, could only stare after him and wonder when exactly Aidan McCullough had claimed her heart.

$$\binom{17}{}$$

s the next week flew by, neither Aidan nor Debbie mentioned the kiss. The atmosphere seemed electrified with tension. While he, himself, would've loved to elaborate on the subject, Debbie wore herself ragged trying to avoid him. Raking a hand through his hair, Aidan sighed. How much longer would this go on? At least she was talking to Maureen. His mind was eased as he rationalized that if anyone could perhaps talk some sense into that headstrong woman, it'd be his sister.

But I'd rather she talk to me, he thought sadly.

He quickly organized the paperwork and set it aside for Debbie to collect upon her departure. Movement from the periphery of his vision caused his head to turn. Debbie confidently cleared the last step and strode toward the empty space behind the free weights. Aidan's whole body began to tingle as he recalled the sweetness of their kiss. He remembered the way she had fit in his arms so perfectly, as well as the stunned expression on her face when he'd let her go. Now, it was a constant battle between his heart and his mind to keep from entwining her in his arms—but this time, not letting go—or allowing Debbie to continue on in her denial until she could admit her affections. The sheer nonsense of her actions caused Aidan to feel as though he were losing his mind.

Dialing Maureen's number, he tapped a pencil spasmodically against the desk. As he waited for her to answer, he realized he didn't know what he wanted to say.

"Hello?"

"Hi, Maureen, it's Aidan."

"How are you doing? Has she talked to you yet?"

"No. She's been playing some strange version of hide-and-seek. If she doesn't want to see me, then I'm not supposed to see her. Understand?"

"Not entirely. As a woman, I can't help but cheer for your method of enlightenment. Honestly, that was something straight from the movies. I know that if Tom had DONE THAT FOR ME—" Aidan smiled, sure that the shouted statement was strictly for the benefit of her husband, no doubt lounging in the next room, "I would've been thrilled down to my toes."

"Yeah, well, I just didn't deal well with the whole, 'You're just one of the girls' thing.' "

"I imagine that had to be painful. I know that I practically choked on my potato when I heard her say that. And all I was trying to do was force the two of you to own up to your feelings. Suddenly, ka-BLAM—I'm caught in the crossfire."

Aidan laughed. "Well, sometimes, it serves you right. So, she's coming by your place tonight, right?"

"Yes, and with my back still acting up, I may ask her to stay and help me out again. Then, hopefully, we can discuss the 'incident.' "

"I hope you can figure out what is going on inside of her mind. I'm really beginning to think that hauling her off over my shoulder is a plausible alternative to talking."

"Well, I can't condone that, of course. But I will keep you posted. Have a good day, Aidan. Don't let her get you down."

"I'm trying. It's a pretty big ego deflation when the girl you're after doesn't even think a kiss like that merits discussion."

❧

Deborah fluidly executed her numerous stretches without so much as a thought to them. Her mind, no matter how she tried to bring her thoughts under control, was consumed with Aidan and his forceful kiss.

"What does it mean?"

Don't be silly. You know what it means. He cares for you. Not just your Christianity. He cares for you as a person.

What about me? Do I care for him?

Of course you do, girl! Think about it!

She continued to argue with herself long after women began to arrive for the high-impact class. The self-examination was frightening, to say the least.

Pressing the "Power" button on the stereo, Deborah skipped any superfluous words and jumped right into the routine. She pictured herself becoming flustered during her usual introduction and inadvertently saying something she longed to keep secret. Something about Aidan. *Wouldn't he get a kick out of that?* she thought bitterly. *That man obviously has no regard for my personal space or my wishes. What an animal!* But thoughts of his assertiveness caused well-recognized tingles to break out all along her spine and throughout her scalp. To counteract the unbidden Sparkles, she doubled the workout pace and lost herself in the irregular thudding of the pop song.

Turning to avoid any conversation beyond "thanks" and "see you next Monday," Deborah closed up the cabinet and headed toward the locker room. Within fifteen minutes, she stood with her bag slung over her shoulder, leafing through the figures Aidan had left out with a note: "Debbie—take these to Maureen at home, like usual. Thanks, Aidan."

"Hey, Debbie, before you go." Deborah froze at the sound of his rich voice.

"Yes, Aidan?" Calm professionalism took over, and Deborah eyed him with cool confidence.

"Just making sure we're still on for Sunday." *He's smirking at me! The nerve!* Deborah fought every instinct in her body. Half of her was screaming for her to grab and kiss him, while the other half demanded she berate him for his actions and run away. In theory, both seemed equally effective. In practice, however, she was unable to move.

"I suppose so," she answered slowly, almost as a resigned sigh.

"Good. Oh, and tell Maureen I said 'Hi.' " With that, he turned on his heel and entered the pool room.

"Some people!" Clutching the papers in a tight fist, she stomped out the door and to her car. The air smelled of snow, and her angry breaths came out in frigid puffs of condensation. The drastically dropping temperature threatened to penetrate the skin of her bare forearms, but undiluted rage fueled a fire within her.

Switching the defroster onto "High," she beat her open palms against the steering wheel. "Why doesn't anything make sense! Why is he doing this to me? I leave in two and a half months. Who starts a relationship with someone who's going away?" A hand slipped, causing the horn to emit a long, loud blast. Looking around in embarrassment, she focused her attention on the front door of McCullough's.

Through the window, she could make out a man—a laughing man who looked a lot like Aidan. Infuriated, she let out a low growl. Throwing the car into gear, she forced the accelerator down as far as it would go and popped the clutch. The Cavalier promptly died. Realizing she was now directly in front of the entryway, she drew a deep breath and gritted her teeth. Stealing a sideways glance, she watched as Aidan seemed to double over in amusement.

"I can't deal with this. He already thinks I'm a fool. Now, I've proven it." Restarting the engine, Deborah willed herself to be calm. This time, she rejoiced as she casually coasted out of the parking lot and toward the Smith residence. "Let him laugh," she declared. "I don't need him. I don't need anybody." But the certainty in her voice failed to bolster her sagging spirits.

By the time she arrived at Maureen's, the sun had fallen behind the horizon. With the air crisp and free of its normal Kansas humidity, Deborah took a moment to breathe deeply and marvel at the sunset. The horizon was ablaze with apricots, oranges, and crimsons. The outer edges of the bowl of the sky were colored an inky blue, and larger stars could be seen, despite the multitude of city lights. For a brief instant, Deborah felt peaceful.

The door opened and Maureen stepped cautiously onto the porch. "How beautiful," she sighed.

"Yes. I sometimes forget how spectacular a sunset can be, though at this precise minute, I can't see how." Chilled, Deborah attempted to warm her arms by hugging herself tightly and rubbing fiercely from her shoulders to her elbows.

"You need to get inside before you freeze to death. I made you some hot chocolate, anyway." Maureen smiled and reentered the house. Deborah quickly followed, after retrieving the stack of numbers and names Aidan had left her.

"So what flavor of chocolate is it? I know you've always got the exotic kinds on hand."

"You bet. It's hazelnut and white chocolate. I remembered your saying that was your favorite." Maureen poured steaming water over the powdery contents of the oversized mug. Deborah stirred slowly while wrapping her free hand around the warm ceramic. Turning the cup, she noticed it displayed an abstract rendition of a woman in several poses.

"This is really unique. Where did you get it?" Deborah traced the indented outline of the woman's hair.

"Oh, I picked it up in New Mexico. I just fell in love with the lost look in her eyes."

Deborah nodded. "Mmm . . . I can see why."

"Marshmallows?" Maureen offered the open bag.

"No, thank you. This will be fine." Blowing into the creamy liquid, Deborah carefully sipped. "Oh, here are the figures for the week."

"Actually, I was hoping you would help me get through those in a hurry, so we could sit and talk. With Tom at the gym all the time, and Aidan consumed with . . . Aidan things—" Maureen winked, "I get kind of lonely. The girls aren't much for conversation."

Deborah laughed. "No, I imagine not. Sure, I'll stay and talk awhile. I haven't seen or heard much from Cali or Chris, so it would be nice to chat."

"Great. Well, you're welcome to take off your shoes and curl up on the couch. Oh, and there's a quilt draped along the back, if you're super cold. My back is so much better, so I won't need to lie down while we work."

The women moved into the living room, and Deborah nestled herself in the corner closest to Maureen's chair. Tucking her legs up under her, she tasted her hot chocolate again and grinned. "This is sooo good."

"Glad you like it. Tom can't stand hazelnut, and so I'm the only one who drinks it, generally. But here lately, I've limited how much I have since it has caffeine. I'm trying to be careful for the babies."

"I'll be more than happy to help keep the supply down for you," Deborah volunteered solemnly.

"Oh, I'll bet you will." Within the hour, the women had completed the bookwork and sat staring into the roaring fire that occupied the stone fireplace, adjacent to the entertainment center.

"So, tell me, Debbie. Are you going back to Grace this Sunday?"

Deborah tensed and searched the woman's face for signs of ridicule, but Maureen's eyes held no accusation, nor humor. Deborah relaxed slightly.

"Actually, I thought I might. I have to admit that the pastor's words stirred me, but I'm still not sure it's the perfect church. I don't feel any differently there than I did at any of the others."

"I don't think there's any such thing as a 'perfect church,' Debbie. Not at least in the sense of man-made institutions. God's church, meaning all of the believers, is perfect, insofar as we are truly led by God. However, sin taints and destroys the pure motives we start out with, and soon, we're creating laws and bylaws and statutes, instead of focusing on worship and prayer."

"No, I don't mean 'perfect' as in unflawed. I mean perfect for me." Deborah's explanation sounded weak in her own ears.

"Do you, Deb? I'm serious. I believe you use this quest you're on to keep you from attaching yourself to anything or anyone. I honestly can't believe you're even here with me now. I'm exceedingly glad that you are, but I am surprised, nonetheless."

Deborah focused her gaze on the dancing flames. She counted out her breaths, attempting to slow them. *Stay calm,* she soothed herself. *Maureen is only trying to help.*

"Debbie?" Her eyes shifted to the back of Maureen's recliner. Deborah hoped the gesture would cause her to continue. It did.

"I'm glad you will give Grace another week. I hope you give it another week after that. I would love nothing more than for you to make Grace your church home, right alongside me and Tom and Aidan. But you can't expect Pastor Riley—or any of us, for that matter—to answer questions you're not willing to ask. Does that make any sense?"

Deborah nodded, knowing it was the response Maureen desired. How could she tell her what was really on her mind? How could she put words to emotions that threatened to consume her?

"Then explain to me what I just said to you. In your own words, Debbie. What does that mean to you?"

Deborah raised the mug to her lips and drank. Slowly, she repeated the question. "What does that mean to me? Hmm . . . I suppose it means you guys aren't mind readers. That's the first conclusion I can draw. Second, I believe it means you are holding me responsible for what I don't know. And, quite frankly, I'm not sure how I feel about that."

Maureen nodded encouragingly. "Go on."

"Well, if you are insinuating, in order for me to receive guidance and explanations, I need to lay everything out for everybody to see, regardless of its relevance, then I think you've got a poor way of doing business."

"Why would it mean you'd have to 'lay everything out,' Deb?"

"Because I don't know what I don't know! How can I come to you and say, 'Well, Maureen, today I'd like to work on x, y, and z,' when I haven't been exposed to the existence of x, y, and z! Therefore, to make sure you can answer my questions, I would be required to expose myself to complete strangers. You could all feel oh-so-enlightened and helpful, while I'm crying and spiritually stripped in a corner."

"I see what you're saying. Makes total sense to me. If I tell you I can't frost your cake until you make it, yet you have never seen a cake recipe, I can't expect you to bake one without help. Right?"

Deborah waved a hand in the air. "Exactly. So, what are you suggesting I do?"

Maureen sipped thoughtfully from her mug. "All right. If I were you, I would first write down the fundamental things I believe I know. I would show these truths to a pastor or to a friend. I would ask for comments and encourage discussion. In the areas where others could prove me wrong, I would highlight those and seek additional material to explain either where I had gone wrong or where the critic had gone wrong. Either way, it would be a learning experience for all involved. Follow me so far?"

"Yes."

"Okay, next, I would ask for recommendations of books and study materials. Say, the pastor's wife talks to you. That would provide a perfect opportunity for you to say, 'By the way, can you suggest a title or two I could pick up at the bookstore? I'm interested in an independent study, and I just need somewhere to begin.' See? Or you could ask me. I have tons of excellent devotionals and Scripture commentaries. Those sorts of things would be very helpful to someone who didn't know what questions to ask. And as you read, write down your thoughts and the issues that confuse you. Bring those to the attention of your church family. I still do. As I've tried to tell you before, God doesn't punish us for seeking answers and knowledge. In fact, He says in His Word that if anyone lacks knowledge, let him ask for it and his heavenly Father will give it to him. Understand?"

Deborah whistled. "Well, okay then. Sounds like you've got quite a plan outlined for me. You know, nobody's ever done that for me before. Usually, they just say, 'Pray and read the Word' or something noncommittal. You're the first person to present me with a solid answer. I must admit, I'm stunned. I never really had a script for what to say beyond this point."

Maureen just smiled triumphantly. "I'll go the distance with you. I don't think you're going to like the process as much as you may believe, but I'll do it. Now, in light of your dumbfounded state, I suggest we move on to another topic."

Sighing with relief, Deborah agreed. "Yes. Let's."

"Good. Want to tell about what happened with Aidan?"

18

*D*eborah nearly choked. "What?" Maureen's green eyes danced with mirth, while her expression displayed the utmost innocence.

"You heard me. Spill it."

"Oh, no, you don't. You have an unfair advantage. The self-proclaimed Romeo is your brother, so you get more than your fair share of information."

"Too bad. You're in my house, on my couch, drinking my cocoa. So I get to pick the subject. Now, talk." She crossed her arms over her ample midsection and seemed to patiently await Deborah's response.

"Fine, but you don't play fair!" She wagged an accusatory finger at her hostess.

"Funny, Aidan says that too." Her singsong tone and wide eyes told Deborah she had undoubtedly met her match.

"All right, Mrs. Smith. Here's how it is." Frustrated at being cornered, yet oddly relieved, Deborah allowed her manner to be comedic in nature. "Your brother—upon driving me home from church, mind you—grabbed me and kissed me full on the lips!" She threw her hands in the air to punctuate the lunacy of it all, only to see Maureen suppressing a giggle.

Clearing her throat, she nodded gravely and commented, "Well . . . it's about time." Deborah's mouth dropped, and her companion burst into an uncontrolled fit of laughing.

"What?" she shrieked. To this, Maureen only grew louder. Realizing her only options were to laugh alongside or be laughed at, Deborah chose the former.

"All right, I guess it is sort of funny."

"Not it," Maureen howled. "You! You are hilarious. You think I don't see how you look at him! Or how he looks at you? You're both gaga for each other, and it took this long for either one of you to make a move. So, in light of Aidan's overcoming his emotional handicap, you, my dear Debbie, are the funny one. Why didn't you grab that boy and kiss him back?"

"Maureen!" Deborah's attempt to sound scandalized came out as a whine. Thinking better of it, she admitted, "I wasn't passive! He just kind of dropped me and ran away. I figured that was the end of it. He hasn't said anything at work."

"Because you avoid him like a vacuum salesman! I've been there before when you tried to skirt around him, unseen. You're afraid he's not perfect either, aren't you?" Maureen's laughing ceased, and her tone became firm.

"I . . . I . . ."

"You, what—enjoy the attention, but don't have the decency to let him know you're not interested? This is my brother you're playing with, Debbie. I may be as big as a house, but I can still protect the ones I love."

Shocked, Deborah exclaimed, "But I am interested!" Upon hearing herself, she blushed.

"Oh. Well, that's different. But, how is he supposed to know when you won't say anything?" Deborah couldn't help but smile at the woman's feigned seriousness.

"Maureen, you're one talented lady, you know that?"

The expectant mother just beamed. "I told you I'd go the distance with you. Not so sure laying your heart out in front of me was your wisest move, now, are you?"

❧

Aidan pulled into the parking space next to Deborah's Cavalier. His sister had never called him back, and he was going crazy without knowing what was said about him. Pausing to pray, he poured out his heart to the Father.

"Lord, I thank You for Your many blessings. I ask You to continue to watch over my family. Father, please help me to keep my spirit in check. I know Debbie has a long way to go where You're concerned, and the last thing I want to do is to distract her from getting to know You better. Please touch her heart and make it willing to be changed. I also pray my heart would be filled with You and not with my own conceit. In Jesus' name, amen."

After stepping down from the driver's side, his powerful strides carried him quickly to her door. He knocked loudly, then leaned against the doorjamb. Seconds later, he heard the sound of cabinets being slammed. Debbie slung the door open wide and greeted him with a beautiful smile.

"Well, hi there, Aidan. How are you this morning?" Her civil manner threw him off guard.

"I'm, uh, just fine." He hurried ahead of her to open the door of the SUV.

"That's great. Oh, and Aidan? I have some questions for you and your pastor, so we might be a little longer than usual."

≈

Deborah held her spiral-bound notebook close to her body. She excitedly recalled staying up late into the night to answer the questions Maureen had posed. Now, all she needed was a volunteer to engage in a spiritual tête-à-tête. Aidan would, no doubt, do nicely.

The service raced by, and Deborah found herself standing before the pastor. "Here, Pastor . . . Riley, is it? If you could look these over, I'd really appreciate it. I'm trying to take a spiritual inventory, of sorts. I'll get back to you." Confident he would find few to no problems with her belief system, she waited with a smile as Aidan picked up more sermon notes for Tom and Maureen.

≈

"So?" Deborah looked expectantly at Aidan.

"So what?"

"So, what's your answer, Aidan? Do you or don't you believe God rewards those who follow His instructions perfectly, while punishing those who don't?" Deborah eyed him intently, sure she had found at least one truth even the great Aidan McCullough couldn't challenge.

"I don't believe that. Not entirely."

"How can you not? Look at Jonah! Look at Noah! Are you blind?" Deborah's heart raced. *Oh no. He's going to prove me wrong again!*

"Well, for one, Jacob. Jacob stole his brother's birthright and the blessing his father Isaac intended to bestow upon Esau, yet God allowed him to live abundantly. I don't think it was God's perfect will for Jacob to be so cruel to Esau, yet a willing heart allowed God to use Jacob to His glory. So, there you are."

How can he sit there so smugly when my entire life's convictions are being shot full of holes! He can't care about me. No caring person would do this.

Tears stung Deborah's eyes. Instead of pursuing the argument, she recalled Maureen's instructions. She was to seek additional information to either correct herself or rebuke her critics. Somehow, though, the task seemed much more daunting in daylight.

Later in the afternoon, Deborah sat motionless in her car, staring at the numerous pages beside her. Pastor Riley had called and said he would like to see her. Certain he was going to commend her on her insight and praise her youthful wisdom, she had been shocked when he had handed her his comments.

"You should feel free to read over this at your leisure, Debbie. I am so pleased you are seeking to grow. I hope this exercise has proven helpful."

Tears began to escape her eyes. How could she be so far off? These people couldn't all be lying. That seemed too conspiratorial.

When she compared the words of Chris and Cali with the conversations she held with Aidan and Maureen, the similarity was too much to stomach. If she was wrong, then her mother and father were wrong. If her parents had erred in their philosophy, perhaps she had been wasting her life, trying to adhere to foolishness.

Unable to voice her intense sorrow and shame, she drove home and unplugged her telephone. Sobs racked her body, though she knew there was no definable reason why.

What if they're right? What if I am wrong? What does that mean? The thought was too much to deal with. Seeking the solace of her bed, she curled up and wrapped her arms around a stuffed tiger. She felt helpless and lost, like a little child who'd been separated from her parents at the fair.

Deciding perhaps her old method of existing far surpassed her current condition, she resolved to ask no more questions. *Questions are dangerous,* she determined. *Questions only stir up doubts, and that can't be right.*

ха

Aidan tapped the steering wheel to the lively beat on the radio. Without thought, he drove the well-traveled route to Debbie's apartment and parked his Suburban. It was hard to believe she'd been accompanying him to Grace Fellowship for almost two months. She really seemed to be enjoying the services and understanding the messages. Aidan felt his heart swell with love for her. *Wait a minute—love? Yes! I do love her.* The realization resulted in an ear-to-ear grin.

Debbie opened her door and cocked her head to one side. "What's going on with you?" Her raised eyebrow and crossed arms made him chuckle.

"Tell you later," he promised. Today would be just for fun. Church, then perhaps an afternoon with Tom and Maureen. Maybe they could all go out to lunch, though Maureen was due at any minute, it seemed. He would discuss the matter with his sister and brother-in-law, then he would find the perfect time to propose. His thoughts raced at a million miles a minute. Reaching out, he took Debbie's delicate hand in his stronger one and spun her into his arms.

"Ooo-kay, then." Debbie's beaming face thrilled him completely. He opened her door, as had become their habit, then gently kissed the tips of her fingers.

"M'lady," he announced, "your green chariot awaits." Debbie seemed amused by his poor English accent, but she said nothing. Aidan turned the key in the ignition, and they sang all the way to the church.

❧

After a terrific day, Aidan came home to find his answering machine light blinking. Curious as to who could have called, Aidan quickly punched the message button. "Aidan, this is Maureen. Please give me a call. I've got some exciting news."

When the message concluded, Aidan dialed the number and waited. With the second ring, Maureen picked up the phone. Aidan prompted his sister for information. "So, the message said 'exciting news.' I'm waiting."

"Aidan, Tom and I have been going over the sermon notes that Pastor Riley gave us. We've been praying about this for awhile now, and I feel like God has given me an answer. I'm going to continue to stay home, even after the babies are born. I may go back to desk work eventually, you know, on an emergency basis, but I feel this is what God wants for me. Tom is fully supportive. What do you think?"

Aidan smiled, amazed at his sister's change of heart. "Wow, Maureen. That's something I never thought I'd hear you say. I think it's great! My only concern—and naturally, this is strictly business—is who's going to take over for you permanently."

"Aidan, she's right under your nose, silly! Debbie loves the gym. She's great at her job. She's changed so much in these last two months; I honestly believe she'll be thrilled."

"You know what? I think you're right. And guess what? I love her!"

"Oh, really Aidan? You think?" His sister's sarcasm tickled him.

"Fine, so you already knew, but I sure didn't. Not until today. I hoped to talk to you and Tom about it before I proposed to her."

"Well, you can rest assured, Tom and I agree that so long as Debbie's right with God and loves you back, you two were made for each other."

"Yeah, I think so, too."

19

avigating her car into the parking lot of McCullough's Gym, Deborah allowed her mind to drift back. Upon deciding to ask no more questions and seek no more answers, she had found the world generally liked her a lot better. Cali and Chris came by more often, and Deborah found she could talk the talk right alongside them. Maureen and Aidan even noted the difference as "positive." Who was she to complain? Her job obligation would be over as soon as Maureen's children were born, and then, she could find somewhere else to hide. *The sad thing is,* she thought, *I'm running low on options.*

"Debbie! I'm so glad to see you. Come here for a second." Aidan's lopsided grin melted her heart, yet she knew he wouldn't follow her when she left. Their "dates," if you could even call them that, were innocent and sweet. He had no feelings for her beyond casual attraction, and Deborah smiled sadly as she realized she'd convinced her heart the same was true for her.

"Here. Sit right here."

Deborah sank into the cushion and painted a bright smile on her face. "What's going on, boss?"

"First, I wanted to tell you the good news. Maureen went in just a minute ago to deliver the twins. It could be awhile, but the contractions have started, and the doctors seem pretty confident this could be it."

"Congratulations! I'm so excited. We should close the gym and go wait for her!"

"Wait, there's more. Debbie, I want you to know how much I have loved having you here at the gym. You've been such a blessing to me. You seem to enjoy yourself, and I know the classes love you."

"Thank you." Deborah felt a tightness in the pit of her stomach. *I've heard this before. . . .*

"Maureen told me yesterday she and Tom have decided she'll stay home with the babies indefinitely. So, you are welcome to stay on as our permanent aerobics instructor."

"Really?" She hoped the forced enthusiasm wasn't discernable to Aidan. *Oh, how I wish things could be different. I would love to stay here with you, Aidan. If only you could truly know and love me. Not for who you wish I was, but for who I really am.*

"One more thing." Deborah watched in horror as Aidan dropped to one knee. "I figured with all that other good news, I might as well keep going." He produced a small velvet box from the pocket of his jogging pants. "Deborah Shaughnessy, will you marry me?"

The last thing she could recall before fainting was how glad she was he'd allowed her to sit down.

➤

"Debbie. Debbie, wake up, sweetheart." Aidan watched her beautiful brown eyes struggle to remain open. "I must admit, I'm growing weary of coaxing you out of unconsciousness." He smiled and stroked her cheek. So soft. She was all he had ever hoped for in a wife. "Guess the Sparkles kind of hit you all at once, huh?"

As she became more aware of her surroundings, he was able to laugh. Helping her to her feet, he drew her close. "Why don't you go ahead and take the day off? That way you can go see Maureen and tell her that you're going to become my wife. After she's finished having her babies, of course."

"I doubt she'd be very excited right now, anyway," Debbie reasoned. "But I think I will take you up on your offer."

As he watched her exit the building, he felt as though he would burst. She quickly jogged to her car and sped away. "She's as excited as I am!" Turning to roll her chair back in place, he noticed the small velvet box, still on the table.

"Uh-oh!" He put it back in his pocket, planning to pay a visit to her after closing.

&

Deborah barely made it through the door of her apartment before the tears began to fall. Rifling through the cupboards, she grabbed a box of chocolate-chip, peanut-butter-chunk cookies and a bag of sour-cream-and-onion potato chips. Setting the junk food on the counter, she poured herself a tall glass of water.

"Gil!" she moaned. "What are we going to do?"

Walking to the front of the microwave, she peered into the bowl. Unable to find him hiding within the plastic trees, Deborah's eye was caught by an object floating at the top.

Sobs racked her entire body. "I've killed Gil! I can't do anything right!" Blindly flailing herself into the living room, she threw her arms up to the sky and cried out to God.

"All right, I can't take anymore of this. What do You want from me? When I ask questions, no one likes me; but the minute I shut up, then suddenly, I'm wife material! You won't let me find the perfect apartment or the perfect job. You show me the perfect man, but then, just to make things interesting, You cause him to care more about my salvation than me! You make my parents miserable for twenty years. You allow them to make me miserable just as long. And now! Now, You take my fish—my one and only accomplishment on this whole planet, and You take him from me! Will You just tell me what You want from me? I fear You—isn't that enough? Do you want me to dance and sing? WHAT DO YOU WANT?"

Collapsing onto the orange shag love seat, Deborah buried her head in its fuzzy warmth. In a voice barely above her wailing, she heard the words, *"Love me."*

"But how can I love You when You don't love me?" Wiping

her eyes roughly, she continued. "How can You take everything from me, and keep me from true happiness, and then claim to want my love?"

"Of course I love you. Don't you see?"

"No, I don't see. I'm tired. I can't keep anything together."

As she continued to rage against God, she began to pull out her cardboard boxes and tape them together again. She packed her books and videos, then set to wrapping her breakables. Slowly, her shouts fizzled into mumbles. Before long, exhaustion claimed her, and she slept fitfully.

Awakened by the knocks at the door, Deborah sat up amidst the boxes and newspapers and rubbed her temples forcefully. "Who is it?"

"Aidan, your fiancé."

"Not right now, Aidan, please." She stood in front of the closed door and willed him to leave.

"I promise I won't stay. I just have to give you something."

Deborah slapped her forehead with her palm. The ring. "Fine, but please don't ask me any questions. Promise?"

"I suppose so. Are you all—"

Deborah pulled the door toward herself and allowed Aidan to come in. "Umm . . . are you sure I can't ask any questions? You don't look too good."

"I'm positive. We can talk about this later." The one thing she could find to praise God about was that since Maureen was having her babies, she technically would not be in violation of her job contract, so she wouldn't have to feel too responsible if she never saw Aidan McCullough again.

"Here, I brought you these." Aidan thrust a bouquet of wildflowers and tiger lilies toward her and smiled shyly. "See? I remembered the whole tiger motif. Get it?"

Sinking to the floor, she cried, "I can't take care of those! Don't you understand what I am? I murder innocent fish, and you bring me flowers and propose marriage? You're obviously not all there, Aidan." His blank stare did nothing to deter her lamenting. She buried her face in her hands.

After what felt like seconds, she felt arms encircle her. She opened her eyes and found Aidan kneeling beside her. "Shhh . . . it's okay, Debbie. I love you. Fish or no fish." He repeated similar sentiments over and over, rocking her back and forth. "Please talk to me. Please let me in."

"No," she wailed. "When you know me, you won't love me! God hates me; don't you see that? He's taken away everything I love. He's taken my fish. I ask questions, and He punishes me. I can't do anything right, Aidan. I can't find the perfect job. I can't find the perfect place to live. Nothing!"

"Debbie, why are you so hard on yourself? Don't you see how God wants to bless your life? His plan is better than perfect. When you yield to Him and allow Him to use you to His glory, you'll find life is beyond perfect. His love is beyond perfect. So is the love I feel for you."

"How can you say that, when all you care about is my salvation? When I stopped bugging you with my stupid questions, then you loved me. Now that you know I'm crazy, you can't love me. Neither can God. He punished me with my mugging. He punished me with my parents. Now, He's punishing me with my own fish! It all seems so cruel." Against her better judgment, she buried her head in his chest.

"I don't just care about your salvation, Debbie. I'll admit, it's important to me that you be saved. And I believe you are. I just don't think you understand the full benefits of being a child of God. I want to help you explore and understand how wonderful it is to be His. I want to help answer your questions and hear your arguments. I want to read the Bible with you and discuss your opinions. I want to pray with you as your husband and as the head of our family. I want you to know that you can have more than you've ever dreamed of, simply by committing your spirit into the capable hands of our heavenly Father. Debbie, He loved you so much, He let Jesus die a horrible death just so you could come home to Him. No one else can ever love you as much as He does. Not even me—but I sure do love you a lot more than you imagine."

When she didn't respond, she heard him sigh. It sounded like her mother's sigh. Slowly, she moved away and crawled over to the couch. Curling into a ball, she struggled to calm her emotions. Aidan stood and caressed her hair for a moment before speaking.

"Debbie, I could hold you in my arms right now, and believe me, there's nothing more I want to do. I ache for you. But that's not what you need right now. Take a couple days off from the gym and think about what I've said. I know you'll be surprised if you just give it an honest chance." Deborah could hear him turn the doorknob and quietly step through the threshold. "Oh, and one more thing, Debbie—could you please unpack? I'm still worn out from your last move." Despite herself, Debbie smiled. He was awfully easy to love, no matter how much she didn't want him to be.

❧

After a long night's sleep, Deborah awoke with a new purpose. Quickly donning olive corduroy overalls over a black angora sweater, she tied her hair back and washed her face. Her eyes were puffy and red, but she didn't care. She had to get to the bookstore.

Turning onto Quivira, she drove past 95th Street and turned right into the strip mall and parked directly in front of the Christian bookstore. Systematically purchasing every title she could remember, along with CD copies of Aidan's praise songs, she racked up a bill well over $130, but she wasn't worried about money. No, this was much bigger. *If Aidan is right,* she thought, *then Maureen is right. So are Pastor Riley, his wife, and Cali and Chris. How* many countless others knew the truth? And could it be too late for her to understand?

Deborah spent the next day and a half poring over every selection. She cried when she concentrated on the treatment of Jesus during the Crucifixion. She found the corresponding verses in her brand-new study Bible. Highlighted entries covered the pages. She even discovered in Ephesians the verse Aidan had referenced when he spoke to her—["For He] is able to do immeasurably more than all we ask or imagine." For the first time ever, Deborah prayed in order to praise, rather than to cower behind forced reverence.

"Oh, Father, how long would You wait for me? How could You tolerate my ignorance for so long? And the people you placed in my life—Cali, Chris, Maureen, Tom, Aidan—will they still be there, now that I've found the truth? Forgive me for taking so long. Forgive me for doubting Your plan for my life. Thank You for Your love and devotion, even to me. In Your Son's wonderful name, amen."

As if on cue, the telephone rang. Deborah reached for the receiver anxiously. Perhaps it was Aidan. Disappointed at the sound of her mother's voice, however, Deborah tried to sound cheery. "Hi, Mom. How are you?"

"We're doing all right, but I hadn't heard from you in some time."

Deborah nodded as if her mother could see. "I know. I'm sorry. I've been busy."

"Oh? What's going on?"

Deborah wondered how much to say. She couldn't very well attack her mother with, "Well, I've just found out that everything you've taught me about God is off base." She drew a deep breath. "I've been doing a lot of soul-searching, for one thing."

"Is this because of those people you've been hanging with at the gym?" her mother questioned warily. "They aren't a part of a cult, are they?"

Deborah laughed. "No, Mom. But this does have something to do with them. Mostly, it has to do with God."

"Oh, Debbie, honey, what have you done? Are you in trouble?"

"No, I'm better than ever. I've just been reading the Bible and learning to have a closer walk with God."

Silence filled the air. "Mom? Are you still there?"

"I'm here. I'm just not sure I understand what you're talking about. I thought your father and I taught you everything you needed to know."

Deborah didn't want to frighten her mother off. There was so much she wanted to share with her. So much about the love of God and the joy of their heavenly Father. So much that Deborah knew they'd never even begun to see.

"You and Dad have always been good to help. I guess I just want to reciprocate."

"What do you mean?"

Deborah happened to notice the stack of books on her coffee table. "I'm going to send you a book, Mom. I want you to share it with Daddy. Read it and then I want you to promise me that when you're done, we can discuss it. Maybe I'll even fly out for a visit."

"Deborah, you know how busy I am."

"I know. But I also know you have time for reading a chapter every night before you go to bed. Please, Mom. Please just do this for me."

"Well, I suppose I can."

Deborah smiled. "Good. I'll put it in the mail today. You won't regret this, I promise. I think this is going to help you with your outlook on life. Maybe even give you some peace about the past."

Confident in the knowledge that she had done all she could, Deborah assured her mother of her love. Saying their good-byes, she quickly ended the conversation before her mother could further question her about the book.

Her heart took flight and enticed her brain to remember Aidan and his proposal. Without a second thought, she grabbed her keys and prepared to tell him her answer. As she locked the door behind her, she heard another door slam shut. Turning, she found Aidan smiling and striding toward her. In his hand, he held a plastic bag. Deborah offered up a quick prayer of thanksgiving and ran to him.

"Wanna try again?" he asked, grinning hopefully.

Taking the bag, she realized it held two large goldfish.

"Maybe it'll be better with two," he added.

"Oh, Aidan!" She threw herself into his arms and kissed him squarely, just as Maureen had suggested. "I do want to try again. And you were so right. It will be beyond perfect, just as the Lord has promised."

"Well, there is something you need to know before you agree to marry me, Ms. Shaughnessy." His tone was solemn, yet his eyes suggested something quite different.

"And what might that be, Mr. McCullough?"

After drawing a deep breath, he continued, "If you marry me, you instantly become the aunt of two beautiful babies."

"Maureen's?" she squealed.

"A boy and a girl. Born just this afternoon. Think you can handle it?"

"Only if you promise she gets to be an aunt, too."

Nuzzling next to her ear, his husky whisper thrilled her. "That, my dear, I think I can do."

Epilogue

*L*izzy, Timothy, come here!" Maureen's voice carried over the din of the audience. The tiny toddlers crawled through the fallen leaves and gurgled happily to one another. Suddenly, their escape was over, as Tom scooped the twins up into his arms. Carrying one over each shoulder, he reclaimed his seat by his wife on the bench.

Deborah anxiously played with her bouquet of wildflowers and orange tiger lilies and recalled the first time she had seen that particular mixture. Aidan had brought them to her after proposing and she . . . well, she had collapsed on the floor, wailing like a baby. The thought made her smile. Could that really have been ten months ago? Turning her eyes heavenward, she marveled at the pristine blue sky. "Thank You, Father, for this glorious day. Thank You also for my husband . . . to be, of course."

Deborah moved gracefully, the full skirt of her layered muslin gown swaying rhythmically to the first strains of "Pachelbel's Canon in D." She'd worked with Chris and Cali to design the dress and loved the great freedom the skirt's many layers would allow her. Her friends insisted upon the net overlay to complete the sweetheart bodice, and they had also created a wreath of wildflowers to hold the wispy veil and satin ribbons to complete the simplistically elegant look.

Tears misted her eyes, and she looked over to find her father crying as well. "Honey, I'm so happy for you. He's a good man, and I know you will both be very happy. And you look . . . absolutely radiant."

She tried to focus on her steps, but her eyes always found

their way to Aidan, looking more handsome than ever in his black suit. This day was something out of a fairy tale. Nothing in her wildest dreams could've prepared her for the flutter in her heart and the look on Aidan's face.

Reaching the front, she smiled as Aidan led her to an ornate bench. Slipping off her white ballet slippers, he placed her dainty feet into a beautiful basin and poured warm water over them. Lovingly, he caressed them—washed them—silently assuring her of his allegiance and of his servant's heart. After drying them, he replaced her slippers and allowed her to repeat the gesture of devotion for him.

Before returning to take their vows, she stopped. Looking deep into his eyes, she whispered, "Pray with me."

"Now and always," he murmured.

Together they knelt and Deborah knew that nothing, not even the Sparkles could equal the feeling they shared in that moment. "Glory to God," she breathed. "Thank You that You truly are beyond perfect."

Far Above Rubies

by Becky Melby and Cathy Wienke

To Brian and our son Michael,
my two paramedics,
and to Michael's beloved
Rebecca Humphreys Wienke.
Cathy

To Bill, my very own pilot and my very best friend.
Becky

1

*P*aige's foot kept time to the music as she pumped the pedal that turned the potter's wheel. Chubby little fingers slid beneath hers on the slick, wet clay. Paige looked up at the mirror and laughed at the wide-eyed expression of the little girl on her lap. Their creation was getting taller and skinnier by the second.

"Annie, are we making a vase or a giraffe?"

Annie's dark brown ringlets bounced as she giggled. "Raf! Make raf!"

"Okay, Sweet Stuff, giraffe it is!" Paige said as she took her foot off the pedal. "But we have to stop now or the poor giraffe won't be able to hold his head up."

"No stop!" Annie's fingertips dug into the thinning tower of clay as it was slowing down. Suddenly, the top half collapsed and thudded onto the table. Paige held her breath, bracing for another temper tantrum, hoping this would be one of the times that she'd be able to distract Annie and ward off her easily-triggered anger. She picked up the broken piece and handed it to Annie. Annie took it, glared at it, looked for a moment like she might throw it across the room, and then began to laugh. "Raf's head falled off! Silly raf!"

"Silly giraffe!" Paige kissed the top of Annie's head and laughed with her, more out of relief than anything. She looked up at the clock. "It's supper time. Should we wash up now?"

"Eat now!" Annie slid off her lap and ran toward the door of the occupational therapy room.

"Annie! Look at your hands!" Paige's warning came a split

second after Annie's left hand flattened against the window and her right grabbed the handle of the locked door. "Look at your hands!" Paige repeated.

The little girl held up her hands as if seeing them for the first time. "Yuch-y!"

"Very yuchy!" Paige stepped on the bar that turned on the water at the half-circle sink. "Let's wash and then we can eat."

Annie giggled again as spots of dried clay on the backs of her hands turned dark, then disappeared under the spray.

Pulling a paper towel from the dispenser, Paige handed one to her. "Wonder what's for supper," she said.

"Don-odes."

"Not today. Tomorrow we're going to McDonald's with Hailey, and then we're going to buy a new dress for Hailey's wedding and go to the zoo and—"

"DON-ODES!" The wadded paper towel hit the sink.

"I think I smell spaghetti!"

"DON-ODES! NOW!" Two small rubber-soled shoes slapped the vinyl floor. Two hands opened and closed, looking for something to throw.

Paige bent down and picked up the slight-built three-year-old and wrapped her in her arms. "Sunshine and rain," she whispered. "So many smiles and so many tears."

There were no commands to stop the tears, just a gentle restraint, a technique taught her by one of the physical therapists. Since self-control was sometimes impossible for children with Fetal Alcohol Syndrome, there were times when the boundaries of loving arms gave them the security of knowing they wouldn't be able to cause harm.

Annie's fists beat against her, but she didn't try to squirm out of her arms. She vented and then grew still, rubbing her wet cheeks on Paige's shoulder. After a minute she looked up and smiled, her eyes sparkling and her dimples deepening.

"You yike sketti, Paige?" she asked.

"I love sketti, and I love you."

Planting a noisy kiss on Paige's cheek, Annie said, "I yuv you, too."

Paige walked slowly to the full-length mirror. Annie's arms and legs were wrapped around her neck and waist, and Paige smiled at their reflection. Three months ago, on a Friday night, she would have been dining al fresco at a sidewalk café or sipping café au lait and listening to music with other art students at an all-night bistro. If someone had given her a preview back then of the thoughts she was thinking today, she would have laughed. But three months ago she was in Paris.

At times she wondered if she would lose herself in this small Wisconsin town. She loved what her brother had started here at the Sparrow Center; from the beginning she had written to him faithfully about it, encouraging him when the project seemed in danger of being sabotaged. David needed something to throw himself into; that's how God blessed him, because that was David's sort of thing. He had always been the one with the tender heart and the desire for order and predictability. Paige, on the other hand, had always been the one with the longing to see the world, the craving for adventure, the one who thrived on change.

Two years ago, when David was still working on the blue-prints for the Sparrow Center, she had volunteered to paint murals on the Center walls—but never in her wildest dreams had she seen herself living here in Milbrooke. Even a year ago, when David and Karlee were planning their wedding and the idea of moving in with Karlee's sister, Hailey Austin, had first come up, she'd seen it as a temporary thing. Living in Karlee's rustic log home was just one more adventure, a chance to experience life in the Midwest . . . for a while.

So how, she wondered, had she reached so quickly the point she was at now? Her life had become filled with her work with handicapped children, fingerpaint and papier mâché, and trips to the zoo. How had it happened?

She stared at her hand against Annie's back, at the pearl ring on her little finger. She hadn't taken it off in five years, maybe she never would. It was there to keep her sights high, to remind her never to settle for less than the best. Five years ago, even three months ago, what she held now in her arms would not have seemed like the best—but then the one thing she had wanted to avoid at all cost was predictability. Little Annie, though, craved the security of predictability; it was one of the things she needed most.

Annie laid her head against her shoulder, and Paige continued to study their reflection. Her own hair was sleek and straight and curved under just below her chin, but it was only a shade darker than Annie's and their eyes were the same deep brown. Annie's skin was darker, but that would only be a problem for those who chose to make it one.

"We look pretty good together, don't we, Annie-kins?" she said.

At twenty-eight and single, Paige Stern was trying on the name "Mommy" for the first time—and she liked the fit.

⁊

The call came in to the Sparrow Children's Center at 5:46 P.M. Karen Jonas, the second-shift receptionist, answered the phone.

"Yes, I was wondering if the executive director might still be in?"

"He's at dinner right now, may I take a message?"

"Yes . . . this is Warren Klug, attorney for Roman Slayder . . ."

Karen's eyes widened. The name would have meant nothing to her if she hadn't just been reading about him two days earlier while standing in line at the grocery store. But what in the world did Robert Worth, their executive director, have to do with Roman Slayder? She took a quick breath and tried to find her professional voice again. "Dr. Worth is just down the hall, Mr. Klug. Can you hold while I get him?"

"Yes. Thank you."

Karen skidded to a stop in front of the break room where Robert Worth was talking with Paige and several employees over pie and coffee. "Phone!" was the only word she could get out.

Robert looked at her with a patiently amused expression. "For whom, Karen?"

"For you! Long distance!" She lowered her voice to a conspiratorial whisper. "It's Roman Slayder's lawyer!" When Robert didn't jump out of his chair, she added, "Do you know who Roman Slayder is?"

Standing up casually, Robert said, "No, I don't."

"He's the lead singer for Quaestor!" She grimaced and almost shivered at the name of the heavy-metal rock band.

"Mm-hm." Robert smiled and picked up his plate. Taking another forkful of pie, he said, "Don't bother me until the president calls, Miss Jonas."

"I'm serious!"

This time, the look on her face convinced him. Wiping his mouth with his napkin, Robert cleared his throat, decided against using the phone in the break room, and walked down the hall to his office. After listening and nodding for several minutes, Robert finally asked a question, to which Mr. Klug replied, "I'm not saying that my client is denying paternity, Dr. Worth, only that there is naturally some cause for doubt. He's willing to have the blood test done and, if the results do not rule out the possibility of his involvement, he would like to see the child."

"Yes. Of course. Are you free to tell me what his intentions are if it is determined that he is Anika's father? Now that the mother has finally decided to release her for adoption—"

"I can tell you honestly," Mr. Klug interrupted, "that I do not believe he would consider relinquishing his rights. But, of course

. . . there is the concern . . . we know, of course, that she has Fetal Alcohol Syndrome, but just how . . . um . . . severe is her case? What is her prognosis?"

Robert rubbed a hand over tired eyes. He'd had a long day, and this was not the first question of this nature he'd had to deal with in the past twelve hours. If only he had the answers. "Anika is a very special little girl, Mr. Klug. She has been diagnosed with Fetal Alcohol Effects, which is less severe than FAS. Her speech is somewhat delayed, she is still in diapers at night, and she has a very short attention span. We know that she will always struggle with learning disabilities, but it is too early to determine just how severe. She is very outgoing, but social and emotional dysfunction in these children tends to escalate in the teen years, so it is very difficult to predict what the future holds."

Robert sighed. "Anika has had a very hard life; she's been in and out of foster homes. Mr. Klug, a stable environment is essential to the well-being of these children."

"Are you implying that my client cannot furnish a stable environment for his own child?"

Robert rolled his eyes. *This guy must be great in court,* he thought. Taking a deep breath and ignoring the challenge, Robert simply said, "We'll take care of the lab tests on our end. We'll be in touch with you when the results come back."

❧

Two hours later, Robert picked up his briefcase, locked his office door, and walked slowly down the hall, past the nursery, and toward the residential wing. It wasn't often that he worked this late, and when he did, he loved to walk down the dimly lit corridors, stopping to peek at sleeping children or giving a word of encouragement to an employee struggling to settle a restless child. At such times, the miracle of the Sparrow Center never failed to overwhelm him again. They had been accepting residents for only ten months and already they were full and making plans for a new wing. He remembered the months of planning, when the Center had been only a vision and a prayer and gave silent praise for God's faithfulness.

This night he stopped in a doorway at the sound of a quiet voice. He looked in to see Paige sitting on the edge of the bed, her back to the door. She bent down to kiss the sleeping child. "Shelly's old room is pink," she said, "but we can paint it any color you want. And there's a barn—maybe we can get a pony when you get a little bigger." Picking up a stack of books from the floor, she whispered, "Oh, I almost forgot to tell you . . . I looked up your name at the library. Anika means 'very beautiful'."

2

It was just after 7:30 in the morning when Paige and Hailey stepped out of the car in the employee parking lot of the Sparrow Center, yet the heat shimmering off the blacktop promised a mid-summer scorcher. As Hailey touched her key to the door knob, the door opened and one of the third-shift nurses stepped out. She greeted Hailey, then smiled at Paige. The coffee-colored skin crinkled around her eyes as she said, "I sure hope your name is Paige!"

Hailey grabbed the door and held it open with her shoulder. "Must be nice to be famous! Marie, this is the celebrated artist, Paige Stern; Paige meet Marie Wassal, third shift nursing supervisor. Marie runs the tightest ship and has the softest heart in the Center."

Paige held out her hand, "Glad to meet you, Marie."

"And I'm thrilled to meet you, Paige." She nodded toward the hallway behind her. "I love your murals, but your fame goes far beyond your artwork today!"

"Oh?"

"There's a little girl in there who's been asking for you nonstop since five o'clock this morning!"

"Uh-oh."

Marie laughed. "The Lord sure knew what he was doing when He made her such a sweet thing. She's been jabbering about 'rafs' and 'yions' and monkeys all morning, but by lunchtime you may have a little terror on your hands! I'll be praying for you two!"

Paige put her hand on Hailey's shoulder. "Nurse Hailey is in charge of tantrum control today."

Hailey gave an unconvincing smile, then turned to Marie. "How's the new baby?"

"Still critical, but I think he'll be okay. Second shift did an IV Rocephin over one hour. His pulse ox is 94%, and I imagine they'll do a repeat chest film this morning, then we'll know more." Marie turned to include Paige in her answer. "Sad case; three-month-old cocaine baby with pneumonia. His mother is only fifteen. She and the grandmother didn't have a clue in the world that he was as sick as he was when they brought him in. They think we can just fix him up and they can take him home again."

"You don't think her case worker will allow that, do you?" Hailey asked.

"I hope not. Let's pray this will wake that little girl up and force her into detox. Well, you two have a lovely day. I'm going home to air-conditioning and a nice, soft bed!"

❧

Annie sat on her knees, stabbing bites of pancake with her fork while she chattered. One of the nurses' aides had fixed her hair in corn-row braids and the pastel beads tapped together as she turned her head back and forth, taking in everything around her.

"What color dress do you want to wear for my wedding?" Hailey asked.

"Red. Or bwack . . . or lello . . ."

"How about pink?" Paige suggested.

Annie nodded vigorously, the beads clicking wildly. "I yike pink!"

Paige exchanged a look of relief with Hailey. "Okay, pink it is!"

Annie fell asleep on the drive to Milwaukee, giving her an hour nap and giving Paige the hope that her good mood could last all day. They woke her gently and cautiously when they got to the mall and Paige carried her in. Annie was ready to run as soon as she saw the waterfall in the center of the mall, but Hailey took her firmly by the hand while Paige went ahead and rented a stroller.

When Paige met up with them a few minutes later, Hailey was lifting Annie up to stare at wedding rings in a jewelry store window.

Paige held her arms out to Annie and shook her head at Hailey. "You already have one of those!"

"We're picking out one for you."

"Swell, then we'll go buy a wedding gown and pick out china and then we'll run over to Penney's and order a groom from the catalog!"

"Don't laugh! It would be just about that easy for you. All you'd have to do is stand on a street corner in Milbrooke and announce that you were ready to get married and you'd have a dozen proposals instantly!"

"Thank you for that comforting advice. And if I stand on the street corner and scream, I don't want to get married! do you think all you match-makers will leave me alone? I mean, does it say 'desperate' on my forehead or something? I got a letter from my mother yesterday telling me that she 'just happened' to run into the mother of this guy I had a crush on in eighth grade and—can you believe it?—he 'just happens' to still be single! What a strange coincidence . . . hint, hint, hint."

Annie, one stubby finger bent against the glass, said, "Buy dat one."

Paige held up her hand and wiggled her little finger. "I already have a pretty ring."

Hailey put her finger on the glass next to Annie's. "But it's not the right kind and it's not on the right finger, is it Annie?"

With no idea what she was agreeing to, Annie shook her braids. "You need one doze wings, Paige."

Paige gave an arrogant sniff and stuck her nose in the air. "Diamonds are so . . . traditional."

"I just read an article that said that other stones are becoming really popular for engagement rings. Look at that emerald marquis, and there's a sapphire . . ."

Paige made a face and bent to put Annie in the stroller. "Annie is getting tired of looking at silly rings. Let's go find that pink dress."

As Paige buckled the belt of the stroller, Annie pointed to her pearl ring. "Dat's a pwetty wing."

Paige kissed her on the cheek. "Thank you, sweetie." Looking at Hailey as she stood up, she said, "I'm glad some people like it."

"Hey! I like it! I just don't want to think of you going through life with nothing but an antique pinky ring from a flea market!" Realizing what she'd just said, she grimaced. "I'm sorry."

Paige shook her head. "I will forgive you on one condition— that if you associate the word 'ring' or 'wedding' or 'date' or 'man' with me even once today you will voluntarily become polar bear lunch. Do we understand each other?"

"Yes, ma'am." Hailey put one hand on the handle of the stroller. "Beeper on?"

"Beeper on."

"Okay, let's go find that pink dress."

As they walked, Paige glanced down at the pearl on her finger. It was such a part of her that, though she looked at it hundreds of times a day, she seldom really saw it anymore. But once in a while the smell of burning leaves or the angle of the sun let her see it with the same eyes that had first spotted it on a dusty table cluttered with knickknacks and gaudy costume jewelry. In those moments she was transported, if only for a fraction of a second, to an outdoor flea market on a warm September afternoon six years earlier.

For an artist with a passion for out-of-print children's books and antique jewelry, it was a place of magic. To Gavin Prentice, it might as well have been the Amazon Jungle. He had tolerated the afternoon, fitting himself into her plans because it was her last day in Milbrooke. When Paige had laughed at the exorbitant price on the ring and tried to set it down, Gavin had grabbed it from her and paid the ridiculous figure without batting an eye.

It was only their second date, and it hadn't been a day worth writing about in her journal or telling her roommate about when she got back to school. It was only months later, when she'd come to know the man behind the cool exterior, that the day, and the ring, became something to treasure.

❧

In less than an hour they were driving through the gates at the zoo. Annie sat in back in her car seat, clutching the bag that held a pink gingham dress with spaghetti straps, smocked top, and layers of eyelet lace. They'd had a near-disaster when they told her she couldn't wear it to the zoo, but peace was restored when Paige handed her a nickel to throw into the fountain.

They rented a stroller again, and as they walked, Hailey pulled a tube of sunscreen from her pocket and applied it liberally to her pale arms and freckled nose. "I wish I had your skin," she sighed.

"Trade you my skin for your fiancé."

Hailey turned slowly, staring at Paige from beneath her brimmed hat. "Wait a minute! Isn't this a taboo subject?"

"Not if I bring it up."

"So, if you bring it up, do I get fed to the bears if I answer you?"

"Maybe." Paige stopped in front of the zebras and pulled a sketch pad and pencil out of her sidepack. She was having trouble with one of her murals for the Center, and she was hoping that a real, live model would inspire her. She squatted down so Annie could watch her draw. The dimples in the little girl's brown face deepened as the animal took shape on paper. "Know what a zebra is, Annie-kins?" Paige asked.

The beads in her hair clacked as she shook her head.

"It's a horse with striped pajamas!"

Annie giggled. "Can I make a horse in jamas?"

Paige flipped to a clean piece of paper and handed Annie the pencil, then leaned against the fence next to Hailey.

Cautiously, Hailey said, "You know, it wasn't much more than a year ago that I remember telling Karlee that I wanted a David. She said, 'You'll get one. I'm praying for him, whoever he is.' Funny thing is, that was just a few hours after I'd met Cody." She glanced sideways at Paige. "I'm praying for your Cody, whoever he is."

Paige looked down at the ground. "I wasn't serious, you know. I'm taking a sabbatical from men. This is the first time in a long time that I haven't had a guy in my life, and I'm kind of enjoying it."

Hailey laughed. "You have three French pen-pals, at least two over-seas calls a week, and who knows how many gallery customers and guys from church after you . . . you're not exactly a wall-flower, girl!"

"But I'm not attached, no one's running my life but me. My time is my own, I don't have to answer to anyone . . ."

Paige caught the worried look on Hailey's face. "Stop that! You look like my mother. I'm fine! It's possible to be happy without a man, Hailey!"

"That's not what concerns me. It's you running your own—"

"Ice cweam!" The sketch book fell to the ground as Annie pointed to two little boys with ice cream cones.

Paige crouched down beside her. "We can have ice cream after lunch. Let's go see the rhinoceros and the elephants and then it will be lunch time."

"No! Ice cweam now!" The pencil went flying.

Hailey bent down. "Annie! Let's go see the elephants!"

"Ice cweam first!"

Annie kicked the stroller and her screams got louder. People were beginning to slow down or stop to watch. A white-haired man spoke to the woman next to him in a voice meant to be overheard. "I'd like to give that child something to cry about!"

The woman answered, "A good hard swat on the behind is what she needs."

Paige clenched her teeth and lifted Annie out of the stroller. She held her tightly and rubbed her back. Through the screams, she sang in her ear, "Hip-hip-hip-hippopotamus. Hip-hip-hip God made all of us . . ." She sang all the verses she knew of the rhyming song until Annie stopped fighting and her sobs became sniffles. Hailey pushed the stroller as they walked away from the critical eyes.

By the time they stopped in front of the elephants, Annie had forgotten all about the ice cream and was laughing at the elephants' huge ears flapping in the heat. Paige slid her back into the stroller and sighed. Hailey patted her back. "You handled that very well," she said. "I feel sorry for the family that adopts her—dealing with that all the time would be exhausting. It makes you wonder if anyone will ever want her, doesn't it?"

Paige turned away. "Someone wants her," was all she said.

3

From the long afternoon shadow of a small cherry tree, Paige glared over the edge of a framed canvas. "I know toddlers that can sit still longer than you can!"

Hailey ran her finger under the collar of the heavy buckskin dress. "Do you have any idea how hot it is in this thing?"

Paige shook her head and tried not to smile. "Do you have any idea how hard it is to paint a moving object? Your mouth is nothing but a blur! Not that Cody would recognize it any other way, but humor me anyway and freeze for five more minutes."

Hailey wiped the dampness from her top lip. "Poor choice of words," she grumbled. "I'm anything but freezing. Anyway—why do you think God invented cameras? Couldn't you just take a Polaroid of me, and then paint it?"

Paige bent to dip her brush, then tossed her head as her hair fell over her left eye. It was a habitual gesture that she knew drove her best friend crazy, and she was rewarded with an exasperated sigh from Hailey. Paige echoed the sound. "A Polaroid! A snapshot just isn't the same. If I don't capture you live I'll miss the real essence of your charm." She gave her friend a grin.

"I'm going to capture you live if—" Hailey's words were interrupted by the insistent beeping of the pager clipped to the fringe at her side. But as she reached for it, Paige yelled, "Don't move!"

"I have to look at it!"

"One minute."

"Can't I at least turn it off?"

"One minute."

"It might be an emergency."

"It's probably just your co-dependent fiancé." Paige's hands moved furiously.

"What if it's the Center?" Hailey protested.

"You're a nurse, not a brain surgeon. They can wait sixty seconds. This is crucial." Paige dipped the tip of her brush in the dab of indigo on her palette. "I'm doing your left eye and it—" She jumped as the beeper in her pocket began an off-beat duet with Hailey's. Her wide brown eyes met Hailey's blue ones. Together they grabbed pagers and read the identical messages out loud.

"This is it!" Hailey sprang up and grabbed the stool she had been sitting on. As she ran across the field toward Paige's compact car, she struggled with the button loops on her back. "I have to get out of this thing first! I can't show up in my wedding gown!" She twisted desperately to reach the loops.

"You can change when we get there! Help me get this stuff in the car!" Paige laid the wet canvas on the roof of the car. With the easel and a coffee can of clean brushes under her left arm, she opened the car door and pushed the button that popped open the trunk. As she backed out of the car, the easel slipped, banging against the inside of the door and scattering brushes on the ground. She slammed the door, threw the easel in the trunk, and bent to pick up the brushes just as Hailey reached the passenger side and yelled, "Unlock the door!"

"It isn't locked! Quit being a baby!"

"If my hands weren't full of your stuff I—" Hailey tried the handle again. "It's locked. Hurry up and un—"

Paige's face rose slowly over the roof of the car like the sun creeping over the horizon. Her eyes squinted and her teeth clenched as her hand found the door handle and pulled, to no avail. Together, they bent and stared at the gold letter "P" shining in the sunlight, dangling from the keys in the ignition. "Nooo!" Paige wailed. "My camera's in there."

Hailey leaned her forehead against the back window and stared down at her shorts and blouse and sandals on the back seat. She looked down at her bare feet, then slowly up from the fringe at her ankles to the blue beads at the waist of her wedding dress. She looked around at the field of tiger lilies behind them and the quiet stretch of gravel road in front of them. A small voice beside her said, "It's only a mile and a half to the Center."

❧

Perspiration coursed down Hailey's sides as they half ran, half walked into the driveway of the Sparrow Center. She let out a yell as her bare foot landed on the hot blacktop. "Now will you wear my shoes?" Paige panted. Hailey summoned her best martyr voice. "No, that's okay. You go ahead and get into the air-conditioning; I'll go around on the grass. It feels better on my ripped-up feet anyway." Paige stopped, took her shoes off, and sunk to her knees, holding her shoes above her bowed head. "Please, please, Pocahontas, take my moccasins!"

Hailey took the dusty shoes, stared at them, smiled wickedly, and said, "Well, if you insist." She sent the shoes flying toward the Center's doorway, and then she followed them across the hot black surface of the parking lot with Paige close behind, gasping, giggling, and shouting empty threats.

At the door they stopped, trying to muster some measure of composure before entering. Hailey stared at her image in the window of the building she had left just two hours earlier in her uniform. Her hand flew to her head, pulling the beaded blue headband from her sweat-dampened temples. She looked at Paige who was running long, slim, gold-and-pearl-tipped fingers through her hair. "Look at you! You don't even sweat! Look at me! Cody's here—what if he sees me? I'm not supposed to wear this 'til our wedding day! I can't go in there like this!"

"Of course you can. Just smile and act normal and walk straight back to the locker room and borrow someone's clothes!"

Paige raised one eyebrow and batted her lashes. "And don't you worry," she whispered as she opened the door, "I'll take care of Cody."

As they sneaked across the carpeted floor leading to the front desk, Hailey whispered, "If my keys weren't locked in your car we could have used the back door!"

"If your keys weren't locked in my car we wouldn't need the back door!"

The day receptionist glanced up, recognized them both, and smiled as she turned back to her keyboard. Then, as the picture registered in her mind, she turned back, then stood to get a better look. Hailey smiled. "Beautiful day, isn't it, Charissa? I just can't get enough of this place!"

On the wall next to the reception desk was a large cherry wood plaque covered with brass plates. On each plate was engraved the name of a person or corporation that had donated money to build the Center. Touching one of the plates had become a ritual with Paige. Even now, in spite of the excitement of the moment, she kissed her finger and touched the words: "Karl and Madeline Prentice—in loving memory of their son, Gavin."

Entering the hallway, they broke into a run, but their flight was short-lived. Just as Hailey reached the women's locker room two men rounded the corner. Cody Worth, legal representative for the Sparrow Corporation—and Hailey's soon-to-be husband—halted abruptly at the sight of her. Robert, who was Cody's adoptive father, came to a stop next to him. Cody's dark brown eyes traveled from Hailey's long tousled hair, down the dress that his mother had been married in, to the dirty bare feet beneath it, then to the guilty expression on Paige's face. Turning to his father, he rolled his eyes and said calmly, "Looks like trouble again."

Robert nodded slowly and rubbed his chin. "Looks to me like you're eloping, son." Running his hand along his jaw in a gesture that mirrored Robert's, Cody agreed. "Bet you're right, Dad."

"Always said that was the way to go—just grab your squaw and run. In this case, it looks like the squaw is about to grab you!"

"Hey, that works. Definitely the way to go. No tux, no bouquet . . . Why waste your money on—"

"Do you mind?" Hailey nailed them with her eyes. "We're in the middle of a crisis, and a little nineties' male sensitivity would be appreciated! This is it and we're supposed to be there, but we accidentally locked the keys in the car so we need to get a ride or borrow your car, but we have to hurry! We've already walked a mile and a half and wasted a lot of time and maybe we've already missed ev—"

"Excuse me, Dad. There's only one thing to do when she gets like this." Cody took a step forward.

Hailey put her hands on her hips. "So if you would kindly just hand over your keys or give us a ride or—"

Cody put one finger under her chin, lifted her face to him, and pressed his lips against hers. Pulling away, he smiled down at her, then at Paige. "Now, is there something we can do for you ladies?"

Paige let out a loud sigh and crossed her arms in front of her, trying not to return Cody's smile. "Well, for starters you can quit being patronizing and chauvinistic."

Cody looked almost genuinely offended. "That really hurts. There's no way a man can win these days! If I offer to help I'm patronizing, if I hand you the keys I'm being insensitive, if I offer to give you a ride I'm chauvinistic, if I give you advice I'm bull-headed, if I don't I'm not caring, if I—"

"Aaah!" Paige clamped her hands over her ears. "You guys aren't even married yet and you sound just like her!"

She turned to Robert. "Dr. Worth, is there a competent person with a vehicle in this building that you could spare for half an hour?"

At that moment the back door opened and a man that neither Paige or Hailey had ever seen before walked in. Cody looked at his father, winked, and said, "Uh . . . just how, exactly, would you define 'vehicle'?"

4

his is awesome!" Paige shouted above the beat of the helicopter's blades. She held her hair out of her eyes and laughed.

"This is insane!" Hailey retorted, as the pale green scrub suit flapped around her in the pulsing wind. The fringe of the dress she had slung over her shoulder whipped the side of her face.

"I thought you were in a hurry!" Cody yelled back over the roar.

"Not this much hurry!"

Paige laughed and tugged at Hailey's arm. "This is an adventure! Think of the story we can tell our nephew someday!"

"You can tell your nephew anything you want! I'm telling my niece that she's lucky to have at least one aunt without a death wish!" Pointing at the man who was running toward them, bent over to clear the spinning blades of the helicopter, Hailey shouted, "We don't even know this guy!"

Robert put his arm around her shoulders and pulled her back toward the building. "You don't have to do this, you know. Cody can't get away for another hour, but I can take you—I don't think they'll mind if I get there a little early!"

The back door of the Sparrow Center flew open and Charissa ran out. "Hailey! David just called! The midwife is there and Karlee's dilated to five!"

Hailey froze, then prayed, then took a deep breath and drew on every ounce of courage she could muster. Grabbing Paige's sleeve, she yelled, "Quit standing around! When my sister finally makes up her mind to do something, she moves fast!"

Cody gave a "thumbs up" sign to the pilot, and stopped Hailey with his arm. As he was about to make introductions, the man nudged him aside, pulled off his mirrored sunglasses, and held out his hand to Hailey. "Glad to finally meet you, Hailey. I promise we'll give you a smooth ride. This'll give us time to talk about why you shouldn't marry this creep!"

Hailey gave a nervous laugh and tugged again at Paige's sleeve. Cody put his arm around her and gently pulled her hand away from Paige. Turning to his friend, he said, "Brant, I'd like to meet Paige Stern, Hailey's housemate. Paige, this is my long lost partner in crime, Brant McCourt."

Paige extended her hand, keenly aware that the smile had faded from the man's face. He took her hand, then released it quickly without any attempt at pleasantries. She felt suddenly judged. For what, she didn't know, but she wasn't about to let this stranger intimidate her. She challenged him with her eyes and couldn't help, as she did, taking in the strong lines of his tanned face, the wavy, dark-brown hair that blew over the collar of his faded blue T-shirt. He wasn't tall, about five-foot-ten, she guessed, but his broad shoulders and muscular arms gave off a sense of power. Given any degree of internal warmth, he would have been incredibly handsome. But Paige judged a man by his eyes, and these eyes, though disarmingly blue, cut through the July heat like icicles.

Robert ran a hand through his thick silver hair and was about to wave good-bye, but suddenly he gave in to his cautious nature. "Hey, Brant, would you mind hanging around over there . . . just in case?"

By the time Paige reached the helicopter, Hailey was in the front seat with Cody buckling her seat belt for her and talking softly to her as if she were a child. Hailey, her hands covering her face, was repeating every "fear not" Bible verse she knew out loud.

Cody smiled and shook his head as Brant got in. "It's just the going up and coming down that bothers her," he yelled.

Brant laughed. "I'll stay as low to the ground as I can!" Leaning forward, Paige put her hand on Hailey's shoulder as they ascended. Considering the number of transatlantic flights Paige had made in her life, it was hard to empathize with Hailey's phobia. But whenever the subject came up, Hailey, the nurse, had only to gently remind her that, though Paige might be able to fly over an ocean, she couldn't remove a sliver or put on a Band-Aid without passing out.

Paige heard only bits and pieces of the one-sided conversation taking place in front of her, but what she did hear only confirmed her conviction that Brant McCourt was a man who was stuck on himself. "I graduated . . . I flew . . . Canada . . . I was . . . rescue . . . then I . . ." Paige gave up counting the number of times he used the first person pronoun and shifted her attention to the bird's-eye-view of the countryside below her.

They were met at David and Karlee's back door by Karlee's best friend, Jody Hansen. "Man! You guys know how to make an entrance! Who's the hunk?"

"He's Cody's best man," Hailey answered. "How's Karlee?"

Before Jody could answer, Karlee's seven-year-old daughter Shelly came running in on tip-toes, followed shortly by a cat, two dogs, and T.J., her ten-year-old brother. T.J. let himself be hugged by Paige, while Shelly grabbed her aunts' hands. "You're supposed to go upstairs," she whispered.

Jody laughed. "Karlee's doing great; still up and walking around. The contractions are about three minutes apart."

"How's my brother holding up?" Paige asked.

"I think he's okay. He's so sweet with her!"

As she was being dragged toward the stairs, Hailey suddenly turned back and smiled at Jody. "Oh, by the way, you get to entertain 'the hunk'!"

At Jody's raised eyebrows, Paige said, "Don't worry, he'll do all the talking!"

Karlee was sitting in a carved wooden rocking chair, wearing an ivory gown, her red-gold hair pulled up in a pony tail. She didn't look up when they walked in, but continued to stare at her focal point, a quilted wall hanging draped over the end of the four-poster bed. Her fingertips moved in slow, rhythmic circles on her abdomen, in the gentle massage of effleurage. She breathed in harmony to the movement of her hands, and the only sounds in the room were the ticking of a gold clock in a bell jar on David's armoire and the soft "he-he-he" of Karlee's breathing.

Paige smiled at David, sitting on a low stool next to the rocking chair, his hand softly stroking Karlee's arm. Behind them, through French doors, was a scene from one of the squares in the wall hanging. Sunlight shimmered on a ribbon of blue that flowed through a grove of dwarf pines. On the opposite side of the creek stood a sugar maple, full and round and green. Instinctively, Paige reached for the camera that should have been around her neck. Looking around, she spotted David's sitting on the night stand and tip-toed across the room to pick it up. She kneeled, focused, then looked up at David with a silent question. When he nodded, she pressed down on the button, capturing the moment. Karlee didn't flinch, so intense was her concentration.

Finally, after another ten seconds, she released a deep cleansing breath and raised her hand to welcome them. As Hailey walked toward her sister, she smiled at the midwife, a thin woman with straight, salt-and-pepper hair wearing a sweatshirt and faded jeans. "Hi, Diane. How's my niece doing?"

Diane leaned back against one of the bed posts and laughed, shaking her head. "Your niece has a good, strong, heart rate of 130."

"Hm. Sounds kind of nephew-ish, huh?"

"Yup. I've been wrong before—but not too often."

Bending down, Hailey kissed Karlee's cheek, then kneeled beside her, putting her face just inches from Karlee's belly. "We have to talk, baby," she whispered. "You see, if you come out with blue booties on, I have to do dishes for a whole month! Pay attention, baby, this is Aunt Hailey talking, the one who buys you presents and—"

David patted the top of her head. "Hang it up, Aunt Hailey. There isn't much he can do about it now!"

Hailey wrinkled her nose at David. "It's not fair! I put my order in long before Paige did!"

Another flash lit the room as Paige said, "Face it, Hailey, they've always liked me best."

"Yeah, well, at least I—" She felt the muscles beneath her hand tighten. "Cleansing breath," she whispered, pulling her hand away and slipping it beneath Karlee's elbow. "Good girl, nice and relaxed. Just go with it, just let your body do what it wants to do." She rubbed Karlee's arm while David did the same on the other side until the contraction ebbed.

"You were saying?" David prodded.

Hailey stared blankly at him. "Huh?"

"You said, 'Yeah, well, at least I . . .' 'At least I' what? I love to hear you two argue. It's better than anything on TV."

"You just get vicarious pleasure out of hearing me win! I bet you never won a single fight with her when you were little!"

Paige laughed. "I never fought with David."

"That's true. I always gave in to those big brown eyes! Now she and our brother Phil were another story . . ."

"Do you have any more film?" Paige asked innocently.

"Are you changing the subject?" he answered.

"Yes, but do you have more film?"

"Top dresser drawer."

As Paige opened the drawer, she said, "So what was this 'At least I . . .' stuff, Hailey dear?"

181

"Oh nothing. It was too . . ." She felt a hand on her arm.

"Remember me, guys?" Karlee said, then shifted her eyes to the wall hanging and blew out a forceful breath. When the contraction was over, Karlee held her arm out to David. "Help me up," she said. Slowly, she waddled over to a window. "I'm not crazy after all!" she cried. "There really is a helicopter in my back yard. What on earth?"

Hailey laughed. "Don't ask. It's a long story. It all started with Paige locking her keys—and my clothes—in the car and—"

"It did not!" Paige protested. "It all started with Hailey dragging me out to this field of tiger lilies to . . . never mind."

David put one hand to his forehead, while the other gently rubbed Karlee's back as she leaned against him. "Could we go back to the 'at least I' thing? That promised to be very entertaining."

Her face pressed against David's chest, Karlee's voice was lost to the others as she asked, "What about the helicopter?"

"Yeah, let's go back to the 'at least I' thing," Paige taunted. "You were about to say . . . ?"

"What about the heli . . ." Karlee asked quietly between pants.

"Never mind, it was too nasty. Even I can be sensitive at times, Paige dear."

"What . . . about . . . the . . ."

"Oh, no, you're not going to get out of it that easily! You had something deliciously rude planned for me and it's only fair that I get a chance at a comeback!"

"What . . . about . . ."

"I'll save it for a time when I really need it. The birth of our niece is a time of happiness and joy and I will not shatter the wonder of this day with—"

"WHAT ABOUT THE STUPID HELICOPTER?!?"

5

When the shock wave finally subsided, Diane smiled at the stunned faces, none more surprised at the outburst than Karlee herself. "I believe," Diane said, "that we have reached the stage of labor known as transition."

Karlee leaned heavily against David and began her breathing again, her pace faster than before. One hand went to her back as the contraction peaked and Hailey noted a momentary loss of concentration as the intensity surprised her. Karlee's other hand gripped David's shoulder and she squeezed her eyes shut. Hailey moved quietly behind them and pressed the heel of her hand firmly but gently against Karlee's lower back as David whispered against her hair. "Just relax, honey, I've got you." He put his hand over hers until he felt her grip loosen beneath his touch.

When the contraction was over, Karlee said, "I think I'll get in bed now."

Hailey smiled at her, recognizing the universal look of a woman in labor, a look that announced she was entering her own private world, focused solely on the work at hand. As Diane readied pillows and helped Karlee find a comfortable position, Hailey drew the room-darkening blinds and crossed the room to turn on a small lamp.

Paige put her hand on David's shoulder. "I'll go get some coffee," she said. Several seconds passed before her words registered with David. When he finally looked up at her, her heart wrenched at the look on his face. Memories, like specters from a never-forgotten nightmare, hovered around him and were mirrored in his eyes. This was how he had lost his first wife, and tears stung Paige's eyes as she wrapped her arms around her brother. "It's gonna be okay this time," she whispered.

His arms tightened around her. "Can we pray before you go?"

Paige stood next to Diane, her hand resting on the sheet covering Karlee's leg. Across the bed, David held Karlee's hand and Hailey stood next to him, her head bowed. Their silence lasted through two contractions. Then, rubbing his thumb across the back of Karlee's hand, David began to pray.

"Thank You, Lord. I don't have words to express how grateful I am for this child and for the family you have given me. Thank You for letting us share this joy at home. Thank You for Diane, for her skill and compassion . . ." He smiled across the bed at the midwife. "And for her patience with me over the past nine months. Thank You for Paige and Hailey, for their constant support and their ability to make us laugh when we need it. Father, You know our past losses and our fears. Help us to leave them with You and remember Your promises." He stopped for a minute, locking eyes with his wife of one year. "Help me to be strong for Karlee, Lord, and help me be a good father."

Karlee squeezed his hand. Before another contraction began, she had time to whisper, "You already are."

Paige pulled tissues from the box on the night stand, kept one for herself, and handed one to Hailey. The understanding in Paige's eyes spoke volumes and Hailey smiled through her tears and hugged her. "What would I do without you?"

"Probably lead a peaceful life," Paige responded. "I'll bring you some coffee."

David nodded toward the window just as Paige was about to step out of the room. "Brant's still here?" he asked.

Paige nodded. "Robert asked him to stay."

David smiled sympathetically. "That must be awkward for you."

Giving him a confused look, Paige shrugged. "He is a bit egotistical, isn't he? But he's Jody's problem right now, I guess." She turned then, missing the questioning look on her brother's face.

At one end of the high-ceilinged great room, T.J. and Shelly were sitting on the floor playing a board game. Just two feet away, Brant half-sprawled on the couch, one leg over the arm, the other foot on the deep-piled rug. He was peering over Shelly's shoulder, giving her advice on her next move.

T.J. was the first to see Paige descending the stairs. His tattling was not totally serious, but the look on his face was a good attempt. "Aunt Paige, tell him to quit giving Shelly answers! They're cheating!"

At the mention of Paige's name, Brant sat upright. Even though Paige's first impression had not been favorable, the prayer time upstairs had put her in a softer mood, and she was willing to give him a second chance. "Who's winning?" she asked.

A robin could have landed on Shelly's pouting lip. "He is," she whined, squinting at her brother.

Paige winked at T.J. "They're cheating and you're still winning? I wouldn't worry about it, Teej." Then she turned to Brant, who was nervously turning his watch back and forth on his arm. "I'm getting some coffee for the people upstairs. Would you like some?"

"Thank you, but Jody is keeping me supplied."

Paige nodded and walked to the other end of the great room where Jody was just walking out of the pantry, her arms laden with bread, corn chips, and a jar of apple sauce. She jumped as Paige reached out to grab the jar from her. "Sorry, just trying to help," Paige laughed.

"Thanks. I'm jumpy, I guess. It's hard being down here and wondering what's going on upstairs."

"She's in transition. Why don't you go on up for a while?"

Jody laughed. "No thanks. As I recall that's the stage of labor where you start throwing whatever you can get your hands on and telling your husband you're putting him on the next plane to Siberia!"

"Jody! You didn't do that to poor Don, did you?"

Setting the bread down on the counter, Jody gave a deep throated laugh. "Why do you think we stopped at two kids?"

Paige shook her head and took two mugs out of the cupboard. Lowering her voice, she said, "So how are you and the fly guy getting along?"

"Fine! Makes me wish I was young and single!" Jody whispered. "Like you, for instance."

"You don't find him a bit grating?"

Jody's brow furrowed. "Not at all! He's fascinating. I take it you don't agree?"

"I don't know . . ." Paige poured coffee from the coffee maker into an insulated pot as she thought about her answer. "There's something cold about him. Maybe it's just the 'been there, done that' attitude."

"I don't see it as bragging—he really has been there and done that! He's had the kids spellbound with his stories since he got here!"

"What kind of stories?"

"Oh, things like finding himself face to face with a grizzly while he was rescuing some lost elk hunters in Canada, and being stuck in a cabin for two weeks with snow up to the roof . . ."

"And you believe all that?"

"Paige! You're so cynical! Just look into those beautiful blue eyes and you'll know he's not capable of lying! He's really sweet— you just got a wrong first impression. Do you know anything about him?"

"No. I've heard Cody talk about him, but I never paid much attention."

"He just moved back here from Canada. He was on a search and rescue team up there. Now he's working part-time as a paramedic for the city and part-time as a Flight-for-Life pilot and he's trying to start his own medical transport company. He inherited a piece of land out on Old Miller Road and he's had it re-zoned and he's planning to start building in the fall. The closest private transport company is in Madison, so our EMTs and rescue equipment get tied up with non-emergency calls. There's a real need for what he's doing."

"And he's going to hire you for PR, right?"

"He wouldn't have to twist my arm too far! I'm telling you, girl, give him a second chance."

Paige rolled her eyes and set the coffee pot on a tray with four cups. Jody threw up her hands in a gesture of exasperation and said, "I'm going to make sandwiches for you guys and set them in the hallway upstairs. If Karlee's anything like I was, she won't be able to stand the smell of food right now."

Paige laughed, picked up the tray, walked three steps, and turned. "Siberia, huh?"

Stopping next to the couch she asked, "Those two still cheating, T.J.?"

"Yeah. But I don't care. I'm still ahead."

Paige laughed and had started turning toward the stairs when Brant McCourt got to his feet. "Can I . . . carry that for you?"

Trying to read the look in his eyes, Paige stared at him for a moment before answering. The arrogance was still evident in the slight tip of his chin, but it was combined with something that made her even more uncomfortable. She could only define it as sheer embarrassment, as if the very act of offering to help a woman was degrading. She tightened her grip on the tray. "No . . . I've got it."

Brant rubbed his hand over the dark shadow on his chin. "Listen, this isn't a good time, but—"

The back door opened and Robert Worth stepped in. He

greeted Jody, then crossed the floor to Paige and Brant. "How's it going?"

"Getting close, I guess. Karlee didn't seem to be in the mood for any more pictures at the moment so I thought I'd do a coffee run."

Robert laughed. "Yeah, David said you were a wimp."

"Hey, we all have our gifts here! Hailey's the coach, Jody's the baby-sitter, and I'm photographer and gopher!"

"In other words, you're the one who gets to run when you can't handle it!"

"Exactly!"

"So, after all those reasons they gave for choosing home birth, it was really just that they didn't want you creating a scene at the hospital!"

Paige laughed and stepped toward the stairs. "Doctors give me hives!"

Robert laughed, then turned serious. "How's David?"

"He's doing all right. We spent some time in prayer. That helped."

"Good." Robert nodded, then turned to Brant, whose gaze was following Paige up the stairs. "Thanks for staying. I'm sure everything is going to go fine, but I've always been the overly cautious type."

They sat down on the couch and Robert talked to T.J. and Shelly for several minutes, and then to Brant. "Has Cody given you any history on this wonderfully strange family he's marrying into?"

As Brant answered, "A little," Shelly smiled and wrinkled her nose at Robert.

"Well, let me fill you in on what you might have missed," Robert began. "David and his wife Shawna built this house, then they were called to Senegal as missionaries. They were there for three years and Shawna died in childbirth. Matthew, the baby, only lived for about an hour. David moved back here and the Lord gave him a vision for the Sparrow Center. It was the only thing that kept him going for awhile. Before the Center was built he met the mother of these adorable kids." This time, both Shelly and T.J. smiled. "They lost their father in a construction accident two years ago. Karlee and David were married last summer. Now Hailey, Karlee's sister, and Paige, who, in case no one's told you, is David's sister, are living in Karlee's house." Robert looked at the kids. "Did I miss anything?"

Shelly wrinkled her nose again, "You have to say, 'and they had a baby and lived happily ever after. The end.' "

❧

Her timing was perfect. When Paige slipped back into the bedroom, she had just enough time to set down the tray and pick up the camera before a loud, clear, incredible cry broke the silence in the room.

"It's a boy!" Diane announced over the wail. "A beautiful, healthy, baby boy!"

Paige watched in awe as the purplish bundle Diane held quickly turned pink and continued to cry until he was placed in his mother's arms. Instinctively knowing that he was where he belonged, Jordan Matthew Stern whimpered twice and nestled against his mother's breast.

6

$\mathscr{H}$ ailey leaned against the railing of the balcony outside David and Karlee's bedroom. She closed her eyes, letting the balmy night breeze soothe her. When she heard the French doors open, she didn't turn around; she knew who it was. Tilting her head back, she stared up at the star-spattered sky and sighed as Cody's arms wrapped around her waist. Softly in her right ear she heard the words only he knew she so desperately needed to hear at that moment.

"I can hardly wait to see our child in your arms someday," he whispered. Two and a half years had passed since her abortion, yet the pain still came in waves, followed always by another small step in her healing journey. This day had been a roller-coaster of emotions in spite of the thought and prayer she'd put into preparing for it. She'd been strong for David and Karlee, slipping easily into her role as nurse and coach. She hadn't needed to pretend to be elated when Jordan Matthew came into the world. It was only in the quiet hours since then that grief and regrets had found unguarded moments to steal back in.

Cody turned her slowly to face him and his arms tightened around her, giving her permission to cry once again. When her tears were spent, she pulled Cody's face down to hers and kissed him. "I love you," she whispered.

"I know," he said. Picking up the two glasses of iced tea he had brought out with him, he handed one to her. "Take a sip." She did, and he searched her eyes, reading her mood. "You okay, Little Foot?"

Hailey nodded. "I'm okay."

"You need to get home to bed."

She shrugged. "I'm off tomorrow; I can sleep in." She tried to stifle a yawn. "It's been a crazy day."

"It's been a crazy year." Cody laughed at the look on her face. "Nice crazy," he added hastily. Putting his lips close to her ear, he whispered impatiently, "Twenty-four days!"

Hailey gently pulled free and turned, staring up at the stars, so he couldn't see her face. "You know, I've been thinking . . . with the baby coming so late, this only gives Karlee three weeks to recover. What if she's not up to it? Her dress might not fit right and she might not have her strength back. Is it really wise to take a three-week-old to a wedding with all those people and all those germs? I've decided we need to postpone it a good month or two. In fact, I think a Christmas wed—" The hand that clamped over her mouth muffled her words but didn't stop them.

Cody's eyes shone with mischief. "Look woman, let's get this perfectly clear. Twenty-four days from today, at three o'clock in the afternoon, I am standing on the riverbank and pledging my life to someone, and then dragging that someone off to a romantic cabin in Montana for two weeks. Now, if you're not interested in being that someone, I'm sure I can ask P—" Hailey's lips landed squarely on his and she somehow managed to kiss him while laughing at the same time.

"Paige is right!" she said as she pulled away. "You're starting to sound just like me!"

"Scary thought!" Cody said under his breath as he turned her toward the door. "Really scary thought!"

⇌

Diane had given orders before she left for David to clear out the visitors and let Karlee sleep. While she slept, Jody kept everyone downstairs fed and entertained. When they were allowed back upstairs, Karlee was wearing a pink gown with a matching hair band. Her legs were drawn up and the baby's head rested against her knees, his tiny feet against her chest. She stroked the fuzzy, inch-long hair that was the color of blackened copper. Paige flashed the camera incessantly as she picked her way across the room, maneuvering around pets and people to capture every move the baby made and the reactions on the faces of his audience. Hailey rolled her eyes as Paige aimed the lens at her, catching her with her head against Cody's arm. Paige smiled and winked. "A good one!" she whispered.

Hours past his bedtime, T.J. was still bouncing off the walls, telling anyone who cared to listen, "I knew it was going to be a boy! I told all of you it was going to be a boy and I was right!" Shelly, who was wound up in her own quiet way, cooed and giggled and couldn't keep her hands off the baby's downy head. But of all the day's picture-memories that would stay in Paige's mind, the look of awe on David's face would always be most precious. When Karlee laid the baby, just minutes old, in David's arms and whispered, "Here's your son," there had not been a dry eye in the room.

The hot mid-morning sun streamed in the open window. Hailey lay buried beneath the sheet with only her left foot exposed. She sat up slowly, then slumped back against her four pillows, yawned and stretched and smiled smugly. It was her first day off in twelve days and she intended to savor the freedom. She opened one eye and glanced at the digital clock: 10:06 A.M. She rose slowly and stretched again. Still sitting on the edge of the bed, she slipped her feet into her teddy bear slippers. She had only one plan for the day—to do nothing that was not convenient. With that in mind, she pondered the immediate options: should she take a shower, call Cody, eat breakfast, call Cody, call David and Karlee, eat lunch, call Cody, or fall back onto the covers?

As she weighed the possibilities, Karlee's eleven-year-old calico cat, Mrs. Patches, slunk into the room, winding her body against the door frame. Hailey had brought her home with her the night before since the feline's curiosity over the new arrival was bothering Karlee. Hailey reached down near the floor and let Mrs. Patches rub her graying face against her arm, then ran her hand along her soft side. "Morning, you old—eeoo!"

Hailey stared at the sticky swirls of green and blue paint on the cat's fur and the matching streaks on her hand. "This better not be from my picture!" She flew down the stairs, checking the easels in the living room and dining room for signs of damage as she ran, and stopped at the door of what had once been Karlee's den. The table and floor were littered with half-painted canvases, paintbrushes, cloths, and easels.

With relief, she realized that her portrait was still in the trunk of Paige's car which Cody and Brant had rescued sometime during yesterday's confusion. Spotting the altered landscape painting leaning against the wall, Hailey laughed and spoke to the cat. "You're a natural, Mrs. Picasso! Looks like the first hurricane to hit central Wisconsin!" Grabbing a can of paint thinner, she back-tracked into the kitchen and listened to the phone messages while she started the coffee pot, then headed for the bathroom, coaxing Mrs. Patches to follow.

Fifteen minutes later, when she walked out of the bathroom with a clean cat at her feet, Paige was walking in the back door, wearing heels and a black suit with a purple satin blouse, and a large leather portfolio under her arm. "Mmm coffee!" she said.

Without a word, Hailey thrust the can of paint thinner into her hand. "Mmm turpentine!" she said. "The cat has been making improvements on some of your work." Over Paige's wail, Hailey yelled, "You two work well together!"

When the last trace of paint had been removed from door frames and chair legs, they finally sat down for their first cup of coffee. Paige, now in tan shorts and red shirt, was just beginning to see the humor in the situation. "I was getting so many interruptions at the gallery; I thought I'd come home and sit on the porch and work in the peace and quiet of my own home!"

Hailey laughed. "Why don't you get settled out on the porch and I'll make some omelets." At the look of horror on Paige's face, she said, "Better I practice on you than Cody."

Picking up her portfolio, Paige muttered, "I guess I can be sacrificed for the cause."

Half an hour later, after donating her first attempt to the compost pile, Hailey handed Paige a plate. To sidetrack any remarks about her cooking, she quickly asked Paige, "Did you get your messages off the answering machine?"

"No, I got a late start this morning. Who called?"

Hailey sat down on a chintz-cushioned wicker chair. Tapping her head, she said, "I'm not sure my computer has that much memory. Let's see . . . Stuart from Sunday School wants to know if you'll go on the church hay ride with him . . . which is only about nine weeks away! Nothing like planning ahead. Then there was Peter calling from Paris again, and . . . who in the world is Pablo?"

Paige stuffed a huge bite of egg in her mouth to avoid answering. Hailey, tired of waiting for an answer, decided to take advantage of the silence. "Karlee said you were asking about buying the house. You gonna marry Pablo the mystery man and settle down here?" When all she got was an irritated sigh, she asked seriously, "What are you waiting for?"

There was no sense pretending she didn't understand the question. Paige shrugged. "Not Pablo!" She squirmed under her best friend's gaze, then suddenly remembered some old business. "That's what that nasty little remark was about, right? 'At least I' . . . At least I got the guy, right? At least I got Cody, at least I'm getting married?"

Hailey's brow furrowed at the defensiveness in Paige's voice.

"It was a joke, girl! You've got guys coming out of the woodwork after you!"

"Marriage isn't for everyone! Who says I have to be Mrs. Somebody to be happy? I don't need to be washing some guy's smelly socks and sharing his checkbook to be fulfilled!"

Hailey leaned forward, wanting to laugh, yet held in check by the passion on Paige's face. "When you put it like that, neither do I! You make marriage sound like a life sentence on the chain gang! Who have you been listening to? It's not like that, Paige! I may gain a new title as Cody's wife, but I don't lose me! I'm deeper, stronger because of him, not weaker!" Her voice softened, sensing her friend's turmoil. "I watched you holding the baby last night. That was not the face of a woman willing to give up her dreams of motherhood!"

Staring out the window at the swing set in the backyard, Paige quietly said, "We were talking about marriage, not motherhood."

They ate in silence for several minutes. Paige set her plate on the floor and picked up her laptop computer. Hailey stood, picked up the plates, and stared at her friend wondering what was behind the recent turmoil of emotions. A thought crossed her mind and she asked softly, "Ever wonder what your life would have been like if Gavin Prentice were still alive?"

Paige looked up, stared out the window again, and smiled wistfully. "Every day. I'd probably be on a cruise right now . . ."

Sitting back down on the arm of the chair, Hailey said, "You never talk about him."

Shrugging her shoulders, Paige said, "Gavin is like a dream, like something that never really happened. It was right after Shawna died and Mom and I flew out here to help David get settled. David was so depressed . . . one day I just had to get away, so I went into town and had lunch all by myself. Until this gorgeous stranger walked up and introduced himself!" Paige sighed.

"I probably saw him for a total of eight hours—two dates—and then I went back to college."

"But then there were the letters . . ." Hailey coaxed.

Paige sighed. "And then the letters. Gavin was smooth in person, almost too smooth, you know? He looked like a tennis player in a *GQ* ad—tall, sandy blond hair, green eyes like you've never seen before. You know . . . the rich, handsome, candy and flowers type; the kind you're attracted to, but don't know if you should trust?"

Hailey laughed. "Believe me, I know!"

"I was sure that the minute I left here, probably before I landed back in Connecticut, he'd be out with someone else. But I wrote to him anyway, just to see what would happen. I was amazed that he wrote back and amazed at his letters. They were so sincere . . . not smooth, just sincere." Paige looked down, sliding her pearl ring back and forth on her finger. "It was like on paper he could forget that his father was a millionaire and that he was being groomed to follow in his footsteps. He could be real and talk about the things that really mattered. We even wrote poems for each other. It was never romantic, but I could tell him anything. It was almost like writing a journal. I sometimes wish I had the courage to ask his family if they ever found my letters. It would give me insight into who I was then. Sometimes I feel . . . I don't know. I guess I miss who I used to be."

Hailey nodded, encouraging Paige to go on.

"He never wrote about what he was doing, the day to day things, it was always deep—questions about God and the meaning of life." Paige turned away from the window and looked up at Hailey. "He seemed so close to accepting Christ. The day before his plane crashed he wrote a poem for me that was almost a prayer . . . but I'll never know for sure if he gave his life to Christ or not—at least not this side of heaven, anyway."

"Can I ask you something?" Hailey asked. When Paige nodded, she said, "Do you think you're comparing every guy you meet with Gavin?"

Paige smiled. "I know I am, and maybe it's not fair, but I'd rather not have a relationship at all if it can't be that open. I want what you've got, but every guy I meet wants to own me or change me! Why should I settle for something less than what I know is possible?"

7

*C*ody glanced again at his watch. Another ten minutes had passed. He lifted a chain saw from the back of Brant's 1946 midnight-blue pickup, then set it down again. He couldn't do a thing until Brant showed up to tell him where to start, and his patience was wearing thin. He'd promised half of his day to Brant to help him clear trees from a parcel of the land he'd just inherited. The other half of the day belonged to Hailey, and there was no way that Brant's time was going to overlap hers! It wasn't like Brant to be late. But then, the presence of the truck next to the old deserted logging road proved that he'd actually been there before Cody. And it was like Brant to get distracted.

Cody walked to the edge of the trees and called his name for the tenth time, but his only answer came from the red squirrel on a limb above him. He walked back and circled the truck again, admiring the workmanship. It was hard to believe this was the same piece of machinery Brant had uncovered six years ago in his grandfather's barn. He'd found it sitting on blocks, the axles gone, the body weather-worn though not badly rusted, and only one window intact. The upholstery had been home to several generations of mice. But what stood before him now looked like a showroom model and ran as smooth as it looked.

Helping himself to the contents of the cooler in the back of the pickup, Cody dug through the mound of ice and pulled out a can of root beer. Easing his long frame to the ground, he rested the back of his head on the running board and drained the can. Then, slamming it between his hands, he lay down on the uncut grass and closed his eyes, relaxing in the growing warmth of the morning light.

As the sun rose higher in the sky, Cody stirred at the sound of a motorcycle approaching, a strange sound on the little-used road that divided the property once owned by Brant's grandfather. To his knowledge, Brant owned nothing smaller than the truck, but nothing about this old friend would surprise him. Fighting his curiosity, he lay still, pretending to be oblivious to the roaring of the ancient engine in desperate need of a new muffler. It had to be Brant.

When the noise and the vehicle finally came to a stop, the narrow, bald front wheel was only six inches from Cody's head. The familiar laugh above him was reward enough for not flinching.

"Red man has nerves of steel. I could have left tread marks on that pretty face, you know."

Cody rolled over slowly, poked his finger at a bulging spot on the tire, and laughed. "Says white man who cries over road kill!"

"Shhh . . . I got a rep to protect!" Brant extended his hand and Cody rose to his feet, shaking off the dust and fine gravel that Brant's approach had coated him with.

"Don't worry, your secret's safe with me—unless I need to use it, of course!"

Brant laughed and shook his head. "As would any self-respecting lawyer! Hey, you know the difference between a catfish and a lawyer?"

Cody rolled his eyes, amazed that there was a lawyer joke he hadn't heard yet.

"One's a scum-sucking bottom dweller. The other one's a fish!"

Cody sighed, threw the crumpled can at Brant, and pointed

his foot at the motorcycle. "So what's this hunk of junk and where have you been?"

Brant pulled a blue bandanna from his pocket and used it to wipe the dust and sweat from his face. "Found this in the chicken coop. I did some work on it and thought I'd bring it out here to try it out. Got just over the hill and she stalled, then I flooded her, so I had to wait it out. Sorry." He caressed the handlebars as he talked. "1957 Harley. It'll take some elbow grease . . ."

"And an arm and a leg," Cody added.

"Yeah, but picture this baby when I'm done. Maroon metal-flake with a gold gas tank . . . she'll be sweet! I could sell her for five digits!"

"Like you'd ever part with one of your toys!"

"I may have to if my business loan doesn't go through. I can't start a business on what I make from selling firewood."

"Are you worried about it? You're a land owner now, you've got collateral."

"Yeah, but I can't even pay taxes on the place if I don't start making some decent money soon! I've spent most of my inheritance on a helicopter that has shrapnel scars from Vietnam and a Cessna that was born before I was!"

"I guess you are a risk, come to think of it!"

Brant picked up a chain saw and handed it to Cody, then reached for the other saw and the gas can. Cody grabbed the cooler and, as they began walking toward the woods, said, "So tell me, in view of your fascination with dilapidated things, how old do you like your women?"

Smiling, Brant answered, "If I could find a woman as good looking and dependable as my truck I wouldn't care how old she was!"

"Good looking and dependable, huh? Any other qualifications?"

"This is not a hypothetical question, is it?"

"Very astute. There is someone I had in mind."

"She's not my type."

"I haven't mentioned any names yet."

Brant laughed. "You were anything but subtle yesterday when you suggested I teach her to fly in exchange for painting lessons. Like I've always wanted to do water color! I fully expected you to propose for me right on the spot!"

"Hey, I was just taking my cues from Jody! Now there's a woman who missed her calling!"

"Yeah, Yenta the matchmaker!"

"I was thinking she'd make a great talk show host!" Cody set the cooler down and held an imaginary microphone at arm's length. "Paige, dear, tell this nice, handsome, single man what a wonderfully warm, talented, and articulate, not to mention single, woman you are!" Picking up the cooler again, he said, "Seriously, I think you and Paige are perfect for each other!"

Brant took a deep breath and looked away. Almost to himself he said, "I wish." Then, with an intensity that surprised Cody, he said, "Look at her! She's rich, spoiled, artsy . . . she had gold fingernails with little pearls glued to them, for heaven's sakes! And the way she kept tossing her hair . . . made me want to chop it off!"

Cody, who hadn't noticed the color of Paige's fingernails, even though he'd been around her for hours the night before, turned away and smiled to himself. "So what are you looking for? Besides reliable and dependable."

"Someone earthy, adventurous."

"She wants to learn to fly a plane! How much more adventurous can you get?"

Brant took out a spray can and marked a blaze-orange X on the tree in front of him, then moved on. "You don't think for a minute she was serious, do you? Pretending to be interested in a guy's hobbies is the oldest trick in the book!"

"So you're saying she was just coming on to you? You think she's interested?"

Brant flexed his right arm. "How could she not be?"

Cody rolled his eyes, but Brant only shrugged his shoulders. "Well? Women like me, what can I say? But for once I'd like to find a girl who's not stuck on herself, someone who doesn't go through withdrawal symptoms if she's away from a mirror for an hour! I want a woman who's low maintenance, you know? Who cares more about inner beauty than peach satin and pearls!"

After several seconds, Cody managed to recall that Paige had been wearing a satin blouse yesterday. Had he been quizzed, he would have guessed it was pink, but obviously Brant had paid closer attention to details. With exaggerated compassion in his voice he quoted, " 'Who can find a virtuous woman? For her price is far above rubies!' "

Not responding to the sarcasm, Brant marked another tree and kept talking. "And I want a family. Just being there yesterday when the baby was born . . . I've done a dozen emergency deliveries, but they never got to me like this one. Hearing that first cry, even from downstairs . . . and seeing the looks on those kids' faces, and David and Karlee together . . . I want that."

Cody stared at his friend as if seeing him for the first time. This sudden bout of seriousness was so out of character it was all he could do not to laugh. Brant unscrewed the gas cap on his chain saw and looked inside. Replacing the cap, he stood still for a minute, then looked beyond Cody, deep into the trees.

"My tastes have changed so much in the past five years. All those years you were talking to me about God and telling me how great it was to be a Christian, you never prepared me for that! That not only would my life change, but I'd change. Who would have thought I'd be looking for a woman who loves kids! I'm plenty ready to settle down, but it's got to be with someone challenging, with real depth, someone who's really passionate about serving God! Are there women like that really out there?"

Finally letting himself smile, Cody said, "Sorry pal, I got the last one." They walked in silence, Brant marked two more trees, and then Cody said, "Don't be too quick to rule out Paige. There's more to her than satin and pearls."

Shaking his head, Brant said, "Hang it up, Code, even if I could get beyond the fingernails and the hair thing, she's got an attitude I can't tolerate."

"What do you mean?"

"I don't know . . . isn't she supposed to be a Christian? But instead all she seems interested in is . . . oh, you know, Paris and the 'Gallery' . . . been there, done that, you know? There's no way that you're hooking me up with Cleopatra!"

Cody turned slowly and stared at Brant. "You just met her yesterday and she told you about that?"

Brant's face blazed red. "Well, I . . . I guess someone mentioned it . . ."

"No way! No one in that house 'just happened to mention' the time Paige was performing as Cleopatra and ended up falling off the stage in a gold lamé dress! When David told Hailey and me about it, we laughed for three hours and Paige didn't talk to any of us for a week! She made us sign an oath in blood not to repeat it! Where did you hear about that?"

"I, uh, well—"

Brant's excuses were drowned in the roar of the chain saw.

8

*T*aking a calming breath, Paige settled herself on a cushion on the floor and began arranging brushes and tubes of paint in front of her. Painting, especially the kind she did here at the Center, was usually relaxing. The whimsical style had always come naturally to her. Before she had been offered a scholarship to study "serious" art in Paris, all she had wanted to do was illustrate children's books. Now she painted landscapes and portraits and collected books illustrated by other artists while her sketch books collected dust in the closet.

She looked up and down the hallway, picturing the finished job. This was her last project until the new wing of the Sparrow Center was finished. She'd spent most of the previous summer covering the walls of the lobby and day room with jungle-theme murals. Then, after returning from Europe in the spring, she had started in on smaller scenes in the resident rooms.

She'd planned to finish weeks earlier, but volunteering to help the occupational therapy team had cut into her time. It had also introduced her to Annie. She looked at the crayon drawing sitting next to her on the floor and sighed. She hadn't planned on painting tonight and the mood she was in wasn't conducive to creativity. What she had planned on was supper with Annie and then curling up together with a stack of Winnie the Pooh books. Instead, she'd spent an extra hour on the freeway when a gruesome accident had backed up traffic for almost an hour and her car had overheated. On top of that, she hadn't thought to check Annie's schedule, and as it turned out, she'd had five minutes with her before a group of volunteer "Grammas" had come to take her and several other residents out for dinner.

Sliding the drawing into her canvas bag on top of the books she'd brought, she pulled out her CD player, hoping a few minutes with Michael Card would soothe her spirits. Adjusting her headphones, she pushed "play," picked up her pencil, closed her eyes, and tried to envision a zebra leaping through a field of tall grass. What she saw instead was the underside of the Flight-for-Life helicopter flying over her and the flashing lights of two rescue squads pulling away from the accident scene. She turned the volume knob on the CD player, and waited, but all she got was silence. Looking down, she saw the CD sitting motionless beneath the player's window. The batteries were dead.

"Rats!" She tore the headphones off and slammed them on the floor. Picking up the pillow, she threw it down the hall and watched as it skidded across the floor and into the break room. Not bothering to go after it, she walked into the store room that David, whose architectural firm had designed the Sparrow Center, was using as a temporary office. She began rifling through drawers, hunting for batteries, and making so much noise she didn't hear David come to the doorway.

"What, exactly, are you looking for?" The amusement was clear in her brother's eyes. Paige mumbled an answer and moved to the next drawer, turning her back on him.

"This is just like old times," David said, "You, in my room, rummaging through my stuff without my permission. If I had the slightest idea what you just said I might be able to help you."

Paige banged a cupboard door shut and threw up her hands. "You'd think in all this junk there'd be a couple measly little double A batteries!"

Putting his hands on her shoulders, David turned her to face him. "Take a deep breath, kid. What's the matter."

"My batteries are dead."

"It's not dead batteries that have you wound this tight." He guided her to a chair and gently pushed her into it. "Talk, woman."

"There was this horrible accident on the freeway tonight and I can't get it out of my head and all my plans for the weekend got screwed up and . . ."

"And . . . ?"

"I want to have a child."

David sat down heavily on the corner of the desk. "Say, what? Are you . . . pregnant?"

"No! David! Of course not!"

"So what are you talking about?"

"Oh, David, you're so traditional, so conventional. You'll think I'm crazy."

"I've thought that before. Try me."

"A child. I want one."

"I assume you're talking about marriage first and then a baby?"

"No! I'm not talking about marriage at all! I'm not even talking about a baby!"

"You're right, I'm way too conventional. I haven't got a clue what you're talking about and you're scaring me. This isn't like you, Paige."

"I'm going to be thirty in two years and I want to be a mother! Hailey got the last decent, marriageable guy in the United States, and besides, I'm not sure I'm the marriage-type anyway. I just want to be a mother." She looked at David's confused expression and turned away from him. "I want to adopt Annie," she said quietly.

"Whoa . . ." David stood, then dropped into the chair across from her. "Have you talked to Robert about this?"

"No. I haven't talked to anyone yet. But I know that her mother is relinquishing her rights, and there's no father in the picture."

David ran his hand over his face. As president of the Center's board, he knew things that Paige didn't, things he couldn't talk about yet. He sighed, hating to see her get hurt. "Adoption can be a complicated thing, Paige; there could be a lot of obstacles in your way. I hate to see you get your hopes up. Have you really thought about it? Do you realize what kind of commitment it would take? Annie is a precious little girl, but raising her would be a minute-by-minute challenge, maybe for the rest of your life."

"I've thought about it, David. Annie needs a real home and I need a purpose in life."

"Have you prayed about it? Keep in mind, little sister, that good will is not always God's will."

"Please. Spare me the sermon, David. I was counting on your love and support. Do I have it or don't I?"

"My love, always. My support . . . I don't know." He stood, then bent down and wrapped her in a bear hug. "But I will pray about it," he said.

Walking into the break room to get her pillow, the first thing Paige saw was a pair of leather boots sitting next to the couch. The next thing she saw was her pillow—wedged beneath Brant's head on the couch. His eyes were closed and Paige couldn't help but sigh in exasperation at his gall. She hoped he would hear her, but not a muscle moved. Opening the refrigerator, she whispered, "Welcome to the Holiday Inn, sir."

Grabbing a can of tomato juice, she let the door slam, and turned to see if it produced a reaction. He still appeared to be sleeping like a baby. "Of all the nerve," she sighed. Pulling the tab off the juice can, she studied him, wondering why he wore wool socks in the summer, what it said on his brass belt buckle, and if he owned anything other than faded T-shirts. She let her eyes travel up to the sun-streaked hair that curled at his neck and the strong jaw.

She took a drink, then looked back at him, and almost choked. His eyes were open, wide open, and the small curves at the corners of his mouth said he was enjoying every second of her discomfort. Recovering as gracefully as she could, she said, "When you're done with your nap I'd like my pillow back."

"No problem," he said, smiling wider as he closed his eyes again.

Paige shook her head in disbelief and headed for the door. She wasn't going to start a fight. Not over a pillow, and not with the likes of Brant McCourt.

His voice stopped her in her tracks and pulled her back. "I don't think your adopting Annie is such a good idea."

"Of all the . . . I can't believe . . ." was all she managed as she stormed back into the room.

"Look," he said, "I know it's none of my business, but—"

"It's one thing to overhear a private conversation, Mr. McCourt. It's an altogether different thing to think you've got a right to get involved in it!"

Brant sat up. Mocking her formality, he said, "Miss Stern, would it be possible for you to cut me some slack? If you really want a reason to be mad at me I can give you one, but if you could just give me one minute . . ."

"Did it occur to you that I might not be interested in listening to your opinion about my future?"

"Just who *are* you listening to these days? Seems to me you don't hear much beyond your own voice."

"How dare you!"

Brant shoved one foot into a boot and said, "I dare because I've been there, Miss Stern! I think you've got your own interests in mind here and not what's best for that little girl!"

Paige gripped the back of a chair. Never in her adult life had she had such a conversation with a virtual stranger. "You've been hanging around here for one week and already you're an expert on the residents' welfare, and mine, too? What do you know about Annie, and what could you possibly know about me?"

Brant put on his other boot, picked up her pillow, and stood. She challenged his arrogant smile with fire in her eyes. But the smile only widened, and his left eyebrow arched. "Well . . ." he said slowly, "I know you love surprises, hate eating alone, don't take phone calls while you're working, and you're allergic to strawberries. Shall I go on?"

Stunned, feeling enraged and somehow violated, Paige could do nothing but grip the chair and let her mouth fall open. Before she could think of the next move, he walked toward her, shoved the pillow at her, and headed for the door, where he paused and turned. "And I know you didn't answer David's question when he asked if you'd prayed about this."

When she could think enough to move, she walked into the hallway, threw the pillow down next to her canvas bag, and headed for the back door and fresh air. Before she got there, she ran into Robert. He gave her a rueful smile.

"Guess I should have found a better place for Brant to take a nap, huh? He was up all night on call, and then just after he got back from transporting a patient for us this afternoon he got another Flight-for-Life call. I told him to sack out on the couch when he got back; I didn't think he was in any condition to drive home. But it sounds like he was having a fairly lively discussion with you instead of sleeping."

Paige's clenched jaws slackened. "I guess you could call it that," she said, then added slowly, "I saw that accident . . . how can anyone deal with that day after day?"

Robert nodded. "It takes a toll. Makes a person a little irritable at times, too, I imagine." He smiled at her. "Go on out and get some fresh air. You look like you could use it."

Outside, Paige took a deep breath and pressed her hands

against her hot cheeks. She sucked in another breath, and then went back inside.

Two double A batteries sat on top of her pillow in the hallway. She was touched by David's thoughtfulness, but there was no way she could paint now.

9

*S*leep was the only thing on Brant's mind as he parked his pickup next to the house. He wanted to close his eyes and erase the last few hours.

He'd been in a foul mood ever since the last accident. Some things you got used to; you learned to wall off your emotions so that cries of pain and the sight of mangled bodies didn't pierce your soul anymore. They were part of the job. But there was no way to harden yourself against what he'd seen today. You never got used to the death of a child.

Had it not been for the accident, he knew he would have responded differently to Paige. He probably would have kept his opinion to himself in the first place. They'd gotten off on the wrong foot from the moment he'd laid eyes on her, and he had a feeling there wasn't much he could do to change it. That fact only added to the darkness that hovered over him like a thunderhead.

The last thing he needed now was another reminder of loss, but that was exactly what was waiting for him, tucked behind the screen door in a thick brown envelope. The package fell on his foot when he walked in. Knowing immediately what it was, he kicked it out of the way and walked up the three steps leading into the kitchen.

He dropped onto a plastic-cushioned chair and slowly unlaced his boots. Too numb to construct words, his mind formed pictures into prayers. He saw the young mother standing alone by the side of the freeway, sinking to her knees in grief. He saw her husband, strapped to a back board, being lifted into the helicopter, reaching out to the covered body of his son.

Tears filled Brant's eyes and he rested his head in his hands and let them fall. He'd long since learned not to ask "why?" but the question that came through the fog of his exhaustion was "how?" How, in the face of such grief, do you survive, how do you put one foot in front of the other, or even take the next breath without the Lord?

He stepped into the shower and turned the water as hot as he could stand it. It pelted his chest with fiery needles, making his skin red. Then, gradually, he lowered the temperature, cooling down until the water felt icy against his back. It was a strange ritual, he supposed, a kind of purging, but it did wonders for the tension in his muscles and the heaviness in his spirit.

He put on a pair of cut-off sweatpants and walked out to the kitchen. He grabbed a soda out of the refrigerator and pulled a jar of peanut butter and a package of crackers from the cupboard. As he unscrewed the jar lid, he glanced down the steps to the back door. The padded envelope stared up at him from the floor, taunting him. He stared back as he spread peanut butter on a cracker and chewed it slowly. He went through half a roll of crackers that way, his eyes still on the package, an imaginary conversation going on in his head. Before he picked it up, he had to be ready with a defense, even though, as always, he'd be the only one to hear it.

He put the crackers away, downed the last of the soda, and turned to the bedroom. The package could wait until morning. Or longer.

He was sound asleep within sixty seconds. For over an hour he was dead to the world, but the phone rang just before ten and woke him. He didn't have a phone in the bedroom and he didn't have an answering machine; if he got up, whoever it was would have hung up by the time he got to the living room. He rolled over and pulled the pillow over his head. His pager was on the night stand; in the event of an emergency, he could be reached.

But as hard as he tried to clear his mind, sleep would not

return. He was plagued with a gnawing sense that he'd left some-thing undone. When he finally quit fighting the feeling and prayed about it, two images flashed in his mind simultaneously. One was the envelope on the floor by the back door. The other was Paige, clutching her pillow, her deep brown eyes flashing at him, cutting him. And suddenly, in the dark room with his eyes closed, he saw what he had missed in his anger: the hurt that she had tried to mask in defensiveness. He thought of the envelope. Maybe he and the girl with the pearls on her fingernails were not so different after all.

He got up and put on a T-shirt. As he slipped into his sandals at the back door, he thought about calling first, but decided against it. If Cody wasn't there, Brant had a key. As he bent down and picked up the envelope, he said out loud, "Ah, the wonders of modern technology. Video parenting—it's the wave of the fu-ture, folks! So much more convenient than the old days of Super 8 Movie parenting!" He wondered what his parents would say if they knew he didn't even own a VCR, that he hadn't owned one the whole time he lived in Canada. Every time they'd sent a tape he'd had to watch it at the ranger station thirty miles from his cabin, usually with half a dozen other guys hanging around.

He knew he was being childish. But wasn't that their fault? Didn't kids get psychologically stuck at some immature level if their emotional needs weren't met? Not that he'd grown up with-out love, he'd had plenty of it. But it hadn't come from where he needed it most. It was hard to soak in love from someone else when your own parents were strangers. When he and his sister were little, "Mom and Dad" had been the people on the movie screen in Gramma and Grampa's basement. They were still down there, reels and reels of "Mom and Dad," all neatly labeled: "Jane and Warren in Peru," "Jane and Warren in Guatemala," "Jane and Warren—Christmas in Mexico City" . . . He sometimes wondered what kind of a parent he'd make without having had good role models. But at least he knew the most important thing—he'd be there.

He prayed as he drove. It was the only way to divert the sarcasm that kept bubbling to the surface. "Forgive me, Lord. You know I don't want this bitterness. Help me to love them. Their eyes are blind without You, they have no idea how they hurt us."

The door was locked when he got to Cody's house, so he let himself in. He had no secrets from his best friend, but still he was glad to be alone. These "visits" with his parents were more painful than he wanted to admit, and it was just easier to handle with no one else around.

He took his sandals off and walked barefoot across the teal carpeting. He smiled to himself as he looked around. There were new curtains in the kitchen. It would only be a bachelor pad for a few more days, and Hailey's subtle touches were already evident.

Brant felt a bit wistful thinking about it; it was the close of an era that he and Cody had made last far longer than either of them could have predicted. Just being in the little bungalow brought back so many memories, even though it had been completely redecorated since the days when they had used it as their "secret hideaway."

As he popped the tape in the VCR and settled on the floor in front of the couch, he realized he hadn't even glanced at the post mark. He wondered cynically what rain forest or mountain top they'd be on this time.

But this was something different. His father sat behind a desk, while his mother, in a skirt and jacket instead of the usual khakis and T-shirt, sat on the corner of the desk. Through the window behind them stretched a city skyline. His mother, her silver hair actually permed, spoke first. "Surprise! Bet you never thought you'd see us like this, did you? We're in Los Angeles!"

The picture zoomed in on his father, and Brant suddenly realized that there was someone operating the camera. Had they always done that? Somehow he'd always pictured the camera sitting on a tripod. It struck his tired mind as bizarre and made him want to laugh out loud.

"We're heading into our biggest project yet, Brant. Starting our own magazine! It's about time, huh? Thought you'd like the idea since you're always talking about going into business for yourself! We're calling it *Sea to Sea*. Catchy, huh? Going to focus on the natural wonders of the U.S.; little-known places, not the usual tourist traps. We'll target environmentalists and the back-to-nature types. Lots of pictures, you know."

The camera shifted again. "And that's where you come in! There's a place in this company just tailor-made for you! You'd have your own plane and be your own boss . . . well almost!" She gave a little-girl giggle; it was not becoming on a sixty-three-year-old woman. "You'd have to answer to us, of course, but that's the next best thing to being your own boss!"

The cameraman panned back to his father. Brant wondered if they were following a script. "Always knew that pilot's license of yours would come in handy some day, son!"

Son. Brant hadn't realized that he'd been digging his fingers into the thick teal carpet until the word made his hands clench. His father laughed and spread his hands in front of him. "We need aerial shots, you know? And we need to be able to be on the move at the drop of a hat. We need a cracker-jack pilot who likes living on the edge; someone who really wants to make a difference in the world. We'd be proud to have you work with us, son!"

At that moment, Cody walked in the back door and ambled into the living room. Brant picked up the VCR controls and paused the video just as the cameraman backed up and got them both on the screen. Cody, who had sat through hours of the McCourts' travelogs over the years, gave Brant a sympathetic look. "Hi, Mom. Hi, Dad. Where's the jungle?"

"Don't ask."

"Want a soda?"

"Sure."

Brant waited until Cody flopped down on the couch behind him before pushing play. "How 'bout it?" his mother asked. "Isn't this just perfect for you, Brant? You could have the whole downstairs of our condo, you'd be right in the city, but you'd still get to enjoy nature. And like your father said, this is a chance to leave your mark on the world, to do something really worthwhile with your life. Have you sold the farm yet?"

His father leaned forward. "Don't worry about it. I know a developer from Chicago that would lap that up in a min—" Brant snapped off the picture.

Cody shook his head. "I have no idea what that was all about, but I totally agree with them. It's about time you quit saving lives and start doing something worthwhile with your life, son!"

Brant pointed the VCR controls at Cody and pushed stop.

10

he next morning, the throbbing inside Paige's head woke her long before the alarm went off. She had spent most of the night replaying first David's words and then Brant's. Over and over she had tried to convince herself that, while David's opinion mattered, the opinion of an egotistical stranger was meaningless. But every time she closed her eyes she saw the look on Brant's face as he'd walked out of the room.

Something else gnawed at her as she walked to the bathroom, trying to rub the knots out of her neck, but she couldn't think what it was. She opened the door of the medicine cabinet, hunting for something to relieve her headache, then slammed it again when she found nothing. Sitting on the edge of the bath tub, she opened a bottle of bath gel, then lit a strawberry-scented candle. *Strawberries.* How did he know she was allergic to strawberries?

Pinning her hair up high on her head, she stepped into the tub and sank into the bubbles. As she forced her mind to concentrate on the mural she had to start, Mrs. Patches pushed open the door that hadn't quite latched and leaped onto the edge of the tub, where she began playfully swatting at the bubbles with her right paw. Scooping a handful of bubbles, Paige deposited them on top of Mrs. Patches' head and laughed as she bent her ear with her paw, trying to get them off. Gradually, the distraction and the heat eased her tension and the headache subsided.

Leaning back, she yawned and closed her eyes, trying to picture a zebra, but seeing, once again, Brant's face. The thoughts of the night resurfaced, floating through her mind like the bubbles on the water. Never had anyone made her feel so explosive, so out of control and vulnerable. She was unaccustomed to feeling herself an open book. She couldn't count the number of times a date had called her "mysterious," a quality she had enjoyed and actually cultivated. Now suddenly this man she didn't even like was staring through her, reading her. She tried to reason that he could have gotten his facts from Hailey or Cody, but the truth of it finally pushed to the surface: Brant McCourt knew things about her that she hadn't even admitted to herself.

Hailey called from work just as Paige was pouring her first cup of coffee. "There's a note for you on the porch," she said.

Paige took a sip of coffee. "Okay."

"Go read it."

"Why don't you just tell me what it says. Save me walking all that way."

"I don't know what it says! Why do you think I'm calling?"

"Didn't you write it?"

"No. I was going down to let the cat out about five this morning when it . . . arrived."

"It 'arrived'? By what . . . car, truck, carrier pigeon?"

"On foot . . . kind of."

"Make sense, girl."

"Go read it."

Paige was already halfway out the door with the cordless phone. Sitting on the round wicker table on the porch was an ivory parchment envelope with her name stenciled on it in gold letters. "Okay, I've got it."

"Well? What's it say? Hurry up! My break's almost over!"

Paige smiled. "Mmm . . . I know how you love a good mystery! I think I'll have to sit down for this one. Let's see . . . the rocker, the chair, or the bench? Which would be most comfortable?"

"Read it!"

Yawning loudly, Paige sat down, opened the envelope, and

pulled out a card in matching parchment. "Okay, let's see . . . my, what pretty stenciling. Someone went through a great deal of trouble just for me. It says 'Dear Paige, How about a bit of lunch with me at The Greenhouse at 1:00 this afternoon? I look forward to seeing you.' "

" 'How about a bit of lunch?' That's weird!"

"Haven't you read *Winnie the Pooh*?"

"Not recently."

"Well, that's what Pooh's always having—a bit of lunch." Paige frowned. "The card's not signed. Who brought it?"

"Well, I want to tell you, but I think it's supposed to be a surprise, but I know you and I know that you're going to be thinking all morning that it's some secret admirer and then you're going to get all dressed up and then you're going to be disappointed when you find out it's only . . ."

"Only who?"

"Oh . . ." Hailey whined. "You have to promise not to tell him that I told you and you have to promise to act surprised."

"I promise."

"Well, it was the weirdest thing. The cat started stepping on my face so I finally got up to let her out and I heard a car door slam out on the road as I was coming down the stairs, and just as I opened the door to the porch, the outside door closed and there was . . . this guy . . . running around the corner of the house."

"Did you recognize him?"

There was a pause on Hailey's end and then a quiet, "Yes."

Paige sighed. "Spit it out! Your break's almost over, remember?"

"You're right. Bye."

"Hailey! I'll hurt you!"

"Oh, this is such a cool thing! Why can't it be some tall, dark, and handsome guy that you'd fall madly in love with? I mean, he was—tall, dark, and handsome—well, maybe not exactly dark, but—"

Picking up the silver whistle that Hailey had taped to the phone for prank calls, Paige let out a long, steady blast, not loud enough to hurt Hailey's ear, but enough to shut her up.

"Okay!" There was another long pause. "It was Robert."

After her initial disappointment had faded, Paige began to address the obvious question, and the only probable answer sent her flying back to her room to change out of painting clothes and into shopping clothes. It was her philosophy that every celebration was cause for a new outfit.

The phone rang as she was ready to walk out the door. "May I please speak to Miss Paige Stern?" said the voice in her ear when she picked up the receiver.

"Speaking."

"This is Sandy from The Greenhouse. I'm calling to confirm your one o'clock reservation."

Paige smiled smugly, "Tell Dr. Worth I'll be there with bells on!"

❧

Paige's right hand smoothed out the wrinkles in the rose-printed napkin on her lap. It was ten after one and still no sign of Robert. It crossed her mind just once as she tried to relax against the chintz-covered chair, that she could have been wrong about the purpose of this meeting, but she dismissed the doubt as quickly as it surfaced. Surely he wouldn't pick such a cheerful setting to dash her hopes.

The Greenhouse had just opened in June and this was the first time Paige had been here. Her artistic eye quickly approved the interior design. The round tables were covered with pastel tablecloths and in the center of each one was a glass bowl filled with clear marbles and a simple arrangement of irises, daffodils, and tulips. The walls were stenciled to depict a flower garden in full bloom, and baskets of flowers and trailing vines hung from trellises mounted on the ceiling. Several sky lights flooded the room with natural light and reminded Paige of lunching *alfresco* at her favorite café in Paris.

Her thoughts were interrupted by the voice of the host who had seated her almost twenty minutes earlier. "Miss Stern? Your luncheon date phoned to say he's terrible sorry but he has been unfortunately detained, but he said you should order if you wish."

She hesitated; she hated eating alone. Reluctantly, she picked up the menu and smiled at the host. "I'm used to being stood up," she quipped.

The man in the black vest stared at her in open admiration, his eyes traveling from her sleek black hair to the white linen dress embroidered with gold tropical fish. The dress had spaghetti straps and its straight lines fell softly to mid-calf with a small slit up the left side. He bowed slightly, in very European fashion. "I sincerely doubt that, ma'am."

Paige offered a smile in return for the compliment. She ordered and told the waiter that she would be in the gift shop.

The small shop adjacent to the restaurant was an actual greenhouse, filled with plants, books, cards, plaques, and knickknacks. It smelled of wet dirt, scented candles, and potpourri. Paige found a tiny Green Bay Packer T-shirt that she couldn't resist picking up for Jordan and a copy of *Mr. Jeremy Fisher,* one of the few Beatrix Potter stories she didn't have in her collection. The book would be her first purchase for Annie's room.

Her salad had arrived when she got back to the table. Holding *Mr. Jeremy Fisher* in one hand, she pierced a cherry tomato with her fork and stuck it, whole, in her mouth. Just as she did, a voice behind her said, "Ah . . . 'are we having roasted grasshopper with ladybug sauce? Frogs consider it a beautiful treat, but I think it would have been awful!' "

With her fork still clamped firmly between her lips, she stared up at the man next to her. She didn't even pretend a smile as he took off his mirrored sunglasses and laid them on the table, then took off the blue and orange jacket with the paramedic emblem on the front and laid it on the back of the chair across from her.

Picking up the book, he said, "My grandmother used to read this to me. I knew the whole thing by heart."

Paige took the fork out of her mouth and laid it carefully and deliberately next to her plate. "Obviously," she said.

He leafed through several pages. "You draw better than this; they should have asked you to illustrate it."

If there was one thing she couldn't stand, it was being patronized. Instead of thanking him, she said, "What are you doing here?"

"Oh . . . I know the guy that bought this place. Cody and I went to high school with him. Nice, huh? Are you waiting for someone?"

"Yes."

He waited for more of an answer; and when none came, he asked, "Who?"

Paige gritted her teeth. "Dr. Worth."

"Mmm. Mind if I sit down until he gets here?"

Reluctantly, she said, "No."

The waiter walked up and set a glass in front of Brant and filled it from a pitcher, then handed him a menu, asking, "Would you like a few minutes?"

Brant shook his head. Handing the menu back, he said, "I'll have the beef stew and a salad with Thousand Island; just water to drink."

Paige's mouth opened in what was becoming a familiar expression whenever Brant was around. He smiled. "You don't mind if I have a bit of lunch with you?"

As her jaw dropped even lower, he reached into his jacket and pulled out a thin branch about six inches long with small green leaves. At the end of the branch was a peach satin ribbon. He handed it to her. Paige took it, touching first the leaves, then the ribbon, then lifting her gaze to his, asked the question with her eyes.

"It's boxwood. I couldn't find an olive tree." He stared at her with a look that made the branch tremble in her hand.

"It's a peace offering; I was out of line yesterday."

Paige fingered the shiny leaves, strangely touched by the simplicity and creativity of his offering. A dozen roses would not have swayed her, but this tiny branch had completely disarmed her. "Thank you," she said quietly.

"Does that mean I'm forgiven?"

She smiled at him and nodded. He extended his hand toward her across the table. "Friends?" When she hesitated for a fraction of a second he said, "Potentially?"

Paige laughed and held out her hand. "Potential friends. I like that."

"Are you always up before five?" he asked out of the blue.

"I'm never up before five! Why?"

"I assumed you saw Robert delivering my message."

"Hailey saw him." Paige took her time pulling apart a hard roll and taking a bite. What she wanted to say sounded too intimate. Her impression of Brant was changing much too fast and she wasn't sure she wanted to risk being mere feed for what she had assumed was his colossal ego. In the end, though, she said the words anyway. "I love surprises."

"I know."

"The card was very creative."

"I bought the paint and stencils for a bike I'm working on. Thought it would add a touch of intrigue. By the way, did the batteries work?"

"You left them?"

"Mmm-hm."

223

The waiter brought their food then and Brant said, "I'll pray." His prayer was simple, but so much from the heart that it made Paige oddly uncomfortable.

"I'm sorry I was so late," he said. "I wasn't supposed to be on call today, but you know how that works. Are you disappointed that the invitation wasn't from Robert?"

Paige hesitated. An honest answer would require some explanation. "I was hoping that David had talked to Robert and that Robert was going to give me his blessing to start adoption proceedings."

Brant nodded. "I'm sorry if I misled you."

"I shouldn't have let myself think like that." She looked at him, wondering what had happened to the ice she had seen in his eyes the first time she met him. "You still think I'm wrong, don't you?"

"I'm not sure I have a right to voice my opinion."

"I think potential friends have that right."

Brant smiled. "I don't want to end the way we did yesterday."

"We won't."

"We might." He took a drink of water, set the glass down, and ran his finger up and down the cut-glass side of the goblet. "It's not my style to soft-pedal things."

"So I've noticed. I'm a big girl, Mr. McCourt. I'll listen, then make up my own mind."

Brant stared at her, then at his watch, and sighed. "I have to be back at the station in twenty minutes. This isn't turning out the way I'd intended. I thought we'd have more time just to get to know each other, and I promised myself I wouldn't touch the subject of Annie today. What are you doing tomorrow afternoon?"

"I'm distracting T.J. and Shelly so David and Karlee can have some quiet time alone with the baby. I promised Annie I'd take her along so she could ride T.J.'s pony, and then we're all going back to my place to watch *101 Dalmatians*. Would you like to join us?"

"Not exactly what I had in mind for our first date, but I'll take it. What are you doing Friday night?"

"I don't know. But I have a feeling you're about to tell me."

"How about your first lesson, then a moonlight flight and dinner?"

"Sounds wonderful." She picked up the branch and turned it over in her hand. Looking up at him, she said, "We just might end up being friends after all."

*P*aige balanced on the top bar of the split-rail fence with T.J. on one side of her and Shelly on the other. "I don't think he's ridden horses much," T.J. observed.

"I think you're right, Teej," Paige answered, snapping a picture.

"What if he drops Annie?" Shelly added.

Paige waved at Annie and watched her dark curls bouncing against Brant's blue denim shirt. "Blacky's just walking; there's no danger . . . I hope."

Shelly looked nervously at the pony, then back at Paige. "Isn't it time to go to your house now?"

"Yeah, I guess it is." She motioned for Brant to steer Blacky in their direction. With T.J. snickering on one side and Shelly holding her breath on the other, she had a hard time maintaining a neutral face when he finally reached them. She held her arms out to a reluctant Annie. "Want to go to my house and watch a movie?"

Annie's head bobbed up and down and she dove into Paige's arms. She waved at the pony. "Bye, Bwacky!"

Paige rubbed her nose on Annie's cheek. "Should we make popcorn at my house?"

"Uh-huh. Can Bwacky have po-corn?"

"I don't think so."

"Why?"

"I don't think he likes popcorn."

"Why?"

" 'Cause horses eat oats and hay."

"Why?"

She was saved from answering when T.J. burst out laughing beside her. When she saw what he was laughing at, she put her hand over his mouth and wished she had a free hand for her own. Brant was trying to turn Blacky away from the fence. What Brant hadn't seen, but Blacky obviously had, was the apple in T.J.'s closed fist.

Giving up, Brant ungracefully dismounted and caught them laughing. "Go ahead and have your fun now," he said. "Just wait 'til I get you three thousand feet in the air and hand you the reins!" He turned on his heel and walked into the barn.

The next sound they heard from him was, "Youch!"

T.J ran into the barn and came running out just as fast. "Paige! Come quick! He's bleeding all over the place!"

Paige felt every nerve ending in the small of her back. She set Annie down outside the fence. "Take her into the house, Shel." Seeing the fear on her niece's face, she added, "You know how T.J. exaggerates." But as she jumped down, Brant walked out, his left hand clamped over his right. Blood was on his shirt and running between his fingers.

Taking a deep breath, Paige put on a competent act. "Let's get you into the house," she said, opening the gate for him.

"It's not as bad as it looks. I don't want to drip blood all over the house. Where's the hose?" Paige felt her stomach lurch, but Brant went on talking. "I couldn't see in the dark and I caught the side of my hand on a nail. It ripped a chunk of skin off, but it's not deep."

Small black spots appeared in front of Paige's eyes. She wasn't sure if she was still walking, but Brant kept talking. "I'm current on my tetanus shots, so I don't have to worry about that." He stopped and turned to her as T.J. handed him the hose and ran to turn it on. "If you could just get me a couple of—whoa!" He grabbed her and eased her to the step of the deck. "Put your head down!" The hose came on and he pulled his shirt off and soaked it with water, then wrung it out and put it on the back of her neck, then wiped her face with it.

After several minutes, she felt the blood returning to her head and she looked up. Brant had his hand wrapped in his shirt and there was no blood to be seen. He grinned at her. "I've been a paramedic for a long time, but I've never seen anyone turn quite that color before."

Paige groaned and pointed to his hand. "Is it bad?"

"No. Wanna see?"

"No!" Paige put her hand over her face. "This is so embarrassing!"

T.J. came with the first-aid kit and Brant began unwrapping his hand. Grinning again, he looked at Paige. "Want to give me a hand with this?"

"Stop it!"

T.J. opened the red and white box and sat down on the step. "I'll help you," he said. "Girls are wimps." Paige covered her face with her hands, but Brant slowly peeled one hand away. "We all have our weaknesses," he said softly.

"You don't. 'Cept you don't ride very well."

Brant laughed. "Well, I have a few other weaknesses besides. Ask Cody about me and road kill sometime."

❧

On Monday afternoon when she came home from the Gallery, Paige found a note from Hailey on the counter. "Robert wants to talk to you when you have time. I don't know what it's about, but this time it's really him!"

Paige flew to the phone, but the tone of his voice as he talked to her let her know that he did not have good news. An hour later she stood in his office listening to something that wasn't sinking in. She couldn't let it.

"He has a right to see his daughter," Robert repeated softly.

"And she has a right to be raised by someone who loves her

228

and understands her, not some freak whose face is plastered over every tabloid in the country!"

"He may not even want her, Paige."

"But if he does? A biological act doesn't make him a father! Robert, did you ever listen to his lyrics? They're so corrupt! He's an atheist and a drug addict! And how do we know he didn't know about her until a month ago? Maybe he knew all along and didn't care!"

Even to her own ears, her voice sounded harsh after Robert's gentle words. Robert settled on the corner of his desk, facing her, and motioned once again for her to sit down. Feeling like a school child, she finally complied, looking up at the thick, snowy-white hair, the strong, tanned face that denied his sixty-four years. His eyes looked tired, but the kindness in them was never dimmed by fatigue. He turned the pen in his hand over, end to end, several times, seemingly engrossed in the action, then cleared his throat. "Can I play the father figure here for a minute?"

Paige gave a weak smile and swiped at a stray tear, then nodded.

"Let's just say for a minute that Roman decides to relinquish his rights. I don't know how much you've actually looked into this, but you could face some huge problems in the adoption process. You're single and Caucasian—adopting a bi-racial child can be difficult. Some people feel strongly that a child should be raised by someone who shares her ethnic heritage."

"But with her disabilities . . ."

"I know. I just want you to be aware that there could be problems. Okay, let's say that all the road blocks are removed. I hope you'll believe that I'm not trying to stand in your way, only that I want to be sure that you know what you're facing. I know you've seen Annie at her worst and I also know that you're as good with her as anyone on staff, but . . ." He stared at her, knowing his words would seem strong and hurtful, but unable to avoid them. "You've only been with her for a few hours at a time. Twenty-four hours, seven days a week with a child like this can seem interminable . . . especially for someone with no parenting experience. And what would you do about work?"

"As of the first of August I'll be the manager of the Gallery. That means a raise and also that I'm in charge of scheduling— and the assistant manager has kids at home and she's interested in job sharing. Annie can be here in day school half-days until she's . . . if and when she's ready for kindergarten. I've really thought it through."

Robert nodded. "What about time for yourself? For painting and travel and all the things you're used to doing?"

Paige stared down at her hands. This was the only area she hadn't completely resolved, but she wasn't about to let on. "I've lived in Paris, traveled all over Europe, spent a summer with David and Shawna in Senegal, and seen most of the U.S. and Canada." She attempted a convincing smile. "I think I've got it out of my system. And I could paint after Annie was in bed."

"If you had the energy left." It was not a sarcastic comment, simply the truth, Paige realized, but she had thought it through, she assured him again. Robert nodded. "What about relationships . . . dating?"

"I couldn't be interested in anyone who couldn't accept Annie."

"Is that fair? A lot of men are hesitant about getting interested in a woman with a child, and for good reasons."

"You weren't."

Robert smiled. "Touché. But Cody's mother was a patient and then a friend for years before I married her."

"But it can be done."

"Yes, it can."

"Marriage isn't for everyone anyway."

"True. Some people are called to be single. Do you think that's your calling, Paige?"

Paige looked away. "Maybe I should just hold a press conference so I can tell everyone at once! No, I don't think I'm called to be single! But I don't think I'm called to get married until the right guy comes along! What if he doesn't show up until I'm too old to have kids?"

With only a hint of a smile, Robert said, "Don't you think God can read your biological clock?"

"I suppose, but—" The buzzer on Robert's phone interrupted her.

"I'm sorry," he said, turning around to push the button. Charissa's voice answered. "Mrs. Welch is here."

Paige stood and Robert reached out to give her a fatherly hug. "Whether you like it or not I'm going to be praying for your future husband. And there's something I want you to pray about."

"What's that?"

"Roman Slayder will be here Friday night. I'd like you to be here. I believe that you know Annie better than anyone here. I trust you to be honest in spite of your own desires, and I also trust you to be objective."

"Objective?"

"About Roman. He has his rights and we will not interfere . . . unless Annie's health and safety appear to be in jeopardy."

❧

Friday came much faster than she would have liked. It had been a hectic week, with the Gallery's manager being rushed off for an emergency appendectomy on Tuesday, and two of the college students employed by the Gallery away on an art class trip. What it had meant for Paige was being there an hour before opening until an hour after closing each day.

After locking up on Friday evening, she kicked off her shoes and carried them to her car. Her feet hurt, her back ached, and instead of the planned moonlight flight with Brant, she had to meet the famous Roman Slayder. It was the last thing in the world she wanted to do.

Taking the scenic back roads instead of I-90 would lengthen the drive to the Sparrow Center to forty-five minutes and give her time to unwind. She prayed out loud for the first fifteen miles, pleading her case before the highest court. But as she turned onto a rustic road just north of Cambridge, the words stopped and, for the first time in a very long time, she began to listen. What she heard in the silence as she passed through the stretched-thin tree shadows on the country road was not a voice, but a conviction, a conviction that the focus of her pleas should not be Annie, nor herself, but Roman Slayder. It was a conviction she did not welcome.

The helicopter was in the field behind the employee parking lot, casting a monstrous shadow on the grass. As she slammed the car door, Paige had the strange sensation that she was acting out a scene from one of Hailey's mystery novels. The helicopter, the near-empty parking lot, the odd hour for visitors, all carefully planned to avoid media attention and keep fans off Roman Slayder's trail. Quaestor was in Minneapolis for a Saturday concert and Roman had been flown by private plane from a small town just outside the Twin Cities to the Madison airport where Brant had picked him up in the helicopter. To avoid the possibility of being seen, Robert had even invited Roman to spend the night at his house. Unlocking the back door with the key Robert had loaned her, she wondered cynically if she'd be met by a guard with a metal detector.

Instead, she was met by total silence. Robert had scheduled a skeleton crew of one LPN, two trusted aides, himself, and Hailey. Hailey would be covering the intensive care nursery and Paige assumed she'd find Robert and Annie in the day room. As she walked down the hall, her heels making light clicks on the vinyl, she wondered if they had gotten Annie to take an afternoon nap. If not, her father's first impression would probably not be favorable.

Absorbed in her thoughts, she jumped at the sight of another person. "Marsella!" The head of the housekeeping department was changing a light bulb in one of the brass wall fixtures that were only turned on at night.

"Miss Stern!" the woman gasped, as startled as Paige. "You like to 'lectrocute me!"

Paige laughed. "I'm sorry! I was just surprised to see you here so late."

"My car. She breaks down on my way and I have to wait for my son to fix it. Tomorrow is my vacation; I am going home to see my mother! But I have things to finish here first. So . . ." She gave a shrug and smiled. "So I stay late. You are late, too. Art classes at night?"

Paige thought fast. "No. I'm on my way home from the Gallery. I stopped by to talk with Dr. Worth. Maybe we can go out and get some pie and coffee later. He works too much."

Marsella nodded. "So does Mr. McCourt. Felicia says he brought a patient in tonight. Very late for admitting a patient, isn't it?"

Paige shrugged, as casually as she could. "Well, have a wonderful trip and don't work too hard tonight, Marsella."

"You should take me out for pie and coffee I think!"

Paige laughed. "I'll do that! As soon as you get back!"

She opened the door to the day room. The scene on the other side of the door was so different from what she'd expected that it took a minute to register. Sitting on the floor, cross-legged, in boots, faded jeans, a forest green shirt, leather vest, and a tightly curled hot-pink wig, was Brant McCourt. He looked up at her, smiled, and said, "Laugh and you die."

As Paige clamped her hand over her mouth, Annie ran up and

wrapped around her knees. "I maked Mr. 'Court pretty!" she said proudly.

"Yes, Annie. You made Mr. McCourt very pretty! But I think he needs a hat and a purse, don't you? Can you find a purse and a very big hat for Mr. McCourt?"

As Annie ran across the room to the costume box, Paige pulled a small chair away from the table and sat down facing Brant. "Pretty in pink," she said. "How'd you end up with this job?"

"One of the kids had a convulsion. He's okay, but it woke up the whole room so every available hand is settling kids. Since I'm better at dress-up than lullabies, I volunteered for this. Robert is in his office with 'Rock Star Dad' going over Annie's file. Robert wanted him to be as prepared as possible."

"What's he like?"

Brant took time out to tickle Annie as she set a huge, floppy hat on his head, then sent her off in search of one for Paige. "Nothing like I expected. He asked a lot about the Center, and we talked about the Packers and how he grew up in Milwaukee. He may have a ring in his nose and dreadlocks down to his waist, but he's just a regular guy! I was prepared to dislike him, but he's not the creep I thought he'd be."

Neither are you, Paige thought. Annie held out a six-gallon cowboy hat and Paige bent over so Annie could put it on her head. "Yee-ha! Ride 'em cowboy!" Paige said, slapping her thigh and sending Annie into a fit of giggles.

"She's a neat kid," Brant said. "How are you handling this?"

"Part of me would like to sabotage this whole thing, but God had a little talk with me on the way over here."

Brant smiled. "The still, small voice. What did He say?"

"That this isn't about me. It's about Roman."

Brant reached up and grabbed her hand. "Let's pray before he comes in."

s Brant prayed, his pink-wigged head bowed, Annie put on a sombrero with dangling tassels and slipped a yellow plastic gun into Paige's free hand . . . and Robert led Roman Slayder into the room. Still holding Paige's hand, Brant stood, pulled Paige to her feet, and without hesitation did a smooth, graceful curtsey. Robert, having dreaded this moment, could have hugged the man in the pink curls for breaking the ice.

Robert introduced Paige, then, following Roman's eyes, said, "And this is Anika. We call her Annie." Annie started to walk toward him, but Paige instinctively bent and scooped her up.

"Hey," Roman said by way of greeting, then shifted his weight from one foot to the other. Paige tightened her hold on Annie, knowing full well she was giving the child non-verbal cues. "I brought you somethin'," he said, producing a wrapped box from behind his back.

He's trying to buy her! The thought blared in her head and she locked eyes with Robert, who read her thoughts loud and clear and returned a look of understanding with just a hint of warning. Once again, she felt like the defiant child and wanted nothing more than to bolt for the door with Annie in her arms and run for all she was worth.

Annie's dark eyes lit and she slid out of Paige's arms, took the package, and sat on the floor at their feet, tearing at the paper. Roman stared down at her, still shifting from left to right. The ringed fingers of his right hand played with the silver medallion that hung from a chain around his neck. Annie struggled with the package, ripping off most of the bright paper, but she was unable to budge the tight ribbon that crossed all four sides.

Robert smiled at Roman. "Looks like she could use some help."

"Yeah . . . sure." He crouched beside her, producing a mother-of-pearl-handled pocket knife that sent chills down Paige's back as it slipped through the ribbon like a razor blade. Annie lifted the lid and pulled out a drum the size of a large coffee can and stared at it, then at the man across from her. Once again, Robert stepped in. "Maybe Mr. Slayder can show you how to use it, Annie."

Paige's hands drew into fists. *Why don't we just write him an instruction book? The Care and Feeding of Little Girls—for Fathers Who Really Don't Care Anyway.* She glared at Robert again. Wasn't it obvious to him that this man didn't have a clue? Roman settled cross-legged on the floor and began tapping his fingertips on the rawhide. Annie stared, mesmerized, until he stopped. Then, slowly, she reached out and tapped, first one hand, then two, and then there was no stopping her.

Robert and Brant perched on the edge of a low table to watch. Paige turned the little chair around and sat down. The braids in Annie's hair bounced, the colored balls on her hair bands making a soft clacking noise. Suddenly, the pounding stopped and Annie pointed to Roman. It took him a minute to understand her meaning, but this time he looked at her instead of helplessly to Robert. Catching on, he played a simple beat, then stopped, pointing back at her. Annie copied his rhythm, beat for beat, flawlessly. And Paige felt like something was slipping through her fingers.

When she walked out of Annie's room and down the hall to Robert's office, she felt drained, her back ached, and she knew she was dangerously close to tears. She was in no condition to be talking to Roman. Stopping outside Robert's door, she ran her fingers through her hair, adjusted her wide red belt, and brushed her hands against the skirt of the black shirt-waist dress she'd put on seventeen hours earlier. Just when she felt almost presentable, she heard footsteps behind her.

"Missing something, Miss Stern?"

She turned around to see her black heels dangling from Brant's fingertips. She stared at him blankly, then down at her stockinged feet. "You left them in the day room." Smiling at her as she slipped into the shoes, he reached out and put his hands behind her neck. Her tired mind glided in slow-motion to the conclusion that he was going to hug her, but thankfully her reflexes were just as slow. She laughed, uncharacteristically embarrassed, as he unfastened a string of purple plastic beads, pulled them off her neck, and slipped them into his shirt pocket. "You look exhausted," he said softly, "but can I ask a favor?"

Paige nodded, responding to both his question and his observation.

"Could you give me a ride home? My truck is at the airport."

"Sure. But I don't know how long this will take."

"No prob. You know where to find me."

"My pillow is in the cupboard behind the door."

"Thanks. I'll be praying for you. This won't be easy."

As she turned toward the office, she wondered momentarily what she would have done if he *had* been trying to put his arms around her.

Robert sat behind the desk, leaning forward on his elbows, his shirt sleeves rolled up. Paige took the swivel chair next to Roman and looked at Robert. He cleared his throat. "I've given Roman as much medical information as possible, and I've filled him in on Annie's history and daily routine. I thought you could—"

A voice shouted over the intercom on his desk. "Dr. Worth, Brandon is seizing again!"

"I'll be right there." He looked apologetically at Roman as he rose from his chair, then almost pleadingly at Paige. It was a look that plainly said, "Be nice."

Yes, Daddy, she wanted to say, but she silenced the sarcastic little voice inside her. She turned to Roman, knowing full well what was expected of her, and disobeyed. "So, is it true you didn't know you had a daughter until last month?"

Roman looked over her right shoulder. "I haven't seen her mother since I moved to California. I had no idea she was pregnant when I left."

"Must have been quite a surprise. Do you have other children?"

For the first time, his eyes met hers. "I suppose the answer you're expecting is 'not that I know of'." He leaned forward, never taking his eyes from hers. "Miss Stern, don't believe everything you read."

Not one to blush easily, Paige was startled by the warmth creeping up her neck. Defensively, she answered, "Well, it can't all be a lie."

Roman sighed and sat back, staring at the ceiling. "Aren't you supposed to be telling me about Anika?"

"It's equally important that we know about you and what kind of situation Annie would be going into."

"Since when is it the job of a volunteer art teacher to make decisions on child placement?"

Paige's mouth opened, then closed before her indignation could form into words. He was right, it was not her job. "I'm sorry. It's just that . . . I want what's best for her. I want to see her raised in a good Chris—"

Roman gave a wicked laugh. "Miss Stern, I was raised in a 'good Christian home'! I had the fear of God shoved down my throat before I was weaned! I learned the Ten Commandments backwards, forwards, and inside-out, never had a TV, and didn't wear jeans 'til I was eighteen. When I was twelve years old my father made me copy the entire Gospel of John as punishment for going to see a Muppet movie with a friend. You have before you a true product of Hell-fire and brimstone! Like what you see, Miss Stern?"

"But that's—"

"That's Christianity, Miss Stern!"

"No, it's not! It's a distortion of the truth. If you'd listened to the Book of John while you were copying it, you'd know those things have nothing to do with the character of Christ!"

"Don't start the God-is-love stuff on me."

"But He is love! Jesus came to set us free! That kind of teaching just puts chains on people; it keeps you from knowing the grace and mercy of God, it steals the joy and the peace!"

He sneered at her. "You're a great example of peace and joy, Miss Stern! If I want preaching I'll go home to my father. I came here to find out about my daughter."

Paige froze, then took a deep breath and let it out slowly. "Ever hear of the group Petra?"

"Yeah."

"They have a song that says, 'Sometimes God's children should be seen and not heard.' I guess this was one of those times."

Quietly, she began to tell him about Annie, her routine, her favorite foods and toys, and how to handle her tantrums. That was the point that brought tears to her eyes. "The strangest things can set her off. Usually it's not getting her way, but sometimes it's something completely unpredictable. One day I wore a yellow blouse; it's not a color I usually wear, maybe that was it, but she wouldn't come near me, she just started screaming and throwing blocks."

"And all you have to do when she gets like that is hold her down until she stops, right?"

Paige took another deep breath. This man was not father material. "You hold her, not hold her down. She needs to feel safe, that she has boundaries."

Maybe it was her tears, but something seemed to soften Roman. The defiance seemed to ebb away into a kind of tired frustration. Shaking his head, Roman said, "I have no experience in this area. I'll have to hire live-in help for awhile and find a specialist in FAS."

"Why are you doing this, Mr. Slayder? Why do you want her?"

"She's my daughter."

"Is it a guilt thing? I don't mean to sound harsh, but is it just a matter of feeling responsible for her? Because if that's what it is maybe it would help you to know that there's another . . . party . . . interested in adopting her."

"Dr. Worth never mentioned that."

"No . . . I don't suppose he would."

Roman walked toward the leather chair across from her. Slowly he sat down, staring at her for a full minute before speaking. "I've made some big mistakes in my life. Anika is the result of one of them, and there are other consequences to the kind of life I've lived." He paused and searched her face. "Can I trust you not to repeat this?" Paige nodded and he said, "Due to . . . let's just say medical reasons . . . Anika is the only child I will ever father. I'm in a serious relationship with a very giving woman who was thrilled to find out I have a child. I may not be your idea of a father, but I want to make this work."

Paige swiped at a stray tear. "I understand," she said.

He leaned toward her. "You're the 'other party,' aren't you? The one who was interested in adopting Anika."

"Yes."

"I'm sorry things aren't working out the way you'd hoped."

Paige sighed. "And I'm sorry I came on so strong. I'm sure it would be best for Annie to be with her own father."

Fingering the silver medallion, Roman said, "Don't apologize; you've said some things tonight that I need to think about. The only thing I'm sure of about parenting is that I don't want to be like my father. I turned my back on God because of him—but maybe I never knew God because of him."

*B*rant was sound asleep when Paige walked into the break room. She fought the desire to kiss him on the forehead to wake him, marveling that the idea seemed so natural. Instead, she whispered his name and he opened one eye.

"How'd it go?" he asked, his voice thick from sleep. "I've been praying for you."

She smiled at him. "It looks like it." She watched as he sat up and ran his hand across his face, then reached down for his boots. "How long has it been since you've had a full night's sleep?"

Brant yawned. "About three weeks, I guess. I haven't had a full day off since I started. I need the overtime. But I'm not scheduled to work tomorrow. How about you?"

"I'm off. I did the scheduling this week, so that's one of the perks."

"Good." Brant put his boots on and stood up. "So how did it go with Roman?"

"Not great. I wasn't exactly salt and light."

"It's hard to let go and let God be God sometimes, isn't it?"

"I guess that's what's at the heart of it, isn't it?—wanting my own way."

"That's what's at the heart of all our problems." Brant followed Paige out the back door to the parking lot. As they walked to her car, he looked up. The sky was velvet-black and sprayed with stars. "Would have been a perfect night for a flight." As he opened her car door he asked, "Do you have plans for tomorrow?"

"No." When he got in on the passenger side, he asked, "Sure you're serious about flying lessons?"

"Yes . . . serious, but a little scared."

"That's normal."

Paige fastened her seat belt and started the car. She was pulling out onto the road before she said, "I had a friend from here who died on his first solo flight in a Cessna. Did you know Gavin Prentice?"

"Yeah, I knew him. He was high before he ever got up in the air; he shouldn't have been flying."

The tone in his voice told her the topic was closed. It wasn't hard to understand. She changed the subject. "So you grew up in Milbrooke?"

"Off and on."

She glanced at him, then back at the road. "I don't think I understand."

"Neither did I," he said ruefully. Pointing to the left when she came to a stop sign, he said, "My parents are photo-journalists. They did assignments for *National Geographic* and several book publishers. They were gone more than they were home. Once in a great while we'd travel with them; we spent one summer in Peru, actually living in the same apartment, but my sister and I were basically raised by our grandparents."

"That must have been hard." She paused a minute. "Is that why you're so against me adopting Annie?"

"Yes and no. I have some pretty intense feelings about parents taking responsibility for their own kids, but in this case I'm not sure Roman is the best one to care for Annie."

"But you're not sure that I am either."

Brant pointed to the gravel drive leading to his house and turned to face her. "I think you have all the qualities of an excellent mother."

Paige pulled the car to a stop in front of a small white frame house. "Are you noticing a pattern here? Why is it that as soon as this subject comes up we're out of time?"

Brant laughed and looked at the digital clock. It read 11:26. "Who says we're out of time? We're off tomorrow. You hungry? I can throw a pizza in the oven."

"Sounds good. Come to think of it, I haven't eaten since noon."

As Brant opened the side door to the house he said, "I'm warning you—think bachelor!"

The warning was well-founded. As Paige walked up the three steps to the kitchen, she tripped over a pair of running shoes with socks hanging out of them.

"Sorry," Brant said, catching her by the arm. "Here, stand here and don't move." Paige obeyed and laughed as she watched him fly through the room, scooping up dirty dishes and papers from the counter and table. When he started taking notes and lists off the refrigerator, she said, "Stop! All you have to do is clear a path! I live with a girl who's never made a bed in her life—I'll feel out of place if it's too clean!"

Looking slightly embarrassed, Brant swept the room with his eyes and, piling a stack of papers on top of the refrigerator, pronounced it passable. Paige walked around the small, linoleum-floored room. Except for the microwave and the cordless phone sitting on the counter, the kitchen could have been a page out of a *Better Homes and Gardens* from the fifties. A gray Formica-topped table with four chrome chairs sat in front of a bay window. Next to the white porcelain sink was a pink stove and a matching refrigerator stood next to the window. Paige touched the pink dotted-swiss curtains. The material was so faded and thin she was afraid her touch would pull them down.

"Quite a museum, huh?" Brant said, opening the freezer compartment on the refrigerator. "My grandparents were not the progressive type. Believe me, I've got plans."

Paige touched the once-white plastic shade on the light fixture that hung low over the table. "I love this!"

Turning from the oven, Brant arched one eyebrow and laughed. "I thought you were an artist!"

"This is so . . . authentic; it's so old it's in! You should leave it just the way it is!"

Brant shook his head. "Clear a place and sit down." Lifting a Bible and a copy of *My Utmost for His Highest* off a plastic-cushioned chair, Paige asked, "How long have you been a Christian?"

He turned to face the counter. "Only about five years."

She stared at his back, waiting for him to say more. "Go on. Did Cody lead you to the Lord?"

Brant took the wrapper off the frozen pizza. "He had a lot to do with it."

"Go on."

"Cody and I have been friends since junior high; we got in a lot of trouble together in high school. He accepted the Lord when we were sixteen. I thought he was nuts, but I guess I had the attitude that everybody's got to do his own thing. We stayed friends even though we didn't have a lot in common anymore. After high school we got together when we were both home on vacations. He kept talking about God and I kept ignoring him."

He was quiet for a long time, and then he turned slowly, crossing his arms over his chest and leaning back against the counter. He stared at her, opened his mouth, then closed it as if changing his mind about what he was going to say. After a few more seconds he said, "Then I got into a relationship with a Christian girl and I guess the timing was right, 'cause I was finally ready to listen. God was so real to her . . ."

Brant's eyes locked with hers and Paige felt the same discomfort she had felt at the restaurant. "She loved Jesus with every ounce of her being. She taught me the meaning of dying to self, of total surrender to God's will . . ."

Paige shifted in her chair and looked away from him. She was ashamed to admit to herself that what she was feeling was envy, not just because of the glowing admiration he had for this girl, but because there had been a time in her life when people could have said the same things about her. "Do you still . . . see her?"

Brant smiled wistfully. "Yeah. But things are different between us now."

"But you still care about her?"

He shrugged. "I owe her a lot. I hope I can tell her that someday."

He opened the oven door and slid the pizza onto the rack. "So what's your story?"

"I was raised in a Christian home, went to Christian schools, camps, retreats . . . you name it, but I went through a weird phase right after high school. I joined an artist's colony for two years and tried on a lot of different philosophies. When I got tired of starving and being around really strange people, I went to college. It was a secular school, but a huge revival hit the campus in my senior year. We had all-night prayer meetings, hundreds of kids accepted Christ . . . it was so awesome. That's when I finally understood that kind of complete surrender you were talking about. A bunch of us were reading a book about the early Christians, and I remember feeling like a kindred spirit with them. Back then I knew that I could be mauled by lions or burned at the stake and never, deny Christ. I knew His grace was sufficient and nothing else mattered."

Again, she looked away from him, feeling too vulnerable beneath his searching eyes. "Before the sun comes up I really do want to hear your opinion about Annie."

"So you think!"

"Well, things look different now. Since there isn't much chance it's actually going to happen, I think I can handle it with a little less emotion."

Brant set the timer on the stove and sat down across from her.

"This is going to sound presumptuous coming from someone you just met." He leaned toward her, and once again Paige had the feeling she was an open book and he was turning the pages. "I think your motives are wrong," he said. "Adoption is a beautiful thing, but I think you're looking at this for selfish reasons. I think you're looking for an easy way to fill a void."

Paige drew back as if he'd slapped her. "There's nothing easy about taking care of a child like Annie!"

"True. But maybe in your mind it's less threatening than the real answer." He reached out and touched her arm. "Paige, let go of your pride long enough to ask yourself if it's the truth."

14

atching the red glow of Paige's tail lights fade into the blackness, Brant ran his hand through his hair and sighed. "You're crossing the line," he said to himself out loud. He'd made a promise to himself the day Cody introduced him to Paige, a promise that he would keep his distance from her, both physically and emotionally. And just an hour ago, with his hand on her arm and his eyes locked on hers, he'd broken it. Not only was his hand touching her arm, but he could feel his heart reaching out to her. He shook his head in disgust at himself.

Back inside, he threw away the paper plates and soda cans and took the pile of papers down from the top of the refrigerator and set it on the table. He put the notes and lists back under the magnets on the refrigerator door and set his flight log back on the counter next to the phone, then picked up his Bible and the Oswald Chambers book that Paige had been looking at.

He opened the devotional book. Halfway down the page he read, "To be a disciple is to be a devoted love-slave of the Lord Jesus. Many of us who call ourselves Christians are not devoted to Jesus Christ." He finished reading the passage and turned to a page that he had highlighted in blue. There he read about being broken bread and poured-out wine, about being nourishment for others until they learned to feed on God.

Closing the book, he turned off the lights and headed for the bedroom. Sitting down on the chenille spread, he turned on the lamp on the bedside table and kicked off his boots. He pulled his shirt off and lay down, still in his jeans and wool socks. A slight breeze was fluttering the curtains and making the lilac branches tap against the window. Brant closed his eyes, but knew that, as tired as he was, sleep would not come easily. His mind was heavy with thoughts of a girl whose words had changed his life.

Was he setting himself up for disappointment by hoping for that kind of oneness again? And what made him think that this woman with the red nails and the hair that fell over one side of her face was even capable of the kind of depth he was searching for? He rolled toward the wall, staring at the magnolia blossoms on the peeling gray wallpaper, trying not to see her face. He'd seen something break in her when he told her to let go of her pride, and the feeling it sent through him had shaken his very being. It was all he could do not to take her in his arms. But he had no right to do that. Any affection he showed her now could, in the long run, just cause them both pain.

Was he wrong to commit himself to helping her figure out what he already knew about her? Was he capable of denying his own emotions for the sake of opening her eyes to the truth? Truth—did he even have the right to use the word? Brant sat up and cradled his face in his hands. "Lord, let me be broken bread and poured-out wine for You, for her. Help me draw her back to You. But if You ask me to walk out of her life, I will."

Still in his jeans, he turned off the light, wrapped the spread around himself, and continued to pray until a pale amber light filtered through the holes in the curtains and he fell asleep.

❧

Paige tip-toed up the carpeted stairs, carrying her heels in one hand. But in spite of her quiet, the lamp in Hailey's room came on when she got to the landing and Hailey called to her. Paige dropped her shoes in the hallway and walked into the room, taking off her earrings as she walked.

Hailey sat up in bed. "Were you talking to Roman this whole time?"

"No."

"Where were you?"

"Well, Mom, if you must know, I was with Brant."

"Oooo! Tell me everything!"

Unbuckling her belt, Paige said, "After I get out of this."

She walked into her room pulling her dress over her head. Opening her top drawer, she tossed her earrings into an open box, but one bounced out and fell onto a stack of books on the floor. Sitting on top was a copy of *The Velveteen Rabbit*. Of all the books in her collection, this was by far her favorite. She had sent a copy to Gavin, the only gift she had ever sent him. In it she had written, "Sometimes it hurts when God makes us real, but it's worth the pain."

She put the earring away, slipped into her nightgown, and went back to Hailey's room. As she flopped down on the bed, Hailey said, "Well?"

Paige threw up her hands. "The man has me completely confused."

With a sarcastic smile and a voice to match, Hailey said, "Poor baby. You've never been confused by a man before, have you?"

Paige picked up a heart-shaped lace pillow and threw it at her. "Do you want to hear this or not?"

Leaning forward, Hailey brushed her hand across her face in an attempt to wipe away the smile. "Okay, I'm serious now. But it's true—this is different for you, isn't it? He's not like most of the guys that trail after you." Quickly holding up her hand, she said, "Sorry, that just slipped out!"

"He's not like any guy I've ever met anywhere! Is that a cliché or what? But it's true! A week ago I had him pegged for an egotistical jerk, and now I'm seeing this whole other side. He's strong—emotionally, spiritually—"

"And physically!"

"Like I need you to point that out, girl! Help me stay a little objective here, please!"

"Sorry—again. Let's concentrate on character. He has a soft side. Cody told me about a time he ran into a deer with his car and cried like a baby."

Paige blinked her eyes and wiped away imaginary tears. "See? That's what's so confusing about him! He's not afraid to say what he thinks, to the point of almost being cruel . . . but he's not. But there's this gentleness in him, too. And his faith is so real, so . . . 'intense' is the only word I can think of. The way he prays . . . he knows God. And he knows other things. Have you been talking to him about me?"

"No, but Cody has."

"I guess that would explain it. What did they talk about?"

"What's it worth to you?"

"Dishes for a week."

"Keep going."

"I promise not to put Limburger cheese on your engine after your wedding."

"You're good, you know."

"I know. Talk."

"This comes from the analytical mind of a lawyer, remember. Cody said that if you just listened to Brant's words you'd think he wasn't the least bit interested, but if you read between the lines you can see that he's fighting some sort of pretty strong feelings about you. He keeps saying that you're not his type, but Cody keeps telling him that there's more to you than satin and pearls!"

Paige sat up. "Is that how he sees me?"

"It's all talk. Cody says it won't take much at all for you to have him wrapped around your little finger if you want."

"I don't want!" Paige pounded her fist on the bed. "That's the last thing in the world I want! And I think Cody's got him figured all wrong—I think Brant McCourt is one of the few men on earth that no woman could wrap around her finger!"

With a knowing smile, Hailey leaned forward and whispered, "And that's exactly what you like about him."

🔊

Since Brant's truck was already at the airport, Paige had agreed to pick him up at two. When she got to his house, he was sitting on the front step with the cordless phone in his hand. He motioned for her to join him.

"Hi! You look nice, not like a woman who was out partying until two in the morning. Did you sleep late?"

She couldn't tell him that she'd spent half of what was left of the night talking to Hailey about him and that the rest of the early morning hours were spent tossing and turning and thinking about him. "Not too late," she answered honestly. "How about you?"

He wouldn't tell her he'd spent the night wrestling with his pillow and his memories and counting magnolias in the moonlight. He wouldn't tell her he'd prayed for her until the sun came up. "Slept enough, I guess," he said. "I'm trying to call for a weather briefing. The line was busy." He pushed the redial button and waited, then said, "Good morning. I'd like a standard weather briefing for a VFR flight from Milbrooke, C48, to Oshkosh, OSH. The aircraft is a Cessna 150, 714 Echo Tango. Departure time 2:30 local. Altitude 3,000 feet." Listening to the response, he nodded. "Thank you. Have a nice day."

Turning to her he said, "Sounds like a beautiful day to fly. There's some rain predicted for the northeast part of the state, but it should be too far north to bother us. There's a light wind, but it should be a pretty smooth flight. I'll go grab a couple jackets."

Paige walked to the car, staring up at the cloudless sky. A surge of excitement coursed through her as she realized that in less than an hour she would be up there. As Brant joined her in the car, she asked, "How long have you been flying?"

"About nine years. I got my license just before my twenty-first birthday. It was something I'd wanted to do since I was a little kid. I was going to EMT school at the same time, but I didn't have any thoughts of putting them together and making a career out of it until a couple years later. In the beginning, I just loved the feeling, the freedom. You really get a perspective of how insignificant we are from up there. Houses and cars shrink into these little Monopoly tokens, and fields and roads turn into squares in a patchwork quilt . . ."

Paige looked at him and smiled. "That's very poetic."

"Does that surprise you?"

"Yes. You don't seem like the poetic type to me."

"But you like surprises, remember."

She gave him a sideways look, wondering again how he knew that. "Have you ever had an accident? A crash landing or anything?"

"Never. A couple scares, but nothing more. Any landing you walk away from is a good one!" He grinned and watched the reaction on her face. "Flying a plane is safer than driving a car. Even if we lose an engine we can still land the plane!"

Brant walked up to the desk in the small office and said, "How's it going, Kip? Would you hand me the log book and the key for *Echo Tango*?"

"Where you headed?"

"Just around here for a short lesson first." He introduced Paige to the man behind the counter. "Then we'll take off to Oshkosh for dinner."

Kip arched his eyebrows and eyed Paige, who was looking at the aerial view pictures on the wall. "I see . . . like you do with all your first time students."

Brant smiled, even while he managed to silence Kip with a warning look, took the three-ring notebook, and opened the door for Paige.

The top half of the two-passenger Cessna was white and the

bottom half was bright red. "Looks like someone dipped it in catsup," Paige said.

Brant shook his head. "You sound like someone who should be illustrating children's books instead of painting portraits." He opened the pilot side door for her. Paige looked inside, then back at him.

"Aren't I supposed to get in the other side?" she asked nervously.

"This is 'hands on' learning." He looked down at her, noticing for the first time the large gold barrette holding her hair away from her face. Tapping it with his finger, he said, "Smart." When she still hadn't made a move to get in the plane, he took her chin gently in his hand and turned her face toward the passenger side. "Look in there. I have identical controls. I'll handle the take-off and the landing and I'll talk you through every step in between. When your yoke moves, so does mine, and I can take over any time I need to."

He turned her back to face him, lifting her chin just slightly. "Trust me," he whispered.

Paige felt her knees grow weak and told herself it was just nerves. She had to turn away from him and the only way to get away from him was to get in the plane.

Brant walked around to the other side. Detaching the key from one of the rings inside the log book, he handed it to her. "Okay," he said, "find the ignition switch down on the left hand side; put the key in but don't turn it. Now, see the red flag behind the yoke that says 'control wheel lock'? Pull that straight up, it'll slide out, then reach around and put it in the pocket behind your seat. Now, see the switch right next to the ignition switch? It says 'master switch.' Switch that on. Over here is the flap control switch, slide it down to ten degrees. Turn the master switch off again and check down on the floor in the middle and make sure that the fuel shut-off valve points to 'on.' Now, get back out of the plane and we'll do the rest of our inspection outside."

Paige waited for him on her side of the plane. When he reached her, she said, "Aren't I supposed to take driver's ed or flight simulation or something first?"

Putting his hands on her shoulders, he said in a mad scientist voice, "Trust me, my dear, I know what I'm doing."

They walked around the plane counter-clockwise, going over each step on the pre-flight checklist, examining all moveable parts, the inflation of the tires, the oil and fuel levels. Then he led her back to the pilot's side and motioned for her to get in. Bending over to show her how to adjust her seat belt, he leaned close to her ear, close enough that she could feel the warmth of his breath against her cheek. "Trust me?" he asked.

Numbly, Paige nodded, grateful she didn't have to walk with her legs turning to jelly. All she had to do was fly a plane. With her hands and feet resting lightly on the yoke and rudder controls, she listened as Brant explained every move he made. As he started the engine and began taxiing down the runway, he picked up the radio microphone and said, "Milbrooke traffic, this is 7-1-4 *Echo Tango* departing runway two niner."

To Paige he said, "You shove the throttle lever all the way in. Watch the air speed indicator. When we reach 55 knots, we're going to lift off the runway by gently pulling back on the yoke. Just feel the movement of the yoke. We'll keep the air speed at about 60 to 65 knots as we climb." He glanced at her face as the wheels left the runway and saw the look of wonder he was hoping to find. "When we reach 1,400 feet, that's about 500 feet off the ground, we're going to make a gentle turn to the north as we continue to climb."

As they leveled off at 3,000 feet above sea level, Paige looked down for the first time and felt her anxiety level begin to lower. *Brant was right,* she thought, *there is freedom up here.*

"Okay, Amelia Earhart," he said, "it's your turn now. I'll talk you through it. I want you to gently pull back on the yoke until the nose of the plane lifts a little. You'll feel a little forward pressure, but just try to hold the yoke steady. Good. You're doing great. Now turn just a little to the right and keep holding a little backward pressure on the yoke."

He guided her in a wide circle, pointing out the Sparrow Center and, a few minutes later, David and Karlee's house. "I don't know where you live," he said, "think you can find it?"

"It's about two miles south of—"

A sudden bump rocked the plane. Paige gripped the yoke. "What did we hit?"

Brant turned to smile at her. "There's not much to run into up here."

"But—"

Suddenly, the aircraft jumped and Paige felt like she was in free-fall for a split second. Instinctively she pulled back on the yoke, causing the plane to climb sharply. Brant pressed his yoke forward, counteracting her move. "Let go, Paige, let me have it."

When his words pierced her moment of panic, she relaxed her hold and he leveled the plane off. "It's all yours again," he said, with no hint of criticism.

"I overreacted, huh?"

Trying not to laugh, he said, "You could say that. A little more to the right."

"It was just turbulence, right?"

"Right."

A few minutes went by and then Paige said, "That wasn't so bad. I'll get the hang of this."

Sliding his left hand over her right, Brant said, "You're gonna do just fine."

15

hen they landed at the Oshkosh airport, Brant reached behind the seat and handed her a leather aviator's jacket. "Here, you might need this. Besides, it makes you look the part."

He had called a taxi before they left Milbrooke and it took them to a restaurant overlooking Lake Winnebago, where Brant had reserved a table on the deck. The late afternoon sun sparkled on the water and the wind feathered the fringe on the umbrella above them. Paige gave the waitress her order, then pulled a pen out of her pocket and began drawing on her napkin. Brant watched in silent interest.

When she finished, she handed him the cartoon that depicted him landing a plane in a pool of catsup. He laughed and tucked it in his pocket as the waitress brought their drinks. "That's your real gift, you know."

Quietly, she said, "Yeah, maybe some day . . ." then sat back and took a sip of the virgin Pina Colada that had been served her in a coconut shell. Lifting an aristocratic little finger, she said, "Well, daahling, shall we do breakfast in New York and then dinner in Miami?"

"Sounds delightful, my dear. I take it you're growing fond of this lifestyle—in spite of a little turbulence?"

"There is turbulence in every lifestyle, sir. One must learn to take the bad with the good."

"Well said, ma'am. And does one take one's own advice frequently?"

"Never!" Paige laughed and bent to take another sip from her straw.

Somewhere between here and the airport, he noticed, she had removed the barrette and her hair spilled over her cheek again. He reached across the table and tucked it behind her ear. "I've wanted to do that for a long time," he said.

Cocking her head to the side so that several strands of hair escaped, she smiled coyly. "Why?"

Reaching out and repeating the gesture, he said, "Because I feel like you're hiding from me."

"I thought men liked a little mystery in women."

"A little, yes. Too much makes a man wonder if he's being pushed away."

He was staring through her again, but this time she didn't look away. He'd made a statement, but it was really a question. "I'm not pushing you away."

She expected him to take her hand then, but instead he sat back in his chair and said, "So how are wedding plans coming on the bride's side? The groom is counting the hours and becoming a real pain to be around."

"As of four o'clock this morning everything was running smoothly, but that was twelve hours ago. Every once in a while I hear her gasp and start talking to herself about something she forgot. I can't imagine what she'd be like if they were planning a big wedding! Actually, for once I've been really grateful for her incessant chatter."

"Keeps your mind off things?"

"Mmm-hm."

"When will you hear about Annie?"

"They'll be starting the home study on Roman soon, then it'll be a few weeks before they make a decision."

"That could get nerve-wracking."

"You're being very understanding for someone who thinks I'm totally off base!"

"All the more reason for me to be concerned!"

"Well, for right now you don't have to worry about me flipping out or anything. After the wedding, who knows . . . I may hijack a plane and fly Annie to Tahiti!"

Brant laughed. "Don't take this personally, but I don't think you'll be quite ready to cross any borders by yourself in two weeks!"

"Fine. Then I'll hijack you, too."

"I could handle that."

The waitress brought a plate of relishes and a bread basket. Paige chewed on a carrot, thinking. Suddenly she said, "Could this just be a test? Like Abraham and Isaac, you know? Is God just waiting for me to give up and then He'll let me have her?"

Cautiously, Brant said, "It could be. Or it could be just like you said—that this isn't about you or Annie, it's about Roman."

"But why would God want her raised by a heathen father instead of a Christian mother?"

The look Brant returned was the look her father used to give her just before grounding her to her room. *He may have a soft side,* she thought, *but the egotism is still alive and well.* "You don't approve of my question?"

"Do you really want to get into this here and now?" he asked. "If this is all we ever talk about I don't think we'll ever get beyond potential friends. By the way, how close are we getting to being real friends?"

"I'll let you know after you say what you're thinking."

"You're a glutton for punishment, aren't you? Keep in mind that you asked for this . . ." He took a deep breath and stared out at the lake, then turned back to face her, leaning his chin on his folded hands. "Humor me for a minute here—I'm going to try to make this an object lesson. Before we hit that turbulence this afternoon, who was in control?"

"I was . . . well, sort of."

"What would have happened if you had ignored me or fought me when I told you to let go of the yoke?"

"I don't know, but it wouldn't have been good."

"We would have continued climbing until the engine stalled and we dropped like a rock."

"I think I don't like what you're implying . . ."

"Don't get defensive on me. This isn't an attack."

"I know, but it's starting to feel uncomfortable."

"Hebrews 10:24 says, 'And let us consider how we may spur one another on toward love and good deeds.' I'm just spurring."

"Spurs hurt."

"So does the truth sometimes."

"Okay, go on. Spur away."

"Remember that bumper sticker that said, 'God is my co-pilot'?"

"Yes. I'm going to take some real offense here if you're saying God is not my co-pilot. In the first place . . ."

"Hold on a minute! If you're going to get mad, wait for what I'm going to say next! There was another bumper sticker that came out after that one had been around for awhile. It said, 'If God is your co-pilot, you're in the wrong seat'!"

The waitress brought their food then. After Brant prayed, Paige turned her attention to her plate of shrimp scampi, but her mind was on Brant's words. After several minutes she said, "To use your own words, 'this is going to sound presumptuous coming from someone you don't know very well,' but I think that you and I may be guilty of the same problem." She answered the question on Brant's face. "Hailey accused me of comparing every guy I meet to Gavin. I gather that you didn't like him, but I think I knew a side of him that very few people saw. Still, it's been five years and time turns people into legends. You know what I mean?"

Brant nodded slowly, looking uncomfortable. It was obvious to Paige that he had expected to stay in control of the conversation. "That girl you told me about, the one that led you to the Lord? . . . Are you sure you're not doing the same with her? The same thing I've been doing with Gavin, expecting everyone to live up to a standard that's not realistic. And passing judgment when they don't." She met his eyes squarely. "I'm not that girl, Brant. I'm quieter about my faith, more private; not everyone runs around saying 'praise the Lord' and 'Hallelujah' every other word! I don't think you've known me long enough to make a judgment on where I'm at with God. And I don't know why you feel compelled to steer every single conversation around to my relationship with the Lord!" Jabbing a piece of shrimp with her fork, Paige felt her face color. Not only was she being defensive, she realized, she was also telling him loud and clear that she was jealous of this saintly legend from his past.

"Paige, I have no desire to fight with you, but you did ask for my opinion."

"About Annie!"

"It's all the same subject. Adopting her would be a kind, generous, noble thing to do, but is it what God wants for your life? Are you listening to Him? Please don't take this as an attack; this is something I challenge myself with every day. Am I completely surrendered? Am I truly dead to self and being clay in the potter's hands? And I think we're supposed to challenge each other that way, don't you? I don't think that's being judgmental. Christ is the standard we're all trying to live up to, not any person. Right?"

"Yes . . . of course." Paige squirmed in her seat, trying to think of the words that would explain her discomfort. "But—but, do you do this with everyone you meet? Don't you have to get to know someone before you start pointing out their weak points?"

Brant pushed his half-finished plate aside and reached for her hand. He ran his fingertip around the pearl on her ring. "I know it doesn't make sense, but I feel like I do know you, and I have this strong feeling that you're going through the motions of faith, but you're afraid to let go of the yoke."

Laying down her fork, Paige moved her drink closer and began stirring it with the straw, watching it swirl like a miniature cyclone.

"Say something," Brant said.

She looked up at him with a weak smile. "Ouch," she said.

16

On the day of Hailey's wedding, Paige was smiling to herself as she walked down the stairs. At the bottom of the steps she stopped and picked up the camera that hung from her neck. Before her, in the living room, was a picture worth saving. Karlee, in a dress that looked like the field of wildflowers next to the house, was sitting in a rocking chair next to the stone fireplace nursing Jordan. The afternoon sun glinted on the diamond in the gold cross necklace that hung down next to Jordan's tiny fist. While Karlee's left hand supported the baby, the other combed her daughter's satiny blond hair.

Shelly, kneeling on the braided rug in a dress that matched her mother's, looked up when the camera flashed and grinned at Paige. Smiling back at Shelly, Paige said, "You're getting to be a regular pro at this flower girl stuff, aren't you Princess?"

Shelly nodded. "Aunt Hailey says I get to be in your wedding next."

"Oh, does she? And I suppose Aunt Hailey has decided who I'm going to marry?"

"Uh-huh. Even I know that! Brant is sooo cute!"

Karlee laughed. "Out of the mouths of babes . . ."

"Has he kissed you yet?" Shelly asked.

Karlee's jaw dropped. "Shelly! That's rude!" But over the top of the little blond head she mouthed, "Well?"

"No, he has not kissed me. We haven't even gone out . . . exactly. We're just friends."

"Uh-huh," mother and daughter said in unison.

The sound of the back door opening saved Paige from further

questioning. Ruth Austin, Karlee and Hailey's mother, walked into the room. "Oh, look at you girls!" she exclaimed. "You all look so pretty!" She walked over to Shelly and hugged her, then touched the top of Jordan's head. "If you need someone to burp him when he's done . . ." she offered. Turning to Paige she said, "I think my girls will be happy to see me leave. I'm supposed to be here helping Karlee with the house and Hailey with the wedding, but I've spent most of the time holding this baby!"

"That's what Grammas are for," Paige said, while motioning for her to stand behind Karlee for a three generation picture.

"Where's David?" Karlee asked her mother.

"He and Dad and T.J. are all dressed and headed over to, as T.J. put it, 'make Cody a nervous wreck.' They dropped me off in the driveway and said they weren't stepping one foot inside a house full of primping women!"

"We've taught them well," Karlee said. Ruth nodded. "How's Hailey doing?"

Paige laughed. "She's upstairs babbling to herself about how happy she is that they decided on a small outdoor wedding without a ton of attendants and hundreds of guests because there's no pressure and it doesn't even matter if it starts raining because they can just wait for the rain to stop because they haven't rented a hall and it doesn't matter what time the reception starts and everything is just so low-key that she's not even the least bit nervous!"

"In other words, my little girl's a basket case!"

"You got it."

With a deep breath, Ruth turned toward the stairs.

"Wait, Mom," Karlee called to her. Reaching down, she picked up a small jewelry box and handed it to her mother. "You should be the one to give it to her." Taking it from her, Ruth blinked back the tears that filled her eyes. Karlee smiled. "Don't fight it, Mom. Just have a good cry and get it out of your system so you can touch up your mascara before the wedding."

Pulling a tissue out of her pocket, Ruth said, "We've just been so lucky . . . no, we've been so blessed—you girls have taught me that. Seeing both of you so happy, and a new grandchild, and Dad feeling better than he had for years before his stroke . . . I guess I have every right to a few tears!" With that, she headed up the stairs.

Several minutes later she came back down, still in tears, leading the way for Hailey. As Hailey descended the open staircase, Shelly let out a long "Oooo!" that was echoed by Paige and Karlee. The fringe from the soft buckskin dress flared out from her sleeves and hem as she twirled before her audience. Her dark auburn hair fell in loose curls to her waist; the blue of her eyes was echoed in the beaded band across her forehead and the polished stones in her copper earrings. From a fine gold chain around her neck hung the teardrop pearl that had been worn by her grandmother, her mother, and twice by Karlee.

Shelly stepped closer and reached out to touch Hailey's sleeve. "You're beautiful," she whispered. "Something old is your dress, something borrowed is Mama's sandals, and you have lots of something blue, but what's your something new?"

"I just got it last night," Hailey said. Pulling her sleeve back, she showed them the braided copper bracelet on her wrist.

"Did Cody give it to you?" Shelly asked dreamily.

"No. I got this from . . ." She stopped, determined not to cry. "I got this from Cody's birth father."

❧

The little stone church had guarded the river bank for more than ninety years. A cobblestone walkway curved from the heavy oak door on its south side to the arched footbridge that connected the church yard with the cemetery. Pink and white impatiens and purple alyssum ran along both sides of the path. Today, five people stood in the mid-day sunlight at the foot of the bridge as guitar music drifted out over the river.

Karlee, standing next to Hailey, smiled at David, who sat in the front row of folding chairs holding Jordan. Then she turned her eyes to the church door where her oldest son stood, straight as a soldier, holding the ring pillow. Finally, she looked at Shelly, her hair shining in the sunlight as she walked toward Cody and Hailey, scattering rose petals from the basket on her arm. Karlee pulled a tissue from beneath her bouquet and wiped her eyes.

Crouching on the grass in a dress of unbleached muslin, Paige focused the camera on Cody's face as he lifted Hailey's hand in his and began to recite the vows he had written. "A cord of three strands is not quickly broken. As you and I come together before our Lord, we will draw our strength from him and we will strengthen each other. You are my best friend, Hailey; your love and your trust are precious gifts . . ." He stopped to steady his voice, and Paige lifted the camera again, but found it hard to clear her eyes long enough to focus.

Giving up, she went back to her chair next to David. She listened to Cody's words, and then Hailey's, followed by the traditional vows, but she found her eyes drawn to Brant. Like Cody, he wore black jeans and a silk shirt with a bolo tie. Cody's shirt was off-white, while Brant's was a bright blue. Even from where she sat, she could see what the color did to his eyes.

After the exchange of rings, Cody and Hailey stood facing each other, holding hands. With his cane in one hand and his guitar slung over his shoulder, Richard Wingreen, Cody's birth father, walked behind them to the top of the bridge and began to sing. The sound of the river backdropped his words: ". . . and I don't even know her name, but I'm praying for her just the same, that the Lord will write His name upon her heart. Cause somewhere in the course of his life, my little boy will need a Godly wife, so hold on to Jesus, baby, wherever you are . . ." The words sent a shiver down Paige's spine.

During a lull between hugging and tears and pictures, Paige

walked to the edge of the water and stood quietly observing. Annie, in the pink dress Paige had bought for her, was running behind Shelly like a baby duckling, never letting the older girl out
of her sight. Little Jordan was being passed from lap to lap, with
Gramma hovering close. Cody and Hailey stood between Robert
and Richard with their arms around both of them. It was a scene
that should have produced nothing but joy in Paige, but as she
stood there by the water, other feelings were creeping in.

As if sensing her absence, Brant began looking around. He
smiled when he saw her and came toward her. He was still ten
feet away when he said, "You look beautiful."

When he reached her, he fingered the flowers embroidered
on her bell sleeve. "I like this. You should be standing in my
kitchen with this on. The time eras would just about match."

"I got it at a consignment shop in Boston called Trashcan
Tessie's. It's a gen-u-ine hippie wedding dress; the original owner
is now a grandmother. I thought it was fitting."

"It's perfect. So how's my potential friend doing today?"

"Feeling a little sorry for herself at the moment."

"That's understandable."

"You know what just hit me this week? Starting tonight, I'll
be living alone for the first time in my life! I've traveled all over
the world by myself, but I've always been going to someone."

"Want a little wisdom from someone older and wiser?"

"Speak, Oh Wise One!"

"When God puts us in a position of having to let go of something, He always replaces it—if we let Him. Sometimes we just
need more of Him for awhile and sometimes He gives us a new
mission . . . or a new friend."

Paige nodded. "That sounds like something I would have said
a few years ago. Lately, every time something starts looking uncertain, I start scanning the horizon for the next job or adventure
or relationship, always making sure I've got a safety net. I guess,

266

in part, that's what Annie's been. Making plans for her kept me from thinking about being alone."

"You realize you're admitting I was right."

"Part right. I really do love her."

"I know."

"I keep thinking about what we talked about. Where did I lose my first love? It happened so slowly; God kept getting edged out by all the attention I was giving my work and the excitement of Paris. Letting go again isn't going to be easy."

"No, it's not." Brant took her hand and headed toward the bridge. They stopped at the top and looked down at the water rushing beneath them. Lifting a piece of paint from the railing, Paige let it drop and watched it drift into the river.

"The scary thing is that I'm not sure I want to let go again."

Brant leaned on his elbows, his arm just barely touching hers. "I have a little sign on my dashboard that says 'Don't wait to want to'."

"You have an answer for everything, don't you?"

"Mmm-hm. Irritating, isn't it?"

"Yes! You're a walking book of proverbs! I feel like I'm hanging out with Solomon sometimes!"

Rubbing his chin and continuing to stare at the water, Brant said, "There are some striking similarities, aren't there?"

Before Paige could formulate a comeback, Shelly came running onto the bridge, towing Annie behind her. "Aunt Paige, Brant!" she called breathlessly. "They're going to cut the cake! You have to hurry, cause you have to take pictures! We have to have a picture cause Aunt Hailey promised she's going to smash cake all over Cody's face and in his hair and who knows what he's going to do to her after that! Maybe they'll start a food fight and everybody will throw cake at everybody! Are you coming?"

"We're coming, Jabber Jaws!" Brant was shaking his head and laughing. Paige joined him.

"It's genetic," she said.

At the bottom of the bridge he took her hand and lifted it to his lips. "I want you to know that whenever being alone gets too much, you can call me. I'd leave my 700 wives and 300 concubines for you any day."

She squeezed his hand. "Thanks, Sol, you're a true friend."

$$\textcircled{17}$$

*L*yn Casey looked at her watch as she left the break room to begin her third bed check of the night. It was 5:03 A.M. Shining her flashlight at the ceiling, she bent over the crib where fifteen-month-old Ryan lay sleeping peacefully. Pulling the blanket up to his chin, she said quietly, "Sleep tight, little one," and walked across the room to peek in the other crib.

In the next room, she reached over a bed rail to pull the covers away from the pillow. "You're going to get too hot like that, sweetheart," she whispered. She pulled the blanket back and gasped, then sighed in frustration at the empty bed. In her two months at the Sparrow Center, this was the third time this had happened. The first child had been found in the hallway asking for a drink; the second she had discovered sound asleep under his bed, so that was the first place she looked this time. Getting down on her knees and shining the flashlight along the floor, she quietly called, "Annie! Annie!"

She swept the light around the room, then opened the closet and looked behind the clothes. She checked the bathroom, then the resident's room across the hall. Zigzagging from room to room she checked every room in the east wing. Running down the hall, she tried the occupational therapy room and then the day room. Both were locked. Backtracking, she turned the corner and ran down the hallway leading to the lobby, peering into the staff break room and every unlocked office on her way. When she reached the dimly lit lobby, she flipped the light switches and circled the room, searching behind every chair and calling Annie's name.

Running back to the nurse's station, she called breathlessly to

269

the night supervisor. "I can't find Annie! Page Darla and Wendy—we have to check the west wing and the cafeteria and nursery. I've checked everything else! I'll start on the west wing."

She was already ten feet down the hall when the voice of the woman behind the desk stopped her. "Lyn, come here." Marie Wassal walked around to the other side of the counter. After thirty-one years of nursing, it took more than a misplaced child to alarm her. Placing both dark hands on the LPN's shoulders, she said, "Calm down, now start at the top."

"Annie's not in her bed, and I've looked all over and I can't find her!"

"Relax, Lyn, we'll find her. This happens. She was probably sleep walking and curled up in a corner somewhere. You check the rooms on the right, I'll do the left. Okay?"

Twenty minutes later, Lyn and three nurse's aides stood at the desk, staring at the head nurse. Marie threw up her hands. "This is ridiculous! What have we missed? We've covered every inch of this building and every outside door is locked. Lyn, you're sure she was there at three?"

"Yes! Her bunny had fallen on the floor and I picked it up and put it next to her and she hugged it in her sleep. Now the bunny's gone."

Without another word, Marie picked up the phone and dialed.

Robert answered the phone with his eyes still closed, but the panic in Marie's voice made him instantly alert. "Has anyone come or gone in the last few hours?"

"No."

"Anyone walk outside on break or run out to their car, anything that might have left the door unlocked even for a few minutes?"

"No. We've wracked our brains to think of any possibility. I've questioned the girls in the nursery and everyone on the floor. No one has left the building."

The red numbers on Robert's clock radio read 5:43. The shift would change in just over an hour. "All right. I'm on my way. I'm going to make a couple calls first. If I come up with anything, I'll call you right back." As he hung up the phone, he turned on the lamp and pulled a phone book out of the bedside table. After punching in the number and waiting, he listened with a sinking feeling to Paige's voice on the answering machine.

❧

At the end of his driveway, Robert turned left instead of right. There had been much controversy surrounding the Sparrow Center before they had even broken ground for the building, but so far they had disappointed their opposition by avoiding any hint of scandal. Annie's safety was more important than the reputation of the Center, but he was not about to report this until he had checked the most obvious possibilities.

A spray of gravel flew from beneath his tires as he turned into Paige's driveway. Jumping out, he ran to the garage and looked in the window, relieved to see her car still there. He knocked on first the back door and then the front, but she was obviously too sound asleep to hear. He walked back to the car and dialed David and Karlee's number. They would have a key to the house.

"David, we've got a . . . situation at the Center. I don't want to talk about it on the cell phone, but I need to talk to Paige right away. I'm at her house now; she hasn't answered the phone or the door, but her car is here so—"

"Is Hailey's Jeep there?"

"No."

There was a long pause on the other end. "A radiator hose broke in Paige's car on Thursday," David said finally. "She said she'd just use Hailey's until I had time to look at it."

This time it was Robert's turn for silence. He fought for a logical explanation. "Do you have any idea where she might be? Could she have gone to work early?"

"I doubt it, but I'll try calling. If she's not there, I'll try . . . she's been kind of strange lately. I'm worried about her."

"I think you'd better meet me at the Center, David."

Robert hung up and dialed the Sparrow Center. "I want you to call the police. And Marie—we need to keep this quiet. Please tell the staff not to talk to anyone but the authorities. Then call Nancy; tell her you can't explain over the phone, but ask her who she can get along without this morning. Then call those people and tell them they can have a few hours off with pay—tell them I've called a special third shift meeting or something. If any of your staff can stay for awhile it would be very helpful; they'll get time and a half. Let's try to have the smallest changeover possible. I'll be there in a few minutes."

A uniformed officer was standing at the nurse's station when Robert walked in, and another officer was walking down the hall toward Annie's room with Lyn. As Robert walked up to the desk, he heard the officer saying, "Mrs. Wassal, are you the only one answering the phone on third shift?"

"Yes."

"Have there been any disturbing calls during the night, anyone you didn't recognize?"

"No. There have been only two calls since midnight. The husband of one of the aides called about 2:30 and one of the LPNs that works in the nursery called in sick. That was all."

"Is there ever a time when no one is at the nurses' station?"

"Yes, not for very long, but there are many times that we're all busy with residents."

Robert held out his hand and introduced himself to the officer at the desk. Sergeant Jim Delaney shook Robert's hand.

"We're going to search the grounds first, then we'll fingerprint her room. Dr. Worth, is there anyone who would have an interest in this child—anyone that would stand to gain from abducting her?"

Marie gasped. "You mean—kidnapping?"

Robert's stomach tightened. Up to this minute he had not said the word even in his head. "Marie, is everything covered for first shift?"

"Yes." She answered with a clear note of pride in her voice. "Everyone's called home and worked it out. We're all staying."

"Thank you. I hate to ask you to do this, but would you please get the schedules and call the kitchen staff and housekeeping, O.T., and P.T.—anyone we can do without for a few hours? Breakfast may be a little late, but I think we can manage. We'll need Charissa to answer phones, I suppose . . ." He went through a mental list, then turned to the officer. "Let's go down to my office."

Jim Delaney's eyes widened as Robert told him who Annie's father was. "You're serious?"

"Yes. We've tried to keep it quiet. There are only eight staff and board members who have been in on it, and I trust every one of them implicitly."

"I'll need a list of their names, and all other employees, past and present. I need to know who has keys or access to them." The leather chair creaked as he leaned forward, holding a clipboard in both hands. "Dr. Worth, what's your gut feeling here? Is there any chance she just slipped out?"

"I don't think so. The doors are always locked at night, and she's a tiny girl; I don't think she could open a door on her own anyway."

"Is there anyone that comes to mind with a motive for taking her—anyone with a score to settle, who quit recently or was fired, anyone who talked about money problems? What about her mother, could she have changed her mind? How about Roman Slayder himself? Was he afraid he wouldn't get custody?"

"Annie's mother is voluntarily relinquishing her rights. She's an alcoholic with serious health problems. From the information we got from Human Services, I think she knows she's incapable of caring for Annie. I don't know about Roman. They're doing a home study on him and we were told we'd hear the decision today or tomorrow. I can't imagine he'd think he could get away with taking her."

Sergeant Delaney made a note on the clipboard, then looked up. "But who has he told? And who's watching him? How much do you suppose he's worth? Several million maybe? There are a lot of opportunists in the world, Dr. Worth."

Robert ran his hand through his hair. "Annie is so trusting, she'd go with anyone when she's awake, but she's an ornery little bear when you wake her up. I can't imagine a stranger walking in here and carrying her out without a fight!"

Sergeant Delaney nodded. "Unless they drugged her, or unless it was someone she knew and trusted . . ." The knots in Robert's stomach hardened. There was something he had to tell the sergeant.

Just as he finished, David appeared at the door. Robert introduced the two men and David sat down. As Robert filled him in, David clasped his hands together and his knuckles whitened. Sergeant Delaney asked David several questions about the early resistance to the Sparrow Center, then sat back in his chair. "Tell me about your sister, Mr. Stern."

The slight widening of David's eyes told Robert that the implications in the questions had shocked him. "Paige would never . . . could there have been a lack of communication, Robert? Maybe she left you a note or thought it had been arranged . . ."

"David, I agree that this would be totally out of character for her, but we have to try to be objective. Annie was sound asleep at the 3:00 bed check. No one broke in, no one heard her cry. I can't by any stretch of the imagination picture Paige as capable of this, but—"

Shaking his head slowly, David finished the sentence for him. "But we can't deny that she does have a motive."

$$\left(18\right)$$

t 7:30 A.M., Charissa walked in with a stack of computer printouts and a pot of coffee. "Time sheets, job
applications, employee evaluations, volunteer lists . . .
everything I could think of that might help."

Separating a stack of foam cups, Robert said, "You're a wonder, Charissa. Thank you."

David hung up the phone and shook his head while taking
the cup Robert offered him. "There's no one at The Gallery yet
and Brant doesn't answer his phone or his pager. He has the day
off but his boss said he usually keeps his plectron and his beeper
on all the time. I called the airport—his helicopter and plane are
still there and they haven't heard from him."

Sergeant Delaney took the pen out of his mouth. "You think
this McCourt is with your sister?"

"I don't know what to think anymore," David answered. "I
drove out to his house before coming here. His truck was sitting
in the driveway, but the Jeep wasn't there—not that I expected it
to be." David rapped his fist on the arm of the chair. "I know what
this looks like, but everything in me says there's a logical explanation. Paige is impulsive, but not foolish. I could see her suddenly deciding to take Annie somewhere overnight, since this may
be her last chance, but . . ."

Sergeant Delaney raised one eyebrow and voiced David's own
question. "In the middle of the night?" David shook his head. He'd
run out of explanations. "Does she have a key?" the sergeant asked.

"No," Robert answered, "she's only a volunteer. But she could
have had one made. I loaned her a key the night Roman was here."

David ran his hand over his face, trying to erase the fear and the incredible sadness that was washing over him. The evidence was getting stronger by the minute. "She has Hailey's keys," he said quietly. Addressing Robert he said, "With the baby and the wedding there's been so much going on. When she talked to me about wanting to adopt Annie, I honestly didn't take her very seriously. I really thought it was something that would pass. You talked to her about Roman; could she possibly have been this obsessed with the idea?"

"She was upset, but—"

A patrol officer poked his head into the room. "We've searched the grounds, sir. Nothing."

Sergeant Delaney nodded and held out a piece of paper. "Run a check on this, then call the station and make sure every squad in the county has it." He looked at David, then Robert. "If we have no leads by tomorrow morning, we'll be contacting the FBI."

Robert nodded. "Will it be possible to avoid this becoming a media circus?"

"The case will remain sealed while under investigation, but I think it would be overly optimistic to think that it won't get out. Between your employees and the people around Mr. Slayder, something is bound to leak. Have you reached him yet?"

"Charissa is trying. She only has his lawyer's office number, and it's 4:30 in the morning in L.A." Almost to himself he said, "I wish Cody were here."

The buzzer on Robert's phone sounded. "Maybe she reached Roman," he said as he pushed the button.

"Mr. McCourt is here, Dr. Worth."

"Send him in!" The three men stood as Brant walked in the room. Robert and David spoke at the same time. "Where's Paige?" they asked in unison.

Startled, Brant looked from Sergeant Delaney, to David, and then to Robert. "What's going on? I went out to the airport and they said you were trying to reach me. I tried calling, but I got a busy signal."

Sergeant Delaney looked at Robert. "That's not good. We have to make sure at least one line is open all the time." Looking back at Brant, he said, "Mr. McCourt, come with me. I have a few questions to ask you."

An hour later Brant walked slowly back to Robert's office. Finding the door open, he went in and sunk into a chair next to David. His thoughts moved slowly through the fog of questions Sergeant Delaney had raised. He stared at the pen in Robert's hand. "I want to say she couldn't do it, but I can't."

Robert nodded and David whispered, "I know."

Silence filled the room until David asked, "Did she ever say anything to you? Did you think she was that desperate?"

"Every time the subject of Annie came up I gave her a lecture about listening to God and not to her feelings. But I should have listened to her! I should have been able to see how intense her feelings were. She said something before the wedding that I didn't take seriously—about hijacking a plane and flying away with Annie. I thought she was joking."

David stared at the phone, willing it to ring. "She'd call, though, wouldn't she? Even if she didn't want us to know where she was, wouldn't she know how worried we are?" He looked up at Robert, feeling more helpless than he had in years. "I thought I knew her . . ."

Almost imperceptibly, Brant nodded. "Me too," he whispered.

Just before nine o'clock, David got through to The Gallery. Brant stopped pacing when David hung up the phone. "She called in sick, right?"

"She called the assistant manager at her home last night and said something had come up and she needed the day off. That's all she said."

Brant walked back to the window, then pounded his fist into

his hand. "I gotta get out of here. I'll go get some donuts or something."

He passed the nurses' station on his way to the back door. One of the nurses was rocking back and forth with a child on each hip, another nurse was power-walking down the hall with a tray of medicine cups. He hadn't been around long enough to know any of them by name. Looking at the name tag of the woman behind the desk, he said, "Mrs. Wassal, put me to work. I can rock babies or read stories, and I look great in a pink wig."

The frazzled look left Marie's face as she stood and put her hand on Brant's arm. "Bless you, son." She nodded toward the nurse's aide who was holding the two toddlers. "Darla could use some help. You can entertain those two or you can come with me and I'll show you where we keep the diapers."

Brant held out his arms for the toddlers.

Taking one hand off the steering wheel, Paige took off her sunglasses and rubbed her eyes, then massaged the tightness in her left shoulder. Her eyes burned from tears and lack of sleep and her body ached with exhaustion. As she reached down and stroked the ear of the stuffed pink rabbit on the seat beside her, she glanced at the clock on the dashboard. It was Annie's nap time.

The sight of the county sheriff's car parked perpendicular to the highway on a tractor path leading in to a corn field startled her. Automatically, she stepped on the brake and watched the needle drop from 62 down to 55, hoping she hadn't been detected by radar. Less than a quarter mile after passing him, she heard the siren. Looking in her rearview mirror, she saw the lights, and even before she pulled over to the shoulder, tears were stinging her eyes once again.

"Can I see your driver's license, ma'am?" Her hands were slow to cooperate as she tried to unzip her purse. Finally, she handed it to him.

"This your car, ma'am?"

"No. It belongs to a friend."

"May I see the registration please?"

She fumbled with the latch on the glove compartment, but finally produced the blue and white paper. The officer inspected it, handed it back, and then bent down to look inside the car. Gesturing toward the pink rabbit on her lap, he asked, "Anyone else in the car?"

"No."

"You look upset. Something wrong, ma'am?"

Paige swiped at a tear. "Just a difficult day."

"Where you headed?"

"The Sparrow Center."

"I see . . . maybe I'll follow you and make sure you get there safely."

It took her three tries to get the right key, and all the while the sheriff's deputy sat in his car, talking on his radio and staring at her.

❧

The hall was eerily quiet as Paige approached the empty nurses' station. Then suddenly David, Robert, and a police officer were walking toward her. The officer stepped out ahead of them, around the U-shaped counter, and took her by the elbow. "Miss Stern, come with me. I have some questions for you."

"What's wrong? David? Robert? What's wrong?"

David walked toward her, but Sergeant Delaney stopped him. David's hand dropped to his side. "We can't find Annie, Paige."

"What? What do you mean you can't find her? Why aren't you looking?" She continued to ask questions as Sergeant Delaney guided her toward the room that David had been using as an office. Before she walked in, she turned and saw Brant at the end of the hall, holding a little blond-haired girl, staring at her.

Sergeant Delaney pushed "record" on the small tape recorder and set it on the table between them. "Why did you come here this afternoon, Miss Stern?"

Paige held up the stuffed rabbit that by now was damp from the palm of her hand. "I was bringing this to Annie. She pulled the ear off her old one and I promised I'd get her a new one."

"When did you last see Annie?"

"Three days ago. Tuesday afternoon I did chalk drawings with her and three other kids."

"You're sure you haven't seen her since then?"

"Yes, I'm sure!"

"Where have you been in the last twenty-four hours?"

Paige's mouth dropped. "What are you saying? I'm a suspect?" She started to laugh, then stopped herself. "Sergeant, I love Annie, I wanted to adopt . . . oh . . ." She sat back against the back of the chair. "I see how it looks." She sucked in a breath. "I needed time to think and pray, and I didn't want to be around when we got the results of Roman's home study, so I took off last night and drove up near Lake Delton. An artist friend has a cottage up there, so I called her. I had planned on staying all day, but I got some things worked out and I wanted to get back and spend some time with Annie."

"Did anyone see you?"

"Yes. Vicky Benton, she owns the cottage. I had to stop and get the key from her."

Sergeant Delaney asked several more questions, then laid a paper in front of her. "This is a list of the people who were working the night Mr. Slayder was here. Other than these, have you heard anyone talking, do you have any idea if anyone else knows who Annie's father is?"

Paige shook her head. Chewing on the end of his pen, Sergeant Delaney switched off the tape recorder. "I'm sorry we had to put you through this. I'd like you to stay here at the Center while we check out your story. There are no charges yet, Miss Stern, but I have to tell you honestly that, at the moment, you're the only lead we have."

Paige walked numbly into Robert's office and fell into David's arms. She was just starting to explain where she'd been when they heard the phone ring at the reception desk. Charissa's voice came over the speaker phone. "Dr. Worth, line two. He won't give his name."

Robert looked from David to Paige, then picked up the phone. "This is Dr. Worth."

"Tell her Daddy he can have her back when we get a hundred thousand dollars. I'll call back in the morning."

Robert repeated the message to David and Paige, and David asked, "Did you recognize the voice?"

"No. He had an accent; Puerto Rican I think, but it wasn't familiar."

Several minutes later, Sergeant Delaney joined them. "It was too short to trace, but we got it on tape and we know he's calling from a car phone. It's a start."

When Paige walked out of the office, Brant was leaning against the wall waiting for her. "I heard," he said, putting his hand on her arm.

"I'm scared. She's so little."

"I know."

"Brant, did you think I had taken her?"

Brushing her hair back, he said, "All I could think about was how I'd given you pat answers and sermons instead of trying to understand you. I'm sorry."

"That was pretty evasive for someone who doesn't soft pedal things."

"Okay, I'll admit I thought it was possible that you were so upset that your emotions took over. I'm sorry." He touched his lips to the top of her head. "And I'm sorry I've been a walking proverb instead of a friend."

Paige squeezed his arm. "Find me a cup of coffee and I'll give you a second chance."

"Deal. They've got chocolate pie in the kitchen."

He started leading her down the hall, but Paige stopped suddenly and pulled away from him. "Pie! That's it! Marsella was here the night Roman was here! Marsella's from Puerto Rico!" Leaving a bewildered Brant, she ran off to find Sergeant Delaney.

19

$\mathscr{S}$ergeant Delaney returned to the Center after questioning Marsella for over an hour. David had gone home and Brant was helping in the kitchen. Paige, holding a fussy four-month-old, joined Sergeant Delaney in Robert's office.

Looking at Robert, the officer said, "Marsella was in the supply closet when you walked past with Roman. She heard enough of your conversation to figure out his relationship to Annie. She knew who he was because her stepson Luis has a poster of him in his bedroom that he uses for a dart board. Evidently he's a fan of some band that has a rivalry with Quaestor. Marsella couldn't wait to get home and tell him who she'd seen! The poor woman was devastated when I told her about Annie. Anyway, it just happens that no one has seen Luis or his girlfriend since yesterday. My guess is one of them sneaked in with Marsella's keys. No one seems to know whose car they've got, probably stolen, but I've got someone searching their apartment. We'll find them. Have you heard from Roman yet?"

"His lawyer finally called. Roman should be at LAX right now ready to fly to St. Louis. He has a concert there tomorrow night. The lawyer said he'd page him and try to have him call us before he left. He was wondering if Roman should fly directly here."

"We need him to get the money together, just in case, but I imagine the lawyer can handle that. I don't think he should change any plans just yet; that would only create media attention. Both these kids are addicts. They're after the money, but there may be revenge involved, too, some perverted fan loyalty or something. Seeing their faces plastered on TV might make them feel like he-

283

roes. We don't need that." Looking over at Paige's pale face, he said. "Go home and get some sleep. Once again, I'm sorry we had to put you through so much."

Paige nodded and stood, running her cheek across the soft hair of the baby who was finally sleeping in her arms. Looking at Robert she said, "I'll be back in the morning to help with breakfast. If anything comes up I'll be at David and Karlee's. I don't want to be alone tonight."

❧

Saturday morning dawned hot and hazy. Stepping out of the air-conditioned Jeep, Paige hit a wall of air almost too heavy to breathe. As she reached the front of the Sparrow Center, she caught a glimpse of a white paneled truck in the back parking lot.

Charissa ran to unlock the door for her. Several feet behind her stood the sheriff's deputy who had stopped her the day before. "Good thing you came to the front door," Charissa said. "There's a reporter and a cameraman out back."

"I guarantee there'll be a lot more before long," the deputy added.

Paige shook her head in frustration and walked across the lobby. Robert's door was closed so she headed for the dining room. The few people she passed made attempts at smiles or greetings, but the tension in the air was palpable.

❧

At just after ten o'clock, she stood by Robert's desk, staring at the phone that he had just set in her hand. She watched his back as he left, closing the door partway, leaving her to talk to Roman alone. Lifting the receiver, she said hello and listened as he said, "I'll be heading out of here right after the concert tonight, but I wanted to talk to you before anyone else does. I just found out this morning that I've been granted custody." He paused a minute to give the news time to sink in. "I'm sorry to have to tell you this now."

Paige nodded, but it took her a minute to find her voice. Finally she said, "Right now I just want her to be safe."

"After she . . . comes home . . . I want to talk to you. I want to do this gradually, for all of us. I'd like your help."

"All right."

"Paige?"

"Yes?"

"I'm praying for Annie."

"I am too," Paige whispered. Thunder rattled the pane of glass in front of her. She hung up the phone and leaned her shoulder against the window frame. The black clouds rolling in from the west announced the coming rain, and the creeping darkness seemed a fitting atmosphere.

Turning to pick up her coffee cup from Robert's desk, she saw Brant standing in the doorway. She didn't pick up the cup; the look in his eyes as he walked toward her stopped her, stopped everything, including the storm of emotions in her head. In the next instant, she was in his arms, sobbing.

With one hand pressed against her back and the other on her head, he held her to him, stroking her hair, then resting his head on top of hers. When she stopped crying, he pulled her hair away from her face and lifted her chin. Softly, he ran his lips across her forehead, then touched them gently to her lips. "What happened while you were gone? Something's different."

Resting her head against his chest, she said. "I found my first love. I walked and I prayed and I cried and I finally let go. God is in the pilot's seat again."

Brant prayed a silent thank You and whispered against her hair, " 'Sometimes it hurts when God makes you real, but it's worth the pain.' "

Instantly, he felt her stiffen against him. Drawing a sharp breath, he pulled his arms away from her. He had said it to himself so many times that he had forgotten where it came from. She took a step back and stared at him, her face turning red, her eyes wide with shock and blazing with anger.

"That's it! That's it! That's how you knew so much about me! Somehow, you read my letters to Gavin!" One hand flew to her mouth, then fell away. "Those were private letters . . . did he give them to you or did you sneak them?" She stared at him. "And then not to have told me? All this stuff about feeling like you knew me, all this talk about being 'real' friends—real friends don't lie, Brant!"

Pushing past him, she headed for the door. Brant grabbed her arm and held her. "Look at me."

She turned, glaring at him through her tears. "There are some things I should have told you," he said, "but I haven't lied to you since—"

"Then what do you call it? All this time of acting like you could read my thoughts! Were you just some kind of voyeur, getting your kicks out of reading someone else's mail? Did he post my letters on the bulletin board at the airport? I suppose it was a group effort, huh? Did you all work together, making up stuff for him to write?"

"No one else read your letters."

"You did!"

He let go of her arm. "Yes, I read them. But I was the only one." He paused, looking down at the floor. "Gavin never read them."

"What?!"

"Gavin never wrote to you. I did."

Paige felt like she'd been slapped. "I don't . . . understand."

"Sit down." She dropped to the couch and he sat next to her. "Gavin had your first letter in his pocket one day when he came in for a flight lesson. He hadn't even opened it. He was dating two other girls at the time he went out with you—all he ever talked about was his conquests, so I heard all about you. I know this hurts, Paige, but I need to defend myself a little, and I can't do that without telling you all of it. Gavin called you a 'pretty little prude.' He had no interest in investing in a long-distance relationship. He threw the letter at me and said, 'Here, you can have her.' "

Paige turned away, her face burning. Brant continued. "Please keep in mind that I wasn't a Christian at the time. I read the letter and I was intrigued. All those little sketches you'd drawn around the borders, and the way you described your roommate and your professors . . . I wrote to you just for fun that first time. I was living in an apartment over the old drug store and getting my mail at the post office at the time, so it was easy to give you my box number and tell you I used it because I didn't want my parents intercepting my mail. I guess my conscience wasn't completely seared because after that I was determined not to lie about anything else."

"Except for one little detail!"

Brant ran his hand across his two-day beard. "I don't even know where to begin apologizing, Paige. Just let me try to explain how I saw it at the time. It started as a joke . . . at that time in my life I did anything that sounded fun, and I didn't give much thought to the consequences. I was in a restless stage; I didn't know what I wanted out of life. I was watching friends who were settling down with families or making big career moves and none of it seemed right for me. Always in the back of my mind were the things that Cody had told me for years, but I always shoved them back when they came to the surface. Then I got your letter and it was full of the excitement of the revival on your campus. You were so passionate! You talked about the freedom in being bound to Christ, about the joy of surrendering your will completely and letting Christ live in you. You were so open about how much you loved Jesus; your faith was so vibrant, so . . . tangible. You challenged me to search it out for myself and I did. I was determined to remain a skeptic until I was convinced, but I bought a Bible and I started studying."

Paige swiped at the tears that were spilling onto her lap. Brant looked down at the floor. "Every letter from you shed a little more light, but it did something else. It let me see inside you; your dreams, your secrets . . . By the time I realized what a horrible lie I was living, I was too scared of losing you."

Standing up, Brant walked to the window and stood with his back to her. "I was Gavin's flight instructor. I had no idea he was high when he came in for his first solo flight. For all I know, he may have taken something after he got in the plane. I was standing out on the tarmac, and by the time he was descending to land I could tell something was wrong. He was coming in way too fast. He'd done it so many times with me . . ."

Paige watched his shoulders rise as he took a deep breath. Her mind was whirling; part of her wanting to comfort him, part wanting to run and never look at him again.

"Gavin's family blamed me. They said I should have known that he was taking drugs and I should never have let him go up. They wrote a few scathing editorials about me and airport policies in general. It was such a big deal in this little town, I was surprised that you didn't seem to know about it."

"No one knew I was writing to . . ." Paige put her hand over her face and closed her eyes, trying to make sense of what was happening. "Mom and I were here trying to help David after Shawna died. David was in his own world that first year. He didn't know Gavin, and I didn't think he even knew I'd gone out with him, but I guess he did, because he called me when he heard about the accident." She remembered the odd look David had given her on the day of Jordan's birth; he'd said something about how hard it must be for her to be with Brant. Her mouth twisted as she remembered; she'd assumed he must have been talking about what she'd thought was Brant's egotism.

Brant was silent for several long minutes. Then he said, "I called David. I just said that I was a friend of Gavin's and that you had met him while you were here and you needed to know about his death. I said it would be easier if you heard it from someone you knew. I was so afraid you'd come back for the funeral."

"I didn't know the Prentices; it wouldn't have made any sense for me to come back."

Leaning his forehead against the window, Brant said, "I left town three weeks after the funeral. The Prentices are very influential people in this town, and every time I walked down the street I felt like people were staring at me, like I'd been accused of first-degree murder. I went up to Canada and got a job with a search-and-rescue team. I kept up my Bible study and reread your letters until they almost fell apart. One day I was alone, flying into the sunset and watching the colors change and suddenly I just knew. I was cruising over the Canadian wilderness at 4,000 feet when I surrendered to Jesus."

He was quiet again for a long time, then slowly he turned. "I don't suppose it means anything to you right now, but I wouldn't have done it without you. You have no idea how many times I wanted to tell you, how many letters I wrote and threw away. It just seemed too hurtful. I knew you wouldn't ever want anything to do with me, and it seemed better to let you go on believing that the man you'd been writing to was dead. I never thought our paths would cross. I was in Canada, I figured you'd be home in Connecticut after graduation or working for a publisher in New York like you'd dreamed of. My grandmother had died and my grandfather was in a nursing home and didn't recognize me. I never thought I'd come back to Milbrooke."

Brant rubbed the back of his neck and said, "When my grandfather died he left the farm to me. I was totally unprepared for that. By rights, it should have gone to my dad, but he hadn't been much of a son. I just couldn't bring myself to sell the farm. After the funeral, I went back to Canada, but all I could think about was coming back here to start my own business. Cody had written me about the Sparrow Center and Hailey and the wedding. He mentioned Hailey's room-mate a couple times; I don't know how it happened that neither your name or David's ever came up. You have to believe that I never would have come back if I'd known you were here."

Rubbing her temples, Paige asked, "But why didn't you tell me when we met? I can understand—no, I can excuse your behavior before you were a Christian, but to continue in this charade while you're preaching to me about being in complete obedience to God! That's such blatant hypocrisy, I . . . ." Dropping her hands to her lap, Paige rose slowly and turned toward the door.

"Wait. Please." He didn't make a move toward her, but his hands reached out, as if he could hang on to her from across the room. "What I did was wrong, but I need you to understand why."

Paige turned back, but kept her eyes on the window behind him, not trusting herself to look at him. "That whole year we were writing . . . it was strange, feeling like I knew you so well, and not knowing what you looked like. But I never asked you for a picture 'cause I didn't trust myself." He looked past her and said quietly, "I told myself that you can fall in love with a face, but not with words on a piece of paper." He sighed and ran his hand through his hair again. "Seeing you was like . . . like being hit by lightning or something. Suddenly there was this beautiful face to put with the words, but you were so different than I had imagined. Maybe I'd always pictured you in a white robe with a halo." For a brief second, he smiled. "All the time we were at David and Karlee's, I studied you. You talked about shopping in Paris, working at this fancy gallery, and buying a new car . . . Something was missing. It wasn't that I expected you to say 'Praise the Lord!' with every breath, but it sounded like you were filling your life with everything but God! You weren't real anymore! I wanted you to see how you'd changed and what you'd lost; I wanted to help you the way you'd helped me. I kept thinking that if we just had a little more time together before I told you, you'd see."

"A noble reason for deceit," Paige said sarcastically. "The end doesn't justify the means, Brant."

He lifted his hands just slightly, palms up, as if ready to begin a defense, then closed them into fists and nodded. "I know." He started to turn away, then stopped. "Only the name was a lie, Paige."

She stared at him, then turned, once again, to the door. This time, he let her go, but to her back he said, "I was wrong about one other thing. You can fall in love with words on a piece of paper. The face just made it sweeter."

$\mathcal{T}$he rain began while she was waiting for Charissa to unlock the glass door so she could leave. It fell in large, heavy drops that dotted the pavement and painted it a darker black.

When she reached the Jeep, the paneled truck pulled around the corner and a woman jumped out and ran toward her, then from the other side of the building came a man in a khaki jacket followed by a cameraman with an umbrella shielding his camera as he ran. Paige unlocked the car door and got in, slamming it just as the woman began shouting questions at her.

As she drove, her thoughts flowed in senseless circles, keeping time to the windshield wipers. Annie was lost, somewhere in the storm. Gavin was dead, but it didn't matter anymore, not to her. She had never really known him. Brant had lied to her, but in a way Brant was Gavin, or at least he was the person she had believed to be Gavin. Brant knew her secrets . . . He could read her like a book, but she couldn't trust him. Roman needed her help, but he was taking Annie away from her. But first they had to find her; she was lost, somewhere in the storm . . .

A strange thought came to her and she wondered why it hadn't hit her while she was talking to Brant. She almost laughed out loud at the irony: She was the too-perfect girl, the saintly legend who had led Brant to the Lord. She was the girl she'd been so jealous of!

She pulled into the driveway, but didn't get out. The house was empty and she didn't want to go in. The rain beat hard against the roof and sheeted on the windshield, blurring the edges and corners of the barn. Reaching in the back seat, she grabbed her hooded sweatshirt and slipped it on, then unplugged her cell phone and stuck it in the pocket.

The rain was cool on her face. Head down, she walked toward the road, watching the water cut through sand and stones, carving out miniature rivers at her feet. She had to think, she had to pray.

Father, none of this makes sense, but I'm not asking for an explanation. I've come back to You and I don't want to turn away again. I don't need to understand, but I need to know what to do. Please don't let my anger keep me from hearing You. My pride is hurt, but I have no right to pride. I know that I have to forgive Brant, but what then?

In the middle of the road she stopped and looked up, then closed her eyes. Her hood fell off and the rain soaked her hair and ran down her neck. She felt her sweatshirt grow heavy and her shoes fill with water, yet she stood, listening. What she heard, mingled with the sound of the rain battering the gravel, were Brant's words. "Only the name was a lie, Paige . . ."

The letters were in the storage area behind her closet. She ran back, unlocked the front door, and ran up the stairs, not taking the time to get out of her wet things. At the bottom of a box filled with sketch pads and photo albums were a year's worth of questions and reflections in white envelopes. Sitting on the floor of the walk-in closet, she pulled the first letter from the bottom of the stack, but as she bent to read it, her wet hair fell over her face. Spotting a headband in a basket behind the door, she pulled her hair back, away from her face.

She read out loud, but it was Brant's voice she heard. When she got to the end of the third letter, she noticed that he had signed it simply "me." After the second letter, the name Gavin never appeared. Somehow, that made it easier to erase him from the picture completely. So much fell into place as she read. Now she knew why her questions about his work and sports and family were always ignored. Now she knew why he had never called even though she'd told him he could. As the stack got smaller, her knowledge of Brant McCourt grew. It was as if she had started with a pencil sketch and then gradually added color. Though he had given none of the details of his life, he had given her bits and pieces of himself with every page.

She dialed the Sparrow Center on her cell phone as she walked out of the closet. Charissa answered with her usual cheery voice, as if nothing was different today. Paige asked to speak with Robert, and when he answered she asked if there was any news.

"Nothing yet."

"Is Brant still there?"

"No, he went home right after you left. Paige, I saw you run out. I wanted to talk to you after you talked to Roman. I'm worried about you."

"I'm okay, Robert. Annie's in God's hands and so am I."

❧

It was still pouring when she knocked on Brant's back door. He came to the door barefoot, in jeans and a white T-shirt. His hair was damp, as if he'd just showered and hadn't combed it yet, and he still had a two-day beard. The look on his face told her she was the last person he'd expected to find at his door. It took him a moment to respond, then, without a word, he opened the screen door for her.

Paige walked into the kitchen. It was more cluttered than she'd seen it the first time, but, she noticed, it was an organized mess. Dishes were stacked in the sink and papers piled on chairs, but they were neat piles. She glanced at the refrigerator. It was plastered with magnets holding scraps of paper: grocery and to-do lists, his work schedule and phone numbers—all in very familiar handwriting. Now she knew why he'd scrambled to take them off—and why he'd stenciled the invitation to The Greenhouse.

She turned to face him and wished she'd thought ahead about

what she was going to say. He held out his hand. "Can I take your jacket?"

Paige looked down and saw the water dripping onto the chipped linoleum beneath her. She unzipped it, pulled the phone out of the pocket, and struggled out of it. "I'm sorry," she said, pulling off her wet shoes and turning to look for a paper towel.

"You're soaked through," he said, taking her jacket. "Come on, I'll get you something dry."

She followed him into the room with the magnolia wall paper. Two clothes baskets of folded clothes were sitting on the bed. He pulled out a towel and a pair of sweat pants, then opened the closet door and said, "Why don't you just help yourself to . . . whatever you need. The bathroom is the next door down the hall. I'll go heat up some coffee." He stared at her for several seconds with no expression in his tired eyes, then walked out, closing the door behind him.

She pulled a flannel shirt from the closet and the basket of dark clothes provided gray socks, a navy T-shirt, and a pair of plaid boxer shorts. She held them up to her and giggled nervously. They would do. Taking the clothes into the bathroom, she peeled out of her wet things, dried off, and put on Brant's clothes. Only then did she look in the oval mirror above the sink. The only signs of makeup left on her pale face were the black streaks beneath her eyes, making her look like a backup singer for Quaestor. Turning on the water, she wet the corner of her towel and did the best she could to remove the mascara. She found a brush in an open drawer and worked through her hair, then, as an afterthought, put the headband back on.

Brant was facing the stove when she came in. Paige stood by the table, feeling like a little girl waiting to be told what to do next, but knowing that the first words had to be hers. He had done his apologizing, it was up to her to accept it.

He turned around, a brown mug in each hand. A hint of a

smile flickered on his face when he saw her, but disappeared as quickly as it came. He set the cups on the table and motioned for her to sit down. Once again, she lifted his Bible and the devotional book and set them on the table.

Picking up the mug, she hugged it between her hands, looked out at the rain through the parted pink curtains, and said, "I read your letters over." She didn't know where to go from there, but she felt no need to fill the silence until she was ready. Finally, she said, "It was always hard trying to hear Gavin's voice when I read them; it never quite seemed to fit. But yours did." She took a sip of coffee, feeling the warmth spread down through her chest, then turned to face him. "Brant, I'm not sorry that it was you I shared my secrets with."

As her words wrapped around him, he reached out, took the cup from her hands and set it on the table. "Come here," he whispered, taking her hands and pulling her out of her chair and onto his lap. Closing his arms around her waist, he kissed her. "I've been wanting to do that for a long time," he said.

She smiled at him. "You haven't known me for a long time!"

He laughed. "I've known you for six years, girl."

Just as he kissed the tip of her nose, the phone rang. Paige slipped off his lap and Brant walked to the phone. "It's Delaney!" he whispered, pointing to the phone on the desk in the living room. Paige ran and picked it up.

". . . somehow they got through to Roman at his hotel. They want him to deliver the money personally at eleven o'clock to-night, knowing full well he'd have to bow out of his concert to get back here by then. Roman didn't want to risk being seen at the airport, so he rented a car. He can get to them by eleven, but that doesn't give us time to brief him and . . . get things ready on our end. Can you fly down and get him?"

"Of course." Brant looked out the window and saw, gratefully, that the rain had almost stopped. "If I take the helicopter I can bring him straight to the Center. Find me a place to land." He grabbed Paige's phone from the counter and pushed a button. "I'm taking Paige with me. I'll give you her cell phone number. If I haven't heard from you first I'll call you from the airport."

After hanging up the phone, he grabbed two jackets off a chair with one hand and Paige's wet shoes with the other. Staring into her fear-filled eyes, he said, "We'll have her back tonight."

*T*hey had been in the air, heading southwest, for less than five minutes when the call came in from Kip at the airport. "Brant, do you have medical equipment on board?"

"Just my trauma bag."

There was a long pause, and then, "That'll do. I have Sergeant Delaney on the phone. There's a medical emergency and he wants you to head for the old tile factory."

"Okay, I'm turning. What's this about?"

"A three-year-old girl—he says you'll know who it is—head injuries. She's bleeding heavily and hysterical, but the guy who has her refuses to take her to the hospital. They want medical help on the spot."

There was another long pause and Brant glanced at Paige. Her eyes were wide and her hand was covering her mouth. Kip's voice crackled over the radio again. "They won't give an exact location. You're looking for a car parked off the road with a red shirt on the roof. As soon as you see them, give me directions. Delaney will have squads close but out of sight. He says they may be armed and you should both get out with your hands up and let them see you're not armed."

Several minutes passed and Brant pointed. "I see it! In a clearing a quarter of a mile south of the lake, southeast of the crossroads. Tell Delaney I've got the cell phone with me if he wants to talk to me after we get on the ground!"

He set down in the middle of the field and took off his headphones and unfastened his seat belt, motioning for Paige to do the same. He pulled his trauma bag from behind the seat and put the cell phone in the pocket of his jeans. They got out and walked slowly toward the car. Brant held his trauma bag over his head in one hand. They were about thirty feet from the car when the driver side door flew open and a boy about eighteen jumped out.

"Stay there!" he yelled. Pulling a gun from behind his back and waving it at Brant he said, "Just her! Hand her the bag and you get over there where I can see you!"

"She's not trained!"

"Just send her with the bag!"

"She won't know what to do! I'm not armed, let me at least examine the girl!"

"No way! How do I know you're not a cop?"

"How do you know she's not a cop?" Brant yelled. To Paige, he said softly, "He's scared out of his mind and probably stoned. We're not going to reason with him. They've got a phone, call me on it and I'll tell you what to do."

"Brant, I can't do this . . ."

"Yes, you can. I'll talk you through it."

The boy turned the gun on Paige. "Start moving!"

"I can't do this!" she shouted.

"You're going to have to, lady, I don't trust him."

Brant held out the bag. "Annie needs you," he said. "Put on gloves before you touch her, then call me; I'll talk you through it," he repeated.

Her legs felt like lead as she started across the muddy, rutted field. When she got within ten feet of the car, she could hear Annie crying. The boy yelled and the passenger door opened. A young girl with short, dyed black hair and thick makeup was holding Annie in the front seat. The boy cursed. "Get over there and do something!"

Paige took two steps and he yelled again. "Wait! Bring the bag here first. Set it on the hood." He felt through the bag with one hand, never taking his eyes off Brant. The gun shook in his other hand. From the bag he pulled a pair of scissors and set them on the car, then handled the bag back to her, following her to the open car door.

Paige set the bag on the ground, opened it, and tore open a pair of gloves. Annie was only whimpering now. Her feet dangled limply over the girl's right arm, her eyes were closed, and the girl held a dark brown towel against the side of her head. "Where is she hurt?" Paige asked.

At the sound of Paige's voice, Annie sat up and let out a cry, reaching for her. The towel fell away and Paige gasped and felt her arms and legs weaken and tiny jolts spread out from the small of her back. The left side of Annie's face was covered with blood. Her curls were matted to the side of her head and her left sleeve was soaked. Running behind the car, Paige bent over and vomited.

Wiping her face with her sleeve, she walked back and sank to her knees, holding her arms out to Annie. "It's okay, baby, I'm here now." Annie shivered in her arms and her cold fingers bit into Paige's skin as she clung to her. Sitting down on the wet ground so that Annie could sit on her lap, Paige said, "Show me where it hurts."

Annie pointed to the side of her head. As Paige pulled back the matted hair, another wave of nausea swept over her. She squeezed her eyes shut and forced herself to breath slowly. *Dear God, give me strength.* She handed the towel to the girl. "Hold this against her head. Does anything else hurt, Annie? Your back or your neck?"

"No. I wanna go home."

"Soon, honey, soon." Looking into the pale face of the girl who looked to be no more than sixteen, she said, "That man is a paramedic. I need to use your car phone to talk to him so he can tell me what to do."

The girl unplugged the phone and handed it to her. Touching Annie's arm, the girl asked, "Is she hurt bad?"

"I don't know yet." She looked into the vacant gray eyes that were outlined with thick black liner. "What's your name?"

"Tammy."

The boy cursed again. "Shut up! Are you stupid?"

Tammy flinched and anger flared in Paige, evaporating the weakness in her arms. She turned to the boy. "They already know who you are, Luis! You're not going to get away with this!"

Fear flashed on the boy's face and the gun wavered. "I'll get away with it if I take you with me!" He waved the gun at Brant. "Get back! Away from the chopper!" he yelled.

Paige's finger shook as she punched in the number of her cell phone. "Hand it to me!" Luis shouted. Brant answered and Luis said, "Just tell her what to do. Once she stops bleeding, we're leaving and we're taking the lady with us. Any cops follow and she's dead!" He handed the phone to Paige.

"Brant?"

"I'm right here. Is she conscious?"

"Yes."

"Okay. Tell me what you see."

"There's a big gash above her ear and there's blood everywhere. It looks bad, Brant." The strength she had felt just a minute before had left her at the sound of Brant's voice. A sob shook her.

"Take a deep breath, Paige. You can do this. Rip open a compress and apply pressure, then wrap bandages around any way you can. Just keep talking to her, it'll help her stay calm."

Paige set the bag on Tammy's lap. "Help me open these bandages, then hand them to me as I ask for them." Tammy complied, and then Paige asked for the roll of gauze. Her hands trembled as she pressed the square bandages firmly against the wound. "I bought you a new bunny," she said, her voice quavering. "When we get home you can have it." Annie nodded, then started crying again as Paige began wrapping the gauze around her head.

"Tell me what happened, Tammy."

"She was sleeping in the back seat. Luis was driving too fast; he always drives too fast. He saw a cop and turned hard. I thought we were going to tip over."

Luis pounded on the roof of the car. "Shut up! Just make her stop bleeding."

Again, Tammy flinched, but kept talking. "She fell off the seat. There's a lot of junk on the floor, bottles and stuff. I don't know what she got cut on."

Before Paige had finished wrapping the gauze, the bandages were beginning to turn red. Her heart began to pound and her vision blurred; she put her head down and picked up the phone. "It's soaking through!" she cried.

"That's okay. Head wounds bleed profusely even when they're not serious. Just keep adding bandages and applying pressure. Is she complaining of pain anywhere else?"

"No."

"Is she alert? Does she recognize you?"

"Yes."

"Okay, listen to me, Paige. I think she's going to be fine, but we have to make them think it's life-threatening. We have to scare them into letting us take her. Check her eyes with the mag light and tell me her pupils aren't reacting, check her pulse and tell me it's thready, check her reflexes. Make it dramatic. You can do it."

Paige nodded and weakly said, "Okay," then set the phone down. She took a few deep breaths and raised her head slowly. Putting her fingers on the side of Annie's neck, she found her pulse. It was fast, but strong. She picked up the phone. In a panicked voice, loud enough for Luis to hear, she said, "Brant, her pulse is weak and thready!"

"Check her eyes."

"Tammy, get the flashlight out of the bag." She shined the light into Annie's eyes and picked up the phone again. "They're not reactive!" She turned to Luis. "She's lost a lot of blood, and it looks like she's got internal bleeding. There's nothing I can do about that, we have to get her to a hospital now! Luis, you're already going to be charged with kidnapping, do you want to add murder to it? Do you want to spend the rest of your life in prison?"

Tammy looked up at him pleadingly. "Luis, please, this is enough, let her go! We can still get away."

Slamming his fist against the side of the car, Luis swore at her again and walked several yards away. Tammy looked at him, then back at Annie. Her hands clenched into fists. With one final glance at Luis she leaned forward and whispered, "I took the bullets out of his gun last night! I didn't want anyone to get hurt! Take her and get out of here!" she whispered.

Paige's arms closed tighter around Annie, but she didn't move. "What will happen to you when he finds out?"

"Nothing that hasn't happened before. Go!"

Her prayer was nothing more than two words. *Dear God . . .* As much as she wanted to run, for Tammy's sake, she couldn't. Looking to Tammy, she said, "Okay. Go over there and distract him!"

When Tammy left, she picked up the phone. "Brant, the gun's not loaded!"

"You're sure?"

Paige closed her eyes. Could it just be part of their plan? She took a deep breath. "Yes, I'm sure. Hang up and call Delaney!"

"All right. Pretend you're still talking to me."

Before she could answer him, Tammy and Luis walked back to her. The look in Tammy's eyes was one of disbelief. Luis yelled, "Get in the car, we're getting out of here."

Paige stood slowly, holding Annie as if she were a porcelain doll, and said into the dead phone, "What will happen if we move her?" Looking up at Luis, she said, "He says the slightest jarring could kill her. Do you want that on your conscience?"

"I'll put something on this guy's conscience!" He ripped the phone from her hand and shouted into it. "We're getting out of here and we're . . ." He shook the phone, held it to his ear again, then threw it at her, striking her arm. His face contorted in rage, and Paige turned and began to run. The gun clicked and out of the corner of her eye she saw Tammy grab Luis's arm and heard her scream as he slapped her. Brant was running toward Luis, and Paige heard the impact as he tackled him to the ground.

As she lifted Annie into the helicopter, the squad cars appeared and the last thing she saw before closing her eyes and giving in to tears was Brant running toward her.

> ❧

Paige was curled on a chair in the hospital corridor with her head on Brant's paramedic jacket and the leather aviator's jacket covering her. Sitting next to her, Brant was stroking her hair. Her headband sat on his knee. He nudged her gently as Robert came out of the room across the hall and she sat up.

"She's sleeping," Robert said. "She's exhausted and dehydrated, but that's all. She'll have quite a scar, but her hair should cover it." He looked down at Paige, still in Brant's blood-stained shirt and sweat pants. "So I understand we can't call you a wimp anymore."

Brant put his arm around her. "You should have seen her—a regular Florence Nightingale!"

Paige rolled her eyes. "I don't think Florence Nightingale ever threw up in a crisis!"

"That happens to everyone the first time! Now that you've got that behind you, I can hire you for my ambulance crew!" Robert laughed at the look on Paige's face. "You two go home. I'll keep you posted."

Pulling her to her feet, Brant asked, "Are you too tired to have dinner with me, Florence?"

⁊ð

Paige wrapped a towel around her wet hair and slipped into her robe. Standing in the closet, she went through her summer dresses one at a time. Pulling out a black satin shift, she smiled, shook her head, and hung it back on the pole. She knew exactly what to wear. Walking back to the bathroom, she took off her ring and laid it on the counter, took only mascara and lipstick out of her makeup bag, then opened the medicine cabinet and took out a bottle of fingernail polish remover.

An hour later, she opened the back door. Brant was wearing a white shirt and a tie with his jeans. He took one look at her and started laughing. Loosening his tie and pulling it off, he said, "I guess I don't need this."

"What were you planning?"

"I thought I'd fly you to Racine; there's a place on the lake front that makes the best roasted grasshopper with ladybug sauce around."

"I can change."

"No you can't." He reached out and tugged at her ponytail, touched her tiny gold earrings, then let his gaze wander down to the white v-neck T-shirt, the faded jeans, and leather sandals. Tipping her chin with his finger, he said, "You look beautiful."

"I wanted you to know there's more to me than satin and pearls."

⁊ð

Brant got in the pilot's side and turned to look at Paige. "Ready?"

"Yup." She smiled at him and grabbed the yoke, gripping it so tight her knuckles turned white.

"Haven't you learned anything through all this?" He put his hand on her arm and tugged. "Let go." When he finally pulled her hand free, he held it up and pointed to the white line on her little finger. "Your hand is naked," he said. "It needs something." He brought it to his mouth and kissed her ring finger.

"Is that what it needed?"

"No. It needs something . . . untraditional . . . something red maybe." He continued to stare at her hand.

"Now what are you thinking?"

"That I love you." He stroked his finger along the back of her hand. "And I was thinking about a Proverb Cody quoted to me a while ago."

Paige groaned. "Go on, Solomon."

" 'Who can find a virtuous woman? Her price is far above rubies.' " He kissed her finger again. "I found one, and I'm willing to pay the price."

Paige wiped a tear from her cheek, then leaned over and kissed him. "So, you think you'll like me better in jeans and rubies than satin and pearls?" she whispered.

"I like you in anything—as long as you're real."

"How long does it take to be real?"

"It takes a long, long time." He wrapped her in his arms and kissed her firmly. "But I'll talk you through it."

FAMILY CIRCLE

BY JANET LEE BARTON

To my Lord and Savior for showing me the way.
To my family for their love and encouragement always.
To my church family for rejoicing with me, and
To the real 'Teddy Bear Brigade' for your inspiration.
I love you all.

1

*J*ake Breland pulled himself out of the nightmare, drenched with sweat and shaking all over. His heart beat so hard he could hear it. That meant he was alive, didn't it?

Slinging the tangled covers aside, he stumbled down the hall to Meggie's room. The nightlight cast a warm glow over the room, and as soon as he heard her soft, even breathing coming from the crib, he let go of the breath he'd been holding. Meggie was all right and he *was* alive. It was just the nightmare. Again. The nightmare was coming so often now, he dreaded going to bed.

Jake bent over and inhaled the sweet baby scent of his daughter. He forced himself not to pick her up and hold her. There was no sense ruining her peaceful sleep. As he watched her, his own heartbeat returned to normal. He leaned over and placed a feather-light kiss on her forehead. Meggie stirred, and afraid she'd sense his presence and wake up, Jake quietly backed out of the room. Pausing at the door to his bedroom, he shook his head and made his way down the darkened hall to the kitchen. He wouldn't be able to sleep after that dream. Besides, he had some thinking to do.

Flipping the light switch on, he looked at the clock and sighed. He might as well call it a night and put the coffee on. Leaning against the cabinet, he waited for the coffee to finish brewing and shivered as the cool night air hit his still-damp back.

He rubbed his temples and closed his eyes. All he could see was a replay of the nightmare, Meggie crying and crying and crawling all over the apartment while he lay unconscious or dead in his bed. It always ended the same—with Meggie crying out, and no one there to hear her cries. No one.

Jake shuddered. What if it were real? What if something did happen to him and no one was nearby to take care of Meggie?

He hadn't been able to find a suitable housekeeper since Mrs. Morrow broke her arm, so he'd had no choice but to put Meggie in daycare. He doubted the staff would check on her if she missed a day. They'd just figure he'd kept her at home. It might be days or weeks before someone would find Meggie. By then what could happen to her?

Jake shook his head, pushing the horrible images from his mind. The thought of Meggie having no one to care for her was more than he could deal with. He poured his coffee and wandered into the living room. Picking up the remote, he turned the TV on, keeping the volume low, but he stared at the screen without seeing.

When had these nightmares started? Not in the first few weeks following Melissa's death. He'd been too busy trying to accept the loss of his wife and be both mother and father to his newborn baby to sleep much at all. In the following months he'd had the dreams sporadically, but not until recently, when there'd been talk of opening an office overseas and putting him in charge, had they started coming almost nightly.

Suddenly he knew that wasn't an option. He wasn't taking Meggie halfway around the world, and he wasn't leaving her. He didn't need a partnership in a prestigious law firm. He needed more time with his daughter.

Back home, he wouldn't have to set up his own practice. His cousin John had asked him to come into partnership with him more than once. With two of them to share the workload, there'd be more time for Meggie.

Jake sighed and ran his fingers through his tousled hair. He'd never planned or wanted to move back home. Now he had his daughter to think of. He couldn't put it off any longer.

He might not have family here in Albuquerque to make sure Meggie was all right, but he had them in southern New Mexico, in his small hometown of Sweet Springs. Family who'd offered over and over to help. He had to make sure that if anything happened to him, she'd have someone right there, right away. It was time. Time to go home.

❧

Sara Tanner tied off the embroidery thread and looked at her work with a critical eye. She held it up for her grandfather's inspection. "How's it look, Grandpa? If you were two or three, would it appeal to you?"

William Oliver lowered the newspaper he'd been reading, looked over the top of his bifocals, and chuckled. "It appeals to me at seventy, Darlin'. I'm sure it would appeal to me if I were a child." He got up from the kitchen table and brought the coffeepot over to refill their cups.

"They are cute, aren't they? I'm so glad we decided to do this." Sara slipped the finished teddy bear into a bag with the others she'd made that week.

"You ladies at church do some real good things. I bet those little bears will mean a lot to the small children brought into the emergency room."

Sara took a sip of coffee and nodded. "That's what we're hoping. The hospital thought it was a great idea. We'll know for sure soon. I'm going to pick up the rest and deliver them tomorrow afternoon."

"Tomorrow?" Her grandfather slapped his forehead. "I forgot to tell you—Nora called. You've been summoned to lunch tomorrow."

Sara sighed and shook her head. "That's an apt description of her invitations, if I ever heard one. I dread going. She's just going to try to convince me to move out to the ranch again."

"That's the last place you need to be."

"I know, Grandpa, and I've told her it's not going to happen. I'm running out of ways to say no, but she was Wade's mother. I can't just tell her to get lost."

Her grandfather grinned and nodded. "Even though that's exactly what you should do."

Sara chuckled. "No, I shouldn't but I have to admit I'd certainly like to at times."

"Well, Darlin', I don't like the way she wants to control your life. You've had enough of that."

Sara reached across the table to squeeze his hand. "I'm not going to let her control me, Grandpa. I promise." She made the promise to herself, too. Her mother-in-law could be overpowering at times. She changed the subject. "What are you going to do tomorrow?"

"I'm not sure. I have my garden planted. Ben and Lydia are away at a livestock auction, so we won't be having our regular chess game. Got plenty of time on my hands. Want me to go with you to Nora's?"

Sara chuckled. Bless his heart. "That's a great idea, Grandpa. Do you think you can put up with her for that long?"

"Nora's no problem for me. I'll be fine. Besides, that cook of hers is worth it."

Sara laughed, circling the table to hug him. "I don't know what I'd do without you."

He hugged her back. "Nope, it's the other way around, Sara. I was just rambling around this old house 'til you moved in. You take real good care of me."

Tears pooled in Sara's eyes. They were a pair, the two of them. She knew who'd been taking care of whom. Until a few months ago, she'd been the one on the receiving end of all the care from her grandfather, her husband's family, and her church family. "Thank you, Grandpa. I love you."

"Guess I'll be calling it a night," he said after clearing his throat. "I love you, Honey. I'm proud of the way you're getting on with things." He nodded his head and pushed away from the table. "Real proud. Just don't let Nora tell you how to live your life."

"I won't. You sleep well." She gave him another hug and took their cups to the sink.

It took only a few minutes to clean up the kitchen. Not yet ready for bed, Sara slipped out to sit in the front-porch swing. Putting it in motion, she caught the delicate smell of the lilac bush behind her.

It felt so good to notice small things again: the sweet smell of the honeysuckle climbing the trellis, the soft feel of the gentle breeze. How bright the stars shone down. Spring was here. Everything was coming to life, and for the first time in a long time, Sara felt alive.

Bowing her head, she said a silent prayer of thanksgiving for Grandpa, all of the Tanners and Brelands, and her church family. It'd taken them all to get her through the past year. She wouldn't have made it without them. Most of all, she thanked the Lord for seeing to it that she'd had them to help her.

She couldn't wait until fall, when she'd be returning to her teaching job at the high school. She'd just have to keep herself busy until then—and convince Nora that she was not moving to the ranch. Period. Easier said than done. Her mother-in-law did not like to take no for an answer. Sara could just picture the two of them living together. Two widows growing old together. The thought drew a shudder from her. Maybe she would cancel tomorrow's lunch with Nora, after all. There would be other lunches. There always were.

Sara kept the swing in motion until her eyes grew heavy. She hadn't had trouble sleeping for several months, but still, she didn't like to go to bed until she was almost asleep on her feet. Entering the house quietly, she locked the door and went upstairs. She'd sleep well tonight. She was sure of it.

❧

Sara felt she'd taken the coward's way out by canceling her lunch with Nora, but her excuse of having to pick up those adorable teddy bears was a valid one. Besides, she didn't want lunch with Nora to put a damper on her good mood.

One more stop and she'd have the last of the teddy bears gathered up. She was excited about taking them to the hospital. All of the ladies had been so eager to help make them, and the hospital was thrilled with the offer. If having a teddy bear to cuddle while receiving medical attention could ease the fear of just one child, their work would be well worth the hours spent.

She pulled to a stop at the curb in front of Ellie Tanner's house and hurried down the walk and up the porch steps. "Gram?" Sara called, opening the screen door. "You here?"

"Back here, Sara. In the kitchen," came the reply.

Bypassing the living room, Sara hurried through the dining room into the sunny kitchen at the back of the house. The sight of Gram sitting at the table watching an adorable baby girl attempt to feed herself stopped Sara in her tracks. Her heart twisted and turned, and she forgot to breathe until Gram turned in her seat and said, "Sara?"

Sara forced the air out of her lungs and tried to smile.

Gram quickly got up and led her to a chair. "Oh, my dear Sara. I'm so sorry. I didn't even think to warn you."

Sara blinked quickly to hide the tears that threatened and shook her head. "No, Gram. It's fine. I . . . I just didn't expect to see a baby at your table." She forced her gaze off the child.

Sara patted the older woman's hand that still rested on her shoulder. "I'm fine, Gram. Really. But who is this little beauty? Who are you doing a favor for now?"

Gram gave Sara a warm hug and took her seat once more, handing the baby another chicken stick and being rewarded with a huge grin.

"This is my great-granddaughter Meggie, Jake's daughter. This is Sara, Meggie." She turned back to face Sara. "He finally came to his senses and decided to move back home. He's going to join John's firm as a partner." Gram handed the baby a cup of milk as she continued her explanation. "They're discussing it all over lunch."

Jake. Back here. Sara's heart seemed to screech to a stop before it jumped into high gear. Her gaze snapped back to the baby. *Jake's baby.* The little girl had his dark hair, his eyes, and his coloring. Meggie grinned at her, and Sara saw a miniature dimple—exactly like the one Jake had. Like the one she used to tease him about, just so he'd grin at her. She'd stand on tiptoe and plant a quick kiss on the dimple before it disappeared. She shook her head to clear the vision she'd conjured in her mind.

Sara wasn't sure she was ready to see her first love after all these years and all that had happened. She started to her feet just as Gram set a cup of tea in front of her. When had Gram made it? How long had she been sitting there staring at the baby?

She tried to sound calm. "I just came by to pick up the teddy bears, Gram. I really need to get to the hospital."

"After you drink that tea, Child. You aren't driving anywhere right now. Not until I know you're all right."

Realizing she was not in any shape to drive, Sara nodded her head and took a sip of the hot, sweet liquid. *Lord, please get me through this. You've helped me with everything else, please help me over this new hurdle.*

"Sara."

Sara pulled her gaze from the baby, who shyly glanced from Gram to Sara and back again.

"Yes, Ma'am?"

"Is it seeing a baby or the fact that Jake is moving back that's upsetting you?"

Gram always did have a way of zeroing in on a problem. Sara was saved from answering when the baby suddenly let out a wail and banged the tray, sending her food flying and milk splashing. The wail quickly turned to giggles, and the baby started bouncing up and down in her seat.

Sara couldn't help but laugh. Milk was dripping off the tray and running down the baby's face, and Gram's lap held an assortment of finger food.

"Why, you little minx!" Gram laughed and looked around as if unsure what to do next.

"I'll clean up the mess, Gram. It won't take a minute."

Sara grabbed the washcloth the older woman had handy and started to wipe off the baby's face while Gram emptied her lap, still chuckling.

Sara's heart turned over as Meggie reached out and clung to her blouse, trying to climb out of the high chair. The baby's grip tightened as Gram tried to take her.

In that moment, Sara's heart melted. "It's okay. I'll take her."

Gram chuckled. "I don't think she's giving you much choice. This one has a mind of her own." She took the cloth from Sara to finish cleaning up the mess.

Sara managed to unhook the safety belt keeping the baby in place, and Meggie lunged, climbing into Sara's arms. The baby held on for dear life and hid her face in the curve of Sara's neck. Sara's arms tightened around Meggie, and she murmured soothing noises to the baby, finding that the one thing she'd been avoiding for months was exactly what she needed. The feel of a baby in her arms. Closing her eyes, she cuddled Meggie close and sighed deeply. *Lord, thank You. You always seem to know what I need, when I need it.*

Finished with the cleanup, Gram turned to Sara. "I can take

her now." She held her arms out to Meggie, but the baby clung to Sara.

"If you don't mind, I'll just hold her a little longer."

"You're sure?" Gram asked, concern etching her face.

Sara nodded and took her seat again. "I'm sure. I think this is just what we both need."

Gram looked closely at the two and nodded. "I think you may be right." She freshened up their tea and peeked at Meggie. "Her eyes are closed. I wonder if she's asleep or just playing possum."

Sara gently tightened her hold on the baby. "Doesn't matter to me. I'll just enjoy holding her close as long as she'll let me."

Gram nodded and tears gathered in her eyes. "Sara, you will have another one of your own, one day. The Lord will see to that."

Sara rubbed Meggie's back lightly, enjoying the feel of the warm little body in her arms. "I hope so, Gram. He brought me here today, and He knew how badly I needed the feel of a baby in my arms, even before I did." She closed her eyes and inhaled the sweet, powder scent of Meggie.

"I guess we all thought it would be too painful for you. Maybe we've been a bit overprotective."

"No, Gram. You've all been wonderful. I don't know what I would have done without you."

"I'm just glad Jake has realized he can use some help."

Not wanting to be rude, Sara forced herself to respond to the change of subject. "Will he be staying with you or at the ranch with Luke?"

"He's going to stay here with me." Gram's smile showed her pleasure at having her grandson back in town. "He says he wants to find a house in town or build one, since his office will be here. He doesn't want to commute back and forth from the ranch."

Although unsure of how she felt about seeing Jake again, Sara still felt curious about his reasons for coming back. He'd said once that he couldn't wait to get out of Sweet Springs. "What made him decide to move back? Did he say?"

"Just that Meggie needed to know her family, and he knows someone will be here for her if something should happen to him." Gram sighed. "He's not the same Jake. He seems bitter, angry."

"That's not so unusual, Gram. I had to get over a lot of that, too."

"But that's just it, Sara. You have gotten on with your life. You are dealing with it. Jake hasn't."

"I had all of you to help me."

Gram nodded her head. "And you let the Lord heal you. I don't think Jake is on speaking terms with Him. And without that, I'm not sure how much help the rest of us can be to him."

Sara pushed thoughts of how much Jake had hurt her to the back of her mind. That was the past and had nothing to do with the present. She could relate to the pain he was going through now and felt only sorrow that he might be at odds with the Lord. "We'll just have to pray. You know the Lord doesn't let go of His children."

The older woman patted Sara's hand. "I do know that, but I seemed to have forgotten for the moment. Thank you for reminding me." She reached over and brushed her fingers through the fine hair of the now gently snoring baby and smiled at Sara. "She's certainly taken up with you. You'll be all right while I gather up the teddy bears?"

Sara glanced down at the sleeping baby and smiled. "We'll be fine. I'm in no hurry to let her go."

As Gram left the room, Sara took in every detail of the sweet-smelling infant. Little hands with the tiny indentations where knuckles would one day be. She rubbed a finger over a soft, pudgy hand, and Meggie smiled in her sleep. Fine, dark hair curled softly around the cherubic face. Thick, dark eyelashes hid midnight blue eyes that Sara knew she'd inherited from Jake. She really was a beauty.

Sara's sigh was ragged. A baby with no mother. A mother with no baby. Each receiving comfort from one another. She brushed her lips gently over Meggie's velvety cheek, and try as she might, she couldn't stop the tear that escaped and slid down her face.

Hearing footsteps in the hall, Sara quickly brushed her hand across her cheek, not wanting Gram to catch her crying. She forced a smile and looked up as the footsteps came to a stop just inside the kitchen door.

The breath caught in her throat as she looked up into the eyes of Jake Breland.

ða

Jake returned to his grandmother's house feeling better than he had in months. He was surprised at how good it felt to be home. He was looking forward to the partnership he and his cousin John were forming. Meggie was with Gram. There would always be someone in Sweet Springs to care for her if he couldn't. A huge weight had been lifted, and he found himself whistling as he entered the house. He heard a noise coming from the kitchen and headed there. Just inside the door, he stopped in his tracks.

Jake had known this moment would come. He'd tried to prepare himself for seeing her again. But no way had he prepared himself for the sight of Sara holding his child. The woman he'd loved so long ago cradling the child of the woman who'd come between them. How could something that seemed so wrong look so right? What was she doing here, holding his daughter so close?

"Sara." His stomach did a nosedive and he clenched his fists. "Is something wrong with Meggie? Where's Gram? Is she all right?"

Jake watched the color drain from Sara's face as she quickly shook her head. "Everything is fine. Gram went upstairs to get some things I have to deliver to the hospital. That's what I stopped by for," she quickly assured him.

Jake nodded and relaxed his fingers, relieved that nothing was wrong. "I see you've met my Meggie."

Sara nodded and looked down at his sleeping daughter. "She's beautiful, Jake. I'm . . . sorry about Melissa. I should have written, called. . . ."

Jake shook his head as he crossed the room. "Don't worry about it." He knew his words sounded gruff. He couldn't help it. He wasn't sure what to say to Sara after all this time. "I'm sorry about Wade."

He watched Sara swallow and saw his pain mirrored in her eyes. She nodded. "I know." She bit her bottom lip before continuing. "I didn't know you were moving back to Sweet Springs. Gram just told me."

Jake rubbed the back of his neck, feeling more uncomfortable by the minute. "I didn't know I was moving back until a few weeks ago, and I didn't tell anyone until I got here," he said, wondering why he felt the need to explain his presence.

Seeing Sara again made him wonder if he'd made the right decision. But one glance at Meggie, and he knew he'd had no choice. It was for her sake he'd decided to come home.

Seeing more questions in Sara's eyes, questions he knew he might never be able to answer, Jake turned away to pour himself a cup of coffee. "She wasn't too much for Gram, was she?"

"No, I don't think so." Sara chuckled. "She got a little exuberant with her lunch and dumped most of it onto Gram's lap, but that was nothing."

Jake smiled, even as he noted the hint of nervousness in Sara's voice. "That's my Meggie. Mealtime is an adventure for her."

Turning back to Sara, he leaned against the cabinet. The years had been good to her. She didn't look much older than the last time he'd seen her. Auburn hair was pulled back into a clasp at the base of her neck, instead of up into a ponytail as she'd once worn it. Her deep green eyes were still as large and inviting as the creek on a hot summer day. Her smile seemed strained, yet her presence was calmer, more serene than he remembered, despite the pain in her eyes.

He looked away and cleared his throat. "I didn't give Gram much notice that I was moving back. I hope it won't be too much for her to help me out with Meggie for a little while, until I can get settled and find a housekeeper." Was Gram all he could talk about? He could remember a time when he'd had no trouble finding things to say to Sara. If there had been a lull in the conversation, he certainly hadn't stood around wondering what to say next. He'd have pulled her into his arms and kissed her. His gaze strayed to her full lips. Yes, that's what he would have done. But he couldn't do that now.

"I don't think there's much that Gram isn't willing or able to take on," Sara said, breaking into his thoughts. "She's delighted to have a baby to make over." She motioned toward the hallway. "She should be back down soon."

Jake knew she was as anxious for Gram's presence as he was. When he'd come into the kitchen to find Sara holding Meggie, it'd been obvious that she felt completely at home. Now she seemed as uncomfortable as he felt. He should know that nothing stayed the same. The easy relationship he and Sara had once shared was a thing of the past. Like it or not, he was going to have to deal with it. Just like he'd dealt with everything else. Alone.

When he glanced at Sara again, he saw that her attention was on Meggie, and the tenderness with which she looked down at his daughter was so compelling, it reached out to him. Suddenly, he felt threatened. Without knowing why, he was filled with a compulsion to hold Meggie in his arms.

He crossed the distance between them in two strides and held out his arms. "I'll take her now," he said abruptly.

Trying not to wake Meggie, Sara stood and quickly shifted the baby into Jake's arms. The flood of longing she felt in relinquishing the little girl didn't surprise her. She knew it was natural. But she was totally unprepared for the flash of awareness shooting up her arm when she brushed against Jake's arm during the transfer. Stepping back, she hoped he wouldn't notice her shaking. She wished she could just leave without the teddy bears she'd come to collect, but that would raise all kinds of questions with Gram—questions she wasn't ready to face. Sara forced herself to sit back down at the table and take a sip of her now lukewarm tea.

"I'll just put her in her crib," Jake said, his voice sounding husky. "I'll see what's holding up Gram while I'm up there." He turned and started out of the room. "Good-bye, Sara."

"Good-bye, Jake."

Only it wasn't good-bye, Sara thought as she watched him leave, his back stiff and straight. She and Jake both lived here now. Sweet Springs was a small town. There was no way they could avoid seeing each other. Obviously he was as uncomfortable around her as she was near him. Wishing things could be different didn't make them so, and she was going to have to get used to running into Jake and Meggie.

Sara took a deep breath. She could handle it. But only with the Lord's help. She knew she didn't have the strength to do it on her own.

"Sara, I'm sorry I took so long. I had to finish up one little bear's face." Gram bustled into the kitchen. She took one look at Sara and plunked down in a chair next to her. "I ran into Jake upstairs. Did he say something to upset you?"

Sara shook her head. Jake hadn't said much of anything. But neither had she. "No, Gram. I think we were both just a little uncomfortable with each other."

Gram nodded in agreement. "That's to be expected. You were both young and in love once. Then you went your separate ways."

"How did you know—"

"You young people. You think we old ones don't have eyes?"

Gram chuckled. "It was obvious. The whole family thought an engagement was imminent. Then Jake went off to college and ended up marrying Melissa, and you married Wade a year later. I always wondered if you married him on the rebound," she stated bluntly.

"Gram! I loved Wade. He was a wonderful husband." Sara's insides churned. She just couldn't deal with this now, not after seeing Jake again. She had to get out of here.

"I know you loved him, Dear. And you were a wonderful wife to him, but . . . I also know you once loved Jake . . . and that he loved you." Gram reached over and patted Sara's hand. "I'm not trying to meddle. I'm just saying that the uncomfortable feelings won't last forever. You and Jake care too much about each other."

Sara stood and gathered up her purse and the bag of teddy bears, shaking her head. "I don't know. I think we've both changed too much." She bent and kissed the top of the older woman's head. "But don't you worry about it. Okay?"

"I'll walk you out." Gram rose from the chair. "You be sure and let me know how they like those little bears, you hear?"

They made their way back to the front door, and Gram gave Sara a hug. "Don't you let the fact that Jake is here keep you away, Sara. You're family too, you know."

Only by marriage. And since Wade's death, not even that. But she loved Gram and didn't want to cause her any pain by reminding her. "Thanks. I'll let you know how our bears go over." After a quick good-bye, Sara forced herself to step sedately down the walk rather than running away like she wanted to.

Starting her car, she took off and tried to shake the sudden feeling of loss that invaded her. She loved Gram and her extended family, but it wasn't going to be the same now. It couldn't be—not with Jake back in town.

છ

Jake stepped back from the hall window and started down the stairs, relieved that Sara was leaving yet feeling like a heel. He'd been rude to her. He knew that. It'd just been such a shock to see her sitting in the kitchen, completely at home, holding his child in her arms. The aura of peace surrounding them had pulled a yearning from him so strong, so unexpected that he'd felt lost, alone, on the outside looking in.

Only holding Meggie close and rocking her for a few minutes before he put her to bed had helped. He was just now beginning to realize that he needed Meggie as much as she needed him. She was the only thing in his life that made it worth living.

He entered the kitchen to find his grandmother sipping a cup of tea. He poured himself a fresh cup of coffee and joined her at the table.

"Is Meggie still sleeping?" she asked.

Jake leaned back in his chair and nodded. "I guess the trip wore her out."

"Changes do that to children, sometimes. She sure took a liking to Sara."

Knowing his grandmother, Jake sensed there was more coming. "Seemed like it. Sara certainly seems to feel at home here."

Gram looked him in the eye. "Why shouldn't she? She was married to your cousin. She's family."

Jake felt defensive. "Only by marriage."

"Jake Breland!" Gram set her cup down so hard, tea sloshed over the side. "When did that ever make a difference in this family?"

Jake knew it never had. He wouldn't have wanted it to. But the bad feelings he'd had for Wade colored his judgment and made him continue. "Well, Wade's gone now."

"Yes. He is. And if it'd been you instead of Melissa who'd died, she would still be a part of this family. Jake, I can't believe how insensitive you've become."

326

"You're right, Gram. I'm sorry." And he was. But he still couldn't come to terms with the past. Not after seeing Sara again.

"Well, that's something. Maybe there is still enough of the old Jake left to feel some compassion. After all, Sara has gone through as much pain as you have. More."

"How could that be?"

Gram closed her eyes and shook her head. "You lost your wife in childbirth, and I know it was devastating." When she opened her eyes, tears filled them. She reached over and covered one of his hands with hers. "I know it still is, Jake. But you have your child. Sara not only lost Wade in that car accident, she lost the baby she was carrying."

2

*J*ake's stomach clenched. Lowering his head, he willed himself to swallow past the knot in his throat and breathe normally. Sara had lost a baby. He hadn't known she was pregnant. No wonder she'd looked so bereft when he'd taken Meggie from her. Tears stung the back of his eyes, and he blinked rapidly to hold them back. Once he thought he had control, he looked at his grandmother. "Why didn't someone tell me?"

Gram ran her hand over her own teary eyes. "You were dealing with your own pain, away from us all. We didn't think you needed anything more to deal with."

Jake propped his elbows on the table and cradled his head with his hands. He thought about Meggie sleeping peacefully upstairs, and for the first time in a long time, he thanked the Lord for sparing him the pain Sara must feel.

"Did she lose it in the wreck?" Jake realized how little he knew about Wade's death. He didn't even know if Sara was with him.

"Because of it, yes." Gram got up to refill his coffee cup. When she sat back down, she clasped her hands together. "Wade was killed instantly, but Sara was put in intensive care. There were internal injuries. I know they did the best they could, but she lost the baby the next day."

She wiped her eyes with her apron. "We thought we were going to lose Sara too. Only the Lord and prayer brought her through."

Jake cleared his throat. "She seems to be dealing with it all very well." Except for when he'd taken Meggie from her.

Gram nodded. "She's come a long way, Jake. A long way. Today was the first time she's held a baby since she lost her own. I didn't think to warn her Meggie was here before she came to get the teddy bears. But they took to each other right off, and she said she'd been needing to hold a baby for so long."

Jake walked over to the open back door. Leaning against the doorframe, he looked out on the backyard and shook his head. "I wish I'd known, Gram."

Maybe he'd have thought before he practically yanked Meggie away from Sara. What must she be thinking? He hadn't even mentioned being sorry about her losing the baby. He was going to have to talk to her, try to explain.

The front screen door slammed, and they heard footsteps and voices heading for the kitchen. His brother Luke and cousin John were arguing over the pros and cons of their favorite baseball teams as they reached the kitchen doorway.

"Shh." Gram put her finger to her mouth. "We have a sleeping baby upstairs and you two sound as though you're trying to be heard over the crowd at that game you're talking about."

The two men looked at each other and shrugged, tiptoeing the rest of the way into the kitchen.

"Sorry, Gram." Luke bent down and gave her a kiss and a hug. He grinned at Jake. "Hi, big brother. When's the little darlin' due to wake up? I sure would like to see her."

"So would I," John added. "We came over just to see her." He pulled two cups out of the cabinet and filled them for himself and Luke. "And to see if Gram would take pity on us bachelors and invite us to supper."

She got up from the table and thumped him on the shoulder. "When have you ever had to ask?"

John chuckled and gave Gram a kiss on the cheek, being careful not to slosh coffee on her. "It's so good to know we're always welcome at your table."

"You are. As long as you remember I just cook. You three have cleanup duty."

Luke saluted her. "Yes, Ma'am!" He kissed her other cheek.

Gram shook her head and went about getting supper started.

"You're awful quiet, Jake. Not regretting moving back already, are you?" John asked.

Jake shook his head in response to his cousin's question, although he was wondering if he'd made a major mistake. It'd been much harder than he'd realized it would be to see Sara again. And now he was going to have to see her sooner than he'd like so he could apologize for this afternoon.

"Gram just told me about Sara. About her losing the baby. I didn't know." Jake looked pointedly at his brother.

"Yeah, well, you had a lot to deal with about that time," Luke replied.

"Still, someone should have told me. I didn't even tell her I was sorry about the baby when I saw her today." Jake saw Luke and John exchange a look.

"I'm sorry, Jake. We just didn't know how to go about it," Luke said. "There was so much grief in the family around that time. Sara will understand."

Would she? Jake hoped so. But he was going to have to explain soon. He couldn't let her think he was totally unfeeling.

A cry from the second floor signaled Meggie was awake. All three men jumped to their feet. Jake was first up the stairs with Luke right behind him. John tried to overtake Luke but was pushed back.

"Hey, John, I'm the uncle," Luke protested. "You're just a cousin. You have to wait your turn."

The conversation drifted down to the kitchen where Gram was busy pulling out a skillet. She rolled her eyes and chuckled. Boys would be boys. Luke and John would be good for Jake. He needed the bantering, teasing love of his family. They'd do all they could to help him adjust to moving back. With the Lord's help, he'd heal.

ð

Sara felt a little better as she left the hospital. At least for a short while she'd been able to push Jake to the back of her mind. The bears had been a big hit with the nurses on duty. She'd even seen how well they would go over with the children when little Ricky Monroe was brought in with a gash on his head. He'd been climbing up to his tree house when his foot slipped and he fell, scraping his head in the process. He'd been really frightened of being sewn up until the nurse handed him the little bear to hold on to. He was so busy checking it out, the stitches were finished before he knew it.

The ladies would be so pleased. She reminded herself to call Gram later, hoping Jake wouldn't answer the phone. *Jake.*

She still couldn't believe he was back in town. Gram was right; he'd changed. He seemed older than his years, aloof and lonely. He was very protective of Meggie; that was obvious. Or maybe she was misreading him. Maybe he just hadn't wanted *her* to hold his child.

Sara sighed. So much had changed. Neither of them were the same people they'd been all those years ago. She didn't know this Jake at all. Still, her heart went out to him. She could understand having to carve a new life out for yourself when all you really wanted was your old one. It wasn't easy, but it had to be done. She knew she'd never be able to do it without the help of the Lord and Grandpa and Wade's family—Jake's family, too. Would he be willing to share them now that he was home?

Sara pulled in the drive and hurried into the house. It was time to start supper, and she couldn't worry about it now. She'd leave it all in the Lord's hands.

The mouth-watering smell of homemade stew greeted her as

she entered the kitchen. Her grandfather turned from checking on a pan of cornbread in the oven.

"Grandpa, I'm sorry I'm late getting home."

"No problem, Darlin'. I was just waiting until you drove up to finish it up. Gave me something to do."

Sara hugged him and started setting the table. "I appreciate it, Grandpa. I would have been finished sooner, but I was at Gram's longer than I expected."

He nodded. "Ellie called a little while ago to see if you were back yet. She told me Jake and his baby girl are moving back." Grandpa took a seat at the table. "Said you two took to each other right off."

"Oh, Grandpa, she's adorable." Sara chuckled and told him about Meggie's lunch as she joined him at the table. "She grabbed hold of me and wouldn't let go. It felt so good to hold her. You know?"

Grandpa patted her hand. "Hindsight is always better than foresight. We erred on the side of caution, I guess, keeping babies and little ones away from you. We were just afraid it would be too painful, Sara."

"I know. But it was just what I needed."

Grandpa cleared his throat. "What about Jake? How does he seem?"

The timer went off, and Sara got up to take the cornbread out of the oven, glad for a minute or two to regroup. She placed the pan on a pad in the center of the table. "He's still struggling, I think."

"I guess he's been trying to deal with it all on his own. Maybe now he's home, we can help," Grandpa suggested.

Sara ladled the stew into bowls and brought them to the table while Grandpa cut the cornbread. Once they were seated again, he offered the blessing and asked the Lord to help them to help Jake in whatever way was needed.

"I hope he lets his family help him now that he's home," Sara said. "I can't imagine how hard the last year would have been on my own." She shook her head.

"Ellie said he's going to look for a house or build one in town."

"That's what she told me. He'll be staying with her for now. He seems a little concerned that Gram might not be up to keeping Meggie all day."

"Ellie? I don't think there's much that woman isn't up to."

"She's something, isn't she?"

"She sure is."

Something about the way he spoke made Sara look at her grandfather more closely. Could it be he was interested in Gram? They both went to the seniors class at church on Tuesday mornings and served on several committees together. Was there romance in the air? Sara tried to stifle a small chuckle.

"What? Did you say something, Darlin'?"

She shook her head. "I was just agreeing with you."

The phone rang and Sara went to answer it, moaning inwardly at the sound of her mother-in-law's voice on the other end.

"Sara dear, did you get the teddy bears delivered safe and sound?" Nora asked.

Sara knew that wasn't the reason her mother-in-law had called, but she went along with it. "I did. They were a big hit too."

"That's good, Dear. I heard something today."

"Oh? What did you hear?" Nora was always on top of anything new that happened around town. She made it her business to know everyone else's. Sara admonished herself for her unkind thoughts, but they were true. Nora seemed to keep up with everyone and everything without having to leave the ranch.

"Jake is back in town."

"Yes, I know."

"Oh?"

"He came in while I was at Gram's picking up the bears she made."

"Humph. I guess he decided he needed some help with that child."

"That child's name is Meggie, Nora, and she's adorable. I'm sure Jake could use some help. He's had a great loss to deal with, as well as trying to be both mother and father to a baby." Sara was surprised at how defensive she sounded, but sometimes Nora's attitude really got to her.

"Well, yes, I guess it has been hard on him. But you've gotten through worse, Dear."

Sara looked up to see her grandfather watching her. She rolled her eyes, signaling that Nora was giving her opinion as always. "Was there anything else, Nora? We were eating dinner."

"Oh. Well, I wanted to see if you were free for lunch tomorrow."

The teddy bears were delivered. Sara couldn't come up with another excuse. She sighed silently. "Of course, Nora."

"Good. I'll meet you at Deana's at noon then. Unless you'd like me to pick you up?"

"No, I have some errands to run afterward. I'll just meet you there."

"All right, Dear. You have a good evening."

"You too, Nora."

Sara hung up and sat back down at the table. "I do care about Nora, Grandpa, I really do. And I know she's lonely. But sometimes she just makes me feel . . . smothered."

"Honey, you're a sweet and giving woman. But you're going to have to be careful that you don't let Nora try to run your life."

"She's already trying to do that, but I'm not going to let her. I just don't want to hurt her."

Grandpa got up to refill his bowl. "I know you don't, Sara,

but she can't cling to you forever. You have your own life to get on with."

"I know." Somehow getting on with that life had seemed easier last night than it did right this minute.

❧

Meggie entertained everyone at supper that night. She grinned and cooed at her uncle Luke and cousin John. Jake held his breath, waiting for her to throw something at one of them, but she was on her best behavior.

"Look, look, did you see that grin she gave me?" Luke asked.

"She's a beauty, Jake," John said. "You'll have to beat the guys off with a stick when she gets to be a teenager."

"Hey, now. Let's not rush things." Jake watched as his daughter soaked up the attention like a sponge in water and knew he'd made the right decision in moving back. Meggie needed to know her family. Luke and John had fought over who got to hold her, feed her, and wipe her face ever since they'd gone upstairs with him to get her.

She'd been crying at the strange surroundings until Jake walked into the room. Then she'd given him that smile that always made his heart turn to mush, held out her arms to him, and said the most beautiful word in the world: "Dada." He'd lifted her out of her bed and gathered her close before turning to introduce her to her uncle and cousin.

When she'd seen Luke and John, she'd plopped her thumb in her mouth and laid her head on his shoulder, shy at first. But after they'd acted like a couple of two year olds trying to get her attention, she'd finally rewarded them each with a smile.

When Luke held out his hands to her and she went right to him, Jake felt much the same as he had when he saw her in Sara's arms. Abandoned. He shook the feeling off as he saw Luke's joy in holding his niece and Meggie's obvious love of the attention. That was why he had come back. For Meggie to have the family connections he'd grown up with. Now as he watched Luke, John, and Gram try to win his little girl's heart, he realized how much he'd missed being around his family. Resentment toward Wade flared up, and Jake worked to smother it. Wade was gone. What kind of person resented a dead man?

"All right!" John's exclamation brought Jake out of his thoughts.

After checking her cousin out all through supper, Meggie had finally lifted her arms to John. Jake cleaned her face and hands, unbuckled her highchair belt, and watched closely as John picked her up.

"I have held a baby before, Jake," John said, lifting Meggie out of the chair. "I know how to do this."

"Guess I'm a little overprotective," Jake admitted.

"Maybe just a little," John teased. "Now let me enjoy her. It took me long enough to get her to come to me."

"None of you have Sara's touch," Gram said. "Meggie took to her right off."

And they'd looked so natural and content; it'd made him almost jerk Meggie out of her arms. Jake couldn't shake the look in Sara's eyes out of his mind. He had to talk to her, try to explain that he hadn't known she'd lost her baby.

"We may not have a woman's touch, but we got Meggie to take to us, just the same," Luke said. "Let's take her into the living room and give her those toys we brought, John."

Jake followed them, glad for the diversion. "Going to spoil her already, are you?"

"That's what uncles and cousins are for, right, Gram?"

Chuckling, she joined them in the living room. "That's right, but Grammies get to spoil them most of all."

"Uh-oh, I can see I have a whole new set of problems moving back here."

Luke slapped him on the back. "You haven't seen anything yet, Brother."

≥

Sara remembered to call Gram before she started cleaning the kitchen. Her heart thudded with each ring. *Please, please don't let Jake answer the phone.* When Gram answered, Sara hoped her sigh of relief wasn't audible. She quickly told the older woman how well the teddy bears had gone over and asked how Meggie was settling in.

"She's having a great time, Sara. Luke and John came over and brought her some toys. I wish you could see all these grown men falling all over themselves trying to get that baby just to smile at them."

Sara laughed. "I bet that is a sight." She could hear exuberant noises in the background and wished she could see them all playing with Meggie.

"I think it's just what they both need. To be around family."

"I'm sure it is, Gram." It was a wonderful family and one she was proud to be part of, if only by marriage. She hoped she could stay close to them all with Jake back.

"Sara dear, I . . ."

"What is it, Gram?"

"Well, I told Jake about you losing the baby. We hadn't told him because of all he was going through at the time."

"It's all right, Gram. I understand."

"I think he feels real bad that he didn't know."

"There's no need for him to. Don't you worry about it."

"Well, you stop by anytime you need a baby to hold, you hear? And don't forget about Sunday night supper."

"Thanks, Gram. I will, and I won't forget. Grandpa wouldn't let me."

The older woman chuckled. "He'd better not. Good night, Dear."

"Night, Gram." Sara placed the receiver back on the phone and began cleaning the kitchen on autopilot. She was sure Gram was right that being around family would help Jake and Meggie. Melissa had had no living relatives, and the only family Meggie had was Jake's. That little girl needed to grow up being close to them. Everyone should know they had a family. Sara didn't know what she would have done after her parents died if it hadn't been for her grandparents taking her in and loving her.

She hoped being back with his family would take that haunted look from Jake's eyes. He looked so lost and alone. She did the only thing she could do for him. She prayed. *Dear Lord, I don't pretend to know Jake's relationship with You, but please help him heal. Please let him and Meggie make a good life here. In Jesus' name. Amen.*

Sara put a pot of coffee on and sat down to call the rest of the women who had made teddy bears. Everyone was thrilled that the bears had gone over so well and promised to have more ready in a month.

She took coffee to Grandpa and joined him in watching a rerun of *Happy Days*.

"Did you remember to call Ellie?" Grandpa asked during a commercial.

"I did. She reminded me about Sunday night supper."

"Did you tell her we wouldn't miss it?"

"I didn't think I had to. I just told her *you* wouldn't let me forget it."

Grandpa chuckled. "You were right. I do look forward to her supper all week."

Was it the suppers or Gram's company that Grandpa looked forward to? Sara admitted to herself that she might worry if Grandpa showed signs of being sweet on any other woman. But she would only rejoice if those two dear people cared for one another. She was going to have to watch the two of them closely Sunday night.

When the sitcom was over, she went into the kitchen and made a batch of Grandpa's favorite cookies. He'd fixed supper for the two of them; the least she could do was keep the cookie jar filled. She wasn't surprised to see him enter the kitchen just as she took out the first sheet of chocolate chip cookies.

"Mmm, those sure smell good." He got a glass and poured them both a glass of milk. "You spoil me, Honey."

He took a bite of warm cookie. "You make them just like your grandmother did. That woman sure could cook."

"Yes, she could. Gram's a pretty good cook too."

Grandpa nodded. "She sure is. Good woman, Ellie."

Sara smiled. "She's one of the best."

"Watching a toddler is going to keep her hopping, that's for sure." Grandpa changed the subject. "But I know she's thrilled to have that baby close."

"She was glowing this afternoon. But I think this must have been a fairly sudden decision. Jake said he didn't give much notice. I'm sure if he'd been planning it for any length of time, he would have let the family know."

"Ellie would have said something if she'd known."

"Oh, I'm sure she would have. Having a baby around is going to be good for the whole family. You should have heard the laughter coming over the phone lines earlier. From what Gram said, I think Meggie's uncle Luke and cousin John are already in love with her."

"I'll have to get over there to see her soon." He paused. "You're all right, aren't you, Honey? I mean with Jake coming back and all. . . ."

"Why wouldn't I be?"

"Well now, Darlin', I seem to remember you doing your share of crying over him years ago."

"That was a long time ago, Grandpa." Sara didn't want to tell him that since seeing Jake, those days seemed closer somehow.

339

The night Jake had been late coming home to celebrate her birthday and had caught Wade trying to comfort her with a kiss had suddenly become very vivid. She could remember Jake yelling and accusing her and Wade of seeing each other behind his back. She'd tried to explain, but Jake wouldn't listen. He'd turned on his heel and walked out of her life.

She got up to take the next tray of cookies out of the oven and bent to kiss the top of Grandpa's head. "Don't worry about me. That was all a lifetime ago."

"I'm not going to worry. With all that you've come through this last year, I don't think there's much you can't handle now."

"Thank you, Grandpa." His vote of confidence buoyed her spirits. It was the way she'd felt when she'd left home this morning. Somehow with all that'd happened during the day, she'd lost the joy she'd started out with.

Grandpa ate one more cookie and got to his feet. "I think I'll go up and read awhile. Don't you stay up too late, you hear? You'll need all your wits about you for that lunch with Nora tomorrow." He chuckled as he headed out of the room.

Sara couldn't stop herself from joining in. He was right. Tomorrow would definitely be a challenge. "Night, Grandpa. I love you."

"Love you too, Darlin'."

Sara took the last batch of cookies from the oven, washed the baking dishes, and put everything away. She was still too keyed up to call it a night and decided to enjoy the early spring weather once more. As she opened the front door, her feet suddenly froze in place. Her hand flew to her throat.

Jake was standing there, his Stetson in one hand and the other raised to knock at the door. "Sara, I'm sorry. I didn't mean to frighten you. I saw your lights on and . . . um, could we talk a minute?"

Sara released the breath she'd been holding. "Of course.

Would you like to come in?" Her heart did a tap dance. What did he want to talk about?

"No, that's all right. I won't take much of your time." He took a step back and leaned against the porch rail, crossing his booted feet.

Sara slipped outside and leaned back against the screen door. Did he feel as tense around her as she did near him? The silence thickened until she could stand it no longer. "Are Gram and Meggie all right? Nothing is wrong, is it?"

"They're fine. Gram was watching the news when I left, and Meggie is asleep. For the night, I hope. Meggie loves all the attention she's been getting, but everything is new to her."

"Your family will help her adjust to the move in no time, Jake. They're wonderful—I don't know what I would have done without them." Something inside her whispered it was Jake who needed them badly now.

"Yeah, they are. Except they didn't tell me. . . ." He looked down at his feet and back up again before his brown gaze settled on her face. "Sara, I'm sorry for appearing so unfeeling this afternoon. I didn't know about the baby you lost. I'm so very sorry. . . ."

"Jake, it's all right," she said softly. "You had your own pain to deal with. This evening Gram told me that they hadn't told you."

"I wish I'd known."

Sara nodded. She could hear the sincerity in his voice. "I know."

"Wishing doesn't change much, does it?"

She knew he was talking about more than the fact that no one had told him about her baby. "No, it doesn't."

Jake looked as though he was going to reach out to her, but then he straightened and turned to go. He cleared his throat and turned back to face her once more. "Guess I'd better get back. Meggie may wake up and be frightened in a new place and all."

"Okay." The awkwardness between them squeezed at Sara's heart. "Thank you, Jake."

He put his hat back on and tipped it slightly before he turned and headed down the steps.

Sara watched him walk to his car, and something about his slumped shoulders reached out to her. The sorrow surrounding him was almost tangible. Her heart went out to him, for she knew the feeling well. But she knew where to turn when those moments of utter misery threatened to drown her. Tears gathered in her eyes. *Dear Lord, please help Jake the way You've helped me.*

She turned to go back inside. Sitting out in the cool night air no longer held any appeal. She'd only think about other times she'd sat on this same porch, in that same porch swing . . . with Jake.

She wasn't going to let herself think about the past. Not about the bad times—or the good. No, she wasn't ready to dredge it all up. Jake was right: Wishing wouldn't change a thing.

$\mathcal{J}$ ake looked down at his sleeping daughter. Dark hair curled around her little face. Every few seconds, she sucked the tiny thumb in her mouth. The other hand clutched a stuffed toy. Her soft, even breathing was music to his ears. He could not imagine life without Meggie. How did Sara find the strength to go on day after day? She seemed to have come to terms with it all, but he didn't know how.

He covered Meggie up and quietly left the room, leaving a nightlight glowing and keeping the door cracked. Making his way downstairs, he let himself out the front door. Gram had gone up to bed shortly after he'd returned from Sara's. He didn't tell her where he'd gone, but he suspected she knew.

Jake lowered himself onto the porch steps and leaned back to look at the starry sky. He thought he'd feel better after apologizing to Sara, but he'd been wrong. Seeing her on the same front porch where they'd spent so much time only brought back memories best left buried.

But how was he going to keep such thoughts at bay now that they lived in the same town again? He hoped they didn't run into each other at every turn. How could he have forgotten that she was now a part of his extended family? Jake ran his fingers through his hair. Had he just blocked out all thoughts of Sara? Had that made it all easier on him?

A deep sigh escaped him. He shook his head and groaned. She'd looked wonderful tonight. Tendrils of hair had escaped from her french braid, making him want to reach out and curl a wisp around his finger the way he used to. He'd had to catch himself to keep from doing just that. And her eyes. How could eyes reflect such deep sadness and serenity at the same time?

There was a quiet peace about Sara that he wished he could find for himself. He would have liked to ask her about how she'd reached that point in her life, but he couldn't. There was a time he could have asked her anything, but not now. He'd felt so awkward around her; he could barely get out the few sentences he'd gone there to say.

Jake got to his feet. Maybe he should have waited for another day to talk to her, but he wouldn't have been able to sleep. He knew he'd changed a lot, but he couldn't live with the idea that she thought him totally insensitive after this afternoon.

Making sure the door was locked, he turned out the lights and headed for bed. Tomorrow he was going to call a Realtor. The sooner he decided whether to buy or build, the sooner he and Meggie would be in their own home. And the less likely he'd be to run into Sara.

❧

Sara glanced at her watch as she parked her car on Main Street. She'd gotten off to a slow start that morning and was going to be late for her lunch with Nora. Her mother-in-law hated tardiness, but it couldn't be helped.

She'd tossed and turned most of the night. Jake's return had shaken her, no doubt about it. There'd been a time when they could talk about anything. But that was then, and this was now, and nothing was going to change that fact. Still, she wished she didn't feel so on edge around him.

The tinkling bell above the door announced her arrival at the diner. Sara spotted Nora sitting in a booth and checking the time on her watch. She hurried over and quickly slipped into the seat across from her mother-in-law.

"I'm sorry I'm late, Nora. I didn't sleep well last night, and I just couldn't get going this morning."

She was rewarded with a half smile. "It's all right, Dear. Was there any particular reason you had trouble sleeping? You aren't coming down with a cold, are you?"

"No, I don't think so. I guess I was just too tired." Or too keyed up after Jake's visit. But she wasn't going to tell Nora that. She grabbed a menu and scanned the lunch specials.

"Well, you do keep yourself quite busy these days. You haven't been out to the ranch in several weeks."

Sara took a deep breath and smiled at her mother-in-law. "I'm sorry I haven't made it out there lately, Nora."

Sara was relieved when the waitress came to take their order, but she realized it was only a short reprieve.

The waitress had no more than turned her back when Nora got to the heart of the matter. "I really do wish you would move back to the ranch, Sara."

"And I wish you'd just move into town." Sara caught her breath as soon as the words left her mouth. She couldn't believe she'd actually said them out loud. She was just so weary of this conversation.

Nora sat up straighter and inhaled sharply. "Why would I want to do that? I have a perfectly beautiful home at the ranch. I can come into town whenever I feel like it, but the ranch is my home."

Sara nodded, knowing she should have kept quiet. "I just thought you might be happier here. There's more to do, you could see more of your friends—"

"I'm perfectly happy at the ranch. It's where I raised Wade. I don't want to move."

Sara reached over and patted Nora's hand. "My point exactly. I can understand that, Nora. I don't want to move, either," she said softly.

Nora jerked her hand from underneath Sara's. She took a sip of coffee and brushed at crumbs only she could see. "I see."

"I hope you do. Nora, you know you'll always be family to

345

me. You've been wonderful to me, and I love you. But Grandpa isn't getting any younger, and I want to be close by. It will be much easier on me when I resume teaching in the fall if I'm living in town. I—"

"There is no need for you to teach. Wade never wanted you to work, Sara. If you invest what he left you, you shouldn't need to work."

"Nora, I want to teach. When Wade was alive, I loved being his wife, but I never felt I had enough to do then, and I need to keep busy. I can't just sit around—"

"Like I do. Is that what you're saying?"

"Nora, no! I—"

A look from Nora silenced her as the waitress approached with their lunch. Sara was torn between relief and frustration when Nora changed the subject as soon as the waitress left the table.

"What are you bringing to Ellie's Sunday night?" Nora asked.

Caught off guard, Sara didn't want to tell her that she was trying to think of a way to avoid going to the regular Sunday night supper at Gram's. For as long as she could remember, Gram had invited family and friends to her home for supper after church on Sunday nights. But now, with Jake back in town, Sara felt the need to bow out. "I'm not sure."

"I think I'll have Cook bake one of her famous chile casseroles." Nora took a bite of her chicken-salad sandwich and chewed delicately.

Sara's appetite was diminishing rapidly as she thought about not being able to spend as much time with family as she liked. But the only way to avoid seeing Jake would be to distance herself from the whole family. It was his family, after all. She picked at the salad she'd ordered and tried not to think about it.

The bell over the door of the diner jingled several times, but it wasn't until she saw Nora's face flush that Sara took notice of who'd entered.

Luke Breland was striding over to the booth, with Jake slowly coming up behind him. Sara's heart started hammering in her chest.

"Aunt Nora, Sara! It's good to see you both." Luke gave them each a kiss on the cheek and motioned to Jake. "Look who showed up on Gram's doorstep yesterday."

The smile Nora gave Luke disappeared when she looked at Jake. "Jacob, I heard you were back in town with your daughter."

Jake looked irritated but bent to brush his lips across his aunt's cheek. "It's good to see you too, Aunt Nora."

Nora's face flushed at his slight admonition. "You decided you needed help, did you, Jacob?"

Sara was appalled at Nora's rudeness. "We all need help from time to time, Nora. I've had to have a lot of that myself."

"I decided it was time Meggie got to know her family," Jake said gruffly.

"Well, I just hope watching her isn't too much for Ellie. She's not getting any younger, you know." Nora calmly took a sip of her iced tea.

Sara couldn't believe Nora was treating Jake so badly. "Nora, you know Gram loves babies. And there are plenty of people around to help out if she needs it."

"Including you, I suppose?"

"Of course, including me." Sara couldn't resist adding, "And you too, Nora. After all, Meggie is your great-niece. I'm sure you'd be willing to step in if Gram needed you."

Nora coughed, almost choking on her tea, and Luke patted her on the back.

"Don't worry, Aunt Nora," Jake said. "I don't think you or Sara will be needed. I'm fully capable of taking care of my own daughter. And I'm sure John would understand if I worked at home."

He clapped Luke on the shoulder. "Speaking of work, we'd

better get those sandwiches we ordered and get back to it. I'll go see if Deana has them ready."

Sara watched him walk away and willed her heartbeat to return to normal. She looked up to see Luke smiling down at her.

"Thanks for the offer to help Gram with Meggie, Sara. I know it wasn't easy for Jake to realize he needed to come home. I sure don't want him feeling like he's putting Gram out."

"I'm sure Gram's loving every minute of it." Sara smiled back at Luke. "But I'll check on her later to make sure she's all right."

Luke bent and kissed her cheek once more. "Thanks, Sara. Good-bye, Aunt Nora." He joined Jake at the door, and they left without so much as a backward glance from Jake.

"Humph! That boy has a lot of nerve coming back here," Nora said as soon as the two men were outside.

"Nora! What is your problem with Jake? He's your nephew!" Sara might not be happy that she was going to run into him at every turn, but he had a right to make his home here as much as she or anyone else did.

"How can you defend his coming back home and just dumping his daughter on Ellie?" Nora asked stiffly.

"Nora, Sweet Springs is his hometown. And I saw Gram with Meggie yesterday. I can assure you, she doesn't feel dumped upon!" Sara looked up in time to catch Nora dabbing at her eyes with a tissue and immediately felt bad for upsetting her.

"I'm sorry, Nora. But it's not like you to be rude to people." At least not to their face, Sara thought. Nora's technique was usually much more subtle.

"I just think he's made a mistake. He's going to let everyone get used to having the baby around and then he'll decide he wants to move back to Albuquerque."

While Nora's reasoning sounded logical, Sara felt that the woman was reaching for any reason to excuse her attitude toward Jake.

"I'm sure they will just be glad for whatever time they have with Meggie. She's delightful."

"Yes . . . I'm sure she is," Nora said, sounding wistful.

Sara immediately felt ashamed of herself for being critical. Although Nora had never seemed that excited about the prospect of becoming a grandmother, Sara was sure her mother-in-law would have loved the baby had it lived. Her heart knotted in pain at the losses they'd both suffered. "Nora, I—"

"I'm sorry, Dear, but I really have to leave. I have a doctor's appointment," Nora said, easing out of the booth.

"You aren't sick, are you?" Sara asked, feeling even worse.

"Just a checkup. Since Doc Edwards married Hilda and retired, I haven't bothered to find a new doctor. But several people have told me that the new doctor in town is good, and you never know when you might need medical care. So I made an appointment. If I think he's any good, I'll have Doc's office send my records to him," she explained, pulling a wad of bills from her purse and laying them on the table. "That should take care of lunch. If not, I'll pay you later."

Sara stood and gave Nora the quick, impersonal hug she seemed to expect but not like. So much for having a nice, calm lunch with Nora, she thought as she watched the woman hurry out the door. She sat back down and pushed what was left of her salad away. What little appetite she'd managed to hold on to was now totally gone.

"Sara, you look like you could use a friend and a fresh cup of coffee." Deana stood with the coffeepot in one hand, two cups in the other, and a smile on her face.

Sara summoned up a smile of her own. She and Deana had been good friends since high school, and Deana could read her all too well. "You couldn't be more right. Can you join me?"

Deana glanced around the diner and motioned to the waitress that she was taking a break. She slid into the side of the booth

Nora had vacated, pushed aside the empty plate, and poured them both some coffee.

"Mmm. Feels good just to sit down. Some days I wish Mom hadn't given me this diner when she got married. I have a whole new respect for that woman, though. She raised us all by working really, really hard. I never realized just how tough it was to run this place until I took over." Deana took a sip of coffee.

"Have you heard from her and Doc lately?"

Deana nodded. "They're camping up in Colorado. She said they'd be coming home in a week or two. I'm ready. I miss them when they're gone months at a time."

Sara nodded and stirred her tea.

"But I didn't take this break to talk about Mom and Doc."

"No?"

"No. I came because you're looking a little forlorn. And I want you to tell Aunty Deana what has you so down in the dumps."

Sara chuckled and shrugged. "A little of this, a little of that. I was curt with Nora because she was rude to Jake, and now I feel bad. I don't know why I felt I needed to take up for him anyway."

"Maybe because it was the right thing to do?" Deana propped her chin in her hand and waited for Sara to answer.

"He just looks so . . . adrift, you know? And I don't know why Nora seems to get so edgy when his name is brought up. But then I got to thinking that maybe it has something to do with his child being all right, while I lost her grandchild."

"Now that kind of thinking is bound to make you feel bad. Quit looking for excuses for Nora's rudeness, my friend. Far as I can tell, she's never needed a reason to be rude. She just is."

Sara tried but failed to contain the chuckle that erupted.

Deana laughed along with her. "Now that's more like it. Don't you let Nora make you feel bad, Sara."

Sara sighed. "I just don't like to upset her."

"Honey, anyone who doesn't think like Nora or agree with

everything she says and isn't at her beck and call upsets that woman. You of all people should know that by now."

"But she's so lonely. And . . . I still feel it was—"

"Sara, the wreck was *not* your fault. You were pregnant. You had a craving for ice cream at ten o'clock at night. You and Wade went to get some. Thousands of expectant parents do the exact same thing every night."

"I know, Deana. I really do know that. It's just that Wade was Nora's only son, and now that he's gone, I feel responsible for her. But she wants me to move back out to the ranch, and I just can't do that."

"Nor should you. Nora can't live your life for you, or hers through you. You are here for her, you care about her, but you have to get on with your life. Personally I never knew how you stood living out there with her when Wade was alive. I don't think I could have done it."

Sara was relieved when the bell on the door jangled, announcing more customers. She didn't want to lie and say it'd been easy living at the ranch, but she didn't want to sound disloyal to her husband's mother, either.

Deana sighed and slid out of the booth. "Break's over. Got to get back to the kitchen."

Sara gathered her purse and prepared to leave. "You take it easy, Deana. I'll talk to you later." She paid the waitress and headed out the door to her car.

So far the day wasn't going as planned. The lunch with Nora had been anything but calming . . . especially after Jake and Luke came into the diner. Sara still couldn't believe how protective of Jake she'd felt. Nora had no reason to be so rude to him. He was her nephew, and he'd suffered a loss in the past year too. How could she have acted so unfeeling toward him?

And why do I feel I have to take up for him at every turn? He's a grown man and perfectly capable of fighting his own battles. He could probably hold his own with Nora better than I could, anyway.

Sara pulled out of the parking space and headed for the grocery store. It was just that he seemed so unlike the Jake she used to know. He was so serious and aloof. And there was a look in his eyes that Sara couldn't name or forget. *O Lord, he needs You so much. Please ease his pain. Little Meggie needs him to be the happy, loving person he used to be.*

Sara sighed as she pulled into the parking lot of the grocery store. She wanted to help Jake, she really did. But all she could do was pray for him, knowing the Lord would listen.

❧

Jake took the last bite of his cheeseburger and crumpled up the sack it'd come in. He aimed and threw, hitting the trash can at the side of John's desk.

"Good shot!" Luke whistled. "You been practicing trash ball a lot, Brother?"

Jake chuckled and shook his head. "I was aiming for Aunt Nora's backside. That woman never has liked me."

John laughed. "Aunt Nora? What did she do now?"

"She was in Deana's when we went to pick up lunch." Luke crumpled his own bag and threw it away. "Wasn't too nice to Jake. Downright mean, if you ask me." He leaned back in one of two leather chairs facing John's desk.

"Nora never has been known for her sweetness."

"I shouldn't let her bother me," Jake explained, "but she made it sound like I just dumped Meggie in Gram's lap." He sat down in the empty chair and raked his fingers through his hair.

"Sara took up for you, though," Luke said. "And we all know Gram can speak for herself. She'll let you know if it's too much for her."

"Sara took up for you?" John whistled. "She rarely takes up for herself around Nora."

"Good thing she moved back in with her granddad after Wade died," Luke added. "Nora would love to call all the shots in Sara's life now." He stood and stretched. "I've got to get back to the ranch, boys. Uncle Ben should be calling me to let me know about the new livestock he bought. Let me know if there's anything I can do to help you get settled in, Jake. It's good to have you home, no matter how Aunt Nora feels about you." He chuckled on his way out the door.

John turned to Jake. "It is good to have you back. Don't you let Nora bother you."

"No, I won't," Jake assured his cousin. "I do want to make sure taking care of Meggie isn't too much for Gram, though. Mind if I take off early? I need to pick up some things at the store for Meggie, and—"

"Jake, you can take all the time you need. I'm just glad you finally agreed to come into practice with me. But there's no hurry. Get your bearings; get sweet Meggie settled in. If you feel you have to, you can take some files home to familiarize yourself with our clients, but you'll get to know them all soon enough. If you hadn't agreed to move back, I'd still be handling it all myself, anyway."

Jake nodded. Maybe he had been in too big a hurry to start working with John. There was no reason he couldn't get Meggie settled in a little better before he started working. "Thanks, John. I think I could use a little time to adjust to being back. And I don't want anyone thinking I can't take care of my own child."

John joined him at the door of the office and slapped him on the back. "Jake, no one is going to think that. After all, you've been taking care of her real well since Melissa's death. You turned down all kinds of help then. Don't let Aunt Nora get to you."

"Thanks, Cousin." Jake felt his tension begin to ease. "It's good to be home."

"And even better to have you here. Kiss Meggie for me."

Jake nodded and grinned. "Now that I can do."

❧

Sara pulled out the list she'd made that morning and grabbed a buggy. She wanted to make Grandpa his favorite meal as a way of thanking him for just being there. If he hadn't owned a home in this town, would she still be out at the ranch, living under Nora's thumbnail? Sara did care about Wade's mother, but there was no way she could live with her, and she hoped Nora would stop asking after today.

Sara's mood improved quickly once she was in the store and running into first one and then another smiling face. Mrs. Mead gushed about how happy she was the bears had been a hit and thanked Sara for coming up with the idea. Ida Connors hadn't helped with the bears the first time around, but after hearing how well they went over, she offered to help with the next batch.

Sara had put the lunchtime episode out of her mind by the time she'd picked up the ingredients for the meatloaf. Smiling, she turned down the next aisle and headed to the checkout lane, picturing the smile on Grandpa's face when he saw what was for supper. She would have plowed right into Jake's buggy if he hadn't swerved to the other side of the aisle.

Sara's hand flew to her mouth as she realized she'd almost hit him. "Jake! I'm sorry. Obviously I wasn't looking where I was going."

"It's all right, Sara. I looked up just in time. We seem to be running into each other today."

Sara noticed the buggy was full of disposable diapers and an assortment of baby food and snacks. There was something endearing about such a masculine man shopping for a baby with ease. "Is Meggie settling in all right? I was going to check on her and Gram this afternoon."

"She's settling in fine. And there's no need for you to check on them. John and I decided to slow down my return to work for a little while, so you can assure Nora that I won't be taking advantage of Gram."

"Jake, I—"

"I'm sorry, Sara. That was uncalled for. I guess I'm still stinging from Nora's remarks. Thank you for . . . coming to my defense earlier."

Sara nodded and tried to hide the sudden hurt she felt that he obviously didn't want her helping Gram with Meggie. It was probably for the best, but it still stung. "It's all right, Jake. I'm sorry Nora was so rude."

"It's not your fault. I hope she didn't give you too hard a time about taking up for me."

"She'll get over it." Sara saw the first hint of a smile from Jake.

"That's what I figured," he said. "But I don't want to give her anything to fuel that tongue of hers. I'm going to make this my home again whether she's happy about it or not."

"I know the family is glad to have you home, Jake. Gram is thrilled." She just wished she didn't feel so unsure of herself around him. It was a feeling that seemed to deepen each time she saw him.

"I want Meggie to know her family," Jake continued.

"She should. It's a good family to know."

Jake nodded. "Yes, it is."

Sara didn't know what to say next.

Jake found his voice first. "I'd better get going and let you finish your shopping."

Sara was almost relieved to be able to put her cart in motion. "I do need to get supper started. Tell Gram I said hi and give Meggie an extra hug for me."

"I will."

"Bye, Jake."

"Bye, Sara," Jake said as he rounded the corner.

Sara paid for her purchases and headed for her car. No, life wasn't going to get any easier with Jake back in town.

$\mathscr{S}$ ara crumbled crackers, chopped onion and bell pepper, and grated carrots, while trying to banish thoughts of Jake from her mind. Adding some of each ingredient a little at a time, she mixed them with a combination of ground beef and bulk sausage before adding the seasonings, eggs, and tomato soup. She was concentrating so hard on keeping her thoughts off Jake, she didn't hear Grandpa slip up behind her.

"Smells good in here already." He looked over her shoulder. "Meatloaf! How did you know that's what I've been hungry for?"

She had to chuckle. "It was a pretty good guess. You're always hungry for meatloaf, Grandpa."

"Just yours, Honey. You make it just like your grandmother did. But I have to admit, I like yours even better with that cheese you tuck inside."

"Thanks. That's quite a compliment." Sara continued to mold the mixture into a loaf, leaving some to the side and hollowing out the center. She then filled it with grated cheese and covered it with the remaining meat mixture. Grandpa was right. It did smell good even before it was cooked.

Sara slid the loaf pan into the oven and added two foil-wrapped potatoes alongside the pan, before turning to her grandfather. "Should be ready in about an hour. Want a glass of iced tea? We could sit out on the porch for awhile."

"Sounds good to me," Grandpa said. But he turned her toward the door. "You go on out and I'll bring the tea. You look a little frazzled."

"Am I that obvious?" At her grandfather's grin, she shrugged and chuckled. "Okay, I'll meet you out front."

Setting the swing in motion, Sara closed her eyes and tried to relax as she swung back and forth. She was going to have to learn how to deal with an unhappy Nora *and* with running into Jake again. She simply had no choice in the matter.

She prayed silently, asking the Lord to help her deal with the changes that Jake's return would cause. Sara knew the Lord would help her through it all. She just had to give it over to Him. With the acknowledgment that He still was in control, the tension she'd felt all afternoon began to drain away.

"You had lunch with Nora, didn't you? Is that what had you uptight?" Grandpa asked as he let the screen door slam behind him. He handed her a glass of tea and sat down in the wicker rocker across from the swing.

Sara nodded. "It sure contributed to it. I upset her, and I didn't want to." She took a sip of tea.

"Oh? Want to tell me about it?" He settled back in the rocker.

"Jake and Luke came in while we were there, and Nora was just plain rude to Jake. She practically accused him of dumping Meggie on Gram, and I found myself taking up for him."

"No!" Grandpa shook his head and chuckled. "Nora probably wasn't too happy about that."

"Especially not after I'd told her I didn't want to move to the ranch."

"Well, Darlin', you did the right thing on both counts. You don't want to move back to the ranch, and she shouldn't have been rude to Jake."

"I even found myself offering to help, if Meggie got to be too much for Gram."

"I'm glad to hear it, Darlin'. I went to see Ellie today. You were right. Meggie is adorable. And she's a handful." He smiled. "She kept us both busy until Jake showed up."

"I think he's afraid she might be too much for Gram."

Grandpa leaned back and started rocking. "Well, Ellie isn't going to admit that she might be, but I'm sure relieved that Jake isn't going to work full time, just yet. I'm afraid keeping Meggie on an everyday basis might just be a little too hard for her."

He shook his head and grinned. "She's pulling up to everything, trying to walk. Ellie says she can say a few words, too. She's something, that Meggie is."

"Yes, she certainly is." Remembering how wonderful it felt to hold Meggie in her arms, Sara almost wished Jake hadn't decided to take his time settling into the law practice. She'd have loved to help with the baby. But it wouldn't matter. Jake had made it perfectly clear that he didn't want her help.

&

"Jake, don't you take anything Nora says to heart," Gram declared. "Meggie and I will be just fine. And there are plenty of people around to help me, if I need them to." She poured them both some coffee and sat down at the table, where they watched Meggie stack blocks in a playpen set up by the back door. "That woman just doesn't know how to mind her own business."

Jake had to chuckle. "Gram, that woman is your daughter-in-law."

"I know. She wasn't always this way. Nora's turned bitter over the years since Mark was killed in Vietnam." Gram sighed and shook her head. "It's sad. The Nora he married was a kind and caring woman. Just don't you let her get to you."

"Don't worry. I'm determined not to let her bother me. I just don't want anyone else thinking that I've come home to dump Meggie on my family."

"Did Will make you feel that way before he left here?"

"No, he didn't." In fact, Sara's grandfather had been very nice, welcoming him back to Sweet Springs.

"And no one else, except Nora, is going to, either. Jake, you're being too hard on yourself. The whole town knows you've been taking care of Meggie ever since Melissa's death—and that you turned down repeated offers of help."

Jake leaned back in his chair and rubbed the back of his neck. "Actually, I think taking a break and getting settled will help both me and Meggie. The move is bound to unsettle her, and I'd like to make it as easy as I can on her."

"Jake, as long as you are in her life, that baby doesn't care where she lives. Children adjust much easier than we adults do. Take the break if you think it will do you some good. Just don't do it on my account."

Jake tried not to smile. His grandmother would never change. She wasn't about to admit that watching Meggie might be too much for her. But looking closely at her, there was no denying the fact that she looked plumb tuckered out.

"I thought I'd bring some of the files home and go over them here so that I'm familiar with our clients when I do start working full time with John. And I can contact a realtor. If I don't find a house I like, I'll just look into building one."

"You know you are welcome to live here as long as you need to."

"I know that, Gram. And I thank you. But the sooner I find Meggie and me a place of our own, the easier it will be to make Sweet Springs home again." He knew he'd made the right decision in coming back, but there were some things he was going to have to work at getting used to. Like running into Sara when he least expected it. And he hadn't expected it today. Not at the diner and especially not at the grocery store.

"Sara offered to help if you needed her. I think that upset Nora even more than my presence did. She looked like she'd sucked on a sour lemon."

Ellie shook her head. "You know, she's going to have to start living her own life one of these days."

"Sara?"

"No, Nora. Sara will get on with hers in time. She's young. But Nora seems to delight in trying to run everyone's life but her own."

"Luke and John said it took a lot for Sara to stand up to her today. Why is that? She's Wade's widow. She doesn't owe Nora anything."

"No, she doesn't. But Sara doesn't want to hurt her, either, Jake. Nora has clung to her since Wade's death, and Sara feels she's all Nora has left of Wade."

Wade. Jake wondered if he'd ever get over resenting the man who won Sara's heart. Chair legs scraped the kitchen floor as Jake got to his feet and tried to bury the past once more. He bent to pick Meggie up and cuddle her.

"Jake?"

He turned his attention back to his grandmother. "Yes, Ma'am?"

"Wade's gone. You're going to have to come to terms with the past. You know things aren't always what they seem."

"I don't have time to think about the past, Gram." He blew kisses on the back of Meggie's neck to hear her giggle. "Making a new life for myself and Meggie is about all I can handle right now. We're going to go play in the backyard. Why don't you take a nap before supper? I'll cook tonight. I can cook, you know."

"Humph! Jake Breland, I've never been a nap taker and I'm not about to take one at five-thirty in the afternoon. I wouldn't sleep a wink tonight. And I'm not ready to turn my kitchen over to anyone, either." Gram got up from the table and walked over to the refrigerator. "I'll call you when supper is ready."

Jake hoisted Meggie onto his hip and headed outside. "Come on, Sugar. I think we've been dismissed."

৵

Sara had just been congratulating herself for managing not to run into Jake for the last several days—until Lydia, John's mother, called inviting her to a welcome home cookout for Jake.

"I'm not sure, Lydia, I—"

"You don't have a thing that's pressing, and you know it, Sara. Now be a good girl and say you'll come. You don't get out enough, and besides, I'm not taking no for an answer."

Sara sighed. She knew Lydia meant what she said. She'd been after Sara to get out more for months. Besides, there'd be too many questions from the family if she didn't go. "I'll be there. Can I bring anything?"

"Just yourself and Will. We're just having hamburgers and hotdogs. And dessert, of course."

"Grandpa will love that."

"You'll both have a good time, you'll see."

Sure we will, Sara thought as she said good-bye and hung up the phone. She'd spent the last few days helping Grandpa with weeding and watering his garden. And she'd done some serious spring cleaning . . . anything to keep from going out and possibly running into Jake again. Seeing him only confused her.

This was the man who'd hurt her all those years ago by dumping her and then marrying Melissa several months later. Why did she feel this strong need to reach out to him now? He just looked so lost and alone the few times she'd seen him. He should be the last person she was thinking of, but she'd thought of little else since his return.

She'd wanted to call Gram and see how Meggie was doing several times during the day, but she'd been afraid Jake would answer the phone. Part of her resented the fact that she no longer felt she could just pick up the phone and call whenever she wanted to, and the other part of her wanted to take the easy way out by staying away. Seeing Jake wasn't easy, it wasn't easy at all.

Well, Lydia had taken care of all her good intentions. Now she'd have to show up or have everyone upset that she didn't.

Sara poured a glass of iced tea and took it outside. She'd asked Grandpa to take a pot of soup and a batch of cookies she'd made over to Gram's for her. She felt she was helping in some way by seeing to it that Gram had a break from cooking a meal here and there. And this way she'd get news of Meggie when he got home.

She just wished she'd get past this overwhelming urge to hold Meggie again. Tears threatened to well up, and Sara forced them back down. She wasn't going to cry. She wasn't going to let herself. She'd spent the better part of a year crying over her loss, and she wasn't about to start crying over what might have been.

She had to get up and get busy doing something, anything to get her mind off the past. She'd get dressed and go shopping, that's what she'd do. Maybe buying something new to wear to Lydia's party would get her out of her doldrums. It'd be fun, and surely Jake wouldn't be shopping in a ladies' dress shop.

Half an hour later, Sara came out of the dressing room wearing a colorful sundress. Catching a glimpse of someone, she sighed. This day wasn't getting any better. While Jake wasn't in the shop, Nora was.

"Sara dear. I thought that was your car outside. If I'd known you were going shopping, I'd have asked you to come with me. We could have had lunch together." Nora's gaze took in the long dress Sara had on. "That's a little bright for you, don't you think?"

It was better to laugh than cry, Sara thought as she chuckled. "I like it, Nora. It feels cool and summery."

"Are you buying it for anything special?"

"Lydia is throwing a party—"

"Yes, for Jake. I was invited too."

"Oh? And you're shopping for something new, too. That's nice, Nora."

"No. I am not buying anything new for that party. I really hadn't planned on going. I just saw your car outside and thought I'd stop in and see you."

"That was nice of you, Nora. The shopping trip was just spur of the moment. I haven't bought anything new in a long time."

Not since she'd bought her maternity clothes. Nora had been with her that day and insisted on buying several outfits for her. They'd had a very good time. Sara had forgotten how excited about the baby Nora had been. Now she wondered if the sadness in Nora's eyes was reflected in her own.

Sara forced herself to put thoughts of the past away. She couldn't let herself start thinking about the pain of the last year. She'd come too far. But still, she felt some of the weight of Nora's sadness. "Why don't you come have supper with me and Grandpa?"

"No, Dear. I have some errands to run. I'll leave you to your shopping." Nora pulled the shoulder strap of her handbag higher up and turned to leave. "I'll see you tomorrow night, though."

"Oh, good. You've changed your mind? You're going to go? Lydia will be so—"

Nora was out the door before Sara finished the sentence. Sara sighed and headed back to the dressing room. She wasn't making Nora very happy these days.

By the time the next evening rolled around, Sara wanted nothing more than to get out of going to the party for Jake, but Grandpa was excited about it. She dressed in the colorful dress she'd bought the day before and joined him downstairs.

"You look beautiful, Darlin'. It's time we had a party around here. You need a change of scenery."

Sara forced herself to smile. Grandpa loved parties, and she wasn't about to spoil his fun. "Thank you. You don't look too bad yourself. And you smell really good. You trying to impress anyone I know, Grandpa?"

"Just Meggie." He chuckled. "You know that little tyke has been playing hard to get. Won't let me hold her at all."

Mention of the baby's name made Sara realize how she was hoping to see her tonight.

≈

Jake took a deep breath as he followed Ellie up the walk. "Be a sweetie tonight, Meggie, and help me through this," he whispered in the baby's ear.

He hadn't wanted a fuss made over his coming home, but he didn't want to hurt Aunt Lydia and Uncle Ben, so here he was. He'd dreaded it all day. But there was no getting out of it. He just hoped that everyone was so enthralled with his daughter that he could blend into the background.

John answered the door and took Meggie and her diaper bag. Meggie was quite happy with all the attention, and Jake had to force himself not to take her back. Luke came up and led him away before he could protest.

"Meggie will be just fine, Jake. If she starts crying, you can rest assured John will find you."

By the time they'd made their way outside, Jake felt like he'd greeted most of Sweet Springs. Everyone was very nice and seemed genuinely pleased that he was back. He spotted Nora holding court, seated in a chaise across the yard, and was thankful that he didn't have to speak to her just yet. What was she doing here anyway? He knew she wasn't here to welcome him home. Run him out on the rails would be more like it.

Just then Aunt Lydia and Uncle Ben rushed up to him and welcomed him home. Lydia wanted to know where Meggie was and immediately went inside to look for her.

Luke helped to nudge Jake's memory by putting names to faces of old classmates and friends who came up to him, and after awhile, Jake began to relax and have a good time. But it wasn't until he spotted Will and Sara coming out the back door that he knew in spite of the past, in spite of trying to block thoughts of her out of his mind, in spite of the fact that she should be the last person he wanted to see, he'd been waiting to see if she would be here, all along. She looked out across the yard and her eyes met his. Sara smiled, and he was struck once more by the peaceful serenity in her eyes. She'd come to terms with the pain she'd suffered, but he didn't know how.

She looked wonderful. Her auburn hair was caught up on top of her head, and she was in an aqua and yellow sundress that looked wonderful on her. He knew from the way family and friends alike greeted her that Sara was special to everyone here. There was no getting around it. As much as he felt he needed to stay away from her, she was a part of his family and this town. Oh yes, he was going to have to find a way to deal with the fact that he was drawn to Sara as much now as he ever had been in the past.

᳀

Sara was glad so many people turned out for Jake's party, especially after the way Nora had treated him in the diner. When she glanced up and caught Jake looking at her, she smiled and her heart seemed to somersault all the way to her stomach when he smiled back. For a moment she wished she could change the past and go back to the time when they'd been best friends and shared everything—

"You look lovely, Dear," Nora said, appearing from nowhere. "I wish Wade were here to see you."

Looking into the cool blue eyes of her mother-in-law, Sara was reminded that there would be no going back to being friends with Jake. "Thank you, Nora. You look wonderful, too. I meant to ask you about your doctor's appointment. How did it go? Did you like the new doctor?"

"Humph! Dr. Richard Wellington is just a little too full of himself. I don't think I'll be going back after I get the results from my blood work."

"Oh, I'm sorry you didn't like him, Nora."

Meggie was brought outside just then, and she claimed the spotlight without even trying. Luke took her from John but wasn't allowed to keep her for long. Sara and Grandpa chuckled as Meggie reached out to first one and then another family member until she got to Gram. She was settling into this family life really quickly.

But when Gram sat down between Sara and Grandpa, still holding Meggie in her arms, Sara's fingers itched to take the baby and hold her once more. She barely noticed Nora's quick departure from her side.

"I think she's getting just a little tired," Gram said. The baby was looking around with almost a glazed look in her eyes. "Meggie, do you remember Sara?" Gram asked as she turned the baby toward Sara.

"Hi, Sweetness. Do you remember me?" Sara smiled at the baby.

Immediately, Meggie reached out to her. "Sawa."

Delighted that Meggie said her name, Sara wasn't sure if Meggie dove for her, or if she grabbed the baby. The next thing she knew, the baby was in her arms and had her head on Sara's shoulder.

"Oh, how sweet," Gram said. "She certainly does remember you, Sara."

Sara rocked the baby back and forth, loving the feel of her in her arms. She couldn't resist planting tiny kisses on her silky soft hair. Meggie was quickly claiming a piece of her heart.

"Well, would you look at that?" Grandpa asked moments later.

Gram smiled. "It seems as though Meggie was just waiting for your arms to fall asleep in, Sara."

Sara chuckled and tightened her hold on the baby. "I'll take that as a compliment."

"Oh, you should," Gram said. "I have to rock her for a long time before she goes to sleep. She'll fall right to sleep in Jake's arms, but not mine."

The bond Sara had felt that first day in Gram's kitchen grew even stronger as she sat and watched the party with Meggie in her arms. She knew she should lay the baby down, but she didn't want to let her go. Not yet.

Jake was beginning to tire of trying to keep names and faces straight. He wanted to find Meggie and make sure she was all right. He wasn't used to letting others take care of her, and he'd made himself stand and make conversation for over an hour now. It was time to find his daughter.

He started across the yard, but seeing Meggie in Sara's arms once more stopped him in his tracks. Sara was rocking back and forth, staring down at the baby. From the looks of it, Meggie was sound asleep. Gram and Will were looking on and talking to her.

His first instinct was to do what he'd done that first day in Gram's kitchen. Just take her from Sara and make a quick run for it. But he couldn't do that. Not here. He wasn't about to make a scene in front of his family and friends.

An invisible link seemed to be forming between Sara and his daughter, and he wasn't sure he liked it. Nor did he understand it. And he didn't have a clue what to do about it. He forced himself to walk casually up to the small group and smile. "She couldn't take any more attention, huh?"

Gram chuckled. "I guess not. She recognized Sara and reached out to her. It took her all of about a minute to crash."

"Doesn't take her long some nights. I guess I should be getting her home," Jake said, hoping his grandmother would agree, but knowing she wouldn't.

"It's early yet, Jake. We haven't even eaten yet. I'm sure Lydia will have a bed Meggie can sleep in for a while," Gram said. "Let me go ask." She was up and gone before Jake could stop her.

"Do you want to take her, Jake?" Sara asked softly.

Yes, he wanted to take her from Sara. There was something about the two of them so close together that pulled at his heart and created a longing within himself that he neither welcomed nor understood. But he was reminded of the look on Sara's face when he'd taken Meggie from her before, and he knew he wasn't going to let himself react that way again. The least he could do was let her hold his child for a few minutes.

"I don't want to jostle her too much. No need to wake her up," Jake said, although he was pretty sure nothing would wake Meggie up, as tired as she'd been lately.

Lydia came back outside with Gram. "I turned down the guest bed. I even have one of those bed rails to keep her from rolling off. She should be fine there. You know which room it is, Sara?"

Sara nodded and looked at Jake.

"Lead the way." He put his hand on her elbow to help her up from the bench she was sitting on and motioned for her to go first.

He followed Sara through the kitchen and up the stairs as she held his child in her arms. She turned to the right in the hall and they entered a small room with a twin bed that had indeed been turned down. A soft light lent a cozy glow to the scene.

Sara laid Meggie down, but the baby had a firm grip on her dress. She gently dislodged the little fingers, rolled the baby on her side, and rubbed her back. Meggie smiled in her sleep and plopped her thumb back into her mouth. Sara looked up at Jake and whispered, "Should I take her shoes off?"

Watching her with his child, Jake suddenly realized how very much Sara had lost and his heart twisted for her. He cleared his throat but still couldn't find his voice, so he just nodded.

He watched her fumble with one small shoe and then the other. Sara seemed to have forgotten he was there as she covered Meggie up with the sheet and caressed her cheek. "Sweet dreams, little Meggie."

She kissed her brow, stood, and backed away while he put the guardrail in place.

Jake bent over and kissed his daughter's cheek before turning back to Sara.

"Thank you, Jake." Her smile was real, but so was the sheen of tears in her eyes. Jake reached out and pulled her into his arms, wanting only to comfort her. Sara's head was on his shoulder, and they rocked back and forth for several minutes.

He wasn't sure what to say, he just wanted to make her feel better somehow. "Sara—"

Sara lifted her eyes to his and smiled through her tears. "Jake, I'm all right. Truly I am." Her voice broke for a moment before she continued. "It's just so good to hold a child."

Knowing he could never fully understand what Sara was feeling, Jake simply nodded, while he marveled that there was no bitterness in her eyes. "I'm sorry I took her away from you the other day."

Sara shook her head. "There's no need to apologize. I've seen you looking for her all evening. I think you're having a hard time trying to share her, and that's understandable. After all, it's just been the two of you since she was born."

That she read him so well came as no surprise to Jake. Sara had always understood him. But it was disconcerting that she still did after all these years.

His eyes strayed to her lips, and he found himself wondering if they tasted the same. Feeling the need to know, his head dipped and his lips lightly brushed hers. Sara responded. Her lips clung for a second, for two, before she pulled away.

Jake wanted to kiss her again, but his eyes met hers and he saw the confusion in them. What could he possibly be thinking? Sara was not in his future. She'd opted out of his past. Hadn't he learned anything over the years?

$\mathscr{S}$ara's heart charged into triple time as she stood there looking at Jake. What just happened here? She'd wanted Jake to kiss her. Wanted him to hold her. The touch of his lips on hers felt familiar and comforting.

What was wrong with her? How could it feel so right to be in his arms? It'd been over between them long ago. She'd loved Wade. How could she be so disloyal to his memory?

The look in Jake's eyes mirrored her own confusion. She wanted both to reach out to him and to flee. She chose to run. "I'd better check on Grandpa," she said, backing out of the room.

Jake cleared his throat and nodded. He turned back to Meggie. Sara saw him bend down and kiss his daughter again before she turned and hurried back downstairs.

Sara didn't realize she was holding her breath until she entered the kitchen and saw that in reality, only a few minutes had passed since she and Jake had taken Meggie upstairs.

Ben was on his way out the door with more hamburger patties to put on the grill. Lydia was slicing onions and tomatoes. She'd commandeered Nora into tearing lettuce leaves and placing them on a big tray. Other family members were busy with the small jobs that always made huge gatherings somehow work. No one seemed to have missed them, or so Sara thought until she met her mother-in-law's chilly glance.

"There you are," Nora said. "I came in the house looking for you, and Lydia put me to work."

Sara hurried over and began helping Nora. "I'll do that for you."

Lydia chuckled. "I thought you came in to help out, Nora. If you'd asked, I could have told you Sara was upstairs putting the baby to bed."

The sound of Jake's heavy footsteps came down the stairs. When he entered the kitchen, Sara willed herself not to look at him, concentrating instead on tearing lettuce.

"Thanks for the loan of the room, Aunt Lydia," Jake said. "If you hear her wake up, please call me in."

"Of course, Jake. She'll be fine," Lydia reassured him. "You go on outside and enjoy your party. We'll listen for her."

"Thanks for getting her to sleep, Sara." Jake stood in the middle of the room, appearing to be waiting for her to say something.

Looking up and meeting his eyes, she said, "You're welcome. It was a pleasure to have her in my arms."

Jake gave a brief nod before heading outside, and Sara watched him go, remembering the feel of being in his arms just minutes ago. It'd felt like coming home, like—

"Sara, are you going to stand there staring into space, or help me with this lettuce?" Nora arched an eyebrow at her.

Sara ducked her head and continued tearing lettuce. She tried unsuccessfully to keep the color from stealing into her face. She'd been reliving Jake's kiss, and now the guilt that she'd enjoyed it washed over her. Wade had been gone over a year now, but it didn't seem right to be attracted to another man—especially when that man was his cousin. Yet right or wrong, she was drawn to Jake.

One glance at Nora told her that her mother-in-law wasn't happy about the short time Sara and Jake had spent together upstairs. The woman's lips were pursed together. Frown lines gathered between her eyebrows. Suddenly, Nora's hand pressed against her chest and she closed her eyes.

Sara reached out and touched Nora's shoulder. "Are you all right?"

Nora shook her head. "I'll be fine."

"You're sure? You look a little pale."

"I think I may be coming down with something. I do have a headache and feel nauseous. I think I'll just get my purse and go on home."

"I'll go up and get your things, Nora," Lydia said, washing her hands at the sink.

"No, no! I can get them myself. I'll see myself out. You see to your guests." She hurried upstairs, leaving Lydia and Sara to stare at one another.

"I'm a little worried about her, Lydia. She hasn't seemed herself lately," Sara said.

"Maybe it's just stress. It's been a hard year for Nora," Lydia said. "I think I tend to forget that sometimes, she's just so . . . Nora." She shook her head. "I doubt I'd have been anywhere near as strong as she's been had I lost my only son."

"I think I'll go up and make sure she is all right," Sara said, wiping her hands. She ran lightly up the stairs and turned to the right to peek into Lydia's room where guests had been instructed to leave the items they didn't want to carry around all evening.

Nora wasn't in the bedroom. The bathroom door was ajar, and Sara could see she wasn't there, either. She came out of the room and glanced down the hall. Nora must have turned on the landing and gone out the front door. She'd call in a little while and make sure she made it home safely.

The door to the room Meggie was napping in was slightly ajar, and Sara quietly peeked inside. Surprise took her breath away. There, on her knees beside the bed, was Nora. Tears flooded Sara's eyes as she watched her mother-in-law reach out and gently smooth back the hair on Meggie's forehead. But when she saw Nora bend over to kiss the baby's cheek, Sara's hand quickly covered her mouth to quiet the sob that formed in her throat.

Knowing Nora thought she was alone, Sara quickly backed

out of the room and tried to calm herself. She must have made some kind of noise, though, because Nora's head turned sharply and she swiftly got to her feet and joined Sara in the hall. Sara's first instinct was to give Nora a hug, but her mother-in-law had never been comfortable with genuine demonstrations of affection or comfort.

"You might ask Lydia if she has one of those gates to put up at the door so that the baby doesn't fall down the stairs," Nora said brusquely as she started down the hall.

"Yes, yes, I'll ask her," Sara answered.

"She could crawl to the end of bed and get down," Nora continued. "If she got out of the room she could get hurt."

On the landing leading to both the front and the back of the house, Nora stopped Sara from turning to go back to the kitchen. "Meggie is a beautiful child. But Jake only came home to find a mother for her," Nora whispered.

"Nora, we don't know that. He just wants Meggie to be raised around his family."

Nora shook her head and whispered more urgently, "Mark my words. He hurt you once before, he'll hurt you again. Only this time there'll be no Wade to pick up the pieces." She pulled her purse strap over her shoulder and took the flight of stairs leading to the front door, leaving Sara standing on the landing, speechless and feeling the weight of her loss all over again.

Nora didn't need to remind her that Wade was no longer here. She lived with that knowledge every day of her life, always wishing she hadn't wanted that ice cream. Oh, she knew that the wreck wasn't her fault. A drunk driver had plowed into Wade's car. Still, she'd been the one craving ice cream, and that was the only reason they were in the car at ten o'clock that night.

Nora had never implied that she was to blame. But in the back of her mind, Sara could never quiet the voice that kept telling her that if she hadn't wanted that ice cream so bad, Wade and her baby might still be here. *O Lord, please help me. I thought I was doing so well.*

"Sara? Nora?" Lydia called from the bottom of the stairs.

"It's me, Lydia." Sara brushed away the tears that'd fallen and hoped Lydia wouldn't be able to tell she'd been crying in the dim light. "Nora just left. She was checking on Meggie and told me to ask if you have one of those gates for the door."

"Oh my. I certainly do. I totally forgot about that." Lydia bustled up the stairs, passed Sara, and led the way to the storage closet at the end of the hall. By the time she'd pulled out the gate, Sara had herself under control.

They both peeked in at the sleeping child while making sure the gate was snug against the door frame.

"Look at that. A thumb sucker. If I remember right, Jake used to suck his thumb, too," Lydia whispered. They started back to the kitchen.

Downstairs, Lydia poured them both a glass of iced tea and led Sara out onto the deck where Ben was grilling burgers and wieners. She handed her a plate. "You eat and go enjoy yourself, Darlin'. Enjoy life a little."

Sara forced herself to fix a plate and eat. She managed to mingle with friends and family for the rest of the evening, taking care not to join any groups standing around Jake.

※

Jake renewed acquaintances and re-bonded with family throughout the evening, all the while trying not to think of holding Sara in his arms and the kiss they had shared. Brief though it had been, it'd shaken him far more than he wanted to admit. He told himself he wasn't interested in starting up with Sara again, even if he could imagine that she might still care about him. All he wanted was to be able to raise Meggie in the same loving atmosphere he'd grown up in and make sure family was close by if anything should ever happen to him. That's all.

Yet when Sara came back outside with his aunt Lydia, Jake found his gaze seeking her out, in spite of the fact that he'd resolved to avoid her as much as possible. She'd looked so vulnerable putting Meggie down for her nap. And when he saw the tears in her eyes, he'd wanted to console her somehow. That's all. Just help her past that moment of sadness.

Now as their eyes met across the yard and Sara glanced away, he knew he'd only succeeded in making them both feel more uncomfortable with each other than they already had. When he realized she was trying to avoid him by joining only the clusters of people he wasn't part of, he tried to make things easier by leaving whatever group she headed toward. It was a cat-and-mouse game in reverse. The last thing either of them seemed to want was to catch up with the other.

Jake wondered which of them was more relieved when the party started to break up.

❧

Sara had never been so glad for a party to end in her life. Trying to avoid Jake at his own welcome-home party had been draining enough, but once they were home, Grandpa wanted to rehash the whole evening over hot chocolate. Thankfully, he did most of the talking so all she had to do was add an agreeable murmur here and there.

"Nora left early, didn't she? I was a little surprised to see her there at all."

"She wasn't feeling well. I meant to call her to make sure she got home all right." Sara glanced at the clock and decided it was too late to call.

"More than likely, she just came for appearance's sake and left as soon as she could. We both know she isn't too happy about Jake coming back home." Grandpa leaned back in his chair and brought his cup to his mouth.

"I don't understand that, Grandpa. She used to ask about him and Melissa at every family gathering."

"That could have been more from curiosity than any kind of concern. Nora doesn't seem to care about many people these days. Just you. And I do worry that she's going to keep you from building a new life for yourself."

"I'm not going to let that happen. But she is Wade's mother, and I do feel a responsibility to her."

"I know you do." He drained his cup and took it to the sink to rinse out. He turned back to Sara. "You know, I think Nora needs to make a new life for herself. She's still a nice-looking woman. If she'd just soften up a bit, she could probably attract a man."

"That'd be wonderful, Grandpa, except I've heard her say she didn't want another man in her life too many times." Sara joined him at the sink and kissed him on the cheek. "But it's a great idea. We'll have to be on the lookout for someone."

The older man patted her on the back and nodded his head. "I'll talk to Ellie about it. If we put our heads together, we're bound to come up with someone."

Sara smiled to herself. *Looks like he's come up with one more reason to see Gram.* She really was going to have to watch those two a little closer from now on. "Let me know who you two come up with."

He crossed the room and started upstairs. "I'll do that, Darlin'. I sure will do that."

Sara straightened up the kitchen and headed up to her own room. It'd been a very long evening. She did hope her mother-in-law was all right. If Nora wasn't in church tomorrow morning, she'd check on her first thing when she got home from the service. Maybe Grandpa was right. A man in Nora's life might perk her up. She'd been a widow a long time.

Sara prepared for bed, still wondering about the tenderness

376

she'd witnessed Nora showing Meggie at the party. She would have made a good grandmother. *And I would have made a good mother.* But neither was to be and she wasn't going to let herself slide into a self-pitying mode again. She'd spent quite enough time there.

There might come a day when she could think of starting a family with another man, but it wasn't now. Yet knowing that fact didn't keep thoughts of Jake at bay. Being in his arms for those few short moments had taken her back to a time when she'd felt completely at home there.

It was probably good that Nora had reminded her of how Wade had picked up the pieces. She'd been shattered the night of her birthday when Jake had accused her and Wade of seeing each other behind his back. He had walked up when Wade was giving her a casual kiss, assuring her that Jake would be there to wish her happy birthday soon. That was all it'd been, but Jake hadn't stayed around to hear an explanation. Instead, he'd flown into a rage and taken off.

She'd cried herself sick for weeks and even tried calling to talk to him. He was never in. Finally, Wade had gone up to college to talk to Jake. When he came back, it was with the news that Jake was getting married to someone else. Sara couldn't remember much of the rest of that year, except that Wade had always been there for her. He'd taken her wherever she needed to go, escorted her to all kinds of events, and helped her get over his cousin.

She'd come to love Wade in a whole different way than she'd loved Jake, and when he'd asked her to marry him, she hadn't hesitated. She'd said yes. There might not have been bells and whistles, but they'd had a comfortable relationship and a good marriage, and she missed him dearly.

Now she felt guilty, angry, and confused for being comforted by the very man who'd hurt her all those years ago.

❧

Jake tossed and turned all night. But it wasn't his old nightmare keeping him awake. He simply couldn't get Sara out of his mind. He threw off the covers and got out of bed. The sun was just coming up. He'd check on Meggie and go put the coffee on for Gram. It wasn't often anyone beat her up of a morning.

Meggie was already awake and playing with one of the stuffed animals in her bed. She looked up at him with that beautiful smile and reached out to him. "Dada!"

Nothing in this world felt as good as having his daughter in his arms. He changed her diaper and carried her downstairs to the playpen in the kitchen. After quickly putting the coffee on, he played hide-and-seek behind one of Meggie's big stuffed toys, while waiting for the coffee to brew. It'd just finished when Gram joined them.

"Well, this is a treat. Not often do I wake to the smell of coffee first thing in the morning." She crossed the room to give both Meggie and Jake a kiss on the cheek. "It's so nice to have you two here."

"I was hoping I'd beat you down." Jake kissed his grandmother on the cheek. "That's not easy to do."

Gram chuckled as she poured two cups of coffee and set his on the table. "I must have slept in this morning."

Jake sat down across from her and cradled the cup in both hands, savoring the rich aromatic smell before taking a sip.

"You haven't forgotten your promise, have you?"

"No, Gram, I haven't forgotten. I'll feed Meggie as soon as I get a cup of coffee in me and then go get her ready." It was Sunday, and he'd promised Gram that he and Meggie would go to Sunday school and church with her. As if he'd had a choice. Anyone who lived in Ellie Tanner's home went to church on Sunday.

He really didn't mind. Taking Meggie to church would be one less thing to feel guilty about, Jake realized as he prepared his daughter's oatmeal and juice, while Gram began working on their breakfast. He'd promised Melissa that if anything happened to her, he'd see to it that their child knew the Lord. And he wanted her to have a good relationship with God. Like he'd had before.

Watching Meggie try to feed herself took all of his attention. She did pretty well until he tried to help. Then she pulled back on the spoon, and oatmeal went flying. It kept him busy, just trying to keep everything from ending up on the floor.

Gram set a plate of bacon and eggs in front of him just as Meggie took her last bite.

"You eat your breakfast and I'll get Meggie dressed," Gram said, reaching to pick at his hair. "I think you'd better jump in the shower. Meggie got more oatmeal on you than on herself or the floor."

"Typical meal time with my daughter. Most of it ends up anywhere but inside her," Jake said, chuckling. He took Meggie from her high chair and handed her to Gram. "Thanks for your help, Gram. You'll know better what to dress her in than I would."

"You do fine, Jake. Meggie always looks adorable, don't you, Sweetie? Let's see. Do we need to wash your hair this morning?" She chuckled and checked Meggie's hair. "No, looks like Daddy got all the mess today."

Jake joined her laughter and watched as she and his daughter left the room. He quickly ate his meal and rinsed off his plate before hurrying upstairs to get in the shower. You had to act fast with oatmeal. It acted like cement if it sat in one place too long.

❧

When Sara and her grandfather took their seats in church that morning, she knew something was up. A bevy of females was clustered in the middle of the aisle.

The last person she expected to see in church that Sunday was Jake Breland. But he was sitting beside Gram, looking very ill-at-ease with all the attention he and Meggie were getting. Meggie, however, seemed to be eating it all up as she sat in her daddy's lap. She looked adorable dressed in pink and white gingham. Luke came in late, took one look at the crowd around his brother, grinned, and then backtracked to enter the pew from the other side. Aunt Lydia, Uncle Ben, and John seated themselves in the pew behind them.

It appeared as if most of the young single women were busy welcoming Jake and his daughter home. If Nora was right in her assumption that he'd come home only to find a mother for Meggie, Sara figured he'd have several to choose from. For some reason that thought didn't set well with her, but she told herself it wasn't jealousy.

Too bad Nora wasn't here to see how many women seemed to be interested in exploring that very subject. Sara made a mental note to be sure to check on her as soon as she got home from church.

Finally, one of the deacons stood at the podium and cleared his throat, trying to get everyone's attention. Sara halfway expected to hear an announcement about an eligible bachelor being back in town. She was glad Jake had come to church, though. She hoped Gram was wrong in thinking that Jake's relationship with the Lord wasn't what it should be.

Sara tried to keep her mind on the service. She joined in the singing and heard Jake's baritone joining in. She'd forgotten what a beautiful voice he had. Meggie kept looking at her daddy's lips move, as if she'd never seen him sing before. She clapped when the first song was over, bringing chuckles from those around her.

More than once during the service, Sara had to force her attention away from Meggie and back to the sermon. The regular minister and his wife, David and Gina Morgan, were away on a missionary trip and were scheduled to return later in the week. Gina was one of Sara's best friends, and the couple had been a source of great strength for Sara over the past year. She really missed them. Gina's father, Tom Edwards, filled in for David, giving a good message on turning one's life over to God each and every day.

When the worship service came to an end, Sara hoped Grandpa wouldn't stand around talking for too long. She hurried out to the foyer ahead of him. Much as she wanted to reach out to Meggie, she didn't want to deal with Jake.

Looking back into the sanctuary, she recognized there was no need to worry about running into Jake. He and Meggie appeared to be held captive once more. Sara hadn't had any idea there were that many single women attending church, and she tried to tamp down the flash of jealousy she felt seeing Jake be the focus of all of their attention. Fortunately she didn't have to sort out her feelings, because just then she was approached by one of the deacons, who asked about the teddy bear project.

As soon as she and Gramps got home, Sara kicked off her heels and sat down to call Nora. But Nora didn't appear to be in the mood to talk. No, she wasn't sick. No, she didn't want company. Sara sighed as she hung up. She just wished Nora would move into town. Uncle Ben ran the ranch from his place. There was really no need for Nora to stay out there. It would make it so much easier for her to check on her from time to time.

Sara finished up the roast she'd put on before leaving for church that morning, but her thoughts kept returning to Meggie and how adorable she'd looked sitting in Jake's lap.

Grandpa said the prayer before the meal and then filled his plate. "What did you think of the reception Jake got at church this morning?"

Sara had been trying *not* to think of it. "Nora told me he'd only come home to find a mother for Meggie. If that's the case, it looks like he'll have his pick."

Grandpa chuckled. "Just 'cause he's got a lot to choose from, doesn't mean any of them would be his pick, Darlin'."

"Well, I'm sure it's none of my business." Sara passed the mashed potatoes to her grandfather.

"None of Nora's, that's for sure." He took a bite of roast and sighed appreciatively.

Sara's appetite had disappeared. She just pushed the food around on her plate. Why did it bother her so much to see all those women converging on Jake and Meggie this morning? She was going to have to get a grip on the situation. Jake was a handsome man, and he was bound to start dating sooner or later.

"This is really good, Sara," Grandpa said.

"Thank you." Sara smiled across the table at her grandfather. He was always so careful to compliment her on her cooking. Grandma had trained him well.

"What are you going to make for Sunday supper at Ellie's?"

Sara moaned inwardly. She didn't want to go to the supper at Gram's tonight. She wouldn't be able to avoid Jake, and she wasn't ready to deal with making small talk with him.

"I'm not sure I'm going tonight, Grandpa. I haven't spent much time with Deana lately, and I thought I'd see if she wanted to do something." Deana loved Gram's suppers, too. Sara hoped she could talk her into taking in a movie instead.

"And miss Sunday night supper?"

His face looked so crestfallen, Sara had to chuckle. "You can go, Grandpa. I'll make that blueberry pie you like so well for you to take."

"Well, all right, but I wish you'd change your mind and go. You love those suppers with the family."

And she did. But they weren't going to be the same now that Jake was back. It wouldn't be long before the whole family picked up on how uncomfortable they both felt around each other. Then everyone would start to feel uncomfortable too. Sara wanted to avoid that as long as possible.

Her heart tightened at the thought of spending less time with the family she loved. She didn't feel she could call Gram just to chat anymore, and now she wasn't sure she'd ever feel comfortable at Sunday supper again. With Jake's return, changes were occurring much faster than she'd anticipated. Part of her wished he'd stayed in Albuquerque, and the other part wanted nothing more than a repeat of last night. A repeat of that moment of feeling she was where she'd always been meant to be. Held securely in Jake Breland's arms.

*W*ith Meggie napping in her playpen close by, Jake sat at the kitchen table shelling pecans for Gram to make pies for her Sunday supper. He wondered how he'd forgotten about Gram's suppers. As a child and young man it'd been one of his favorite things about Sundays.

He'd probably blocked it out during his period of self-exile. He'd been so unhappy ten years ago. Crushed by Sara and Wade's betrayal, marrying Melissa and trying to make their marriage work despite the way it began—it had all been much easier to handle from Albuquerque.

For years, he'd avoided family gatherings, telling his grandmother they were going to Melissa's parents for all the holidays. They had spent some time with her family, but then her parents had been killed in an airplane crash. By that time, he was so used to not being in Sweet Springs, he had felt no desire to come home for the holidays. On those rare occasions when he'd made plans to come back, he had made sure word got out early. It seemed that Wade wasn't anxious to see him, either. He and Sara were either gone or busy with something else, and the result was that they'd never had to deal with seeing each other.

Now Jake sat at his grandmother's kitchen table, wondering if Sara and her grandfather would be there for supper and feeling disloyal to the mother of his child for even thinking about Sara. The familiar guilt that he'd never loved Melissa as much as she loved him washed over him. He'd tried. He had learned to love her, and he truly did miss her, but he'd always been suspicious about the way their marriage started. When Melissa came to him and told him she was pregnant, he did what he knew he should. He took responsibility for his actions and asked her to marry him. And when she'd lost the baby a few weeks after their wedding, he'd kept his vows and promised Melissa they'd stay married and work to make it a good one, but in the back of his mind, there'd always been that question. Did Melissa trick him into marrying her? Had she ever been pregnant?

In spite of his suspicions, they had turned their marriage into a good one. Only Melissa had done most of the work that built their relationship, and Jake knew it. She'd been a good wife, and she would have been a wonderful mother to Meggie. He wished he could have loved her more. Now she was gone, and he could never go back and say the things she would have loved to hear from him.

Jake cracked another pecan, but his mind wasn't on what he was doing. He'd made so many mistakes. Oh, he'd tried to make things right. He'd taken responsibility for his actions and he'd asked the Lord for forgiveness. But he'd always felt he should do more to earn it, and now with Melissa gone, he never would be able to. All he could do was be the best father to Meggie that he could be. That he was determined to do. *Please, God. Let me do that right.*

"Tom had a good lesson today," Gram said, bringing him back to the present.

Jake nodded in agreement. "I didn't know Tom was the minister here."

"Oh, he's not. His son-in-law, David Morgan, is. He and Gina are due back from Guatemala this week some time."

"David Morgan? He's a preacher?" Jake remembered David Morgan from high school, but he'd never have thought his friend would become a minister.

Gram came over to the table and patted his shoulder. "He is.

One of the best I've ever heard, too. I'm sorry, Jake. We really didn't keep you up to date very well, did we?"

"Well, Gram, it's not all your fault. I didn't show much interest in what went on in Sweet Springs." He reached up and patted the hand that rested on his shoulder. "I'm sorry."

"You're home now, though. You'll catch up in no time." She looked into the bowl of freshly shelled pecans. "That's probably enough for now."

"You sure? I haven't had a piece of your pecan pie in years. I could probably eat a whole one by myself." Jake grinned at her.

"No way, big brother," Luke said, coming in the back door.

Both Gram and Jake shushed him, and Luke took care that the door didn't slam behind him. He crossed the room to kiss his grandmother's cheek. "If you get a pie to yourself, so do I," he said to his brother.

"Help Jake shell a few more pecans, and I'll make an extra pie for you both to share."

The brothers grinned at each other and started working on the pecans. "Meggie sleeping?"

Jake nodded toward the playpen over in the corner and glanced at the clock. "She should be waking up any minute now."

"All that attention at church must have worn her out," Luke teased and then dodged the pecan Jake threw at him.

"I know it wore me out," Jake admitted. "I didn't know there were that many single women in all of Sweet Springs."

He had noticed that Sara hadn't approached him and Meggie. She seemed to be avoiding him, which he knew was for the best. Still, it rankled. He hadn't been able to sort through his feelings from the night before, and right this minute, he wasn't in a hurry to figure them out.

"I know what you mean," Luke said. "And I sure didn't know they were all so hard up they'd be fighting over my brother."

Even Gram joined in the laughter that time. "There were quite a few young women around our pew today."

"Well, if you'd like a clear field, Luke, you can get the word out that I'm not interested."

"Nah, you can let them down all by yourself, big brother."

"I didn't know we'd raised you two to think so highly of your-selves." Gram stood facing the two men with her hands on her hips. "There were some fine young women in that group—some of whom might not want either of you, if they could hear the way you are talking right now."

"Aw, I'm just teasing Jake, Gram. You know how we are."

"Too bad some of those nice young ladies don't," she said, then shook her head and went back to her piecrusts, chuckling to herself every now and then.

෨

Jake wasn't aware he was looking for Sara until Will showed up that night after church without her. He heard his grandmother ask Will why Sara hadn't come, but he couldn't quite make out the answer from across the room.

He didn't welcome the sharp pang of disappointment he felt. What was wrong with him? His mind warned him to stay as far away from Sara as possible, but the rest of him ignored the signals and looked for her at every opportunity.

"What's with you, Jake?" John joined him in a corner of the large wraparound porch. "You look like you've lost your best friend."

He had, Jake thought, a long time ago. For that's what he and Sara had started out as. Best friends. Both orphaned at early ages, they'd found they had much in common, and they'd formed a close friendship. There was nothing he hadn't been able to talk to her about, until the night he'd found her and Wade kissing. He shook his head. "No, I was just thinking back to when we were all young and how so much has changed."

"We had some great times, didn't we? This is a great family to be raised in. And Sweet Springs is a good town to grow up in. I can't imagine living anywhere else," John said. "I don't know how you stayed away as long as you did."

Jake shrugged. What could he say? That he was too immature to handle seeing Wade and Sara build a life together? He couldn't do that to Melissa's memory.

But he did have some questions he'd like answers to. "John, why didn't you and Luke—anyone in the family for that matter—tell me Sara and Wade were seeing each other behind my back?"

Luke walked up just in time to hear the question and spoke up before John could say anything. "What are you talking about, Man? Sara was heartbroken when you married Melissa."

Jake shook his head. "No, she wasn't. She and Wade were seeing each other long before that."

"I think you're mistaken, Jake," Luke said.

"I saw them kissing!"

Luke and John looked at each other and shook their heads. "When was this?" John asked.

"On her birthday. I was late getting home. I'd had a flat tire."

Luke nodded. "I remember Sara was upset because you never showed up."

"But I did show up. And Wade and she were kissing."

Both Luke and John shook their heads. "I never even knew you were here," Luke said. "You went on back to school?"

"Yeah, I went back. I saw no reason to stay." Not then. But now, he knew he should have stayed to hear Sara out.

"Maybe Wade was just trying to comfort her."

Jake met John's eyes. "Yeah, right."

"Did you ask them about it?" John asked.

Jake turned away. He should have. But would that have changed anything? He shook his head. "From where I stood, there was no reason to ask. I saw them kissing."

"But you married Melissa just a couple of months after that." Luke looked closely at his brother. "We all thought you broke up with Sara because of Melissa."

"You thought wrong," Jake said. He wasn't going to tell them just why he'd married Melissa—there was no reason to now. But was it possible he'd been wrong about Wade and Sara? *Oh, dear Lord, could I have read everything wrong that night?*

"If there was anything going on between Sara and Wade before you married Melissa, we didn't know about it, Jake. We'd have said something if we did," Luke insisted. "You know we would have."

More family and church members began to arrive, and the conversation came to a halt. But Jake did feel closer to his family than he had in years. Until he felt the anger fading away, he hadn't even realized he'd been holding a grudge, thinking they'd covered up for Wade and Sara. At least if Wade and Sara had been seeing each other, his family hadn't been trying to keep it from him.

He managed to enjoy the Sunday supper. The only glitch in the night was hearing so many people ask about Sara, especially when he had a feeling that he was the reason she was staying away.

૨�

It'd taken some talking, but Deana did agree to go to the movies with Sara after church that night. Sara knew Deana was curious about why she was so determined not to go to Gram's, but Sara was given a reprieve from talking when, as they took their seats, the lights dimmed and the coming attractions started.

After the movie, they made their way out to the parking lot. "Well, the movie was okay, but I'm not sure it was worth missing one of Ellie's suppers. You going to tell me why we had to go tonight?" Deana asked as they walked to their cars.

Sara shrugged. "You never know how long a movie will be here."

"You know I'm not buying that answer, don't you? I think we need to talk."

Sara sighed. Deana knew her too well. "I'm not ready to talk about it yet."

Deana nodded. "Okay. You know where I am."

"Thanks, Deanie. For going with me tonight and for letting me off the hook."

"Oh, I'm just letting you off for the time being. Don't count on my forgetting."

"I know you won't." Sara chuckled as she got into her car, but she knew she was in for a lengthy question-and-answer session one of these days.

She'd barely gotten the door unlocked when Grandpa pulled up. He'd brought her home a plate of sandwiches and various desserts, and she felt bad for not asking Deana over for coffee.

"Everyone asked about you, Sara. Said to tell you they missed you." He set the plate on the table.

"That's sweet. It's nice to know you're missed," Sara said, taking a seat at the table.

"Ellie said to tell you that she's taking no excuses next week. Said she expects you to be there."

Knowing Gram, she probably had already figured out why Sara hadn't made an appearance. Sara made a noncommittal sound before biting into a sandwich.

Grandpa poured himself a cup of coffee and sat down across from her while she ate.

"How was Meggie tonight?"

"The main attraction, of course. She laps up all that attention, but only to a point. Several of the women who were so attentive at church came to supper, but Meggie wouldn't have much to do with them. She's very selective about who she lets hold her." Grandpa laughed. "Linda Plunket tried to take her from Jake, and

Meggie started crying. Jake had to take her upstairs to calm her down."

"Poor Linda. I'm sure that made her feel awkward."

"Ellie made her feel better by telling her that Meggie was just now getting used to the family holding her."

"She'll adjust to having new people around soon." Sara chuckled. "As a member of the Breland/Tanner family, she won't have much choice."

"They're a good bunch of people."

"Yes, they are." Sara bit into a chocolate brownie.

She loved the family she'd married into. She'd missed being there tonight. But the tension between her and Jake was so strong that everyone in the family would be picking up on it. Nora had certainly not kept it a secret that she didn't like Jake being home. Any time spent in his company was bound to cause more tension between her and Nora.

Nora was right about one thing, Jake had hurt her in the past. She couldn't chance letting him hurt her again, and the easiest way to keep that from happening would be to see as little of Jake Breland as possible.

"You all right, Darlin'?" Grandpa nudged her hand.

"What? Oh, I'm fine, Grandpa." Or she would be—if she could just stop thinking about Jake.

❧

Sara called Nora first thing the next morning, but it seemed she was feeling much better. So much so that she wanted Sara to meet her for lunch. Relieved that Nora wasn't feeling worse, Sara agreed.

Just as she hung up the phone, it rang again. "Sara dear," Gram said, "I missed you last night."

"I'm sorry, Gram. Deana and I went to the movies. Grandpa had a real good time, though."

Gram chuckled. "Your grandpa always manages to have a good time. Did he tell you that we're in cahoots together?"

"Oh?"

"We're trying to find a man we can introduce Nora to. Probably should be someone she's never met. You know, someone who hasn't been the victim of her sharp tongue?"

Sara couldn't contain her laughter. "Gram! You and Grandpa better watch yourselves. I don't think Nora will take kindly to you meddling in her life," she teased.

"Well, someone needs to. Maybe it'd stop her from meddling in everyone else's. Anyway, that's not what I called to talk to you about. It's time to start planning our annual family reunion, and I could use your help if it wouldn't be too much trouble."

Sara's newfound resolve to see less of the family melted. "Of course, I'll help you. What do you need me to do?"

"I thought maybe you could come over today, and we could map out a few things."

For once Sara was grateful for one of Nora's lunch dates. "Well, I am having lunch with Nora at noon."

"That will work out just fine. Meggie takes her nap around two o'clock. Would that work for you? Should give you plenty of time with Nora."

More time than she needed, actually. But she didn't want to run into Jake, either. She hesitated.

"Sara dear, Jake is going into the office this afternoon. You won't have to run into him."

Sara didn't know what to say. She didn't want to lie to Gram, but she knew the older woman would see through any excuse she could come up with. "I'll be there around two."

"Thank you, Dear. I knew I could count on you."

Sara hung up the phone with a half-smile on her face. Gram knew everything. Good thing one could trust her not to tell it all.

❧

This time Sara beat Nora to the diner. It was crowded when Sara got there, and Deana was busy in the back. Sara sighed with relief. One more reprieve from a heart to heart.

"Hello, Dear," Nora said, sliding into the booth opposite Sara. She picked up the menu and began to study it. "How was Sunday supper?"

"Grandpa said there was a good turnout. I didn't go." Her answer seemed to pique Nora's interest.

"Oh? Why not?"

Sara shrugged. She certainly wasn't going to tell Nora it was because Jake had held her in his arms and kissed her on Saturday night and she wasn't ready to try to look into his eyes and pretend it didn't happen. "Deana and I took in a movie."

Nora seemed pleased. "That's nice, Dear. I'm glad you are getting out more with friends like Deana."

Yes, of course she was, thought Sara. *As long as it wasn't a man— especially one named Jake Breland.* She immediately regretted her attitude.

"What are you doing this afternoon?" Nora asked as soon as they'd given their order to the waitress.

"Gram called and asked if I'd help plan the family reunion."

When she saw Nora's face tighten up, her first instinct was to assure Nora that Jake wouldn't be there. Her second was to tell herself that she didn't have to explain her actions to Nora, and her third was to wonder if she'd imagined the tender scene between Nora and Meggie that she'd seen the other night. It certainly wasn't in evidence today.

"Is it that time again?" Nora frowned. "Seems like we just had a reunion."

"Actually, there wasn't one last year. There was too much grieving. But Gram doesn't want her family losing touch, and I'm glad she's going ahead with this one. I love the Breland/Tanner reunions."

"Well, I'd think she'd have enough help with Jake home. He could help her plan."

"Nora, you know men don't really like to plan these kinds of things." Sara was relieved that their lunch was served just then. Her mother-in-law's tone was turning chillier by the minute. Sara sighed and wished she'd just kept quiet about helping Gram. But Nora wouldn't like it if she thought she was being kept in the dark. Sara was going to have to keep these lunches with Nora to a minimum. All she seemed to get out of them lately was a bad case of indigestion.

≈

"Come in, Dear. Thank you so much for offering to help me with this." Gram met her at the door and led the way to the kitchen, where she checked on the contents of a large pot simmering on the back of the stove. She poured two cups of coffee and brought them to the table, where a plate of chocolate chip cookies rested. "I put a roast on before Jake left for the office, Meggie just went down for her nap, so we should have several hours of uninterrupted time."

"Looks like you have everything under control, Gram. How are you doing? Remember my offer to help with Meggie if this all gets too much for you." She took a sip of coffee and watched the older woman gather tablets and pencils before joining her at the table.

"I do remember, and I'll keep it in mind," Gram said, sitting down. "Right now, with Jake here of a morning, and Meggie sleeping in the afternoon, it's working out pretty well."

She certainly looked none the worse for wear, but she always had seemed to have the energy of a woman half her age. Sara could only hope that she aged as well.

Gram pulled out the list of family members and handed it to Sara. "I'm really hoping Laci will be able to come home for this reunion. I haven't seen that child in two years, but she's promised to try."

Laci was John's sister, and she'd moved to Dallas several years back to study design. Now she owned her own interior design company. Starting a new business had kept her extra busy, and she hadn't been able to make it home in quite some time.

"What date are you targeting? It's the end of May now."

Ellie nodded her head and looked at the calendar. "I know I'm cutting it close, but I'd like to try for the Fourth of July. A lot of family may have already made plans, but I'd dearly love to have as much of my family together as I can this Independence Day."

"Well, let's go for it. What do you want me to do?"

"Sara, I don't know what I'd do without you. I guess the first thing is to call my sister and brother in Arkansas and see if they can come. Then, there's Bill's brother and family. . . ."

The next few hours flew by as they kept the phone busy. Almost everyone was as anxious to pick up with the family re-union as Gram was. She had plenty of room in her home, but there was no way she could put everyone up. Sara called both motels in town for information about reserving rooms. She'd just poured them both a fresh cup of coffee when the back door opened.

Luke entered and gave both his grandmother and Sara a kiss on the cheek. He turned to his grandmother with a wide grin. "It sure smells good in here. Think you could set a plate for one more?"

Gram grinned up at him. "Since when do you have to ask?"

Realizing that Jake would be coming in soon, Sara quickly gathered her things together and crossed the room to kiss the older woman on the cheek. "I didn't realize it was getting so late. I'd better check on Grandpa. You call me if you think of anything else you need me to do, okay?"

"I will, Dear. Thank you for helping today."

"You're welcome," Sara said as she headed for the door.

"Hey, where's my kiss?" Luke asked.

Sara shook her head and turned to kiss him on the cheek. "Night, Luke."

He reached out and tousled her hair. "Night, Sara."

She pulled the door shut behind her and sighed with relief that she'd been able to leave without running into Jake again. If only she could feel as comfortable around him as she felt around Luke.

7

*A*fter several days had passed without running into Jake, Sara began to relax. Since Gram had told her that Jake went to the office each afternoon, Sara timed her visits with the older woman when she was sure that he wouldn't be there.

Plans for the reunion were moving along. They'd contacted Laci, and she'd promised she'd try her best to come. A couple of Gram's great-nieces and nephews had let her know they were coming as well. Sara loved hearing the excitement in Gram's voice and was glad things were coming together so well.

Nora hadn't expressed much excitement about the reunion, but she didn't get excited about too much these days. Sara was beginning to think Grandpa and Gram were right: Maybe Nora did need a man in her life.

Sara had just finished making calls to remind the ladies of the church about the next teddy bear-making meeting and poured herself a glass of iced tea, when the phone rang.

"Hi, Sara," the voice on the other end said after Sara had answered the phone. "I hear you've been quite busy since we've been gone."

"Gina! You're back. When did you get in? Did you have a good trip? When can we get together?"

"We got in last night, the trip was really rewarding, and anytime is good for me. I missed you!"

"How about the diner?" Sara looked at the clock. The lunch crowd would have cleared out by now. "In about thirty minutes?"

"I'll be there. I can't wait to get caught up on what's been happening in Sweet Springs."

A short while later, Sara parked at the diner. Gina was already waiting in a booth but got to her feet as soon as she spotted Sara. The two friends hugged and grinned at each other before taking their seats.

"A month is just too long for you and David to be gone. I really have missed you."

"We're glad to be home. But the trip really was such an eye-opener for me. We take so many things for granted here, Sara. The orphanage is growing so fast, I'm just glad we've been able to help down there. The children will steal your heart."

"I'm glad you were able to do it. Tom did a real good job while y'all were gone."

"I'll tell him you said so. He and Mom are going down to Guatemala with the next work group."

The waitress came for their order, and they both settled for apple pie and coffee. As soon as they were left alone, Gina grinned over at Sara.

"I hear we have a couple of new faces in town—and that they caused quite a stir in church on Sunday."

Sara chuckled and nodded. "Jake and Meggie. He's going into practice with John. They're staying at Gram's for now."

"That's what I understood." Gina turned serious. "How is he doing as a single parent?"

"He's very good with Meggie. And she's adorable, Gina. I know exactly what you mean by stealing your heart. She stole mine the very first day."

"It hasn't been too hard on you, seeing her . . ."

Sara shook her head. "The first day at Gram's, she reached out to me, and it was as if God gave me what I needed, a child to hold, even if only for a few minutes. It was time."

Deana came out from the kitchen, bringing their pie and coffee, and joined them for a few minutes before the coffee-break crowd descended upon the diner. "What was time?" she asked Sara.

"For me to hold a baby."

"Ah, Meggie, right? Jake brought her in with him the other day, and she really is a cutie. It won't be long before she's walking. I hope she's not too much for Ellie then."

"So do I. Jake is only working part of the day now, but that can't last forever."

The bell above the door tinkled, and the three of them looked toward the door.

Deana grinned. In came David, Jake, and John. "Do you think they have radar and know when we're talking about them?"

She stood up and stretched. "The afternoon crowd arrives. It's back to the grindstone for me. One of these days, I'd like to sit down and have a real gab session."

"We'll have to get together soon and have a real hen party," Gina said.

Deana nodded on her way back to the kitchen. "Sounds good to me. Let me know when."

David slid in beside his wife and kissed her on the cheek, while John pulled a chair to the end of the table, leaving the space beside Sara for Jake.

Sara scooted over to give him more room, knowing she'd congratulated herself too soon for managing not to run into him. From Jake's quick shrug and half smile, she surmised he hadn't expected to run into her, either. She hoped the flurry of greetings everyone else was involved in would help keep them from noticing how uncomfortable she and Jake were.

"I thought you were catching up in the church office this afternoon," Gina quizzed her husband.

"He was," John said. "But word had it that you two were back, and Jake and I searched him out and convinced him to take a break with us."

"Jake, it's good to see you again." Gina smiled across the table at him. "But I'm really looking forward to meeting your daughter. I've heard she's really something."

Sara watched Jake's smile turn into a proud-papa grin.

"She is that. You come by anytime. I'm always happy to show her off."

"Oh, we'll be there for Sunday supper, if not before," David said. "Ellie is one of our favorite people."

"How's she making out, keeping up with Meggie?" Gina asked.

"So far, so good. But I'm hoping it won't be for too long. I know Gram isn't getting any younger. I've been in contact with a realtor, and I'm going to look at a few places this weekend. But what I'm really going to need is a housekeeper to watch over Meggie for me. Any ideas on how to find one?"

"Have you tried the employment office?"

"Not yet. I was hoping to find someone through recommendations from people I know and trust."

"Let me think on it," David said. "Maybe I can come up with someone."

"In the meantime, if Ellie needs help, feel free to call," Gina offered.

Jake glanced at Sara and back to Gina. "Thanks. A lot of people are willing to help Gram, and John is letting me take my time getting settled."

"There's no hurry," John interjected. "I'm just thankful you've agreed to come in as a partner." He looked over at David and Gina. "Now, we want to know all about your trip. How is Guatemala?"

David and Gina didn't need any more coaxing to talk about their experiences in Guatemala. Sara tried to listen intently as they explained the ongoing work at the orphanage, but part of her was attuned to each and every breath Jake took. She was relieved when the impromptu gathering came to an end.

> &

Jake had enjoyed the afternoon. He liked getting to know David and Gina all over again. From all he'd heard, David made a wonderful minister. He found himself looking forward to hearing him on Sunday.

The only rough spot in the afternoon had been when they'd first entered the diner and he'd found himself sitting next to Sara. He felt like a fumbling teenager as he drank coffee and ate his pie, trying very hard not to let her know how totally aware of her he was. Obviously they were going to be running into each other more often. They had family and friends in common, and Sweet Springs was not a large city where he could lose himself in the crowds. Hopefully he and Sara would soon get used to being around each other. He was back to stay, and he certainly couldn't see Sara moving away.

When Jake got back to the office, a message from Gram was waiting for him, and he quickly punched in the number. She answered on the fifth ring.

"Gram, is anything wrong?"

"I don't think it's serious, but Meggie's been a little fussy this afternoon. She doesn't have a fever, but I can't get her to eat a thing and she's been crying off and on. Do you think she might be cutting a new tooth?"

"Probably her first molar. I'll stop on the way home and get some of that stuff that numbs her gums. Maybe that will help."

"That's what I was going to ask you to do. Poor baby."

Jake could hear Meggie crying and Gram making soothing noises to her. "I'll be home as soon as I get it, Gram."

Jake hurried down the street to the drugstore. It hadn't changed much from when he was young. It was probably one of the few drugstores left that still boasted a real soda bar. Jake grinned, remembering all the fun he'd had here as a kid. It was nice to know that some things stayed the same. He'd have to bring Meggie in for a soda when she got a little older.

"Jake?" a soft voice inquired. "Is Meggie sick?"

He turned to see the concerned look in Sara's eyes. "Not sick, really. We think she's teething."

"Oh, that's good. Well, not good for Meggie, but I'm glad it's nothing more serious."

"Thank you, Sara." He motioned to the shelf in front of him. "I think one of these will help."

Sara nodded. "I'm sure it will."

"If I can only figure out which one to buy." He pulled two different brands off the shelf and turned to her. "Do you have any idea which one I should go with?"

Sara looked at both and shrugged. "I think either one will be all right. I'm sorry, Jake. I really don't know which brand to go with."

"Don't feel bad, Sara. Neither do I, and I've bought it before." He put one back on the shelf and turned to her again. He wanted to say more but didn't know what to say. "I guess I'd better get it home."

"Yes. I hope it works quickly. Give Meggie a hug for me?"

Jake nodded. "I will." He hurried to the checkout counter. It seemed to be the day for running into Sara. Maybe with time, it'd get easier. But somehow he knew that wasn't gong to happen until they'd confronted the past, and he wasn't looking forward to that conversation at all. Not one bit.

❧

Sara had left the diner with the beginning of a headache and had stopped at the drugstore to pick up some aspirin. She left with a full-blown headache and started home wondering when and where she was going to run into Jake again.

She'd certainly made up for lost time today. She would have

to try harder if she was going to manage to miss running into him at every turn. Was it even possible to avoid him? And was running into him, being in close proximity to him, ever going to get any easier?

That evening while fixing supper, Sara told Grandpa about David and Gina's trip as well as about running into Jake at the drugstore and learning of Meggie's teething difficulties. When they sat down to eat, he thanked the Lord for bringing David and Gina home safely and asked that Meggie feel better real soon.

Sara couldn't help but smile. She knew Grandpa was as taken with Meggie as she was.

All through supper, she told herself not to worry about the little girl, but she kept wondering if the problem involved more than teething. Could she have a cold or maybe a childhood disease?

After she'd cleaned the kitchen, Sara could stand it no longer. It didn't matter who answered the phone. She had to know how Meggie was. She picked up the phone and dialed Gram's number.

"Hello?" Gram answered.

"Gram? How is Meggie? I saw Jake in the drugstore—"

"She's fine now. That teething medicine worked like a charm. We even managed to get some supper down her. Jake's giving her a bath now. We think she'll be okay."

"Oh, good. I just wanted to make sure it was nothing more serious." Sara pictured Jake bathing Meggie and putting her to sleep. He really was a wonderful daddy.

"No, we're sure she's teething. Her little gum is real swollen. We'll doctor her good before she goes to sleep. Hopefully that tooth will come right on through."

"I'll pray it does. If you need anything, you call, okay?"

"I will, Sara. Thank you for checking."

Sara sighed with relief as she hung up the phone. Life was complicated enough without Meggie getting sick.

That Sunday morning, Jake listened closely to David's sermon. At first he listened mostly from curiosity about how someone he had known back in high school would preach. But soon the content of the sermon gripped his attention. It was on forgiveness—how we should forgive others as Jesus forgives us and forgive ourselves once we've been forgiven. David went on to describe the importance of going forward rather than dwelling in the past.

Jake wanted to move forward with his life. He was tired of living in the past. He wanted a better relationship with the Lord. He left church feeling for the first time as if maybe that would be possible. If Sara was at Gram's supper that night, he was going to talk to her. It was time to mend the past.

Sara knew she couldn't get out of going to Gram's Sunday supper, and she really didn't want to. It was a sort of welcome home for David and Gina, and she would never hurt them by staying away. She spent the afternoon baking a cake and making a platter of sandwiches to take. Wanting to help Gram as much as she could, she and Will took separate cars to church that evening so she could hurry over as soon as services were over.

Thankfully, others had already arrived when she got there, so Sara went straight to the kitchen to help Gram get things on the table. The turnout was large, as she knew it would be. Everyone wanted to welcome David and Gina home. Sara was hopeful that she and Jake could mingle without running into each other.

Somehow they managed to do just that. Or at least she did. By keeping a careful eye on which direction Jake was headed, she was able to move from one room to another just a step before or behind him.

She helped Gram keep the table full, took a turn washing up dishes, and still managed to visit. She even got to hold Meggie for a minute before Lydia claimed the little girl. All in all things were going better than she'd expected. Even Nora seemed to relax and enjoy herself.

Sara was headed back around the living room to pick up empty plates and cups when someone tapped her on the back. She turned to find Jake smiling down at her.

"Sara, can we talk?"

"Now? Here?" Sara hated sounding so breathless.

Jake looked around. "How about out on the porch?"

"All right," she said, doubt coloring her voice. She and Jake had been trying to stay out of each other's way ever since he came home. Now he wanted to talk?

Jake steered her to the side door, and when they got outside, he led her to a quiet corner. "I don't quite know how to go about this," he said, running his fingers through his hair. "But Gram says it's time."

"Time for what, Jake?"

"To try to call a truce or something so that we can co-exist in this town without making everyone around us uncomfortable. And today, David's sermon was on forgiveness. I just—"

"Jake, is that what this is all about?" Sara smiled up at him. "Because if it is, I forgave you for dumping me, long ago."

Jake's dark eyes glittered in the dark. "Dumping you? You were the one who was seeing my cousin behind my back."

"What are you talking about, Jake?" Sara whispered hoarsely. "I wasn't seeing Wade behind your back."

"Well, tell me who it was you were kissing that night. It certainly looked like Wade."

Sara gasped and turned around. She headed down the steps and ran out to her car, but Jake caught up with her before she got the door open.

"Sara, answer me." Jake's hand kept her from opening the car door.

"You lost the right to ask that question when you turned and walked away without listening to me that night." Sara looked back at the house and was relieved that no one seemed to have noticed them.

"Then it wasn't you I saw kissing Wade that night?"

"There was nothing going on between us, Jake. Nothing."

"That's not the way it looked to me. Not after I'd received several anonymous notes telling me different, that very week. And especially not after I saw you in Wade's arms."

"What are you talking about? I don't know anything about any notes. And Wade was just comforting me when I got upset because you hadn't shown up."

"Yeah, right."

"I don't owe you any explanations, Jake. You wouldn't listen that night. It wouldn't make any difference now. But I did *not* cheat on you. Wade and I didn't even start dating until after you married Melissa. From where I stand, it looks like you were the one doing the cheating."

Jake turned Sara to face him. "I never dated Melissa until after I saw you and Wade kissing that night."

"But you married her just a few months later."

"Yes, I did. But I wasn't seeing her before that night." Jake couldn't bring himself to tell Sara the full story—that after he had returned to college he had gotten drunk for the first and only time in his life and that weeks later Melissa had told him that she was pregnant with his child from that night.

"Wade said you admitted dating her when he went up to college to tell you there was nothing going on between us."

"Then he lied to you. And he never told me there was nothing going on between you two. He said that you didn't want to hurt me, but that you and he were in love. That he'd been in love with you for years."

"No! Wade wouldn't lie to me. He went to talk to you because I was so upset and I could never get you on the phone. He said he'd straighten everything out. Then when he came home, he said you were getting married."

"That much was true," Jake admitted. "I was getting married." He could never betray his dead wife by telling Sara that he got engaged because of Melissa's pregnancy. Besides, it would probably seem like a lame excuse. No one else knew of the pregnancy; Melissa had lost the child shortly after their wedding. He shook his head. Nothing he could do or say was going to change the past. The only thing he and Sara had was the future.

"Sara. Please. Can we call a truce? Can we put the past to rest and start over?"

"You're telling me my husband lied to me. How can you expect me to just put that to rest, Jake? I don't know that I can." Sara pulled on the door to the car, and Jake moved his hand away.

"I'm sorry, Sara."

"So am I, Jake." She got in the car, started the engine, and pulled away.

Jake watched her leave, feeling a mixture of regret and relief. Regret that he'd brought her more pain, but relief that the past was finally in the open. His heart felt lighter in the knowledge that while his cousin had betrayed him, Sara hadn't—at least not knowingly. But that relief ended when he realized that while Sara was innocent, he and Wade had chosen to act in ways that damaged many lives. And the pain from those actions lived on.

$\mathcal{A}$ll Sara wanted to do was keep driving—east to Roswell, west to Las Cruses—anywhere away from Sweet Springs. But she knew Grandpa would worry if he came home and she wasn't there. He'd be worried enough already that she hadn't told him she was leaving Gram's.

So she drove home the long way, up and down one tree-lined street after another, until she thought she had herself under control. Then she went home and dialed Gram's number.

Thankfully, Luke answered the phone. It was easy to convince him she wasn't feeling well without raising too many questions. He promised to tell Gramps she went home early and told her he hoped she felt better real soon.

Sara hoped so too, but somehow she doubted it. Jake had just told her that Wade had lied about them. How could she accept that her whole married life had been based on a lie? *Dear Lord, how could that be?* Wade had been a good husband, faithful and loving. He wouldn't have lied to her, would he?

She shook her head. No. He wouldn't. And it didn't matter, anyway. Wade wasn't here to defend himself, and she wasn't going to start doubting him now.

She put the water on to make some hot tea and paced the kitchen while she waited for the kettle to whistle.

No matter how hard she tried to suppress them, questions about the past kept surfacing. How could Jake have thought she was seeing Wade back then? She'd been crazy about Jake from their very first date. That was what had hurt so much. He hadn't trusted her. It'd taken so long for her to get over him. Wade had been there, that was true, but it didn't mean he'd been in love with her all that time or that he'd been trying to break her and Jake up.

No, Jake was mistaken. Or making excuses for his actions that night. Wade was her husband, and she knew him.

The kettle whistled and Sara quickly made a cup of tea and took it up to her room, but the drink sat untouched as she sat in the rocker by the window and looked out. How could she and Jake possibly bury the past when a whole new set of questions had just been raised?

❧

Jake shook his head as he watched the taillights of Sara's car disappear. If he could manage to physically kick himself, he would. As it stood, he was seriously thinking of getting his brother to do it for him. Luke would oblige, but he would have questions Jake wasn't ready to answer. It seemed he'd made more of a mess of things than they were before he'd started.

He slowly walked back into the house and went up to check on his sleeping daughter. He'd just put Meggie to bed when he'd come back downstairs earlier and spotted Sara in the dining room. He'd been looking for a chance to talk to her all night, but she seemed to be in any room except the one he was in. So he'd quickly grabbed the chance presented to him and sought to clear the air between them. Oh, yeah, he'd cleared things up all right.

Fat chance of any truce being called now. He should have just asked that they start over, instead of actually going into the past with Sara. Now it looked like he was trying to excuse his actions by blaming a man who was no longer around to defend himself.

And wasn't that exactly what he had done? He was the one who hadn't given Sara a chance to explain anything that night. He was the one who'd gotten drunk and couldn't even remember what he'd done that night. All he knew was what Melissa had told him, and that had resulted in their marriage.

Oh, Wade may have used everything to his advantage, but it was Jake who'd given him that chance by not trusting Sara in the first place. Even if Wade had told him the truth, Jake knew the outcome wouldn't have changed. By then it was too late. Melissa had told him that she was pregnant.

Jake felt sickened by his behavior. He'd blamed everyone around him for his own mistakes. Oh, he thought he'd accepted responsibility for his actions by marrying Melissa. But he'd continued to blame Wade and Sara for his reactions to seeing them together that night.

He looked down on his daughter as she slept peacefully and marveled that the Lord had allowed him to be her father. To Meggie, he was just "dada," and she loved him unconditionally. Of course she didn't know what a mess he'd made of so many things. Jake hoped she'd never have to know.

He wished he could just stay upstairs by himself. But plenty of people were still visiting, and Gram could probably use his help. He bent down and kissed Meggie's softly scented cheek before heading back downstairs.

David looked up from refilling his coffee cup when Jake entered the dining room. "Been checking on Meggie?" he asked.

Jake nodded and chuckled. "She's sleeping soundly, thank goodness. She's been teething this week, and she's still not used to having quite so many people around."

"Changes can be tiring for a baby," David agreed. He took a sip of coffee. "I saw you walk Sara to her car a little while ago. Was she not feeling well?"

Surprised by the quick change of subject, Jake looked around and was relieved that they had the room to themselves. "I think she was fine before she talked to me. Sara and I have been finding it a little difficult, being part of the same family."

David nodded. "I noticed the two of you seemed a little uncomfortable the other day at Deana's. Anything you want to talk about?"

Jake saw only genuine concern in David's eyes. But he shook his head and nodded toward the doorway, where Gina and Lydia were entering. "Thanks for the offer. Maybe one of these days. Now's not a good time."

"Just so you know, I always have the time."

Jake smiled and nodded. "I'll remember that."

He greeted the two women and went through to the kitchen to see if Gram needed anything. It was the least he could do after running off her best helper.

&

Funny how when you didn't want to run into a person, you couldn't seem to miss them, but when you wanted to run into someone, they were nowhere to be found, Jake thought. He'd been to Deana's at lunchtime two days in a row. He'd made several grocery runs for Gram and even strolled Meggie to the ice cream parlor last night, but Sara was nowhere to be found. He'd even checked out the drugstore to no avail. He was beginning to wonder if she'd left the country.

His search for a house wasn't turning up anything, either. He wanted an older home in town, in good condition. So, it seemed, did everyone who owned one. The ones that were available were either too little or too big.

Several lots were for sale, however, and after an initial meeting with a local architect and builder, it looked like he'd be at Gram's until he could have plans drawn up and a home built. Now, if he could just convince her to let him hire a housekeeper to help her out.

He approached the subject again at supper, when he had Luke to support his efforts. "Gram, I think it's time we put an ad in the paper to see if we can find a housekeeper to help you out."

Gram looked up at him, her knife poised motionless above a

half-buttered biscuit. "Jake, I told you, I don't want some strange woman taking care of my house or helping me with my great-grandchild."

"But I know Meggie is a handful." Jake cut the chicken-fried steak into bite-sized pieces for his daughter and handed her a child-sized fork. She loved spearing food and feeding herself. He looked back at his grandmother and continued, "She's going to be walking and climbing before long. I don't want her wearing you out."

"Jake's right," Luke chimed in. "Meggie will run you ragged in no time once she starts walking. You are going to need some help."

"Lydia has been coming over some."

Jake nodded. "Uh-huh, and John said she told him that you practically run her off every time she mentions helping out."

"She has a house of her own to run and a husband to take care of."

Jake spooned some mashed potatoes onto Meggie's plate, and she gave him a cheesy grin.

"Anyone want more tea?" Gram started to get up.

"You sit, Gram." Luke got up and brought the pitcher over to the table. "Jake and I can certainly wait on ourselves."

"You'd think I was an old invalid, the way you two talk," she grumbled, lifting her glass for a refill.

"No, we don't," Jake answered, "and I certainly don't want our being here to turn you into one. How about this?" he added as he handed Meggie her sippy cup. "Do you think there might be a teenager or two from church who would want a part-time job? One who could come in afternoons and on Saturdays to help out?"

Gram looked over at him and smiled. "Now that I might be willing to think about. It just might work. I think there are one or two who could use the money."

Jake breathed a sigh of relief, and he and Luke did a high-five. Their grandmother could be one stubborn lady.

≈

Sara had been trying to keep busy. She'd helped Grandpa in the garden, she'd made ten more teddy bears, and she'd rearranged the living room. She'd stayed away from Deana's, the grocery store, and downtown in general.

But while she'd successfully avoided Jake, she hadn't been able to put him and what he'd said out of her mind. She kept going over the conversation with him. What bothered her the most was her reaction to the knowledge that Jake hadn't been seeing Melissa all along like she'd thought. He truly did seem to think that she and Wade had been seeing each other, and if that was true, then he had cared about her. Even though it shouldn't matter after all these years, she wanted to believe that Jake had loved her. And that's what troubled her most of all—the realization that she still felt something for Jake.

Recognizing that she had to talk to someone who might give her some insight into the past, she invited Gina and David to supper. Grandpa and David were out inspecting the garden before starting a game of horseshoes. Gina insisted on helping Sara do most of the dishes before they served dessert.

"Okay, my friend. Open up," Gina said, as she helped clear the table. "I know something is bothering you."

"You're right about that." Sara smiled at her friend. "What gave me away? The panic in my voice as I issued my last minute invitation?"

Gina chuckled and shook her head. "No, I think it was last week at Deana's. The tension between you and Jake."

Sara sank her hands into the hot water and started washing a plate. "So much for thinking no one could tell."

Gina gave her a quick hug and took the plate from her. "I take it it's not been easy to adjust to him being back?"

"Loving his family so much doesn't make it any easier. They all mean so much to me, I don't want to have to give them up."

"As if they'd let you! Jake hasn't told you to stay away or anything like that, surely—"

"No." Sara shook her head. "In fact, he'd like us to call a truce. To get past our past, so to speak."

"Well, that's one way to put it. Can you do that?"

"Oh, Gina, I want to. I really do. Obviously we're making it hard on everyone around us. We have the same family and friends. It's not fair to you all."

"But?"

"But Jake told me something the other night that I find hard to believe."

"What was that?"

"Remember when Wade went up to college to talk to Jake? And he came back and said Jake was getting married?"

Gina leaned against the counter and nodded. "I remember."

Sara scrubbed another plate. "Jake says that Wade told him that we—Wade and I—were in love."

"Ah . . ."

"Jake said that Wade had been in love with me for a long time before that."

"Does that surprise you? Surely you knew that."

Sara closed her eyes and shook her head. "No, I didn't. I thought he was just my good friend."

"Oh . . ." Gina took the plate from Sara and dried it. Then she turned Sara around and led her back to the table. "And now you're wondering if Jake is telling the truth about what Wade said to him?"

Sara nodded. "I never knew Wade to lie to me."

"Did he ever tell you he didn't love you while you were dating Jake?"

"Well, no. He knew I was crazy about Jake. But if he told Jake that we were in love with each other, he lied to Jake."

Gina nodded. "That's true." She rubbed Sara's tense shoulders. "Sara honey, I don't know what to tell you. I can tell you that I always had the impression Wade was in love with you. Not that he was actively trying to break you and Jake up, but that he'd be there in the wings if you ever needed him."

"Why didn't I see that?"

"All you could see back then was Jake."

"Well, I'm not sure the same could be said about Jake. He said he didn't start seeing Melissa until he found Wade kissing me that night. But that's pretty hard to believe."

Gina shook her head and went back to the sink. This time she washed. "Not to me."

Sara took the plate she handed her and began to dry. "Why not?"

"Because I saw the way he looked at you, Sara. I think Jake was crazy about you."

Sara shook her head and continued drying dishes, mulling over what Gina had said.

"I'll never know for sure, will I?"

"I don't know, Sara. But I do know one thing from experience. None of us can redo what's in the past. All we can do is go forward."

Sara took the dishcloth from Gina and wiped down the counter. "I know you're right. It's just not easy."

"No, it's not." Gina drained the dishwater and turned to Sara. "You haven't asked for my advice, but I'm going to give it anyway."

"You know I always value your opinion."

"I'd say put the past to rest, call a truce with Jake, and go forward. Wherever that takes you."

Before Sara could answer, the screen door opened and

Grandpa stuck his head in. "Sure is nice out here. You girls going to join us?"

"We'll be right there, Grandpa."

❧

Jake watched his daughter staring at the room full of other children. Meggie didn't seem to be sure she wanted to stay with the other toddlers. The woman who cared for them on Wednesday evenings at church showed Meggie a toy and introduced her to another little girl. Jake stayed until his daughter seemed to relax and become curious about the other children. He started to ease out the door and felt his heartstrings tug when Meggie casually waved her little hand and said, "Bye, Dada." Pride in the fact that she was handling his departure so well warred with the ache in his heart from realizing that she seemed so unconcerned about where he was going.

He took a seat in the pew with Gram and Luke in the adult class. Quickly he became immersed in David's lesson. The minister encouraged everyone to ask questions, and the discussion went beyond surface issues.

When the bell rang to end class, Jake got up to bring Meggie in for the song service. His heart gave a sudden lurch when he spotted Sara and Will two pews behind him. He nodded in passing, but hurried on up the aisle when he noticed Meggie's teacher bringing her out of her class.

"How'd she do?" he asked, as Meggie threw herself into his arms.

"She did really well. I think she liked it. It takes them a little time to adjust, but she didn't cry at all. That's a good sign."

Meggie waved good-bye to the teacher and looked around as Jake carried her back to his seat. She liked the singing, and to Jake's surprise, she stayed quiet through the closing prayer.

Before the service ended, David invited everyone to adjourn to the fellowship hall to celebrate the eightieth birthday of one of their members. Gram offered to serve the cake and ice cream, so Jake had no choice but to stay.

"Meggie, want some cake and ice cream?" Luke asked, holding his arms out to her.

She reached for her uncle. "I-ceam!"

Jake laughed and handed her to his brother. "Yeah, you can go with Uncle Luke. And he can clean you up afterwards."

Luke made a face at him, and Jake watched the two of them head up the aisle. Just inside the fellowship hall, Luke and Meggie caught up with Sara and Will. Their words drifted back to Jake.

"Hi, sweet Meggie," Will said. "You going to get ice cream? Can I go with you and Uncle Luke?"

Meggie nodded and looked at Sara. "Sawa comin'?"

Jake saw Sara smile at Meggie and look back at him. "I am. But first I'm going to talk to your daddy, okay?"

" 'Kay."

Jake stood at the doorway of the sanctuary, his heart hammering in his chest. Now was his chance to apologize. What better place than a church, he thought fleetingly, as he strode across the foyer to join Sara at the door to the fellowship hall.

He took a deep breath. "Sara. I was hoping for a chance to talk to you."

She arched an eyebrow and smiled. "Oh? So was I. Wanting to talk to you."

"I'm sorry for upsetting you the other night. I was wrong—"

"Jake." Sara held up her hand and shook her head. "Do you still want to call that truce?"

"If we're going to live in the same town, I think it would be a good idea." Could she really be considering a truce after the way he'd hurt her on Sunday night? "What do you want?"

"What do I want?" Sara repeated his question and paused. She looked around at all the friends and family they shared. She smiled, seeing Luke help Meggie with her ice cream. And she saw Gina glancing their way from across the room.

"I think it might be easier to tell you what I don't want."

Jake nodded. "All right."

"I don't want our friends and family, especially your sweet Meggie, to feel the tension we feel. I don't want them to be uncomfortable every time the two of us are around." Sara looked him straight in the eyes. "And I don't want to rehash the past to get to that point."

Jake couldn't believe she was willing to bury the past and what he'd said the other night. He'd accused her of being untrue to him, he'd called her husband a liar, yet here she was offering to forget it all and go on.

"Jake? What don't you want?"

He never wanted to forget this moment. "I don't want to go back. I'd like to go forward, but do you think we can?"

Sara tilted her head to the side. "We won't know until we try, will we?"

Jake was ready to try. More than ready. He was tired of the past. All it had ever done was pull him down. He nodded. "No, we won't."

"Truce?" Sara asked, sticking out her hand.

Jake covered her small hand with both of his. "Truce."

They smiled at each other for several seconds before Sara gently pulled her hand from his. The tension between them was by no means gone, but there was a subtle difference to it.

John walked up to them, a plate of cake and ice cream in his hand. "What are you two discussing so seriously over here? World peace?"

They both chuckled, and Jake shook his head. "No. Just our little corner of it."

"Cake looks good. I think I'll go try it myself," Sara said. "Catch you two later."

Jake watched her walk over to the cake table, then scanned the room for Luke and Meggie. He nudged his cousin, and they both laughed. Luke was letting Meggie feed him, and from the looks of it, he was the one who'd need his face cleaned when the evening was over.

☙

Sara took her plate from Gram and turned to find Gina at her elbow.

"Come on. I have a spot all picked out for us."

Sara knew she was going to be quizzed on her and Jake's conversation, but at least Gina waited to bring up the topic until after they'd taken seats off in a corner where, hopefully, they wouldn't be disturbed.

"So . . . how'd it go?"

"Truce is called and hopefully we'll be able to co-exist in the same town without all of you wishing we'd both move away." Sara grinned at Gina and took a large bite of cake.

"Nah, before we'd get to that point, we'd probably lock the two of you in a room together. Or knock your heads together."

Sara chuckled. "Well, maybe you won't have to resort to those tactics now."

"You look better all ready."

"I thought about what you said. You were right."

"Only because experience taught me a few things."

Sara knew Gina was referring to her own relationship with David and how the couple had been forced to deal with a past of their own before they found happiness together. "Well, just don't expect Jake and me to turn out the way you and David did."

"No?"

Sara wasn't happy about the way her heart sped up at the thought of a future with Jake. That was not what this truce was about. "No. You can't compare Jake and me to you and David."

"You think not?" Gina quirked an eyebrow and nodded across the room to where Jake was sitting.

Sara looked up to find Jake's gaze on her. Her breath caught in her throat as he smiled, and it felt like a hundred butterflies were let loose against her ribs. She smiled back before turning around to answer her grinning friend. "No."

Gina chuckled. "Okay. I won't compare. I'll just sit back and watch."

9

"Would you look at that?" Luke paused in cleaning frosting off his mouth and nudged Jake's arm.

"What?" Jake was busy wiping cake off Meggie's face and hands. Evidently forks and spoons didn't work when feeding Uncle Luke. Only hands would do.

"Gram and Will," Luke said. "He's making her take a break from serving. I thought he was getting seconds, but he was fixing a plate for Gram."

Jake turned to look across the room at the older couple. He saw Will pull out a chair for Gram and place a plate of cake and ice cream in front of her. Then he took a seat beside her and patted her back. They were either the very best of friends, or—

"Have I missed something?" Jake asked his brother.

"I think maybe we both have. Is that our grandmother blushing?"

Jake chuckled and nudged him. "Well, don't gawk at them."

"Gwalk, dada? I walk."

"I know you do, Sweetheart." Jake chuckled as he put Meggie on her feet and took her hands in his. "Let's go get you a drink."

Meggie hadn't quite gotten up the courage to let go yet, but her greatest joy was trying to walk. Jake led her past the table his grandmother was seated at, and a quick glance told him that the older woman's cheeks did appear to be a little rosier than usual.

Jake helped Meggie climb up the steps to the toddler fountain and held her while she drank. The thought that Gram and Will might be sweet on each other didn't really bother Jake. It did create one more reason that he and Sara needed to make their truce work. But just because they'd called a truce didn't mean everything would be smooth sailing from here on out. He was sure that he and Sara would go out of their way to keep from making the people they cared about feel uncomfortable in their presence. Who knew? Maybe one day they wouldn't feel so tense around each other. But it wasn't going to happen until he could find a way to curb the attraction he felt for her.

Watching Sara and Gina deep in conversation, Jake admitted to himself that past or no past, he was attracted to her. And he knew it wouldn't matter if he had never met Sara before—he'd still be drawn to her. Yes, she was beautiful, but there was more. There was a depth to her that hadn't always been there; a light that seemed to come from deep inside. Suddenly Jake knew that her relationship with the Lord set Sara apart and gave her the peace he so desperately wanted.

❧

Sara watched Jake walk Meggie to the water fountain and help her get a drink.

"He is crazy about that baby, isn't he?" Gina asked.

"He certainly is." Sara nodded. She loved watching Jake with Meggie. The love shining from his eyes when he looked at his daughter was so strong it was almost tangible. "It was just the two of them until he moved back here, and I think he's had a little bit of trouble letting others help him with her. Not that you'd know it to hear Nora talk."

"Oh? Nora isn't happy about Jake being back?"

Sara shook her head. "She thinks he came back just so he could dump Meggie on Gram, to hear her tell it." Sara instantly felt sorry for gossiping about her mother-in-law. "I shouldn't have said that. I'm sure she is just concerned about Gram taking on too much."

"Maybe that's what all of that was about, earlier." Gina looked thoughtful as she scooped up a bite of cake.

"What are you talking about, Gina? What happened?"

"Well, Nora was serving earlier, and when she saw you and Jake talking, she said something to Ellie, and I heard Ellie tell her that it wasn't any of her business. Then Nora left in a huff."

"I'd wondered where she was. She probably won't be happy with me. I've upset her several times over Jake. I guess this is another one."

"Sara, you can't let Nora bother you. You and Jake are part of the same family, just as Nora is. Getting along is a good thing. It makes life easier on everyone."

"I know. I just don't like upsetting her." She chuckled. "Grandpa and Gram think she needs a man in her life."

"Ah, that explains what those two have their heads together about. They're hatching a plan to get Nora together with someone?"

"Well, now, it might have something to do with Nora, and it might not. I've been wondering about those two." Sara shook her head and grinned. "Don't they make an adorable couple?"

Gina laughed and nodded her head. "They do. My word, David and I go away for a month and come back to all kinds of matchmaking."

"Don't hold your breath to see if any of it is successful. Far as I know, those two haven't come up with anyone for Nora."

"What's this about someone for Nora?" Lydia asked, coming up behind them. "What a good idea!"

Sara and Gina both laughed.

"Grandpa and Gram seem to think so," Sara said. "We think that may be what they are talking about over there." She unobtrusively motioned to the table where the older couple was seated.

"Oh." Lydia sounded disappointed. "I thought maybe there was a romance brewing between those two."

"I wouldn't rule that out yet, either." Sara gathered up her plate and cup and led the way toward the kitchen to help with cleanup. "We've been wondering the very same thing."

❧

The next few days gave the tentative truce a chance to work. Jake and Sara smiled hesitantly at each other in the grocery store and waved at each other from across the street. It felt like progress when they graduated from trying not to make eye contact to actual conversation during the next few days.

On Thursday, Jake was just entering the diner as Sara began to leave. He held the door open for her. "Good morning, Sara," he said. "Nice day we're having."

"Good morning, Jake," Sara answered. "Yes, it is."

The next afternoon Jake was leaving just as she and Gina entered Deana's.

"Good afternoon, ladies," Jake said. "How are you both today?"

"Doing well, Jake," Gina answered.

"That's great. Thank you for the names you gave Gram. She said she was sure she could pick one or two girls to help out from the list you gave her." He turned to Sara and grinned. "And you, Sara? Have you had a good day?"

"Hi, Jake. I'm just fine. How are you? And Meggie and Gram, how are they?" Sara couldn't help it. She chuckled at their exaggerated politeness.

"We're doing just fine, thank you." His deep chuckle joined hers as he walked out the door.

Sara was still smiling when she took her seat across from Gina.

"Looks like the truce is holding," Gina said.

"Well, I don't think it's been tested yet. We've only seen each other in passing."

"You're both laughing at the situation. That's always a good sign."

"A sign of what?"

"Oh, come on, Sara. You two genuinely like each other. You always have."

Sara couldn't argue with her friend on that one. She and Jake had always liked each other. They'd been relaxed around each other whether they were talking or silent, and she did miss that closeness. Sara was relieved when the waitress interrupted their conversation. She didn't want to talk about her present feelings about Jake. She wasn't quite ready to admit how strong they were—even to herself.

But she did want to know about these helpers for Gram, and after the waitress left with their order, Sara turned her attention to Gina. "What's this about a helper for Gram? Is she having problems keeping up with Meggie? I offered to help anytime." If they were looking into others lending a hand, apparently Jake didn't want to take her up on her offer.

"Now don't get all riled up, Sara. From what Ellie told me, she still doesn't think she needs help. But Jake insisted she get someone. They finally compromised on getting one or two of the teens from church to come in after school to help out, at least until Jake gets into his own place and can hire a housekeeper."

"I could help out easily," Sara said. Some truce they were going to have if Jake didn't even trust her with his daughter.

"Sara, you know how independent Ellie is. She only agreed to this plan because she knows there are several girls who could use the money. It's her way of helping out. You know if it was more than a few hours a day or if she was sick or something like that, you're probably the first person she'd call."

Sara nodded. Gina was right and she was sure that Gram would call her. What she wasn't sure about was that Jake would ask her to help.

That same afternoon, she'd agreed to meet with Gram again to firm up some of the plans for the reunion. Truce or no truce, she was a little apprehensive as she knocked on the door and breathed a sigh of relief when Gram answered.

"Come in, Dear. Meggie is down for a nap, and I'm just putting a roast on for supper." She led the way back to the kitchen and poured Sara a cup of coffee.

Gram finished browning the large roast and slipped it into the oven before joining Sara at the table. She gathered her lists together, looked through her glasses at Sara, and smiled. "Let's see, where did we leave off?"

The rest of the afternoon flew by as they made more phone calls and went over menus and shopping lists. Gram was as excited as a child about the coming reunion. They worked steadily until male banter and laughter alerted them that Jake and Luke were entering the kitchen.

"Sara! It's nice to see you," Luke said, crossing the kitchen to give his grandmother and Sara a kiss on the cheek.

Jake barely had time to smile at her before a squeal was heard from upstairs and he rushed to check on Meggie.

"Oh my, it's later than I thought," Gram said, looking at the clock. "Sara, why don't you call Will and tell him to come on over? This roast is big enough for all of us, and I just didn't seem to know when to stop peeling potatoes."

Sara noticed several more pots on the stove and realized Gram must have finished her meal preparations while she had been tied up on the phone. "That's all right, Gram. I'll go home. Grandpa may have already started supper."

The older woman picked up the phone. "Well, there's only one way to find out." She dialed the number just as Jake came back down the stairs with Meggie on his hip.

"Will, it's Ellie. Darlin', I'm afraid I've kept Sara here too long today. I've asked her and you, of course, to eat with us, but she was afraid you might have started supper already."

Apparently both Luke and Jake caught the change in their

grandmother's tone as she talked to Sara's grandfather. Luke raised an eyebrow in Sara's direction and motioned toward Gram. Jake looked on as Sara shrugged and grinned. Luke raised and lowered both eyebrows as they heard Gram's side of the conversation continue.

"I'll tell her. We'll be eating in about a half hour. We'll be looking for you."

Sara quickly hid her smile as Gram turned to her. "Your grandpa said he hadn't started a thing and he'd be glad to give you a break from cooking. He'll be right over." She looked down at her apron and reached up to fluff her hair. "Sara dear, would you check the roast? I need to go freshen up just a bit."

Luke, Sara, and even Jake could barely contain their chuckles until they were sure Gram was out of earshot.

"Did you hear that? Gram sounded all of sixteen on the phone," Jake said.

"From the sound of it, we may have to ask your grandfather what his intentions are," Luke added.

"Don't you dare embarrass those two wonderful people!" Sara said, but her giggles increased.

Meggie looked from her daddy to her uncle Luke to Sara and back again. Finally she giggled and clapped her hands, not wanting to miss out on any of the fun.

All three adults struggled to get their laughter under control before Gram came back downstairs, but they were still chuckling when she returned.

"My, my, I haven't heard this much laughter in a long time," she said as she entered the kitchen. She'd changed into a dress, put on lipstick, and coaxed her hair into soft silver waves around her face. "What has everyone's tickle bone turned on?"

Jake seemed to recover first. "Oh, Meggie got tickled about something and it just snowballed. You know how that goes. One person giggles, then another, and pretty soon, you have a whole roomful of people laughing and no one can tell you why."

"You look awfully nice, Gram. You wouldn't be sprucing up for any reason we need to know about, would you?" Luke asked.

Sara shook her head at him. What was he doing? Trying to embarrass Gram? How she and Grandpa felt about each other was none of their business.

"Lucas, I do not feel that question deserves an answer other than the obvious one. We have company coming for supper." She turned from the stove and arched an eyebrow at her youngest grandson. "Do I need any other reason to comb my hair and put a clean dress on?"

Jake and Sara couldn't help chuckling again, only this time their amusement was brought on by the look on Luke's face as he realized his grandmother had just put him in his place.

"Uh, no, Ma'am, you don't." He crossed the room and kissed her cheek to make amends. "You look quite lovely, too."

"Thank you. Now you can mash the potatoes."

Luke saluted and rolled up his sleeves. "Yes, Ma'am. I'll get on that right away."

Gram grinned at him. "Good."

Her attention turned to Jake and Sara. "Jake, will you sharpen the carving knife for me?"

"Yes, Ma'am," Jake said, plopping Meggie in her playpen until suppertime.

"And, Sara, would you be a dear and set the table in the dining room?"

The three exchanged glances and tried to hide their smiles as they went about the chores they'd been given, feeling properly disciplined.

A few minutes later, Sara stood back and looked at the table. It looked nice. The doorbell rang, and Gram called out, "Sara dear, please let your grandfather in."

Sara hurried to do just that, wondering if her grandpa had taken the time to spruce himself up as well. She opened the door and caught a strong whiff of his aftershave. She'd never seen him look so nice except for when he went to church. While he didn't have a suit on this evening, he'd dressed in a nice pair of slacks and a white shirt. His hair was slicked back, and his bushy white eyebrows actually looked tamed. He'd even trimmed his moustache. *Oh my, this does look serious.*

"Why, Grandpa, don't you look nice."

"Thank you, Darlin'." He looked around. "Where's Ellie? In the back?" Not waiting for an answer, he headed for the kitchen. Sara followed, a half smile on her lips. Grandpa seemed to feel even more at home here than she did. She noticed Gram blush as Grandpa walked over to her and took her hand in his.

"Ellie," he said, "thank you so much for inviting Sara and myself to supper."

Gram reached up and patted his cheek with her free hand. "You're very welcome, William."

They stood looking into each other's eyes until Luke called from by the stove, "Mashed potatoes are ready, Gram."

"Oh." Gram turned her attention to getting the meal on the table. "Yes, well, Jake, you get Meggie set up in the dining room. Luke, carry those potatoes in, please. And Sara dear, please get the rolls from the oven."

They all jumped to do Gram's bidding, feeling a little like intruders waiting to see what the older couple was going to do next. It wasn't until they'd reached the dining room and taken their seats that the three realized their respective grandparents were still in the kitchen. They looked at one another. The silence was deafening.

Several minutes passed before Gram led Grandpa out to the dining room. He put the nicely sliced roast in the center of the table before pulling out Gram's chair for her.

The relief was almost tangible when Meggie broke the silence by clapping her hands. "I hungy, Gma!"

"Will, would you please say grace, so we can feed this baby?"

"Dear Father, we thank You for this food we are about to eat, for those who prepared it, for this family and these friends. We thank You for watching over us and seeing to our needs daily. In Jesus' name. Amen."

Jake quickly dished up some mashed potatoes and watched as his daughter filled her spoon. She managed to take her first bite without spilling any. And her second. It looked like his daughter had finally conquered using a spoon. "Meggie, you did it!"

Meggie put down her spoon and clapped her hands. From then on the evening was hers. She flirted and giggled between each bite. But as soon as she finished eating, she reached out to Sara.

"Sawa, hode."

When Sarah looked at Jake for permission to hold his daughter, he knew he'd never be able to deny her. He unbuckled Meggie and started to hand her to Sara, but Meggie said, "I walk."

Jake put her on her feet and steadied her. Meggie held on to his hands for a second and then let go. Everyone at the table silently watched Sara get out of her chair and kneel on the floor, holding her hands out to Meggie. Then, hands outstretched, Meggie took one . . . two . . . three steps straight into Sara's arms.

Sara hugged her. "Meggie, you did it! What a big girl you are!"

Meggie had to walk back to her daddy and then take turns walking to everyone else at the table while Uncle Luke took pictures. But she ended right back with Sara when she tired of showing off.

"Sawa, hode now."

It was impossible for Jake to keep his eyes off Meggie and Sara. Like it or not, they'd bonded to each other. It didn't bother Jake as much as it had when he'd first returned to town. Sara was wonderful with his daughter. She finished the rest of her meal with Meggie sitting in her lap as if she belonged there. When she brushed the hair from Meggie's cheek and kissed her, Jake was reminded of the night she'd put Meggie to bed. The night he'd held her in his arms and kissed her. His gaze strayed to her mouth, and he looked up to see color stealing up her face as her eyes met his. Was she remembering too? He liked the thought that she might be.

Meggie seemed content to stay right where she was, and Jake couldn't blame her. When the meal was over, the only thing that got her out of Sara's lap was the promise of a horsy ride from Uncle Luke. Sara insisted on clearing the table and doing the dishes, leaving Gram and her grandfather to visit while Jake and Luke played with Meggie.

It wasn't until Sara and her grandfather had left and Jake was upstairs giving Meggie her bath that he realized he was no closer to knowing how serious his grandmother and Will were about each other than he'd been before supper. While he'd meant to pay special attention to how they reacted to each other during the meal, it seemed his focus had been elsewhere. His attention had been taken by his daughter . . . and by Will's granddaughter.

❧

Sara was tired but still too keyed up for sleep. She made some hot chocolate and took it to the front porch. Setting the swing in motion, she smiled, thinking back on the evening. The truce had held and she was glad. She and Jake had done the right thing by agreeing to it.

Now if she could just find a way to keep her heart from going into overdrive every time she was around him. Sara sighed and closed her eyes, but all she could see was the look in Jake's eyes while she held Meggie. She hoped that hadn't been pity she'd seen, because pity was the last thing she wanted from him. She couldn't deny it anymore. She was falling in love with Jake all over again.

$$\large 10$$

*J*ake sat in Meggie's room, still rocking the baby long after she'd fallen asleep and thinking back over the evening. After the awkwardness before Gram and Will came into the dining room, the evening had been a true delight. Now that she had let go of his fingers and gone off by herself, his daughter was officially a toddler.

He was actually glad she'd taken those first steps to Sara. He'd been able to watch them both, and it'd been hard to tell who'd been more excited, Meggie or Sara.

The truce was holding, and he was pleased, even with the stipulation to stay away from the past. There were only two reasons he'd ever want to visit those days again—to find out if Sara had truly loved him and to explain about Melissa.

But as he looked down at his sleeping child, Jake wasn't sure he could do that. Melissa had given him Meggie. And telling Sara that he suspected Melissa's first pregnancy might not have been genuine—that it actually was a trick to get him to the altar— seemed disloyal to the mother of his child. Not to mention that it would seem that he was laying the blame for the end of his relationship with Sara at someone else's feet, when he knew it was the result of his own choices.

For years he'd blamed Sara, Wade, and Melissa for messing up his life. How wrong he'd been. He was the one who had been so hot-headed that night that he'd refused to listen to Sara. He was the one who'd gone against all he'd been taught when he got back to college that night. Jake groaned in disgust with himself and nearly woke his sleeping child.

432

He stood up and carried Meggie to her crib. Laying her down gently, he patted her on the back to keep her asleep.

He propped his elbow on Meggie's crib and buried his face in his hands. *Oh, God, please forgive me for blaming others for the mistakes I've made. Please help me to truly take responsibility for the pain I've caused them and to mend my relationship with You. I'm not even sure how to go about it, so I just ask You to show me the way. In Jesus' name. Amen.*

Jake bent down to brush his lips over Meggie's brow, thanking the Lord for blessing him with this child.

❧

Sara was enjoying her second cup of coffee when Nora called the next morning. Somehow she knew it would be her mother-in-law before she answered the phone.

"Sara dear, I called last night but you weren't at home."

"No, Grandpa and I were at Gram's. I'd been helping her with—"

"With that baby. I knew she would be too much for Ellie."

"No, Nora. It wasn't Meggie. We were working on the reunion. We lost track of time and Gram asked Grandpa and me to eat supper with them." Sara wished she didn't constantly feel the need to explain everything to Nora.

"Oh. I see. And I suppose Jake was there too?"

"Yes, he and Luke were both there."

"I see."

Sara didn't like the condescending tone her mother-in-law was using. "No, Nora, I don't think—"

"Sara, remember, I warned you about Jake. I saw him seek you out Wednesday night. He's got his sights on you as a mother for Meggie."

"Nora, Jake does not have his sights set on me." Sara knew her voice sounded as irritated as she felt, but she couldn't help it. Sara trembled just at the thought of being married to Jake and becoming Meggie's mommy. But having to hide those feelings from Nora and everyone else wasn't easy. And Sara knew it wasn't going to get any easier.

As if she sensed Sara's mood, Nora quickly changed her tone. "I'm sorry, Dear, I just don't want to see you hurt. I want the best for you, you know that."

"I do know that, Nora. But Jake has moved back here. He's part of the family. You can't pretend he doesn't exist."

"Yes, well, I don't have to condone his dumping his child on Ellie."

"Nora, Jake has not dumped Meggie on anyone. He's hiring several of the teens from church to come in and help out. And I think he had to talk Gram into agreeing on that. Has it ever occurred to you that she's enjoying keeping Meggie?"

"I'm sure she's a joy. But Ellie isn't getting any younger."

Remembering the tenderness Nora had shown with Meggie, Sara sighed and shook her head. Maybe Nora was truly concerned about everyone. If so, it was a shame that she never came across that way.

"You're right, she isn't. But she's enjoying herself right now, and that's a blessing." Sara changed the subject. "How are you feeling, Nora? Have you been back to the doctor to get the results from your tests?"

"I'm fine. Just under a lot of stress, as if I didn't already know that. You know what kind of year it's been. I don't know why everyone expects me to act as if life is just rosy and I have no cares."

"Nora, no one expects that from you."

"Yes, well, Dr. Wellington seems to think I've grieved quite long enough. He had the audacity to tell me to find another doctor so that he would feel free to ask me out."

"Oh my." Sara grinned. Maybe Gram and Grandpa weren't needed in the matchmaking department after all.

"Well, I have no intentions of going out with the man."

"I've heard he's very nice, Nora. Gina thinks the world of him. And it'd be nice for you to get out occasionally."

"I'm too old for all of that dating nonsense."

"Nora, you aren't too old at all."

"Well, when you've been a widow as long as I have, then we'll see how old you feel."

Suddenly Sara's life, as Nora painted it, loomed out in front of her . . . long and lonely. Just as suddenly, she knew she didn't want to settle for being alone the rest of her life. She wanted a home and family. She wanted someone to love and take care of.

But there was no way she could tell Nora that. No way at all.

&

David's sermon that Sunday focused once again on trusting the Lord to forgive and then demonstrating that trust by forgiving ourselves and going forward instead of dwelling on any past wrongdoings.

Jake wondered if David might be preaching straight at him, because he'd never thought about forgiveness in quite that way before. He knew that he'd had a hard time forgiving himself and forgetting the past. Sometimes he wondered how God could love him after he'd strayed from all he'd believed and been taught.

He sought David out the next morning, showing up at his office with coffee and donuts.

"Does that offer to talk still stand?" he asked, waving the bag of donuts across the desk.

David laughed. "Sure does. It'd stand even if you didn't have something delicious in that bag. Come on in and sit down."

After they'd downed a couple donuts and most of the coffee, David leaned back in his chair and got to the point. "What do you want to talk about, my friend?"

Jake leaned forward and clasped his hands together. "I liked your lesson yesterday. About forgiveness."

"I'm glad. Was there anything particular about it you'd like to discuss?" David pulled his Bible to the center of the desk.

"The part about forgiving ourselves, forgetting the past, being . . . an act of trust?"

David nodded. "Many of us have problems with that. Sometimes it's hard for us to believe we're truly forgiven even after we've asked for that very thing."

"That verse you quoted from Philippians—"

"Philippians 3:13–15," David said as he opened his Bible and flipped through the pages. " '*Brothers, I do not consider myself yet to have taken hold of it. But one thing I do: Forgetting what is behind and straining toward what is ahead, I press on toward the goal to win the prize for which God has called me heavenward in Christ Jesus. All of us who are mature should take such a view of things. And if on some point you think differently, that too God will make clear to you.*' Is that it?"

Jake nodded. "That's it. I know I've dwelt in the past way too much. I'm tired of it weighing me down."

"Sounds to me like you're just about there, Jake." David chuckled. "Maybe God's making it all clear to you."

"I certainly hope so. It's about time I figured it out, don't you think?"

"Well, I was a late bloomer myself," David said. "Sadly, it seems to take some of us longer than others."

He got up and refilled their Styrofoam cups from a coffee pot he had set up in the corner. "How are you and Sara doing? Gina mentioned something about a truce being called."

"Ah, well, we decided it was time to try to get along. This town isn't going to grow so large that we can keep from running into one another. And we have the same family and friends."

"Want to talk about why you two feel so uncomfortable around each other?"

"Nah, it's in that past I'm trying to get past." Jake grinned.

"Yeah, Gina and I had one of those kinds of pasts ourselves." David nodded. "We did have to visit it a time or two before we were able to forgive each other."

Jake shook his head. "One of the amendments of the truce was that we don't 'rehash the past.' "

"Your amendment or hers?"

"Hers."

"That might make it a little harder to put to rest."

Jake looked down into his coffee cup and sighed. "That's what I'm afraid of."

David shook his head. "My friend, notice I said harder. Not impossible. Take it to the Lord and let Him handle it."

Jake grinned and got to his feet. "I think I'll do just that. Thanks, old friend."

David stood up and the two men shook hands. "Any time."

ॐ

The Teddy Bear Brigade, as they'd taken to calling themselves, had decided to meet each Tuesday at the church for lunch and an afternoon of bear making. With one of the teens keeping watch over Meggie, Gram was free to join the group. Everyone brought their favorite dish, and David found one excuse after another to come into the fellowship hall, until finally the ladies insisted he join them for lunch.

Sara laughed, overhearing Gina admonish her husband at the same time she set a plate in front of him. "You are pitiful, you know? Taking advantage of these wonderful ladies, just because you're the minister." The sting was removed from Gina's words by the smile she bestowed upon her husband.

"I know, my love, I know." David nodded. "But you weren't in my office trying to endure the tempting smells wafting in from all this food. Why, my stomach was growling so loud I couldn't concentrate on tomorrow night's lesson."

Sara and Gram burst out laughing, and Gina just shook her head.

"Well, since you're here, would you be so kind as to say the blessing for us?"

David smiled at his wife and looked at all the ladies. "I'd be delighted. Please pray with me."

He bowed his head. "Dear Father, we thank You for all this food and for each of those who prepared it. Thank You for letting these sisters invite me to join in this meal. And thank You for the response they've had from these little bears they're making. Please continue to bless their work and each of their lives, dear Lord. In Jesus' name. Amen."

Everyone enjoyed the meal, and David even helped with the cleanup before going back to his office.

"You've got a good man there, Gina," Gram said as the ladies settled down to their sewing.

"Yes, Ma'am, I do." Gina threaded her needle. "It took us a long time to get it all together, though."

"Well, good things are usually worth the wait." Gram pinned a bear pattern to a short length of material. "How's Nora doing?" she asked Sara, changing the subject. "I haven't heard from her in several days."

Sara shook her head. "I'm not real sure. She had an appointment with that new doctor in town—"

"Dr. Wellington?" Gina asked. "He's supposed to be a very good doctor."

Gram winked at Sara. "Is he married?"

"No. He's never been married, from what I hear," Nell Schneider offered from across the table.

Sara got up and went to the kitchen, just off the fellowship hall, to put on a fresh pot of coffee. It was hard to keep from telling everyone that this Dr. Wellington was interested in her mother-in-law.

Gram followed her into the kitchen and pulled some Styrofoam cups down from the cabinet. "Might be a nice match for Nora," she whispered to Sara.

"Not if she doesn't like him," Sara whispered back.

Gina joined them in the small room. "What are you two cooking up now?" She grinned, as it seemed to dawn on her. "Oh . . . now, that might be a good match. He's very plain spoken. Doesn't impress me as the type to take much guff from anyone. He could be just the kind of man Nora needs."

Sara sighed. She couldn't keep it in any longer. "Well, we're halfway there. It seems Dr. Wellington is interested enough in Nora that he told her to find another doctor. He wants to ask her out."

Gram chuckled. "Now that does sound promising."

"Not as much as we'd like," Sara admitted. "Nora says she isn't interested."

"You think that's so?"

Sara shook her head. "I don't know. We were talking on the phone so I couldn't see her face. She says she's too old for a relationship."

"Oh, hogwash," Gram said. She went to the refrigerator and brought out some cream.

Sara grinned over at Gina. She had a feeling that would be Gram's opinion. At least it should be, if she and Grandpa were starting to care for one another.

"Maybe I'll just have me a talk with Nora," Gram continued.

"I think that's a great idea," Sara said.

"So do I," Gina added.

"I'll try to get with her in the next few days, and we'll have us a good long talk." As if that settled everything, Gram raised the service window facing the fellowship hall. "Ladies, coffee's ready."

Sara gave Gram a ride home. When they arrived, they found Meggie outside with Maria Bellows, one of the teens Jake had hired to help out. Enjoying the warm afternoon sun, Maria and Meggie sat together in the tire swing hanging from the large cottonwood tree in the backyard.

"Hi, Meggie," Sara called as Gram went inside to take care of her teddy bear supplies. "Are you having a good time?"

Meggie nodded and reached out to her. Sara dropped her purse to the ground. "Want me to swing you?"

Maria vacated the swing, and they laughed as Sara clumsily tried to seat herself in the tire swing. Once she felt halfway secure, she reached for the toddler. "Let's see if I remember how to do this."

Meggie giggled and clapped as they swung back and forth. Sara heard the back door slam but kept her eyes on the child, for fear of dropping her. "Maybe Daddy needs to look into getting a regular swing set for you," she observed.

"Daddy has been thinking the very same thing."

Sara's heart skipped more than a few beats as she recognized Jake's voice.

"Afternoon, ladies," he said, his smile taking in all three women.

"Hi, Mr. Breland. Meggie's been a really good girl this afternoon," Maria said. "If she's like this all the time, babysitting her will be a piece of cake."

Jake laughed. "Well, I can't guarantee she won't give you fits some days."

"That's all right. She's a sweetie anyway. We'll get along just fine."

"Thank you, Maria. There's a check for you on the kitchen table."

"Thanks." Maria waved to Meggie. "Bye, Meggie. I'll see you on Monday."

"Bye-bye." Meggie waved back.

"Bye, Mrs. Tanner, Mr. Breland." The young girl hurried across the lawn to get what Sara was sure was her first paycheck.

Sara let the swing gradually slow and brought it to a halt.

"Dada, hode me."

Jake took his daughter from Sara and grinned. "So, you think I should get a regular swing set?"

Sara struggled out of the swing as gracefully as she could, feeling Jake's eyes on her. She tried to ignore whatever it was that had her heart hammering against her sides. "Well, it might make it a little easier to swing her, unless . . . you know, they have those baby swings that Meggie would fit in, and you could attach it to the tree until she got big enough to sit in this one."

Jake scratched the back of his head. "Oh, yeah. I think I've seen those at the toy store. That's a good idea, Sara. I kind of hate to have to put up a swing set here, just to take it down in a few months when we move to our house."

"How's that going?" She wondered what kind of house he was going to build. Long ago they'd talked about the house they'd build some day, and she could still remember the floor plan they'd decided on.

"I'm supposed to meet with the builder tomorrow to go over some plans. Another week or two and hopefully I'll have the plans nailed down and he'll have all the subcontractors lined up."

"Jake Breland, what is this you have in my kitchen?" Gram called from the back door.

"Oh, that's my surprise for Meggie." He handed his daughter back to Sara. "I'll be right back."

He ran across the yard and into the house. When he and Gram came back out seconds later, he was carrying a large box. Sara watched as Jake knelt down and pulled an adorable golden retriever puppy from the box. Then he reached up for Meggie.

"Doggie, doggie!" Meggie said, as Jake held her close to the puppy and let her pet it.

Sara and Gram looked at each other and laughed, trying to figure out who was the most excited, Meggie, the puppy, or Jake. Gram kneeled down to pet the dog. "Now I wonder just who you bought this for, Jake—Meggie or yourself?"

Sara laughed at the injured expression on Jake's face.

"Now, Gram, you know I put my daughter's interests first." He reached down and helped his grandmother to her feet.

"Yes, I do. I'm teasing, Jake. It's a pretty dog."

"He is, isn't he?" Jake reached down and picked up Meggie while they watched the puppy run around. "We can keep it then?"

Even Meggie looked at her great-grandmother, as if she knew who had the final say.

"It can sleep in the utility room. But it stays out here during the day."

Jake grinned and bent to kiss his grandmother's cheek. "Thank you, Gram."

"Now, I'm going in to start supper." Gram smiled at Sara. "Want to stay and eat with us, Sara?"

"Thanks, Gram, but Grandpa is making stew." She reached out and tweaked Meggie's nose. "I'd better be going."

"Maybe another time," Gram said, heading for the house. "Thanks for bringing me home."

The puppy decided to run rings around the older woman, and Sara and Jake laughed as she made a game out of pretending to turn and chase it. The puppy would stop in its tracks and yap at her before running around her again.

But Gram made one move a little too quickly, the puppy tumbled between her feet, and Gram tripped. Jake handed Meggie to Sara and ran toward his grandmother, but he wasn't fast enough and his grandmother landed on her ankle. By the time Sara and Meggie got there, Jake was tenderly checking Gram's foot and leg.

"I'm so sorry," he said to the injured woman. "I should never have brought that puppy home. I should have waited until Meggie and I were in our own place."

Gram patted his hand, although she was in obvious pain. "It wasn't the dog's fault, Jake. I shouldn't have been teasing it. Every once in awhile, I forget I'm nearing eighty instead of eighteen."

Jake nodded and looked at Sara. "Maybe we should call an ambulance."

"Jacob Breland, I do not need an ambulance. Just get me in the house."

"No, Gram," Jake lifted her into his arms and looked at Sara. "Would you mind watching Meggie, Sara? I think I'd better get Gram to the hospital."

"Of course I'll stay. We'll be here when you get back."

Their eyes met, sharing unspoken concerns.

Sara and Meggie watched Jake gently ease Gram into his car and take off. Sara took the baby into the house and went to the phone. She dialed her home number, all the while praying, *Dear Lord, please let there be no broken bones. Please let Gram be all right.*

*A*fter telling Grandpa about Gram's accident, Sara called the rest of the family to let them know what had happened. She was surprised when there was no answer at Nora's, but she left a message on her answering machine and hoped to hear from her later.

Grandpa came right over, bringing his Crock-Pot stew with him. But he paced so badly he made Sara even more nervous than she already was, and she finally sent him to the hospital to check on Gram.

Sara tried not to watch the clock and kept herself busy by entertaining Meggie and making her a supper of macaroni and cheese. She made sure it was cool enough before setting the bowl in front of Meggie, but when she began to fill the fork with macaroni, Meggie reached for it.

Sara relinquished the small utensil to her and chuckled as Meggie slowly forked several pieces of the cheesy pasta and deftly plopped them into her mouth.

Remembering the first day she'd watched Meggie make such a mess with finger food and a sippy cup, Sara marveled at how fast the little girl had caught on to the intricacies of feeding herself.

Grandpa called from the hospital to let her know that Gram was still waiting to see a doctor. There'd been a wreck earlier, and the doctors were tied up. He promised to call and update her as he could.

Sara had bathed Meggie and rocked her to sleep before the phone rang again. Jake was calling to update her and check on Meggie.

"How is Gram?" Sara asked. "Is anything broken?"

"Can you believe she didn't break a thing? But she does have a nasty sprained ankle and will be down for awhile," he answered.

"Bless her heart. She's not going to like that at all."

"No, she's not a happy camper. And it's all my fault. I should never have brought that puppy home."

"Oh, Jake, I'm sure she doesn't blame you."

"No, she doesn't. But I blame myself." He changed the subject. "How's my girl? Did she give you any problems?"

Sara chuckled. "Not one. She fed herself, had a ball in the tub, and went right to sleep."

"Well, I just wanted to let you know that we'll be on our way as soon as we can get Gram released."

"Okay. I'll have supper on the table."

"You don't have to do that, Sara."

"It's no problem, Jake. Grandpa brought over the stew he had cooking. All I have to do is heat up some rolls and set the table."

"All right. Thank you, Sara, for staying with Meggie—for everything. I really appreciate it."

"You're welcome . . . hurry home. With Gram," Sara added quickly before hanging up the phone.

She set the table and put on a fresh pot of coffee. She'd just finished placing the rolls in the oven when the phone rang again. Nora had returned home and wanted to know the latest. Sara was glad that she could at least give her an updated report on Gram.

"I just got back from town," Nora said. "I wish I'd known. I could have gone to the hospital with . . . ah, to see about her."

"Well, they'll be home any minute now. I'll be sure and tell her you called to check on her," Sara said, wondering who Nora might have gone to the hospital *with*.

"Yes, please do, Dear." Nora's tone cooled slightly. "I suppose this means you'll be helping her with the baby."

"Of course I'll help, Nora."

"Yes, well, I figured as much."

Sara heard a car pull up outside. "Nora, I think they're home now. I'll be sure and give Gram your love."

"Please do."

"I'll talk to you tomorrow and let you know how she's doing. Night, Nora." Sara hung up and ran to the door.

Her heart ached at the sight of Gram struggling to get out of the car. But she had to smile, hearing Jake try to convince his grandmother to let him carry her inside. "Gram, you have plenty of time to get used to those crutches tomorrow. Let me carry you into the house."

"No, Jake. I want to do it myself."

"Won't you let me carry you, Ellie?" Grandpa asked.

"Will, you aren't any younger than I am. You'd drop me or trip over something, and we'd both end up back at that hospital. Now both of you move out of my way. I can do this."

Sara could tell Gram was tired and hurting from the abrupt way in which she talked to two of her favorite men. They'd probably been hounding her about what she could and couldn't do all the way home. She had to chuckle as she watched Gram make her way to the back porch, with Jake and Grandpa right beside her. But as she watched the injured woman maneuver the steps on crutches, Sara was sure she knew how the two men felt. Her fingers itched to reach out and help. They breathed a collective sigh of relief when Gram made it through the back door and into the kitchen.

"Are you hungry?" Sara asked as Gram took her seat at the table.

"I am starved, Dear, thank you."

"Me too," Jake said. "The cafeteria was closed, and all they had were those awful vending machines. After you told me Will's stew was waiting, I just got hungrier." Jake chuckled. "What can I do to help?"

"You can put ice in the glasses and get the tea," Sara answered, bringing the stew to the table.

She dipped out a bowl for everyone while Jake took care of the drinks. Grandpa was busy finding an extra chair for Gram to prop her foot up on.

Once they were all seated, Jake offered the blessing and thanked the Lord that his grandmother wasn't hurt any worse.

"My, this stew is tasty, Will. Thank you. I didn't realize just how hungry I was," Gram said.

They'd barely finished eating when Luke, John, Lydia, and Ben showed up to check on Gram. Amid hugs and kisses, she tried to assure everyone she was fine, but the telltale black and blue inching up from her ankle to her calf said otherwise.

"I think I should stay here tonight, just in case you need help," Lydia offered.

Gram shook her head. "I'm perfectly capable of getting myself to bed. I don't need anyone to look after me, but I'll have to admit, I'll need some help with that little tyke upstairs."

"Don't worry about a thing, Gram. I can stay home with Meggie," Jake said.

John nodded. "He can. Or he can bring her into the office."

"I . . . I'd be glad to come over and watch Meggie. I'm only a few blocks away, and I'd love to help out, if it's all right with everyone." Sara looked at Jake to gauge his response. She wasn't sure what his quick frown was saying.

Grandpa chimed in with his two cents. "That's a good idea. Lydia would have to come in from the ranch. We live much closer, and I can come over and help out too. There's no need for Jake to stay home all day when he has all of us to lend a hand."

"This is true. No matter how we work it out, Jake, we're family and we're here to help," Lydia said.

"Well, if I have any say in all this planning, I'd like to take Sara up on her offer," Gram said. "We're in the middle of planning the reunion anyway, and Meggie has taken to her from the very first. I think she'll be happier if Sara is around."

Everyone seemed to be looking at Jake for his approval. He looked around the room and knew this was exactly why he'd come back to Sweet Springs—having family nearby to help with Meggie when he needed them. He smiled and nodded.

"Thank you all. I know Gram and Meggie will be in good hands no matter who is with them." He hadn't expected to be turning to Sara for help, but his family would never understand if he turned down her generous offer. "If you really don't mind, Sara, I think Gram is right. Meggie will be thrilled to have you here each day."

Their eyes met, and for a brief moment he wished he could retract what he'd just said. Not because he didn't want Sara around, but because he did. He knew having her close by on a daily basis could lead to more heartache. Yet he wanted to be able to see her every day. He held his breath, waiting for her answer.

"I'll be here first thing in the morning. Just tell me what time you need me."

✪

Early the next morning Sara let herself into Gram's sunny kitchen with the key she'd been given the night before. Jake had told her she didn't need to be there before nine o'clock, but she'd awakened early and couldn't see any sense in sitting around waiting when Gram might need help with something.

She quietly put the coffee on and went upstairs to check on the patient.

"God bless you, Sara," Gram said as she entered the room. "I'm a little stiffer than I thought I'd be this morning. Could you help me get out of this bed, please?"

"Of course I can. I should have slept here last night," she said, feeling bad that she hadn't insisted on staying. She helped Gram slide her legs to the side of the bed and put an arm around her to steady her while she balanced on the crutches.

"There was no need for you to stay here last night," Gram insisted as she slowly made her way across the room. "I slept fine. That pain pill put me right out. But I've been awake for about an hour and I didn't want to wake Meggie too early by yelling for Jake to come help me."

Sara stood outside the bathroom door in case Gram needed her, but the older woman managed just fine. She refused to get back in bed, and took a seat in the easy chair beside the window.

"You know me, Sara. I can't stay in bed. In fact, once Jake is up and around, would you ask him to help me downstairs? I'll be much more comfortable there than up here."

"Gram, you really ought to rest that ankle for a few days."

"I'm going to rest it. Just not up here. I want to be down where you and Meggie are."

Sara tried to talk her into staying in bed, but Gram could be stubborn, and Sara finally gave in.

They heard a knock on the door and looked up to see Jake sticking his head around the corner. "Good morning. How are you feeling, Grams?"

Sara caught her breath at how handsome he looked first thing in the morning. He was dressed in a maroon robe, but his eyes still had that sleepy look and his jaw was dark with an overnight beard. His smile had her heart tripping over itself, and she was glad Gram answered him.

"I'll feel much better once I get downstairs," she insisted. "I'd like you to help me get there. I don't like feeling cut off from everything."

Jake raised a questioning eyebrow at Sara. She shrugged and found her voice. "I think she's going to get downstairs one way or another. The safest way would probably be for you to help her."

Jake nodded. "Can you wait until I shower, Gram?"

"Of course."

"Then I'll hurry." He looked at Sara. "I think I hear Meggie stirring. Would you mind bringing her down to her playpen in the kitchen? She's used to playing in it until I get her breakfast ready."

"I'll be glad to," Sara said. She turned back to Gram. "Do you need me to get you anything first?"

Gram shook her head. "No, I'm fine until Jake comes back to get me. You go see about our little darlin'."

Sara didn't have to be prodded to check on Meggie. She followed Jake down the hall to the baby's room and watched his grin turn into a full-fledged chuckle as Meggie looked up and greeted him. "Dada!"

Twin sets of dimples greeted each other as Jake picked up his daughter. "Mornin', Precious."

Meggie looked over his shoulder and spotted Sara for the first time. "Sawa!"

"Hi, Meggie. Can I get you ready and take you downstairs while Daddy takes his shower?"

Meggie reached out to her. Jake chuckled and kissed his daughter before handing her to Sara. "Well, I guess that answers your question."

"I think we're going to get along just fine, Jake. Don't you worry about us." Sara took Meggie over to the changing table and set about getting the baby ready to go downstairs.

"No, I won't," Jake said. He turned to the hall. "I'll be down to get her breakfast ready as soon as I get cleaned up and get Gram down there so she can oversee everything."

But by the time he got downstairs with Gram, Sara had bacon and eggs on the table and Meggie was in her chair, nibbling on toast and bacon.

"Oh, this is nice, Sara," Gram said as she shifted to get comfortable in her chair and prop her foot up on a small footstool Jake had found.

"Yes, it is," he said, taking his seat next to Meggie.

"I wasn't sure what to feed Meggie," Sara said, pouring three cups of coffee and taking a seat across from Jake. "I thought she could probably handle this."

Jake spooned some scrambled eggs onto Meggie's plate and handed her the small fork she liked. "This is fine. She loves bacon."

Sara sat back with her cup of coffee and watched Jake lift four pieces of bacon onto his plate. "And I can see her daddy does too."

Jake chuckled and nodded. "She comes by it honestly."

"Tomorrow, have Will come on over for breakfast," Gram said. "No sense in him having to cook for himself while we're all enjoying each other's company."

"Yes, do," Jake added. "We've taken his cook away from him, the least we can do is have him join us."

"Grandpa doesn't mind. He—"

"Is a good man. But there's no sense messing up two kitchens when one will do," Gram said with a tone of finality.

Sara grinned and looked at Jake. He shrugged and nodded. "I'll be sure and ask him to come with me tomorrow, Gram. I'm sure he'll be showing up anytime now, anyway."

"Oh, Jake," Gram said, changing the subject, "before you go to work, did you buy any dog food?"

"It's in the back of my car. I'll be sure and get it before I leave." He looked at his grandmother. "If you're sure about keeping him. I really do feel badly, Gram."

A small whine was heard, and they looked up to see the puppy looking through the screen door. Meggie clapped her hands. "Doggie, doggie!"

"Now, how could I tell you to get rid of that puppy after that?" Gram asked. She shook her head. "I told you it wasn't the puppy's fault. Of course he can stay."

"Thanks, Gram." He went outside and was back in just a few minutes. "I fed the dog and gave him water, too. Do you need anything brought back down from upstairs?"

"No, my medicine is in my pocket, the crutches are right here—"

"And I'm here if she thinks of anything she needs," Sara added.

"And you're the only reason I can even think of going to work today. Thank you, Sara." Jake smiled at her from across the room.

"You're welcome. I'm glad I can help. I've had a lot of it given to me from this family."

Jake nodded and headed upstairs. He came back down only minutes later with a jacket slung over his shoulder. He kissed the top of Gram's head, "You take it easy today, you hear?"

"I will."

He bent down and kissed Meggie on the cheek. "You be a good girl for Sara, okay?"

Meggie nodded. "'Kay."

Jake straightened and looked over at Sara, wishing he could kiss her too. "I'll see you this evening. If you need anything, just call the office."

"I will." Sara smiled and nodded, motioning toward the door. "Shoo, Jake. We'll be just fine. I promise."

And they were. Grandpa came over and entertained Gram for most of the day, making sure she took a nap both morning and afternoon. While she slept, he took Meggie out to play with the puppy so that Sara could straighten up the upstairs rooms and do some wash.

The phone rang on and off all day with relatives, church members, and townspeople wanting to know how Gram was and offering to help in any way they could. By noon, Sara knew not to start supper, because several of the ladies from church were arranging to bring over a series of meals. The outpouring of care and concern for Gram reminded Sara of how lucky she felt to be part of such a wonderful church family.

But the best part of the day was, without a doubt, Meggie. Sara loved interacting with the toddler. At nap time, Meggie came to Sara with her blankie and crawled into her lap. Holding the baby close and rocking her, Sara envisioned her own child being cuddled close and rocked to sleep in heaven. She gathered Meggie just a little closer as the pain she always carried eased.

$\widehat{12}$

$\mathcal{T}$he next week flew by for Sara as she tried to see that Gram took it easy and worked to keep up with Meggie. Sara kept her camera close by so she could get snapshots of an adorable Meggie toddling around, falling, and picking herself up.

Gram's ankle seemed to turn a different color each day. It went through varying shades of black, blue, and green before settling into a yellowish gray. But as always, the older woman's attitude inspired Sara. Gram didn't let the pain or the awkward use of crutches keep her down. Sara could only hope she'd be as full of life and living when she neared eighty.

While Meggie napped, she and Gram either worked on the plans for the reunion, or sewed and stuffed more teddy bears. Meggie woke up early one afternoon, and Sara brought her down to her playpen in the kitchen while she finished up one of the bears.

"Wat dat?" Meggie asked, pointing to the little bear.

"It's a bear, Sweetie." Sara made one last stitch, tied it off, and cut the thread. She carried the brightly checkered bear over and showed it to Meggie. "Do you like it?"

Meggie dropped the blanket she'd been holding and grabbed the little stuffed animal. "Thanky, Sawa."

Sara's heart melted and she wondered why she'd never given the child one before. "You're welcome, Sweetie."

Sara drove home unsure of which time of day she liked best lately. The mornings when she let herself in the back door, brought Meggie down, and started breakfast while Jake showered, dressed, and helped Gram get downstairs. Or the evenings, when he came home from work and they all ate supper at the big table in the kitchen.

She had no doubts about which part she liked least. She hated leaving at night. She always felt as if she'd left a big chunk of herself back at Gram's. As she pulled into the driveway at home, she was pretty certain it was her heart she'd left behind.

The next morning, Sara was delighted to see both Jake and Meggie already downstairs when she let herself in the back door. Jake had the coffee on and was holding Meggie on his hip while he stirred something on the stove. The little girl grinned widely when Sara greeted her.

"Sawa!" She held up the little bear Sara had given her the day before. "Ted-bear seep wif me."

"He did?" Sara looked around for the child's blanket and, finding no evidence of it, looked questioningly at Jake.

"It appears Meggie has given up her blankie for Ted-bear. She slept with him all night and had him clasped in her arms when I went in to get her this morning."

"Oh, how sweet. I kind of hate to see the blanket go, though."

Jake chuckled. "I know. She didn't even ask for it last night when I rocked her to sleep. But thank you for giving her the bear. She loves it."

He turned back to the oatmeal he was cooking for his daughter and poured out a bowl. "This just needs to cool. Would you mind taking Meggie while I go up and help Gram down? I'm meeting with the builder to finalize the house plans this morning."

"Of course I don't mind." Sara reached out and took Meggie into her arms. "Hi, Sweetie. You ready to eat?"

"Ted-bear eat too?"

"Hmmm," Sara said to herself as she settled Meggie into her high chair. "I can see that we might need a spare bear around here. I'll see if we have enough of that material left to make another one."

By the end of the day, Meggie had a spare bear in her room, but she still hadn't asked for her blanket.

Jake came home from work that night with the plans to his and Meggie's new home under his arm. The rest of the family had been invited over to take a look, but they all had to wait until after supper when the table was cleared to get a look at them.

Jake spread the plans out on the table, stood back, and waited for comments. He answered question after question about this room and that. Then he noticed Sara looking intently at the plans, color flooding her face. She bit her bottom lip. Suddenly he realized what he had done. His plans matched exactly the plans he and Sara had talked about when they were young. He hadn't even been aware that he'd duplicated them.

The house would be a large two-story with a wide wraparound porch. The kitchen stood along one end with windows on the front, side, and back of the house. He remembered how Sara had commented years ago that she wanted to be able to look out and see their children playing no matter where she was in the house.

This house would have nooks and crannies much like Gram's house—all the little touches that builders usually didn't bother with anymore but that gave a house character. The same touches he and Sara had decided they wanted when they were young and in love. Suddenly he remembered that years ago he and Sara had walked along the very block where he was now building and how he had commented that he'd like to build a house there some day.

"I like it, Bro," Luke said, bringing Jake out of his reverie.

"So do I. It's going to look especially good on that block. It'll look as though it's been there forever," John said. "It'll blend right in."

"It's going to be a lovely home for you and Meggie, Jake," Lydia agreed.

Jake was glad they all liked it, but he knew there was truly only one opinion that mattered to him.

Sara turned to him with a smile. "Well, it goes without saying that I love it."

That was the only reference she made that came close to touching on its similarities to their dream house, but it was enough to make Jake realize that his dream home wouldn't be complete without Sara in it. He wanted them back together. Not just as friends. While he'd been crazy about the younger Sara, he was head over heels in love with this one.

He looked into her eyes. "I was hoping you'd like it," he said, but his mind skittered all over the place. How could he let Sara know that he'd loved her all his life, without feeling disloyal to Meggie's mother? Was it possible that he ever could? Jake didn't know how much he could reveal to Sara about his and Melissa's relationship, but he did know one thing. He was in love with Sara, he wanted her in his and Meggie's life, and he was going to do everything in his power to make her see they truly were meant for each other.

Jake went to bed that night with a new determination. He was going to try to get Sara to fall in love with him again. He knew he was putting his heart on the line, but he also knew that he had no choice. He loved Sara, plain and simple. Now he just had to do his best to convince her they were meant to be together.

The first phase of Jake's plan went into action the next morning. He didn't have to do much talking to convince his grandmother and Will that Sara needed a break. But he knew persuading Sara might be a different story. So he did the only thing he could think of. He called Gina and David and enlisted their aid.

Jake dawdled over breakfast that morning so long that finally Sara asked him if he was taking the day off.

"No. But I can if you need me here to do anything."

"No, Jake, we're coping very well. I'm just not used to you being here after nine o'clock. Are you feeling all right?"

"Sara, I'm fine. I just wasn't in a hurry today. Actually, I—"

The phone rang right on cue and Jake answered it. "Hi, Gina. Yes, she's right here."

"It's for you." He handed the phone to Sara and poured himself another cup of coffee, trying not to let on that he was listening to Sara's side of the conversation.

"Oh, Gina, that sounds nice, but I'm not sure how I could leave Gram."

She was quiet for a minute and then said, "Well, yes, Grandpa is here."

Jake had his back to Sara and grinned at Will and Gram.

"What is it, Darlin'?" Will asked Sara. "Does Gina need me for something?"

Sara asked Gina to hold on and turned to her grandfather and Gram. "She wants me to go to lunch with her today. I just don't think I should leave—"

"Now there is no reason you have to be chained to this house, Sara," Gram interjected. "Will can stay with me while you go have lunch."

"Well, then, with Grandpa here, I could take Meggie with me—"

"There's no need to take that baby. I can take care of her and Gram just fine," Will said.

"Or I could get one of the teens in to help this afternoon." Jake offered. "You need some time off for good behavior, Sara."

She held the receiver back to her ear. "Gina, I can make it. You'd think they all wanted to get rid of me today."

She smiled and nodded. "Yes, I know they are trying to take care of me. What time do you want to meet at the diner?"

Jake gave Will and Gram a thumbs-up sign and hoped the rest of his plan went half as well.

"Thank you all," she said when she got off the phone. "I do want to stop into the drugstore and pick up some pictures I took of Meggie anyway."

Satisfied that the first part of his plan was working, Jake kissed his daughter good-bye and headed out the door. But he turned back to Sara. "You have a good lunch, Sara, okay?"

Sara promised him she would and found herself looking forward to lunch with Gina. By one o'clock, she'd fed Meggie her lunch and put her down for a nap. Gram and Grandpa should be able to handle things for a few hours, but she felt bad leaving them with no lunch fixed.

Grandpa shooed her out the door. "I'm perfectly capable of making us a grilled cheese sandwich or heating up leftovers in the fridge, Honey."

"I know, Grandpa."

"You just have a good time."

Gina was waiting at the diner when Sara got there. She'd made Deana promise to take a break and have lunch with the two of them when Sara showed up. Deana cooked most of the daily specials herself, but she did have two short order cooks and several waitresses, working two different shifts, to help out.

Deana brought their lunch to the table herself and turned to her help. "It's all yours. At least for an hour."

They just laughed at her.

"They know you too well, Deana," Sara said. "They know that all they have to do is give you that pitiful 'we need help' look, and you'll be on your feet and behind the counter in two seconds."

"Yeah, well, that's how it is when you own the place," Deana said.

"How is business these days, Deana? It always looks busier than ever when I'm in here." Gina took a bite of her roast beef sandwich.

"A little too good, some days. But I enjoy it." Deana grinned at her. "Oh, guess who was in here yesterday for early coffee?"

"David?" Gina asked.

Deana shook her head. "Nope."

"Luke and Jake?"

"Oh, they came in. But they aren't who I'm talking about."

Sara shrugged. "Okay, I give up. Who came in?"

"Nora. And she wasn't alone."

"Oh? Who was she with?"

"Dr. Wellington. And they were in very deep conversation until Nora seemed to get angry and flounced out of here."

Gina raised an eyebrow. "Well, so much for getting the two of them together."

Deana looked from one to the other. "You're wanting to play matchmaker?"

"Well, we'd thought they might make a good couple."

"They seemed to be getting along real well until Jake and Luke came in. Don't know what happened then. But the next thing I knew, Nora was hightailing it out of here."

"And what did Dr. Wellington do?" Gina asked.

"He chuckled and shook his head. Then he asked for another cup of coffee."

"I am going to have to meet this man," Sara said. "If Nora doesn't run him off, he may be just the man for her."

"I don't think he'd take any of her guff," Gina said.

"Exactly. I think she needs someone who isn't intimidated by her." Sara shrugged. "You know, someone who could let her bad moods roll right off of his back."

"That's a pretty tall order, Sara," Deana said. "I'm not sure that kind of man exists."

They all laughed and Sara sighed. "Well, we can hope."

The afternoon passed quickly. Deana wouldn't let either of them pay for lunch, and Gina wouldn't let her go back to Gram's.

"Ellie called me right after you left the house and said to tell you to make an afternoon of it. She called Maria and asked her to come over this afternoon."

"Maybe I've been crabby lately and they wanted a break from me."

Gina laughed. "You know better. They just don't want to wear you out."

At Sara's forlorn look, she relented and let her call to make sure Gram and Meggie were all right.

Once Sara heard Gram's voice and was assured all was well, she was able to relax and enjoy the afternoon. She and Gina went window shopping and stopped to pick up the pictures she'd taken of Meggie earlier in the week, and of course they ended right back at the diner for afternoon coffee. They were poring over the pictures of Meggie when a shadow fell across the table. Two shadows. David and Jake stood next to them, grinning.

"Now why does it not surprise me to see the two of you here?" Gina asked.

"Probably because we planned to meet here this morning," David grinned and slid into the booth alongside his wife.

Jake smiled down at Sara and she slid over to make room for him. "And were you in on this plan, Jake?"

He chuckled and joined her in the booth. "You could say that. It took everyone to get you to take a break. You've been putting in some long hours lately. I just wanted you to know how much we—I—appreciate you."

"I . . . thank you, Jake." Taken aback by the compliment, Sara didn't quite know what to say. She slid the packet of snapshots over to him. "Here are those pictures of Meggie."

Jake grinned and pulled the packet closer. "Oh, Sara, these are wonderful. I haven't been the best at taking pictures of Meggie. Now I wish I'd taken more."

Sara pointed to one with Meggie asleep, her thumb stuck in

her mouth and the teddy bear held tight in her arms. Another was of her playing with the puppy outside with Grandpa, and yet another had her sidling up to Gram and trying to share a cookie.

Jake looked at each picture and handed them to David. When he'd gone through them all, he looked into Sara's eyes. "Thank you."

"You're welcome. Would you like me to buy a photo album for them?"

"Let me look in Meggie's dresser. I'm pretty sure there's one there or in a box somewhere."

Sara nodded. "Okay. If you can't find one, I'll pick one up."

"Pssst, Sara," Gina whispered.

Sara looked over and saw Gina motioning to the other side of the diner.

"That's Dr. Wellington."

Sara turned her head and saw a tall, silver-haired man, about six feet tall and nicely built, sitting at a small table. He looked up at the waitress, and Sara could see that he had a wonderful smile.

She looked back at Gina. "He and Nora would look stunning together, wouldn't they?"

"What are you two up to now?" David asked.

"We aren't up to anything. Just hoping."

"About what?" Jake looked across the room. "Oh, he was here with Nora yesterday, I think it was. She didn't stay long, though. She left right after Luke and I came in."

"We're hoping there might be a little romance in the air for them."

"Then you'd better pray about it," Jake said. "From what I saw, Nora wasn't too happy when she left here."

"But then it's hard to tell when Nora is happy, isn't it?" Gina asked.

"Sure is for me," Jake replied.

Gina looked over at the doctor and sighed. "Still, they would make a stunning couple."

"Wife of mine," David said, "you know it takes more than looking good together to make a good couple."

"Oh, yes, that I know," Gina grinned. "It takes love and trust and faith and God's blessing to make a good couple."

"And sometimes it takes years to get there," David added.

Gina leaned into the arm that surrounded her and nodded. "Sometimes it does."

Sara and Jake chuckled, knowing their friends were talking about themselves.

"And sometimes it takes knocking some chips off shoulders and rehashing old hurts to get to real healing." David winked at his wife.

"Sometimes it does." Gina repeated softly. They both shot Sara and Jake pointed looks.

"What?" Sara and Jake asked at the same time.

David slid out of the booth with Gina right behind him. He looked at Jake and Sara and smiled. "Dear friends, I think maybe it's time to bury that past of yours so you both can get on with the future. To that end, Gina and I are providing supper for Ellie, Will, and Meggie. Take your time."

With that, they walked out of the diner, leaving Jake and Sara at a loss for words.

Jake found his voice first. "I think my plans have just been sped forward." He shook his head and laughed out loud, bringing curious glances from nearby tables.

"Jake? What's so funny? And what plans are you talking about?" Sara asked.

He met her eyes and his laughter stopped. He reached out and twirled a piece of Sara's hair around his finger and smiled at her.

"I wanted to have a chance to talk to you without Meggie

interrupting us, without you having to see to Gram and Will, without any of the hundred and one things you keep busy with at the house. So I came up with the plan to let you have an afternoon off."

"You had me spend the afternoon with Gina so you could talk to me? Jake, that doesn't make much sense." Sara pulled back and the tendril of hair slid through Jake's fingers.

"You needed an afternoon off. And it seemed the easiest way to get you to the diner. My plan was just to have coffee and then maybe stay awhile after Gina and David left. I didn't know they were going to add clearing up our past into the mix."

"Why didn't you just tell me you wanted to talk to me?"

"I was afraid you'd find something you just had to see to. It seems every time we're alone together for more than a couple of minutes, you find something that needs to be taken care of."

He was right. Sara was afraid that if they were alone for more than a few minutes, Jake might become aware of the love she felt for him and tried so hard to hide. She sighed lightly.

"Well, here we are," Sara said softly. "What do you want to talk about?"

He stared down at his coffee cup.

"Jake?"

He took a deep breath and looked into Sara's eyes. "I was wondering, if we could, well, if you would go to dinner with me one night."

"To dinner with you?" Sara looked confused.

Jake nodded. "You know, as in a dinner date?"

"A dinner date," she repeated. "With you?"

"Yes."

"Oh." Sara's heart seemed to do a double somersault before she could speak again. "I'd like that."

"You would?" Jake grinned. "I mean, you will?"

She nodded, feeling the color steal up her cheeks. What was

wrong with her? She felt like a teenager being asked out for her very first date. "When?"

"How about Saturday night? Anywhere you want to go."

Sara smiled. Jake was as nervous as she was. "Anywhere is fine. You plan it."

Jake nodded. "All right. I'll pick you up at six-thirty if that's okay?"

"That'd be fine."

They were both silent for a minute.

"Jake?"

"Yeah?"

"I don't know if I'm supposed to go home now, or back to Gram's house to pick up Grandpa."

Jake smiled and shook his head. "Neither do I. I'm afraid my planning hadn't gotten much past asking you for a date."

Their eyes met and they burst into laughter, spontaneous, shared, and comfortable.

13

*J*ake followed Sara back to his grandmother's house. True to their word, Gina and David were already there, and they asked Jake and Sara to join everyone for the pizza they'd had delivered.

Although Jake noticed several curious glances, no one asked why they'd returned early. And no one said a word when Jake asked Will if he was up to babysitting on Saturday night while he and Sara went out to eat.

Will just grinned and said, "You bet I am."

That was it. No teasing remarks or nosy questions. Just acceptance.

After everyone left and Jake put Meggie to bed, he remembered to look for the photo album he was sure he'd packed. Melissa had made it, and he'd like to at least get all of those first pictures of Meggie in the album her mother had created especially for her.

A quick look through Meggie's dresser drawers told him it wasn't there, so Jake took down the two boxes he'd put in the top of the closet when they'd first moved back. The first box held clothes Meggie had grown out of before they left Albuquerque, but the second one held the album. It was covered in baby print material, with a covered heart that a picture could be slipped inside of gracing the front.

Jake took the album downstairs to the kitchen where he'd left the photos of Meggie. He knew he hadn't put any pictures in the album, so he was surprised when he opened the album up and saw a photo of himself and Melissa on the very first page. He remembered when the photo had been taken—right before Meggie's birth. An envelope had been slipped in behind the photo.

Jake pulled it out and turned it over in his hands. It was addressed to him and Meggie in Melissa's handwriting and was dated only a month before she'd died. He opened the envelope and drew out a letter.

All the guilt he'd ever felt for not loving Melissa enough came to the surface as Jake unfolded the single page and read the very first line:

To my two loves, Jake and Meggie,

I pray you never have to read this, because it will mean I'm not with you. I've been told it's a normal thing to be afraid of childbirth, and I am. And no, Jake, there is nothing wrong that I know of. But just to put my mind at ease, I'm writing this in case something should happen to me during delivery and I don't have a chance to tell you both how very much I love you.

My dear sweet Meggie, how I looked forward to holding you in my arms and being the best mother I could be to you. But it's not to be, if this letter is being read, so I have to tell you and your daddy a truth.

Jake, my love, I'm sorry. For I did deceive you in the beginning. I was not pregnant when you married me. I took advantage of your honor because I wanted so much to be your wife. I'd loved you for so long, and yet I knew you didn't love me. You tried your best. I know that. And it's not your fault. I robbed you of your chance for happiness by grasping at my own. I'm sorry, Jake. I pray that you will forgive me and find that happiness with someone who will be a loving mother to our daughter.

Precious Meggie. Please listen and learn. Never try to trick someone into marrying you. Your daddy has been a

*wonderful husband and has tried to make me happy in
every way possible. But the one thing I wanted, his love, is
the one thing he couldn't completely give me. You see, it
always belonged to another. Yet your daddy gave up the
happiness he could have had for me. For what he thought
was his responsibility. I lied to him to get him to marry me.
And he stayed with me when there was no reason for him to
do so, because of his beliefs and the faith that I took
advantage of. So instead of one person being unhappy, there
were three or more. I tell you this now, my sweet Meggie, so
that you will be happy for your daddy when he finds his
own happiness after all of these years. And to keep you from
making the same mistakes I did.*

*I've asked God for His forgiveness, and I know that I
have it. Now I ask your daddy to forgive me. He has
promised to take you to church and teach you all the things
I didn't learn until I was an adult. If we can show you how
to always look to the Lord to lead your way, you'll be fine,
my love. I could leave you in no better hands than those of
the Lord above and your daddy. I love you both with all my
heart,*

Mommy Melissa

Jake pressed his eyes shut against the sudden sting of tears
and took a deep steadying breath. Finally he knew the truth.

ॐ

Sara tried to stay busy to keep from getting nervous about her
date with Jake. But it didn't work. And Nora didn't help matters.
She called bright and early the next morning, and Sara could tell
from the tone in her mother-in-law's voice that she wasn't at all
happy.

"Sara, just what kind of hold does that man have over you?"

"Pardon me? What are you talking about, Nora?"

"I heard about you and Jake cozying up at the diner yesterday. I told you he only wants a mother for Meggie. Are you honestly going to let yourself be hurt by that man once more?"

"Nora—"

"I just can't stand by and let you do that without warning you, Sara. You are going to be hurt badly." With that, Nora hung up.

Sara stood looking at the receiver, shaking her head, at a total loss for words. She hung up the phone and sighed deeply. She truly didn't want to upset her mother-in-law, but the only way to avoid that would be to move to the ranch and never come into town, thereby avoiding running into Jake and Meggie at all. Sara knew that never had been an option.

Still, Nora's warning repeated itself over and over in her mind. Was Jake's only interest in her as a possible mother for Meggie? While she would love to have that role, she didn't want it without Jake's love.

She lost count of how many times that day she picked up the phone to cancel the date with Jake only to change her mind and hang up before the call went through. The truth was that she wanted to go out with him. She wanted to see where they were headed. Wanted to see if what she thought was happening between them really was. She hoped she wasn't in for more heartbreak.

Grandpa left for Gram's about thirty minutes before Jake was due to pick Sara up. Gina had called earlier to let Sara know that she and David were providing supper again for the two older people and Meggie, so she wouldn't have to worry about anything.

When Jake arrived a few minutes early, Sara was relieved that she didn't have time to get nervous. But when she opened the door to him, she knew she'd only been faking her serenity.

She'd decided to wear the aqua-and-yellow sundress she'd bought for his welcome-home party. As his glance took in what she was wearing and zeroed in on her mouth, she knew she'd worn it because it reminded her of the night when Jake had held her in his arms and kissed her. Noticing his eyes darken as he pulled his gaze away from her lips to her eyes, Sara was pretty sure he was also remembering that night.

"You—" Jake cleared his throat. "You look lovely."

"Thank you." He seemed almost as nervous as she felt, but he certainly looked handsome in dress slacks and a crisp white shirt, with his hair still damp from the shower. "You look very nice yourself."

She grabbed her purse and the wrap that came with the dress and locked the door behind her. They headed for Jake's car, and she savored the feel of his hand at the small of her back. He made her feel protected and special. "Where are we going?"

"Well, the choice is still yours, but I've been told there's a new restaurant just outside of town, Los Hacienda, that's very good. We could still go into Roswell or Ruidoso, if you'd rather."

"No. No, Los Hacienda sounds wonderful. I haven't been there yet, and I've heard the food is excellent."

"Well, I have to admit, I'm a little nervous about going too far away from Gram's right now."

Sara laughed as Jake opened the passenger door and she seated herself. "You must have read my mind. I kept thinking that we might want to be close by. Although Gina and David will be there, I'd still feel better if we don't go too far."

Jake smiled as he went around and took the driver's seat. Sara was already so protective of Meggie. Melissa couldn't have hand-picked a better mother for their child. But Jake knew Sara's mothering abilities had nothing to do with his asking her out. He wanted to be with Sara, the woman he'd come to love even more than the teenager he'd planned to marry.

Jake had been told to ask for a river table, and he'd done that when he'd made reservations the day before. Now he was impressed when they were led to the second floor and shown to a table set in its own little alcove, with a small balcony off to the side, overlooking the Hondo River below.

The waiter lit the candle on their table, filled their water glasses, told them of the day's specials, and left them with menus. He returned quickly with a basket of tortilla chips and salsa. They both decided on the special of the day and were left alone once more.

"Oh, Jake. This is really beautiful," Sara said, looking around at the warm interior and back out to the river.

"A fitting setting for a beautiful woman." Jake didn't take his eyes off her as she turned back to him. She was beautiful, her green eyes glowing, her auburn hair on fire in the candlelight. She took his breath away.

"Jake—"

"I mean it, Sara." Jake reached across the table and took her hand in his. "You are beautiful, inside and out. You always have been."

Jake could see the color rise in her face even in the dim candlelight. He felt the tremble of her fingers in his hand, but she didn't pull away. Feeling a hope he was almost afraid of, Jake reached over with his other hand and raised her chin so that her eyes met his. "I love you, Sara. I always have."

Sara's hand slid out of his and covered her heart. She shook her head and looked around as if she wanted to escape. She bolted from her chair and ran out to the private balcony.

Jake was right behind her. He turned her to face him. "Sara?"

"Jake, you don't mean what you are saying. You loved Melissa—"

"Sara, I know you didn't want to go into the past, but we have to. I was so wrong to lose my temper and leave so long ago. Can you ever truly forgive me?"

"You know that I already have forgiven you, Jake. There's no need for this—"

Jake's fingers gently touched her lips to quiet her. "Sara, please, hear me out. I need you to know that I understand I was the one who threw our relationship away. I was the one who didn't trust you, myself, or the Lord back then. And I ruined it all. I don't even remember the drive back to the university that night, but I know there was a party going on when I got there. I remember taking one beer, then two. I don't remember much after that. I got drunk, Sara. For the first and last time, yes, but I got royally drunk."

"Jake, we all make mistakes. You really don't have to do this."

Jake looked out over the vista before him, but saw nothing of its beauty. He rubbed the back of his neck and closed his eyes. He knew what he said next might end any chance he ever had with Sara, but he had to say it.

He opened his eyes and looked into hers. "By the time I came to my senses and realized I needed to apologize to you, it was too late."

"What do you mean, too late?" Sara asked.

"I know now that you didn't betray me that night. But I betrayed you. And that betrayal changed the course of my life." Jake reached into his pocket and pulled out the letter from Melissa.

"I didn't feel free to tell you this until I found this letter the other night." He handed it to Sara. "I'm not sure I'll ever give it to Meggie to read. Maybe the best thing to do is to leave it all behind. But I want you to read it, Sara. I want you to understand."

Sara unfolded the piece of paper Jake handed her, and he stood still, his heart pounding as he waited. When she looked back at him, her eyes were overflowing with tears.

"Oh, Jake." She handed the letter back to him and brushed at her wet cheeks. "I don't know what to say. I truly thought you'd broken up with me for Melissa. But I didn't know—"

Jake looked down into her shimmering eyes. "I'm so sorry, Sara. If I hadn't been so stubborn and jealous that night—"

"You wouldn't have Meggie now," Sara finished. "And neither of us would want that."

Jake never knew who reached out first, but suddenly, Sara was right where he wanted her to be—held tightly in his arms.

"I know you loved Wade and had a good life with him, Sara. I learned to love Melissa, and I will be eternally grateful to her for giving me my Meggie. But I've always felt we were meant to be together. I do love you, Sara. I know that I always will. Is there any way . . . do you think it is possible for us to start over and go on from here? Could there be a second chance for us?"

Sara released a sob and a joyful chuckle all at once. "Oh, Jake, I hope so. I truly hope so."

Jake crushed her in his embrace and claimed her lips. At her unhesitating response, he deepened the kiss with sweet promise. The past was buried and the future begun.

*S*ara could never remember enjoying a meal more. She knew there were stars in her eyes and she didn't care who saw them. Jake loved her. Had always loved her. She was sure the joy she felt was obvious to anyone looking at her. It had to be.

If anyone asked her later what she'd eaten, she wasn't sure she would be able to tell them. All she knew for certain was that Jake loved her and she loved him. Nora had been wrong. Melissa's letter had put all her doubts to rest. Sara thanked the Lord for letting Jake find the letter and have her read it.

Jake paid the waiter and they were getting ready to leave when Sara turned to see Nora near the doorway, staring at them. Nora was with Dr. Wellington, but she pulled away from him and approached their table.

"I knew there was something going on between the two of you! I knew it!"

Dr. Wellington approached the table, looking apologetic, and put a hand through Nora's arm. "Nora, our table is ready. Please—"

Nora jerked her arm away. "Not until I've said what's needed to be said ever since Jake came back to town."

"Nora, please," Sara said. "You are creating a scene." She knew Nora would hate herself once she realized how she had behaved in public. Appearances meant everything to her.

"I don't care. I'm going to say this. Of all the people in the world for you to take up with, don't you know that Wade would turn over in his grave to know it was Jake? He worked so hard to win you. Even had me writing those anonymous notes to get Jake to doubt your love—"

"Nora!" Sara couldn't believe the woman's horrible rudeness or her awful admission.

Jake put his arm protectively around Sara.

"Nora, that's enough!" Dr. Wellington said. He pulled her to face him. "We are going to our table now. Or we are going home. Your choice."

Nora looked around as if she only now realized where she was and what she had done. Her hand grasped her chest, and she crumpled into a heap.

Sara knelt at the doctor's side as he checked Nora's vital signs. He picked her up.

"I'm taking her to the hospital right now. I don't want to wait for an ambulance."

Jake pulled Sara to her feet and gathered her purse and wrap. "We're right behind you."

᙮

Hours later, Sara and Jake sat in the hospital waiting room, still uncertain of Nora's condition.

"Sara? Are you all right?" Jake asked. "Do you want me to get you some coffee, hot chocolate, anything?"

"No, Jake. Thank you, I'm fine. I just wish Dr. Wellington would let us know how she is. I knew she was stressed, I knew it. I should have spent more time with her."

"Sara, you can't blame yourself for this. Nora must have some kind of underlying problem. You are not to blame."

Sara sighed and lowered her head, rocking back and forth on the waiting room couch. "I don't want to take the blame, but I—"

"She's going to be fine, Sara." Dr. Wellington crossed the room and held out his hand. "I'm Michael Wellington. I wish we could be meeting under better circumstances."

"Nora? She's going to be all right? Did she have a heart attack? A stroke?"

The doctor shook his head. "No, she didn't. I am going to keep her in here at least overnight for observation, but it wasn't a heart attack or a stroke. She's put herself under a lot of stress in the last few years, but of course you know that."

Even though his arm encircled her, Jake felt Sara pulling away from him inch by inch.

"Do you think she has a heart problem, Doctor?" he asked.

"No. At least not now, and none of the tests we've run show anything wrong with her heart. I do want her to undergo a stress test to be certain, but stress can cause a lot of problems when it's not under control, and it's obvious that the last year has taken its toll on Nora. I do apologize to you both for the scene she caused tonight."

Sara shook her head. "No, I should have seen this coming. I should have checked in on her more often. I should have seen that she was struggling."

"Sara. None of this is your fault. Nora brings a lot of this on herself."

Sara shook her head. "I should have known she needed me."

Jake exchanged glances with the doctor. He shrugged and shook his head.

"Well, right now Nora needs rest," the doctor said, "and I'll see that she gets it. You two should go on home. You can see her tomorrow."

Sara nodded and Jake shook Dr. Wellington's hand.

They walked out to Jake's car silently, but when he'd settled Sara and taken his seat, he turned to her before starting the car.

"Sara, Dr. Wellington is right. This isn't your fault."

Sara nodded. "I know. And it wasn't my fault that Wade and my baby were killed in the wreck. But if I hadn't wanted that ice cream, they might still be alive."

She looked over at Jake with tears in her eyes. When he reached to take her in his arms, she pulled back and shook her head. She sniffed and brushed at her tears.

"Jake, I'm not sure we can see each other again. I cannot take feeling responsible for something happening to Nora. I can't."

He wanted to yell and tell her she couldn't throw away what they had. Not now. But a quiet voice stopped him. *Trust in Me, always,* it said.

Jake listened and tried to stay calm. "Sara, I love you. I want to have a life with you."

Sara turned her face to the window. "I want that too, Jake. But right now I'm not sure it's going to be possible."

Jake took a deep breath. He'd waited this long, surely he could wait longer. And this time he was going to put his trust in the Lord.

๛

The next few days were some of the longest Sara had ever endured. Nora seemed to have slid into a deep depression, and she wasn't talking. At least not to Sara—even though Sara spent most of every day in Nora's room, reading to her, talking to her, anything to get her to respond.

Sara knew that Nora could talk if she wanted to. She'd heard her speaking to the nurses. But as soon as Sara walked into the room, she clammed up.

Dr. Wellington had ordered a battery of tests, but so far nothing unusual had shown up. Sara knew he cared for Nora, but at the same time he seemed frustrated with her.

Gram was getting around without the crutches now, and Lydia took over planning the family reunion, while Gina and the church family stepped in to help so that Sara could be with Nora.

But Sara missed being at Gram's. Her heart cried out for Meggie, and she was afraid the baby would feel she'd abandoned her. Her heart twisted each time she thought of what Jake must be feeling. He'd laid his soul bare for her, and she'd left him without an answer.

She'd never felt so torn in her life, Sara thought as she walked down the hospital corridor from Nora's room to the cafeteria. She and Jake had been on the verge of staking out a future for themselves and Meggie, but now, with Nora in the hospital and knowing how she felt about Jake, the future seemed bleaker than ever.

Sara wanted to be with Jake and Meggie, but how could she possibly start a new life when her mother-in-law refused to even talk to her about anything, much less her relationship with Jake?

Sara ran into Dr. Wellington in the cafeteria line, and he bought her lunch and himself a cup of coffee and asked if he could join her. Sara was glad to have a chance to talk to him. "Have any of the test results pointed to what is wrong with Nora, Dr. Wellington?"

"No. And they aren't going to tell us anything we don't already know. Nora is basically healthy. She's just let the stress in her life take over, instead of handing things over to the Lord."

"You're sure she didn't have a heart attack?"

"Yes, Sara, I'm sure. Her heart is healthy."

Sara tried to blink the tears of relief away. Dr. Wellington reached out and took her hand. "I know you care deeply for your mother-in-law. So do I. But we can't take on the blame for Nora's stress. She's gone through no more than you have in the last year, Sara. You can't let her health rule your life."

"But I don't want her to think she doesn't matter to me."

"Then tell her that she does and get on with your life. You have that right."

"I want Nora to be happy."

The doctor nodded. "So do I. And I'm going to do everything I can to see that she is. But in the end, Sara, I can't make her happy. You can't make her happy. She has to learn to let herself be happy."

"I know what you are saying is true. It's just so hard to walk away and start a new life, knowing I'm hurting her."

"And what she's done hasn't hurt you? And Jake?" He shook his head. "No wonder you're the one who has rings under her eyes. Look closely at Nora when you see her again."

"I think I know what you're telling me. I've been praying about it. I'm sure the Lord will let me know what to do."

Dr. Wellington looked at his watch and stood up. "I'm sure He will. I'm going to look in on Nora now. You relax and enjoy your lunch."

Sara tried to do just that. But mostly, she just prayed.

Jake headed down the hall to Nora's room. He didn't know what else to do. If he waited for Sara to tell Nora to go fly a kite, he'd have a long wait. Yet all of this was taking its toll on her. He knew she loved him and Meggie. He could hear it in her voice when she called at night to see how Meggie and Gram were doing. He reassured Sara, but he didn't tell her that Meggie asked for her at least ten times a day. He couldn't put that kind of pressure on her. Neither could he ask her to marry him, knowing that Nora would never give them her blessing and would try to make Sara as unhappy as she could.

He'd just realized how very important family was to his daughter and to himself. And Nora was family. He had to try. But he dreaded the confrontation he knew was coming, and he stopped outside her room to gather his thoughts.

A male voice Jake recognized as Dr. Wellington's could be heard coming from the half-opened door. "Nora, you have got to get past this. You have to for Sara's sake, for your own sake. For our sake."

"I know I do, Michael," Nora cried. "It's just that Sara is all I have left of Wade, and she has been a daughter to me. But she loved Jake before she ever loved my son. I don't want to lose her, but I can't help but feel pushed aside. And I'm jealous. I wanted a grandchild so badly, and now Sara will get to be a mother, but I'm never going to be a grandmother."

Jake could hear sobbing from the other side of the door. His heart went out to his aunt, while at the same time he was appalled at her petty jealousy.

Judge not. Trust Me. The small voice made itself heard. Jake nodded. "I hear You, Lord," he whispered.

He needed the reminder. His jealousy had been the cause of his and Sara's first breakup. Now Nora's threatened to do the same. But this time, he was going to trust the Lord to lead his way. He bowed his head and said a quick prayer and then walked into Nora's room.

Nora's hand flew to her throat. "Jake! What—"

"Good afternoon, Jake," Dr. Wellington said, interrupting Nora, but he reached out and touched her shoulder. "It's good to see you again."

"Aunt Nora, Dr. Wellington." Jake strode into the center of the room. "I couldn't help but overhear part of your conversation."

His aunt's face paled as she looked at the doctor, who smiled at her and took her hand.

Jake cleared his throat. "I have a little girl who has a great-grandmother, and I'm hoping the woman I love will become her mommy. But every little girl needs a grammy."

The color began to return to Nora's face. "How about it, Aunt Nora? Want to make a deal?"

≈

Sara finished her lunch, thinking over what Dr. Wellington had said. Nora didn't have heart trouble. She was going to be fine. All Sara could do for Nora was let her know she cared about her and would always be part of her family no matter who she married. If Nora would think rationally about it, she'd realize that marrying Jake would keep her in the family.

Sara disposed of her dirty dishes and headed back to Nora's room. She was going to take the doctor's advice and reassure her mother-in-law. Then she was going to Jake and Meggie and get on with her own life.

When she turned onto the corridor that led to Nora's room, Sara was surprised to see Jake outside the woman's room. He bowed his head before opening the door and entering. What was he doing? He knew how Nora felt about him. She hurried her pace until she arrived outside the room.

She entered quietly behind Jake, and what she heard sent a warm wave of love flooding through her heart. Jake was declaring his love for her and asking Nora to be a part of that love by being a grandmother to Meggie. He'd put his heart on the line with Sara, and now he was trying to make peace with Nora so that they could have a future.

Sara broke the silence that fell on the room. "Nora, if I were you, I'd take Jake up on his offer." She walked up to Jake and wrapped her arms around him. "I certainly plan to."

Jake's smile lit his face as he gathered Sara close. "Nora, I meant what I said. Meggie needs a grammy. Think about it."

Nora's mouth opened and shut, but for once, nothing came out. Dr. Wellington stood at her side, grinning.

Jake and Sara backed out of the room. "You can give us your answer later, Aunt Nora," Jake said. "Right now, we have a few things to settle." He pulled Sara into the hall and looked down into her eyes. "Did you mean it? Will you marry me and be a mommy for Meggie?"

"I will."

Jake picked her up and twirled her around right there in the hospital corridor. He bent his head and sealed her answer with a kiss that healed the past and promised a lifetime of love for the future.

Epilogue

*D*ressed in lace, with her auburn hair swept up into an elegant french twist, Sara waited in the fellowship hall to begin her walk down the aisle behind her attendants, Deana and Gina. More nervous and happy than she could ever remember, she clung to her grandfather's arm, thinking back over the past few weeks since she and Jake had announced their engagement. Her heart filled with love for Jake, Meggie, their extended family, and friends, and she thanked the Lord for the blessings He'd bestowed on her.

There hadn't been any debate over the wedding date. As Gram stated, "What better time to have a wedding than on the Fourth of July? Everyone will be here for the family reunion, and by then your new home will be ready to move into."

Sara and Jake weren't about to argue. They'd waited such a long time to start their life together.

Nora had wasted no time in taking Jake up on his offer. She'd come to realize that the guilt she'd felt about sending Jake those anonymous notes all those years ago had surfaced when he'd moved back home. The fear and worry that he and Sara would discover what she had done had taken its toll on her health, but with the truth revealed and having received Jake and Sara's forgiveness, Nora began to count her blessings. By the end of that week, she was out of the hospital, helping Gram and Sara take care of Meggie while everyone in the family helped plan the wedding.

Sara let the school know that she wouldn't be teaching that fall. She and Jake had talked it over, and because Meggie had gone through so many changes in her young life, they decided that making sure she felt secure and loved was one of their top priorities. There would be plenty of time to teach once the toddler started school. Besides, Sara could think of nothing she'd rather do than enjoy the blessing God was giving her—to be Jake's wife and Meggie's mommy.

But the blessings hadn't stopped there. Nora was a different person. She'd turned into the woman Sara had only been given a glimpse of the night of Jake's welcome-home party. She was absolutely crazy about Meggie, and Meggie had taken to her as well. Nora would stay with Gram and help take care of Meggie while Jake and Sara went on a brief honeymoon to Santa Fe. And much to the delight of the whole family, Nora and Dr. Wellington had become an item around town.

Gram and Grandpa kept everyone guessing about their relationship. They seemed to be inseparable—chuckling and whispering together any time they were around each other—and Sara and Jake were sure they must be plotting and planning on how to add Dr. Wellington to the family.

"We're going to have to do something about those two," Sara had whispered to Jake the night before, as they'd watched their grandparents during the wedding rehearsal.

Jake nodded. "As soon as we get back from Santa Fe, we're going to have to do a little matchmaking ourselves."

Sara took a deep breath when she and Grandpa were given their signal and began their walk down the aisle. Her smile was tremulous, but she kept the tears of joy at bay by focusing on Jake.

With Luke and John by his side, Jake tried to hide his nervousness. But when Sara started down the aisle, he was sure his sigh of relief was audible. He couldn't take his eyes off her as she made her way to him, and he barely heard David ask who gave Sara away, or Will's answer. Finally she was standing by his side, and the moment he'd spent a lifetime waiting for had arrived.

Jake and Sara turned to David and exchanged their wedding vows in front of family, friends, and what must have been half the town. They were pronounced husband and wife, and Jake's lips claimed Sara's in a sweet promise to love her for the rest of their lives.

David introduced them as Mr. and Mrs. Jake Breland, and the two turned to face the loved ones who had just witnessed their promises to love, honor, and cherish each other. Jake smiled at his Meggie sitting contentedly in her Grammy Nora's lap, saw his grandmother and Sara's grandfather sitting side by side and Aunt Lydia and Uncle Ben behind them. The smiles of his and Sara's family and friends reflected their shared joy.

Jake pulled Sara's hand through his arm and looked down at his new bride before starting up the aisle. The love shining from her eyes had him swallowing the sudden lump in his throat, and he thanked the Lord for bringing him home, for bringing him and Sara together again, and for their ever-widening family circle.

Will nudged Ellie and whispered in her ear as they watched their grandchildren walk back up the aisle together. "Look at those two. We finally did it, didn't we, El? We finally got those two together."

"Oh, I think we had a lot of help from above, Will. We can't take all the credit ourselves," Ellie said softly, leaning closer to Will so that he could hear.

"That's true, El. Very true," Will nodded. "But, now that they are together and it looks like Nora has found a man who can handle her, maybe it's time we concentrated on ourselves for awhile. We aren't getting any younger, you know."

"I've been wondering when you were going to realize that, William Oliver. It's about time you made this courting you've been doing official," Ellie said, patting Will's cheek.

He quickly captured her hand and brought it to his lips. "Consider it done, my sweet Ellie. Consider it done."

The wedding party spilled out onto the church grounds just as the first fireworks from the Independence Day celebration began crackling in the night sky. Jake pulled Sara close to his side, and as he bent his head to kiss her once more, the fireworks surrounding them reflected the pure light of love bursting forth from their hearts.

THE WEDDING'S ON

BY GAIL SATTLER

Dedicated to Lil Sattler,
my mother-in-law,
just because I love you.

1

*O*h, Janice! I'm getting married!"

Janice Neufeld nearly dropped her coffee cup onto the kitchen floor. She watched Laura, her best friend, spin around, raise her hands above her head, then flop backward against the wall.

"Married?!" Janice sputtered. "To whom?"

Laura's eyelids fluttered shut, and she sighed. "Why, to Frank, of course."

Janice blinked and shook her head. "Frank? Frank Magnussen? How can that be? You two barely just met! How long have you known him? Two months?"

Laura lowered her arms and hugged herself, opened her eyes, then sighed again. Her dreamy expression almost made Janice want to throw up.

"I know it hasn't been long, but it's just so . . ." Laura sighed again. "So right!"

"I don't believe this," Janice muttered, shaking her head. Suddenly, she froze. If she thought she felt sick before, she really felt sick now at the thought of one reason why her friend would be rushing to get married. Even though it was wrong in God's sight, Christians were not immune to temptation. "You're, uh—not— you know."

Laura giggled. "No, silly. We're just in love. But he'll probably want to start a family pretty soon."

"Probably? You don't know? Just how much *do* you know about him?"

"Enough to know that we're going to be very happy together."

Janice fought to think rationally. She had known Frank longer than Laura had. Because of that, Janice knew him much better—so much so that Janice didn't see how a relationship between Frank and Laura could possibly work. Knowing Frank as well as she did, Janice didn't know how Laura and Frank managed to stay in the same room without arguing. While it was said that opposites attract, Laura and Frank were one pair that were too opposite in things that really mattered.

However, it appeared Laura and Frank did have one thing in common. Apparently, they both wanted to get married.

Janice doubted that was enough to last the test of time.

She forced herself to keep a grip on her coffee cup, when what she really felt like doing was waving her hands in the air in utter frustration. "But you hardly know Frank. Do you know his likes and dislikes? His hobbies and interests? His future goals? Does he even like kids or even want kids at all—never mind right away? How does he feel about your rabbit? Not all guys like caged pets, you know."

Laura waved one hand in the air. "You're worrying for nothing. Just be happy for me."

Janice sucked in a deep breath. She never thought one word would be so hard to force out.

"Congratulations," she said.

She only wished she meant it.

❧

Trevor Halliday choked on his coffee. "Laura Merring? Are you nuts?"

Trevor's best friend raised his arms in the air, linked his fingers behind his head so his elbows stuck out to the sides, then flopped back against the doorframe. "Yeah." Frank sighed lazily. "Maybe I am. But I am serious. We're getting married."

Trevor wiped his mouth on his sleeve as he finished sputtering, then rested the coffee mug on the kitchen counter. "I thought you two just met not long ago."

Frank grinned. "We did. I can't explain it."

Trevor shook his head. "Yeah, well, neither can I. Does insanity run in your family? I didn't know you knew her that well."

Frank's grin turned so sappy that Trevor wanted to shake some sense into him. "I know her well enough."

Trevor doubted that. He'd known Laura for a couple of years, which was about a year and ten months longer than Frank had known her. And knowing the two of them as he did, Trevor didn't see this as a match made in heaven. "I don't know about that. How much time have you really spent with her? I mean, quality time. She's never even been here, to our home, has she? How does she feel about Freddie?"

"Don't worry, Trev. She's cool. She won't mind Freddie."

Trevor had his doubts about that too. He wasn't too fond of Freddie, himself. He had a sneaking suspicion that Laura wouldn't be too fond of the nine-foot Burmese python either, especially on feeding day, as he knew Laura tended to be squeamish. "If you say so, Frank."

"I say so." Frank walked to the calendar hanging on the wall, paged through it, and circled a day in red.

Trevor peeked over his shoulder. "What are you doing?"

"Circling my wedding day, my friend. You gonna be my best man?"

Something in Trevor's stomach went to war with the coffee he'd just swallowed. "That's only four months away. You're only twenty-four years old. You don't have to rush. Unless . . ." A sick feeling settled in the pit of his stomach. His friend was a good Christian man who was supposed to be waiting for marriage, just as Trevor was.

Frank grinned. "Don't worry. It's not that. We booked the church today because we don't want the same thing to happen to us as it did to my sister. Remember the mess when she took too long to make arrangements when she got married?"

Trevor shook his head. "But you hardly know Laura! God wants us to love our wives, to treat them with respect, and be partners, sharing everything." He couldn't see Frank and Laura being partners in anything, least of all marriage.

"This wasn't the response I was expecting out of you. I thought you'd be happy to get the place to yourself."

Trevor swallowed hard. Instead of criticizing his friend's judgment, as the future best man he knew what he should say. One word had never been so difficult.

"Congratulations," he choked out.

"Thanks." Frank smiled ear to ear. "Are you busy tomorrow night? I think maybe it would be a good time to get together and discuss stuff. Laura's friend Janice Neufeld is going to be her maid of honor. Do you remember her? Short little thing. Brown eyes, brown hair. Wears glasses."

He remembered Laura's friend. Laura was everything Janice was not. Laura was tall, blond, thin, and always in the center of the action. Janice, on the other hand, struck him as simply ordinary. "Yes, I've met her a few times."

"Great. I'm not sure what goes on behind the scenes in a wedding, but I know there'll be lots to do. You two should probably sit down and talk about stuff."

Frank stuck his hands in his pockets and sauntered into the living room, whistling the wedding march.

Trevor remained in the kitchen, his hands glued to his ceramic coffee mug. He couldn't let his friend set himself up for the heartache of an unhappy marriage. He didn't know what he was going to do, but he had to do something.

❧

Janice followed Laura, Frank, and Frank's friend, Trevor, into the mall. Once inside, they stopped a few feet beyond the entrance.

494

Frank pointed to the left. "If you guys don't mind, Laura and I are going to go to the sport shop."

Laura pointed to the right. "Don't you think we should go to the jewelry store first, Darling?"

"Oh, yeah. I guess. We'll meet you back at the food court in ten minutes."

Laura shook her head as she checked her watch. "Make that half an hour."

Frank grinned like an idiot and followed Laura to the right.

Janice had never seen Frank act so complacent before. It wasn't like him at all.

As soon as Frank and Laura left, she lowered her head. Trevor lowered his head at the same time.

"It's not going to work," they whispered in unison.

Any other time, Janice would have laughed. Today, nothing was funny. Not only had Laura and Frank booked the church, but over the next months, she was supposed to start helping her friend make all the wedding arrangements. And that meant spending a lot of time with Trevor Halliday, a man she barely knew.

She struggled with the fact that this was really happening. Now, while she was expected to sit and talk to Trevor over coffee, Frank and Laura were off to buy the rings. For the wedding. The wedding that shouldn't happen.

Even though it was Saturday, the food court wasn't crowded, allowing Janice and Trevor to select a relatively private table once they purchased a cup of coffee apiece.

Trevor leaned back in the chair and folded his arms across his chest. "If you're going to be Laura's maid of honor, I guess that means you know her pretty well. Is she really serious?"

Janice arched one eyebrow. "I was going to ask you the same thing about Frank."

They both stared at each other until Trevor cleared his throat. He leaned forward, lowered his head, and studied his coffee cup very intently as he spoke. "This probably isn't going to sound too great, but I'm really concerned that Frank is making a mistake." He raised his head but didn't release the plastic cup. "Not that I have anything against Laura. I like Laura. I just think they should take more time to get to know each other." He didn't break eye contact as he picked up the cup and sipped the hot coffee, then slowly lowered it to the tabletop.

"In other words, you think that if they got to know each other better, they'd see that getting married is a dumb idea."

Trevor's ears turned red, and he stared down into his coffee cup. "I wouldn't have put it quite so succinctly, but yes, that's exactly what I meant."

Janice froze, then stared down into her own coffee cup. "I didn't mean that quite as badly as it sounded, but I'm glad you agree. The trouble is, I don't know what to do about it. I can't sit back and let Laura make what could possibly be the biggest mistake of her life." Janice felt the heat rising in her cheeks as she lifted her face to look back at Trevor, who was now looking up at her too. "Don't get me wrong. I like Frank. I really do. But knowing Laura, I don't know how those two even stay in the same room together. I can't imagine them being married. I really don't know what to do. All I know is that I have to do something."

"Same here. I don't want to see Frank make a mistake about something so important either."

Janice looked more closely at Trevor. Even though he didn't attend the same church as she and Laura, she knew he did attend regularly at his own church, with Frank. From past times she'd met him, she considered his faith to be solid and believed he lived his life according to God's direction to the best of his ability. Knowing that he felt the same way about their friends' upcoming marriage gave her more conviction that she was right. Or, if not right, at least she had just cause for concern.

Not wanting to get caught talking about their friends, Janice glanced over her shoulder to make sure Frank and Laura weren't on their way back yet. They weren't, but she lowered her voice to a whisper anyway. "So, what do you think we should do?"

Trevor also lowered his voice. "I don't know. I thought about it all night, ever since I found out, and I can't think of anything. Normally, I'd be inclined to let time take its course, but I don't know if that's such a good idea in this case."

She nodded, then adjusted her glasses when they slipped down her nose. "I know what you mean. The wedding is four months away. That gives us some amount of leeway but not a lot. Maybe we should just watch them closely for a month and see how it goes. Although I hate to start making arrangements and putting down deposits and down payments when the outcome is still uncertain."

"I know what you mean. Do you have any idea how much it costs to rent a tux?"

Janice grinned wryly. "Do you have any idea how much it costs to have a bridesmaid dress made? It's even worse spending all that money and knowing you're only going to wear it once. Or in this case, hopefully never."

"I never thought of it that way. Why don't women just rent the dresses?"

At his question, Trevor grinned. Janice's breath caught. She'd been with Trevor in a group many times before today but never realized how attractive he was when he smiled. He wasn't old enough to have laugh lines, but she could see little crinkles starting to develop at the corners of his eyes, something she'd always found attractive in men.

Really looking at him for possibly the first time, she reevaluated him. He wasn't exactly movie-star handsome, but despite his big nose, he wasn't bad-looking. That she'd never been attracted to the blond-haired, blue-eyed types before probably explained why she'd never taken notice of him. Frank was the one who was tall, dark, and handsome, although he wasn't quite as tall as Trevor by about an inch. Now that she did decide to pay attention to Trevor, he wasn't hard on the eyes at all.

Janice shook her head. She wasn't there to ogle Frank's friend. Also, just because he was good-looking didn't mean she had to like him or pretend that she wanted to become friends with him. She was only there to make sure her own friend wasn't heading into the biggest disaster of her life.

She glanced over her shoulder once again. "Never mind about the clothes. We have to think of something before they get back."

They both sat in silence, staring at each other, thinking.

An idea popped into Janice's head. She opened her mouth to speak, but before she could get a word out, a familiar voice sounded behind her.

"Hey! Janice! Look what Frank gave me!"

Her mouth snapped shut. Automatically, Janice looked down to Laura's hand. Her ring finger was still bare.

Janice tipped her head up to meet her friend's eyes, but a sparkle around Laura's neck caught her attention.

"A diamond necklace! It's beautiful!" She jumped to her feet to examine it. If Frank could buy an engagement ring at the same time as such an expensive trinket, he had more money than she realized.

Trevor stood as well, but he didn't appear to be as interested in the necklace as Janice. "Why did you buy a necklace? I thought you two were going to buy an engagement ring."

Laura slipped her arm around Frank's waist. "We did. We bought both. And wedding rings too. We have to wait a couple of days for the rings to be sized. But look what Frank got me to make up for it."

Dollar signs flashed before Janice's eyes. "Don't you think that's a rather large expenditure just before a wedding?"

Frank shrugged his shoulders. "That's okay. I charged it. I don't have to pay for it for a long time."

"You . . ." Laura's voice trailed off, and her eyes widened. "You didn't tell me that. I hope you intend to pay for all this before the wedding."

"I don't know. I'll have to see how much overtime I get."

"Overtime?"

"Yeah. You know I have to work a lot of overtime. Trev loves it. He gets first dibs on the television."

"But . . . ," Laura sputtered.

Before she could say another word, Frank turned to her. With his index finger, he lifted the center of the diamond necklace, then smiled. Laura's mouth closed, and she tipped her head up to gaze back at Frank with stars in her eyes.

Janice wanted to throw up. She leaned toward Trevor. "Just how long does Frank work each day? I don't think Laura wants to get married so she can stay home alone and watch television. She doesn't even watch that much television."

Trevor lowered his head and whispered back. "He's teasing. He doesn't work late that often. It's just that when he does, it's long hours. Neither of us watches much television since most of the shows are junk. We recently talked about canceling the cable service."

Janice's eyes widened. "Really? Us too."

"Hey, you two!" Laura said as she tapped her foot on the hard floor. The noise echoed down the mall. "Quit whispering. I'm hungry."

Frank rubbed his stomach with one hand. "Yeah. Who wants pizza?"

Laura rested her hand inside the crook of Frank's elbow. "Mushroom and pepperoni? At Alberto's?"

Frank smiled. "My favorite."

Janice whispered to Trevor out of the corner of her mouth.

"At least there's something they agree on. Maybe there is hope, after all."

He mumbled something she couldn't hear, which was probably just as well.

Together, the four exited the mall to their cars.

Janice had come to the mall with Laura in Laura's car, and Trevor had arrived with Frank in Frank's car. Somehow, instead of being with her friend, Janice now found herself traveling with Trevor, and Frank had taken her place in Laura's car.

She didn't want to ride with Trevor. She needed to talk to Laura.

They had to discuss the necklace. Issues about money commonly affected the success or failure of a marriage. Laura was best described as "thrifty." Frank's impulsive and extravagant gift came at a time when the money could have been spent more wisely, especially when he didn't really have the money in the first place. If this was an indication of Frank's spending habits, already things didn't bode well for a good start to their impending marriage. What she didn't understand was that Laura seemed genuinely pleased Frank had bought the necklace. Knowing Laura's eagle eye for price tags, Janice had no doubt that Laura knew the cost before Frank bought it.

Trevor's voice broke into her thoughts. "What if we're wrong? What if they're more suited to each other than we think? Frank is my best friend. I don't want to ruin the relationship if it is the right thing. But if it's not, I can't stand by and let him make a big mistake."

Janice stared out the window of the moving vehicle, unable to look at him as she spoke. "I'm just as confused by this whole thing as you are."

"Every time I think one way, they do something to confuse me. The bottom line is that they obviously like each other. But

I'm not sure if liking is enough of a basis for marriage. They've known each other such a short amount of time."

Janice turned to him and nodded. "I know exactly what you mean. I've known you longer than Laura has known Frank. And I'm not about to marry you." Janice slapped her hands over her mouth. "Oops! I didn't mean that the way it sounded."

"That's okay. I don't want to marry you either."

Janice felt her mouth drop open as she turned and stared at him. He didn't turn his head. Instead, he paid more attention to the road than he had the entire trip so far. He clenched his teeth on his lower lip, and Janice could see the corners of his mouth quivering.

She steadied her glasses on her nose with her index finger. "You are sooooo not funny," she muttered, then cleared her throat. "What I meant was, Laura isn't flaky or anything. She's had only two serious boyfriends since high school. She's not the type to fall in and out of love easily. The relationship with the one guy she claimed she had fallen in love with didn't last, but while it was on, she never stopped talking about him. What makes this so strange is that I never heard any declarations of being in love with Frank. I didn't even know she had been seriously dating anyone. When she told me she was getting married, I didn't know who the lucky man was."

All traces of humor instantly left Trevor's face. He emitted a strangled, choking sound, quickly glanced behind them, pulled the car to the side of the road, and stopped abruptly.

"The same happened with Frank. I didn't know he and Laura were dating either. The next thing I know, he's circling a wedding date on the calendar."

A throbbing sensation started above Janice's left eye, which usually meant the beginning of a migraine. With all the tension of the day, she shouldn't have been surprised. First, she had been nearly overwhelmed with guilt at her wish to stop Laura and Frank from getting married, at least right away. Then, she let herself hope against hope that Laura and Frank really could be happy together, even though she didn't see how. Now, an impending sense of doom washed over her as she pictured that in the not-too-distant future, she would be helping Laura deal with the pain of divorce.

While divorce was frowned on in the church, no one could deny that it happened—and to good people. Despite the apparent ease of divorce in today's society, she had witnessed its effects on people she knew, both Christians and non-Christians alike. Divorce was painful and difficult, leaving much devastation in its wake.

When the day came for her to get married, Janice vowed she would be obedient to follow God's direction. She fully intended for her own marriage to last forever. Following God's guidelines meant that when she met her Mr. Right and agreed to marry him, there could be no doubt that she was making the right decision. In order to be prepared, she planned to know the man who would be her husband far better than Laura knew Frank. She also would need to be assured in concrete ways that they shared common interests and goals. She would have to know beyond a shadow of doubt that their compatibility would withstand the test of time.

Janice lowered her voice, although she didn't know why. It was just the two of them in the car. Slowly, she massaged the tender spot above her left eyebrow with her fingers. "We've got to show them how unsuited they are for each other. I have an idea." She stopped and looked Trevor straight in the eyes. She could see him stiffen with the intensity of her gaze.

She cleared her throat. "But I'm going to need your help—and lots of it."

*S*uddenly, the air in the car became unreasonably stuffy. Trevor turned off the motor and rolled the window down. Without breaking eye contact with Janice, he moved his face closer to the window and inhaled a deep breath of the cool evening air to clear his head.

He didn't know what he'd been thinking, but it hadn't been to make plots and plans behind Frank's back. However, he didn't know how he had thought the end result would have been anything different. Realistically, he knew that agreeing about Frank and Laura's unsuitability as mates with Laura's friend wouldn't make the problem go away, nor would merely discussing the problem solve it. He just hadn't thought about it to the logical conclusion, which was to be prepared to actively do something about it.

His vision blurred, not really seeing Janice even though he was looking straight at her.

A voice in his head echoed that he had no business interfering with Frank's love life. Worse than interfering, he was now involving himself in making a secret scheme that would no doubt hurt his best friend.

Another little voice battled the first little voice. What kind of friend was he if all he did was complain to Janice, agree that his friend was making a mistake, and then watch it happen? The answer was: a rotten friend. It was his duty and responsibility to guide Frank if he saw Frank doing something wrong.

Not that getting married was wrong—the issue was Frank's judgment in his choice of Laura as the perfect wife. Not that there was anything wrong with Laura. Trevor just didn't see her as a good match for Frank.

Trevor exhaled deeply and refocused on Janice. The second she saw she had his attention, she started listing numerous reasons she thought Frank and Laura weren't suited to each other. As if he needed convincing.

Nothing of what she outlined came as a surprise. Still, the more she said, the heavier the weight of guilt settled on his shoulders at what he had to do. Over and over, he reminded himself that both he and Janice were only trying to do what was best for their friends in the long run.

A verse from Matthew ran through his head, the one about every matter being established by the testimony of two or three witnesses. The more he listened to Janice, the more he became convinced that they were justified in their concern—justified enough to do something about it.

In the end, if Frank and Laura were suited to each other, then what Trevor and Janice were about to do would strengthen the relationship and thereby help to cement the basis for a strong marriage. If what they were about to do broke up the relationship before the wedding, then it was right that the wedding should never take place. Either way, Janice's concerns strengthened his growing convictions that they were doing the right thing after all. What they were doing, they were doing out of love for their Christian brother and sister, who also happened to be their best friends.

Janice cleared her throat. "Well? What do you think? Do you think that's a good idea?"

All Trevor could do was blink. Basically, her plan was for him to make an extensive list of Frank's personality traits, good and bad, as well as Frank's likes and dislikes. At the same time, Janice would make a similar list for Laura. Then, they would trade lists. Trevor was to sit with Frank and ask Frank his needs and wants of the woman who would be his wife, as well as what Frank thought he would bring into the relationship that Laura would want. Trevor would refer to Janice's list about Laura to either prove or disprove whether Frank and Laura were a match. At the same time, Janice would do the same with Laura and the list Trevor made about Frank.

He cleared his throat. "I know we don't know each other very well, and I hope you'll take this in the spirit in which it was meant. I think it's a lousy idea."

She crossed her arms and leaned back in her seat. "Oh? Why?"

"You're on the right track, but I don't think it's going to work. I don't ever question Frank about women he's dating, and especially not if the relationship is serious. Not that there have been many, you understand. I don't think asking him to provide a list of characteristics he would like in the woman he wants to marry is going to do anything except make him mad. I can tell you that if I suddenly start spouting negative answers to questions about Laura in comparison to what he thinks he should be hearing, he won't believe me. At least not when I read the answers off a list that *you* wrote. He has to learn that stuff for himself, right from Laura."

She leaned closer. Even in the dark, he could see her eyes widen behind her glasses. "But don't you see?" she asked. "There isn't time for that. I don't know why they can't see those things about each other, so we have to show them."

He shook his head. "I'm no psych major. I can't analyze and mix and match personality traits from a list. Pointing out to the two of them that Frank wants to live in an apartment close to downtown where the action is, and Laura's dream is having acreage on the outskirts of town in order to be closer to the cows doesn't mean they're going to agree that they wouldn't make good marriage partners. I don't know enough about stuff like that to know what things make opposites attract and what things drive a person nuts about another person."

"But we've got to get them to see this realistically. To talk about it. Right now, Laura can't see past the stars in her eyes."

Trevor dragged his palm down his face. "Right. Get them to talk about it. And how do you suppose we're going to bring this up in conversation?" Trevor cleared his throat and deepened his voice while he waved one hand in the air. "Hey, Frank, old buddy. Janice and I made a list of the things Laura wants in a husband. And guess what? You don't match up with a single one." He let the silence hang.

Janice made some kind of strange snort, which Trevor thought quite unfeminine. "And what's wrong with that?" she grumbled.

Trevor ran his fingers through his hair. "I can't believe you're being so pragmatic about this. You're completely missing the point here. Didn't you see the way he was looking at her? They think they're in love, and maybe they are! And you're adding up lists of personality traits in a tidy package. Like the mathematics of the negatives will outweigh the positives. It doesn't work that way. You're a woman, for crying out loud! Think *romancey* stuff!"

"You're shouting."

Trevor bowed his head slightly and pinched the bridge of his nose. "Sorry," he mumbled.

She crossed her arms over her chest. "So, you have a better idea, I suppose?"

Trevor started the engine. "No, I don't. But I do know one thing. If we don't get to the restaurant soon, they're going to think we were in an accident and call 911. We'll have to think of something else later."

They made the rest of the trip in silence.

He'd barely stopped the car before they pushed the doors open and ran across the parking lot. They skidded to a halt at the entrance, stiffened their backs, and tried to appear carefree as they entered the dining area.

Frank studied his watch and raised his eyebrows as Trevor

and Janice lowered themselves into the waiting chairs. "We were getting worried that you'd had an accident or something. Is everything okay?"

Trevor nodded. "Everything is fine. We just stopped to talk for a couple of minutes."

"Stopped to talk?" Frank glanced back and forth between Trevor and Janice, then smiled. "Oh. To talk. That's cool."

Without clarifying what he meant or dwelling further on it, Frank turned to Janice. "It looks like you'll be seeing me at your church tomorrow. I've decided to make Laura's church my home, since we have to decide between the two. It wouldn't be right for us to go to different churches. Besides, we booked the ceremony at your church." He turned back to Trevor. "So it looks like you'll be going alone tomorrow morning, old man."

The gears started whirring in Trevor's head. He didn't know why it took so long, but it suddenly dawned on him that Frank didn't believe that he and Janice had stopped to simply talk. With that in mind, he formulated a plan of his own.

A plan that would work.

Now if he could just figure out a way to let Janice know what he was doing without Frank and Laura catching on . . .

ક

Janice stared at Frank, trying to think of what this new development would mean. She and Laura always went to church together. They usually sat together, but not always. Still, no matter where they sat, since they always arrived in the same car, one never made plans without the other. Now, since Laura had invited Frank, she didn't know if she would be included or not. Nor did she know how to ask if she would be going alone to church or if she would be the odd man out and make it a threesome. Neither held much appeal.

She tried to think of a way to ask the question without sounding stupid when Trevor spoke up beside her.

He smiled politely at Frank. "I won't be going alone. I'm going to be joining Janice tomorrow morning, so it looks like we can still drive together after all, at least to Janice and Laura's."

Janice turned to stare at Trevor.

Before she had a chance to ask him what he was talking about, he turned his head and reached toward her. Gently, he rested his palm on her forearm. At his touch, her words stalled in her brain. All she could do was stare at his hand, his touch warming her.

Trevor's voice came out in a low rumble. Despite his hushed tones, she knew Laura would still be able to hear him. "I know you said you wanted it to be just the two of us, but would you mind if we sat with Frank and Laura? Maybe they can join us for lunch afterward?"

"But . . . ," she sputtered, letting her voice trail off. "I never . . ."

Something tapped her sharply at the ankle. To prevent herself from saying anything stupid, she took a long sip of her coffee to give herself some time to figure out what was going on.

Trevor continued. "If you want, we can still go alone. But maybe it would be fun—you know, like a double date, for lunch after church."

Janice nearly choked on her coffee, something she noticed had been happening a lot over the last couple of days. To imply there would be a change to make it a *double date* meant that a single date had been planned, and it had not.

"Janice!" Laura chimed. Janice turned her head to face Laura, whose fingers were firmly intertwined with Frank's atop the table. "I didn't know you and Trevor were seeing each other. How exciting!"

Janice blinked repeatedly. The only reason she'd seen Trevor at all was because of Laura. She certainly would never have chosen to see him on her own.

She turned back to Trevor, who had quit touching her arm.

He was now nonchalantly leaning back in his chair, his arms crossed over his chest. He was also grinning like an idiot. Beneath the table, Trevor's foot kept nudging her ankle.

Janice sucked in a deep breath. "It kind of caught me off guard too," she grumbled.

The rest of their time together passed quickly and smoothly. Still, even though Frank and Laura didn't argue or disagree about anything verbally, Janice could see that they were worlds apart on many of their discussion topics. More than ever, she knew she had to do something to get Laura to see their differences.

Not for the first time, the guilt at what she wanted to do assailed her. All she wanted was for her friend to be happy. If that meant for Laura to marry Frank, then that was well and good. However, the more time she spent with Laura and Frank as a couple, the less she could foresee them being happy together on a day-to-day basis.

The more she thought about what Trevor had said in the car, the more she could see he was right. Pointing out to Laura that Frank was not the man of her dreams would not work. The only way for Laura to change her mind was through direct interaction with Frank to discover their differences for herself.

As partners, she and Trevor could gently point out areas of compatibility or incompatibility while Frank and Laura were together. Maybe if they did it right, Frank and Laura might not realize their involvement. Done carefully and correctly, Frank and Laura might even think that they came to the realization that they really weren't suited for each other by themselves.

Again, Trevor was right, in theory. Certainly, she and Trevor would have to spend time with Frank and Laura as a couple in order to do this. However, trying to disguise it as a double date was going about it in the wrong way. If it weren't for her friend, she wouldn't be with Trevor at all. She most certainly wouldn't be dating him. She didn't know him very well, but she knew him well enough to know that there was nothing about him that she specifically liked and much about him that she didn't like.

First of all, he was too pushy and impatient. Janice always preferred a man who was gentle and soft-spoken. The first time they had ever been alone together he had shouted at her. She hated being yelled at, especially when all she had done was express her opinion and subsequent thoughts on a plan of action.

She also wasn't too fond of his thrown-together strategy to double-date in order to get closer to their friends without discussing it with her first. Janice thought her idea made much more sense because at least she had a specific plan. Despite the fact that it wouldn't work, it was still a well-thought-out plan. He'd blurted his plan out and put it into action before he'd logically reasoned it out. Janice knew without doubt that spending Sunday afternoon together under the guise of a double date wouldn't solve the problem.

However, what was done was done. She had no alternative but to follow through with Trevor's plan—already set in motion. For now, it was the best they could do in their quest to show Frank and Laura their misconceptions about each other.

They didn't have time to lose. A wedding date of four months down the road was now circled on the calendar in her kitchen.

Therefore, she had no alternative but to pretend to be dating Trevor Halliday.

Janice steeled her nerve and smiled at Trevor, who was smiling at her, making her realize she had missed most of the conversation and had no idea what he'd just said.

"Great," Trevor murmured. "I can hardly wait until Tuesday, then, when I can see that new dress. You're so pretty in blue."

She forced herself to keep smiling. She seldom wore dresses, even to church. She only owned two dresses, and neither of them was blue. The only blue things she owned were blue jeans. Instead of showing everyone that she hadn't been paying attention, she would ask Trevor later what they had allegedly scheduled for Tuesday. She would also tell him whatever it was she'd agreed to, she had no intention of wearing a dress.

When the pizzas came, they paused to pray over their meal. Conversation continued on neutral and insignificant topics, giving Janice a chance to study the man whom she was supposed to be dating. On the bright side, Janice reminded herself that dating was the way to get to know someone better. Since she was supposed to be dating Trevor, she could show Laura how the process of getting to know a man was supposed to be done. Not that she intended to get to know Trevor that well. She only had to know him well enough to accomplish their mutual purpose.

By the time they left the restaurant, she couldn't say she knew Trevor any better than when they went in, despite the change in their relationship status. Thinking back, she'd dated the one man she'd ever come close to being serious about for nearly a year before she got to know him reasonably well. And over that year, she'd never considered marrying him.

The four of them walked together into the parking lot. Janice doubted she would get the chance to talk to Trevor privately because this time, instead of getting into Trevor's car, she was destined to be Laura's passenger since they were all going home.

Once they reached the cars, she knew without a doubt that no matter how quietly she spoke, Frank and Laura would hear every word she said. She needed to ask Trevor a few things about himself in order to make it look like she really was dating him. As it was now, she could barely recall the color of his eyes.

Laura and Frank stepped to the side, but not out of hearing range.

Laura's voice dropped to a husky whisper. "Good night, Frank," she purred, shuffling closer to him. Frank lowered his head and gave Laura a chaste, but long, kiss.

Janice squirmed. If she was officially dating Trevor, she wondered if she was supposed to kiss him good night too. She wished she knew how long they were supposed to have been dating so far. And even if she had been allegedly dating him for awhile, she still wouldn't have kissed him in the middle of a parking lot.

Trevor grinned and stepped closer. Janice's stomach dropped to somewhere below her shoes. She really didn't want to kiss him. She barely knew him. What little of him she did know, she wasn't sure she liked, especially in light of his ridiculous masquerade.

Suddenly, she was toe-to-toe with him. He lowered his head. Janice gritted her teeth. She was well practiced in the art of self-defense, and she wasn't afraid to use it. If Trevor tried anything funny, she considered decking him, regardless of what Laura and Frank would think.

His lips brushed her hair at her temple, but instead of kissing her cheek, his palms rested on her shoulders. He whispered in her ear, "We have to talk."

Janice tipped her chin up, not to kiss his cheek but to whisper closer to his ear. In doing so, she made a mental note to remember that his eyes were blue. "You've got that right, buddy boy."

"Loosen up," he continued to whisper. "I should probably look like I'm kissing you, but you're so stiff it looks like you're ready to run the fifty-yard dash."

Running wasn't exactly what she had in mind, but it was probably better than the violence currently formulating in her head. "Where did you get this harebrained idea that we should let them think we're dating?" she hissed between her teeth.

"It came to me in a stroke of genius," he whispered back.

Janice wondered about his IQ level.

He continued to whisper. "I should phone you when I get home, but I don't want Frank to overhear. I'll think of something later."

Before she realized it, he'd backed up. However, he didn't release her shoulders. One finger gently brushed her lower cheek.

She narrowed her eyes and glared up at him. He removed his hands a split second before she would have smacked them off.

"Good night, Janice," he said softly, but loudly enough for Laura and Frank to hear. "I can hardly wait for tomorrow morning."

For the first time in her life, Janice didn't want to go to church.

If she didn't feel guilty enough for what she was trying to do, now more guilt piled on her head.

Trevor started to step away but stopped when they saw Frank and Laura talking in hushed tones, not separating.

He shuffled closer again, but fortunately, not as close as before.

"Sorry about earlier, but the idea just kind of hit me," he said softly. He quickly glanced at Frank and Laura, then turned back to Janice. "If they think we're dating, then we'll be able to be with them most of the time. You know, to keep tabs on them and stuff. But this won't work unless you're a little more convincing. You should act at least a little bit romantic if we're supposedly seeing each other."

Janice nearly choked. She didn't want to think of acting "romantic" toward Trevor when she didn't know him beyond the realm of a casual acquaintance. She knew her best friend's fiancé better than she knew her alleged boyfriend. However, since she didn't figure she had much time before Frank and Laura were finished talking, she focused on their primary concern. "Why are you doing this? We're never going to fool anyone."

"Don't worry about it. You saw them today—they couldn't agree on a single thing. I'm sure they're on the verge of seeing this isn't meant to be. We won't have to pretend we like each other for very long."

As Trevor backed up, his words echoed in her head. *Pretend we like each other.* Never in her wildest dreams or worst nightmares would she have foreseen the magnitude of what she had agreed to do.

Frank and Laura separated, and the two men quickly slipped into Frank's car.

Janice stood in one spot, her feet refusing to move. She pressed the fingertips of both hands to her throbbing temples. If she was lucky, maybe her headache would develop into a full migraine, then she would have a legitimate excuse for missing church and their scheduled "double date."

"Come on, Janice," Laura said as she opened the car door. "It's late, and we have to get up early in the morning."

3

*A*s he stood with Frank on Janice and Laura's doorstep, Trevor strained to hear what Janice was trying to tell him.

He couldn't hear her over Laura's giggling.

Janice stepped away from Frank and Laura, so he stepped closer to Janice.

"What in the world are you wearing?" she ground out between her teeth in a stage whisper.

"Is this a trick question?" he asked as he raised one hand to the knot of his tie. As he did, he studied Janice, who was wearing fashionably snug jeans and a fluffy pink sweater. He looked further down. Instead of dress shoes, she wore sneakers.

Trevor cleared his throat. "Aren't we going to church?"

"Of course we're going to church. But it's a regular Sunday service. Not a funeral. You'd better come in. If you don't take off that suit jacket, everyone's going to stare at us."

A very bad premonition washed over him. He'd automatically chosen what he would have worn to his own church, which was his best monochrome pants and shirt ensemble with a matching sport coat and a plain tie. He'd grown up in a traditional church where all the men wore suits—or a reasonable facsimile. What he wore today was quite appropriate for a warm spring Sunday service.

It appeared her church was more laid-back than his.

Again, he looked down to her sneakers. He could almost see wearing jeans to a service if they were new and of a reasonably good quality brand name, but hers were neither. In addition to the condition of her jeans, he thought the sneakers were a bit much, no matter how relaxed the setting. "Are you seriously going to church like that? Or were you out in the park for a walk first?"

She laughed, probably thinking he was joking. "Of course not. I was right here, waiting for you."

Trevor checked his watch. "I guess we'd better get going."

As he turned, Janice grabbed him by the arm and pulled him inside. She held out her hand. "Wait. I'm being serious. You can't go like that to church."

"But . . ." He let his voice trail off at her stone-faced expression.

"No one ever wears a suit to Sunday service. You're going to look silly."

He opened his mouth to tell her that he was quite appropriately dressed for a Sunday service, but before he could form an argument, he stopped himself. He didn't know Janice well, but he did know from previous occasions that once Janice set her mind to something, she stuck to it like a dog with an old bone.

He sighed as he shrugged off the jacket and handed it to her, telling himself that he was doing this for Frank, not for Janice.

She slung the jacket over one arm and held out her free hand. "Come on, Trevor. Lose the tie."

Automatically, he rested his palm in the center of his chest, over his tie. "No. I haven't been to church without a tie since I was a kid. I can't go to church without a tie." The only times he didn't wear a tie to church was once a year at the church picnic, when they had the service in the park. Even then, it felt funny.

"Quit fooling around. We don't have time for this."

He stiffened his back and shook his head. "I'm not fooling around. This has gone far enough. It's not proper to go to church without a tie."

She sighed loudly and tilted her head toward their friends. "Look. Frank is taking off his jacket and the tie too. Can't you just do the same, nicely?"

Trevor gritted his teeth and slipped off the tie, even though it went completely against his grain. Knowing Frank really didn't know much about Laura, he should have guessed that Frank wouldn't have known anything about her church either, even though he should have. After all, this was supposedly the church Frank had chosen to get married in and attend after the wedding.

The four of them went together in Frank's car, leaving Trevor to share the backseat with Janice. Conversation was stilted, and Janice spent most of the trip seated as close to the door as her seat belt would allow. Trevor chose not to comment. If she chose to be in a snit because he didn't agree with her dress code, that was up to her. He wasn't going to ruin his time of worship by arriving at church in a foul mood.

They soon arrived at a massive parking lot adjoining a large multifaceted brick building. The main entrance consisted only of plain double doors, which were at the base of what was probably the modern version of a bell tower. However, instead of a hollow space and a bell at the peak, a huge white cross graced the top. The building itself was a three-story structure graced with tall, rectangular, starkly plain glass windows. A large flat section extended to the back, which Trevor guessed would contain the classrooms.

As they walked in, Trevor could barely believe the size of the place, which somehow seemed even larger from the inside. Music drifted from the sanctuary—not hymns, but a contemporary chorus played by a whole band.

"How many people attend here?" he asked, leaning down so hopefully Janice was the only one who heard his question. His own church had a regular attendance of approximately three hundred people. He liked being a member of a congregation where he could know everyone, by face if not by name.

"I don't know. I suppose about twelve hundred people. There are two services Sunday morning, plus one in the evening. In the summertime they have a Saturday night service too. And on Friday, they always have youth and young adult functions. Lots of times I come here Friday night to play volleyball. There's a gymnasium down the hall."

It shouldn't have surprised him that there was another huge room he hadn't accounted for.

Just as Janice had said, everyone he could see was dressed casually. With the exception of a few of the older men present, most of those in attendance were under thirty years of age and wore jeans and a casual top. He did appear to be on the verge of overdressed. He would never admit it to Janice, but now he was grateful she'd made him take off his tie.

He continued to study the people milling about the foyer.

"Look," he whispered as he leaned down to Janice. "There's a guy in a tie." He jerked his thumb over his shoulder to direct her attention to the right person, as if she could miss him. He was the only one in the place wearing a tie, even if he wasn't wearing a jacket.

Janice poked Trevor in the stomach, making him bring both hands down to protect himself.

"Don't do that! He's the only one here who ever wears a tie, but he can do whatever he wants. He's my boss, Ken Quinlan. The woman with him is his wife, Molly. She's the one who led me to the Lord two years ago."

"Really? That's amazing. There's an older man who goes to my church named Walter Quinlan. I know that Walter never had kids, but I wonder if they're related? It's not a common name. Can you introduce me?"

Janice shook her head. "I can answer that. Walter is his uncle, and he used to be my boss. He still owns the company, but Ken started running it when Walter took an early retirement. Maybe I'll introduce you later. We're supposed to be with Frank and Laura, not socializing."

He followed her into the sanctuary. Unlike the ornate wooden benches in his church, the seating consisted of padded stacking chairs. Like the outside, the sanctuary was also void of any decoration except for a single cross at the front. Even the wooden podium was rather plain.

A few people in the front rows appeared to be praying and readying themselves to worship. Other than that, most people talked freely in the sanctuary.

Still, despite the lack of formality, the place held a certain appeal. Since it wasn't in the surroundings, Trevor figured the charm of Janice's church had to be in the spirit of the people present—all believers obviously happy to be in God's house on a Sunday morning.

His attention wandered to the speakers mounted near the ceiling at the front, which piqued his curiosity about the band's sound system. At the same time as he checked the place out, he reminded himself that this was the church Frank was getting married in. As much as the place was growing on him, it still made him wonder how Frank could have agreed to such a thing without seeing and experiencing the congregation first. This church was very different from theirs.

He felt a tug on his sleeve. "Come on. There they are. We'd better sit down now if we want to get seats beside them. This place fills up fast. The service starts in five minutes."

They took their places, and as Janice predicted, the service started exactly on time at ten o'clock.

To his surprise, he enjoyed the worship time, unexpectedly being able to forget about the crowd around him as he praised God in song. Still, he didn't lift his hands like most of the people around him, including Janice. He listened politely to the testimony of a teenaged girl who had recently come to the Lord through the church's extremely active youth group. In addition to being moved by her testimony, he greatly admired the girl for being able to speak so freely in front of a large group, something he knew he wouldn't be able to do.

The pastor was a dynamic speaker, moving the place up another notch on Trevor's scale. During the pastor's message, a number of people boldly called out "amen." One man called out a few comments that made many in the congregation laugh. Even the pastor laughed. For such a large place, Trevor was amazed that it could be so friendly.

At the close of the service, he didn't want to admit it, but he kind of liked the place. Still, he knew he would never consider attending on a regular basis. As nice as it was for a change, the informal atmosphere wasn't his style for a house of worship.

This time, he and Janice stuck close to Frank and Laura as they mingled with the people milling about. He recognized a few of Laura and Janice's friends from having met them before. Janice introduced him to everyone as they chatted for a few minutes and carried on the conversation, just in case he didn't remember their names, which he appreciated.

They were almost on their way out of the building when another couple joined them. Laura introduced them as Rick and Sarah, who were brother and sister.

Sarah and Rick remained close together, chatting with Janice in such a way that seemed to deliberately omit everyone else from the conversation. As the only relative stranger in the crowd, Trevor stood back to watch.

Trevor noted with amusement that much of Sarah's conversation centered on her brother and all his finer attributes. Rick had very little to say while his sister dribbled on and on, mentioning Rick at every opportunity, slipping little plugs into the conversation about what she considered Rick's best qualities.

Before long, Sarah began prompting Janice to say something. When Janice finally started adding more into the conversation, Sarah poked Rick in the back, much to Rick's annoyance, forcing him to step forward and participate more as well. At that point, Sarah shuffled slightly back, starting to edge out of the little group, leaving Rick talking solely to Janice.

Any other time, Trevor would have found such lack of subtlety in matchmaking hilarious. This time it wasn't funny.

Glancing out the corner of his eye, Trevor noticed Frank looking back and forth between himself and Rick as Rick's actions and conversation began to cross the line from small talk into serious flirtation. Laura stared unwavering at Janice. Neither of them made any attempt to break into the conversation.

Janice giggled at something Rick said.

Trevor gritted his teeth. Without warning, he stepped forward, placing himself directly between Rick and Janice, purposely standing much too close to Rick, invading Rick's personal space. He made a point to take advantage of his height, noticeably tipping his head to look down at Rick, who was only about average height. Rick quickly backed up a step, and his voice trailed off as he finished his sentence.

Trevor gave a lopsided grin and quirked one eyebrow. He sidestepped until he was side by side with Janice, then slipped one arm around her waist. "Sorry to interrupt, Rick, but we were just on our way out for lunch. Maybe we'll catch you and Sarah another time. Nice to meet you."

He heard as well as felt Janice's sharp intake of breath. On his other side, he heard Frank clearing his throat.

"Yeah," Rick mumbled. "Nice meeting you."

Trevor nodded toward Sarah, who he noted was very pretty, although she did talk a little too much for his preference. He made a mental note when the whole fiasco with Frank and Laura was over to get Sarah's phone number. "Have a nice day," he said to Sarah.

Without waiting for either of them to respond, he removed his arm from Janice's waist, picked up her hand, and linked his fingers through hers. "Come on, Shorty. Let's go." Not waiting for a response, he gave a slight tug and led her outside. Frank and Laura followed at a distance.

The second they arrived at Frank's car, Janice yanked her hand away. "Shorty? And what did you think—"

He placed his index finger in front of his lips. "Shh. Here they come."

On the way to the restaurant, conversation in the backseat of the car was even more stilted than on the way to church.

Trevor didn't mind. The silence gave him time to think.

He stared absentmindedly out the car window as they drove to the restaurant, unable to believe what he'd done. He'd issued a nonverbal warning to Rick—and to any other male in the vicinity—to keep away from Janice.

He'd acted like some macho jerk, publicly staking his territory. And he'd done it in God's house.

Trevor squeezed his eyes shut. The only way he could justify his actions would be that he had to show any man who might be interested in Janice that she was taken. He had to perpetuate the illusion that they were dating so they could continue with their mutual mission with Frank and Laura.

He didn't care about himself, but this instance made him realize that he hadn't been fair to Janice. Rick seemed like a pretty decent guy. He appeared to be truly interested in Janice—interested enough that his sister had acted as a matchmaker for him, preplanned or not. Trevor couldn't tell if Janice was interested in return, but she hadn't exactly turned Rick away. She certainly appeared to be enjoying Rick's company.

A pang of guilt settled in his gut. He had prevented Janice from seeking the companionship of someone who might come to love her someday for real. Trevor knew he had come across too strong. By doing so, he had caused Rick to look weak in Janice's eyes, and that was wrong. Because he couldn't tell Rick he wasn't really dating Janice, there was nothing he could do, but he did know that he would have to apologize to Janice. With some luck, when they finally managed to convince Frank and Laura to either postpone or hopefully call off the wedding, maybe enough time would have passed for Rick to be able to face Janice again. If he was still interested. Trevor hoped he hadn't scared Rick off permanently.

When the car came to a stop, Trevor forced himself to stop thinking about Rick and start thinking about the reason he'd made such an effort to show the world that he and Janice were an item.

Frank and Laura joined hands as they walked into the restaurant. Janice wouldn't come near him, and he couldn't blame her. However, he had worked too hard to arrange for this time they were to be spending together so they could talk in a nonthreatening environment. He couldn't allow his mishandling of the situation with Rick to spoil it.

He would take his lumps later. For now, they had more important things to deal with.

While they waited for a table, he shuffled Janice to the side to speak as privately as possible amongst the crowd in the restaurant's lobby.

"We have to talk." He almost asked why she was mad at him, but he couldn't bring himself to do it. Besides, he already knew the answer. Instead, he tried to think of something to say that would calm her down. It didn't take a rocket scientist to see how she felt. Her whole body was stiff. Behind her glasses, her brown eyes absolutely flashed. She wasn't just a little mad at him. She was furious.

Before he could think of the right thing to say, she leaned toward him. He tried not to cringe.

"You called me 'Shorty,' " she ground out between her teeth.

Trevor blinked, then stepped back as he looked down at her. He was six feet tall, and judging from the height difference, taking into account her footwear, he figured Janice was only five foot two. She *was* short. It was a fact that couldn't be denied. "It was supposed to be an endearment . . ." He let his voice trail off.

Janice crossed her arms over her chest and glared up at him. "Oh? Really? Would calling an overweight person 'fatty' be termed an endearment? Or because I wear glasses, would 'four eyes' also be an endearment, in your estimation? Should I be flattered that you address me by my most prominent physical fault, something I can't do anything about?"

Trevor stiffened from head to toe. He had been teased relentlessly as a child about his big nose because that was the problem everyone could see. Through his struggles in school, often the teasing about his big nose had been the straw that broke the camel's back. No one but his mother knew how often as a young child he'd come home crying. As a teen, to his dismay, to top everything off his nose grew proportionally to his height. With the years, his fellow schoolmates became better at inventing creative insults. Short of plastic surgery, his big nose was the one thing he couldn't hide. This was the way God had made him. Fortunately, now no one ever bugged him about his big nose, and it was a welcome relief, although he was sure many people thought about it.

"Uh . . . I never thought of it that way. I'm sorry." He let the silence hang until he finished fighting his personal demons of his youth. When he finally returned his attention to Janice's face, her expression had softened. He could see on her face that she'd forgiven him.

He cleared his throat. "I thought we should talk about Rick."

Her eyebrows rose. "Rick? Why do you want to talk about him? That was quite a little performance you put on, by the way. If I didn't know better, I would have thought we were together. You were quite convincing. I hope you can handle the gossip. You should have seen everyone watching you. It was really funny. Oh. They just called our table. Come on."

Their time together progressed much the same as their pizza dinner the night before. Together, they did manage to point out a few things to Frank and Laura that made the outing a worthwhile expedition, but for the moment, nothing changed. Not that he expected them to realize how wrong they were for each other in only one day. Trevor only hoped and prayed that they'd planted the first of many seeds today that would make them think about things more realistically as time went on.

When they were done and the bill and tip were paid for, Trevor was pleased that Janice and Laura invited him and Frank to their house for the afternoon. It was another opportunity Trevor couldn't turn down.

He stayed with Frank in the living room while the women went into the kitchen to make coffee. He realized too late that he should have offered to go into the kitchen with Janice, as he wanted to talk to her privately about a few things that were said at lunchtime. He didn't need more time with Frank. They lived together and saw each other every day.

Frank's voice jolted him out of his thoughts.

"What did you think of Laura's church? It sure is different, isn't it?"

Without thinking, Trevor's hand went up to his throat, to pat the knot on his missing tie. "Yeah. It sure is. And you've already decided to get married and attend there, huh?"

Frank smiled and gazed out the window. "Yeah. It's big, but I figure I'll get used to it."

Other than the informal atmosphere, Trevor couldn't see anything else wrong with the church. The congregation all appeared sincere. Despite his personal preferences, he knew there was benefit to getting together with a large group to worship God. Therefore, he couldn't say anything.

He decided to change the subject because Laura and Janice had returned.

Frank covered Laura's hand as soon as she sat down beside him. Fortunately for Trevor, he'd sat in the armchair, so he didn't have to sit beside Janice.

He looked across the room to Frank and Laura, who were all snuggled up. "Have you two decided on a guest list or anything?" Trevor asked. "And what about the size of the wedding party? As far as I know, Janice and I are it."

Laura smiled at Frank as she answered him. "I thought we should have a small wedding. You know. Something private. Sunday is the time for a large gathering."

Frank's eyebrows rose. "I know guys aren't supposed to care about stuff like this, but I've always wanted a big wedding. This is a celebration of the start of our new lives together. I wanted to invite lots of people."

Trevor tried not to gloat. Here was something else they disagreed on. He and Janice exchanged sly glances.

"You know, Laura," Janice said, folding her hands demurely in her lap, "this is something you should have agreed on first. It doesn't look like you discussed the guest list either before you booked the church."

Frank and Laura gazed lovingly into each other's eyes. The last time Trevor had seen such sappy expressions was in an old B movie an old girlfriend once forced him to watch.

"That's okay," Laura said as she sighed airily. "We can meet in the middle. Isn't marriage all about compromise?"

Trevor nodded. Of course he knew compromise was a necessary ingredient for a successful marriage. However, he'd always thought that the more a couple agreed on in the first place, the less compromise was necessary and, therefore, the better the chances that the relationship would survive the test of time.

"Okay," Frank said. "I had figured on five hundred guests and four attendants."

Laura's eyes widened. "Are you counting Trev and Janice? So that means one bridesmaid and one groomsman besides them?"

Frank shook his head. "No, I mean besides them. Four attendants each."

"But I didn't want a big wedding party. How about this? If you reduce the number of attendants, I won't mind more guests."

"How many guests?"

"I only wanted a hundred guests. But you can have fifty more guests for each less attendant."

"Each?"

"Total."

"Then three hundred guests, two attendants. Each."

"Only Janice and Trevor, you can have three hundred and fifty."

"Deal."

"Done."

They shook hands, then turned and smiled at Trevor.

Trevor wanted to shake his head. They'd reduced the planning for a wedding to a bartering exchange. This wasn't exactly the way he'd pictured a couple in love discussing their upcoming wedding ceremony.

Trevor cleared his throat. "Have you at least decided where you're going to live when you get married?"

Frank nodded. "We'll rent an apartment downtown, close to our jobs. A high-rise."

Laura's smile disappeared. "But I wanted a house in the suburbs. With a big yard and a garden."

Frank shrugged his shoulders. "We'll have lots of time to discuss that later."

Laura shrugged her shoulders. "I suppose . . ."

Frank turned to Janice and smiled. "That coffee smells great. Is it ready yet?"

*J*anice stood. She glanced at Trevor, hoping he would follow her, but Laura jumped to her feet instead and accompanied her into the kitchen.

Janice didn't know what to do. It appeared that Laura and Frank were going to have their first argument about the wedding in the company of herself and Trevor. This was exactly the opportunity they were striving for. Not only one, but two obvious disagreements had risen to the surface.

Now was the perfect time to gently point out to Laura how ill-suited she and Frank were for each other.

But Janice couldn't do it. Laura was her best friend. She wanted to console her friend—to tell her that their disagreement would blow over and that everything would be all right. However, that wasn't what she was supposed to do. Not that she didn't want Laura and Frank to kiss and make up—her ultimate goal was for her friend to be happy. For today, she and Trevor would strive for Laura and Frank to understand their disagreement in the perspective of the big picture.

When Laura and Frank passed the stage of the warm fuzzies, it would take more than a quick smile to solve their issues. When their relationship developed into making choices instead of simply flowing with the attraction, Frank and Laura would never make it. They were just too different, and their needs in a marriage partner too far apart.

She expected Laura to say something about the wedding plans gone askew, but she didn't. Instead, Laura rummaged in the fridge for the cream while Janice poured the coffee into four mugs.

As soon as Laura closed the fridge and stood upright, Janice knew she had to say something, but she didn't know what. She didn't want to rub her friend's face in her failures or her bad choices. Besides, not only Laura's feelings were involved. Frank was also her friend, and she didn't want to hurt him either.

Janice cleared her throat. "Laura, I've been thinking. You two haven't had enough time to plan everything out. You know what I mean. All those nitpicky wedding details. Also, you two really should discuss other important things beyond the wedding. Not only where you want to live but also all the practical day-to-day stuff. Don't you think maybe you should set the wedding back for awhile and work all this stuff out first?"

Laura smiled. "But we did work it out. We only have to make the actual guest lists."

Janice forced herself to smile. She didn't consider the bartering exchange she'd witnessed working it out. Also, Frank never did settle the issue of the downtown apartment. He'd simply dismissed Laura to get the coffee, which rankled Janice.

"But what about where you're going to live? It's important that you both agree."

"I don't care where we live, Silly. We're in love. We'll be happy wherever we are."

"You say that now, but there's more to it than that."

"Not really. Love conquers all, you know."

Janice shook her head. "But love isn't blind, deaf, and dumb, Laura. It's complicated."

Laura picked up the mugs meant for herself and Frank. "Love is only as complicated as you make it. Come on. Before the coffee gets cold."

Balancing two mugs in one hand and a plate of cookies in the other, Janice followed Laura into the living room. Judging from Trevor's expression, she could see whatever reasoning he'd attempted with Frank had netted the same result.

She rested the plate on the coffee table and handed one of the mugs to Trevor.

He sipped the coffee slowly, then sighed. "Thanks. I see you remembered how I like it."

"It was easy. You take it the same way as I do. Double cream, no sugar."

He nodded. "Frank and I were thinking that it would be fun to do something after work tomorrow. You interested?"

She wasn't really, but Trevor mouthed a "please" at her when no one else was looking at him. She had no idea what he had in mind. However, neither of them had made any progress in their quest so far. "Sure, that would be nice," she said, trying to smile and make it look like she meant it. "What have you got in mind?"

"I dunno. Something we can do together. I don't feel like sitting in a restaurant. I want to do something. You think of what we can do."

Her mind went blank, especially with the three of them staring at her. "Well," she mumbled, letting her voice trail off while she rested her hand under her chin and tapped her cheek with her index finger. "How about bowling?"

Trevor blinked and continued to stare at her. "Bowling? I was thinking more of wide-open spaces."

Laura's face lit up. "Bowling! What a wonderful idea! I haven't been bowling for years."

Frank turned to stare at Trevor. "Yeah. That's a good idea. I love bowling."

Trevor's eyes widened. "I haven't been bowling since junior high school. But if that's what everybody else wants, I guess I can do that."

Laura nodded and glanced at the clock. "You know, it's nearly five o'clock. Do you guys want to stay for supper? I think we can scrape something together. Maybe I should put the cookies away."

Trevor rested one hand on his stomach, which Janice thought kind of cute. He smiled brightly. "I'd love a home-cooked meal."

Frank turned to him. "What are you talking about? You cook pretty good, and we eat at home all the time. There's nothing wrong with the stuff we eat."

Trevor grinned. "Food always tastes better when someone else makes it, no matter what it is."

Janice nodded. "I know. Laura does most of the cooking here, and everything she makes definitely tastes better than my cooking."

Frank nodded too. "Trev does pretty much all of the cooking at our place."

Janice didn't know how it happened, but somehow Laura and Trevor disappeared into the kitchen, leaving her alone in the living room with Frank. Not that she felt like cooking, but she had thought this would have been a good opportunity to talk to Trevor. To her surprise, they returned, both grinning and winking at each other, to announce that they were going to make a surprise for supper. They instructed Janice and Frank to stay in the living room until they were done and disappeared as quickly as they had come.

Janice gritted her teeth. Again, another opportunity to talk to Trevor in private where they could come up with another plan had been lost.

Still, if she had to see something as good instead of as a loss, she could take this as an opportunity to talk to Frank. She hoped that Trevor was doing the same with Laura.

She started out by talking about the things she had in common with Laura, then steered the conversation over to Laura's hobbies and choices of entertainment. It came as no surprise that many of them were news to Frank. For recreation, Laura enjoyed crafts and other sedentary pastimes. Laura's idea of strenuous exercise was a trip through the mall during the holiday season. Laura's only form of outdoor recreation consisted of a walk through the park if the weather was just right.

On the other hand, Frank enjoyed more strenuous pursuits such as skiing and cycling. Unfortunately, he didn't seem to find anything wrong with the fact that Laura didn't share his interests. He only laughed and said that if one of her hobbies was cooking, then he had no complaints.

The whole time Janice tried to explain to Frank that Laura wasn't about to suddenly take up hang gliding, she heard Trevor and Laura laughing and goofing around in the kitchen.

By the time they returned, Janice could barely believe that nearly an hour had passed. She'd tried her best with Frank, but one look at Trevor and Laura told her they hadn't talked about anything important or done anything except cook supper and make a mess in the kitchen.

"Whatever you're cooking smells great," she said, trying her best to be gracious. Not that she wasn't telling the truth. She didn't know what Trevor was like in the kitchen, but she knew Laura was a great cook. Laura was just as creative in the kitchen as she was with her crafts, while Janice had two left thumbs.

"I'm not telling what we made, but you'll probably guess pretty soon."

Janice tried to think of what they had on hand, but she wasn't sure since Laura usually did most of the grocery shopping. "Sorry, I haven't a clue."

Trevor checked his wristwatch. "You don't have time to guess anyway. We still have stuff to do, and supper will be ready in ten minutes. Laura told me it's your favorite thing."

Janice gritted her teeth. They weren't supposed to be discussing her favorite things. They were supposed to be comparing Laura and Frank's favorite things.

Everyone was watching her, probably expecting her to immediately guess what they had made. "You made chocolate chip cookies for supper?"

"Well, maybe your second-favorite thing."

Immediately, she knew they'd made lasagna. "You're kidding. Right?"

"Wrong."

"I thought it smelled like lasagna for awhile, but there's something else."

Trevor grinned. "We fried an onion to mask the smell of the lasagna. Pretty smart, huh?"

Now she knew what at least some of the laughter had been about.

She could have mentioned something Trevor could have done that would have been smarter, but she chose to bite her tongue. In silence, she followed everyone else into the kitchen. Immediately Janice and Frank sat down. Trevor and Laura brought everything to the table.

They prayed together and began to eat. Janice had never tasted such delicious lasagna in her life. Not only had they made a big salad to go with the lasagna, they had also taken a loaf of bread and cooked it with garlic butter. Everyone laughed at the accompanying side dish of sautéed mushrooms and onions.

"Pretty good, huh?" Frank mumbled around his mouthful.

Laura beamed. "Trevor was the head cook here today. It was a real treat to let someone else take charge in my kitchen. And now I know his secret ingredient. Next time, I'm going to use it."

Janice nodded while she swallowed her mouthful. "Laura does most of the cooking here, in case you can't tell." She turned to Trevor. She didn't want to say anything about how surprised she was, not only that he could cook but that he did it so well. Still, she couldn't not say anything. He'd done too good of a job to let it go. "This is great, Trevor. My compliments to the chef."

"You're welcome. But don't thank me too much. We did it together as a team."

When everyone was so overstuffed they couldn't eat another bite, they all rose from the table.

Instead of leaving the room, Trevor helped himself to another glass of milk. "By the way, we've already discussed it, and since Laura and I did the cooking, you and Frank are doing the dishes."

Janice surveyed the mess. Beyond a total lack of culinary talent, this was the biggest reason she avoided cooking any more than she had to. Usually, the quality of the meal was inversely proportional to the mess produced to create it. More important than the dishes, she wanted to talk to Trevor, not spend more time with Frank. But after Trevor had made such a wonderful dinner, she could hardly refuse.

She shrugged her shoulders. "I guess so. It's the least I can do after all your hard work. I had no idea you were such a good cook."

Trevor grinned and placed one hand over his heart. "My daddy always told me that the way to a woman's heart is through her stomach."

Every thought in Janice's head deserted her. All she could do was stare at him.

Frank cleared his throat behind her. "Remember when I washed your car for you last week?"

Trevor glanced behind her to Frank, then shrugged his shoulders. "I think I owe Frank a favor, and he's calling me on it. I guess this means that you and I are doing the dishes, and Frank is off the hook. I don't mind. This gives us a chance to be alone together, although I could think of a few things I'd rather be doing alone with you other than the dishes."

It took a few seconds for what Trevor said to sink in. She opened her mouth to ask him what in the world he was alluding to when Frank spoke up.

"That doesn't get any argument from me. Come on, Laura. Let's go."

Frank and Laura disappeared in seconds flat.

Janice tapped her foot, crossed her arms, and glared daggers at Trevor. "What in the world are you trying to do? Do you know what that sounded like?"

Trevor turned his back to her and returned the milk carton to the fridge. "Relax, Janice," he said from within the fridge. "I'm teasing you. We're supposed to be dating, remember? Don't you think that's what couples should do? Get away from the crowd to be alone every now and then?"

"Frank and Laura aren't a crowd," she said to his back as he continued to move things around in the fridge. Nor were they really a "couple." Still, being alone with Trevor in the kitchen was exactly what she wanted in the first place. She convinced herself that it was only the rebel within her that no longer wanted it to happen.

She cleared her throat. "We have to talk."

He left the fridge door partway open, picked up the pan of leftover lasagna from the counter, and worked it into the empty space he'd made. Janice heard more banging and shuffling as he attempted to make more room for the large pan.

His voice came out muffled as he spoke. "Hey. You've got a chocolate bar ditched in here."

"What I've got put away in a safe place in my fridge is none of your business. What's supposed to be your business is this issue with Frank and Laura. Will you get out of there?"

Slowly, he backed up and straightened. As he turned around, he waved the chocolate bar that was supposed to be in the fridge back and forth in front of her. He grinned and quirked up one eyebrow. "Mmm. My favorite. If you loved me, you'd share."

Janice opened her mouth, but no sound came out. Before she said something she knew she'd regret, she stomped forward and grabbed her chocolate bar out of his hand. She straightened her glasses on her nose, narrowed her eyes, and glared up at him. "I don't know what you think you're doing but stop it. We have important stuff to talk about."

His focus remained glued to the chocolate bar the whole time she reprimanded him. She whipped it behind her back.

Trevor's posture sagged, and he lost his smile. "All I wanted was one little bite. But that's okay. I have three sisters. I know from experience what happens when a man comes between a woman and her chocolate bar."

All the fight left her. She held the bar out to him and sighed. "If you need it that bad, take it. I have a feeling we don't have anything to talk about, anyway. I heard you and Laura goofing around the whole time you were making supper. Didn't you think that it would have been a good time to talk to her about Frank?"

Trevor removed the chocolate bar from her hands, tore open the wrapper, and took a bite. He closed his eyes as he chewed slowly, savoring it like he hadn't tasted chocolate for years. As he swallowed, he opened his eyes and smiled. "This is my favorite kind. You want some?" He tore back the wrapper but didn't actually give it to her. Instead, he held it out as if she should take a bite while it was still in his hand.

Janice shook her head. At her indication that she didn't want any, he took a second bite, then proceeded to talk with a mouthful.

"I may not have directly pointed out how wrong they are for each other, but I was working on something else. I've known her for a couple of years but only as a casual acquaintance. We don't really know each other very well, at least not where it counts for true friendship. Before she trusts me, she's got to learn that I'm on her side. Then she'll take what I say more to heart." He paused and pointed at her with the half-eaten chocolate bar. "You know, like witnessing to someone you don't know that well. First you have to earn the right to be heard."

"I never thought of it that way. That's probably a good idea. But I did have a nice talk with Frank. Even if I couldn't get him to agree with me on the whole thing, he did admit that he and Laura don't share many common interests."

"I guess that's a start. But you know him better than I know her. You at least knew where to start."

"Yes. And speaking of starting, we should start these dishes, or we're going to be stuck here in the kitchen all night. Since this is my house and I know where everything goes, you wash, and I'll dry."

Trevor tucked the remainder of the chocolate bar into the torn wrapper and laid it on the counter. He then rolled up his sleeves and began rinsing the dirty dishes that were stacked beside the sink. As Janice gathered everything else that needed to be washed, she watched him, glancing out the corner of her eye.

Until today, every other time she'd met him, she'd always considered Trevor to be the quiet type. Today she'd seen a side of him she'd never seen before. She'd been especially surprised by his little performance with Rick. Once Trevor warmed up, he really wasn't very quiet at all. In fact, she wondered if it would be hard to turn him off once he got started.

Also, once he got started and opened up, his warm smile changed his whole countenance. He may not have been handsome in a classical sense, especially since he had such a large nose, but when he smiled, his smile came all the way from his heart.

This morning, she couldn't believe it when he'd arrived for church all dressed up. In all the other times she'd met him, he'd been wearing jeans and a comfortably worn T-shirt, like her. Today, in the pristine monotone jacket, shirt, and pants ensemble, she couldn't believe the difference. The contrast between the dark clothes and his blond hair came across as quite striking, adding to his overall appeal.

Apparently, clothes did make the man.

She'd meant to talk about Frank and Laura, but as they worked together to wash and dry dishes and clean up the kitchen, they talked about everything except their friends. He told her wryly how even though it wasn't what he was used to, her church service had pleasantly surprised him. It pleased her that he enjoyed it. Before she realized what she'd done, she agreed to attend the service at his church with him the following week.

When they were done, they joined Frank and Laura in the living room. Instead of talking, the four of them sat together on the couch and watched the second half of a television drama. Part of Janice told her that they were wasting the evening, but another part of her just wanted to relax and enjoy the quiet time without pressure.

At the end of the program, Frank stood. "I think it's time to be going. Everyone has to get up early for work tomorrow."

Trevor rose to follow as Frank and Laura walked outside, and Janice rose to follow Trevor. One step beyond the doorway, Trevor stopped. Not realizing he'd stopped, Janice walked into his back, bumping him forward. He tottered slightly but corrected his balance as he spun around and grabbed the railing with one hand.

As he faced her, Janice covered her mouth with her hands. Her heart pounded at the thought of what almost happened. Through her carelessness, she'd almost sent him flying down the steps. She would have been the cause of him breaking his neck. She may not exactly have liked him, but she certainly didn't want to kill him. "I'm so sorry!" she squeaked out with her heart in her throat. "Are you okay?"

Her breath caught as she realized that they were only inches apart. He couldn't back up, or he would go down the steps for real. She could have backed up, but her feet seemed glued to the porch.

His voice came out in a low rumble. "Don't worry. I'm fine. Are you okay?"

She nodded. "Why did you stop?"

The words barely out of her mouth, she glanced past Trevor to see Frank and Laura wrapped in each other's arms, locked in a kiss.

"Oh," she mumbled. "Never mind."

Trevor broke out into a wide grin. "We're supposed to be officially dating, you know. Good night, Janice." Before she had a chance to speak and bid him good night, he closed his eyes, placed his hands behind his back, leaned slightly forward, puckered his lips, and made a loud smooching sound in the air.

Her mind went blank, and she broke out into a cold sweat. "Get real," she hissed. Miraculously, her feet became unglued from the porch floor. Before he could respond, she backed up into the house and pushed the door closed inches from his face.

She stood staring at the closed door, unable to believe what she'd just done or what had nearly happened.

Trevor's laughter echoed through the heavy wooden door.

Her mind raced as she tried to think of what she should do. Certainly, she had no intention of opening the door and talking to him after this. Nor could she afford to take the chance that he would open the door and come in. The clock above the fireplace ticked, nagging her that it wouldn't be much longer until Laura would return.

Janice didn't want to be near the door when it opened in case he was still there, so she turned and ran. Not thinking of where she was going, she found herself in the kitchen. And since she was in the kitchen, she stared straight at the fridge, which held her emergency chocolate bar.

She had the fridge door partway open when she remembered

that Trevor had absconded her secret stash after supper. However, she didn't recall him actually finishing it.

She turned her head, and sure enough, the half-eaten chocolate bar sat on the counter near the sink, all nicely wrapped up and tucked to the side.

Praising God for small miracles, she pushed the fridge door closed with a muffled bang. Without delay, she strode across the kitchen, scooped up the chocolate bar, and ran into her bedroom. In the privacy of her room, she nibbled away at the remainder, savoring it bite by bite, letting the soothing chocolate calm her shattered nerves. However, she knew that from this moment on, she would never be able to think of her favorite chocolate bar without picturing Trevor nibbling at it and waving it in her face between bites.

She stared through the window into the dark night for a few seconds, then yanked the curtain shut.

Tomorrow was another day. Unfortunately, it was another day she would see Trevor Halliday.

5

*T*revor lay on his back, staring up at the dark ceiling. Not for the first time, he turned his head to check the glowing green numbers of the clock radio.

Four twenty-seven. In only three hours he had to get up for work, and he'd barely slept.

He squeezed his eyes shut, but the self-imposed blackness couldn't stop thoughts of Janice from cascading through his mind.

In an attempt to block Janice out of his consciousness, he draped his forearm over his eyes. It didn't help. In his mind's eye, he could still see her.

He couldn't believe how he'd behaved. He couldn't say he was trying to be funny, although he had to admit that he'd certainly enjoyed himself in an odd kind of way. He would never have foreseen himself deliberately provoking a woman, yet that was exactly what he'd done. He couldn't remember the last time he'd laughed so hard as when she'd closed the door in his face. The entire way home, Frank had caught him still snickering about it. Trevor was at a loss to explain why, because he didn't understand it himself.

Now, in the silence of the night, the more he thought about it, the less funny his actions became.

He'd met her many times before Frank and Laura's engagement, but he'd never paid her much notice. Not that there was anything specifically wrong with Janice. It was just that between the ordinary brown hair, the ordinary brown eyes, her total lack of height, and the quiet and studious demeanor which her functional glasses only magnified, she'd never done anything to make him take notice.

Today, though, he'd seen the fire in her eyes, and it mesmerized him. In spending so much time so close to her over the past few days, he did something he'd never done before. He'd looked at her. *Really* looked at her. He'd seen past everything that made her appearance ordinary and beyond everything she did to fade into the background. Her eyes truly were the windows to her soul. Her thoughts and reactions to everything he'd done couldn't have been clearer if the words were written in neon pen across her forehead.

Janice was doing the exact opposite to him as Frank and Laura were doing to each other. Frank and Laura only put their best foot forward with each other. For whatever reason, they chose not to show anything that might disturb the status quo of their relationship. The end result, intentional or not, was that they were not being honest with each other in their actions—or their responses.

Through Janice's unpretentious reactions, Trevor couldn't help but see how she felt about everything he'd done.

She was furious when he called her Shorty, even though he'd originally misjudged the reason for her anger as his leading Rick to believe they were seriously together. But the more he thought about it and the more he came to know her, he realized that she had accepted all facets of letting Frank and Laura believe they were truly a couple. Looking at the big picture, the rest of their little universe had to also perceive them as a couple. She had already accepted that for the time being, she wouldn't be pursuing relationships with other men, regardless of who started it, as part of the package. Not only did she not have a problem with him acting like a jealous boyfriend, she'd expected it. He realized he hadn't given her enough credit.

He also saw in her face that she thought he was too stuffy

when he arrived for church appropriately dressed. Normally, he would have been annoyed for being judged like that. However, in the end she'd been right. He would have felt very self-conscious if he'd arrived at her church in his true Sunday best while everyone else around him, with the exception of her boss, wore clothes fit for little better than a Sunday picnic.

After lunch, when they'd returned to her house, her annoyance when he was joking with Laura in the kitchen couldn't have been more obvious. But by that time, he'd been just as annoyed with her as she was with him. The woman never let up on anything. He wanted to take a little break and relax. She didn't. All he wanted to do was enjoy a good meal, especially when he'd worked so hard to prepare it. She remained steadfast and focused on the reason they were together in the first place, which was to straighten out their friends. Nothing more and nothing less.

Then he'd taken her chocolate bar. The reason he'd taken it wasn't because he wanted it so bad. By that time, he simply wanted to see what she would do when she lost something, because she'd won at everything else all day.

Without specifically calling them arguments, she'd beaten him on every issue. She'd won the argument about his clothes. She'd certainly convinced him that calling her Shorty had not been an endearment. She'd also been right about him goofing off with Laura in the kitchen, regardless of his justifications for his behavior.

He was being childish, but he wanted to, for once, get one up on her. He wanted to see what would happen if she lost a small battle in her quest to win the war. He'd chosen his wording for getting the chocolate bar from her in such a way that she couldn't say no. Then he'd made a grand show of savoring and enjoying every bite.

Somewhere in the middle of his little performance, something changed. At first he'd thought he was only teasing her, watching her watching him eat her treat—which she'd surrendered to him. By the time he got halfway through, he'd felt so guilty he couldn't finish.

Trevor rolled over and buried his face in the pillow. At the time, he hadn't really thought about why he'd wanted to challenge Janice. Now, after much introspection, the reason behind his actions hit him. It had been more than friendly teasing.

He was measuring her up against Brenda, his ex-girlfriend, comparing them.

He'd once done something similar to tease Brenda, but instead of it being a treasured, hidden treat, he'd made a game of holding back something useless and frivolous—the toy from a fast-food kid's meal, something Brenda couldn't have cared less about. Even though the battle itself was meaningless, she still cared about winning.

He'd previously experienced Brenda's crocodile tears when she wanted to convince him to do things her way. He'd pointedly ignored Frank's jibes about being a sucker and giving in every time Brenda turned on the waterworks. On that occasion, though, she hadn't cried, but he hadn't been prepared for what Brenda did.

At first she had playfully pouted, acting coy and cutesy. When that failed to net the toy, she had gone on to distract him, using his interest in her against him. At the time, he'd had a hopeless crush on her, and she knew it. When she couldn't reach the toy as he held it over his head, Trevor had laughed. But he stopped laughing when she started touching him suggestively. To entice him, she ran her fingers down his cheek and through his hair. Then, when she saw that she was having an effect on him, she started planting little kisses on his chin until he couldn't think. Then, her teasing little kisses moved closer to his mouth, like she was going to kiss him for real. As soon as he lowered his arms to embrace her properly, she snatched the toy from his hand, stepped away, and laughed. The game was over. She'd won. He had been goofing around, but Brenda had been more than serious.

Watching her wave the toy in front of his nose in triumph, everything had come together with shocking clarity. Brenda hadn't kissed him as a sign of affection. She kissed him as a means to get what she wanted—as a tool, even a weapon. She was playing dirty. Knowing how he felt about her, she'd used her feminine charms to make him weak, then used his weakness against him. It hadn't been that she'd managed to take the toy from him that bothered him; it was how she did it. She'd manipulated him with no thought or concern for his emotions or his heart—with a clear conscience. That day had been the end of his relationship with Brenda.

And now, he'd used Janice's chocolate bar against her, teasing her with it in order to test her. He'd dared her, challenged her, yet she'd done the honorable thing, which was nothing.

Realizing how he was testing her and comparing her when she'd done nothing to deserve such treatment made him feel lower than a common earthworm. What started as a game had suddenly turned into something else.

Instead of trying to manipulate him like Brenda would have, with sad eyes and crocodile tears, Janice only stared at him in unmasked disbelief when he'd actually started eating her chocolate bar. He'd seen in her face that she really didn't think he'd do it. Then, in a split second, her face had hardened, and she'd bluntly told him they should have been dealing with the problem at hand, which was Frank and Laura. She never mentioned the candy bar again, everything was back to normal, and they'd started cleaning up the kitchen.

He'd never enjoyed doing dishes before, but the time had gone surprisingly fast as he and Janice completed their chore. He could almost have forgotten that they were only pretending to like each other to fulfill their mutual goal.

He'd tested her twice that evening. Once with the chocolate bar and again at the door as they parted.

He honestly didn't know what would have happened if she had called his bluff and actually kissed him.

Trevor flipped over on his side and pulled his blanket up to his chin. The more he thought about it, the more he thought that Janice wouldn't have kissed him, and she would never kiss him. He didn't know her tremendously well, but well enough to know that Janice would only kiss a man if she meant it, which was as it should be.

Tomorrow, he would figure out how to make things right for taking her chocolate bar and eating it in front of her. Then, all would be well with his soul.

☜

"Good morning, Quinlan Enterprises," Janice singsonged. As she spoke, she knocked over a stack of purchase orders one of the supervisors had just deposited on her desk. She struggled to grab the pile and not let the phone fall from her shoulder where it was precariously balanced.

"Hi, Janice. It's me. Trevor. I hope you don't mind me calling you at work."

"Trevor?" She gulped. The phone slid off her shoulder anyway, and she scrambled to catch it before it hit the floor. Her desk sat alone in the entrance to the office building, but she lowered her voice to a whisper anyway, since it was a personal call. "How did you get my number?"

"I phoned Frank at work, and he phoned Laura at her work and left a message. Then she phoned me back on her coffee break and gave me your number. You won't get in trouble, will you?"

"My boss is really nice, but I can't abuse taking personal calls on company time. What do you want?"

She waited for his reply, which stretched into a long, heavy silence. She wondered what he had to think about so hard before he spoke. While she waited, she glanced up at the clock. It was exactly noon, so it was unlikely that a call would come in to interrupt him once he got started, if he got started. She would have liked to hear that something had transpired from her little talk with Frank the night before. However, the longer the silence dragged on, the less optimistic she became.

Finally, he spoke. "I wanted to know if you were free to go out to lunch with me. How long do you get for your break?"

A knot formed in the pit of her grumbling stomach. She had no idea what could be so important that couldn't be said over the phone or couldn't wait until evening, when they met to go bowling. If it was good news that Frank and Laura were starting to appraise their relationship in a realistic light, Trevor should have just said so. Instead of the encouraging news she hoped she would hear, a cloud of discouragement settled in—maybe the situation had become worse instead of better.

She looked up at the time again. "I get half an hour for lunch, starting at 12:30. I don't know where you work. Are you close by? I'd offer to meet you halfway, but I take the bus to work and leave my car at home."

"It's not too far. Well, maybe it's a little ways away. Okay, I guess it's not that close. I work in the industrial park, and I know that you're downtown. It will probably take me about twenty minutes to get there, which would work if I leave right now."

The sudden silence told her Trevor was waiting for her to accept or decline his invitation.

She looked up at the clock again, calculating his travel time in addition to the length of time they would need to eat. Even if he got an hour for his lunch break, he would still exceed his allotted time allowance.

Now she knew it had to be important.

Janice cleared her throat. "Yes. If you're in a rush, we can grab a quick lunch at the place down the block."

"Great. If you wait out front, I won't have to waste precious time and go into the visitor parking lot. See you at 12:30. Bye."

Janice found herself staring at the handset while the dial tone buzzed. At the sound of footsteps echoing on the tile floor behind her, she fumbled with the phone and hung it up quickly, then returned her attention to her work.

Right on time, Susan arrived to relieve her. Janice dashed outside at the same time as Trevor's car pulled over to the curb in front of the building, in a no parking zone.

She scrambled into his car in three seconds flat, barely fastening the seat belt before the car was once again in motion.

"Did you have to circle around the block, or did I make it?"

He checked over his shoulder as he pulled into the downtown lunch-rush traffic. "I should say I had to circle a few times, but that would be lying. Your timing was perfect. I just got here. Where should we go? I seldom come downtown and never for lunch on a weekday."

Janice pointed straight ahead toward the fast-food restaurant. "There's the place I usually go when I don't bring a lunch. One block that way—on the corner. They have a nice variety, it's fast, and best of all for you, they have ample free parking for customers."

"I'm not going to argue with that. That's a big part of the reason I never come downtown. No parking. And I don't like the crowds."

"I know what you mean. If it weren't for my job, I wouldn't come downtown either. Everything I want is close to home. Why should I go miles and miles for the same thing I can get right next door? I've never considered shopping an adventure."

He nodded and steered the car into the parking lot. Janice pointed to an empty spot, and soon they were standing in line at the counter.

She couldn't wait until they sat down. If what he had to say was so important that he'd gone through such trouble to come all this way, she wanted to know now. "Is Frank starting to change his mind about the wedding yet?" she blurted out, not caring about the proximity of the other people in line around them.

"I don't know. I really haven't talked to him since last night. I don't know what things are like at your place, but on a workday morning, Frank and I kind of grunt at each other as we get ready to run out the door. But he did remind me that we're all going bowling tonight."

She waited for him to say more, but when she turned toward him, he was looking up and reading the menu board.

"It's the same for me and Laura in the morning too. You talked to Laura on the phone today, didn't you? Did she reconsider this thing with Frank?"

He stepped forward with the line as he continued to study the board. "I don't know. She really only had time to give me directions how to get here and your phone number. I don't know if you could call that talking. I'm going to have the number six. What do you want?" He turned and grinned at her. "My treat."

The rest of her question about talking to Laura caught in her throat. Those little crinkles she liked so much were back at the corners of his shining blue eyes. Combined with his heart-stopping smile, the man would have been absolutely great in a toothpaste commercial.

Janice reached up and straightened her glasses, just in case they were crooked. "I always have the number three."

He glanced back up to read her choice. "Aw, you don't need that diet junk. Come on. Have a number six with me." He turned his entire body toward her. Slowly, he reached forward. With a touch so light she barely felt it, he ran his index finger along the back of her wrist. One eyebrow quirked up, and his voice dropped to a low, husky whisper. "Just for today, you can live dangerously."

Janice forced herself to breathe. She didn't know what just

happened, but suddenly the danger became more than a high-cholesterol, artery-clogging, mega-calorie, fast-food meal.

She tried to clear her throat, but her voice still came out all funny. "Then I'll have the number five."

Trevor turned to the clerk. "Two number fives, please. And make one of them the super size. With two coffees."

As he fished his wallet out of his back pocket and paid the clerk, Janice kneaded her lower lip between her teeth and watched him. She still couldn't believe this was really happening. She'd lain awake in bed for hours last night, going over and over in her mind how Trevor had stepped between her and Rick at church. Even though it probably wasn't politically correct to act that way, she had secretly been flattered by his actions. She'd never had a man care enough about her to be possessive, and it was a new experience, even if it was only in her mind. One day, in God's timing, a man who would be her perfect mate would cross her path, and she could live happily ever after. Until then, she was stuck with Trevor Halliday and her overactive imagination. Still, even though he wasn't tall, dark, and handsome like Frank, two out of three wasn't bad.

He lifted the tray and tilted his head to one side. "I see an empty table. To the left."

Janice followed him through the small cafeteria-style restaurant. Because she was so short, she always had difficulty finding an empty table. However, Trevor stood nearly a head taller than most of the people present, making her slightly jealous of the advantage his height gave him.

She tucked her purse under her chair while Trevor removed the food from the tray and divided everything between them. After a moment of silence, he said a short and quiet prayer of thanks for the food, and they began to eat.

Trevor nodded once while he chewed. "This is good," he

mumbled through the food in his mouth. "Coming here was a great idea."

"Everything here is good. Even the 'lite' meal."

He smiled. "Maybe. But I'm not a rabbit. Men need real food."

She almost started to say that the high-cholesterol mayonnaise blend in his sandwich and deep-fried potatoes on the side didn't exactly qualify as "real food" on a consistent basis, but she stopped herself. Even though he hadn't yet let her know what he wanted to discuss in person, she knew it wasn't to argue about nutrition basics.

"I have no doubt that you're really going to eat all that, plus half of my potatoes, which I won't be able to finish."

He stopped midchew. "Really?" he mumbled, then swallowed. "You don't think you'll finish those? But it's so good. I wish we had a place like this in the industrial park."

"I don't even know where you work or what you do. If we're supposed to be seeing each other, I should probably know what you do for a living."

"It's kind of hard to describe. In my official job description, they call me a mechanical engineer."

"I'm sorry. I don't know what that is."

Trevor shrugged his shoulders and laid his sandwich on the paper plate. "It's a fancy term for a high-tech handyman. I work for V. L. Management, the company who oversees the Valley Lane Industrial Estate. Sometimes I'm an electrician, sometimes I'm a roofer, and sometimes I'm an inspector. Whenever there's a problem with one of the leased buildings, it's my job to go fix it, and if I can't fix it myself, it's my responsibility to contract it out and oversee the project."

"That sounds like an interesting job."

"I guess. No two days are alike, that's for sure. What do you do?"

Janice hunched her shoulders and stared down into her coffee cup. "I'm just the receptionist for Quinlan Enterprises. And I do the accounts payable."

"There's nothing wrong with a desk job. If you like to work inside, it's steady, and you don't mind shuffling paper, that's what counts."

She nodded. "Yes. I like working with people. Basically, I talk on the phone most of the day." Janice grinned.

Trevor returned her smile. "I like working with people too. Except, often they're angry people because the only reason I see them is when something has gone wrong. Like if the roof is leaking and there's a puddle in the lobby. Or in the center of the boss's desk."

Janice listened intently as Trevor entertained her with stories of the interesting and unusual disasters he'd had to deal with in his history as a mechanical engineer. Before she knew it, half an hour had passed—and then some. They abandoned their unfinished fried potatoes and half-cups of coffee and literally ran to Trevor's car. Fortunately, the one-block trip from the restaurant to her office building took less than a minute.

When Trevor stopped at the red light, Janice opened the door to get out. "Don't circle the block. The office is just across the street. I'll just cross at the intersection and run in. You can keep going." She had one foot out of the car before she realized that in all the time they'd spent together, they hadn't discussed whatever it was he came for in the first place. Now, not only was she returning late, Trevor's half-hour break was over by more than double, and he still had a twenty-minute drive ahead of him.

She exited the car but didn't close the door. Resting her hands on the roof of the car, she leaned in to talk to him. "I guess I'll see you tonight at the bowling alley," she said.

"Yeah. At seven?"

She glanced up at the light. The cross street's light had turned amber. Her time was up. She nodded. "Seven sounds good."

As she started to back up, Trevor leaned toward her, over the top of the stick shift. "Wait!" he called out. "I have something for you." He reached into a bag between the seats, pulled out a chocolate bar, and handed it to her. "I got this for you. See you later."

She slammed the door closed just as the light turned green.

Janice stood at the curb, staring at the chocolate bar in her hand. It was her favorite kind. The kind Trevor had half eaten last night.

She raised her head and watched Trevor's car as he drove down the street and turned the corner.

She still had no idea why he'd come.

When the light changed, she ran across the street and into her office building. Whatever the reason, she had no choice but to wait until seven o'clock and hope for the best at the bowling alley.

A t least I hit something last time, which was better than you did."

"Yeah," Trevor mumbled back to Laura as they watched Janice steadying her bowling ball while she took aim. "She's pretty good, isn't she?"

"Yes. She was in the bowling league where she works last year, so she used to bowl a lot."

Trevor watched Janice do some strange little dance as she pranced to the line, ending with a quick hop before she released the ball, sending it in a straight path down the lane. With an echoing bang, the ball knocked down six pins on her first shot.

He thought she bowled like Fred Flintstone, but then again, she had nearly double his score.

"Bet she gets a spare," Laura said, leaning closer to him so he could hear over the din.

"Probably," he muttered.

Laura then leaned into Frank and ran her hand up and down his arm. "But Frank got another strike last time."

Frank didn't reply. He just turned to Laura and smiled.

"Frank has been bowling in a league for three years," Trevor muttered. "He should be good."

Once again, Trevor watched Janice as she watusied to the line, did her little hippity-hop thing, and sent the ball on its trajectory. The clatter and talking and banging coming from the other lanes continued on, but their own group remained silent as they mentally cheered Janice's ball to success.

At the last second, the ball curved, missing the mark by a

fraction of an inch. Three pins went flying. The last one tottered back and forth, causing everyone to hold their breath, trying to will it to fall over. The wobbling slowed and stopped. The last pin remained tauntingly upright.

Trevor smiled as in his mind's eye he pictured himself walking up the long wooden lane and personally kicking the pin down, just so Janice could have scored a spare.

He cleared his throat, his face solemn by the time Janice turned around. "Better luck next time," he called out.

Frank stood and retrieved his ball while Janice approached and sat down at the bench. "I didn't know Frank was this good," she said.

Trevor nodded. "Yeah. He's got his own ball and everything. Last year he got a trophy when his team won some kind of tournament."

"No wonder he was so anxious to go bowling."

He glanced over to Laura, whose attention was totally fixed on Frank as he took aim. Trevor leaned closer to Janice, hoping he could speak quietly, yet still be heard over the racket around them. "Speaking of bowling, how in the world could you come up with an idea like this? The reason we were supposed to get together in the first place was to talk to them, to have them get to know each other better and identify their conflicting interests and personality traits. This place is so noisy and distracting we haven't said a word about anything important, nor are we likely to."

She leaned closer as she spoke, also lowering her voice as the clatter around them continued. "You wanted me to come up with something we could all do together."

"But you were supposed to think of something quiet and romantic!"

In the blink of an eye she turned her face toward his, not giving him time to move or respond. Her face was so close they could almost rub noses. He blinked a few times and managed to focus beyond the reflection of the overhead lights in her glasses. For the first time, he realized her eyes weren't completely brown but were flecked with minute quantities of some kind of olive green.

Her eyes narrowed. "This was the best I could come up with on short notice," she ground out sharply. "I couldn't think with everybody staring at me like that. I'm not a mind reader. If you wanted to do something specific, you should have said so in the first place."

The close proximity made it difficult to maintain his focus. As her face blurred, he had two choices. He could either back up a few inches to see properly, or he could close his eyes . . . and kiss her.

Trevor backed up and shook his head.

"And another thing. You all keep talking about tomorrow night, but I have no idea what it is you've got planned. The other day you said something about a blue dress, and I don't even own a blue dress. You better not have planned something late, either, because we all have to get up for work in the morning."

Trevor shook his head again and held up one palm in the air to silence her. "Relax, Janice. I only suggested we go out to dinner—a nice little place I know about that's quiet and has relatively private tables. I thought it would be nice if you and Laura wore dresses. You know, like a date."

"What makes you think that I'd wear a dress out on a date? I don't even wear a dress to work. You already know I don't wear a dress to church. I own exactly two dresses, neither of which have been worn in a very long time, and neither of them is blue."

Glancing out the corner of his eye, he saw that no pins remained upright in the lane. Frank had turned around and was returning to take a seat, meaning it was Trevor's turn to bowl.

He stood, then leaned down to Janice. "If you don't wear a dress on a date, what do you wear?"

"Just the same thing I always wear, either jeans and a matching top, or whatever I wore to work. I don't fuss and play with my hair either. What you see is what you get."

Behind him, Frank cleared his throat. "Come on, Trev. Your turn," he called from the scorekeeper's chair. "Quit yapping and start bowling."

Absently, Trevor selected a ball. He stepped into the center of the approach to the lane, wiggled his fingers into the holes of the bowling ball, and took aim. While he was supposed to be concentrating on the pins, Janice's words echoed in his mind.

What she said was truer than she probably realized. The woman didn't appear to put on airs for anyone or anything, even to go so far as to not even dress up for church. Of course God accepted everyone as they came to Him in every aspect of their lives; however, Trevor thought a woman should be a little different when it came to men. Not that he was anyone special that she should dress up for him, but every other woman he'd dated had always put her best foot forward and tried to impress him, at least when they first started dating.

Again, he thought of Brenda. Every time they went out, Brenda had worn nice clothes, and her hair had been perfect, usually with some frilly thing tucked into her curls. Brenda's tastefully applied makeup had always been just right. So far, he couldn't remember Janice ever wearing makeup, except for a little light-colored stuff on her eyelids when he'd picked her up for lunch. He remembered once bumping into Brenda unexpectedly at the grocery store late at night. She'd been embarrassed to have him see her without makeup, even though he'd seen nothing wrong with her, especially considering the time and where they were.

The more he thought about it, the more he realized he would

have liked seeing what he was getting with Brenda a lot sooner. He'd only had a superficial view of her—it took quite a bit longer to see her heart, deep down, where she kept everything hidden. He'd gone out with her for a few months before he realized she had a hidden agenda behind much of what she did. Because she had pretended to be someone she was not, it had taken awhile for him to figure her out.

The complete opposite of Brenda was Janice. Everything she thought was as plain as the nose on her face, every opinion bluntly expressed with no guesswork needed. Her home was functional, and she conducted her life in a similar manner. The woman even took the bus to work instead of taking advantage of the freedom and comfort of her car. He thought she could take a few lessons on being at least a little mysterious for a man, unless she planned on being single all her life.

Trevor gave his head a mental shake. He wasn't there to think about Brenda or analyze Janice. He was, unfortunately, there to bowl, and he wanted to get it over with.

He positioned himself at the foot of the bowling lane and sucked in a deep breath. He exhaled, walked in a nice, simple straight line, took a simple aim, and let the ball go. Instead of traveling down the lane in a straight line, the ball curved in a big arc to the left, visibly spinning as it rolled. Then, halfway down the lane, just when he thought the ball would drop into the gutter, it started curving to the right. By the time the ball reached the pins, it knocked down only one, the one on the far right.

Three loud groans echoed behind him.

Frank called out, "I can see why you haven't bowled since junior youth group days, Trev! You're pathetic!"

The reason he hadn't been bowling since junior youth group days was because he hated bowling. It naturally followed that he wasn't very good, but he didn't want his failures announced to the entire population of the bowling alley.

Trevor turned around, about to tell Frank so, but as he did, Janice jumped to her feet.

"Stop that, Frank. He just needs to develop a better delivery."

Trevor could tell that Janice was about to show him how she thought he should bowl. In front of everyone. He didn't care how he bowled. He just wanted to finish the game so they could leave.

He raised both palms in the air as she approached. Janice's rented bowling shoes made a squeaking sound on the polished wooden floor as she skidded to a halt.

"Forget it," he said. "Even though you bowl better than me, there's no way you're going to get me to do it like that."

She crossed her arms over her chest. "And what's wrong with the way I bowl?"

He raised one hand and walked two fingers in the air. "That little thing you do."

"What do you mean, 'thing'?"

Trevor gritted his teeth. Without another word, he turned around, grabbed one of the bowling balls, positioned himself at the beginning of the runway, or whatever they called it, and prepared to roll the ball.

He glanced briefly over his shoulder. "You bowl like this." As he made his way up the lane, he swiveled his hips from side to side while making short little steps, waggling the ball in front of him as he walked. When he got right to the line, he imitated Janice's dancing little two-step jump, drew the ball back to wind up, and pitched it forward while standing on one foot, making sure to flex his wrist the same way Janice did, just as he let the ball go.

He didn't even wait for it to hit the pins. Trevor twirled around.

Frank was laughing so hard Trevor didn't know how Frank stayed on the seat without falling down. Beside Frank, Laura sat stiff as a board, her eyes wide as saucers, with both hands clamped over her mouth.

In front of Trevor, Janice hadn't moved. But every thought was expressed clearly on her face. Her eyes were narrowed into little slits, her eyebrows were all scrunched in the middle, and her lips were pressed together so hard some of the skin around her mouth had turned white.

Then her foot started tapping. Behind him, he heard the bang as the ball came in contact with the pins.

"That's how you bowl. Like a girl," he said.

"Then you should bowl like a girl more often, because if this would have been your first ball, you would have just gotten a strike. Smarty-pants."

"Really? Are you kidding me?"

Her stone-faced expression told him she definitely wasn't in the mood to kid.

He spun around to face the pins once more, and sure enough, not one remained standing.

Trevor grinned from ear to ear as he turned back to Janice. "Hey. I got a strike. How about that?"

"I said, if it was your *first* ball it would have been a strike. That makes it a spare."

"Still. That was pretty good, don't you think?"

"That was horrible. How could you embarrass me like that?"

Trevor crossed his arms, matching her stance. He smirked. "Sorry, Darlin', but you do just fine at embarrassing yourself without me."

"I don't look nearly as stupid as you did."

"That's 'cause you're a girl. When girls do stuff like that, most guys think it's cute. If I did that, which I did, I just look ridiculous."

She didn't answer. She only continued to glare at him.

As the silence drew on, Trevor realized that Frank and Laura were watching them, as were the people in the lanes on either side of theirs. The longer they continued to stand there, the more he realized that he really had embarrassed her, maybe not by imitating her, but by arguing with her about it where everyone could see.

Trevor stepped forward and raised one hand to touch her shoulder so he could usher her to a more private setting. Since it was the first time they were standing so close together since they arrived, Trevor hadn't realized how far down he had to look at her. Wearing the flat-soled bowling shoes, she was shorter than ever.

Before he could guide her away gently to a less public location, she flinched away from his hand and glared at him even more intently.

"Don't touch me," she hissed between her teeth. She spun around so fast her hair flopped. Without breaking the flow of the movement, Janice stomped off to the bench and plunked herself down beside Laura.

He grinned weakly at Frank and Laura, who were both staring at him. "I think she's mad at me," he mumbled as he passed them and sat beside Janice. He saw Laura whisper something in Frank's ear.

Trevor cleared his throat and sat as close to Janice as he could without her shuffling away. "I don't know what you're so mad about. I really don't like bowling, and I was getting frustrated. Maybe I did get a little carried away, but it was me who everyone was staring at, not you."

"It's not that everyone was staring at you. You were imitating me. Is that really what you think of me? I look that stupid when I bowl? And even if I do look that dumb, it wasn't very nice of you to make fun of me."

Laura leaned forward and glanced nervously between the two

of them. "It's okay, Janice. You don't really look like that when you bowl. Trevor was totally overdoing it."

Frank stepped in front of Janice. "Yeah, Janice. He's just jealous 'cause everybody else bowls better than he does. Come on, give him a break. He didn't mean to hurt your feelings. Did you, Trev?"

Judging from her expression, she was more angry than hurt, but he supposed there was some of that too. "Would it help if I said I was sorry?"

Janice heaved a sigh. "I don't know why I'm so angry. That's okay, Trevor. I probably do look a little silly when I bowl. Other people have teased me about it, but no one has ever done such an active demonstration. I guess that's why it kind of hit me between the eyes. Now let's finish up this game and get out of here. The leagues are going to be starting soon, and we don't have much time left."

Laura rose and selected a ball to take her turn.

While Janice watched Laura, Trevor watched Janice out the corner of his eye.

He'd made her angry again, with the same result as the last time. Everything blew up on the surface quickly, they settled it, and the disagreement was over within minutes.

Also the same as the last time, he'd crossed some kind of line he didn't know existed. He'd hurt her feelings, but instead of making him guess what he did wrong, she let him have it, holding nothing back. She did nothing to manipulate him by piling guilt on his head for hurting her feelings, and she didn't test him with guessing games. She didn't appear to be holding a grudge. He didn't need to make it up to her. There were no tears. They dealt with it. It was over.

The incident was both forgiven and forgotten by Janice, but Trevor wasn't going to soon forget. He'd never seen a woman handle hurt feelings like that before. He'd seen his sisters hold a grudge for weeks. Their boyfriends, and later their husbands, often went through extreme measures in order to make things right. Only when enough time had passed and proper restitution accomplished could the incident be sufficiently laid to rest. Like most men, he couldn't handle a woman's tears. He'd had girlfriends do the same to him, particularly Brenda. He'd seen it so often, in varying degrees, he thought it was normal.

Having a spat with Janice was almost like having an argument with Frank. Except, for some reason, when he fought with Janice he felt like doing something special for her to make up for it when it was over—not because he had to, but some deep little inner voice made him want to.

Janice rose as Laura approached the bench. "Good going, Laura. You're getting better already. I wish we had time for another game."

Trevor harrumphed under his breath. "Yeah, what a crying shame that we have to go. I just love bowling so much," he grumbled sarcastically.

Janice turned, scowled at him, turned back to Laura, smiled once again, and walked away to select her ball.

This time, when Janice wound up and did her walk up the approach area, her motions lacked the fluidity of her prior efforts. Trevor tried to convince himself that it was only his imagination that she didn't score as well as she had in previous rounds. Yet, she only smiled politely after her second throw and returned to her seat.

Frank rose for his turn, so Trevor shuffled closer to Janice. "You're pretty good."

"Not really. But I'm better than you." She closed her eyes, turned, and briefly stuck her tongue out at him, then turned back in time to watch Frank bowl a strike, allowing him to have another throw on their last turn.

"Yay, Frank!" Janice called.

Laura simply clapped her hands.

Trevor didn't care about Frank's score. He only cared that the bonus throw gave him a minute longer to sit with Janice.

"Are we going to do something else after this?"

She glanced at her watch, then spoke with her face turned straight ahead, watching Frank. "I don't think so. There really isn't time to do anything. We have to get up for work in the morning."

He sat in silence while Frank threw his last ball.

"Okay, Trevor, it's your turn," she said, still not looking at him as she spoke.

He wanted her to turn to him, with her eyes open this time. He wanted to see if those little green flecks were still there once she'd calmed down.

"Do I have to?"

"Yup." She nodded but didn't turn her head.

He leaned closer. "I think I'll forfeit my turn. I've got the lowest score anyway, so who cares?"

Suddenly, she did turn to him. Through her lenses, he could see the flecks were still there. When she realized how close his face was to hers, she tilted her head back as she spoke. "Quit being such a coward. Just because the whole place was watching your sterling performance last time and will be watching you again this time, you don't have to be nervous. You can bowl like a man now."

He couldn't hold back his laughter. "I had that coming, didn't I?"

She smiled. Something strange happened in his stomach, making him wonder if he was getting hungry.

"Yes, you did. Now get up there."

He continued to snicker to himself as he wound up and took his turn. He didn't bowl a strike or a spare, but he scored better than he had the entire game.

As he changed spots with Laura so she could take the last turn of the night, Laura whispered to him. "Good going, Trev, but I still beat you."

He grinned. "Ask me if I care."

While they returned the rented shoes, Trevor struggled to keep quiet and not comment about the size of the shoes Janice laid on the counter. Next to his size twelve shoes, hers looked like a child's. Since he already knew that she was touchy about her height, or rather the lack thereof, he didn't want to take the risk that her sensitivity extended to her shoe size. He also didn't know why in the world he would find her shoe size so fascinating.

He didn't mind the distraction when Frank slapped him on the back. "Hey, Loser. How's it feel?"

"I really don't care. If nothing else, tonight was a good reminder of why I hate bowling."

Laura linked her hands through the crook in Frank's elbow. "I know what you mean. I don't exactly hate bowling, but I don't think this is going to become a favorite weekly thing for me either." Laura turned to Janice. "I don't feel like going home yet. How about if we go next door and grab a donut or something?" Laura then released Frank, leaned closer to Janice, and whispered something in her ear.

Trevor turned to watch Janice. Her cheeks darkened, she shook her head, and she suddenly stared at the floor. Something strange happened in his stomach again. Now he knew he had to be hungry.

He pasted a smile on his face. "Yeah. A donut sounds good. I've got to do something to make me forget about bowling."

The donut shop was considerably quieter than the bowling alley. First, Janice slid into the booth. He prepared to slide in beside her, but Frank pointed at something out the window. Trevor couldn't see whatever interested Frank so much, and when he turned back around, Frank had already lost interest and taken the seat beside Janice. Laura slid into the other side of the booth, then patted the vinyl seat beside her, encouraging Trevor to sit beside her in what should have been Frank's spot.

Trevor shrugged his shoulders. Rather than make an issue of their strange behavior, he slid in beside Laura.

Now that they finally could begin with the issue at hand, he waited for Janice to start the conversation. However, Frank began monopolizing her attention, talking in hushed tones, not giving her the chance to speak to the group as a whole.

He felt Laura poking him in the ribs. She spoke in hushed tones as she leaned closer to him. "Trevor? If you ever need help with Janice, you can ask me anything. Did you know that her favorite color is purple?"

He blinked, rested one elbow on the table, and rested his cheek on his fist. "Really? Do you know what Frank's favorite color is?"

"It doesn't matter about Frank's favorite color. We have to talk about Janice."

"I think I can handle Janice just fine. Why don't we talk about Frank?"

Laura shook her head. His peripheral vision caught Janice shaking her head at Frank at the same time. Trevor thought it was kind of funny.

"No, we have to talk about Janice. She may have a few little quirks, but she's got a heart of gold."

Trevor struggled to keep a straight face. "Quirks? Janice? No. I hadn't noticed."

Laura nodded so fast her hair bounced. "It's true, and I only mean that in the kindest way. We've been best friends since elementary school, and I'd do anything for her." Laura's voice lowered in volume even more, forcing Trevor to lean closer to her in order to hear. "For starters, I warn you not to get her talking about junk food. Not that she's a health food nut—but she's very careful about what she eats."

He recalled Janice's comments on their lunch choices earlier in the day. Now he felt more than ever that he'd made a good decision in changing his selection from the greasy burger to the healthier submarine sandwich. "No kidding?" he asked, trying to keep the sarcasm from his voice.

Realizing he was fighting a losing battle, especially since Frank seemed to have Janice's attention completely tied up, Trevor listened politely to Laura as she told him everything about Janice and her likes and dislikes. The more he listened, the more he realized that Janice had been right. Laura should have known all Frank's likes and dislikes the way she knew Janice's. He wanted to point out to her that since Laura felt it very important that he knew all about Janice, then she should know the same about Frank. However, Laura didn't allow him the opportunity to change the subject.

The second Laura finished her donut, she cleared her throat. Trevor wondered if this had been a prearranged signal because Frank instantly pushed his coffee cup aside and stood. "Sorry, guys. I just noticed the time. Laura's got to be up at six. We should go."

Before he knew it, Trevor was in the passenger seat of Frank's car, and they were on their way home.

He only hoped Janice's efforts had obtained better results.

$\mathscr{J}$ anice, while you were gone for lunch, someone called for you. It sounded important. It was . . ." Susan picked up the yellow note. "Mr. T. Halliday. He's some kind of engineer at V. L. Management."

Janice stuffed the bag and her purse under her desk while she mumbled her thank-you to Susan for relieving her.

The second Susan disappeared around the corner, Janice dialed the number.

He answered in one ring. "Maintenance."

"It's me—Janice. What do you want, Trevor?"

The echoing drone of traffic in the distance drifted through the phone along with his voice. "There's going to be a slight change of plans tonight. I hope you don't mind."

Janice glanced down at the corner of the bag peeking out from beneath the desk. She'd spent her entire lunch break shopping for the coming evening. She could probably say she hated shopping as much as Trevor hated bowling.

She sighed. "No, I don't mind. What's the matter?"

Trevor didn't speak while the wail of a siren blasted in her ear through the handset. "Frank's got to work late tonight. Would you mind if you and Laura came here and picked us up instead of us picking you two up? That will give Frank the time he needs to shower and clean up before we all go out for dinner tonight at a decent time."

Another siren wailed through the phone. Janice waited until it passed before she spoke. "That's fine. I guess Laura's got your address?"

"Believe it or not, she's never been here. I'd better give it to you. You can't miss the mailbox in front. It's one of those red antique kinds on a post."

As she scribbled the address and made a note about the mailbox, another siren wailed.

"Where are you?" she asked after it passed. By the number, she knew he was on a cell phone. Not only did he seem to be outside, it sounded like he was in the middle of a busy intersection.

"I'm on the roof of one of the buildings removing a bird's nest from an air-conditioning intake duct. I'm having an easy day today. But judging from the fire trucks that just went by, I'm going to have a bad day tomorrow. But so far no ambulance, so that's a good thing."

She didn't want to think about cleaning up and rebuilding in the aftermath of a fire. Suddenly, she became more satisfied with her uneventful desk job. However, the thought of spending part of a workday up on the roof of a tall building did hold a certain amount of appeal. She wondered how much of the city he could see from his present perspective and if he ever took his camera with him.

Janice pictured a vivid pink and purple sunset from the vantage point of the roof of a tall building in a quiet section of town, businesses closing as people went home for the night. At nightfall, the glowing colors would be striking, but fading quickly. The evening air would blow a cool, refreshing breeze. The lights of the city would be slowly blinking on, just like a scene from an old romantic movie . . . a young couple in love, sharing a rare, quiet time together, hidden from the hustle and bustle of a long and hectic day, alone on the roof. . . .

Janice shook her head and cleared her throat, sending her foolish thoughts from her head. "So you want us at your place at six, then?"

"Six would work with our reservations. See you then."

"Okay. Oh, Trevor?"

"Yes?"

She opened her mouth but snapped it shut. "Nothing. See you at six," she said, then mumbled a quick good-bye and hung up.

Janice stared blankly at the door. She'd almost asked him if he was going to wear the same thing he'd worn to church on Sunday. Only this time she wouldn't have asked him to take off the suit jacket or the tie.

Janice buried her face in her hands. She didn't want to know what Trevor was going to wear.

Now she only had to convince herself that she didn't care.

ॐ

Laura knocked on Trevor and Frank's front door, then turned around and called to her down the length of the sidewalk. "Come on, Janice. You look fine."

"I'll be there in a sec," Janice muttered around the key fob she held between her teeth. Somehow, the elastic waistband of her slip had become twisted, and when she slid out of the car, the left side of the slip slid up and became entangled at the waistband beneath her dress. Now the wretched garment wouldn't go down without a little convincing.

She tried to position herself discreetly, standing in the vee between the open car door and the car itself while she tried to grip the slip and pull it down through the fabric of her skirt.

If she had been in a more private setting, she could have simply reached under her skirt and yanked it down. However, not only was she on public display in the middle of Trevor and Frank's neighborhood, but soon Trevor would see her.

This was one of the reasons she hated wearing a dress.

Finally, she managed to tug it down properly into position, so it now lay flat beneath the skirt. Quickly, she swiped her hand down the front of herself to smooth a wrinkle that had appeared from being scrunched up while driving and made her way to Trevor's front door.

Her ankles wobbled as she tried to maintain her balance in the high heels while hurrying up the sidewalk. She felt more comfortable, and safer, in her sneakers.

This was another reason she hated wearing a dress.

Trevor opened the door just as her foot reached the first of the three steps leading to the porch.

He smiled when he saw Laura, but when he looked at Janice, his eyes widened, his smile dropped, and his mouth literally fell open.

Janice could almost feel his gaze as he scanned her from head to foot and then back to her face.

Her face flamed. While she wasn't fat, she'd never been thin, especially compared to Laura. All her life she'd been cursed with a flat chest, a big rear end, and chunky thighs, something the fitted waist of her dress only accented.

Another reason she hated dresses.

Trevor cleared his throat and reached up to fumble with the knot of his tie.

Janice's heart stopped beating for a second. He really was wearing the tie. And a different suit jacket. With matching pants. He'd also recently shaved.

"Wow . . . ," he mumbled, his voice trailing off.

Laura shrugged her shoulders and walked past him while Trevor stepped forward. He stood at the top step and extended his hand toward her to help Janice up the few steps.

Janice couldn't move her feet. All she could do was stare up at him.

"I'll go right in," Laura said, already inside the front door.

Not really wanting to, but not wanting to embarrass herself any further, Janice decided to throw dignity and decorum out the window. She grabbed the sides of her skirt at midthigh with both hands, hiked it up a couple of inches to allow her sufficient leeway to move her legs, and put one foot on the first step.

Obviously, women's clothes were designed by men who never considered that sometimes a woman would have to walk up stairs.

Another reason she hated wearing a dress.

Trevor broke out into a wide smile. Little crinkles appeared at the corners of his shining blue eyes. "This is a—"

Laura's scream pierced the air.

Trevor spun and ran into the living room. Janice hiked her skirt up even more and ran behind him, doing her best not to stumble in the ridiculous shoes.

"What is that?!" Laura shrieked, pointing to a five-foot-wide aquarium set prominently against the living room wall.

Janice studied the aquarium. Instead of water and brightly colored fishes, gravel lined the bottom of the unit. The whole aquarium floor was scattered with rocks and sticks and numerous tropical plants.

She stepped closer. In the corner, one of the rocks was a strange color, not gray, but markedly brown and tan—with distinct geometric lines differentiating the color variations and patterns.

And then the rock moved.

Janice stepped closer. It wasn't a rock at all. The "rock" was merely a length folded in half, both halves extending along in a flowing line down the side of the aquarium and then along the back.

"It's a snake," she said. "And it's big."

Trevor stepped beside her. "This is Freddie, Frank's Burmese python."

Laura didn't move. She stood at a safe distance from the snake, her eyes wide, both hands pressed to her heart, and her purse on the floor, its contents scattered at her feet.

"It's ugly," Janice said softly. "Why would anyone want such a thing?"

"Frank's had it since he was a kid. It wasn't nearly this size when he got it, oh, about twelve or thirteen years ago. When he moved out—strange thing—his mother told him she didn't want Freddie in the house any longer, so he had to take Freddie with him. Imagine that, huh?"

Janice stepped up to the aquarium, steadied herself by touching her palms to the glass, and then bent at the waist to see the snake better. With her nose nearly touching the aquarium side, she studied the monstrous creature. "How long is that thing?"

Trevor hunkered down, squatting beside her near the aquarium. "I guess it's about nine feet. Maybe ten."

"I don't think I want to know what Frank feeds it."

"Nope. You don't."

"That's what I thought."

Before she had a chance to ask about average life expectancy and molting patterns, Frank's voice sounded from behind them.

"Sorry about this. I don't usually have to work late on Tuesdays. Are we all ready to go?" Frank paused for a couple of seconds. His voice dropped to a low whisper. "Who is that?" he asked, directing his question at Laura, who remained a healthy distance from the snake habitat.

Janice squeezed her eyes shut. Of course Frank couldn't recognize her. Not only had he never seen her in a dress in the whole two years she'd known him, she was bent over studying his snake. All he could see of her was her too-wide behind sticking in the air.

She stood and turned around slowly.

"Janice? You look great! Doesn't she look great, Trev? Did you tell her she looks great?"

Trevor stood as well, and Janice noticed that his cheeks had darkened. She seldom saw a man blush, and she thought it quite endearing.

"Uh, no, I didn't. But I meant to."

Janice felt her own cheeks darken as well. "You guys both look good too." Especially Trevor, who was taller and not as stocky as Frank. Frank's hair was still slightly damp from the shower. He also wore a sport coat like Trevor, but Frank's top button on his shirt was unfastened, and he wasn't wearing a tie.

Trevor checked his watch. "We should be leaving in a couple of minutes. Are you nearly done, Frank?"

Frank ran his fingers through his hair, then glanced at Trevor. "Do I need a tie? Give me another minute, and I'll be right there. I'll meet you at the car."

Janice allowed Trevor to escort her outside and down the steps while Laura waited inside for Frank.

"We have to talk," she said as they neared the car.

"You've got that right," Trevor mumbled.

At the same time, they both glanced toward the house, confirming Frank and Laura both remained inside.

"By the way," he said, "you really do look nice. I thought you told me yesterday that you don't own a blue dress."

"I went out and bought it on my lunch break," she said, once more turning her face to the front door. She still couldn't believe that she'd bought a new dress, never mind that she was actually wearing it. Most of all, she couldn't figure out whatever had possessed her to do such a thing for a single occasion. "But never mind this dumb dress. We've got to discuss what we're going to do tonight. Last night was a disaster."

Trevor nodded. "I know. Laura didn't give me a chance to talk to her about Frank because she was too busy giving me a list of all your good and bad points. Just like what you said we should do for them. I couldn't get a word in."

Janice felt her face flame. She deliberately focused far too much attention on inserting the key into the door lock. "Frank did the same about you. Laura's also been bugging me, asking if you and I have kissed and made up yet. Tonight, we've got to get them talking about themselves and each other. If the conversation starts to drift, point it back to the wedding to get them back on track."

He nodded again. "I agree." Once more, he checked his watch and glanced toward the house. "They still haven't come out. Maybe we're worrying for nothing while they're fighting about Freddie, and the wedding is off. Did you see her face?"

"Yes. I thought she'd seen a ghost or something. You have to admit that a snake isn't exactly a normal pet."

He continued to watch the front door. "I know. I'm a dog person, myself. One day, when I get married, I'm going to get a nice, fuzzy, ugly-type mutt. Maybe I'll rescue a dog that's going to be put down at the animal shelter. I've always wanted to do that. I think mutts make great pets. Especially for kids."

Janice nodded as she secured her purse strap more firmly over her shoulder. "Me too. Here they come. Oh dear. They're holding hands. It looks like Laura recovered from her fear of snakes."

Trevor sighed. "I guess that would have been too easy. Here goes nothing."

Since it was her car, Janice drove to the restaurant, which ended up being much more luxurious than she had anticipated.

Instead of durable, industrial-type carpet or tile, the lobby floor was constructed of rich, dark hardwood flooring. Muted shades of pale green and dark burgundy served as the main colors of the decor, blending with assorted hand-painted pictures of both meadow and mountain scenery framed with dark antique wood the same color as the flooring. Fine lace curtains covered the windows, allowing some light to enter the room while providing a barrier from the outside world. Strains of classical music echoed in the background, loud enough to be pleasant, but soft enough to allow quiet, private conversations at each table. A flickering candle graced each table, and a single, low-wattage overhead lamp cast a soft glow on the patrons' faces and just enough light to read the menu, giving each table a distinctly intimate atmosphere.

The servers and the hostess were clothed in black slacks or skirts, black shoes, and starched, pleated white shirts adorned by a black bow tie, completing the elegant mood of the establishment.

While Trevor gave his name to the hostess, another couple entered, also dressed to the nines, making Janice suddenly grateful for her impulsive decision to purchase the blue dress for the occasion.

The hostess smiled and led their group to their reserved table. Frank and Laura followed first, and Janice lagged behind. She slowed her pace, then poked Trevor in the ribs to get his attention so he would walk slower with her to create a space between them and Laura and Frank, allowing her to speak candidly.

"Look at this place," she ground out in a stage whisper. "How much is this going to cost?"

He bent toward her as they walked. "None of your business," he replied. "Frank and I already discussed it, and we're paying. Don't even think about it. It's our treat. Besides, this is supposed to be a date. You're supposed to smile pretty while we all make nice to each other at the table."

"Don't worry. I'm not going to wreck the evening arguing about money. We can deal with that later. The point is that we're supposed to be getting them to assess their relationship realistically. This place is too . . ." She struggled to find the right word. "Romantic!"

He turned toward her for a brief second, not altering his pace. "Shh. Trust me."

Strangely, she did.

The hostess seated them at a table by a large window overlooking a small pond full of lily pads and a flock of ducks happily floating about.

True to his word, Trevor did manage to steer the conversation toward points of mutual interest, as well as conflicting interests, without allowing the discussions to become dissonant. Janice thought that if it were herself instead of Laura, she would definitely have started to have doubts about her compatibility, or incompatibility, with Frank over the long-term by now.

However, Laura wasn't Janice. Laura just didn't get the message. Nothing she or Trevor said seemed to make a difference.

Instead of getting even more frustrated with Laura's inability to see the situation realistically, Janice changed her focus to trying to figure out why Laura was so intent on marrying Frank, a man with whom she had little or nothing in common.

Janice had met Laura in elementary school, and they'd been inseparable since. Laura was intelligent and exercised good judgment, except for the current situation, and showed a promising career as a design consultant. At the same time, Laura also had an interest in children, and Janice knew that Laura intended to put her career aside for a few years to raise a family.

Laura's hobbies and interests also revolved around her creative bent. She enjoyed crafts and making things. Laura sewed much of her own clothing—but not because it was less expensive to sew a garment with the high cost of the designer fabrics she selected. Laura sewed because she loved the process of creating something with her own hands. Laura also enjoyed cooking. However, neither of them enjoyed cleaning. Still, when their home was a mess, it bothered Laura much more than it bothered Janice.

In many ways, they were like a female version of the Odd Couple. In the same way as Laura and Frank, many of Janice and Laura's likes and dislikes were opposite. However, their differences were complementary opposites, not opposites that would drive each other nuts in the long run. Besides, Janice only lived with Laura. She wasn't married to her. They both knew their arrangement of sharing the house was only as permanent as the first one of them getting married and leaving.

The relationship Laura planned with Frank was for keeps. Therefore, there had to be a different set of rules.

Even though she didn't know Frank that well, Janice knew him well enough. Now, as Trevor did his best to point out the differences between Frank and Laura, she knew more than ever that Frank and Laura were not suited for each other.

The night progressed pleasantly due to Trevor's quick wit and persistent patience. The more they talked, the less Janice could understand what Laura saw in Frank as a marriage partner. Neither did she see what Frank saw in Laura.

Despite Trevor's efforts, nothing changed. Janice could tell the minute he gave up for the evening. He turned the subject to a topic totally unrelated to relationships or anything anyone was specifically interested in, and they simply enjoyed the rest of the evening as four friends out together.

The drive home turned out to be equally pleasant and uneventful.

When Janice stopped in front of Frank and Trevor's house, her mind went blank. Officially, the evening had been a date. She'd never driven a man home after a date; she had always been the passenger. At the end of the date, he would walk her to the door. Depending on how well they knew each other, how long they had been seeing each other, and how much she liked him, the night would end with a peck on the cheek or a short, chaste kiss at the front door.

Since she was the one dropping Trevor off, Janice didn't know if she was supposed to escort him to the door or if he was simply supposed to leave her at the car and go into his house alone. Either way, she didn't know if she was supposed to kiss him good night or if he was supposed to kiss her good night. She wondered if she could get away with simply shaking hands and going their separate ways.

Frank and Laura exited the car and walked to the door, leaving her alone with Trevor, making her more uncertain than ever. Even though she'd been alone with him before, that had been at lunchtime, in the middle of the day, in the middle of downtown. This time, they were parked on a dark street, and they'd just been on an official date. As they now sat, it would have been a simple matter for him to lean toward her and kiss her good night.

Janice cleared the car so fast she didn't know how she didn't slam her skirt in the door. She praised God for the small miracle that her slip didn't ride up under her dress this time.

Trevor exited the car slowly and began walking around to her side. She glanced at the porch where Frank and Laura were standing, facing each other, talking quietly, their hands clasped between them. She couldn't interrupt Frank and Laura, but she had no place else to go, so she remained beside the driver's door of her car.

By the time Trevor arrived beside her, she couldn't stop her knees from trembling.

He stood so close to her, their toes almost touched.

He shrugged his shoulders. "I tried, but this didn't exactly go as I'd hoped."

"I know."

Trevor glanced at Frank and Laura, who hadn't moved from their spot on the porch. "I think we'll have to try another double date. Next time, I'll have to approach things differently, though."

Janice nodded. "I agree."

He continued to look into her face. One eyebrow quirked up.

"Frank is really concerned that you're still mad at me. You're not still mad, are you?"

She shook her head. No words came out.

He smiled. "Good."

Even in the indirect light from the streetlamp, she could see those adorable little crinkles forming at the corners of his eyes. Blue eyes. At least, normally they were blue. In the muted light, she could only see a slim ring of the light blue around his pupils. Standing so close, she had to tip her head up to see better.

Before she realized what he was doing, Trevor lowered his head slightly. Slowly, both hands came up, and his palms cupped her chin. "I know it wasn't a real date, but I had a really nice time. Thank you."

As she continued to stare up into Trevor's eyes, they drifted shut. He lowered his head.

He was going to kiss her.

She was too stunned to move away.

With the utmost gentleness, his warm lips covered hers.

She couldn't help it. She closed her eyes too.

And then the kiss was over, or at least she thought it was over. However, instead of pulling away completely, he tilted his head, and his mouth found hers again, this time the contact slightly firmer.

She lifted her hands to his chest, meaning to push him away if he tried anything more than a simple kiss, but the feeling of his heart pounding beneath her palms stopped her. Instead of wanting him to stop, the warmth of his chest beneath her hands and her awareness that his heartbeat had quickened only made his kiss sweeter.

Suddenly, his mouth left hers. He released her chin and stepped back. With the loss, despite the warm spring evening air, she felt strangely cold.

He backed up exactly one step. "Good night, Janice," he said, his voice lower pitched than usual, and oddly rough sounding.

"Good night, Trevor," she mumbled back.

In the still of the night, the soles of Trevor's leather shoes tapped as he walked up the concrete sidewalk. Laura walked down the three steps of the porch at the same time as Trevor walked up.

Janice hustled back into the car and drove off the second Laura closed the door. Laura stared out the window in silence for the entire drive home, which was fine with Janice.

She didn't know what had just happened with Trevor, but one thing she did know.

It would never happen again.

8

*T*revor knocked on Janice and Laura's door and waited. Once again, he glanced to the street, noting the absence of Janice's car, which was not a bad thing. Part of him wanted to see her, but part of him wanted to run for the hills.

He still couldn't figure out why he'd kissed her. It hadn't even been a real date, and they both knew it. Still, when she looked up at him like that, he couldn't not kiss her. One little peck hadn't been enough, either. He'd gone and kissed her twice.

Not that she had acted any different than usual, but Trevor wondered if she realized how attractive she was in that dress— not in the sense of a model's perfect features kind of beauty, nor was she as pretty as Laura, at least on the outside. Janice's beauty lay in the richness of her smile and the sparkle in her eyes behind her glasses. At first he'd scoffed at her "what you see is what you get" statement, but the more he came to know her, the more he appreciated it. What Laura had called a quirk made Janice more attractive than any woman he'd ever dated for real.

Because of the quasi-date status of the evening, in the back of his mind he'd kept trying to figure out if she'd gone out and bought that special dress just for him. He knew that he'd chosen his own clothes very carefully last night, not just because they were going to a fancy place. He'd dressed extra special for Janice.

When she'd shown up in that dress, it had thrown him for a loop. He'd been so rattled that he'd missed telling her how pretty she looked before Frank dragged it out of him. The omission bothered him.

To top it off, his last words before they parted echoed in his head. He squeezed his eyes shut and sucked in a deep breath. "I had a really nice time," he'd said. He couldn't believe how lame that sounded. He should have told her he'd had fun, but they'd only gone out for dinner, and "fun" was the wrong word too.

He could have said the evening had been enjoyable, but that felt too stuffy. He didn't know what the evening had been, but "nice" certainly wasn't the right word.

The sound of the door opening drew his thoughts back to where they should have been in the first place.

"Trevor?" Laura tipped her head to one side to look behind him. "What are you doing here?"

"Frank didn't come with me. He had to work late. I found this on the floor." He paused and held up a pink address book. "I knew it had to belong to either you or Janice because it sure doesn't belong to me or Frank."

"That's mine. It must have fallen out of my purse when I saw that horrible snake," she mumbled. "Come on in. Janice should be home in a few minutes."

Trevor glanced behind him to the street, confirming that Janice's little red car really wasn't approaching quite yet. "Sorry, I really should be going. Everyone has to get up early in the morning."

He started to turn around, but Laura grabbed him by the wrist. "Nonsense. You can stay for a couple of minutes. I'm sure she'd be disappointed if she knew she missed you. She should be home any minute."

Trevor wasn't as sure as Laura, but he didn't want to look like a coward and run since Laura had already pulled him inside and closed the front door.

"You want some tea? It's made."

"No, thanks. I'm a coffee person."

Laura shrugged her shoulders. "Suit yourself. If you don't mind, I'm going to refill my cup. I'll be right back."

With that, she disappeared into the kitchen, leaving Trevor alone in the living room.

Prior to his arrival, he hadn't thought about the possibility of being alone with Laura. He had simply planned to return the address book and leave. He hadn't thought about the opportunity the situation provided to do what he had missed doing on the weekend, which was to talk to Laura privately.

As he sat thinking of what to say, the doorknob rattled, the door opened, and Janice walked in. Despite the dry weather, her T-shirt appeared damp. If he didn't know any better, and if she were a guy, he would have thought he saw sweat stains extending from beneath her armpits. Besides the dingy T-shirt, her jeans were ratty and had a hole in one knee. Her hair hung limply in clumps, and even from across the room, he could see a big fingerprint smear on one of her lenses.

"Trevor? What are you doing here?"

He tried not to let his mouth gape open. If she hadn't been so calm and collected, he would have asked if something was wrong. If nothing were wrong, his next question would have been how she could be out in public like that. As she was now, Trevor could barely believe that the untidy person before him was the same delicate woman he'd so gently kissed last night.

Not wanting to say or do the wrong thing, Trevor chose to say nothing about her appearance. He leaned back on the couch and crossed his arms over his chest. "When I got home from work, I found an address book on the floor. I knew it had to belong to one of you, so I brought it over, and Laura asked me to stay. She said you would be mad at me if I left without seeing you. I don't ever want to make you mad."

"Very funny." Janice kicked off her sneakers, wiggled her toes, and walked into the room but didn't sit down. "Okay, you've seen me. Now you can go."

Instead of leaving, he stretched out his legs and crossed his ankles. It was killing him. He couldn't help it. He had to ask. "Where were you? You look like you've just crawled out from beneath a rock."

Her lower lip protruded over her top lip and she blew out a puff of air to blow her hair out of her face. When that didn't work, she reached up and swiped her hair back with her hand. He didn't want to notice, but now he was positive she really did have sweat stains under her arms.

"I was at my exercise class. I go once a week and most Saturdays. Once a month we wear street clothes instead of our regular uniform so we can get used to the restricted movement."

Trevor blinked. "Uniform? I knew women wore those spandex thingies, but I didn't know they were called uniforms."

"It's really a women's self-defense class."

Trevor blinked. "And you need a uniform for that?"

For the first time, he noticed what was on her T-shirt. It pictured a woman wearing a martial arts uniform, one leg extended at waist height and her fists close to her body beneath her long, flowing hair. Below the picture, in bold, black letters were the words "Yes, I really do kick like a girl."

Trevor stood. He took one step toward Janice, but she raised her palms in the air toward him. "I warn you. Come near me at your own risk. I stink." She wiggled her toes inside her socks again to further emphasize the point. Her words "what you see is what you get" once more echoed in his head.

He grinned and approached her anyway, appraising the size of her. For the moment, since Janice was shoeless, he now stood a full foot taller than she did, maybe more. She was so short, he wondered if her legs were much longer than his arms. He couldn't see her successfully defending herself against anyone older than twelve, and even that was doubtful.

He couldn't hold back a snicker. "You say you stink, but I think you need more for self-defense than body odor."

Her eyes narrowed. Suddenly, Trevor knew he'd crossed that line again.

"It's a martial arts class, and I have my red belt. If we weren't in the middle of my living room, I could really hurt you. You're lucky that as a Christian, I abhor violence."

"Then why are you taking such a thing?"

Her eyes widened. Silence hung in the air for a long, few seconds. Laura, teacup in hand, walked into the room.

Janice's voice came out so soft he barely heard her. "Because I work downtown," she squeaked. Without elaborating further, she turned and ran out of the room before he could say a word.

Something in Trevor's gut clenched. He had a bad feeling there was more to the story than simply the location of her workplace. The possibility that she'd once been attacked on a downtown street being the reason she would take martial arts for self-defense nearly made him sick. She could have been really hurt . . . or worse. He felt even sicker knowing he'd teased her about it.

"Janice! Wait!" he called out, totally ignoring Laura. He ran to the entrance of the hallway and stopped, not knowing if he should go farther. Janice hadn't exactly invited him in—Laura had. Actually, now that he thought about it, Janice had specifically told him to leave.

A door down the hall slammed shut, making his decision for him. "I don't care that you stink!" he called out louder. "We need to talk!"

"Blew it again, huh, lover boy?" Laura muttered behind him, sipping her tea as she spoke.

Trevor sighed. "Apparently," he mumbled.

She sat on the couch, rested her cup on top of a magazine on the coffee table, and picked up a church bulletin that was on the arm of the couch. She opened it, and one finger trailed down the right side. "Janice thinks that Frank and I should take this couples' course our pastor is running. The little blurb says it's not just for couples who are about to be married. It's also for anyone who is considering getting engaged or even for someone who isn't necessarily thinking about getting married but wants to explore their current relationship. Frank and I talked about it, and we're not going to go, but maybe you and Janice should. You two really seem to need it. If you don't mind me saying so."

Trevor stared blankly at Laura while Laura reread the course outline. "It says it starts this week. It's on Friday nights, for twelve weeks."

Trevor turned his head and continued to stare blankly at the vacant hallway. He didn't need to take such a course. He and Janice weren't even dating for real. As soon as Laura and Frank split up, he would never see Janice again except when they bumped into each other with mutual friends, just as they always had.

For some reason, he didn't want that to happen. The thought of hardly ever seeing her again gave him a stab of loss in the pit of his gut.

He didn't want to date her, but he did want to be her friend.

A light bulb went on in his head.

He turned to Laura. "We'll go if you go."

Laura knotted her eyebrows and lowered the bulletin to her lap. "I beg your pardon?"

"I have three sisters who got married. Even though they're older than me, I could tell that when they took those premarital things, it was really good for their relationships. I'm not sure entirely what goes on, but all three of them said they got to know their future husbands much better and much faster than if they'd only been dating and hadn't taken the premarital sessions. These things are all about sharing and mutual needs and getting to know a person, really deep down, where it counts. I think it would be really great for you and Frank to go. That way, you could get to know each other really, really well. Before the wedding."

"I don't know. I don't think Frank would want to go. We planned to opt out for one single session where we would sit down with the pastor only once just before the wedding."

"I think Janice is right. Taking a twelve-week thing is a great idea. Besides, what's twelve short little weeks in the span of an entire lifetime?"

"I don't want to go if we won't know anyone else there."

Trevor grinned and struggled not to rub his hands together with glee. "You won't be alone. You guys will be with me and Janice."

Laura picked up the bulletin and read it to herself once more.

Trevor glanced again to the vacant looming entranceway to the hall, which led to the room Janice was now hiding in.

If the only way Frank and Laura would go to the couples' course was if he and Janice went, then that was the way it had to be. They both had failed in their quest for Frank and Laura to see each other in a realistic light. Janice had the right idea in trying to convince Frank and Laura to attend. It was time to call in the experts.

"I guess we'll go, then," Laura muttered, still reading. "But only if you guys go."

He wondered what Janice would say when she found out.

❧

"Good evening and welcome, everyone. Let's all introduce our-selves."

Janice said her name in turn as the introductions went around the big circle. Including themselves, eight couples were in attendance, and one more couple who couldn't make it tonight was scheduled to join the following week.

Pastor Harry smiled at everyone and folded his hands in his lap. "Before we start, I want each of you to hold the hand of the person you came with and look them in the eye as I say this." He paused while everyone in the room shuffled. A few of the young women giggled.

Trevor reached for her hand and gave it a gentle squeeze. He smiled and spoke softly, barely moving his lips. "It's okay. It's only twelve weeks."

She forced herself to smile back, knowing these were going to be the longest twelve weeks of her life.

Pastor Harry cleared his throat. "Now that you're looking at each other, I want you to listen carefully to what I'm saying. Everyone brings their good traits and their bad traits into a relationship. You are the person you are, just as the person with you is the person they are. This is the person you have fallen in love with. Look at them carefully. Most likely, they are not going to change very much as the years go by, just as you are not going to change that much either. Some of you have wedding plans in the near future, and some of you don't. But I think that you all recognize the possibility, and that's why you're here.

"If you think you are going to change your partner after the wedding, you're wrong. Tell yourself right now, it's not going to happen. One of the biggest mistakes people make when they get married is thinking that they're going to change their partner and make them into what they want their partner to be after the wedding.

"So if your partner drives you nuts with the remote control and never-ending channel flipping . . ."

A number of the ladies giggled.

"Or if it drives you bananas when your partner thinks they need five hundred pairs of shoes when one or two will do—"

"Hear, hear!" one of the men called out, followed by more giggling and a light smack on the man's knee.

"Then I'm afraid you'll have to get used to it because it's not going to change. Welcome to our Getting To Know You, Spring Session."

Janice leaned closer to Trevor. "Are you a channel flipper?" she asked softly.

Trevor tipped his head down so he could whisper in her ear. "No. How many pairs of shoes do you own?"

She grinned. Maybe, just maybe, this wouldn't be so bad after all. "Three if you count my sandals. Plus my sneakers and my boots."

Trevor grinned back. "I like you better already."

The pastor handed a booklet to each person.

"We're going to start out with this as an introduction. This centers on what you are willing to put into a relationship versus what you expect to get out of one. Above all, I want everyone to be honest, because you are fooling no one. This is for you and you alone and sometimes, for your partner. There are no right or wrong answers. I'm not going to ask anyone to share anything they don't feel comfortable talking about in a group. We'll have eleven group sessions, and for the last one, I'll see every couple privately. If anyone feels they want to speak to me in a private appointment at any time, just ask. That's what I'm here for. Does everyone have a pen?"

Janice dug two pens out of her purse, one for herself and one for Trevor, and they started writing. She found she didn't know the answers to a lot of the questions because she didn't know Trevor well enough. In the back of her mind, she wondered how Laura and Frank were doing, which was the reason she was here in the first place.

She really and truly hoped they were doing better than she was. Her point was not to rub it in their faces that they didn't know enough about each other well enough to delve headfirst into a marriage relationship. Her goal was for them to discover more about each other, and along with the discoveries would come the realization that they were not suited to each other for the lifelong commitment of marriage.

When everyone present answered all the questions, they had an open session for discussion. Janice had nothing to contribute, but many people present did share their answers with the group. Listening gave Janice quite an insight on the development of interpersonal relationships with men in general. She decided to keep some of what she learned in a little file in her head for future use, for when she finally did meet the man who would be her Mr. Right.

At the close of the session, the pastor thanked everyone for coming, then encouraged all the couples to discuss their answers with each other, first to get to know each other better, and second, as a side benefit, for everyone to get to know themselves better. He invited everyone to stay for coffee and goodies, which were set out on a table in the lobby, so everyone in the group could continue to talk in the less structured atmosphere.

If things continued the way they were, Janice had a feeling that by the time the twelve weeks were over, they would all know each other a lot better, regardless of coffee and snack time, by the nature of the reason they were together.

Janice walked to the coffeemaker to help herself. While she poured her coffee, she quickly glanced over her shoulder at Trevor, who was standing near the doorway yakking with Frank and Laura, coffee and donut already in hand.

Specifically, she knew that she and Trevor would get to know each other much better through the material provided. So far, in the concentrated time they'd spent together before the course started today, she'd already come to know him much better. He wasn't at all what she expected.

She again thought about her first impression of him being the quiet type. Now, she definitely knew better. After he warmed up, he had a delightful sense of humor and a sharp wit, even if he did tend to go a little overboard. But then, if she had to look deep down inside herself, which this material Pastor Harry gave everyone was forcing her to do, she had to admit that she enjoyed egging him on. Since they'd started spending so much time together, she had to admit that she kind of liked Trevor, as a friend only, of course.

She lowered her head and smiled to herself, thinking of his response to her "I stink" comment. She would have completely lost all respect for him if he hadn't responded in kind. Of course he rose to the challenge, even if his response had been a bit insensitive. Still, she'd had it coming. She'd fully enjoyed the banter until he asked the one question that had sent her running to her bedroom like a scared rabbit. Now, a couple of days later, he thankfully hadn't brought the subject up. However, she feared this wasn't the end of it.

The whole purpose of the course was to get to know each other better, whether she wanted to or not. That being the case, she had no doubt that the subject matter would back her into a corner, and she'd have to tell him.

Maybe she could come down with a killer flu that night.

For now, she hoped that he would forget about it if she became less outspoken and behaved herself. She would miss the verbal banter, but it was now time to play the girlfriend role, which meant not doing what others might perceive as fighting, no matter how much fun they had doing it.

Later, when they no longer had to concentrate on the situation with Frank and Laura or what people thought, she could once again enjoy countering him in a battle of wits.

She hadn't realized how long she'd been standing still at the coffeemaker until one of the men whom she recognized from the Friday night young adult group appeared beside her.

"Hi, Janice."

"Hi, Dan. It's good to see you here. I heard that you and Allyson were recently engaged. Congratulations." This time, Janice found she meant it, unlike the last time she nearly choked on the same word.

A smile flitted across Dan's face. He quickly glanced down at her left hand, then at Trevor, who was still with Frank and Laura, along with another couple. "It's nice to see you here—quite a surprise." He jerked his head toward Trevor. "Sorry, I forgot your boyfriend's name; there are so many people here tonight. Seeing you here with another guy is a real surprise. I thought you were going out with Rick."

Janice quirked her eyebrows. She'd been with Rick in a group, but she'd never been out with him alone. "Rick? What makes you say that?"

Dan shrugged his shoulders. "Oh, just stuff I heard."

She opened her mouth to ask what he'd heard, but before she could get a word out, Trevor appeared beside her. She nearly spilled her freshly poured coffee when Trevor slipped his arm around her waist.

"Hi . . ." Trevor scanned Dan's name tag, then smiled at him. "Dan. Nice to meet you. I assume you already know Janice?"

"Yes. We were just talking about being here. I didn't know she was engaged."

Janice turned her head to gauge Trevor's response.

Trevor's smile widened, and his grip around her waist tight-ened. "Well, we're not officially engaged, at least not right now. But you never know, right?" He gave Dan an exaggerated wink.

Janice grabbed Trevor's hand at the same time as she forced a smile at Dan. "Excuse us, please. We have to talk."

Without waiting for Trevor or Dan to respond, she dragged Trevor away, holding firmly onto his wrist.

"Have you noticed we seem to need to do a lot of talking?" he asked as soon as she positioned him in a relatively private corner of the room.

Janice crossed her arms over her chest. "Just what did you think you were doing back there?"

"Did I do something wrong?"

"Didn't anyone ever tell you not to answer a question with a question?"

"Why do you ask?"

Janice dragged her hand over her face.

His goofy smile dropped. "Seriously, don't you think that since we're here, we should give people the impression that we're having a serious relationship? Face it. The few people who are here who aren't officially," he paused, making quotation marks in the air with his fingers for emphasis, "*engaged* are right on the verge of popping the question. They just want to tie up a few loose ends and answer a few questions first before they make the big decision. You know, the opposite of what Frank and Laura have done?"

Janice exhaled a long, deep sigh. "I suppose you're right. You just caught me off guard with your little performance. Have you ever gone to acting school?"

He puffed out his chest, pressed one palm, fingers splayed, over the center of his chest, and cleared his throat. "Hey. I'm a multitalented kind of guy."

After promising herself that she was going to be more demure and act the girlfriend role, Janice bit back the comment that was on the tip of her tongue. "Never mind," she grumbled as they started walking back to join their friends. "I guess you're right; that is what people are thinking. We'd better get back there before everybody thinks the wedding's off and we won't be coming back for the next fun-filled eleven weeks."

He nodded. "Oh, by the way, the four of us are going on another double date tomorrow night. Laura wants to go see that new chick flick with what's-his-face."

Janice's feet skidded to a halt, and she spun around, forcing Trevor to stop as well. "I know which one she's been wanting to see. I forget the name, but I heard it's bad. I hope you didn't say we would go."

"Uh . . . I've got some good news and some bad news."

She squeezed her eyes shut, sighed, then continued walking.

With any luck, all four cars would get flat tires and the buses would go on strike so they would have to walk to the video store and rent a good action movie instead.

9

revor couldn't believe what he was seeing. He leaned back in the chair and folded his arms over his chest. "Aw, that's so fake. You can tell it's a backdrop. The same tree keeps reappearing as she's running in a supposedly straight line. See that leaf pattern over there? You'll see it again in a few seconds."

"Never mind that. I bet a log magically appears, and she's going to fall. Oh! Told you so!"

Suddenly Janice jumped in her chair. Trevor quickly glanced to the side to see Laura poking Janice in the ribs. "Will you two shut up?" Laura whispered roughly between her teeth. "You're ruining it!"

"Sorry," Trevor and Janice mumbled in unison.

Trevor leaned closer to Janice's ear. "I'm not really sorry. Are you?"

She giggled, and it was a lovely sound. "Nope. This movie isn't so bad after all. If you know what to watch for."

He leaned closer until his lips brushed her hair as he spoke. He could smell some kind of herbal shampoo. It suited her. "Bet she has a sprained ankle, and he has to help her run now."

She tilted her head more in his direction and turned so she now whispered in his ear. "Of course. Next he's going to fight the rabid wolf with his bare hands and win. Just wait and see."

Trevor shook his head. "No. She can't appear too weak. She'll stand and scream for a bit, but that would be too stereotyped if he just fought off the wolf that way. Besides, they need to fill in more time. There's still twenty minutes left in the movie. They'll fight for awhile, then at the last minute the wolf will overcome him. I'll bet just as the wolf is going for his throat, she's going to whack the wolf with a stick and save the day. See the stick? It's just sitting there, too convenient. I can almost see the sign on it that says 'grab me.' And you'll notice her ankle won't be so sprained anymore."

They continued to watch as the scene continued to unfold. Janice gasped and brought both hands to her mouth as the movie heroine, a terrible actress whose name Trevor couldn't remember and didn't care to remember, eventually did exactly as he predicted.

"You're right! How did you know? Did you read a review or something with some animal activist group complaining about this cruel mistreatment?" Janice turned and glared at him, but he could tell she was only pretending to be angry.

Trevor grinned and pointed as discreetly as he could to the corner of the screen so as not to disturb others around them. "Naw. The wolf is as fake as the boulder that nearly hit them. Look at the tail."

They put their heads together, ear to ear, and Trevor described the many flaws of the fake animal, as well as the mathematically perfect tear that suddenly appeared in the hero's shirt, exposing his manly hairy chest for the female viewing audience.

Janice giggled again.

"Will you two knock it off?" Laura hissed. "I'm trying to watch this!"

Trevor slipped his arm over the back of the chair behind Janice, just so he could lean over more easily to whisper in her ear again. "I think we'd better behave, or we're going to be in trouble."

Janice raised her index finger, pressed it to her lips, and nodded.

Since she didn't flinch away from him, Trevor neglected to remove his arm. When she didn't complain after a minute, he moved just a little and rested his palm on her shoulder. To his surprise and delight, she still didn't protest, so he decided to keep it there and just be quiet and watch the rest of the movie.

As the scene progressed, once the hero and heroine were assured the big bad wolf was dead, they hugged and kissed to end the traumatic life-threatening episode. Both Trevor and Janice had to muffle their laughter as the evil forest ranger villain, rifle in hand, appeared conveniently and predictably too late, only to find out he didn't get the girl in the end.

Beside Janice, Laura sniffled at what was probably supposed to be a very touching scene. Beside Laura, Frank appeared to be on the verge of falling asleep.

And then the credits started to roll.

Despite the pathetic special effects, the questionable acting, and the nonexistent plot, Trevor couldn't remember the last time he'd enjoyed a movie so much.

Janice leaned toward him, so he leaned toward her to meet in the middle.

"That was really funny. You know, if we rent that someday to watch it again, we'll probably wonder why we thought it was good the first time around."

"Probably." He smiled, thinking about her use of the word "we" and wondering if she realized what she'd just said.

"The arm around me was a nice touch. However, the movie's over. Now move it off before I smack it off."

Trevor hesitated. Part of him wanted to keep his hand there, just to see if she really would smack it off. But then again, she had some kind of higher belt in martial arts. Instead of hitting like a pansy, she could probably deliver a punch that broke bones as well as boards. Then again, if she said she wouldn't flatten him in the privacy of her living room, she likely wouldn't flatten him in a public movie theater.

Thinking of the incident in the living room, he remembered

how he'd unwittingly reminded her of something that had frightened or hurt her very badly in the past.

In the blink of an eye, Trevor removed his hand.

Frank became more alert once people started exiting the theater, then fully awake by the time they walked outside and into the fresh evening air. Fully invigorated and refreshed after his nap, Frank suggested that instead of taking the women home, they detour to the local donut shop. They all piled into Frank's car, Frank and Laura in the front, and Trevor in the backseat with Janice.

Trevor scanned the distance on the seat between them, and for a second he experienced a fleeting sense of jealousy. When the four of them had gone together in Janice's small economy import car, Frank and Laura were forced to sit close together in the backseat. In the back of Frank's large car, Janice positioned herself almost squashed against the door, and there seemed to be miles between them. He started daydreaming about taking Janice's car the next time they went somewhere, only asking Laura to drive so he and Janice could get the backseat.

As Trevor realized where his thoughts were leading, Frank pulled into a parking spot. They all piled out and went into the donut shop. Back on track, Trevor tried to point the conversation to Friday night's couples' counseling sessions and the upcoming wedding. Instead they talked about everything else, most notably nothing that could in any way be important.

Not that he didn't have a nice time, but he wasn't there to have a nice time. Even though the wedding was still a little over three months away, he was starting to see that Janice might have been right to be so worried so soon. Nothing they had done was making any headway between Frank and Laura. Neither one of them had changed, nor did they appear likely to in the near—or distant—future. The worst part was that they both acted so out of character with each other. As the pastor had said, thinking you were going to change your partner after the wedding was a dangerous notion because it wasn't likely to happen.

Worse for Frank and Laura, neither of them knew there was anything to change. Both of them were acting totally out of character, yet they were the only ones who couldn't see it. When the day came that they stopped being so accommodating to each other and more like themselves, they were both in for the shock of a lifetime. More than ever, Trevor became determined to be sure that happened before the wedding.

The next time the four of them went together to a show, he would pick something he knew Frank liked, then watch how Laura dealt with it. He would bet that with all the action, Laura wouldn't fall asleep like Frank had. He also doubted she would enjoy such a movie, although he thought Janice might.

Trevor watched Janice and Frank play-arguing about the chocolate sprinkles on the donuts while Laura stirred her coffee and stared out the window at an animated billboard. While the movie was understatedly bad, Trevor couldn't imagine himself falling asleep with Janice beside him like Frank had with Laura. Janice may not have been the most charming date, but she was fun to be with, and there was never a dull moment.

Laura stood, and Frank and Janice fell silent. "I hate to be a party pooper, but we all have to get up for church in the morning."

Trevor nodded as he also checked his watch. "That's right, and we're going to our church this time." He turned, making direct eye contact with Janice as he spoke. "And remember, my church is a little more conservative than yours." He didn't elaborate further. The slacks she wore to the office would have been fine, but what he really wanted was for Janice to wear that dress again.

Janice didn't comment. Trevor knew he'd fall asleep dreaming of Janice in that blue dress.

The trip back to Janice and Laura's house seemed too short. Before he knew it, Frank and Laura were sharing a short good-bye kiss in the front seat, and Janice was standing outside the car with the door wide open.

Before closing the door, she rested her hands on the roof of the car and leaned down, speaking to him from across the length of the backseat. "Conservative, huh? I hope I don't have to wear a tie."

His mouth tightened. "Not funny," he grumbled. "You'll have to wear something nice, though."

Suddenly, her frown turned into a smile that was a little too bright. "Don't worry. I'll try to find some good jeans that don't have a hole in the knee," she said and hopped backward a step.

He leaned over and opened his mouth to tell her not to wear jeans at all, but the car door closed in his face. Janice ran into the house, with Laura walking slowly behind.

Suddenly, the donut he'd previously thought so delicious went to war with his stomach.

Trevor climbed into the front seat with Frank, and they drove home.

He knew it was going to be a long night.

❧

Trevor stood beside Frank on Janice and Laura's doorstep and raised his fist to knock. At the exact same moment as he started the downward motion, the door opened. He stepped back quickly, barely missing whacking Laura on the head as she ran past him.

"Sorry," she mumbled, only slowing slightly. "I just got a call to do an emergency fill-in at Sunday school."

Frank turned in an instant. "I'll go with you. Do you need some help in the class?"

"That would be great. Let's go. I have to set up, and people will already be arriving."

Trevor turned and watched Frank and Laura jog down the sidewalk. "But we were supposed to go to my church today. I'm helping with the offering, so I can't go to your church today."

Laura hopped into the passenger's seat of Frank's car, calling out to him as she closed the door. "Sorry. You and Janice can still go, though. See you sometime during the week. Bye."

Both doors closed with a muffled thud, and Frank drove off.

"Trevor? Is that you?" Janice called from within the house.

He stepped inside and shut the door behind him. "Yeah. I guess it's just you and me. Apparently, I'm at your mercy for transportation. Frank just left with Laura."

He could hear Janice's footsteps in the hall. For an instant, a vision of Janice wearing jeans and her ratty sneakers flashed through his mind. He steeled his nerves and waited.

Trevor's breath caught as Janice stepped into his sight. Instead of the jeans he'd half expected, she wore a casual skirt and blouse. After he got over the shock, he noticed it was a denim skirt. A jean skirt.

He couldn't help but grin. "You are a brat. I should have expected something like that out of you."

She grinned back. "I hate wearing skirts, but it was worth it just to see the look on your face. I'm ready. Let's go."

While he waited for her to lock up, Trevor couldn't help but think back to what he'd said the night before. He should have realized Janice would have taken his request that she wear something nice as a challenge. Part of him told himself never to make that mistake again, and part of him thought it was hilarious.

He also wondered what he could do to make the most of it.

During the drive to his church, he did his best to answer her questions. Many of them served as a reminder that Janice had only been a Christian a few years, whereas he'd been in a Christian family all his life, as had Frank. They had both made their decisions to follow Jesus in their teens.

He heard Janice inhale deeply the second he turned into the church's parking lot.

"This is where you go?"

He'd attended this same church with his family all his life. He gazed up at the grand old stone building and tried to think of how a newcomer would see it. Without a doubt, the building was impressive. The stained glass windows alone were breathtaking. As a child, when he was bored with the service, he often let his attention wander to the craftsmanship of the colorful antique windows. From an adult's perspective, now that he knew the time and workmanship involved, especially in the day they were made, they impressed him even more.

"Yeah. Pretty nice, isn't it? Wait 'til you see the inside. It's a heritage building, and it's very well cared for. Up until about a year ago, an elderly lady even played the big old pipe organ on Sundays. But she retired, and now we have a piano and a guitar. No drums or anything like at your church, though. It's just a big, black, grand piano and an amplified acoustic guitar. I also want you to take notice that every male over the age of thirteen is wearing a tie."

When they made their way inside, Trevor had to bite his lip and not laugh. Janice didn't say a word. She just looked around the building, in complete and total awe of her surroundings.

He didn't know why he did it. Maybe because she was so pretty wearing nice clothes for a change. Maybe out of respect for his surroundings. Admittedly, most of the members of his congregation were older, and with their age, old-fashioned. It just felt right. Trevor picked up Janice's hand and tucked it into the crook of his elbow, resting his hand on top of hers as he gave her a tour of the building.

From a distance, as they walked around, Janice saw her old boss and his wife. They waved at each other pleasantly, and Trevor led Janice into the sanctuary, where they took their seats in the polished wooden pews.

Pastor Gregory soon welcomed everyone present, highlighting a few items from the bulletin, and the worship leader stepped forward. Janice participated eagerly in the worship time, during which the congregation sang mostly hymns and a couple of contemporary choruses. Trevor felt bad about leaving her while he helped accept the morning's offering. In their original plan, she wouldn't have been left alone because Frank and Laura were supposed to be there too. However, her graciousness impressed him. He didn't think he'd ever forget her cute little smile and wink when he passed the basket by her, and she tucked something inside.

She remained quiet beside him for the rest of the service, paying rapt attention as the pastor spoke. At the close of the service, he led Janice into the lobby.

Perhaps because he'd had her holding onto him before the service, she automatically did the same as they walked around afterward. The contact of her warm hand on his arm made him in no rush to leave.

As they continued to walk around, they alternated between making small talk with people he knew to privately discussing more of the points of interest in the heritage building and features of the church as a body of believers. He'd always enjoyed the majesty of the old place and felt the surroundings greatly added to the mood of worship to his Lord and Savior.

The more they continued to walk around, the more Trevor noticed people's heads turning.

He tipped his head to talk softly to Janice as she checked out a table of featured books from the church's library. "You know, I think people are looking at us funny."

"They are? Why? I'm properly dressed."

Trevor shook his head. "I don't know. Maybe it's because I've never brought a woman to church before. That's kind of an indication of a serious relationship, which no one knew I was having. Of course, I didn't know I was having a serious relationship either."

Janice stopped flipping pages and turned to smile up at him as she spoke. He hadn't noticed before that moment that the room had been getting a little warm.

"That's okay," she said. "I suppose this is the kind of thing we should expect if we're going to pull this off with Frank and Laura. Just be sure to act suitably heartbroken when we break up, and everything will be fine."

He'd already thought about officially splitting up with Janice after Frank and Laura finally saw the light. Suddenly, a queasy feeling settled in the pit of his stomach. He raised his wrist to check his watch to see if it was close to lunchtime.

While he stared blankly at his watch, he heard someone calling his name.

Suddenly, his stomach felt even worse. "Oh, no," he mumbled. "This is something I hadn't thought about."

"Huh?" Janice mumbled as she continued to page through the book in her hand.

"It would have been different if we were here with Frank and Laura, but we're alone."

"So?" She closed the book and returned it to its place on the table.

"It's totally obvious we're together."

"I thought that was the point." She picked up another book and started reading the back cover.

"It's my parents. They see that we're together, and they're coming to talk to us. I have a bad feeling they're going to invite us over for lunch. When they do that on Sunday, I always go."

She smiled so sweetly, his poor stomach didn't know how to feel. "What's wrong with that? They're your parents."

"You don't understand. By now, they will have talked to my sister, who can never keep her mouth shut. I can tell by the way my mom's walking toward us that she's got something on her mind. That means Melissa told them I'm going to a premarital course. Since I haven't told my parents I was even seeing someone on a regular basis, they're going to want to know what's going on. I'm twenty-five years old, and Mom's been hinting for awhile that it's about time I got married."

Janice stiffened from head to toe. "Uh-oh . . . ," she muttered.

Trevor dropped his voice to a whisper. "Here they come. Remember. We're supposed to be in love."

*J*anice forced herself to breathe.

Love.

She didn't know what it was like to be in love. Her heart didn't do silly flip-flops when she was around Trevor. She didn't count the minutes and seconds until the next time she would see him again. She didn't dream about him; at least she didn't dream about him very much.

She tried to give herself a crash course on being in love. She tried to think of everything listed in 1 Corinthians 13, but she'd never actually memorized it.

"Love is patient; love is kind. Love doesn't boast. It is not self-seeking."

Mentally, Janice shook her head. She couldn't remember any more, and what she did remember was undoubtedly in the wrong order with many traits missing. The order didn't matter anyway. She didn't know how those things actually related to the way someone felt in their heart about a person they were supposed to be in love with. She thought she'd been in love once before; but after she and her boyfriend split up, she realized it wasn't love at all but an infatuation, over as quickly as it began.

As Trevor's parents approached, she could see they were both tall and both fairly good-looking for their age. She estimated them to be in their early sixties, both by their appearance and because Trevor was the youngest of four children. She could also see that Trevor got his nose from his father's side of the family.

"Hi, Mom. Dad. I'd like you to meet Janice. Janice, these are my parents, Ed and Kathy."

Janice tried to smile politely, and they smiled back.

Suddenly, she was extremely grateful for the book in her hand. She didn't know if she was supposed to shake their hands or if there was something else she should have done. Also, since she was supposed to be having a serious relationship with their son, she didn't know if she was supposed to call them by their first names, their last names, or . . . Mom and Dad.

"Pleased to meet you, Mr. and Mrs. Halliday," she mumbled through her forced smile.

Mrs. Halliday glanced back and forth between them, and Janice couldn't help but wonder what she was thinking.

"It's a pleasure to meet you, Janice. Melissa told us all about you and Trevor. To tell the truth, we didn't even know that Trevor was seeing anyone, so it's good to meet up with you today."

Trevor didn't speak, but his face said, "I told you so."

Janice found herself waiting for the lunch invitation, undecided about what she should do. She thought it might be fun to accept, just to watch Trevor's response—after all, he was the one who had gotten them into this situation.

Then again, she didn't want to put Trevor in an awkward position. Even though they hadn't known each other well at first, only being casual acquaintances at the beginning of their supposed relationship, things had changed. She now appreciated and valued his friendship.

All she did was smile. Whatever happened, she would let Trevor handle it and go along with his decision, although she suspected that he was looking to her to give him an easy out.

Mrs. Halliday glanced at Trevor, then back to Janice. "Any other day, we would have loved to have you both over for lunch. However, we've already accepted an invitation from Walter and Ellen Quinlan."

Janice nearly choked. She wasn't going to tell them that Walter was her boss before he retired and gave the company reins to his nephew, Ken.

Trying to be discreet, she glanced to the side. She couldn't see him now, but Walter had already seen her with Trevor. Knowing Walter, she had no doubt that if Walter thought about it, an invitation to them would be forthcoming, especially since she already knew him, and Trevor's parents had already accepted their invitation. If Walter found out how allegedly serious her relationship with Trevor was supposed to be, Walter would tell Ken because Ken was now her boss.

Not that Ken spread gossip, but Ken would certainly tell his wife Molly. Janice had worked closely with Molly—Molly had been the one to lead her to Jesus. Janice had also been awarded Molly's job when Molly and Ken got married. Janice had no doubt that news of her personal life would be welcome news to Molly.

While Molly no longer worked for Quinlan Enterprises, she often showed up at the office and remained friendly with all the staff. Once Molly got wind that she and Trevor were an item, Janice easily pictured Molly orchestrating a surprise bridal shower at the office.

Besides misleading Trevor's parents, this was another complication neither of them needed.

Janice cleared her throat. "You know, Trevor, we really should be going. We're going to be late. I didn't notice the time."

Trevor's eyebrows arched. "Late?"

Janice nudged him in the ankle with her toe. "Yes. We're going to be late."

"Oh. Yes. You're right. Excuse us, please, Mom and Dad. We've got to go. Maybe we can get together another time."

Both Mr. and Mrs. Halliday smiled brightly.

Mr. Halliday patted Trevor on the shoulder. "Catch you another time, Trev."

Guilt a foot thick piled on Janice's head. She remained silent.

She also made a mental note that Trevor's father didn't seem to talk much, and she wondered briefly if once he got started, he too would be hard to turn off.

Trevor's mother smiled sweetly and rested her hand on his father's arm. "We'll have to make plans to get together for coffee one evening, or maybe after church next weekend?"

"Sure, Mom. Now if you'll excuse us."

Janice smiled, returned the book to the table, then hustled out of the building with Trevor, straight to her car without speaking to anyone else.

Trevor didn't speak until they were standing beside her car. "What is it we're late for?" he asked.

"I don't know. Lunch, I guess." Janice heaved a huge sigh of relief.

Trevor checked his watch. "I wonder if we should try to find Frank and Laura."

"I don't know." Janice grabbed the door handle but didn't open the door. "Part of me says we have to try harder to get them to see each other in a more realistic light, but part of me says to leave them alone for awhile. Maybe they need some time without us, so they can start some of this discovery stuff mentioned in that booklet we got on Friday night. I honestly don't know what to do anymore."

She slid inside, reached over to unlock the passenger door for Trevor, and they drove off. Glancing out the corner of her eye, she realized Trevor had turned toward her and was watching her intently as she drove.

"What?" she asked, glancing quickly at him, then returning her attention to the traffic around them.

"I know we keep saying we have to talk, but you know what? We never do. I mean really talk. There is something I feel we should discuss, and I don't want to do it in a moving car or with

Frank and Laura or anyone else we know looming. I also don't want to need to watch the time."

"What are you saying?"

"Instead of going to where we know Frank and Laura will probably be, let's do the opposite. Let's go someplace we know they won't be. Someplace private, where we can talk uninterrupted and without an audience. For as long as it takes."

Her grip on the steering wheel tightened. "You mean, go to my place? Since we know Laura won't be home?"

"No. I'm not positive they won't go straight to your place after lunch. Same thing with my place. Maybe they'll go there; maybe they won't. Trouble is, I don't know where to go. I really don't want to go to a public restaurant either. Or anywhere that there's a crowd."

"You're not leaving a lot of options here. If you want private, it's not going to happen. If you've got something to say, say it now, in the car. But I don't want to get into a heavy discussion that will compromise my concentration on my driving. And I'm starving. Stress always makes me hungry."

Trevor snapped his fingers. "The car! That's it!"

"Pardon me?"

"Let's go to a drive-in restaurant. We can still get our lunches served to us but not be in a room full of people. We won't have to worry about being interrupted by someone we know because we'll be sitting in the car. No one will bug us, and we can take as long as we want. It's perfect."

Janice grinned. "Great idea. I haven't been to a drive-in restaurant since I was a kid. I always go to the drive-thru window and take it home."

Immediately, she turned and headed for the drive-in restaurant she'd gone to as a child. She picked a spot on the end, away from the majority of the other cars, and killed the engine. They

Beyond Perfect

didn't waste any time, quickly decided what they wanted, and ordered.

The second the carhop left, Janice turned in the seat toward Trevor, resting one arm over the top of the steering wheel. "Okay. Here we are, all alone. Talk."

Trevor cleared his throat and paused, giving her a bad feeling that she wasn't going to like what he was about to say.

"I've been thinking. What if we're wrong? What if Frank and Laura really are more suited to each other than we think?"

At his words, Janice didn't know which she felt more: hungry or sick. She removed her arm from over the steering wheel and clasped the steering wheel with both hands.

Her voice came out in a strange squeak. "This is scary. I've been thinking the same thing myself. For everything we point out to them, they don't seem to think any of it matters. What if those things aren't as important to a relationship as I always thought? If God has put them together, who are we to separate them?"

Trevor's face tightened. "I know. But there's another side of it too. What if we're right, and they're only fooling themselves for reasons we can't figure out? What kind of friends would we be if we stood back and just let them set their lives up for heartbreak and misery?"

Janice nodded. "I know that in any relationship, realistically, two people will never share every common interest. If they did, then life would eventually become too boring for words. But those two have taken the 'opposites attract' thing to the extreme."

He nodded. "There has to be a middle ground, but those two aren't in it—at least not that I can see. But I'm not as sure that marriage isn't what God wants for them as I was a couple of weeks ago."

"Then I suppose the best thing to do is what we've already been doing. To point out where couples should agree, where it's good to have a different approach, focus on common interests and personality traits, and let them discover the truth for themselves.

612

We'll have to support them whatever happens, whether they get married, or they split up. We're doing everything we can."

"Not really. There is one thing we've been missing so far."

Janice frowned. "What? I've thought so carefully about this. I've participated with you in what we agree is the best course of action. We've got them involved with the pastor and a good, in-depth session that's exactly what they need to get to know each other deep down. I'm continuing to pray about Laura and Frank every day. I don't know what else to do."

He leaned back in the confines of her small car, shuffled his feet, then crossed his arms over his chest. Oddly, the action made him appear even larger. "We've both prayed about Frank and Laura separately, but we haven't prayed together. I think it's long overdue."

She gulped. Of course he was right. They did need to pray together. They should have prayed together when they first began their efforts.

A tap on the window brought their attention to the carhop holding their tray of food outside, another stark reminder of being constantly interrupted. However, this time, when the carhop left they were finally, exclusively alone in their own, enclosed world.

Trevor wasted no time and immediately prayed over their meal. While they ate the conversation changed. They didn't talk at all about Frank and Laura, which Janice found a welcome diversion and a much-needed break.

Lately, the strange mismatch had been occupying her thoughts day and night. Whenever she had been able to free her mind from thoughts of Frank and Laura, her thoughts strayed to Trevor. She didn't know why, but she attributed the phenomenon to his proximity and involvement with the situation.

When they were finished eating, Janice moved all the wrappers and empty mugs to the tray hanging on her window, but she didn't turn on the headlights to signal the carhop to come.

They were finally ready to do what should have been done a long time ago.

"I want to pray intelligently," she said as she rolled the window up most of the way, leaving it only open enough to give them some fresh air. "I also want to be sure that we're both praying for the same thing before we start. After all, it's been some time since this whole thing blew up in our faces. Since then, I'd think a few things have changed, even if our bottom-line goal hasn't. I have to admit it feels very strange, praying with someone else about being a part in trying to break off the engagement of my best friend."

He nodded. "I know. I've been feeling the same way. Maybe that's why we've put off praying together for so long."

All Janice could do was nod back.

Trevor smiled for only a brief second, then became serious. He reached over the stick shift and grasped her hands in his. "First and foremost, we want to be sure we are in God's will for this. Whether they break up, or whether they actually do get married, I want to be obedient to do whatever God wants to happen here in this situation."

"Yes, that's most important. We do have to accept the possibility that they'll stay together, even though we think it won't work. God's plan is bigger than our plan, and He sees things we don't."

Trevor nodded again. "Sometimes I forget that. I need the occasional reminder, I think."

Janice thought she needed reminders too. However, with both of them more aware of each other's weaknesses, she became more confident that they could keep each other on track by working together more and being less independent. "I still think we're doing the right thing. We're not openly or aggressively trying to make them split up. We're only helping them get to know each other better, which is a good thing, especially if they do decide to go through with the wedding. That couples' course was a great idea. I think it may even have been God's timing. I'm almost positive that will be what they need to show them they're not right for each other. All we need to do is keep after them and make sure they do the assignments and really talk about stuff, like Pastor Harry says to do. That's the only way they'll get to know each other properly. But you know that means we have to do the same thing, right along with them."

For a minute, he remained silent. "I know," he said, then became silent again.

Janice waited for him to say more, but he didn't, nor did he appear to be waiting for her to say anything. They simply sat there, staring at each other within the closed car, the only movement being the slow back and forth motion of his thumbs on her wrists as his large hands completely enveloped hers.

They were kind of holding hands, but kind of not, since he was the one doing all the holding. Yet, she could have pulled away at any time because he really didn't have any grip on her. His big hands were more wrapped around hers than holding them. She should have felt strange, touching like that, sitting with no words between them, but in a strange way Janice enjoyed it. They had all the time in the world. Not needing to speak and not feeling awkward about it felt strangely right. Comfortable. His lazy half grin told her that he felt the same way.

The more time they spent together, the more she'd come to appreciate him. Spending so much time together and digging deep into both her psyche and his, as the couples' course required, wasn't so scary anymore. Despite his size, he was kind and gentle. Yet, at the same time, when he really wanted something, she had sampled his dogged determination firsthand. While he didn't have an upper-management career, he accepted much responsibility with his various duties and seemed to be proficient at a job he enjoyed. Most of all, she thoroughly enjoyed his offbeat sense of humor and often wondered why Laura didn't seem to have much patience with him, which had been obvious at the movie theater.

As the minutes passed, his lazy-cat expression turned into more of a grin, and those adorable little crinkles she was becoming so fond of appeared at the corners of his sparkling blue eyes. Watching the little crinkles appear made her aware that she had been staring into his eyes for quite some time and hadn't realized it. She didn't know when or why she had become so fascinated with Trevor's eyes. She'd always thought that the typical female attraction to men with blue eyes was highly overrated.

His quirky little grin became infectious. Before she knew it, Janice felt herself starting to grin too, even though she didn't know why.

Finally, Janice couldn't stand it anymore. She had to break the silence. "What are you thinking about?"

The smile dropped. He cleared his throat, dropped her hands, and sat straight in the seat. "Nothing. Is there anything else we need to talk about before we pray?"

The brusque way he switched moods to the business at hand left her with her mouth gaping open. Abruptly, she snapped it shut and turned to stare out the windshield as she tried to figure out if she'd said or done something to make him angry. Not that he appeared angry; she'd never seen him angry. The problem was that she didn't know what he felt, and it bothered her that she might have been the cause of it.

She turned back to face him. "I can't think of anything else."

"Okay," he mumbled.

Silence hung between them.

Janice focused all her attention on his hands, which were now folded in his lap. She wanted the same thing they had only a few minutes ago. Not only did she want to join their hands while they prayed, something deep inside her needed to do so. She also wanted the warmth between them back.

If he wasn't going to take the initiative, then she was left with no alternative.

Janice leaned forward, lifted up his hands, tried her best to cover his hands with hers, and gave them a gentle squeeze.

She smiled. "You ready?"

Trevor smiled back and moved his hands so their fingers were intertwined. "Yeah."

Something funny happened in her stomach, which Janice couldn't figure out because she'd just eaten a wonderful meal and her tummy was well-satisfied.

She cleared her throat. "You want to start?"

"Sure."

They both bowed their heads, taking a minute to clear their minds and hearts, and Trevor began to pray for their situation. He prayed for God's continued guidance, for Frank and Laura to respond to God's leading, and for themselves—to be within God's will, and to be able to accept the outcome of their efforts, whatever it might be.

All Janice could do was agree and say "Amen."

For the first time since she'd heard the news of Frank and Laura's engagement, Janice felt at peace.

Their fingers separated, and they both sat straight in their seats.

Janice turned on the headlights. Within minutes, a carhop removed the tray from the window, and they were ready to go.

"That's it, then," she said as she started the engine. "Now we continue to do what we've been doing, but this time it's in Someone else's hands, where it should have been all along."

Trevor nodded. "Yup. So, tomorrow's Monday. Any idea what we're all supposed to be doing?"

Janice bit back a grin. "I heard rumors of bowling."

"Bowling! Please, don't do that to me!"

Janice pulled into traffic. "But think of how much fun we had last time."

Trevor groaned. She simply listened in silence as he complained the entire trip back to his house.

*G*ood afternoon, Quinlan Enterprises."

Trevor turned to try to block the sound of a truck going by. "Hi, Janice."

"Trevor? Are you on a roof somewhere again?"

He grinned openly, even though he was technically alone. "Can you tell?"

"Yes. Why are you calling? Do you have good news? Laura didn't say anything to me this morning. Everything was all normal."

His grin dropped. "Actually, I was calling to see what you're doing tonight."

A silence hung over the phone for a few seconds.

"I didn't think we were doing anything this evening. Laura has a Sunday school teacher's meeting. Remember?"

Trevor blocked the mouthpiece with his hand as another truck approached on the street below. "I didn't forget. I wasn't thinking of going out with Frank and Laura. I was just asking you."

This time, the silence on the phone seemed to last forever.

"Me?" she finally squeaked out.

"Yes, you."

More silence loomed.

He'd hoped for a more enthusiastic response, but he supposed he had this coming. It had been two months since they began their mission to talk some sense into Frank and Laura. In all that time he'd only been out alone with Janice once, the day he took her to his church, and their time together that day had been far from planned. All they'd done was sit in her car to eat and pray, which had been badly needed at the time.

That had been a month ago. Since then, the only other time they hadn't been with Frank and Laura they had gone to visit his parents, and that didn't count. He'd been so nervous he hadn't been able to think straight.

He'd introduced Janice as his girlfriend, but he could tell that his parents, especially his mother, had been sitting on the edges of their seats, waiting for him to hint at promises of future wedding bells. Of course, it didn't happen.

Janice had handled the uncomfortable evening better than he had. Instead of letting them dwell on the disappointment that their son wasn't announcing an engagement after all, she cleverly turned the conversation to the progression of plans for Frank and Laura's wedding, which sufficiently distracted his mother. Before he knew it, they were in the car, waving their good-byes.

All the way home she'd teased him mercilessly about his predicament with his parents and even laughed. He'd thought the evening had been anything but funny. In retrospect, he appreciated it more, now that some time had passed.

Fortunately, they wouldn't have to deal with her parents, since they lived in a different city about five hundred miles away. By the time they arrived for Frank and Laura's wedding, if it happened, everything would be over, and life would be back to normal.

And now, he didn't want life to get back to normal. The better he got to know Janice the more he enjoyed being with her, even with Frank and Laura present every time they did something together. However, he could do something about that, if he really wanted to.

Since she still hadn't said anything, Trevor decided to forge ahead anyway.

He cleared his throat. "I thought it would be kind of fun to go out, just the two of us, for a change."

Another silence hung on the line.

If he had to be honest with himself, he had been thinking of what it would be like to go out and do things without Frank and Laura present for a long time. However, they'd been so busy going out as a foursome the opportunity had never come up.

Last night he had sat home alone waiting to call her after she got back from her exercise class. After realizing what he was doing and why, he came to the conclusion that sometimes opportunities had to be made.

"I guess . . . ," she mumbled.

"Great. I'll pick you up at six, and we'll go for dinner. And wear jeans. Okay?"

"Uh . . . Okay. . . . Oops. I have another call coming in. I-have-to-go-bye."

A click sounded, and the dial tone buzzed in his ear.

As he pushed the End button on his cell phone, Trevor caught himself smiling at her rushed end to the conversation.

For the rest of the afternoon, he found himself anticipating the evening. He already knew where they were going to go and what they were going to do. He only hoped he was ready.

At six o'clock sharp, he knocked on Janice's door with one hand behind his back.

She answered, wearing a plain pink blouse and a nice pair of jeans—without a hole in the knee. He'd seen the blouse before as something she wore to work. The simplicity of it suited her.

"Hi." Trevor smiled and brought his hand forward.

Her eyebrows raised, and she tipped her head up to make eye contact. "What's that?"

Trevor sighed. "They're called flowers, Janice."

"What are they for?"

"When a man gives flowers to a lady prior to going out together, it's usually taken as a sign of affection."

"Oh." She stared at them like they were made of toxic residue. Then her cheeks darkened. "Thank you. I guess I should put them in water or something. Come in for a minute."

He stepped inside and waited beside the door until she returned.

"Where are we going?"

"I thought we'd go to that café in Stanley Park for a nice little dinner, then walk around the park for awhile. The weather is warm and the days are getting longer, so I thought that would be a good end to a nice spring day."

Her little smile warmed his heart. "That sounds nice."

They made pleasant small talk on the long drive to the park. The parking lot had many wide-open spaces, and the restaurant itself was busy but not crowded, exactly as he expected for a spring weeknight.

He'd never been inside, but he'd heard the restaurant was quaint, the food good, and overall, it was a great place to take a woman for a quiet and informal evening.

She tugged on his sleeve as soon as they walked in the door. "Wow. Look at this place. Are you sure about this?"

He grinned down at her. "I hope you like seafood."

"I do, but this place is so, well, you know. If we're just going to walk around, why don't we go to the concession stand by the beach and get a couple of hot dogs?"

"Why don't we get a nice cozy table for two on the patio and walk around later?"

She shuffled to stand closer to him as she continued to study the decor. Her voice dropped to a near whisper. "I don't know, Trevor. This place seems so, I don't know, kind of romantic."

"What's wrong with that?"

"But it's just us."

"I know. That's why I picked it. I thought it would be a nice change. And I don't want to hear any arguments like you usually do about paying. This is my treat because it was my idea. And since I'm driving, one word from you about money and you can walk home."

"If you want to waste your money, that's fine with me. Just don't complain when I pick the most expensive thing on the menu."

He grinned and said nothing, knowing she was kidding. He actually wouldn't have minded if she did order something expensive. He wanted tonight to be special—for a number of reasons.

After they were seated at a table and had placed their order, Trevor pulled the booklet from the previous session of the couples' counseling course out of his back pocket. "I also thought this would be a good place to do our homework."

"Good idea." Janice pulled her rather scrunched-up booklet out of her purse, then began to dig to the bottom for the two pens she always carried. "Class is tomorrow, and I haven't even looked at the assignment yet," she muttered as she dug through her purse. "The days are sure going fast, aren't they?"

"Yes." He watched as she began pulling stuff out of her purse in her quest for the pens. First she pulled out a notepad, then a collapsible umbrella, a fork, a map, a squashed-up church bulletin from a month ago, a screwdriver, her day planner, an empty mesh shopping bag, and a computer disk. She located one of the pens, then continued to pull out smaller items, including a couple of Scrabble tiles and other items. He couldn't for the life of him figure out why the last few items were in her purse.

She did the same thing every time she hunted for the pens, only not to this extreme. He didn't know why she didn't clip the pens inside the day planner, which was always one of the first things out of her purse. Every time she went through the same process to find something, he wondered, even anticipated, what else got loaded in there over the past few days. Judging from the volume of clutter on the table, the thing was a bottomless pit.

He knew he'd seen something most men never saw—the contents of a woman's purse. One of life's timeless mysteries, solved.

Trevor plunked his elbows on the little remaining visible tabletop and cupped his chin in his palms. "Why don't you just carry a suitcase? Then you could really take along everything you need from day to day, including a change of clothes. Unless you have that in there too, but you haven't got that far down yet."

She grumbled something he wasn't sure he wanted to hear.

She found the second pen and shoved everything back into her purse only seconds before the waiter arrived with their meals. After Trevor led with a short prayer of thanks, they both paged to the assignment and rested the open booklets on the table and began to eat. He didn't want to remind her that it was rude to read at the table when with someone. He'd been the one to prepare ahead and had already reviewed both the lesson and the assignment.

"I remember now," Janice mumbled through her mouthful as she flipped the pages, scanning the material from the previous week. "The last lesson was on trust, and we were supposed to practice trusting each other."

Trevor fiddled with his fork, then laid it down so he wouldn't appear too nervous. "I know we don't have the same kind of relationship or the future plans as everyone else in that class, but over the last couple of months I think I can safely say we've at least become friends. With any friendship there is a good degree of trust. So it's kind of the same but kind of different. When I read what we're supposed to do this week, I found I do trust you like that."

She smiled and laid her own fork down. "That's so sweet of you to say that. I trust you too."

He forced himself to smile. "Before you say that, you should really read what the book says to do."

Janice scrunched her eyebrows, reached up to adjust her glasses, then flipped a few pages forward. "Hmm . . . I haven't read the whole thing, but this first part is so basic it's childish. They ask if I trust you with my safety. It says that I'm supposed to close my eyes and fall backward and trust you to catch me. What a silly thing to do."

"Maybe, but it says to do it. I trust you to catch me when I fall backward."

Janice made a very unladylike snort and closed the booklet.

"Then we can do our homework after supper. That's not something we can do in a restaurant. Is that why you wanted to come to the wide-open park? So I would land on the soft ground if you missed me? I know I'm going to catch you."

Her little grin eased some of the growing tremor of anticipation in his stomach. He sipped his water and nibbled on his salmon to try to ease the sensation a little more. It was the second part of the assignment that was the reason he'd brought her to the park.

"Very funny. I wanted to be completely alone in a relaxed atmosphere, and there's nothing more relaxing than being outside in the middle of the beauty of God's creation. You know; the breeze and the fresh ocean air in our faces, the sounds of the seagulls squawking overhead, and the waves lapping up the shore. The promise of the new growth of spring in the trees around us . . ."

Her eyes widened, as if she couldn't believe what he was saying. "I guess," she muttered, then lowered her head and resumed eating.

Trevor grinned. Between the cozy dinner for two and the romantic setting of the ocean park, most women would have been eating out his hand. But not Janice. He'd never seen a woman so unromantic as Janice. She hadn't gushed over the flowers, she never seemed anxious to see him, and she never tried to impress him. He remembered back to the evening she'd closed the door in his face when he'd playfully tried to kiss her good night. Janice was also the most pragmatic person he'd ever met. He'd never known a woman could be so focused and determined once she set her mind to something, whether it was to straighten out Frank and Laura or if it was to follow the manual and change the spark plugs in her own car.

Since theirs was not a typical dating relationship, he couldn't expect her to do the usual things, but Janice was not a woman to be stereotyped. He couldn't even say she did the opposite of everything he expected because now, knowing her as he did, he did expect most of her reactions and opinions. He also accepted that hers were different than any other woman he'd dated.

At the thought of dating Janice, he nearly choked on his mouthful and had to quickly take a sip of water. He wasn't dating Janice. The relationship had been fabricated from the beginning. However, one thing could not be fabricated, and that was the growth of their very real friendship.

"This was delicious. Thank you, Trevor."

"You're welcome. Would you like dessert?"

"No. I think we should just go outside, catch each other, and then go for a walk before it gets dark out. I don't come here very often, and this is a real treat."

Trevor led Janice to a quiet, grassy spot beneath a large patch of cedar trees. "The book says that this is supposed to demonstrate trust in our physical needs, to show we trust the other to help when we need it."

She made that snorting sound again and dropped her purse to the ground. "If you say so. Okay, here I come. You ready?"

Because she was so short Trevor lowered himself to one knee. When he held his hands out in front of him, she smiled, closed her eyes, spread her arms, and let herself fall backward. He caught her with ease and lowered her to the ground gently, leaving her lying flat on her back on the thick, green grass.

On his hands and knees above her, Trevor's heart caught in his throat. He didn't think the exercise was supposed to turn out this way, but with her lying on the ground, almost helpless beneath him, he wanted to scoop her up and kiss her.

Before he could make sense of the misfiring in his brain, she scrambled to her feet. Turning, she brushed the back of her pants free of a few blades of loose grass, then looked down at him. "Okay. Your turn."

He pushed his errant thoughts to the back of his mind, stood, closed his eyes, and extended his arms to the sides, just as she had. "You ready?" he asked.

"I'm ready, but are you sure you want to do this? You're a lot bigger than I am."

Trevor smiled, not opening his eyes. It was true—he stood taller than Janice by ten inches, and he surely outweighed her by sixty pounds. "I'm fine. With that red belt and all your martial arts training, you have to be stronger than you look. Here I come."

Without another word, Trevor let himself fall backward. Sure enough, both her arms slid under his arms and around his chest, cradling him as he came down. He let himself remain completely limp as she lowered him to the ground, although he felt himself slipping down much faster than he'd let her down.

With the speed at which the whole transaction occurred, she didn't pull one of her arms out from behind him quite fast enough. He landed on the ground with her wrist trapped beneath his shoulder blade and her forearm resting behind his neck, effectively pinning her so she was positioned almost on top of him.

In the position they were in, it would have taken no effort at all for him to wrap his arms around her, pull her down the last six inches between them, and kiss her. With very little effort, he could have embraced her with both arms and rolled over, pinning her on the ground beneath him, where he could have kissed her well and good.

But the whole exercise was a lesson in trust. If he did such a thing, she would never trust him again.

He ached inside with the loss, but lying flat on his back, Trevor twisted to raise his right shoulder off the ground to allow her to pull her arm out from beneath him, which she did.

He now understood that the silly exercise was a lesson in trust in more ways than he'd originally thought.

"You okay?" he asked as he stood.

"I'm fine," she mumbled, but Trevor was sure he heard a tremor in her voice that indicated she wasn't.

Now he was more certain than ever that they had to do the second half of the assignment.

With a quick swipe, he brushed a few pieces of grass from his backside and off the backs of his legs. "Let's discuss the rest of the lesson as we walk. You haven't read it, so how would you like to read it out loud as we walk, and you can refresh my memory."

"Okay."

As they walked, she read a short paragraph about trusting your partner with your heart as well as your body. "The assignment is to tell your partner something either you've never told anyone before, a deep secret, or something you're too scared to tell anyone else. Something no one else knows. And you have to be able to trust the other person, first, to keep your secret, and second, not to use it against you." She kept her face facing forward as she walked, focusing only on the path straight ahead. "Do we really have to do this?"

He lowered his voice, although he didn't know why, because they were alone in that section of the park as they made their way to the ocean shoreline. "Yes. I think we should." His next words were almost painful. "Unless you don't trust me. It's okay if you don't. After all, we haven't known each other very long."

They arrived at the shoreline, but instead of stopping and sitting on the bench like he'd originally planned, they turned and began walking slowly on the seawall walkway.

"But I do trust you, strange as that sounds. I don't know why, but I do. I just don't know if you want to hear my silly problems."

She didn't stop walking, so neither did he. "I do want to hear them. I think trust goes hand in hand with honesty, so I'm going to be honest with you. When you told me about that self-defense class you've been taking, I wondered why you would take such a thing. Not that it's unusual for a woman to take such a course. I think that's a great idea. But when women take self-defense classes, most take a short thing that teaches a few basic self-defense moves, and then they carry bear spray and stay away from dark places at night. You've gone way beyond that. You've been doing this for years, and you're good enough to flatten a man with your bare hands. I want to know what happened to you that made you go to such extremes. I'm going to be honest with you and tell you that I've already asked Laura what happened, but she told me she doesn't know. She only told me that one night you came home really scared, and the next day you signed up for that martial arts thing and haven't looked back."

She remained silent as they walked. Trevor held his questions, knowing she needed the time to think and trusting that if she wanted to tell him, she would. If not, he would have to live with not knowing.

When she wrapped her arms around herself as they continued on, Trevor didn't think that was a good sign. Still, he waited for her to have the first word, even if she didn't speak until they finished their walk and returned to the car.

Her voice came out so soft he barely heard her over the pounding of the ocean waves on the sand.

"I haven't really talked to Laura about it. I don't know why. I guess I felt too stupid, like it was my own fault. I know that's dumb. It's never the victim's fault."

A lump went to war with the good meal he'd just eaten. Now he hated himself for what he had started. He didn't want to hear what he suspected was true, but at the same time, he had to know

if she had been a victim of a brutal attack, or worse. . . . He found
he couldn't speak, so he waited for her to continue.

"Don't worry. I'm not going to break down and cry on you.
I'm okay."

He found it difficult to keep walking. He slowed to see if she
would also slow and maybe stop, but she didn't. Therefore, he
continued to walk. "Are you sure? It's okay if you're not."

"But I am okay. I wasn't hurt or anything, if that's what you're
thinking. I was just scared. More scared than I'd ever been in my
life. If it hadn't been for God's timing, though, I don't even want
to think about what would have happened."

"Do you want to tell me? You don't have to."

Janice kept her focus straight ahead and continued to walk
with her arms wrapped around herself. "There's not a lot to tell.
I had to work late one night. I missed the bus, so I decided to
walk to another bus stop to take an alternate route. That ended
up being a bad decision because on the way to the bus stop a
couple of guys jumped me. At first they only wanted my money,
but when they so easily overpowered me, I think they got different
ideas. They dragged me between two buildings, but a police officer
happened to be driving by and saw my purse lying on the ground.
He stopped the cruiser, turned on the flashing red and blue lights,
and then the two men dropped me and ran. I couldn't identify
them, so they were never caught. But I truly believe that God sent
that cop there at the right time. There was no other reason for
him to notice my purse on the ground on a dark street. That's
about it."

"Are you sure you weren't hurt?"

"Positive. Please don't worry about me. And don't ever believe
it when someone tells you there's never a cop around when you
need one. He also gave me the card for the martial arts studio I
go to."

Trevor tried to tamp down a growing anger. "And you still

take the bus back and forth to work every day? After what nearly happened?"

Suddenly, she stopped. Since he hadn't expected it, Trevor stopped three steps ahead of her, turned, and walked back, resulting in speaking to her face-to-face.

She unwrapped her arms from her waist and crossed them over her chest as she glared up at him. "I'm not going to live in fear for the rest of my life. I'm going to continue on as normal, a little more careful, and a little more prepared. Besides, cars sometimes break down, you know. For your information, I did take my car for awhile, until I figured I could take care of myself if anything like that happened again. I'm also much more careful around strangers. For awhile, I was afraid of everything, that someone would jump me from around every corner. Do you know what it's like to walk around like that, always being afraid? It's awful. I won't live like that again."

Being male and six feet tall, Trevor figured that even though he was sometimes nervous out at night in a strange area in a rougher end of town, he would never truly know the fear women faced when out alone, where danger could lurk around every corner. Also, he knew that in actual fact cases of women being attacked by a stranger were rare. More women were hurt by men they already knew, which only made it worse, because they didn't know who to trust. He couldn't imagine the trauma she'd experienced while working through the horror of being attacked and all the complications that went with it.

He didn't know what to say, so he said nothing.

She turned and smiled at him. "So, now it's your turn. What are you going to tell me about yourself that no one else knows?"

12

*J*anice turned around and started walking back to where they came from, trusting that Trevor's secret would take the same amount of time to share as hers. He quickly caught up with her, and they walked side by side in silence.

She still couldn't believe she actually told him. She hadn't told anyone, not even Laura, her best friend, how much that one incident had affected her. Until a few minutes ago, she hadn't realized herself how much it had affected her whole life, even after all this time.

While men who knew nothing of martial arts did come into the class as volunteers so the students could test their skills on someone besides their teacher, she'd never been able to truly use her skills outside the studio. More importantly, she'd never put her confidence to the test.

Today, when Trevor had unwittingly trapped her she knew beyond a shadow of doubt that she could have escaped if she had wanted to. If it hadn't been Trevor, she could have and would have done what she needed to do to be safe. Because it would have meant hurting Trevor, she hadn't reacted. But the important thing was that she knew she could have and would have, if necessary.

Nothing had happened, but in the event itself a question had been answered.

She had finally conquered her fear, fully and completely. She would never stop being sensible and careful, but from that moment on, she knew she would never have to walk in fear again.

"Come on, Trevor. Being able to share that with you lifted a great weight off my shoulders. I never would have thought it would feel so good to tell you, and now I don't have to carry it alone. You can tell me something close to your heart. Let me help you carry your burdens."

His voice dropped to a gravelly whisper. "I have to admit that a few people already know this. My parents and my doctor, but no one else. Not even Frank."

Something inside Janice went numb when he said "doctor." If something was seriously wrong with him, she thought she just might die inside. In everything they'd done together, he'd seemed healthy and fit. From his dietary habits, she knew he wasn't diabetic. However, being diabetic or anything like that was nothing anyone needed to keep secret. In her mind, she conjured up all the things that could be wrong with a person when they appeared normal on the outside but would be fatal in time.

All she could do was wait for him to tell her in his own time.

They walked in silence for a couple of minutes before he finally spoke. "I'm dyslexic."

She turned her head to study him as they walked, but his attention strayed everywhere except to her.

"I don't know much about dyslexia, only that it's some kind of learning disability that involves mixing up letters and things."

"Well, sometimes it's kind of like that, but not always, and there's more to it than that. It's a neurological dysfunction. All my life I've struggled with reading. I did graduate from high school, but I had to work very hard, and I didn't do very well. It still affects me, but it's not as bad as it used to be. I think I can safely say that I'm never going to go to a university and get a degree in anything. I'll probably be the maintenance guy for V. L. Management all my life."

She tried to encourage him with a smile, but she had a feeling he knew her smile was forced. "I much prefer your official title of

Mechanical Engineer. Not everyone goes to the university. I'll probably never go either. I like my office job."

He turned to her. "I like my job too, but no one is ever going to talk about you behind your back and say you're stupid."

"But you're not stupid! I've also seen you read. You haven't had any difficulty with the lessons at the couples' counseling classes."

"That's different. Those aren't real books. And remember, much of the lesson assignments are read out loud during class. I don't have any trouble with oral instruction or problem solving when it's spoken, just when it's written down. It's hard to explain. I still read the occasional novel, and of course I read my Bible every day. But reading takes me longer than anyone else, and sometimes I don't understand what I read so easily. It's not always consistent, and some days are better than others. I don't have any trouble with anything else, just reading. I'm only a mild case, but it's there, and it will always be there. I've actually got a better memory than most people, and maybe that's why. You'll never believe what a relief it was when my parents had me tested and we had an explanation for it. We never told any of my teachers because my doctor told my parents that if I worked hard, I could probably pass on my own. Back in school I developed the most amazing ways to hide it, and I suppose I still do. Otherwise, I risked being treated differently than the rest of the kids. So instead of being labeled as mentally deficient, I was just labeled as lazy and a problem child. Praise God, my parents knew how hard I worked. They helped me as best they could and stuck up for me when I needed it."

"What about your sisters?"

"Statistically, it affects boys three to six times more often than girls. My sisters are fine."

"Is it genetic?"

"No one else in my family seems to have it, but who knows

about past generations when they didn't have a name for it. Anyway, God loves me, I'm happy with my life, I have good friends and a good job I enjoy, so it really doesn't matter anymore."

She doubted that it didn't matter to him, especially if he'd never told anyone about it, not even Frank. Right then, Janice didn't care that she had to get up early for work. Tonight, before bed, she would do some significant searching on the Internet for more information on dyslexia.

He stopped and pointed to the ocean. "The sun is setting. Want to stand on the shore for awhile and watch?"

"Yes, I'd like that."

She stood at his side to watch the sky brighten with the pinks and purples of the spring sunset reflecting over the crystal surface of the endless ocean. With the fading light, the temperature continued to drop quickly. Even in her jacket, Janice couldn't suppress a shiver.

"Cold? Want to go?"

She wrapped her arms around herself. "No. Not yet."

Slowly, Trevor's arm wrapped around her shoulder, and he pulled her in close to him. "Better?"

It was better, not just for the warmth. The tender but firm way he cradled her spoke volumes—he didn't think less of her for her weaknesses, and the reassurance touched her deeply. She wished that she could somehow do the same for him.

The more she thought about his disability, the more she respected him. Even though he admitted to struggling at times, he *had* made a good life for himself. After more than two months of seeing him nearly every day, she still would never have guessed he had a learning disability. With his quick wit and eye for detail, she didn't know how anyone could ever perceive him as stupid. She would never have known he had a problem if he hadn't told her. She couldn't imagine the challenges he had overcome growing up.

To be trusted with such a painful and personal secret was a staggering responsibility and a vivid statement of how much he really did trust her, not just for the sake of the assignment, but for all time.

When the sun sank below the distant shore, leaving only a dull red glow in its wake, Janice turned her head to speak to Trevor. "I've had a lovely evening, but I guess it's time to go home."

"Yes. Tomorrow night is the class. How would you like to join me for lunch? I can pick you up."

Janice smiled. He'd joined her for lunch many times in the last two months, and she'd enjoyed it every time. "I'd like that very much."

Just like every other time he announced he would be joining her, she could hardly wait.

&

"Well? What do you think?"

Janice lowered her chin while she studied the fabric, trying to gauge if the green color suited her or not.

She heard Trevor clearing his throat. "I think it makes her look short."

Janice pushed the shiny fabric away and glared at him. She'd teased him about so many things she could no longer be angry with him for teasing her about her height. "How can a length of fabric make me look short? You're just saying that because you're mad that you had to come."

He leaned back in the chair, stretched his long legs out in front of him, crossed his ankles, then lifted his arms and linked his fingers behind his head. Those adorable little crinkles appeared at the corners of his striking blue eyes as he grinned. "I dunno. I can't think of a more manly place to hang out than the local fabric store. How about you, Frank? Are you having fun yet?"

"Oh, sure," Frank grumbled as he hunched in the chair, trying to hide so anyone walking by wouldn't see him through the store's large window.

Janice picked up the dress pattern and studied the picture. Having both the men's shirts and the maid of honor's dress made of the same fabric would look sharp, but she couldn't see it happening. "I can't believe you've left these things for the last minute like this. I know you've already altered your mother's wedding dress, but how are you going to make the two shirts and a dress for me in three weeks?"

Laura crossed her arms. "I can do a shirt in one day and the dress in two. There's lots of time."

Trevor held up a bag to shield himself as he spoke. "We have to make sure the photographer gets lots of pictures. Janice in a dress, especially a fancy dress, is going to be the eighth wonder of the modern world, and we're all going to be there when it happens."

Janice thumped the pattern on the top of the cabinet. "How dare you! I wore a dress a number of times when we went out. I've also been to your church a few times, and I wore a dress every time."

"That was a jean skirt you wore every time, not a dress. Doesn't count."

"Children! Stop fighting!" Laura interjected as she wrapped the fabric back around the bolt. "After we pay for this, Janice and I are going to go down the mall to pick up the napkins and stuff, and you guys have to go reserve your tuxes."

Trevor and Frank wasted no time in leaving the fabric store, so Janice helped Laura gather everything she needed for her rush sewing project and proceeded to the cutting table.

It was the opportunity Janice needed. She stood close to Laura while they waited their turn in the checkout line. "We always seem to be together with the guys, and then when we finally get home it's so late we hurry off to bed. I can't remember the last time we sat and talked, just the two of us."

"I know," Laura mumbled as she ran her finger down the notions list of the pattern, checking one last time that she had everything she needed. "I guess with the wedding approaching, everything we've done has been centered on getting ready for that."

"I was thinking, have you ever wondered if you're doing the right thing? There's only a few sessions left of that couples' counseling course, and I've sure gotten to know a different side of Trevor. Surely you must be seeing Frank in a different light since the whole thing started."

Laura simply shrugged her shoulders. "Not really. Some stuff, I guess. But not a lot."

Janice gritted her teeth, then turned to smile at Laura. "But what about when the topic of the week was romance versus routine? What it's like to really live with someone after the glow of the initial romance is over? The day-to-day stuff of living together and getting along when neither of you is at your best? When you no longer try to impress and when your partner no longer cares about impressing you? Do you really think you and Frank can be happy together?"

Laura shrugged her shoulders again. "Sure. Why not?"

Janice felt like dragging her hand down her face but restrained herself. While she struggled to think of the right thing to say, Laura raised her hand and rested it on Janice's shoulder. "You're not having problems with Trevor, are you?"

Janice blinked. "Problems with Trevor? No, there's nothing wrong between me and Trevor. But since the course began, we've gotten to know each other much better."

Janice had come to learn a lot about Trevor that no one else knew. She'd learned a lot about his dyslexia, and he'd told her what it was like to grow up with it. The whole time he'd been adamant about her not feeling sorry for him. They'd both found it funny that Janice hadn't wanted him to feel sorry for her due to her long-standing and recently resolved paranoias and fears about being out at night. He'd even agreed to be the aggressive male at one of her self-defense classes, risking his healthy male ego by getting beat up by a bunch of women.

In many ways, she now knew him better than Laura, who had been her best friend since elementary school. Likewise, she'd opened herself to Trevor completely, holding nothing back, even sharing many things she'd never told Laura. And he still liked her anyway.

"I guess the same thing has happened with me and Frank, now that I think about it. We've learned a lot about each other we didn't know, but nothing has changed."

Janice couldn't say the same. Everything had changed. Originally, she and Trevor had planned not to see each other again unless their paths crossed after Frank and Laura either split up or got married. Both of them had expressed regret that everything would soon be over and they wouldn't need to see each other every day. In doing so, they discussed the direction their friendship had taken and decided not only to keep in touch but to continue in their friendship as they were doing, just not every day.

Laura and Janice's turn to pay came before she could resume the conversation, so Janice had to tell herself that she'd planted a sufficient seed for the day and leave it in God's hands. She knew Trevor had experienced many of these same frustrations with Frank and suspected he was having another one at this same moment.

The girls couldn't see Frank and Trevor waiting for them when they walked out into the mall, so they headed for the men's shop to meet them.

"Janice?"

Janice turned at the sound of a male voice that sounded only slightly familiar.

"Rick! I haven't seen you for a long time. How are you?" She quickly glanced over his shoulder to see if Sarah was with him, but she wasn't.

"I'm doing fine. I see that blond guy isn't with you. Dan told me you were going to that couples' thing Pastor Harry is doing. I see you're not officially engaged yet, and the class is almost over. I was wondering if anything has changed?"

"Well, actually—" A squeak escaped her mouth as an arm slid around her waist.

"Hi. Rick, is it? If I'm the blond guy you're referring to, the name is Trevor."

Rick's ears reddened. "Hi, Trevor. I didn't see you."

Trevor's one arm tightened around her waist, pulling her in closer to him. He extended his free hand to Rick.

As Rick grasped Trevor's hand, Trevor lowered his chin, drawing particular attention to the fact that he stood three inches taller than Rick. He met Rick's gaze with a stony stare. "Yeah. I can see how I'd be hard to miss."

Very slowly, their hands moved up and down in a brief handshake. By Rick's slight wince, Janice could tell that Trevor was squeezing a little too hard. When Trevor finally released Rick's hand, Rick backed up a step and flexed his fingers at his side.

One corner of Trevor's mouth quirked up. "Maybe I'll catch you some Sunday at church, Rick. You'll probably be seeing me there more often. Just look for Janice, and I'll be there."

"Uh, yeah. Well, it was nice meeting you again, Trevor. See you, Janice." Rick turned and walked away. Frank, Trevor, and Laura stood in silence, watching Rick go. Janice watched Trevor. His mouth was set in a grim line, and his eyes narrowed as he glared at Rick's diminishing form.

Laura glanced at Janice, then turned and tugged on Frank's sleeve. "There's something I want to show you. Over there."

Without another word, Frank and Laura disappeared into the bakery a few doors down.

Janice pulled out of Trevor's grasp. She crossed her arms and tapped one foot, the sound echoing on the floor. "That was rather immature, don't you think?"

Trevor crossed his arms as he continued to watch Rick walk down to the end of the mall. "He annoys me."

"That was no reason to be rude."

"I wasn't rude. Name one thing I said that was rude."

"You know what I mean."

Trevor turned to face her. He rested one fist on his hip and jerked his other thumb over his shoulder in the direction Rick had gone. "He had no right to ask you if I'm past news. None. Not while we're still taking that course together."

Janice blinked and stared. If it had been anyone else, she would have said he was jealous. But this was Trevor. Her friend. They were pretending to be a couple only because they had a specific purpose in mind. They both knew that.

"And another thing. He knew my name perfectly well. We were introduced before, and I remembered his name just fine, especially considering the circumstances of our original meeting. He was just trying to diminish my position as your official boyfriend by calling me 'that blond guy.' "

"You're taking this awful personal, Trevor."

"That's because it *is* personal."

Janice dearly wished she could have asked him why, but Frank and Laura returned, cutting their conversation short.

Together, they browsed through a few more stores, bought the supplies to decorate the hall and tables at the wedding, and then went home.

Since they had gone out as two couples most evenings, they

had developed a pattern to allow themselves a minute of privacy from each other as they parted. Since it was Frank's car, Frank and Laura stayed at the car to say their good-byes, and Trevor escorted Janice to the door of the house.

She didn't want to spoil the evening, so Janice decided not to question him further about the incident with Rick. However, when this whole thing was over, she knew she would have to seek Rick out and talk to him, because now the same thing had happened twice.

Standing nearly toe-to-toe, Trevor grasped both of her hands between them, as he often did. "I can't remember whose church we're going to tomorrow. I guess yours, since there's only two Sundays left before the wedding."

"That's right."

"Okay. I'll see you tomorrow."

He released her hands but didn't back away. Instead, he shuffled closer and cupped her chin with both hands. His voice dropped to a low, husky whisper. "Good night, Janice."

His head lowered.

Janice's heart stopped beating.

His eyes closed.

Her heart started pounding in double-time.

Janice tipped her chin up without his prompting.

His lips touched hers softly, barely touching, then lifted. Before the disappointment fully sank in, his hands drifted to her back, his mouth settled in for a full contact, and he kissed her for real.

Janice couldn't do anything else. She reached around his back to embrace him and returned his kiss.

Too soon, he released her mouth and stepped away. His hands drifted from her back and grasped her hands between them once again, as he should have in the first place.

Janice cleared her throat. "What was that for?"

"I don't know. I guess I like you. Isn't that a good enough reason?"

"I thought we were supposed to be just friends. Friends don't do that."

"Then maybe we should be special friends."

Janice shook her head. "No. I've heard that a romance that isn't meant to be will destroy a friendship. I value what we have too much to risk ruining it. I want to stay just plain old friends and nothing more."

"Are you sure?"

She had to force the words out. "Yes, I'm sure. I've never been more sure of anything in my life. What we have is good and unique, and I want to keep it that way."

A long silence loomed between them.

She couldn't have it any other way. The fear that gripped her soul over the thought of something going wrong terrified her unlike anything she'd ever experienced. Trevor was the sweetest man she'd ever known. His gentleness when she needed it only emphasized his strength where it counted. They could share anything and everything—and did. She'd never known anyone like him and knew she never would again. What they had between them was too valuable to do anything to risk it.

She had to keep him as her friend forever.

"If that's the way you think it should be, then that's the way it is. Besides church tomorrow, do we have anything else planned with Frank and Laura?"

She'd never been so grateful for a change in subject, but she had a feeling Trevor had done it on purpose. "Yes. Dinner on Monday. Tuesday and Wednesday Laura's going to sew Frank's and your shirts. Thursday you guys are coming here for dinner to try on the shirts and then we're doing more shopping. Then Friday is the last class."

"That means we're almost out of time. Do you think this wedding is really meant to happen?"

She shrugged her shoulders. "I don't know. We should really get together some time without Frank and Laura and pray about it some more."

He nodded. "I'll call you at lunchtime Monday, and we'll set something up without those two listening in. In the meantime, I'll see you tomorrow."

$$\text{\Large 13}$$

$\mathcal{W}$ elcome to week eleven of our Getting To Know You, Spring Session. This is our last class together as a group. For next week we'll have individual sessions for every couple. There's a sign-up sheet in the back. If you don't see anything suitable, please speak to me privately after class.

"Last week we talked about conflict and resolution. Today we're going to be talking about the causes of successes and failures in a marriage. Brittany, can you hand out one of these booklets to everyone, please?"

As he accepted a booklet, Trevor glanced at Frank and Laura. This was it, the last session of the class that was supposed to help Frank and Laura get to know each other beyond the smiles and warm fuzzies. Even after all that had been discussed and all the weekly assignments, Frank and Laura openly held hands and gazed at each other with such starstruck expressions that Trevor thought he might be sick. Over the past four months, he and Janice had become even more convinced than when the whole fiasco started and they first began their quest of how ill-suited Frank and Laura were for each other. If it wasn't his imagination, he also had the impression a few others in their group also thought the same way.

When everyone had opened the newest booklet to the first page, Pastor Harry began.

"Experience has taught me that one of the major causes of the breakdown of a marriage or any kind of relationship is the lack of effective communication. How do you communicate with your partner?"

He paused to let his statement sink in around the room.

Trevor bit back a smirk. Since Frank and Laura announced their engagement, he'd seen Janice almost every day. When together, they tended to talk a lot. In those days they hadn't been with each other in person, they somehow usually ended up spending a fair amount of time on the phone. Most of the time he called her, but sometimes she phoned him. The conversations always started the same, clarifying upcoming plans to be with Frank and Laura. Then they always seemed to drift onto something totally unrelated to the original topic. A number of times they'd talked so long that Frank gave up and went to bed, then yelled at him to shut up so he could sleep.

He hadn't spent as much time on the phone in the past four years as he had in the past four months. In that short space of time, he'd come to know Janice better than Frank, his best friend whom he'd known all his life.

The sensation of being poked in the ribs brought his thoughts back to the class.

"Pay attention!" Janice whispered through her teeth. "This is about communication, and you're sitting there daydreaming."

Trevor turned to Janice and grinned at her like a Cheshire cat, showing all his teeth. She made a disgusted grunt, then turned to watch Pastor Harry as he continued to talk.

Of course, Trevor agreed with everything the pastor said, especially when the topic centered around disagreements and arguments. He'd never seen Frank and Laura have a single disagreement, which made him doubt they were communicating effectively. However, he'd had a few humdingers with Janice.

When she was mad at him, she let him have it right between the eyes. There was no guessing that she was angry, nor did he ever have to guess at why. He simply knew it. He also liked it that way. They could deal with the problem, and life went on as usual.

So far, Janice had done nothing to make him angry, so he

wasn't quite sure what would happen in that case. However, that was no surprise. All his life, Trevor tended to be even-tempered, and he didn't become angry often. He also tried to act intelligently when he was angry. Instead of roaring off in his car or punching holes in the walls like some of the men he knew, he went for a walk until he calmed down and could think rationally.

The pastor's words interrupted his thoughts. "I'll give you ten minutes to answer the questions, then ten minutes to talk about your answers between yourselves. Then we'll open up for sharing before we go on to the next chapter."

He started scribbling down his answers. In the middle of question three, Janice poked him again.

"What?" he muttered as he tried to complete his sentence.

"I have to go," she whispered.

Trevor raised his head and glanced toward the door. He could never figure out why women couldn't go to the washroom alone when in a crowded room or restaurant. "So? Go. You don't need me to hold your hand if Laura's busy."

"I meant leave. I have to go home. Now."

The pen froze in the middle of a word. "Now? Is something wrong? Are you all right?" He narrowed his eyes and studied her face.

"No, I'm not all right. In twenty minutes, I'm going to be sick. I've got just enough time if we leave right now."

He laid the pen in his lap. "I've never seen someone be sick on a stopwatch before. What's really wrong?"

She lowered her head and pressed the fingertips of both hands to her temples. "I just saw a flash of light, and I'm getting a really bad headache, very fast. That means I'm getting a migraine. I have to lie down in the dark, and if I can do it fast enough, maybe I won't be sick. But since I'm out and can't go straight to bed, it's going to be too late to ward off the progression. Within twenty minutes, I'm going to be throwing up."

Trevor had never had a migraine in his life, but he'd heard they were awful.

He turned to Frank. "We've got to go. Now."

Frank laid his pen down and glanced up at the clock on the wall. "What are you talking about? Class just started."

Still sitting, Trevor bent at the waist and leaned closer to Frank so those around him wouldn't overhear. "Janice is getting a migraine."

Laura leaned closer and covered her mouth with both hands. "Oh, no," she said from between her fingers. "You've got to get her home right away." She reached into her purse for her keys, then froze. "I forget. How did we get here? We didn't take my car this time, did we?"

"I drove this time," Trevor said. "You've either got to come with me right now or find someone else to drive you back."

Glancing out of the corner of his eye, he saw Janice get up and leave. He wanted to call out to her that he'd be there in a minute, but he didn't want to disturb the class any more than he was already doing. He also didn't know the severity of her headache, so he didn't want to make any sharp or sudden noises.

He turned back to Frank. "Make up your mind. You have fifteen seconds, then I'm leaving whether you're with me or not."

Pastor Harry watched the door close behind Janice as she went outside. "Excuse me. Is something wrong?"

Trevor glanced around the room. Everyone was staring at him. He tried to smile to everyone but failed.

He stood. "Janice doesn't feel well, and we've got to go. Can someone give Frank and Laura a ride home? Otherwise, they've got to come with me."

"I can drive them home," Pastor Harry said. "Give Janice my best, and we'll all pray for her."

At the pastor's words, Trevor darted across the room. He

opened the door and let it slam behind him as he increased his speed and ran as fast as he could to the car.

He unlocked the car door and stepped aside. As Janice slid in slowly, his stomach did another flip-flop. In only a few minutes, the pallor of her skin had become alarming.

They both remained completely silent as he drove as fast as he could back to her house, trying his best not to make sudden movements or get a speeding ticket. They arrived in thirteen minutes. Counting the three minutes it took to get moving in the first place, that meant she had four minutes of grace.

He watched her hand shake as she fumbled with the key in the lock. Without asking for her permission, he removed the key chain from her hand and opened the door.

She didn't say a word as she hurried through the house and into her bedroom, her head down and her fingertips pressed to her temples.

Trevor remained standing in the living room. The bedsprings creaked, and then, except for the hum of the fridge, all was silent.

He didn't know what to do. He thought he could remember something about a cold facecloth helping in a case like this, but he wasn't sure.

Since it couldn't hurt, Trevor walked into the hallway to the linen closet. The second he touched the knob to pull the bi-fold door open, the bedsprings creaked again. Janice stepped out of the bedroom, one hand pressed to her temple, the other over her mouth. She ran all the way into the bathroom, and the door banged shut.

A soulful moan drifted through the closed door, and she started to retch.

Trevor thought he might be sick too.

He stood in the hall, his hand still on the linen closet doorknob. He couldn't just stand there and do nothing. She needed him.

He walked softly to the bathroom door and tested the doorknob. It turned, so he slowly pushed the door open. Janice was hunched over the toilet, one arm wrapped around her stomach, the other palm still pressed to her temple. Her complexion had faded to a ghastly pale gray. It also dawned on him that she wasn't wearing her glasses. He'd never seen her without her glasses before, not even the time they went swimming.

"Go away," she moaned. "You can go home now."

Trevor stepped beside her, hunkered down, and wrapped one arm around her waist. He could feel her trembling all over. In addition to her cheeks being without color, they were also wet with tears.

"Shh," he whispered. "I'm not going anywhere."

He expected her to tell him to leave, but before she could speak, she retched again.

Trevor did the only thing he could, and that was to hold her until she got everything out of her system, then he led her back to bed.

When she was lying down and still, Trevor walked across the room, trying to ignore the fact that he was in her bedroom. He closed the blinds to make it as dark as possible until the sun fully set. He remained beside the window and turned. "Would a cold facecloth help?"

She lay on the bed with her arm over her eyes, her whole body unnaturally still. Her voice came out in a low mumble, barely discernable. "There's an ice bag in the freezer."

Trevor tiptoed as fast as he could out of the bedroom and ran to the kitchen. He located a gel-style athletic ice bag, wrapped the dishtowel around it, and hurried back to the bedroom. When he stood beside the bed, Janice lifted her arm from her face and raised her hands to accept it from him. Tearstains lined her cheeks, and a few new tears trickled through her tightly-closed eyelids.

He felt like he'd been dealt a sucker punch to the gut.

Instead of handing her the ice bag, he gently placed it over her forehead for her, making sure the towel covered it properly. "Is this right?" he whispered, barely able to choke the words out.

She pressed the ice bag down with her fingertips and spoke so softly he could barely hear her. "Yes. Thank you. You can go now."

He didn't go. He wanted to touch her, to gently smooth away the hair from her forehead. To brush away the wetness from her cheeks. To help reposition the ice bag to put the coldest part over her forehead. But he was too afraid.

Trevor rammed his hands into his pockets. "I'm not going anywhere," he whispered back, not knowing how loud he could speak, hoping she heard him. "What causes this?"

Her voice trembled when she spoke. "It doesn't happen that often, but there are some food triggers that I try to avoid. Chocolate is my weakness. I don't know what started it today. I've been so careful with what I've eaten."

Trevor shuffled his feet but otherwise didn't move. He stood beside the bed with his hands still deep in his pockets.

"Is there anything I can get for you? Some medicine or something? Do you take that kind of thing? I don't know what to do, but I'm not leaving you like this. At least not until Laura gets home."

"In the medicine cabinet. In the bathroom. It's the only prescription bottle with my name on it."

He returned in a minute flat, a pill in one hand, a glass of cool water in the other. Very carefully, he helped her sit up and supported her back while she swallowed the pill with a tiny sip of water. As gently as he could, he slowly lowered her back down. He let her adjust the ice bag on her forehead by herself, and then he stood beside the bed.

Another tear escaped her closed eyelids. She sniffled, then winced. "I didn't want you to see me like this," she mumbled.

This time, he couldn't help himself. She still wasn't wearing her glasses, and their absence made her seem totally vulnerable. With as soft a touch as he could manage, he brushed the errant lock of hair back from her forehead. "Don't worry about it. Now you be quiet and see if you can sleep."

Trevor stood and watched in silence for a full twenty minutes before her breathing slowed and became shallow and perfectly uniform. Even knowing she was sleeping, he couldn't leave her side.

This still, silent creature on the bed had last week threatened to flatten him in the middle of the parking lot after he'd teased her about something insignificant. And he had no doubt that she would have done it if he hadn't run, laughing, calling back to her that she couldn't hurt him if she couldn't catch him. Of course, she had been laughing too, which made it harder to take each other seriously.

Frank and Laura had watched them in total disgust. Trevor had never had so much fun in his life.

Janice now lay completely immobile. Defenseless. A wounded angel. And there was nothing he could do about it.

He'd never felt so helpless in his life.

As he continued to stand beside her still form, the revelation struck him. In some ways, it had happened so fast; but in another way, it snuck up on him slowly, a little bit each day, so gradually he didn't see it happening. But now he couldn't deny it. He hadn't known her long in the overall scheme of life, but since they started spending so much time together she'd become his very best friend in the whole world. Their relationship had gone far deeper than mere friendship. Trevor had totally and completely fallen in love.

The front door creaked open, and soft footsteps approached behind him.

"Is she sleeping?" Laura whispered.

"Yes," he whispered back.

"We should get out of here. Want some tea?"

He followed Laura out of the room. "No, thanks. I really should be going. Is she going to be okay tomorrow?"

"Usually she is, but that medication makes her real dozy. She's not going to be good for much until sometime in the afternoon. Good thing tomorrow's Saturday."

"I understand. Tell her to phone me when she's feeling better."

"You bet. Good night, Trevor."

౸

Trevor leaned his hip into the doorframe of Janice's kitchen. "How long do you think they'll be?"

She poured the water into the coffeemaker and turned around. "I'm figuring they'll be back in about an hour. That gives us just the right amount of time."

As he continued to prop himself against the doorway, Janice fidgeted with everything she laid her hands on, something she never did.

Tomorrow was Thursday, the wedding rehearsal, and then two days after that, Saturday, the wedding. Frank and Laura had done their private appointment with Pastor Harry, and they were really going through with it. Trevor had a feeling he and Janice were going to pray about it one more time, talk, and then leave it in God's hands and let whatever happened, happen, just as they'd discussed and agreed a million times.

Such being the case, he didn't know why Janice seemed to be developing a case of the nervous jitters. She picked up and put down everything she could possibly touch until the coffee was ready.

When she poured the coffee into two waiting mugs, Trevor found the cream in the fridge and topped off both cups.

As soon as they sat on the couch and placed their hot mugs onto a magazine on the coffee table, Janice folded her hands in her lap and turned to face him.

"Before we pray together about Laura and Frank, there's something I have to say to you. It's about us."

Trevor's heart pounded. He crossed his arms over his chest, so she wouldn't be able to see his hands shaking.

He'd hoped and prayed for this moment, the moment she told him that she loved him as much as he'd come to love her. Since they'd already discussed so many times the what-ifs of Frank and Laura actually going through with the wedding, he had already prepared himself for whatever happened afterward. If they were happy together, he would praise God, and life would go on just fine. If Frank and Laura weren't happy together, Trevor would be the best friend he could be to Frank and help him through whatever life threw at him.

Either way, the wedding would be over, and he would be free from his agreement with Janice to pretend to be a couple.

The minute everything was over, he planned to tell Janice that he was through pretending. He wanted to make their relationship as a couple real. She had tried to feed him some song and dance about friendship and romance not being compatible, but Trevor didn't agree. If they tried dating and it didn't work, he would gladly go back to the friendship they had developed, but he wanted them to try. If it didn't work, even though it wouldn't be the ideal solution, he could love her from the distance of a safe, platonic friendship. But if it did work, he would be the happiest man on earth.

Janice leaned forward in her seat. "As you know, the wedding is in three days. It looks like everything we tried hasn't worked, and they're going through with it after all. I guess you know that after the wedding there will be no need for us to keep pretending as we have been."

Trevor bit his lip to stop himself from blurting out his feelings and to let her finish talking. "Yes, I know."

"I've thought long and hard about this, and I thought you should know what I've decided. I'm going to go talk to Rick."

Trevor knotted his brows. "Rick? What for?"

"First of all, I have to explain to him why you acted the way you did in front of Frank and Laura. I know he won't be angry,

653

but I do feel I have to explain. And then, if he asks me out, which I think he's going to do, I'm going to say yes."

Trevor's whole body went numb. All his hopes and dreams came crashing down around him. "What? Why?"

"I'm getting too mixed up about what's happened with us. We've known each other such a short amount of time, and everything is happening so fast. I need some time, and I need to distance myself and sort everything out. Since we agreed to remain just friends, I think I should pursue other romantic relationships. If Rick is still interested, that allows me to sort myself out while I see where that leads."

Trevor jumped to his feet. "I don't understand. I thought we had something special between us. Why do you feel the need to see someone else?"

Janice remained seated. She looked up at him from her place on the couch as she spoke. "It's not that I feel a need to see anyone. I just feel really mixed up, and I need time to figure some stuff out."

The front door creaked open.

"We're ba-ack!" Laura singsonged.

"Hey, Buddy," Frank said as he approached the couch. "We gotta go. There's a problem with my cummerbund, and if they can't get it fixed, we have to pick new ones, which might mean some quick alterations. That means you would have to try it on. They close in twenty minutes. We have just enough time if we go now."

"But . . ." Trevor let his voice trail off as he turned to Janice. "We were talking about something important."

Janice stood and shook her head. "It's okay, Trevor. We can talk more about it tomorrow after the rehearsal. Go now."

Trevor stood and left. It was the hardest thing he'd ever had to do in his life.

$\mathcal{A}$s the maid of honor, Janice walked up the aisle first, humming the wedding march to herself.

"Janice! Slow down!" Laura called from behind her. "It's a wedding, not a race!"

Janice slowed her step and continued to walk slowly, as she'd been told to do.

She couldn't believe this was really happening. It was Thursday, two days before the wedding. They were actually going through the rehearsal, and Frank and Laura really were getting married on Saturday. Most of the church had been decorated. They only had a few things left to do on Friday, and all arrangements were in place. It was really going to happen.

Neither she nor Trevor thought Laura and Frank were doing the right thing. So she and Trevor had found a little time before the practice started while everyone was doing the decorating and prayed together one last time, agreeing that they had left it in God's hands, and even though it wasn't what they wanted, it was done.

As she stepped to the side, she smiled weakly at Trevor, who was already standing beside Frank. They then waited for Laura and her father to position themselves and start their walk up the aisle.

While they worked on setting Laura's hand on the right place on her father's arm, Janice watched Trevor out the corner of her eye.

She wasn't looking forward to the wedding, but she sure did want to see Trevor in a tuxedo. She knew she was setting herself up for a disappointment by dreaming about Trevor in a tux. Rick would also be at the wedding, and she had decided not to waste any time and to talk to him right away. As difficult as it would be for her to see Trevor with another woman, she had to accept that as friends, and friends only, they both would have to watch each other date.

The thought stabbed her where she didn't think she'd heal. She really didn't want to date Rick, nor did she think she would survive watching Trevor date other women. However, since she didn't know what else to do to get on with their lives and remain friends, she couldn't see any other alternative.

Janice did her best to push those thoughts out of her head and tried to concentrate on going through the motions of practicing for the wedding ceremony.

After they were done, Pastor Harry took Laura's parents to the side and talked to them privately. Janice and Trevor joined Frank and Laura, who were pointing to the podium and the potted fern arranged in front of it.

"You know," Laura said, sighing as she spoke, "I can almost see Bunners peeking through the leaves and wiggling his cute little nose at me."

Frank groaned. "I can't believe you named a rabbit Bunners. I still don't know where we're going to put that dumb bunny, either. You better not let it run around loose because Freddie will be watching it. I don't want you to be mad at me if one day that thing is gone."

"Pardon me?" Laura squeaked.

"I usually feed Freddie rats I buy from the pet store, but when a snake gets that size, people often feed them rabbits."

Laura's face paled. "Then I think you should get rid of Freddie."

Frank's face hardened. "I'm not getting rid of Freddie. You should get rid of that rabbit."

"And while we're on the topic of getting rid of things, I don't like the way you seem to think that you can tell me to get rid of my stuff. My stuff is just as good as yours."

"Forget it, Laura. You're just tired. Actually, I'm tired too. Knock it off. Your constant whining is getting on my nerves."

"Constant whining? You're being unreasonable, which you are a lot of the time."

"I'm not unreasonable. You have your head in the clouds on a regular basis. I'm just trying to be practical."

"Practical?" Laura sputtered. "I'm not the one who thinks nothing of living on credit, then wonders why the only thing you can afford to eat for a week is macaroni and wieners."

"Laura, if there's one thing I'm going to do with you after we're married, it's going to be to teach you not to be so cheap."

"And I'm going to teach you how to be more sensitive. How dare you say that about me in front of my friends!"

Janice felt Trevor's hand on her forearm. "Uh-oh," he mumbled as he gently guided her back a few steps.

They stood back and watched as Frank and Laura began hurling insults at each other.

Frank stiffened from head to toe and crossed his arms over his chest as he spoke in low, harsh tones. Tears started to stream down Laura's cheeks, and her voice skipped as she responded.

The pastor stopped talking. He didn't move, but he did watch Frank and Laura as the argument escalated.

Janice felt more than saw Trevor lean down to whisper in her ear. "I don't think they're doing that right. The book says they should communicate effectively, but that's not doing it very constructively."

Janice nodded and said nothing as the conversation continued to deteriorate exponentially. Even though it was what she and Trevor had been striving for over the past four months, it gave her no joy to hear Frank and Laura tossing back and forth opposing personality traits and conflicting characteristics that weren't necessarily bad, just not compatible for a permanent relationship, especially when discussed in anger.

Suddenly, the room fell silent, except for the sound of Laura's sniffling.

Both Frank and Laura turned to their guests—the pastor, their parents, and to Janice and Trevor.

Laura swiped her arm across her face, but it was Frank who addressed everyone.

"I don't think Laura and I are going to get married after all." He swept one hand in the air to encompass the decorating. "I know everything has all been set up. We'll be back in a minute to decide what to do about it. For now, Laura and I have to go talk in private."

A stunned silence hung in the room as Frank and Laura walked out.

"Wow," Trevor muttered. "Who would have thought it would come to this?"

"Yeah," Janice mumbled. "This is what we wanted to happen. Why do I not feel very happy about it?"

"I know. It's like that old saying in reverse. We've been trying and trying to get them to see each other realistically all this time and couldn't get them to see it. Now they do. We lost every battle but won the war. Still, there is no victory here."

The backs of Janice's eyes burned, and her throat clogged up. Her eyes welled up, and a couple of tears escaped. "No, I don't feel particularly happy about this either. With the heartache to Frank and Laura, all this wedding stuff around us just seems to rub everyone's noses in it too. I know it's better in the long run, but it's awful to see it around me right now."

Trevor stepped in front of her. Very slowly, he brushed his thumbs up under her glasses and wiped the tears from beneath her eyes.

"You know, dating for a long time before getting married isn't what builds a good marriage. My Great-Grampa Elliott and Grammie Louise don't talk a lot about their courtship, but I do know that they didn't know each other very long before they got married, only a few months. The old codger is going to be eighty-eight this year, but you should see the old guy go, especially when Grammie calls him City Boy. I've been trying to get them to tell me the story of that for years, but all they do is laugh. My point, though, is that they've been happily married over sixty years after a very short courtship."

"I don't understand what you're trying to say. What does this have to do with Frank and Laura?"

"I wasn't thinking about them. I was thinking about us. How do you feel about me, Janice? Do you really want to stay friends and date guys like Rick? Or do you want to be with me every day, sharing what we know is good? Living together and spending the rest of our lives together, in friendship and in love."

"Living together?"

One corner of his mouth quirked up, and his voice dropped in pitch. "This is coming out all wrong. I love you, Janice. I don't know when I started loving you, but when we were going through the motions of the ceremony before Laura and Frank called it off, I found myself thinking about what it would be like if this were my wedding. Our wedding."

"Our wedding?"

"I guess I'm asking if you'll marry me."

Janice's heart stopped, then started up again in double-time. She did love him. Like Trevor, she didn't know either when she started loving him, but she couldn't bear the thought of them going their separate ways. The only reason she thought it would be a good idea to date others was to avoid a romance between them that might spoil their friendship. All last night she'd lain awake, thinking about Trevor and his reaction to her words.

Of course he was right. She wouldn't be able to watch him

date other women when she loved him to the depths of her soul. Nor did she think he would be able to stand watching her date other men. Without words, she already knew he loved her; and she suspected he already knew she loved him, or he wouldn't have asked her to marry him.

"Of course I'll marry you. You knew before you asked."

"When? I don't want a long engagement, and we've already been through the premarital counseling thing."

"Yes, but we missed the last private session. We'll have to at least do that."

"Yes, we will." His hands slipped to the sides of her waist, and she put her hands on his. "Look at all this around us. Do you think our wedding will be anything like this?"

Janice thought about what was all around them—all of it going to waste. Everything was in place for a wedding that wasn't going to happen. The church was decorated, the minister present, the caterer booked, the limo reserved . . . Everything was ready, and it was too late to stop it.

"I suppose I'd do much the same. I even like Laura's green color scheme. I guess you and I are going to have to deal with everything tomorrow. I hope it's not too late, and they won't lose all their deposits. I know the one for the caterer was really big."

She heard as well as felt Trevor's sharp intake of breath. "Unless we use everything ourselves. What if *we* get married on Saturday?"

"Us? Just like that? I've never done anything impulsive in my life. I don't think this is a good time to start."

"Well, it's up to you, of course. All I know is that Laura's friends are your friends, and Frank's friends are my friends. Both sets of our parents are already coming. When our wedding comes, there will only be a few minor changes to the guest list. Not a single person I'd like to invite to my wedding who isn't already coming wouldn't drop everything and come with a day's notice. All it would take is a few phone calls. What about you?"

"I suppose . . . But what about the marriage license?"

"My cousin Benny works for city hall, and he's good friends with his supervisor. If we call him tonight, I'll bet he'd be happy to rush it through tomorrow so we could have it by Saturday afternoon."

"I don't know . . ."

She didn't want to rush such an important decision, but when she knew beyond a shadow of doubt that it was right, there was no need to wait.

Janice reached up to run one finger across the tip of Trevor's chin. The little gesture gave her goose bumps. "I can't make such a decision so fast. I think we should pray about it first, don't you?"

Keeping his hands on her waist, he lowered his head until their foreheads touched. "Dear heavenly Father, this day has taken such an unexpected turn of events, but yet I can see Your hand in it as for the best for Frank and Laura. I now ask for Your guidance and Your wisdom in the decision Janice and I now face."

Janice softly cleared her throat. "Father, I'm not impulsive. Deep in my heart, I do want to marry Trevor, and I do want to marry him right away. But Your will is not always the same as our will. I'm scared to be heading into such a life-changing decision so fast. I too ask for Your wisdom and guidance and for confirmation that this would be the right thing. Please help us make this decision. I ask this in the name of our Lord and Savior, Jesus Christ, amen."

They both sighed deeply and released each other.

"So now what?" Trevor asked.

Before she could reply, Pastor Harry joined them.

"I hate to see it end like this for Frank and Laura. To be honest, I've had my doubts about them all along. Not that this makes me happy, but I firmly believe that their decision was for the best. As a pastor, I've seen a few weddings canceled but never at the last minute like this. I look around and see everything is ready to happen, but with no bride and groom, the wedding's off. By the way, what about you two? We never had that last appointment to discuss your wedding. Have you set a date yet? Because I can hardly wait to see you two married. It's been a pleasure to have a couple like you with such a solid relationship and strong potential for a great future together in my class."

Trevor smiled at Janice so sweetly she thought she might melt. All she could do was smile and nod.

"What about your dress?" he asked. "You can't get married in a green dress."

"That's okay. I'll just wear my jeans because they're blue. I have a white blouse and white sneakers."

"I don't think so," he grumbled. "I've heard that wedding ditty about something borrowed and something blue often enough in the past month. There's no way jeans legally count as the blue thing. I don't care if you wear your sneakers underneath whatever you wear, but can't you borrow a real wedding dress? What about your mother's dress? You said you're short like her. Has she still got it? I hear women tend to keep those things. Or can't you just buy a dress off the rack tomorrow? They have things like that, don't they?"

Janice couldn't tamp down her smile. "I was planning on wearing my mother's dress when I get married because it was her mother's dress too. I don't expect Laura to start sewing for me, considering what happened, but my mother sews. I'll bet she could do any alterations that need doing in one day. I wouldn't think there's much to be done."

His arms circled her waist, and he broke out into a wide smile. The adorable little crinkles at the corners of his beautiful blue eyes had never looked so wonderful.

Slowly, his smile faded, and his mouth opened like he was

going to say something, but no words came out. Instead he smiled again, bent down, and brushed a slow, gentle kiss to her lips.

When they separated, he spoke to Pastor Harry but kept his eyes fixed on hers. "There's a different bride and groom and a few changes to the seating arrangements, but you're wrong. Pastor. The wedding's on."

Epilogue

*T*revor turned the doorknob slowly so Janice wouldn't hear him coming in. With as much stealth as he could muster, he poked his head in to first determine where she was.

Clunking noises echoed from the kitchen. Trevor closed the door slowly behind him and tiptoed inside with his hands behind his back.

"Honey, I'm ho-ome!" he chorused as he rounded the corner.

Janice squealed. She turned around in a flash at the same time as she whipped something behind her back.

Trevor grinned. He could see she hadn't forgotten either.

He brought out the flowering hibiscus plant from behind his back.

She didn't bring forward whatever she was hiding behind her back. "What are you doing home so soon?" she squeaked. "And what is that for?"

Trevor sighed. Maybe she had forgotten. "Today is our anniversary, remember? Flowers are supposed to be a sign of affection, and this is something that won't die after a few days, so you can be reminded every day of how much I love you."

"Oh, brother," she mumbled. "Like I need a reminder." Instead of bringing out whatever she was hiding from him, she quickly glanced at the back door, then back to him. "You're home early. I wasn't expecting you so soon."

He cleared his throat. "I have to admit the plant wasn't my first thought. I've been checking every couple of days for a suitable dog to rescue, and today they got one in that sounded so perfect.

I got off early to go to the pound and see him. If he was right, I was going to bring him home for you. But when I got there, someone else had got there first. I just thought that it would have been a nice anniversary surprise. I guess we'll have to wait."

He leaned toward her to give her a kiss, but she turned her head, only allowing him to kiss her cheek.

"Why do you keep looking into the backyard? And what's that strange noise?"

Suddenly, the door thumped. Trevor plunked the plant on the counter and ran to the back door.

"Trevor! Wait!"

He opened the door. As he looked into the yard, something bumped into his leg. He looked down in time to see a blur scoot past his feet. As Janice squatted down, she dropped a blue dog bowl on the floor and scooped up a rather matted, little, hairy brown dog.

Trevor's throat clogged. Words failed him.

Janice stood with the dog in her arms. "I can't believe this. After we talked about it, I've been checking at the pound every couple of days too. It looks like I was the one who beat you to him. I was going to bathe him and try and do something with his coat before you saw him. He doesn't have a name. He sure doesn't look like much and he's a little shy, but he's housebroken. He seems so much like he needs a friend."

Slowly, she handed him the dog. He cuddled the forlorn little creature, petting him very gently, since he could see the dog was nervous. He suspected the little dog had been neglected, but Trevor knew that soon this dog would be very spoiled and very happy. Almost hesitantly, the little dog squirmed, his tail made an uncertain wag, and he licked Trevor on the chin.

"I don't know what to say," Trevor choked out as he wiped his chin with his sleeve.

Janice rose on her tiptoes and gave him a peck on the cheek. "Happy anniversary. You ruined my surprise, you know."

He couldn't stop his grin, which he didn't think would leave his face for the rest of the day. He'd wanted a dog for years. They both had. Not long after they were married, they had agreed that they would rescue a dog, and now they had.

"Believe it—you really did surprise me." He gave the dog one more hug, then stepped closer to Janice, trying to figure out some way to embrace her and the dog at the same time. "We've bought a house, and now that we've got a dog, you know what's supposed to happen next, don't you?"

Janice grinned and rested one hand over her stomach. "Uh, Trevor, speaking of surprises . . ."